内

羊老师吉祥

富源

2024.3.13

Tiergarten Berlin.

18.8.56

Ref. 5617

Wild Fox Ridge

Xue Mo

Tranaslated by Howard Goldblatt and Sylvia Li-chun Lin

RUXUE INTERNATIONAL MEDIA INC

First Edition 2023

ISBN 979-8-88991-003-9
US$37.00
Copyright © 2023 by Xue Mo
Published by Ruxue International Media Inc
332 S Michigan Avenue STE 900 Chicago, IL 60604
Tel:+1(773) 648 5522   (86)13434375544
http://xuemo.com
E-mail: ruxuemedia@gmail.com   xuemo1963@163.com

Contents

Prologue	*1*	*Fourteenth Session*	*349*
First Session	*6*	*Fifteenth Session*	*379*
Second Session	*21*	*Sixteenth Session*	*405*
Third Session	*66*	*Seventeenth Session*	*434*
Fourth Session	*86*	*Eighteenth Session*	*458*
Fifth Session	*133*	*Nineteenth Session*	*478*
Sixth Session	*171*	*Twentieth Session*	*512*
Seventh Session	*203*	*Twenty-first Session*	*537*
Eighth Session	*230*	*Twenty-second Session*	*553*
Ninth Session	*254*	*Twenty-third Session*	*569*
Tenth Session	*268*	*Twenty-fourth Session*	*591*
Eleventh Session	*288*	*Twenty-fifth Session*	*625*
Twelfth Session	*311*	*Twenty-sixth Session*	*638*
Thirteenth Session	*332*	*Twenty-seventh Session*	*663*

Prologue

Wooden Fish Valley beneath Wild Fox Ridge
Pots of gold and silver falling into a pond
Go look for the key at the Hu Family Mill
                              ——*Liangzhou Children's Song*

A hundred years ago, two camel caravans disappeared at Wild Fox Ridge.

They were both well-known caravans in the West at the time, one Mongolian and one Chinese, each with over two hundred camels. They had traveled the thousand-mile trail countless times, wearing down the stones on the mountain path and leaving deep ruts on Baosui Road, a route of great importance to the camel drivers. They had survived natural disasters and man-made calamities, equipped with the strongest camels they could find, and guarded by skilled marksmen armed with the best weapons available. Moreover, they aspired to change the world—transporting gold, silver, and tea to Russia to trade for arms and ammunition so they could overthrow the imperial court called Qing. A Liangzhou gazette had a detailed account about the trek, but the two camel trains simply vanished like smoke. As a child, I often heard the story from camel drivers; it became an unsolved mystery in my mind, and that was the major impetus for my later visit to Wild Fox Ridge.

I saw them often in my childhood fantasies: one afternoon a hundred years ago, two formidable camel caravans made a magnificent start on their journey to a place they called Luocha. Naturally, they did not know that, despite the similarity in pronunciation, Luocha was quite different from Russia. In the folklore of Western China, Luocha is a malevolent demon, a kind of raksha, capable of raining down blood and raising noxious winds in the universe. Over a thousand years ago, the all-powerful Guru Rinpoche had gone to the country of Luocha to vanquish the rakshas, but he did not make it back. Later an accomplished master of arcane knowledge told me that, judged by their genesis, the caravans going to Luocha had an inauspicious beginning; he said their disappearance had to have been caused by interference from Luocha (the Luocha of which he spoke were those demonic rakshas). On the surface, he said, many of the calamities appeared to have been caused by humans, but actually resulted from the power of the Dharma realm, whose power was called malevolent demons and evil spirits by our ancestors. It is said that terrible things inevitably happen on days when these demons and spirits are on duty, which in a way acknowledges the ancestors' belief in auspicious days.

On those many occasions when I carelessly enter a trance-like state, I can see that legendary tale. The departing caravans look mightily impressive; the rings from camel bells are so loud they shake heaven and earth, and hundreds of camels cry out in a prolonged monotone, loud enough to be heard throughout Liangzhou. It was the most exciting and moving scene in my childhood imagination.

Following a trail used for thousands of years, the drivers made their trek, the camels' flying hooves kicking up enough dust to blot out the sky.

They entered Wild Fox Ridge a few months later.

Then they disappeared, as if vaporized.

Few people knew what had happened in the mysterious Wild Fox Ridge.

In my young mind, there often appeared the camel drivers who entered Wild Fox Ridge. At the time, I told myself that I would solve the mystery when I grew up. Later my teacher (an old lama with an unusual, ancient face) gave me an enigmatic look and said, "You don't need to go there. The truth will reveal itself to you once you've attained the capacity to comprehend past lives."

Yet one winter many years ago, I went to Wild Fox Ridge anyway. In the days before my departure, I dreamed about the camel caravans every night, the details crystal clear and the people life-like, as if it were an important life experience for me. I asked the lama who was adept in that capacity, but he only smiled inscrutably, saying it was a memory from a previous lifetime.

"Go to Wild Fox Ridge then," he said. "Maybe you'll meet your unknown self."

So I did, taking with me two camels and a dog. One of the camels, a white one, carried me; the other, a yellow one, transported water, food, and other necessities.

I chose winter, because I wanted to avoid the scorching summer heat in the desert, but also because the camel caravans too had started their journey in winter, which was very common in China's West.

Following the storied camel trail, I eventually located the drivers by an unusual method. It's important to know that many things in the world appear to have vanished, although considerable information about them remains. They might change or transform into something else, but never disappear completely. So-called "eternal causal relationships" in Buddhism are considered to be the "conservation of mass" in modern science. As a result, the location of Wild Fox Ridge is the spiritual homeland of many camel drivers. Lingering concerns and longing bring forth souls with all sort of desires, which is why a children's song has spread across Liangzhou: "Wooden Fish Valley beneath Wild Fox Ridge/Wandering souls fill the nine ditches and eight ponds/Go look for the key at Hu Family Mill."

On an afternoon saturated with the smell of blood, I finally made it to Wild Fox Ridge, where I spent dozens of days and nights. It was a memorable juncture in the first half of my life.

You must have heard the wind sing under a desert moon, that and the sound of waves. How can there be the sound of waves in the desert? You might ask. Believe me, it's there. The sand trough was once the bottom of an ocean, the underworld too is our world. This seemingly illusory locale is an intangible, alternative realm, but also an omnipresent reality.

All the grains of sand have experienced the sound of waves. At the instant we met, they abruptly released all their life's memories. I organized twenty-seven interview sessions at the mysterious place, sessions intended not only for the interviews, but also for people to meet. The duration of each session varied. We chatted longer if we had much to say and ended early if we found the topics boring. So I'll use "session" for each of the divisions of this book.

Since there are many characters vying to talk, at first glance the novel may seem disorganized, but if you calmly read on, you may see a different landscape.

What left the deepest impression on me among the abundant interviews was the course of the caravan's life, while the afternoon of the destruction was the most memorable . . . if you look through the lens of life's twists and turns, you'll see that that afternoon had long ago turned into an oil painting that was soaked in water, its colors faded, blurred, and yellowed. But the inconstancy of life fermented, like wine, growing stronger as it aged. And yet, strong or weak, I don't feel like fussing about it. It's a waste of effort; oftentimes memory has its own authority.

Of all the narratives on life's uncertainties, the blurred afternoon was what I later cared most about. At dusk the most dazzling sight was a lonely white sun hanging above the vast desert, looking solitary and forlorn. It happened after every wind storm. Like the inconstancy of life, the wind sweeps away many things, but never the giant corona around the white sun. I clearly saw several men in rags stumbling along beneath the corona. They had managed to escape the sandstorm that entombed their camels, but could they walk away from their destiny?

A mill by the corona made a rumbling noise. The millstone was being pulled by a white camel, trailed by a man and a woman.

An aged voice was singing—

High up on the mountains a clear, fresh spring,
Winding its way down, has for thousands of years,
Everyone comes to drink the spring water,
Some taste bitterness, some taste sweet . . .

First Session
Specters' Personal Accounts

Night was deepening when I first entered Wild Fox Ridge. The sky above the great desert was sprinkled with a multitude of stars, making the horizon seem low, like the folded wings of a large bird.

I walked on sandy ground toward the mysterious locale. Along the way, the sand dunes underwent constant changes; I saw many indistinct figures, which I glimpsed out of the corners of my eyes. They vanished when I looked closely at them. I also noticed an old man supported by a cane who forced out a string of coughs through his aging throat in the night wind. I wasn't able to make out whether he was a desert poplar or a ghost from the stories. You know that at the time I was listening for the rustle of feet on the sand, which is the best way to be vigilant on night journeys.

Noise constantly assailed my ears, like the groan of a desert poplar or a woman's shriek, similar sounds that are hard to tell apart on a quiet night. At times I heard a wolf's doleful cry that resembled a widow's weeping at her husband's grave.

A pale crescent moon splashed its faint, misty light all around. The outline of sand hills came first into view, as a massive silence enveloped me. Sometimes shadows shot past like arrows, but it was impossible to know if they were foxes or were galloping or scattering specters.

I started calling for the specters when I reached my destination, using a rite that had been in secret circulation for a thousand years. I performed the ritual nightly for ten winters. Starting in October, I walked to the hundred and eight evil spots one by one, where I pitched a tent and began summoning the spirits before carrying out a special ritual. The specters never failed to appear before me, so I could give them either sacrificial offerings or deliverance. The method, passed down from the Dakini of the Joyul sect of Tibetan Buddhism, was what I used that night.

First, I lit a yellow candle, and then I recited an ancient incantation. I was calling out all the specters associated with the camel caravans—to be sure, not just specters, but any life forms who possessed the information I needed. Scientists believe that human visual perception can detect less than four percent of the world, with the rest existing in the forms of dark matter and dark energy. What a massive information field that is. To prevent unrelated spirits from appearing, I created a shielded sphere. That, too, was an arcane ritual; I asked guardian spirits to guard my altar every night when I conducted the interviews, so that only invited guests could enter. The shielded sphere was very much like the circle drawn by the Monkey King in "Journey to the West." Only those associated with camel caravans were allowed entrance, thus guaranteeing that the topics were relatively focused.

The candle cast a muted yellow light, under which the sand trough was reflected and turned into a different world. The atmosphere was somewhat eerie.

The first to appear at the first session was the murderous aura of a killer. It was an oppressive force, which, compared to other elements, did not dissipate easily. That is one of the reasons why humans are constantly plagued by wars. And which is why our ancestors said, "If you want to know if there are wars in the world, just listen for a butcher sharpening his knife."

Then orbs of light began to gather. Depending on the disparate nature of the mind, the orbs were imbued with various colors, some white, some yellow, some gray. In a word, they were all different.

Over the first few days, except for some special cases, I saw mostly orbs of light.

I was keen to know who I had been in the lifetime mentioned by the lama.

In response to my eager anticipation, my guests narrated descriptions of themselves, using unique forms, of course.

One. Killer

I went looking for death in Wild Fox Ridge.

I wanted to die there. I was afraid of dying, but I wanted to die in that place because I knew I could not get out alive, and neither could they.

Those who did make it out could not escape the Wild Fox Ridge of their destiny.

I had to die, because, based on the Kālacakra, the end of the world would occur during that trip.

Since the end was near, I obviously had to carry out what I was born to do. At the place called Wild Fox Ridge, I wanted to fulfill my destiny of killing Ma Zaibo, him because he was a descendant of the Ma family. Killing him was the reason for my existence. It would be my way to tell the world that evil-doers will suffer retribution and that calamities will reach into future generations.

I would kill him and then wait quietly for the inevitable.

Look. The thing is coming from a distance. It is a giant wooden fish. Despite its shape, it is actually made of two millstones, the upper one as extensive as the sky, the lower one expansive as the earth. From the opening between them comes the unique clacking sound of a beaten wooden fish, in quick tempo, fast-paced as galloping horse hooves. I can even feel the wind whirl when the wooden fish turns.

You might not hear it. You're a bunch of blind and deaf idiots. You are licking the honey off a knife blade, you have a ferocious tiger over your head, and below your feet is an abyss where a giant crocodile, its mouth agape and its teeth bared, is waiting for you to fall. You are suspended by a rope that has been gnawed at by rats; it is about to snap, but you, you're still thirsting for the dewdrops on the rope. You don't know that the dew will dry once the sun is out and that your rope is ready to snap.

You truly have no idea that the rope of your life will snap at any moment.

The colossal millstone is turning, and countless creatures will be crushed to death.

Unless, that is, you can find the Wooden Fish Incantation.

I really don't like Killer's tone; there's something about it that annoys me. It is a reminder of me as an angry youth. That was me for quite a long time; I hated everything, I wished for something better. Later, I found it in a type of thangka, the furious-looking tantric deity. The old lama explained the face to me, "It is a sad, angry look, upset over the failure of all sentient beings to make themselves better." I detected the sentiment in Killer's tone of voice, along with something I find it hard to describe.

So I asked myself, could this be me during an earlier lifetime?

I didn't dare say no, because, before physically being in Wild Fox Ridge, my spirit had been here with the old lama, who introduced me to the specters. "This is the reincarnation of Xingtian after five hundred years' retreat," he said, "becoming rare beyond words, with a murderous aura that can reach a distance of thirty-five thousand li." The haughty specters looked at me with deep veneration after hearing the lama.

This spiritual experience both pleased and upset me. I do like the ancient deity who, after the Yellow Emperor lopped off his head, used its nipples as eyes and wielded his axe to continue the battle, but I'd much prefer to be a reincarnated Buddha.

When he saw my dejected look, the lama told me that Xingtian was a primordial god of war, the incarnation of Mahakala, also known as Daheitian in Eastern lands.

Two. Qi Feiqing

I'm Qi Feiqing; style name Zhenlu, from Liangzhou. History books call me a national hero, because I organized an anti-Qing uprising. In the so-called uprising, people rushed into action and dispersed in confusion—that wasn't my fault; it was the nature of Liangzhou people—a riot that ran the risk of beheading. And that was exactly what happened to me. A few months after the Wuchang uprising, one of the Qing court's magistrates lopped off my head. There have been quite a few stories in Liangzhou about my beheading. In one of them I was said to be a Qigong master, and the sword was fast as the wind, but only managed to leave a few white marks on my neck. So the Liangzhou residents said I knew impregnable Qigong. In another version, the executioner was rumored to be a sympathizer—some said he was paid by my family—so he smeared jute bark on the blade and thickened it several times. The sword could not slide into my neck easily. The two versions shared the same outcome: my neck was sawed through by the executioner, a hair-raising sight, which could be the reason why my reputation spread in Liangzhou—I was almost treated as a martyr.

A very popular story had me assuming the position of the local temple god in charge of Liangzhou.

Before I died, I said something that would become quite well known:

"The people of Liangzhou have a right to be poor." "Have a right to be" is a Liangzhou expression, meaning "should be." The phrase said everything I felt for that land, as I truly wished it would be a better place.

There was more lore accompanying my emotional outburst; it involved the Qing code regarding beheading, which is to be carried out in a single chop. When the first swing of the sword, with the help either from the executioner or from my Qigong skill, did not lop off my head, someone from Liangzhou would have shouted at the presiding official over, "Dai! The Great Qing code stipulates one chop for the crime. Do you know the law or not?" It was said that the shout would have saved my life—heh-heh. It was actually just people's wishful thinking. If the government really wanted you dead, would they care about the law? All the laws they set up were just excuses to take your life.

But the citizens of Liangzhou who had illusions about the law sighed over my fate for more than a hundred years: Ai! So many spectators and yet not a single one shouted. So the executioner said, "Master Qi, you have outlived your people." What he meant was, I did not have a single friend who could speak up for me. Then he wiped off the sticky jute bark and sawed on my neck until I died.

I also heard about a provincial scholar called Yang Chengxu, who pissed at Liangzhou's main crossroads after my death. His grandson said:

"Grandpa, there are people out on the street."

"No people live in Liangzhou!" Old Mr. Yang replied, as a rebuff of all residents of the city. A hundred years later, Xue Mo shouted at Old Mr. Yang:

"Dai! Are you not a Liangzhou resident? Why didn't you go save his life?"

The question exposed Yang's hypocrisy.

But this would happen later, so let's put it aside for now.

What happened at Wild Fox Ridge constituted the experience of a lifetime for me. I will be the leader of the camel caravans in this story.

I never imagined that we would have such chilling, thrilling encounters at Wild Fox Ridge.

Three. Lu Fuji

I am Lu Fuji, also from Liangzhou. I don't know what to say about myself. In terms of literary talent, I can't compose poetry or write decent lyrics, nor was I proficient enough in martial arts to gain an official post. All I have is the hot blood coursing through my veins and my dreadful strength. In Liangzhou lore, I merely count as a friend of Qi Feiqing's. What has circulated among the people mostly deals with my righteous acts. The most famous one concerns a blacksmith who stole the sword from Master Guan's Temple in the village. He turned it into a hoe and a scythe, but later was caught. In the villagers' eyes, he'd committed a cardinal offense. Who is Master Guan, but a deity recognized by countless emperors? Master Guan's Temple in our village could do wonders, could grant all wishes. Wasn't it strange that it could not even safeguard the deity's own sword? Obviously, Master Guan meant for the blacksmith to have it. If he hadn't, even a hundred blacksmiths could not overcome his magical power and get away with the sword. Hei-hei. That's how I defended the blacksmith. I was right, wasn't I?

The villagers let the blacksmith go. Later he opened a forge in Lanzhou, and much later was the one who collected my body after I was beheaded by a running dog official of the Qing court at Xiaojiaping. It was the perfect manifestation of "a good deed begets another and evil incurs retribution."

There are so many stories like this in Liangzhou. Some are true and some are false, until eventually the fabricated stories seemed more real than the true ones.

I still played a supporting role to Feiqing at Wild Fox Ridge, helping him with the Chinese camel caravan. But seriously, that really was a chilling, thrilling life experience.

Four. Ma Zaibo

The experience at Wild Fox Ridge elevated my life to a higher level.

I'd never even heard of all the countless miracles, the countless hardships, and the countless encounters, let along savor them over several lifetimes.

I'm from Zhenfan, a town with a derogatory name, for it means "vanquish the barbarians." It is close to Mongolia, across a desert some eighty *li* wide. Called Eighty Li Desert, it is what is known as the Tengger Desert in books.

For as long as there have been records, Mongolians have raided our area. Dressed in fur, they crossed the desert on camels to seize food and property, women too. Chinese women with fair, tender skin, unlike theirs, who are exposed to the elements out on the steppes. The Mongol warriors zipped over and returned loaded down with what they wanted. The imperial court relocated a large group of people over here, and they were my ancestors. The successive dynasties had hoped that my ancestors would guard the border and vanquish the warriors riding on massive horses and shooting long bows. The township of Zhenfan was established under the jurisdiction of Liangzhou Prefecture.

Our Ma family was a prominent Zhenfan household.

How did the Ma family gain its renown, you ask? I'll tell you. You've probably heard of Nian Gengyao and Yue Zhongqi, who launched a westward expedition, haven't you? Yes, it was during the Yongzheng reign of the Qing dynasty. When many thousands of soldiers went west, the provisions were sent on ahead of them. I tell you, those provisions were transported by Ma family camels. At the time, the line of camels stretched across the whole Eighty Li Desert—eighty *li* in width only, for in length it reaches all the way to the horizon, and no one knows where it ends. At the time, white camels were rare, usually one in a thousand. We had three hundred of them. Just imagine how impressive that looked.

When General Yue returned victorious from the expedition, he gave a factual account of the Ma family's contribution to the Imperial court. Emperor Yongzheng was elated, proclaiming that the Great Qing court would guarantee a hundred years of prosperity for the Ma family. Sure enough, our family's fortunes rose like the sun at high noon over the next hundred years, until the time of the Empress Dowager. Then the Eight Nation Alliance fought their way into Beijing, and when the Empress Dowager fled the attack, she rode on a camel supplied by who else? The Ma Family.

Look at me, see how I get all excited when I talk about my ancestors. I seem shallow, don't I? I can't help it. It's a habit of mine. I've been practicing self-cultivation over several lifetimes. Worries are easy to shed, habits are hard to change, even for the Bodhisattvas. Habits are like the smell of a chamber pot. When the pot is emptied, you still must scrub it many times to get rid of the smell. Look at me, here I am, defending myself again.

I knew nothing about self-cultivation until one day several monks came from the Mongolian side. They told me I was the reincarnation of a Pandita, which means "great scholar" in Tibetan. From that moment on, I felt that I was a practitioner. But I refused to be enthroned right away; instead, I promised that I'd go over to them once I found what I needed.

I'm not sure if I really am a lama reincarnate, but I was different from other boys in one sense. As soon as I was old enough to know what was going on, I discovered that everything in the world is constantly changing, from existence to nothingness, from good to bad. I couldn't find a single thing that never changed, and that frightened me. It's truly frightening if everything in world must deteriorate, so I've been searching ever since.

What happened at Wild Fox Ridge was the experience I sought. I followed the camel caravan to find the place called Hu Family Mill. There's an ancient rhyme in Liangzhou that goes like this: "Wooden Fish Valley beneath Wild Fox Ridge/Souls filling the nine ditches and eight ponds/Go look for the key at Hu Family Mill." According to ancestors, when you find the Hu Family Mill, you'll find the real Wooden Fish Incantation, which in turn will help your mind perceive everything in the three realms, and every one of your wishes will be granted. To be sure, I never quite understood the concept, but you should know that some things in this world are beyond comprehension.

Five. Patul

I'm a Mongolian camel driver.

Some Chinese camel drivers remembered me as a cruel, brutal fellow. As a child, I tortured and killed many cats. The cruelest thing I've done was not taking human lives, but torturing cats. I often took kids up to people's rooftops to search for old cats. The old ones are often demonic. Haven't you seen an old cat curled up somewhere mumbling a sutra? It would keep doing that for a few decades and, in the end, gain magical powers that told it what I had in mind. So, whenever I tortured a cat, I told myself it wasn't torment, but a compliment. They could read my mind, and thought that since I was saying wonderful things about them, they let down their guard enough for me to pounce and cover their heads with a shirt.

But even then, my success rate was still very low. I found out that the old cats could tell what I had in mind. They saw right through me. I stopped hiding my cruel nature. I just took the village kids up and went after them with cattle whips. Numbers mean power, and as our whips snapped in the air, the old cats eventually fell exhausted into my hands, no matter how cunning they were.

They cried like crazy when I chased and beat them, like a baby being burned. I wondered if they had been humans in previous lifetimes. But that insignificant thought did not erase my murderous intent. The whip in my hand would snap and weave a black net. The cat would die, but it wasn't a real death, since they have twelve lives and this was only one of them. It would come back to life soon enough. An old cat had to die twelve times before it was truly dead. Understand? That's why I loved torturing old cats. They don't die so easily.

Hell, it was lots of fun.

Six. Huozi

I'm a huozi. Sure, you can call me Harelip, but Liangzhou people customarily call someone like me a huozi.

So Huozi it is.

I'm a younger cousin of Qi Feiqing's. I've never done anything worthwhile. I've done a lot of things, all but one of them has been buried in the passing of time. I sent Qi Feiqing to the execution block, and that is the only thing history remembers. So many people in the past have wanted to leave a good name behind, trying so hard their heads turn pointed, but they all failed, like a fart hitting your beard—in other words, delusional. Just think, whose fart can reach all the way up to his beard? I never wanted my infamy to spread, but by chance I became famous throughout Liangzhou, the same way people talk about accidentally planting a willow branch that grows into a huge shade tree. I heard of a prostitute in the Song dynasty who wanted to be famous, so she wrote the great poet Su Dongpo a letter. Su responded and, sure enough, she is remembered down through history. I didn't want to be remembered. What I really wanted was to get my hands on some money while I was alive. I was surprised to see that what I did to Qi Feiqing got my name into the Liangzhou gazette. Heh-heh, I guess the power of my ancestors must have worked.

My family wasn't rich or anything, but Feiqing was a wealthy man. His many pawnshops provided him with untold riches. People always thought I did that to him because I resented his wealth. That's not true, not at all. There were plenty of rich men out there, why didn't I do something to them?

I didn't like him because he wasn't a good man. Sure, he could claim some degree of righteousness, but that didn't concern me. What got me involved was the very reason I wanted to harm him. You know, many talented people are extremists, and that's what Feiqing was. Here's a story for you: he had a dog, the one he cut on the lip to turn it into a harelip. It was clearly modeled on mine. Then he called out to the dog—Huozi, Huozi—and the dog would come to him.

You see, that's what he was like.

On the stage at Wild Fox Ridge, my role was as steward for the Mongolian caravan. The Mongols weren't good with numbers, so they usually hired Chinese to take care of their accounts. I didn't have much education, but I'm pretty smart and I can do math in my head. I don't need an abacus to put complex numbers in neat order. But Heaven has no eyes. Why can't a smart man like me get rich?

Everyone says wealth is a karmic accumulation from previous lifetimes. I don't believe Mengzi—that's the old thief Qi Feiqing's nickname—did a better job accumulating good karma in an earlier lifetime than I did.

Shit!

Seven. Sha Meihu

I'm known by many names, but for now I prefer talking to you as Sha Meihu.

Sometimes a name represents a person's identity, so I'll tell you a Sha Meihu story. People in Liangzhou all knew that Sha Meihu was a well-known desert outlaw. My fame was real, and I remained famous even after I died. I'm one of the few desert outlaws who made it into the local gazette. Later, as I traveled to countries like Japan with the gazette, even the foreigners knew about a big-time outlaw in the Tengger Desert called Sha Meihu.

Sha Meihu is a sand cyclone, a desert storm, a nightmare for camel caravans —see how literate I sound? Only literary talent like this could elevate me above all the other, crude, desert outlaws.

Yes, I had a hard life. Everyone in my family died tragically in fierce revenge killings. I became a desert outlaw so I could kill as many enemies as I wanted. I had dozens of brothers, whose mouths opened as wide as a stove, demanding to be filled every day. I often engaged in a little side business—seizing tea and cooking oil. Later some petty thieves did their dirty deeds under my name, which was why I had such a far-reaching, impressive reputation. I didn't mind it when they did that; any small-time robber could use my name, but I wouldn't allow any of my men to lie— that is, they couldn't deny they worked for me, even it meant they'd lose their heads.

Just like that, my name was on everybody's lips.

Eight. Yellow Demon, king of the Han Chinese caravan, speaking for all camels

I have nothing to say.

I wanted Brown Lion to speak for us. You were a camel king at the time, but you act like you're dumb, not a word passing through your teeth. I know what's on that sneaky mind of yours; you're afraid to go down in history with a bad name. Heh-heh, what are you afraid of? Don't you all say that everyone leaves a name behind? So why worry if it's a good one or a bad one?

Actually, I can't represent the other camels, and I don't want to speak for Brown Lion, the male camel in the Mongol caravan. I can still feel the rage inside me when his name comes up. I'll take him on again, if there's a next life. It's what they call an injury for an injury.

I can only speak for myself, but you say you want me to speak for you, well, there's nothing I can do about that. Why don't you speak for me?

What I really want to say is, I want to be a camel in my next life.

Why?

Why not?

That's all.

Nine. Wooden Fish Girl

I've had many identities. People called me a beggar when I was out on the streets begging. When I sang wooden fish songs, they called me Muyu Mei, or Wooden Fish Girl. I did many other things, and each new thing brought a new name.

But whatever identity I assume, to me, I'm just a woman, a woman who knows how to sing wooden fish songs. All the other identities were given to me by fate or by someone else; the only one I'm happy to be is Wooden Fish Girl.

Naturally, it's the name I like best of all. I'm an heir to the tradition of wooden fish songs, and I can sing many of them. You can even say they were the reason I was born, and why people call me Wooden Fish Girl.

Wild Fox Ridge was a man's world, a place overflowing with rousing masculinity. You know, women are just ornaments in a man's world. What's a woman? A woman is the spice in a man's life. Without a woman, a man's world would be bland and dull. With a woman around, it would feel like seasoned mutton; the spices might not cover up the gamy smell, but they add a different flavor—that's it; that's what women are.

At Wild Fox Ridge, I was a prop, an important prop, but a prop nevertheless. On the other hand, just about everything in the world is a prop, isn't it? The world is an enormous stage, where you, I, and he are acting out a drama, like in the song—

> *The sun and the moon are two lamps,*
> *Between Heaven and Earth is a stage.*
> *You and I will act for a thousand years,*
> *But who understands what it means?*

Do you?

Second Session
Setting Out

Drive the camels, go to work, reach the first stop.
Leave parents, abandon a wife, unconscionable.
Look at me, this is, driving camels,
It's really no way to make a living . . .

——*Song of a Camel Driver*

The yellow candlelight envelopes the broad sand trough. I look quietly at my interviewees. At first, all I sense is one excitable specter after another; I can't get a clear look at their faces.

I wonder which of them would have been me, if I'd really had a previous life. I'm dying for a definitive answer, but I must admit I don't want to be any of these.

At the moment, the tiny sliver of a moon sends down faint circles of light. Every once in a while, I hear a wild fox barking. The number of foxes around is how this place got its name. Foxes are furtive animals, you can't see them in other deserts. But here at Wild Fox Ridge, they're everywhere. Sometimes on a moonlit night, I even see them praying to the moon for self-cultivation. I've heard that many foxes have attained immortality.

I conduct my first interview at a spot where the camel caravans stopped soon after reaching Wild Fox Ridge. Here there's a section of a city wall. When it first came into view, I saw a woman at the base of the wall. Dressed in red, she was combing her hair, casting a captivating silhouette. I knew it was a transformed fox. I fired a shot into the air and she vanished at the sound. I heard a fox cry out, first from the wall and soon after, several li away.

I entered on my camel, followed by my dog. But I left them behind when I conducted my first interview, though I certainly wished for their company—I was more than a little frightened of the specters at first—but I left my animals behind because I'd heard that animals' overwhelming yang can affect the results of a séance.

At the first interview, I recall, there was pervasive quietude as well as agitating turbulence. The sounds of their souls were clearly audible.

First I interviewed Killer.

I couldn't see him clearly, but the murderous aura was palpable; menacing, sinister, and chilling, it had a texture, like the air you'd feel when a sharp knife presses down on you. His voice, too, was an icy undercurrent of gloom.

Later, I shuddered whenever I thought back to the interview on that cold night.

One. Killer

1

I was once a killer.

My identity changed later, but I prefer the old me, so I'll talk to you as a killer. Since you want to know what happened back then, the me telling you the story will be the real me of that time.

I'll show you the true heart of a killer. For a long time in my life, being a killer was the reason for my existence, so, let me speak as a killer.

I told you already that killing Ma Zaibo was one of the reasons for making the trek. He was an important member of the camel caravans. In fact, when I laid my eyes on the person I wanted to kill, something had its gaze on me too. It was my fate.

So many of us can't fight our fate, which we usually understand only when we're near the end of our lives. Many people don't even know it until they breathe their last. Before then, they scheme and haggle, and they don't give up until all hope is lost. They think they'll live a thousand, maybe ten thousand years. They have no idea that their lives are but a spider thread beneath an eyelid that will break off at the slightest movement of the wind.

I've seen armed fights between local villagers and Hakka outsiders. People who had bickered nonstop died in droves. Of course, they'd never thought they would die so soon.

I've seen more than my share of revenge killings. The grim, brutal scenes stick in my mind.

Several earlier generations in my family have died in revenge killings. The seeds of hatred and my own unique experience turned me into a killer. For a long time, my identity kept changing, but the heart of a killer remained in me. I could hear my family's screams before they died, and their anguished cries never faded from my hearing. Then there were the children's moans, the smell of blood, a raging fire, and my relatives' blood-curdling screams in the flames.

I've seen too many bloody scenes, like murderers opening up a pregnant woman's belly, spearing the unborn, and waving it around; or like skinning someone with sticky jute, using strong glue to paste on threads of jute and, when it dries, pulling the threads off along with skin and flesh; or like pulverizing someone by grinding him with a giant pestle, such as crushing someone under a stone roller—that's how several people in my family died.

My first aunt developed a tremor after viewing one of those scenes; she shook uncontrollably, head to toe, so badly she could not hold a bowl or chopsticks. Her children had to feed her like a baby for the rest of her life.

Here's a scene I see during inadvertent moments. Terror in the eyes of people who were bundled up like rice stalks and laid out on a drying ground. Their eyes were wide open, the size of clay bowls, turning green. A giant stone roller pulled by horses were coming at them, the rumble reaching into the sky, like a massive millstone turning with nothing below it. The roller's axle ground against the stone, the sound like a demon's whistles boring into their veins and on their nerves, where they squirmed like earthworms. Most terrifying was the sound of the approaching horse hooves. The killers had borrowed the horses from the military. They were newly shod, semi-circular metal horseshoes fastened by six nails, like tiny iron fists. My ancestors' backs were bitten by these nails first, a savage invasion by the force of the powerful. The hooves trampled their bodies, as if stomping in mud. I saw splashes of blood stuck to those hooves.

The hooves splashed more and more blood until their night-eyes—the eye-like crusty spots on their legs, which are rumored to make night travel possible for horses—were covered. Each steel hoof opened up a bloody hole, until countless holes accompanied the screams from bodies on the ground. But they would not die; they could only shriek, making inhuman sounds, as the stone roller got louder. Strangely, though, the roller was nearly silent when it crushed the bodies—perhaps drowned out by the noise of the axle rubbing against the stone—but I heard the roller sound like grinding a millstone, a sound that made my teeth ache. It stayed with me throughout my life. Each time it came, I saw millstones turning in a carousing frenzy, large or small, shaped like a wooden fish.

In an endless void, the millstones turned forever, and I wondered if they might be the flying saucers people talked about later. I refuse to believe that they only existed in my wild imagination; I am convinced of their empirical existence.

As horse hooves trampled on my blood relations, their bodies twisted, though they did not die, since the horses were unaware of the locations of vital organs. Wanting to know where they would put down their hooves first. I discovered that many of them shook their heads and swished their ears, reluctant to step on people. Whips wove a net that landed on their heads, sending clumps of hair flying, so they had to walk to where they were expected to go. They wanted to avoid the bodies, but had no choice. The ground was strewn with bodies and the horses could not avoid walking on them. Pulling the stone roller, they advanced like a surging wave, closer and closer. The roller seemed as imposing as the raised end of a coffin being carried out of the village. You must have seen a coffin like that, symbolizing death, incomparably powerful. A power that pulverized so many people.

After the hooves came a stone roller weighing over two hundred *jin*. But it failed to flatten all the bodies; that would have been better, for it made no difference to the dead whether they were flattened or pulverized. But not so for the living. Those who weren't flattened were mostly still alive, and the roller had only crushed their bones, which poked through their skin, as horrendous a sight as the bloody holes made by the hooves, similarly accompanied by horrifying screams that had long stopped sounding human. You cannot find screams like that anywhere else in the world. I can't describe it. You can imagine how it sounded, though what you imagine was not the real sound, but the sound you thought you could imagine.

The ground was carpeted in blood after the horse hooves and stone roller's first pass. First Uncle, who was hiding in a nearby kindling pile covered my father's mouth—Father told me about it later. He said he did not hear any sound. He couldn't think, his mind a blank; all he felt was a monstrous fear looming above him.

I saw another group of men who were reveling joyously, for they felt a visceral hatred for those shrieking people. They would have liked to slice and dice them. Their own families had died at the hands of those on the ground, though in a different manner, mostly skinned alive. Rumor had it that their skin had been sent to Tibet to make human snare drums in exchange for weapons and ammunition. But the killers were screeching beneath the roller before the weapons arrived. It was because of what they had done that I did no killing before I arrived at Wild Fox Ridge, for on many times late at night I heard the agonizing cries from those who had been slaughtered by my ancestors. Every massacre resulted from a previous revenge killing.

You see, this is how I am different from most other killers.

I heard that some bodies were still twisting after the horse and stone roller passed a second time. The bodies were thrashing in blood, like the drowned struggling to survive.

2

In my memory, those people were turned into a gigantic meat patty spread out on the drying ground, shrouded in a massive silence. I did not hear a sound, but the heavy smell of blood followed me everywhere, like flies.

The village dogs were the first to pounce; they chomped on the meat patty, fresh blood dripping from their mouths. It was the best food they'd ever tasted. Their eyes turned red from the feasting frenzy, their backs arched like millstones, broad enough for children to ride on. Years later, a dog that was used to feasting on human flesh would sometimes gobble up a child riding on its back, and the villagers would then eat the dog. Which is why I contend they were incidental cannibals. The bodies of the elders turned into nutrients to feed the dogs, through which they entered the enemies. You will probably say that my elders merged with their enemies. Sure, you can say that, but that's not how I see it, for that would erase my hatred, which, for a killer, is indispensable. Without it, I would not be a killer.

The hatred nearly left me on a number of occasions. For instance, when I was studying the Kālacakra, the hatred in my heart receded like ice melting at room temperature. I was reminded of the many colossal celestial bodies and the boundless universe, a vast background against which the people, the nation, and the earth are so minute, so insignificant, tiny as a dust mote, that they can be completely ignored. Just think, in this limitless, mighty universe, where time has no beginning and no end, doesn't it seem meaningless for one group of men to be tangled up with another group of men? The association enlarged the capacity of my mind, day by day, a change that put me on guard, for I realized that the earth shrank to a tiny dot as the capacity of my mind expanded. According to Buddhist teaching, the universe is but a dust mote in the palm of the Mahavairocana Buddha. Viewed in this fashion, the hatred brought on by the death of my ancestors naturally began to fade, sometimes growing so faint, I felt it had nothing to do with me, and I found that appalling.

Appalling because I did not want to forget my destiny, which included two missions, one assigned by my uncle, the other by my father. As soon as I was old enough to understand him, Uncle told me about fights between the locals and the Hakka outsiders that had occurred years before, a killing spree that went on for years. Many in my grandfather's generation were murdered by the Hakkas. Like reciting a sutra, Uncle repeatedly exhorted me to seek revenge. Even when my brothers and I were very young, he'd planned to turn us into killers, starting with shooting sparrows with our slingshots. My second younger brother was the best in our generation at that, and was always after those noisy birds. He missed a lot at first and cursed through clenched teeth as he pulled the rubber band and fired stones. But soon the birds were doomed if they came within range; they became delicacies at our table. He hitched every one he killed on a hemp rope around his waist. Once it was full, he looked as if he'd grown a feathery tail. After he died in the fire, I often recalled the image of him dragging a feathery tail behind him.

We loved roasted sparrows. They quickly turned into charred feathery balls after we put them in wood fires. I parted the feathers to reveal the bright yellow meat inside. I usually went first for the innards, for they were easy to spot, wrapped in coiled intestines. You can eat them too—if that doesn't gross you out, because there could be rice kernels or insects in them, depending on the season. Sparrows eat insects in the spring and summer. Actually, you can eat insects too, since there are even people who eat other people.

The bright golden meat of a roasted sparrow had a wonderful taste, despite the burned odor. I chomped on them, bones and all, so did Uncle, who cursed while he did so, I'm eating a Hakka's flesh, I'm eating a Hakka's flesh. He told me to follow his example, but my little mouth was so stuffed with sparrow, I could only mumble. What he didn't realize was that I was actually mumbling about the delight in eating a delicious sparrow.

Sparrows can be cooked many ways. People say they're better than ginseng when caught during the first nineteen to twenty-seven days after the winter solstice. Two or three sparrows can produce a pot of nice broth and a single bowl of that makes you feel great all over. That's why I've been strong and healthy since childhood.

Without telling Father, who wanted us to forget the hatred, Uncle taught us to kill frogs. He showed us how to skin one alive. We learned how to do it so fast a skinned frog would keep hopping. He also showed us how to snap little insects in half, followed by skinning rabbits and other small animals. In our childhood, we skinned lots of rabbits, relieving them of their skin intact as they squealed. Then we set them free. I'll bet you've never seen a skinned rabbit run for its life. I can tell you it's like a bloody streak. The thing is, you don't blind them, although you do get a more interesting sight if you do. You'll see a screaming ball of flesh running amok. For a child, there was no more exciting sight in the world, it was our favorite entertainment.

My heart was hardened like that little by little. You can say cruelty has become a secret code in my life.

Uncle once caught a dog belonging to a Hakka family and told us to skin it alive. You have to know that skinning a dog alive isn't easy, especially around its mouth. If you muzzle it, you can't have a complete skin, but if you don't, it'll bite you. You have to be nimble, and use a bunch of techniques. Not even a profession furrier would have an easy time of it.

This was the training we received from Uncle during our childhood. After the Hakkas, he hated the Ma family the most. He said that what he wished for more than anything was the chance to skin a Ma offspring alive, so he could write an ancient sutra on the skin and make it into a book. Father was different; he did not think children should be responsible for their elders' actions. He even went to Ma shops to sing wooden fish songs, and he did not stop Mother from working at Ma's draft bank to earn a little extra money for daily necessities. He was opposed to Uncle's hatred and constantly repeated that enmity should be lessened not deepened. If revenge breeds revenge, when does it end? I think he must have been trying to blunt the hatred Uncle instilled in us.

Uncle had a cache of three human-skin books, behind each of which was a chilling story. I'll tell you about them when I'm in the mood. Uncle took one with him, and left one each to his son and Father. Father gave me his copy because he was averse to stories of murders. My copy had no sutra on it; instead, Uncle had engraved the names of family members who'd died during battles against the Hakkas. He was so good at it they looked like tattoos. I don't know if he'd tattooed the names before skinning the man or the other way around. I forgot to ask him, and he was dead by the time I thought about it. I later went down to the underworld to look for him; I even asked for help from deities hiding in people's ears, but they couldn't find him either. I don't know where he went, and his whereabouts remain an unanswered question.

Those books had a semi-transparent quality after the skin went through a special curing process. Strangely, though, the hair continued to grow on the book. I recall that it was bare when I was a kid, but later on I began to see stubble, which grew into a profusion of hair. It was prickly when I carried it next to my chest.

Then I discovered that something abnormal occurred any time the hair turned prickly, either I forgot my destiny, my life was in danger, or I encountered someone from the Ma family.

And later, alerted by the body hair, I was able to counteract the corrosion of the Kālacakra —I nearly became its captive.

Besides the hair, the book also reeked of the smell of blood. I don't know if it came with the book, since it had been around since the day I was born, but it nearly made me retch.

Uncle said that a blood bath was how you washed off the smell of blood. Only when my hands were covered in a Ma's blood, he said, would the smell disappear. And only through revenge and the offer of Ma's blood would the souls of those in our family who had died unjustly be delivered. Before that, they would just be ghosts of wrongful deaths. Sometimes, when it was really quiet at night, I actually heard them cry, sobbing pitifully, many of them. Uncle said that whoever could hear them cry was the one to avenge them.

From then on, I knew it was my destiny.

And much later, I realized that time, not a butcher's knife, was the best medium to exact a large-scale revenge. After the passage of decades, those who had slaughtered the locals were all dead, without my wielding a knife. Time used its knife to kill off all creatures who embraced desires.

I would really like to tell others about my discovery.

When a killer has finally found an even more lethal killer, he possesses an incredible sense of enlightenment.

Two. An Old Mouth

The dim candlelight flickers. I'm shivering from the cold.

It's already winter; I'm cold even though the city wall has blunted some of the wind.

I wish I could light a bonfire. Just thinking about a fire on an icy-cold desert warms me up. But I'm worried that the specters will be afraid of the fire. When I was a kid, Mother always had a fire going before our gate when Father returned from a long trip. She'd make him step over the fire, to burn off everything "unclean."

Sometimes for Liangzhou people, the "unclean" things were ghosts. When the children had a headache or a fever, the adults would say "something unclean was following them," and they'd burn a few pieces of paper or circle the air above their heads with a lit oil lamp to frighten it away.

I didn't dare light a fire at first, even though I was freezing, for I didn't want the fire to alarm the specters. That was my initial concern, of course, because I didn't know at the time that some ghosts aren't afraid of fire, especially the aged ones. The average ghost is intimidated by the flames, but not the embers. When I was a kid, I actually saw ghosts crouching to warm themselves like monkeys at a fire people left behind.

As I'm lost in thought under the flickering light, I suddenly detect the smell of tobacco and follow it to see an old man squatting like a monkey. He was the first one during that interview to willingly show his face at the time. The others I encountered at first were merely coronas of light or air. They had strong functionality, but their shapes were indistinct. Later I was able to see their features from that earlier time.

The old man wheezes, as if he has asthma, but that's just how I feel—

1

I'm an old camel driver. If you count back carefully, you and I are related. Liangzhou residents call people who are related "dang jiazi," meaning we're almost family. Your grandfather called me "Old Grandpa" when he was little. At the time, I wasn't that old, but my mouth was so big some pesky kids nicknamed me Big Mouth Grandpa behind my back. If they had a fight with kids in my family, they'd drop Grandpa and just call out in a singsong voice, "Big Mouth—Big Mouth—" To Liangzhou kids, it was intolerable that someone should call their father by his name or nickname.

Back then I often sat by the base of a wall to tell the kids stories about the camel trail. I remember that the ruts created by camel feet along Baosui Road were less than a *cun* deep, when I first took up the profession. But when I got old, the spongy feet had worn down the stone slabs by more than five *cun*. How many trampling camel feet did it endure!

I was in my early twenties when I entered Wild Fox Ridge. The drivers naturally didn't call me "Grandpa." I was just Big Mouth to them.

I used to be called Zhang Yaole. A fortuneteller said I'd be a killer and then be killed. My father was worried sick about me until he had a profound understanding of the "truth of suffering" in the four noble truths of Buddhist teaching, and named me "Wule," without happiness, as an interpretation of the notion that "all worries bring suffering."

As a result, I had a childhood without happiness. I kept encountering inauspicious occurrences when I grazed sheep or camels for the steward. And the wolves in the desert never forgot me; they kept coming to take a lamb now and then or drag out a camel's guts. I tasted the landlord's whip every time. One day I heard Young Master Ma—Ma Zaibo, that is— reciting a sutra, and the beautiful melody kept pounding against my heart. Young Master Ma was always saying that suffering and happiness were nothing but manifestations of the heart. Little by little, I stopped suffering. The reason for that was my discovery that there were life forms who suffered more than I did. Such as camels. They had to carry a load of two hundred *jin* or more as much as several dozen *li*. That's suffering, don't you think? Or a donkey, turning a millstone around and around from the time it's little till it's an old donkey. Hard, wouldn't you say? And there's an old ox, tilling the land and pulling a stone roller all its life. When it's old, it gets the knife. Now that's suffering.

There are more, but you'll have to find them out for yourself.

With all these examples, I finally realized that I wasn't suffering, so I changed my name to Yaole, to have happiness. Ever since then, whenever I'm free, I sneak in something to be happy about. I was pleasantly surprised that a new name did bring me happiness. I saw so many things to make me happy—a cool breeze, birds singing, lush mountains, emerald green rivers, all to be happy about.

One day I noticed a fire raging somewhere in the desert. Its flames shot into the sky. But I didn't see a thing once I got there. So I started digging at the spot and unearthed a metal griddle that contained a pile of oxcart chains—the metal strips on the cart axle. They were made of copper, so I took them home and gave them to the landlord. He was jubilant. I didn't know they were gold ingots. He started treating me well after that, and switched me to herding camels instead of sheep. I heard he got very rich after I gave him the gold, but his offspring suffered because of it, designated as landlords to suffer at struggle sessions for over a decade.

I'm getting ahead of myself. Let me continue with the idea of happiness. At the time, I even forgot what the fortuneteller had said about my fate. I didn't believe a happy man like me could ever kill.

I didn't believe a word of it.

2

When it first set out, no one could have predicted the disaster that would befall the caravan.

I did not, and could not know that we would run into a calamity that destructive.

Don't ask me if I knew, I can't tell you. But to be honest, it did occur to me. Not because I could see into the future, though. I just knew that the weather was unpredictable and that something unexpected could happen at any moment. Things are never clear, so it's really hard to tell. Nothing in the world is more significant than life and death, which is determined by a single breath. If you breathe in but don't breathe out, then you're bound for another world. I've been through a lot of changes in life. Have you ever heard that a poplar has three thousand years of memories? Standing in the desert, it lives a thousand years; when it dies, it remains standing another thousand years, and when it finally falls to the ground, it doesn't decay for another thousand years. I haven't lived as long as a poplar, but you can't tell how many lifetimes I've had or how many cycles of transmigration I've gone through. No one has a clear idea of how many thousands of years he has traveled in the tunnel of transmigration. I've experienced a great deal. I found that those who want to laugh ended up crying, and those who want to go east go west. What started as one thing turns into something else. I can't give you an answer if you want to know if I'd had a sense of the subsequent disaster. I'm not a prophet, but every time we set out, I knew some of the camel drivers would be a pile of bones on the camel trail. Haven't you seen all the bones along Baosui Road? Even the limestone surface is worn down a *chi* or more. Generations of camel drivers have been lost on the limestone. Wooden Fish Girl said she didn't believe me, that she was dubious that many thousands of camels could travel in such a deep trough. She can believe it or not, but all camel drivers know.

Every time when we left, I wondered if I'd still be alive the next spring, when the camels are let out to graze. I couldn't stop wondering, and was still thinking about it even when we got on Baosui Road. Besides, on this trip, we were going to a place a lot farther than Baosui Road. Well, that would go beyond the heart, so who could have predicted what dangers awaited along the way?

I'd better start with the time we set out.

With the arrival of Autumn, the camel farms get busy. You know that when the camels return in the spring, it's called returning to the farm, and when they leave in the fall, it's called setting out. Setting out is a major event, the reason for herders to raise camels. Only when you set out do you get paid for transporting goods. You'd have to drink the wind if you stayed home. That is why autumn is the busiest time for camel farms. You should never underestimate a camel farm, as that was where the Ma family fortune got its start. Based on your current usage, you can say that the Ma's primitive accumulation was accomplished by their camel caravans. Herds of camels that died of exhaustion built up their enormous wealth, the tea shop would come later. Without the caravan, there would be no Ma family. For over a hundred years, the caravans supported the

Ma family's vast business and brought them prestige. Whenever someone mentioned the Ma family, they'd say, Ai-yo, what's there to say? They've got three hundred white camels.

Ever seen a white camel? With hair like snow, they cut an impressive figure. They are the most valued camels, one in a hundred. And the Ma family owned three hundred of them. When the Eight Nation Alliance attacked Beijing and the Empress Dowager fled to Xi'an, the Ma family sent three hundred white camels to transport provisions. You can see how powerful they were.

I've worked as a camel driver, been a clerk at a draft bank, once ran a camel farm. In those days, it was usually a seasoned camel driver who ran a camel farm. When you're old, you're worse than a piss ant; you can't fart without shitting your pants. You spew more words than there are lice and fleas, and you wet your shoes when you pee. When you're old, you're old; there's nothing you can do about it. When you're too old to wear heavy shoes, you have to work on a farm. To be sure, not every driver can hang on to work on a camel farm when he's old; some die before they get there. Even fish die from crashing waves. It's his good fortune for a camel driver to perish on the camel trail. Later, I began to envy those who died that way, because I didn't work many years on the farm before a different "hat" was clapped on my head: a member of one of the despised "four elements." I lived under the label for years and was depressed most of the time. When I think back now, it was sort of like walking on a rock-strewn gobi at night—the endless kind, of course.

But I kept busy on the farm. There was so much to do when fall arrived, things like animal fattening, that is, feeding the camels with nutritious food to build up a storehouse of fat in their humps. Without it, a camel can't travel, and if it barely manages to survive the perils of winter, it won't make it through the scarcity of spring.

The camels return to the farm in the spring, exhausted after months of hard work. You've probably seen a tired camel. Its humps droop, like the breasts of a sickly women who's nursed three dozen babies. When it walks, it looks like a jaundiced monkey or a donkey that's been overworked at the mill, or a listless man in early spring or early fall. At a time like that, it can barely support itself, let alone carry anything on its back. But by then the grass has sprouted and the water is fresh, so the drivers let the camels rest and return them to the farm, where they graze through the spring and summer. They can eat to their hearts' content, chewing the tender grass into a green liquid, gnawing dry kindling to bits. They get plenty of nutrients that grow into fat, and they leave their waste on the farm.

In a word, it's time for them to rest and eat until their bellies are full.

Humps that looked like old women's breasts slowly change until they perk up, fuller than those of a young girl. Then the male camels start getting ideas. A man thinks about sex when he's full and warm, so do camels. The males' eyes turn red, like young men in later days who watched porno videos, and their lips flap at high speed until they're foaming at the mouth. They grunt as they chew their lips, the sound as hard on the ear as a red-hot poker—right, it's a kind of drawn-out, lusty sort of thing. Their eyes shine bright, with a lecherous look, and you know what they're looking for. Actually, they don't have to look far, because sometimes female camels in heat will come looking for them to have their seed planted in their wombs. Naturally, these are mature camels, those that have had offspring already; they're so experienced that giving birth is easier than taking a leak. They won't actually throw themselves at the males, but once a male bites her leg—you can compare this with humans kissing—the females will take the cue to lie down docilely and raise their tails for the males. See, that's how all those baby camels are born. The Baosui limestone trail has worn out generations of camels, but the females' wombs stubbornly give birth to generations more.

But young females are different. They're like virgins in the human world, and the hardest to take care of at the farm, though male camels like them best. Think about it, even an animal prefers a virgin. That's really weird. But it is what it is—an animal's nature is out with the old and in with the new. Young female camels are too inexperienced to know there's something better than fresh water and lush grass. They freeze when they see a young male, its mouth covered in white foam, coming at them; leg biting that is the human equivalent of kissing feels like a battle to them. They're also afraid of the powerful body of a young male, like Yellow Demon. It certainly isn't light. So, a young female will run away. There's enough room at the farm for her to run. The male gives chase, which you'd think was all about its desire to mate, but it's also a form of training. A young male builds up stamina by chasing after a female. They're always the strongest in a caravan, and I'm curious to know if it may not have something to do with chasing a female.

You see, a young male will eventually catch up with a young female, bite her hind leg, pull her down to the ground, and mount her. At that moment, her tail serves as her last line of defense, for a female like that won't let the male get his way too easily. I usually walk up and pat the female, telling her not to be shy. It's time for her to have babies. I pull the tail away and put the male's throbbing organ where it belonged.

Camels, like humans, need to procreate.

Sometimes some male camels will fail to find a rape target; their organs have an angry look, but they cannot find any female after searching around, so they're reduced to hitting it against their own belly. It won't take long for it to splatter the ground with white sticky stuff, which should be taken seriously, because it's part of what builds the fat. Once or twice is fine, but its hump will collapse if it does it a hundred times. Then I have to take a rope and tie a knot around the playful organ to stop its owner from wasting energy.

My job at the camel farm was to help the females get pregnant.

Every day I made a round of the farm with my eyes wide open. When I saw a camel looking tired, I put it in a separate stall from others. When I saw a male pull a female to the ground, I ran over to move the tail aside for him to carry out his mission successfully. Without my help, some of the impatient ones would rub against the female's crotch and spew the treasure all over. Now, that's a waste.

In the fall, when the frost hasn't yet killed off the last sign of life, and desert plants, pea shrubs, and needle grass still retain a hint of green; the camels are in a frenzy chewing on the signs of life on plants that in turn stubbornly send forward new vitality for them. Just like that Sisyphus you're always talking about, these plants carry out their own destiny in the cycles of transmigration.

The same goes for camel drivers.

The thousand-year-old camel trail wore away countless young men, turning them into piles of bleached bones, but group after group of men still followed in their footsteps. Heaven might be changeable; it can do what it wants. But they have their ways to deal with it. Their ancestors eked out a living in that tiny corner of the desert for generations, didn't they?

I could almost physically feel the great changes. I never stopped seeing piles of bones on the trail and on the farm, some human, some camel, but it didn't matter which. They were just bones, left behind by the Angel of Death. The most jarring were the skulls; the dark holes where the eyes used to be seemed to be asking questions, inquiring after their fate. But I know they weren't anywhere close to an answer, no matter how they asked.

Later, when Wooden Fish Girl arrived in the West, sometimes she visited the camel farm, where she laughed and pointed, looking at a young camel chasing after a female. That girl had no shame. The local girls would cover their faces when they saw that sight, acting shy, but not her. She was always clamoring for me to help the camel out. I ran so fast I could always catch up. By the time an impatient male was about to spew its seed from all the rubbing, I'd be yanking the female's tail away. The male was barely in when we heard the angry grunts from the female and the happy shouts from the male.

I helped many female camels through the process before they became mothers.

3

On the day we set out, the moon was wearing a halo, which was common in those days. A sandstorm was all but assured when that happened; there was nothing we could do, so we endured it. When the wind blew, it was like your mother getting married again, unstoppable, so you let it happen. I was surprised to find, I recall, a wooden fish twirling in the moon's halo, like two millstones put together. Later the twirling wooden fish repeatedly appeared above the village, and after that, you people changed the thing's name, calling it a flying saucer. In fact, it wasn't a saucer; it was two millstones. To the villagers, a millstone is an enormous object they call a white tiger. Every house has something heavy, maybe a millstone, at the corner of a wall as a symbolic anchor.

Finally, someone noticed the twirling millstones in the halo.

"Oh, no, a white tiger!" Cai Wu cried out.

Everyone said it was a good sign.

But I wasn't so sure, because I saw rays of light shooting out from the millstones; they looked blood-red to me. I asked someone, but he said he didn't see any. It wasn't until later that I realized it was blood shed by the drivers.

It was my first time seeing something like that before setting out, which had always been on an auspicious day. There wouldn't be any bad omens on days like that, since the felicitous deities would never let the demons have their way.

But Feiqing treated the millstones as a good sign. "Millstones are great," he said. "They're big, heavy things that can anchor everything securely." He believed the profits would be great this time; that is, we'd make lots of money.

Later I learned the back story behind our trip. Someone had paid not only for the transport, but for the camels too. So, if we lost any of them on the way, the loss would be his, but if the camels survived, the camel farmers would earn extra.

I'd never met a client like that; no wonder even the Mongolian caravan wanted the job.

I knew that he was aware of the countless dangers lurking along the way, a new route no one had traveled before. I had no idea how long it would take. You know that we traveled day and night, but the destination seemed forever beyond reach.

It felt to me in a way that the twirling wooden fish in the halo were hinting at something, but, unfortunately, I was unaware of what it could mean at the time. When we finally understood, it was too late.

I echoed Feiqing's tone of voice: "Yes, it's a good sign." I'd heard from the elders about the importance of initial reactions, which must not be undermined. On many occasions, what one says can determine the direction of fortune.

Yet my positive response did nothing to avert the calamity that occurred.

To reassure myself, I took along a protective talisman passed down from my ancestors. It was a wooden fish made of scented rosewood from Hainan. When you struck it, the sound seemed to dance in your heart. Why did my ancestors use a wooden fish as an amulet? I don't know.

The ancestors are all dead; they were humans when alive and deities after death, and we mortals are not privy to the private activities of these deities. I took it along even though I had no idea why they'd chosen a wooden fish.

Later, I figured out that the twirling object in the air appeared in different forms to different people; some thought it was millstones, while others saw it as a wooden fish. I don't understand why; what were the mysterious causes behind it?

What I wanted to tell you was, the three eccentrics showed up again before we left.

Those three old men made frequent appearances in our village in those days. Everyone said they were crazy, and they sure looked it. Our village had seen its fair share of crazy people. They were in rags, which wasn't unusual, since no one had anything decent to wear back then. What stood out about them were the strange props they brought along: the first one shouldered a pole, the front end carrying a straw hat and the back a millstone. The pole was perfectly balanced even though one end was so much heavier than the other. The second man held a pestle, which he smashed down in a mortar, and the third one had a long pole with a persimmon hanging in front him.

That's about it.

They walked along and shouted:

"All even. It's all even."

"Stone on stone. Stone on stone."

"A persimmon in front. A persimmon in front."

No one had any idea what they meant, me included.

It was too late by the time I figured it out.

4

As we left Liangzhou, a strange sensation welled up inside me, for I realized I was walking into a giant unknown, like a skiff being tossed about in the ocean.

It was new to me.

I'd been a camel farmer for many years, and I'd always felt as happy as a fish in water every time I left on one of these trips. My father once said I was born to be a camel farmer. Endowed with impressive strength, I could easily lift a litter that weighed two hundred and forty jin at the age of sixteen. Being the restless type, I'd longed for the life of a camel farmer since I was little. I'd worked with four senior drivers. I'd never been one myself, but not because I couldn't, I didn't want to. A driver's authority was awesome. He could choose where to stay, and wherever he ended up, the women there would fawn all over him to get on his good side. Sure, I envied the feeling of having warm soft flesh in my arms, but I knew that with pleasure worries often follow. I wasn't a driver, but no driver could survive without me. I knew how to read animal tracks and I never got lost, no matter how big the desert or how deep into it we'd traveled. I could rattle off all the stops along Baosui Road with my eyes shut; I knew where to find fresh water and lush grass, the areas frequented by desert outlaws, the spots where wandering ghosts caused trouble, which inn could be dangerous, and which woman was an outlaw's informer. All these should not be underrated, for there are traps everywhere on a long camel trail. If you aren't careful, you'll fall into one and turn into a ghost.

I'd never had that sensation before.

I wondered if Ma Zaibo felt the same. I didn't know why he sold his farm and came on the trip with us. Did he want to settle down in the Russian area? On the other hand, we weren't told we'd be heading into the Russian area when we left Liangzhou. Our ancestors called the place Luocha or Eluosi, something like that. I didn't know where Luocha was, except that it was to the west, farther and farther west. I was told that Feiqing had a map that marked the route, but I never laid eyes on it.

The camel bells clanged, but they portended neither good nor ill. I once was able to tell from the sounds of the bells. When I heard what sounded like "fortune! fortune!" we'd surely strike it rich, and you couldn't stop that from happening. If I heard something like "crumble! crumble!" then it was hard to say what would happen. We might run into outlaws or soldiers, or the market would slump. It was hard to say, in any case. I couldn't tell what we'd encounter this time, I didn't hear "fortune" and I didn't hear "crumble." More like a miasma, actually. I was curious to know if the bells were ringing the same strange way on the Mongolian caravan that was setting out from the other side of the desert.

Twenty camel drivers went on this trip. The transport fee was high, so the Mongolian and Chinese vied to take the job. Afraid of antagonizing either one, the party involved decided to hire ten from each side and each driver would be in charge of eleven camels. The two caravans agreed to meet at a certain spot three days after departure.

The Mongolian caravan was as well-known as the Ma family's, and they had a long history of antagonism, for neither was willing to give in to the other. Later, when I thought it over, I had to wonder if the outcome would have been different if the Mongolian caravan hadn't been involved. But there are so many things that are beyond conjecture. You only live once and you can't start over, so when it's done it's done. The affairs of this world can't always be explained clearly.

What concerned me was the issue of provisions when the two caravans set out together. It was a mighty doubled caravan, a chorus of bells, and we had a dozen marksmen, so small-time outlaws wouldn't get any ideas. But it wouldn't be easy finding an oasis that could provide enough water and grass for several hundred camels. You always read about a chorus of bells in books, but that's only in books. In fact, the fewer drivers the better when traveling down a camel trail, for there will be no problem with water and grass. It was beyond me why the client wanted to use so many camels. I'd like to know what the man was like who could afford to pay for several hundred loads of goods.

But the drivers were the ones who had to worry about provisions. Where there's a cart there's a road, a road opens up when the cart reaches the mountains. Worst case, we'd divide the caravans into several groups. They would stay together at spots with enough water and grass and disperse when there was less to eat and drink. One must be flexible. You can't die from holding back urinating, can you?

As usual, I put on my heavy shoes, which I did all the time. Taking long reins and wearing heavy shoes are what a camel farmer does. Everyone knows about taking the long reins, but few have any idea what wearing heavy shoes is all about. I bet you're not aware that camel drivers in those days weren't allowed to ride their camels. The animals were meant to carry goods, and the drivers had to keep up with them no matter how fast they walked. The sick ones were exceptions. We wore heavy shoes when we traveled. They were made of donkey pelts at first, but cowhide was then used to patch worn spots, layer upon layer, over and over, until it was absolutely solid and absolutely clunky and unsightly. How heavy were they? Hard to say; it depended on their age, some lighter and some heavier, but usually at least five *jin*. Our ancestors said heavy shoes could prevent blisters on your feet, which might make sense, but I preferred to take it as a form of training. Just think, if you're in a pair of shoes that heavy in all seasons and in whatever you do, wouldn't your legs grow strong and powerful after a long time? I wore them even when I was back working on the camel farm. Maybe I was born to do that.

To me everything is tied up with fate. I was born to wear heavy shoes, and I wouldn't know how to walk in lighter ones.

Generations of camel farmers wore heavy shoes like that, and we measured tens of thousands of *li* as we walked. Except this time the trail seemed too long. People say the sun is closer than Chang'an, but there are places farther than that, like Beijing, Tianjin, plus that place beyond the horizon, Luocha, where the Russians live. That was so far, it hardly existed, I thought.

Fear gripped me at first, when I thought about a destination as far off as the horizon. Later, Father told me that camel farmers never think about destinations, they only worry about the next stop. On the first day, they set their eyes on Baigeda, the second day Duqingshan, the third day Hongshagang . . . They walk on day after day, passing one stop after another, and that is how they take measure of a trip of tens of thousands of *li*.

I often think about the trails I've walked, and it amazes me each time, until I hit upon a concept: our legs last longer than the road. We are born to walk far. Once we set our mind on a goal, we walk toward it one step at a time, and eventually we reach a destination as far as the horizon. That was how the white dragon-horse carried Tripitaka, the renowned monk of the Tang dynasty, to the West. Compare that with people in Liangzhou who walk every day too, but they just make circles, like a donkey in a mill. They turn round and round all their lives, but never manage to move beyond a palm-size area. Like them, I walked day after day, but I had a goal, so I made a path for my life's trajectory.

On that afternoon, I did feel like I was walking alone on the endless camel trail. I was surrounded by other camel farmers, but I had the feeling that there was no one around and desolation as far as I could see. I didn't know why.

The camel bells clanged away, loud and monotonous. I didn't know where we were going, nor where I'd end up. But I did know I must keep going.

For I was born to walk, and walk I must, no matter what road lay ahead.

And that was my destiny.

Three. Eyes of a Killer

1

I saw the caravans stop.

It was time for the camels to relieve themselves. After traveling five *li* they needed to stop for their first break. It was critical for them to urinate. Drivers often said that letting the blood of their feet was more important than shoeing them, and letting them urinate frequently was more important than letting the blood.

Let me start with shoeing. Camels must be shod each time before the caravan sets out. It's like shoeing a donkey or a horse. But you know that horse hooves are hard as rocks, so before shoeing, you have to put the horse hooves on a wooden bench to file them, trim off the worn parts, and hammer the nails in to fasten them on the shoes. You can't do that with camel feet, because they're soft. You need to cut a piece of cow hide about the same size as a foot and sew it on with an awl and hemp thread. Naturally, the best of the new pads are those from a dead camel.

The drivers pampered their camels by sewing the pads on, letting the blood, and letting them urinate, the last of which is most critical.

I saw the camels relieving themselves, which they did intermittently, maybe because they knew all too well that water was precious. Certainly, it could also be due to its unique physiological structure, for the urine slowly seeped out of its urethra to drip into the sand, then stopped before starting again, and so on.

It takes about the time to smoke a pipeful for the camel to finish the job. One driver, a heavy smoker, took the opportunity to enjoy a pipeful. He was addicted to his pipe, and the other camel farmers called him Chain Smoker. I realized he was looking at me with a questioning gaze. He surely did not know the heavenly secrets, which must not be revealed. I heard that heaven would punish whoever revealed those secrets. The question was, who cared about celestial repercussions when the sky was about to fall?

Hu Gala, a Daoist priest, discovered the outcome one night. He was adept at Kālacakra, for he had studied with a lama between the ages of twenty and thirty. You probably haven't heard about the Kālacakra, and surely wouldn't know a thing about the Kālacakravajra. Let me tell you, the Doctrine of Kālacakravajra is the way to reach Buddhahood. I don't harbor any expectations to become a Buddha, but I study the Doctrine anyway. It took me several years to learn most of Hu Gala's expertise. In any case, I've never failed, not since I mastered the theory.

But don't confuse Hu Gala with run-of-the-mill fortunetellers. You can't. Some of them might well be charlatans, but not him. Hu is an expert in Kālacakra. He has predicted over a dozen lunar eclipses over several decades and was never wrong. I can understand it if you're dubious, but I'm a believer, because I, too, have predicted several eclipses, lunar and solar, using his method. It's like fish know the temperature of the water they're in. I know Hu's skills are the real deal.

A month before they set out, I did a divination and concluded that a comet would hit the earth one day a few months later. I still recall how my hair stood on end at that moment, for I knew what it signified. Unsure if I had got it wrong, I repeated the process a few more times, all with the same result. To verify what I'd found, I went to the Su Wu Temple, where, before I even opened my mouth, Hu Gala gave me a letter in which he confirmed my prediction.

Those were the circumstances when I got on the road.

I plan to finish what fate wants me to do during the time I have left. It has weighed me down for years and wakes me late at night, when all is quiet. The earth and the human race will turn to ashes one day years into the future, but I don't want to meet my parents as an unworthy child.

I have my eyes set on Ma Zaibo, to whom I have a complex emotional reaction. I wish he weren't from the Ma family; I wish Lü Erye didn't care so much for him; I wish his death wouldn't cause Lü Erye lots of pain; I wish nothing had happened in the earlier days. But seeing these "wishes" come true is unlikely. Don't waste your time, because that's what fate is, and also what life is.

Look, he just stuck his lean face out the window of his sedan chair to watch the camels urinate. When I lay my eyes on him, I have to keep reminding myself that he's my enemy. He's my enemy. If not, I could hardly bring myself to hate him.

The camels are peeing, first a line, then drops.

I've yet to see another animal pee like that. Are they savoring the sensation? Camels are really interesting creatures. Like humans tasting the tea in their mouths, the camels are appreciating the process of urination.

Ma Zaibo's face is pale. Is the pampered young master of the Ma family having trouble enduring the long, bumpy ride?

He's likely unaware that he'll soon become a wandering ghost.

But on second thought, once the comet comes, everything will turn to ashes, whether he stayed behind or not.

Because of my prediction, I've been wondering if it's still necessary to carry out the task entrusted by Uncle.

He made me swear that, during my lifetime, I would take the head of a Ma family relative and use the blood as a sacrifice to our ancestral tablets.

I picked Ma Zaibo.

I picked him because of something else too; I'll tell you about it later. If it hadn't been for that, I would definitely have chosen someone other than him.

2

I learned about the tragic, gruesome event from the stories Uncle told. Father rarely said a word about it, as he didn't want our hearts to be immersed in hatred. He was always avoiding the past, trying to occupy his mind with other things to crowd out the wretched memories of his life.

Regarding hatred, I don't know who's right, Father or Uncle.

What Father wanted to forget and Uncle frequently brought up is a major historical event known as the battle between the locals and the Hakka outsiders. Grandpa died during the battle, along with thousands of others. At the time, the locals slaughtered many Hakkas, who in turned murdered a great number of locals. The bloody conflict lasted years and, I heard, eventually took over a million lives.

Later Uncle and Father managed to survive by fleeing into the mountains. Grandpa's open eyes kept flashing in Father's mind, though he knew that Grandpa had died without eyes. He and several hundred locals were tied up, like bundles of rice stalks, and laid out on the threshing ground, where the enemies borrowed horses from the government to flatten them all into meat patties with stone rollers.

As blood spewed and splattered, Grandpa had shouted, Revenge! The single shout had sounded in Uncle's life for years. Later, every spring, on Tomb Sweeping Day, he would gather us to retell the story and make us take a vow.

Those who ordered the stone rollers had a backer, a general, who had close ties to the Ma family. They donated a hundred thousand taels for troop provisions, so he sent his soldiers. Without the money, there'd have been fewer dead locals.

Uncle blamed the Ma family.

Uncle sought revenge for the rest of his life. Over and over he sneaked into the Ma's house to kill someone, but was captured and released each time. The Ma people said the money was to help the general repair a fortress, and it had nothing to do with his dispatch of soldiers. Uncle didn't believe them. "No matter what, the commander wouldn't have sent the soldiers without the money," he told us. "And without the soldiers, your grandpa would have lived."

Uncle didn't make it into the Ma's house after a while, because everyone knew he was an enemy of the family. When he neared their fortress, husky men would lunge at him and drive him far away.

Later Uncle made us swear a vow to our ancestors, promising to kill one person from the Ma family to avenge them. "Only using the blood of a Ma family member as a sacrificial offering to the ancestors will the souls of wrongful deaths be delivered." So after that, I carried a red wrapper with me wherever I went. In it was an ancestral tablet Uncle had made; he and several close family members had pricked their fingers to smear blood on the wood and infuse the tablet with spirituality.

But there are lots of people who think the Ma family is just fine. They can list the good deeds they've performed. I've lived all these years conflicted and uncertain. Other things happened later—I won't go into them now. But then, based on the Kālacakra, Ma Zaibo would not make it out of Wild Fox Ridge alive, even if I spared him. So why not let me kill him and fulfill the vow I made?

I've got my eye on Ma Zaibo.

I plan to kill him at Wild Fox Ridge.

3

The camels are urinating again.

"What animal pees like that?" I say. "A drop at a time, more like leaking."

"It's not a big deal," Feiqing says. "They know how precious water is, so they don't dare let it all out. Squeeze a drop out and check how it feels. Then squeeze out another drop and check again. Once they're comfortable, they won't waste another drop."

"Not at all," Lu Fuji responds. "It's because their bladders are shut so tight they can't just pee all they want."

Water drips from under the camels' bellies, and rings of wetness slowly spread on the sand. The drivers take the opportunity to check the camels' feet. It's a part of the process. Sometimes they pick up thorns or sharp pebbles. The drivers pluck them out one by one, eleven camels per driver. Once the inspection is done, they lie down on the sand to smoke their pipes.

The camels take a long time to pee, long enough for the drivers to finish smoking a pipe.

"When the camels pee, the drivers get to sleep," Feiqing says. They've just set out, so the drivers want the camels to rest more.

"Let's go," I say. "We'll never get there at this pace."

"We've barely started, and you're already getting impatient." Lu Fuji says with a laugh. "The trip will take decades, so you can celebrate your sixtieth birthday when we get there."

"I don't want to live that long," I respond with a laugh. "I'll be so ugly, with wrinkles and white hair."

I glance at the litter on Ma Zaibo's camel. The curtain is down.

What is he thinking?

Can he feel the murderous aura coming at him?

Four. Feiqing

Feiqing appears, accompanied by the sound of a horse neighing and a few coronae. Could he have actually become a local temple god? The coronae stay outside the barrier. In the dark night, they look agitated as they drift here and there.

Of all the people I interview, Feiqing is my favorite. I feel indescribable excitement when he tells his story. I'd be honored if he were me in my previous lifetime. But I can only choose my future, not my past. I'm sure I wouldn't be able to do what he did, because I'm absolutely sure the violence he worshipped had little effect. I've felt nothing but changes in my life; everything is undergoing constant change, and everything is mutable. I will never waste my life on meaningless things. I would never choose to be him, even if I could start my life over.

On the other hand, what we like in this lifetime doesn't necessarily correspond to our previous life; maybe I think this way now precisely because of what I've been through in the previous life.

I want to ask him about it, but I know sometimes mouthing off can ruin a good conversation.

1

I'll pick up where you left off to keep the story straight. Too many details and too much complexity to the journey, like a tangled skein. In the meantime, I've never experienced anything so unforgettable as the trip to Wild Fox Ridge. For you it was a life-and-death voyage, for me too. I did manage to escape from being buried alive in the sand, but I've failed to overturn my fate, haven't I? If I'd been born to have my head chopped off, then I wouldn't have the good fortune to be buried in the desert.

Years have passed, but I still clearly remember what happened along the way, for, after all, it truly was a life-and-death voyage, no matter how you look at it.

I'll start with the first time we stopped for the camels to relieve themselves.

I remember that Chain Smoker rolled up his tobacco pouch after the camels finished.

The time it took him to smoke a pipeful determined how long we stopped for the camels. He was a smart old man, shrewd as can be, the one I admired most. He was so addicted to his pipe he let the smoke swirl in his lungs for a long time before reluctantly blowing it out. In as a thick plume, out as nearly invisible vapor. Camel drivers are all pipe smokers, the smell of tobacco serving as a kind of insect repellant, but none of these were as addicted as he was. There was a pungent tobacco smell around him at all times. After traveling down Baosui Road for three decades, he was said to have smoked enough tobacco to pave the road. He was too old to handle a camel litter, but I was hoping he'd make the trip. He knew the camel trails like the back of his hand, and he had an intimate knowledge of where we could find the best grass and water, where Tong members would lurk, and which campsite had poisonous insects. He'd been to Luocha, so he knew some Russian; he was a special talent, someone you wouldn't find easily if you searched with a lantern, as we say.

I heard that he didn't smoke when he started out as a driver. One night a snake slithered into his bed and treated his rear end as the entrance to its pit, so he became a smoker for the next four decades. He was well known for his addiction. When anyone mentioned Chain Smoker on the trail, the camel farmers would say, "Hell yes, we know who he is. The old guy who smokes a lot."

I remember the sun rose up over the sand dunes to the west shortly after we started out after the first break. It was late autumn. The grass was frosted over, and the camels would have gotten diarrhea if they'd eaten it. You know the last thing you want on long distance transport is for your camels to suffer from diarrhea. As the saying goes, If you're big and strong, you don't run; the same for camels. Diarrhea causes a camel to lose its fat, and it will be too weak to carry its load. You know a camel usually carries a load of two hundred and forty *jin*. If one has diarrhea, its load has to be shared by others, and that's a problem. The drivers usually travel at night so the camels can graze during the day; they don't mind a bit of suffering, so long as their camels can get to good grass and water in the daytime. It's imperative for a driver to pamper his camels. When traveling a long distance, they shoulder all the hardships and avoid adding unnecessary exertion by their animals.

We set out two hours earlier that day to get a good start. According to our elders, if we rested too long on the first day, the schedule for the rest of the trip would be too tight. We'd traveled five *li* when the sun decided to pack up and go home. That's the most enchanting moment in the desert. I remember there were no fiery clouds, and the setting sun was pale and dim, giving off little light as it hung above the dunes, looking lonely and scrawny. Against the rays of the sun, Artemisia, bunchgrass, cacti, and buckthorns were jet black, as if cast in iron. Their branches spread out in all directions, tattooing the monotonous desert and adding signs of vitality. The creased, shaded slopes also looked stained in ink. The desert resembled a large, freehand painting.

Listen to me. I'm always talking about painting. I've liked to paint since I was a child. Hu Gala said I was a painter in my previous life. I enjoyed it when I was attending a private village school. One day the Master—that's what you call the teacher—saw me doing it and punished me by making me paint a hundred figures, all with different expressions. So, I did. I painted and wrote on them, and they turned out to be worth a lot. You don't believe me? Go to the Confucius Temple in Liangzhou and see for yourself; they've got some of my works there.

You might not know it, but paintings and calligraphy to me are always just trivial playthings. Anyone who's content with composition on a foot-long scroll is an ordinary man. A man of character treats the world as his canvas in order to create a brand-new design. This is probably not something you want to hear, but I can't help it. It's the way I was born. Liangzhou people say I was born to be undependable, destined to stir up trouble and cause destruction. Otherwise, I wouldn't have lost my head.

Want me to continue?

On that afternoon, as the sun set, a white fog-like steam rose above the sand dunes. The misty hills looked unreal, like a dream. Packs of camels walked in that dream; their bells had a high, distant ring to them, and their silhouettes towered in tranquility. A desert wind blew over to ruffle the hair under the chins, making it and the heart quiver with a frisson. On many afternoons, I was moved by the unique beauty of camels walking down a desert trail, so much so that I felt its impact on my soul. Time and again I felt that I might as well be walking out of the Tang dynasty toward eternity amid the clanging camel bells.

Lu Fuji opened his mouth to bellow out a song, in his yak-like voice—

Lead camels, up at dawn, walk to the second stop.
Abandon children, leave brothers, I suffer all kinds of hardship.
Take a look. This is the life of a camel driver,
No way to make a living . . .

"No way to make a living." Qi Lu and the others howled like wolves.

Night sneaked up to envelope us and cloak the earth, as the camel bells rang.

2

We stopped the second time for the camels to pee after we'd traveled thirteen *li*. Now you know how important it is for the camels. Some of the second-rate drivers only knew to work their camels without letting them relieve themselves, and ruined their animals that way. We say to let them pee, but I'm sure it's also meant for them to take a break. One year four Liangzhou porters carried salt from Zhenfan to Wuwei. They walked fast, like the wind, and when they got to Erba, two of them were panting like cows and dropped dead. The other two split the loads of salt, convinced that they had made out like outlaws, raced back home. To their surprise, they didn't go far before they too were panting like cows and dropped dead. Their bodies were left on the road for days, stinking up the area and drawing swarms of greenbottles. In the end, Ma Siye put up the money to bury them.

What I'm saying is, the four men died of exhaustion. Like they say, their minds were willing, but their bodies were weak. You'll die like that if you don't take good care of yourself. The same goes for camels, so, besides letting the camels relieve themselves, the constant stops actually mean for them to rest, not to be overworked. You see?

The camels peed three times between stops, once at five *li*, once at eight, and a third time at a dozen or so *li*. But not long after that, we sped up to reach the next stop.

The first stop was forty or fifty *li*.

We made over a hundred stops altogether. Do you know how far it is from Liangzhou to Wild Fox Ridge?

The sky turned into a giant black pot when we stopped the second time. All was quiet around us, except for the camel bells. The camels' feet were supple and made a soft rustling sound as they walked across the sand. In the quiet night the bells sounded almost deafening, overwhelming the noise underfoot. There was nothing between heaven and earth but the tingling camel bells, though occasionally a camel snorted or some things came loose and banged against one another on their backs. We heard a wolf howl once in a while too, but at least ten *li* away. Ordinarily a wolf pack doesn't dare attack a camel caravan, but sometimes when hungry, wily sneaky wolves will tail from a distance, their eyes on the baby camels traveling with their mothers. A baby camel can get sidetracked and stray too far from the caravan, turning it into wolf food in the end.

It's hard traveling at night. You can't see rocks or potholes clearly, and there is nothing to distract you. If you have something to see along the way, you can make the next stop before you know it. But at night everything fades into the dark. The night swallows up the sand hills, the dunes, the yellowed grass, and other things city folks rarely see. You can't even see outlines. Your mind is on the travel. Yet when you walk in the desert, you feel your legs getting leaden if you pay too much attention to them. We're used to wearing heavy shoes, and the first two weeks are the hardest. Our legs seem to scream and throb like our hearts. To conserve energy, to save the calf muscles, and to prevent leg pain, the drivers wrap their legs with strips made of cow hair, but that does nothing to lessen the weight on the legs on long journeys. On quiet nights, in particular, the legs remind you they're working by constantly rebelling against you with soreness, fatigue, and aches. This is like a rite of passage we go through every time we set out, and not even experienced drivers are spared. After three weeks, we turn lean and muscular, what those in the trade call, "losing the fat." After that, the going gets easier.

Wooden Fish Girl sat in a wooden box, an uncomfortable way to travel. But it couldn't be helped, because it cost too much money to make a sedan chair. The poor can't worry about a little discomfort.

It was still early in the night when we stopped the second time, seven in the evening at the latest. But it felt as if we'd never reach the end. On dark nights the camel trail seems to extend into infinity. At moments like this, I was overwhelmed by strange thoughts; doubts crept into my mind. Was it worthwhile to waste my life on this tedious trail?

Big Mouth, Zhang Yaole, and I were different. He was a hopeless optimist, always comparing his life with the dead or with animals. He was constantly saying, "Ai-ya, I'm still here. Compared with the dead, how lucky am I!" Or, "Ai-ya, I'm fortunate to be human, compared to these camels with their hard life." Like that. He was always laughing, and I envied him, but I could never be that optimistic. I was pessimistic about life and about the world, and my heart was constantly invaded by an emotion unique to the angry youths of today.

The distant sand hills recede into obscurity, leaving only a faint outline; the stars hang low, which is how night travelers through the desert feel. In open space, the stars are always twinkling, tempting you to reach out and pluck one away. Also, you can touch a kind of grandiosity with your heart; it's a quality found only in the desert. Sometimes you feel it pour into your soul and you're imbued with lofty aspirations; at other times you sense your own insignificance, and you're plunged into a profound sadness.

Suddenly a sound came up out of the darkness. I could tell it was Wooden Fish Girl singing, her voice low, like gossamer, threading its way through the night—

The spot of red in the rising sun,
Shines down on Nanshan city decorated in snow.
Stands of trees in the pine forest roil,
A dragon uncoils at every level of the pine pagoda.
Since my little man left home, snow comes and the wind blows.
After a cold blast of wind and a blanket of snow,

Who knows if he's cold or warm.

3

We reached a lodge by dawn. A lodge is like an inn where camels are fed and watered and the drivers find rest. Along the lengthy Baosui Road, there are plenty of lodges or inns where there is no water or grass. The structure is simple: dig a well, throw up a few rooms, and get some animal feed for the owners to make a living by supplying camels.

The bells alerted the lodge owner, so some women came to greet us as soon as we rounded a corner. There were several lodges at this spot. Those who were too weak to be camel drivers, with no land to till, or with no marketable skills set up a shop to make a living.

"Feiqing—Feiqing—come over here." Someone shouted before we got close. It was a fat, flirty girl called Lhamu, unmarried but "with her own household." Her Tibetan father had no son to take charge of their family affairs, so when she turned eighteen, he hosted a banquet for relatives and neighbors and announced, "My girl is setting up her own household, so she will not marry." From then on, she could have any man she wanted; she'd invite anyone she liked to live with her, and they'd go their separate ways if things did not work out. Lhamu was a sweet-talker, fearless, and flirtatious, so many camel drivers loved to stay at her lodge.

"Come here, come stay with us—stay at our lodge." Women, young and old, crowded up. It did not cost much to open a lodge, but they had to have one lure: either there was a pretty woman or they provided top-rate board; otherwise, they would have no customers.

Before I said anything, the lead drivers went to Lhamu's camel pen, where her helpers came up to take the camels, brush dust off the drivers, or bring water for them to wash up. They were smiling broadly. Women from the other lodges walked off unhappily. "Look at that flirt.

Disgusting," one of them said, and another one joined in, "She got the meat and I don't even get to taste the broth." "She knows what to do with her body, that's all," offered a third one.

Lhamu laughed provocatively and said to one of them, "What about you? You've got something going with Sha Meihu. I never say a word about that."

I had to hide my surprise. The woman had nice features and fair skin, though she was cross-eyed. When Lhamu got closer, I murmured to her, "That woman, is she really involved with Sha Meihu?"

"Who knows? That's what everyone says." Lhamu said. "She always gets visitors at night, it could be Sha Meihu, maybe not."

"Ai-yo, Lhamu. Go ahead and eat what you want, but you shouldn't say whatever comes to your mind," the woman said in a sing-song voice. "I don't know any Sha Meihu or Sha Meilang, tiger or wolf. Besides, you'd better watch out or I'll give you a fat lip. People who know what's what can see you're just popping off, but those who don't will believe I share a pair of pants with that outlaw. If someone gets robbed and blames me, I'll come looking for you to stuff his mouth with those big breasts of yours."

Lhamu giggled. "Sure. You can tell whoever spreads rumors about you to come see me. This pair of white doves of mine are eager to take wing."

The drivers chortled, but Wooden Fish Girl frowned.

When the drivers went to the pen, a woman came up to untie the camel belts, "Dai! What do you think you're doing?" Lu Fuji roared. She shrank back. She was new, obviously. Anyone used to dealing with camel drivers knew that after entering the pen, the camels must be left alone for their sweat to dry before the litter is removed. Otherwise, they could catch a cold. She wasn't pretty, but she had a nice fleshy figure.

After the camels sweated enough, the drivers removed the litters. They took care of their own camels and no one touched anyone else's.

Each litter weighed two hundred and forty *jin*, which, with eleven litters, meant a driver must carry over two thousand *jin* each time they loaded and unloaded. It was not a job for the weak.

After the litters were removed, the drivers checked the camels' feet, something they had to do each time they stopped. If they were worn raw, they had to be tended to; if there were blisters, the blood had to be let right away; if pebbles were caught between toes, they had to be removed. Lu Fuji took down a basin and told the fleshy woman to bring some water. He tossed bits of grass into the water. When the camels' backs were completely dry, he led one over and stayed to watch it drink.

It looked happy when it drank. First it rinsed its mouth, then it smacked its lips as it blew air, like a connoisseur tasting tea of the highest quality. Chain Smoker also smacked his lips at moments like this; they parted and flapped like those on his camels, as if he too was enjoying the soothing sensation of the water. This stop only had dry kindling, but the water was good, which Lu Fuji nicknamed "bean water," meaning it was as nutritious as beans.

The camel blew on the grass bits as it drank; that way, it couldn't drink too much too fast, which was critical when a camel was heated. It could choke if it drank too fast. Sometimes it was worse for a camel to choke on water than on food, so as a precaution, the drivers sprinkled bits of grass in the water to prevent the camels from gulping down too much water. Lu Fuji, who was the cautious type, did that each time the camels drank.

Lhamu walked into the pen. She was a robust woman with a large, round face, a sexy look, her body exuding something that made a man restless. My instinct told me she was different from other women, including her life experience.

She was smiling. Despite the serious look on her face, she projected a sensuous quality. With a sideways glance at me, she said with a smile,

"What are you looking at? I'm not a flirt like her, so you won't find me interesting."

"You're wrong. She's a flirt on the surface, but you're a tease from inside out," Lu Fuji said. His accurate assessment made me laugh.

"So what if I am?" She was laughing too. "You can't get inside to see how it is."

Lhamu got her helpers to unload the sedan chair. Wooden Fish Girl had obviously just woken up, looking worn out, her hair disheveled. I was surprised to see the liveliness gone from her face. Lhamu took her into a thatched hut, from where we heard Wooden Fish Girl grumble, "It stinks. I can't sleep in here." "My dear lady, please don't be so picky. In a few days, you won't even be able to dream about a room like this." Wooden Fish Girl walked out and got into her wooden box. "I'll sleep in here."

There were plenty of huts in the pen, all very crude, made mostly of local materials. Wood stakes plastered with wet cow dung formed walls, with wheat stalks on top for roofs. Walls might be rammed earth, and some of the huts were even made with sheep droppings. It was common to raise sheep on camel farms, where the sheep stepped on their own droppings, turning them steel hard. The hardened droppings were then cut into squares to form the walls and, with dry grass added to the top, a so-called hut was created. Inside was usually a large *kang* with a wood plank on top; the better ones had a wool blanket. But the odor of sheep droppings was overpowering, so no wonder Wooden Fish Girl could not stand it.

The girls tethered the camels to long rows of troughs and added grass. Some of the drivers went inside, while others took down their bedrolls and spread them out on a smooth spot before lying down and snoring away.

Lhamu got her helpers to start cooking.

After checking around to make sure everything was in order, I was about to take a nap when I heard someone make a hei-hei sound. I followed the sound to see Wooden Fish Girl waving at me from her box. I walked over. "Feiqing, Young Master Ma is sleeping inside, so I'd like to sleep in his sedan chair. The room is filthy and smells of sheep droppings."

"Sure," I said. "The walls are made of sheep droppings. But you should know she did that for your benefit. Sheep droppings can kill bugs. The other huts are overrun with bedbugs and fleas, this one is clean."

"Clean? My head almost exploded when I walked in. I'll sleep in the chair."

I didn't like sleeping in the hut either, so I got my dog skin and blanket from the litter and spread them out in a nearby sand trough. I undid the leggings, took off my jacket, and lay down. Soon I was dozing off as thick cooking smoke rose from the chimney. Some time later—not too long, though, because dinner wasn't ready yet—I woke up. The dog hair was prickly and scratchy against my skin. This was a bad omen, meaning outlaws or thieves had their eyes on our caravans.

Who could be spying on us, I wondered. Sha Meihu, or other outlaws?

"Enough! That's enough. We'll continue tomorrow." I cry out.

I'm freezing. The night air has bored into my marrow, and I'll turn into an icicle if I don't leave.

"Sure, sure," they reply, though obviously eager to continue.

"We're not going anywhere, so don't wear him out," Chain Smoker says.

I thank them all.

Then I blow out the yellow candle. Silence reigns all around the sand trough.

I walk to the other end of the city wall, my temporary "home." My dog runs up happily when it sees me, and barks softly a few times to show he's excited to see me back. I spread out my bedding on the sunny side of the yellow camel, and pull the white one over for it to lie down. With my arms around the dog, I wrap myself in a sleeping bag and tuck myself under the camel's neck for its long white chin hair to cover me. The sleeping bag, designed for outdoor use, is supposed to protect against extreme temperatures below zero, but I still feel a chill bore into my bones.

I hear many sighs that night.

But from whom, I don't know.

Third Session
Pa's Wooden Fish Songs

I wake up early the next day. The night air feels nippy. The sleeping bag has kept me warm enough, but still I feel a chill. If not for the white camel's chin hair, I may not have made it through the night. I've brought a big fur coat that I could use if it gets too cold, though it's so heavy it could be uncomfortable.

After looking around to enjoy the early morning desert scenery, I worm my way out of the sleeping bag and reflect on the events of the night before, feeling as if they were a dream.

I gather enough kindling to boil water and make a bowl of instant noodles. The smell makes me want to gag, but there's nothing I can do about food. Wild Fox Ridge has been deserted for a long time, and this spot is so far from human habitation; it's beyond imagination.

My camel can't carry much more than water, potatoes (which keep a long time without going bad) and me. Instant noodles are light and last a long time, so I brought a lot.

I'd have liked to come with more camels and some friends, like adventurers of earlier times, but that would make it impossible for me to enter the world I wanted to visit, according to the old man who could communicate with that world. "When there's too much yang, these yin life forms will stay away," he said.

I've seen signs of lodges, a bit like guest houses of a later time, but much smaller and quite crude. Some camel caravans stopped here when they traveled past Wild Fox Ridge. There aren't too many here at Wild Fox Ridge though, because most caravans don't enter the Ridge, just pass through. The drivers would likely say, "better to make a turn at ten li than pass through danger." By making a turn, they mean a detour that will make the trip longer. Of course, they wouldn't be bold enough to enter. In the stories told by camel drivers, Wild Fox Ridge has gained a status similar to the Bermuda Triangle, where strange things happen.

Under the bright sun, given the dream-like quality of last night's events, I write down what they've told me, in ways comprehensive to my contemporaries.

With enough to occupy me, the day passes quickly.

By the time the sun rolls off the western sand hills, my potatoes are roasted—compared with cooking a real meal, roasting potatoes saves water. I eat one and put one in my pocket. When I'm too cold to keep going, I say to myself, it can replenish energy.

I plan to conduct as many interviews as possible. Past interviewing experience shows me that it goes well sometimes, but can get tough on occasion. I perform rites to summon the dead, but don't always succeed in bringing up the specters I want to see.

I light the yellow candle and create a barrier, as the night before.

The dim candle light blurs the drivers' images, but I feel surging emotions in them. I can even hear the camels panting and smell the horses' pungent sweat.

"Were there horses too?" I ask.

"Of course, there were," Chain Smoker replies. He has the most distinct image of all of my interviewees. He crouches like a desert monkey, resembling the root of an old poplar.

The other specters are mostly drifting coronae, some brightly white, some dim and gray.

I hear the occasional hoot of a night bird, likely an owl, but I'm not sure.

Wooden Fish Girl is tonight's storyteller.

I'm surprised to see her, for I thought neither of the two caravans would travel with a woman. And the gazette in Liangzhou made no mention of women.

I tell her, "I just want to learn about what happened at Wild Fox Ridge. I don't want to get distracted and waste pages. I need to finish my interviews before harsh winter sets in. Otherwise, I'll turn into an ice pop."

"You won't get a true understanding of the place without knowing my story. You want to know why we couldn't make it out of Wild Fox Ridge, my story will tell you why we entered it. They're interconnected," she says. "In fact, coming in here has already determined our departure."

And that's how Wooden Fish Girl becomes an important figure in my interviews. She tells me something I hadn't considered, and at some point, I'm even pleasantly surprised. Such surprisingly positive finds have been pretty common in my previous interviews, and they always exceed my expectations.

Oddly she uses some Western slang in her narration. Later I learn that she spent the second half of her life in the west, after growing up in Lingnan—south of the Five Ridges.

Her participation complicates the structure of this book. Her life starts from the south and moves to the west, while the story of the caravans begins in the west and heads to Wild Fox Ridge. You can certainly understand it this way: the former proceeds from death to life and the latter life to death. Life and death thus form a different kind of transmigration.

One. Wooden Fish Girl

1

I have to start from the beginning.

The beginning I'm going to tell didn't happen at Wild Fox Ridge, but without it, you won't have a complete picture of the place. Only through my story of why we entered Wild Fox Ridge can you uncover the truth.

Let me first sing you a tune called "Story of the Whip," which I learned in Liangzhou. It's a realistic description of the time; that is, Liangzhou and Lingnan at the time were both exactly as related in the lyrics. Once you understand this, you'll know about our time—

Li Tesheng, like a juicy plum, rotting Fatso Wang too big for his coffin.
Riding around atop a white horse, collecting money in villages far and wide.
Feasting on chicken and deep-fried cakes, as well as tasty noodle soup.
Sleeping on patterned sheets, under a nice fur blanket,
Wanting to borrow your wife at night.
When the three old donkeys are tethered to a trough,
All the people will suffer.
They chatter and whisper together,
The people's taxes on all things will multiply many times.
It doesn't matter what it's for; there's always a tax to pay.
But it's forced taxation.
It could be for a death, a natural disaster, or a funeral,
Or it could be for getting the son a wife or marrying off a daughter.
Tax for leasing a plot or selling the land, buying a plot or building a house,

Tax for grazing livestock, tax for raising children.
Children pay a tax to crawl around; old men pay a tax for their canes.
Women pay a tax for rouge and powder; bachelors pay for whoring.
Widows pay a tax for the crotch in their pants.
So many taxes, all exorbitant, the people can't keep going.

Get the picture?

The people in Lingnan couldn't keep going. My Pa—my heart aches when I think about him—such tough times we lived in. And there were so many Li Teshengs and Fatso Wangs around us.

2

My love for wooden fish songs comes from my Pa.

So I'll first tell you about him.

Pa was an educated man, but he wasn't famous. You know how terrible life can be for an unknown educated man. Someone with an education must be well known to enjoy a good life; if not, he'll suffer in poverty, especially if he turns into a pedant, which is what people mean when they say "poor pedant." An educated man turns into a pedant when he's poor, but he's poor because he's a pedant.

I hear you've studied the Dharma of Sarasvatī, so you should know that anyone who studies this Dharma will gain wisdom easily, but may end up poor. The goddess in charge of wisdom and the one who metes out wealth have never gotten along, so if the Wisdom Goddess favors you, the Bodhisattva of Abundance will withhold wealth from you. This is highly symbolic. You can undo the curse only if you're exceedingly wise; otherwise, "a talented man always incurs the wrath of fate," as Du Fu wrote. My father's life is a perfect illustration.

He devoted his life and energy to wooden fish songs. We have song books passed down by our ancestors generations ago, so they're very old. In addition, he inherited some land from his father. If he had been content to work the land, he could have lived in relative comfort, but he was restless, and a sense of mission to continue a family tradition solidified his dedication to the songs. He spent his days with blind storytellers, so what do you think he could accomplish?

To collect old song books, he sold the family plot without telling my Ma. When she found out about it, the field was already planted with someone else's crops. She was thrown into total despair. You mentioned Tolstoy in his old age, and I completely understand how the aristocratic lady felt. Just think, a family has to eat, but if you sell your means of a living, they will eat nothing but the wind.

Pa turned the family property into crates of ancient song books, which were said to be rare and valuable. If you ask me, I still think they're precious. Without his effort, those books would have long been used by rats in their nests. What puzzled me was, if the family treated the books as treasures, they would have taken better care of them, such as storing them in better crates, instead of tossing them onto the rafters to be ravaged by rats. Later, I learned that the family hadn't cared about the scraps of paper, and that it was Pa's surprised cries that alerted them to demand a sky-high price. They knew, too, that Pa could not obtain the books anywhere else, no matter how much he was willing to pay. On the other hand, Pa should also have been aware that no one else would have bought those tattered books, even after he alerted them to the value. But he sold the family land without hesitation in exchange for piles of scrap paper, for he was sure that rats would want them, if no one else did. Without proper care, the books would soon be food for the rats or reduced to piles of garbage in the humid weather. When I think back now, I have to say he performed a great service, an act of boundless beneficence. Without him, those precious song books would have been lost to oblivion.

A few of them are so rare they have never been circulated.

Over that summer, Pa got a pot of paste and, under the sun, restored the ancient song books bit by bit, page by page. Using the best rice paper, he pasted the fragmented, scattered, yellowed, and moldy paper into one book after another, and bound them in yellow silk when finished. Ma lent a hand when he worked on them. At the time, she did not know he'd traded the family land for them; Pa had told her they were very valuable, and she'd believed him when she saw the look in his eyes. But what was valuable to her was quite different from what he meant; to her, it was monetarily valuable, which was why she was convinced. Over the next many months, she helped him glue a pile of scrap into bright, yellow books of wooden fish songs. She only happened upon the truth in the following spring, when she saw someone else planting in our field.

She was fit to be tied.

Ma brought out the books and dumped them in the yard; she wanted to burn them up. She was so livid I knew it wasn't an empty threat. But before she could touch a match to it, he sent her to the ground with a vicious slap.

I still recall that it was the first time he'd ever slapped her. She had been his beloved up to that day. Born with good looks, she was a famed beauty locally. Before she married Pa, many young men from wealthy families had pursued her, but she'd chosen father for his talent.

She never forgave him, but didn't try to burn the books either, for he promised her he'd sell them to someone who truly knew their value. He stressed over and over that a real expert would pay at least ten times the property value for them. And that became something she looked forward to all her life.

But the man Pa was waiting for never showed up. It had to wait many years for someone who truly understood how priceless they were.

That person was me.

To be sure, my aunt, Pa's sister, knew that before me. She had committed many of the lyrics to memory, but one night she disappeared under mysterious circumstances. There were many versions of what happened; some said she eloped, some said she died, and yet others said she became a nun after seeing through the vanity of the world. She was a Buddhist, like Pa, and I became one at young age because of them. So naturally, I'm convinced that what happened to me later was a kind of cause and condition.

My aunt's disappearance remains a mystery.

3

I'll never forget how Pa hanged himself.

On that day someone in the village asked him to sing wooden fish songs, something the villagers considered auspicious. Over holidays or when a new house was being built, someone would ask him and some of the blind storytellers to sing for good luck. Pa knew lots of those songs, like "Story of the Two Lotus Girls" or "Faithful Lovers," by heart. But he did not sing them the way others did. His were more elegant, for he employed his talent and cleansed them of all "vulgar" elements. The earlier wooden fish songs tended to be off-colored, and to Pa they were too lewd, so he decided to remove and revise them. He ended up cleansing all the traditional songs. Later, when the great German poet, Goethe, praised "Faithful Lovers," it was my father's version that he read. Since the version was truly infused with high literary qualities, no wonder Goethe lauded it as "magnificent verse."

But Pa was getting poorer by the day. Maybe, when the Goddess of Wisdom blesses someone with talent, she should take away some of the poverty at the same time. Later, I saw the same thing happen to quite a few people. Back then we were utterly destitute, except for the bundles of bright yellow song books. I remember none of us wearing pants. Father gave mother his pants when hers were worn out, so she and the children had to stay home whenever he went out.

On the day Pa was asked to sing the songs, Ma was out working at the Ma family's draft bank. He couldn't wait for her to return, so he put on the special outfit of wooden fish song singers—a long gown—and left. Only his partner knew about it. When Pa told him he had no pants to go out in, the man said, "Just put on a long gown. No one will crawl under to check if you're wearing pants."

Pa sat with his legs crossed to sing that day, and no one noticed anything unusual.

Later, when he was getting up, he rested a hand on his partner's shoulder to hoist himself up, but, unexpectedly, the man tilted his shoulder just as Father stood up so he fell down on the bed. And everyone saw that Pa wasn't wearing anything under his gown. It was a huge loss of face, a crushing embarrassment.

When he got home, Pa tied a rope to one of the beams and stuck his neck through the noose. Luckily, someone came to see him just as he kicked over the stool.

I was out gleaning wild greens at the moment. When I got home, from a distance, I saw a crowd outside our door. I got closer and heard Uncle trying to talk some sense into Pa, "How could you do that? A good death is never as good as the worst life. Once you're gone, what is your widow going to do with all the kids? Just come see me whenever you're in a tight spot, all right?" Uncle had brought with him a bolt of fabric. His family was doing well; like Pa, he'd also inherited some land. Pa's was gone, Uncle still had his and life was much easier for him and his family. Ma was crying silently, soaking her handkerchief. My younger brothers were half-naked, their legs caked in dirt.

I burst out crying when I saw Pa's wooden expression. The onlookers parted to make way when they heard me crying. His face was a pall of gray, his eyes devoid of expression, but he was clearly alive. I breathed a sigh of relief, but tears were still running down my face. I recalled how he would recite a poem when he was drunk, and only then would his face come alive. As if he were all alone, he would chant a Qing poem loudly, "Too poor to have bamboo to lean on/With sorrowful thoughts I want to plant a poplar/Wind surrounds my family/It's the ninth month and we have no winter clothes." Sometimes tears coursed down his face as he recited. When that happened, I knew what was worrying him.

The villagers also tried to talk him around, suggesting that he learn a skill. But he just sat there impassively. It was clear we couldn't go on like that. Without a plot of land, there would be no harvest; without a marketable skill, there would be no money; without enough physical strength, he could not find manual work. All Pa had was a stack of yellowed song books. He locked them in a book case that was two *chi* wide and three *chi* tall, and would bring them out now and then, swaying his head as he sang. In the case were some other books, which he said were written by generations of our ancestors; they recorded, in the format of wooden fish songs, major events over the past hundreds of years. It was history, as well as proof of a village's existence. He continued the record whenever necessary and noted changes in weather, such as an earthquake on a certain date, a flood at this time, or something significant at another. The imperial court had its historian, but not the commoners, though they had their own history books. I naturally could not imagine that the books managed to escape a big fire and that someone would discover them half a century later and take them to Japan, where they became a huge international sensation. I heard that it was the world's very first family chronicle, so valuable that only the ancient books excavated in the Dunhuang Caves were its equal. By then, Pa had long been reduced to a pile of bones. The work he wrote in his impoverished state eventually helped support many scholars who studied it.

The glory the books would garner a hundred years later could not fill Pa's belly. Every time he returned from singing, slightly tipsy from the liquor the family offered, he would brag about his irreplaceable role at a particular historical juncture. Besides writing his never-ending book, he also composed poems of indignation and bitterness. By then I could read a bit, but I couldn't understand his poetry; however, I could feel the expansive sentiments in them, which were also found in the wooden fish songs. He infused the sentiments into his poems to nurture his children. Every night my three younger brothers and I would recite his poems from memory. He also offered free lessons to teach village children the songs, at one point even bringing out his cherished three-string zither for them to pluck. They didn't understand the songs, but loved playing the zither, so they memorized the songs for a chance to touch the instrument. And that was how many of the village children learned the wooden fish songs. Pa called teaching the children songs tilling fields of books, fields that would not produce a crop. He couldn't even afford to wear pants. Ma once offered to make the gown into a set of clothes, but he wouldn't let her, because, for one thing, a long gown was the symbol of a scholar, and, secondly, he needed to wear it to sing the songs. To him it was pretty much his rice bowl. Naturally, no one could have imagined that he'd be stark naked under the gown, impossible but utterly shameful.

Our neighbors talked on for a long time before Pa finally let out a long sigh, and his blank eyes regained life as they swept across their faces. When his eyes met mine, I thought I saw the hint of a smile on his face.

I knelt and took his hands.

Later he wove all the village events and incidents into his songs, exalting the good and vilifying the evil ones, which was why the wounds on his face never fully healed. Some of the evil-doers, after hearing his songs disparaging them, would come to our house to slap him viciously. It didn't take many years for him to lose his front teeth, the result of face-on fist blows. And people stopped asking him to sing, because he slurred his words.

To help support the family, he sent me to herd sheep for the Ma family and also taught me to sing the songs. I had a good memory, so in a few years I'd memorized all the songs in his treasured ancient books, as well as those he composed, which would later be recognized as "magnificent poetry." Now people near and far knew about "Wooden Fish Girl."

After that, Pa found another cache of rare books, whose owner demanded a high price that Pa couldn't meet. He looked so despondent that I was afraid he might fall ill, so I said to him, "You can sell me."

He couldn't do that, but I tried to talk him around by saying, "Sooner or later I'll have to marry someone. You can't provide for me forever. The books will be ruined by the time I'm married. If a woman can't find her true love, it doesn't matter who she marries."

Finally, I convinced him, and that was how I went to live at Lü Erye's house as a child bride.

All the villagers were saying that Wooden Fish Girl had fallen into a den of riches, Pa included.

I naturally had no idea at the time that Lü Erye's youngest son was not quite right in the head, and that Lü Erye wasn't so much looking for a daughter-in-law as finding a personal maid for his son.

I accepted all that had happened. Everything was predetermined by karma.

4

Before I moved in to live with Lü Erye's family, Lü Erye was forever asking Ma to help out in his kitchen, and before long she was hired on as a regular kitchen hand, with an annual salary of one *dan* and two *dou* of husked rice, the same pay as that for a strong farmhand, and Pa agreed right away, with no hesitation.

Ma was known as a good cook, which is a lot like being adept at writing articles, for which natural talent counts a great deal. Some can cook all their life and still produce a pot of pig swill. Ma had several unique skills; for instance, she could make thirty-six dishes out of taro, each looking wonderful and smelling great, but all different. Her Hakka dishes were special too, and were among Lü Erye's favorites.

But poverty continued to eat away at Pa's mind and body, like aged vinegar corroding metal. He looked much older than a man not quite forty, frail and emaciated, often appearing sickly. Only when he had something to drink—Uncle sometimes invited him over for a few cups of rice liquor—would he sway and sing the songs in a loud, full voice, oblivious to his surroundings. When our neighbors heard him, they would say, "Listen, the bookworm is singing the songs again." But they refrained from laughing at him. In my hometown, no one would ridicule a scholar; their scorn was always reserved for the ignorant and incompetent.

Feeling the loss of face, Pa stayed inside for days after his failed suicide attempt. One day, his partner, who had pulled the prank on him that day, brought over a piece of fabric, but Pa could not forgive him, and refused to join him when the man asked him to sing together. Pa knew he could sing and make some money to provide for the family, but he would rather go hungry than partner with the man again. I suppose life lost all meaning for him when he thought about it; maybe "the meaning" of life was more important than being alive.

"What meaning are you looking for?" Ma asked him. "A pedantic scholar is always looking for a reason. In fact, it's the process that counts. In life there's sweet and bitter, happiness and sorrow, and you have to taste them all and go through all sorts of experiences. Don't think too much and back yourself into a dead-end corner."

Ma had once been a Cantonese opera singer, so she could read and write. Quite a few young men from wealthy families pursued her, but she wouldn't even give them a glance; instead she fell for a bookworm. At the time, people were always praising Pa's literary talent, saying he would pass the imperial exam and become a *zhuangyuan*. Ma didn't care if he passed or not and married him; at the time, he wasn't too poor either. Later, he sold the family land for the purported last copy of the block-printed song books. Then a substantial fire burned off whatever was left in the family. He risked his life to save everything, but only managed to drag out the book case. A fire leads to instant poverty, and that was how we became destitute. Luckily, he could sing, so he was always asked to perform at village sacrificial rites to the Earth God, after which he received several *sheng* of grain for his effort. We were forever eating up next year's food, but at least our throats were never left empty.

When he got better, Ma went to work at Lü Erye's shop, a branch of the Mahesheng. I heard there were many branches all over the country. When the time came to distribute bonuses, camels would carry gold and silver along the long camel trail to Lü Erye's hometown.

I heard that he had two homes, one in Lingnan and one in Liangzhou. In the south, he lived in a watchtower, a fortress-like house with high walls, a big yard, and a blockhouse atop that was fitted with locally made cannon and guarded with marksmen. When the locals and the Hakka outsiders had a fight, the locals sometimes got into a killing frenzy, leaving pools of blood, and could take down some townships. But Lü Erye sneered at them, infuriating them so much they gathered more locals to attack his house. They failed to make any headway after months. Later, the rioters came together to kill officials and stage uprisings, slaughtering so many that blood ran in rivers. But they could not make it into his fortress. Several hundred people were living there at the time to avoid the strife of war. When the Governor-General came to inspect, he could not stop marveling over the sturdy watchtower and even wrote on a plaque for it, "A Step Back." It was a puzzling phrase that had people scratching their heads for decades.

Lü Erye's high watchtower was protected by battlements and gun slots all around so marksmen could fire from all directions. It was designed by a Hakka man who had studied in Japan; it later became a famous scenic site, an eye-opening wonder to foreign visitors.

I remember what Ma said about her first visit. She said she'd felt how oppressive the imposing structure was. The meter-thick main gate, with its brass rivets and steel cover, the blockhouse atop of the wall, where the private guards patrolled, and the red, odd-looking flying eaves, they were all talking to her, saying things that made her uncomfortable.

Lü Erye was never without his water pipe. He was a scrawny old man, with a pointed chin, slitty eyes, and a few whiskers that quivered in the wind. According to someone who could read faces to tell fortunes, he had the typical face of a man born to poverty and little fortune. So his wealth must have been a result of riches accumulated by previous generations of his family. It had to be. His elders were merchants of good will who were generous with donations and handouts, benefiting people all over, which was why they had enjoyed more than a hundred years of prosperity. A lucky man can spread his fortune to many. Everyone said he prospered in his ancestors' glory.

Ma said his small eyes were bright, and when he first laid his eyes on her, she felt as if he were stripping her naked. Once, when she went into the mountains to collect kindling and met up with a wolf, she untied her head scarf to wave it around while shouting, "Help, help!" The scrawny old man happened by on horseback, fired a shot to scare off the wolf, and pulled her up onto his horse. Still badly shaken, she nevertheless felt his claw-like hand around her chest. Not good on horseback, she didn't dare try fighting off his hand, which stayed pawing her all the way back. He didn't let her off until they reached the village, where he said, "Damned weird. You've had a few kids, so how come your breasts are so nice and plump?" She never told Pa, but she retched every time she thought about it. Ever since she walked into the watchtower, she felt those beady eyes on her back the whole time.

Later she did tell a female friend of hers in the village—what's called a boudoir confidante. She wanted her friend to watch out for Lü Erye, out of good intentions, but her friend was such a gossip that she told someone else, who told someone else until it became well known, though luckily only among women. Pa was still in the dark.

At the time, I had no idea that many of our family catastrophes would involve him.

5

In those days I often saw camel caravans transporting tea. Pa liked the camel drivers, but he especially liked the folk songs they sang. Actually, he pretty much liked them all, including storytelling songs of Liangzhou and drum lyrics of Wenzhou. His fondness for them made his wooden fish songs even more inclusive. When Ma was formally hired on at Lü Erye's house, I went with her to check on the Ma family shop, where I saw several drivers working out with stone dumbbells shaped like old-fashion padlocks. They tossed them back and forth among themselves to build up their muscles until they looked like land-tilling cattle. Muscles are the mother of physical strength, which was critical for camel drivers, who needed to load and unload two to three hundred *jin* of litters. Back when he'd reached the end of his rope, Pa had thought of making a living with a camel caravan. We'd heard that a driver was paid very well; a common farmhand earned two *dou* of rice monthly, while a camel driver got four, the equivalent of two silver coins. Besides supporting us, he also wanted to travel, but unfortunately, the best period of a driver's life was between the age of twenty and thirty-five. A man in his forties could no longer do the work, and Pa was almost forty when the idea came to him. Picking up a litter would be like an ant trying to topple a mountain, which was what eventually made him give up hanging out with camel drivers.

The caravan brought goods to Lü Erye's shop, tea and salt, and transported salted seafoods to the West.

I never liked Lü Erye, but I enjoyed visiting the shop and watching the drivers work out. They lifted and tossed weights and dumbbells to keep up their physical strength, almost like camels building fat. Between transporting goods and collecting the cargo to take back with them, the drivers also had to work on their muscles; if they missed three days in a row, they'd be rusty, they said. Once someone got lazy and stopped for several months, they could no longer lift a litter and had to hand the job over to someone else. With that as a lesson, the drivers didn't dare let up, and whenever they had time, they were huffing and puffing, working on their strength.

When the clerks at the shop and the camel drivers saw me back in those days, they always broke out in smiles and said, "Sing us a song, Wooden Fish Girl."

If I was in the mood, I'd sing one for them. My favorite at the time was highlights of "Story of the Two Lotus Girls" and I always sang the best parts for them.

Since Ma started working for Lü Erye, the drivers would comment on what a good cook she was when they saw me. It embarrassed me a bit. I don't know why, but Ma working for him felt somewhat shameful to me. He had dozens of clerks and five or six cooks on his staff, but for reasons unclear to me, it felt degrading for her to work there.

I was worried the whole time, gaining a premonition that something terrible would happen. When I'd gone out with her at a younger age, some men often grinned cheekily and made suggestive remarks. When Lü Erye came to our house with his water pipe sometimes, he'd look at her with fire in his eyes. Pa noticed it too, but poverty chills ambition, and the hair looks long on a skinny horse; he could not stand straight in front Lü Erye. The only way Pa could maintain his dignity was not to ever borrow money or grain from him. He would look elsewhere for solutions when we had nothing to eat. He would go without pants if we didn't have money, but refused to pawn or sell the gown—it wasn't worth much anyway. Lü Erye had tried repeatedly to hire Ma to be his cook, offering a pay comparable to that of a male worker, instead of the meager salary the other cooks would get. But each time Pa turned him down with a resounding, "No!" He didn't want her to enter that watchtower compound, but this time she went, to which he reacted with not even a sigh; instead, he wore a blank look and stared at the rafters all night. My heart was in my throat all night too.

I felt reassured, however, when I went to the shop, for the clerks and camel drivers were all so familiar, as if they were part of my life. When I saw them, Lü Erye didn't seem as frightening any longer. When a camel farmer told a story, I thought I could see waves of sand rippling into the distant horizon. I tried to imagine camels dotting the creases of the sand and grazing sheep drifting like clouds in the sky. It always brought me an unusual sense of tenderness and warmth.

When I was little, my favorite stories were all about caravans. Every time the drivers asked me to sing, I'd demand a story from them.

The caravans set out when they had enough salted seafood. The drivers picked the strongest camels to carry the loads, leaving the frail and sick ones behind. They said an underperforming camel would mess up the long-distance trek; a sick camel put too much strain on the whole team and tired the others out. Hence, it was critical to select the best.

They herded the chosen camels into another yard to dehydrate them, which, I heard, was a necessary step. Camels must lose their fluid before getting on the road. During this period, they were fed grass, but no water. They were used to eating as much as they wanted, and enlarged their stomachs, which would suffer if they were made to work with all the fluid in them. It usually took a couple of weeks of dehydration before they were fit enough and could have water again.

I learned all this from Big Mouth, a favorite conversation partner of Pa's. He didn't understand the songs, and Pa explained them line by line. Slowly Big Mouth learned quite a few of them and said some of the stories could be found in Liangzhou's folk song tradition as well.

It was Big Mouth who told Pa about the abuse Ma suffered under Lü Erye. He was a veritable "big mouth." After spending enough time in Lingnan, he could speak some local languages. He just could not keep a secret. I know he told Pa about Lü Erye for his own good, but I still think he talked too much. Even in those days, I learned that what you don't know doesn't exist on some level.

Pa's world grew dim when he heard Big Mouth.

I wonder if Big Mouth's gossipy tendency was partially responsible for what later happened to my family.

Wooden Fish Girl suddenly falls silent.

I sense she's sobbing. A wind blows over the vegetation, making a choking sound.

"I can't go on," she says.

"It's all right. I can wait," I tell her.

She says she feels awful. She is surprised that, after all these years, she still feels so bad when she recalls the past. For years, she's repressed the pain and suppressed the past, like pushing down a leather ball in water. It obviously never disappears from her life's memories.

I notice the sliver of a moon lighting up in the east amid sparkling stars. I hear something rushing like water. Could it be the river in the sky? Or noise from other life forms?

The flame of the yellow candle shifts from side to side with a roar.

I say to myself that she'll continue if I wait awhile, but a long time passes and she remains silent.

I blow out the candle.

I'm up very late on this night; the stars are so noisy I have trouble falling asleep.

In my dream there's a girl with a nice face smiling at me. I think she's Wooden Fish Girl, but I realize it isn't her when I get to see Wooden Fish Girl in person.

The identity of the girl remains a mystery.

I even wonder if she could be me in my previous life.

Fourth Session
Camel Fights

Drive the camels, up before dawn, head to the third stop.
Go to the farm, catch camels, a northern wind pours down my neck,
You see, this is, the life of a camel driver,
No way to make a living.

——*Song of a Camel Driver*

On this night, what I want most is to call forth Wooden Fish Girl, but I barely start my incantation when a pack of camel drivers show up. They have so much to say, for they've lived a hundred years of loneliness. Everything they remember tells a story about what happened in an earlier time.

The night is bone-chilling cold, as before. Looking at the sparks of coronae, I sense there is too much yin in the night air, so I light the yellow candle even though I can do without it now. As the candle is lit, the coronae dim, so do the souls eager to pour their hearts out.

It takes a great deal of effort to halt those eager souls, who are still agitated, judging from their impatient tone of voice. I know very well that *what they want most is someone to listen to them, but more than that, they want someone who can listen and understand them. I'm obviously the best candidate, but I made the trip not to be a mere audience; I have a purpose. I want to know what happened to the camel caravans at Wild Fox Ridge.*

"All right, all right," I say to them. "We have plenty of time, like leaves on a tree. You'll have your chance later. Some other time, all right? If any of you want to share your story, you can always come look me up. But for now, I want to focus on the story at Wild Fox Ridge."

A muscular man, whom a Liangzhou resident would call "a pillar stone," speaks up. I spot him the moment he opens his mouth and try to understand him in the way I read the camel drivers. A clear image of the man stands out in my memories of the specters. "Stop it, all of you. You're so noisy you make my balls hurt. Keep your mouths shut and let me talk first."

He's Lu Fuji.

The clamor dies down slowly and he starts—

One. Lu Fuji

1

The nightmarish journey started out just like any others. We left late in the afternoon and traveled all night, covering about fifty *li*, before resting at a lodge or a camel farm. The early part of the trip was mostly along camel trails, which were paths connecting camel farms or oases. Everything looked normal, nothing out of the ordinary—one day was truly like a hundred years.

I recall that Feiqing told you about the lodge last time. They're all the same. If you know one, you know a hundred, so I won't say another word about it.

Over those three months or so, Sha Meihu, who kept us in constant fear, did not make an appearance, and we only saw an occasional petty thief. The one surprise was caused by the musk Wooden Fish Girl had brought. One night, when we slept out in the wild, her tent was crawling with snakes. Luckily for her, they weren't poisonous, but just red, meaty snakes. There were so many, and they were so noisy, like songbirds, it was as if they were having a festival. I had no idea snakes could make that kind of sound. The girl was fast asleep. Feiqing was startled awake by the noise and took a lantern to check on her tent. You have to know that something like that is a job for the lead driver; ordinary drivers will stay out of it. No matter how you look at it, it was unseemly for big men like them to enter a woman's tent late at night. Heh-heh—it was all right for me though; I was too old for what went on between men and women. Actually, I didn't care much for that even when I was younger. Never could do anything about it, was born that way.

I thought he was being overly concerned when he told me about the noise from the tent. Women are prone to make noise, and camel drivers should just let them be. We couldn't be worried about other people's this and that; all we needed to do was deliver them to where they should be. They could do whatever they wanted, and we couldn't object, so long as they didn't do anything to breach safety. I could only keep the drivers in line; no, I could only keep the drivers in the Chinese caravan in line; the Mongolians had their own lead driver.

The Chinese caravan merged with the Mongolian one shortly after we entered the desert. I told you about the inconvenience of merging two large caravans, like not enough water and grass. But we were clever enough to make sure the two caravans weren't too far apart when we stopped to rest, and that was good enough. With the two caravans merged, outlaws would think twice about harassing us, which was the biggest advantage. Think about it. The din raised by all those camel bells could be heard miles away, so the average highwaymen wouldn't even dare show their faces. Almost all the drivers were big, hulking men who worked daily with heavy loads and litters, and after a while built up incredible strength. Moreover, quite a few of them knew martial arts, so most raiders wouldn't get near us, even if they'd borrowed extra courage.

But as the size of the caravan grew, trouble brewed. First, we had to pick a lead driver for a joint caravan. The Chinese side decided on Feiqing, the Mongolian chose Patul; after a few rounds of negotiation, Feiqing was chosen as the lead driver. When we ran into problems and a decision had to be made, the lead driver would take charge. With him, we now had one large caravan, the sum of its Chinese and Mongolian components.

Feiqing had a talk with the Chinese camel drivers, telling them not to argue with the Mongolians if something came up. Fortunately, nothing serious happened.

That was why I thought he was overreaching when he told me about the strange noise from the tent. Someone from the Mongolian caravan could have gotten the idea to go in there to get something going with that girl. We just had to turn a blind eye to stuff like that; besides, Wooden Fish Girl looked like a trouble-maker to me. I noticed she'd been eyeing Ma Zaibo, while Big Mouth kept looking at her. Luckily for us that Ma Zaibo didn't seem to care; it could have gotten ugly if he'd been the rash type and argued with Big Mouth.

"Let them be, as long as you aren't the one who made the noise," I said to Feiqing. "Worse case, we add a few babies to the caravan when we reach Luocha. Where's the problem?"

"That weird noise didn't sound human. It was some animal."

Sure enough, we were barely at the tent when we heard Wooden Fish Girl's frightened, trembling cries, "Snakes! Snakes!"

We stormed in and saw the ground crawling with red-banded snakes. I don't know if they were really red-banded snakes, but that's what I called them. Feiqing bent over to pick up the fleshy reptiles and tossed them out one after another.

"Light a lantern!" I shouted.

Other drivers quickly gathered at the tent. Wooden Fish Girl had swooned in Feiqing's arms, likely from fright.

"Use the whip," Feiqing said.

Qi Lu raised his whip. You may not know that whips are the best weapon against snakes. A powerful wrist can snap them in two.

It took no time to slice the snakes to pieces.

After a night like that, Wooden Fish Girl gave up her musk, an irresistible attraction for snakes that gather around it like market goers. From then on, before bed time, I pinched some used tobacco from my pipe for her to spread by her head. No poisonous vermin ever entered her tent after that.

In my memory, this incident seemed to have been the only incident that left an impression over those three months.

Granted, everyone has his own memorable event. For instance, if you'd slept with a woman on one of those nights, naturally, you'd find that unforgettable. What I mean is, over those three months, every day felt like the days on all the earlier trips.

That's life for you.

I was a camel farmer for several decades and traveled Baosui Road at least a hundred times, but I've managed to remember only a few incidents.

In my recollection, the truly memorable happened after we entered Wild Fox Ridge.

2

After spending over a hundred nights at lodges, we finally entered Wild Fox Ridge, a spot in the desert with many foxes, according to legend. But they'd all vanished by the time we got there. It was called a ridge, but it was nothing special, with alternating sand hills and valleys, though the topography seemed more expansive than elsewhere.

I was against entering the Ridge and would have preferring taking the long way around. The detour would mean an additional few hundred *li*, but it was safer. My nickname is Sand Fox, and that would clash with the name of the place if we went in there. I'm superstitious about things like that. You've probably heard that Pang Tong, who was also called Fengchu, died at Luofeng Slope, Xue Rengui, a white tiger incarnate, perished at White Tiger Pass. Sometimes you just have to believe in these things, though maybe not wholeheartedly. I didn't try to stop them. For one thing, going through Wild Fox Ridge was a true shortcut, one used by many camel caravans in history to reach Luocha. On the other hand, quite a few camels had died there because they ran out of water, because the paths went this way and that and they got lost, or because, rumor had it, there were demons.

I heard of Wild Fox Ridge when I was little. Back then every Liangzhou child could sing: "Wooden Fish Valley beneath Wild Fox Ridge/Wandering souls fill the nine ditches and eight ponds/Go look for the key at the Hu Family Mill." The elders in my village said there was treasure galore that had supernatural power and made its way to a family in good luck. Based on what they said, that was how the Ma family got their wealth. They said, one night a farmer saw some large wagons coming over the hill. He stopped them when they were about to cut through his wheat field. "We're delivering riches to the Ma family," they said. "Why won't you let us through?" They offered the man a wagon load of wealth, but he wanted more, which annoyed the carter, who raised his whip and sent his wagons roaring off. He hastily grabbed a brick off the wagon and found out the next day it was gold.

The story attracted camel drivers to the ridge. What I found odd was, Feiqing agreed to take the shortcut too.

That was how we went in. The drivers, who were thinking about all the treasure, put another story out of their minds. We'd heard that Wild Fox Ridge was a strange place with unusual occurrences all the time, and that a few caravans had gotten lost in there. Some called it Dead Camel Valley for that very reason, though no one had actually used it, because it was so inauspicious.

Now I don't want to say who was right and who was wrong. Right or wrong, the final outcome was the same. Everything is right or wrong only for a time, and when you place an event in a longer period of time, you'll see that everything ends up the same. Whatever is right or wrong will pass in the end.

The road into the Ridge was littered with rocks, and not ordinary rocks. They were black. I'll bet you've never seen a desert covered from end to end with black rocks. A boundless black, with no end in sight, and you feel dizzy when the sun shines down on it.

We spent three days walking through the black rocky desert. It felt no different from any of the other days of our trek, but I did notice something unusual at the end of those three days. Many of the camels' feet were pierced by nameless rocks.

To protect the feet, Patul had gotten enough cow hides to make covers for them. He did that with the best of intentions, but it very nearly caused the collapse of the caravan.

As the camels walked, they kicked up pebbles, which were then carried along on a mysterious force into the covers. None of the drivers knew about it until a few days later, when the camels were laid up at Wild

Fox Ridge. The pebbles in the covers nearly ruined their feet. I remember that was the beginning of our nightmare.

Two. Ma Zaibo

I was the one who came up with the idea of covering the feet. It wasn't Patul's fault.

I got the idea from Feiqing's "Dark clouds blanketing the snow." You see, he tied leather guards to horse hooves for them to gallop down the desert as if on wings. I just didn't realize that horse hooves are so tough that pebbles could not damage them even if they were stuck in cracks.

I just wanted to protect the camels' feet. I never imagined that the pebbles would sneak in and chew them into a bloody mess.

We really can't blame Patul. I'll take full responsibility. I thought we'd just take a few days off, since their feet had suffered injuries before. No big deal, their feet would heal after a few days' rest. Everything would be fine then.

Naturally, I hadn't realized that the damaged feet were mere blasting fuses and detonators ready to ignite explosives created by many causes. When I think about it now, however, it was hard to say how everything would turn out, even if the camels' feet hadn't been hurt. When one's heart refuses to change, some outcomes are inevitable.

When we first entered Wild Fox Ridge, I was mesmerized by the scenery. I hadn't expected that dangers lurked behind the pretty sights.

My guru told me long ago about the Ridge deep in the desert, where an old city once stood. Yet after reading a great deal of history, I learned nothing about any dynasty building a city around here. Not a single one. I haven't even come across any reference to the city. It obviously only existed in our elders' stories.

According to the guru, in a place called Wild Fox Ridge was a secret locale that was connected to the sacred land of the Dharmadhātu. At that spot, positive energy enters one's central channel easily, and by reciting incantations and self-cultivation, one can gain massive amounts of good karma.

Don't look at me like that, Lu Fuji. That was what our ancestors said. It's just like practicing cultivation during solar and lunar eclipses to increase one's merits millions of times. In our daily lives, we have more negative energy than positive. But during solar and lunar eclipses, the changes in celestial bodies affect the three channels in our bodies, and we have more positive energy than negative. You have to know that positive energy can enter the central channel more easily and bring fundamental changes to your nature. You can increase your merits infinitely if you practice self-cultivation during solar and lunar eclipses. You can find this concept in the introduction to the Kālacakra Mūlatantra, Taoist Priest Hu Gala told me.

It's the same with the secret locale. From influences of veins in the earth, or what people call dark energy and dark matter, you can more easily encounter positive energy, and since it has easy access to the central channel, you can obtain great merits, blessings, and wisdom.

My guru told me that with enough confidence and the right karmic opportunity, I could go to the Hu Family Mill with no trouble and find the Wooden Fish Incantation. The real purpose of my decision that time was to find the incantation, for with it one's every wish is fulfilled. Granted it was just hearsay, but I believed it, though I didn't tell anyone at the time. On the surface I was going with you to Luocha, but my true goal was to find the incantation.

But not many people knew about it even in Liangzhou—some well-traveled camel drivers, and that's it.

Later I discovered that there had indeed been a city, not too big, but a real city. I think it must have been buried in the sand. When gales blew on it throughout history, the loose sand on the surface was lifted to reveal the city.

Everything is dead there now, only a few desert poplars remain alive. The biggest one is as tall as a white poplar, and it later saved my life—though I wondered if it could count as life-saving, for you can't really save a life, since all lives will end eventually.

The camels fell to the sand with their legs stretched out when we entered Wild Fox Ridge. The drivers removed the leather covers and the bloody mess of feet caused by the pebbles came into view. Everyone looked grim, as we all knew that it would be at least ten days before the camels could walk again. Lu Fuji cursed Patul, which was not surprising, because he never thought Patul was all that great a driver. But as I said, it wasn't entirely Patul's fault. He suggested protecting the feet of their Mongolian camels, an idea welcomed by the Chinese drivers, who followed suit. And that was why the camels on both sides had worn feet pads. Strangely though, the Mongolian camels healed faster than ours, probably owing to the difference in genes. Their camels seemed stronger and dealt better with minor problems.

"Stop it," Feiqing said. "At a time like this, you're just wasting your breath. It might be a good thing for the camels to rest for a few days."

The drivers unloaded the litters that carried mostly tea leaves, though there were also gold and silver. Most of the Mongolians litters had bricks of tea. Their camels were stronger, capable of carrying a litter that weighed two hundred eighty *jin*. With heavier loads came better pay. Both sides had spent everything they had in bidding for the trip, and, as you know, the client decided that each would carry half the goods. The loads were about the same, but the Chinese caravan had to use over two dozen more camels than the Mongolian. We had no choice, because the camels had different genes. A human can't expect to be better than others, and there's a limit to what a camel can carry, so we had to avoid overexertion.

The litters were gathered and placed at a higher spot under canvas covers to keep out of the rain, and the camel farmers pitched their tents. More than ten days had passed since we last saw a lodge, which meant we'd deviated from the normal camel trails. Feiqing had a map and a compass; he drew lines on the map for us to follow all the way to Luocha, where we'd trade the goods in the litters for something else.

Many people in the five provinces in northwest China were waiting for the cargo we'd bring back.

Fewer people would have died so tragically if we'd managed to accomplish our task.

The Ma family had dug up great quantities of silver from their archway that we could exchange for the cargo.

I knew Feiqing chose the route so we could carry out the trade via a shortcut.

Three. Feiqing

Feiqing picks up the narration.

He has his own speech pattern and style, sprinkling his narration with local usage, which I work on to make it easier to read.

After this session, Feiqing shows up during most of my interviews, accompanied by a whinnying horse. I find it odd. I wonder if his extraordinary steed called "Black Clouds over Snow" has stayed by his side all these years.

But I only see him, never his horse. In fact, I'd really like to talk to his horse too, since it was his most intimate companion during those days. I failed to talk to it because I couldn't call forth its spirit; it remained hidden beyond the barrier. Later, when I stop setting the barrier, I still couldn't see it. To me it feels like a magic dragon; we can see only its head, nothing else.

The whinny I hear is unique. It rises straight into the sky, like rending fabric, curls upward like a whirlwind, and lingers for a long time.

Whenever Feiqing shows up, there'll always be the unusual horse sound. Like the weeping sound of the woman by the desert poplar, it continues to reverberate in the depths of my soul.

Feiqing sounds composed, like a wise man who has been through too much.

1

In those days, I often delivered goods to the Ma shop mentioned by Wooden Fish Girl.

Let me first tell you about the Ma family's camel farm. Actually, Wild Fox Ridge felt like a camel farm to me.

In fact, we're the ones who name things, so it's a camel farm when we call it that, and it's Wild Fox Ridge because we say so. As far as this is concerned, I have to agree with you that everything related to humans is merely conceptual.

When I realized that the camel caravans had to stay put for a while, the place turned into a camel farm in my mind. It was a remote spot, but with plenty of water and grass, so I started doing what I normally did at a camel farm. You have to know that we have different concerns at different ages.

Have you ever been to a camel farm?

Want me to tell you about it?

All right, we'll start with the Ma family.

They made their fortune during the Yongzheng reign of the Qing dynasty, when the Yongzheng emperor bestowed the shop with the name "Ma Yong Sheng" or "Eternal Ma." Then, the family grew and branched out. When General Zuo Zongtang went on his Xinjiang expedition, the

Ma family donated a hundred thousand taels of silver and was given the title "Patriot Counselor" and then "Major Merchant" by the Empress Dowager. Later, the family members agreed to change Eternal Ma to United Ma and, working as one, spread their reputation by stamping their tea bricks with "Major Merchant United Ma."

Ma Zaibo was one of the Ma's young masters.

The Ma family ran its business differently from other merchants. Customarily in Liangzhou, a shop was owned by a father and son team and employed family members; rarely would they hire any outsiders. But not the Ma family. They brought talented sons into the business; the mediocre ones were shunned but provided for. They hired capable outsiders to help run the business. A manager was assigned respectively to take charge of tea-buying, tea-making, tea-selling, camel-transport, and the draft banks. I was a manager once, in charge of camel transport. Ma Zaibo was one of the young masters, well versed in the classics, but he appeared somewhat strange to others, because he was forever looking for the Hu Family Mill. To us he seemed to suffer from delusions. They had draft banks all over the country. Lü Erye was assigned to Lingnan but was rarely involved in running the shops. Employing only the best was the key to the Ma family's century-long prosperity.

The camel farm got busy when fall arrived. The whole Ma family business depended on the animals, so they couldn't let them stay idle. For over a hundred years, the camels had brought them incredible wealth and glory. Whenever the family was mentioned, people would say, "Ai-yo. What can you say about them? White camels alone, they have three hundred." In fact, where there was water and grass there would be camels from the Ma family. Their camels had traveled the Baosui road for so long and so frequently that the soft-padded camel feet wore down the limestone some three *chi*.

I've seen it with my own eyes. But Wooden Fish Girl said, "I don't believe it." She could believe it or not, I wasn't about to explain it to her. Why? Not in the mood.

What we did most often at the camel farm was fatten up the animals. Without plenty of fat, they couldn't travel far, live through the depths of winter, or survive an early spring of scarcity. We also had to put the sick or frail ones in a separate pen, so they wouldn't fertilize the females with their inferior genes, and we had to match male with females.

We grazed the camels in the spring. They were fatigued after working for months, so once the new grass sprouted, instead of working them, the drivers set them loose on the farm. Spring and summer were the seasons to add fat. The males grazed at will, chewing mercilessly on tender green grass until it turned into emerald juice, then they gnawed on dry, hard kindling, sucking out the nutrients to turn into fat, and released the impurities into the farm.

When their humps slowly grew fuller with fat, the males started to get ideas. They chewed on their lips until foam appeared and called out in a lusty voice as they looked for females. At times like this, the drivers had to pay attention. If the female had already given birth, it would go well, for it would quietly lie down for the male when it bit her on the leg. If it was a young female that had never had babies, it could spell trouble. It would run like crazy; when it could no longer run after the male had pulled it to the ground, it would tuck in its tail to reject the male.

Oftentimes the "seed" was sprayed on the tail.

Some of the males that failed to get a female would whip their organs against their belly and spew the sticky stuff onto the ground, wasting their body fat. A driver then had to tie up the recalcitrant organ to stop the waste.

Making sure the camels reproduced was the camel farmers' business, which was why they got busy during this time.

The Ma family caravan usually got on the road in the eighth lunar month. Around the time of the Mid-Autumn Festival, the supple camel feet would tread in all directions, accompanied by their bells, taking along tea leaves, wool, and opium, and bringing back silver and other goods. They would be kept busy for seven or eight months, until the third month of the next year, when they were let out to graze again.

Grazing camels meant to let them out and put fat on them. After working for seven or eight months, their towering humps slumped, and even the strongest ones turned weak and scrawny. They entered the most critical period of the year for camels, the so-called early spring scarcity. As the desert was usually colder than elsewhere, spring was chilly, with frequent snowstorms that blanketed the farm, and many camels could not survive. At a time like that, thousands of camels would freeze to death in any given small area. Moreover, the females would be giving birth or getting in heat in late winter and early spring, so the first two months after the spring festival were a critical time on a camel farm, when the manager must pay attention and work hard.

Does that make sense to you?

Heh-heh, I hope you don't find this boring. What I'm saying is indeed quite dry, not very interesting at all.

To ensure that the camels would live through the early spring scarcity without a hitch, most farms raised lots of sheep. Big Mouth was once a shepherd for the Fourth Master of the Ma family. We raised sheep at a camel farm for more lambs, but most importantly for their milk. When a camel looked listless, a driver would make it drink sheep's milk. A considerable number of them were saved by ewes. Camels have uncanny human-like qualities, and know how to repay kindness, so they bravely charged at any wolves that came to attack the sheep.

But spring was also a time of scarcity for sheep. Those that failed to add enough fat in the fall and winter often died after an early spring cold spell. To make sure the camels and sheep would live through the period safely, a farm must have a large reserve of feed, mostly black beans roughly milled into smaller pieces called bean bits. The camels were given the feed when necessary. In addition, the farm had to have a huge quantity of vegetation, such as Artemisia, needle grass, desert thorns, camel thorns, or desert rice. There was usually someone in charge of gathering plants. They bought kindling from local farmers by the weight, which prevented camel starvation, while it helped the landless farmers survive. It was stored away from the farm, as a precaution against fire.

Camel mating season usually started after winter; it was a long period that lasted from late winter into the following spring. Besides adding fat to the camels, the farm had another important task—raising more camels. The Ma family had several thousand camels on farms scattered in Shaanxi and Chengde, and they used only those from their own farms. During the Guangxu reign, when the Eight Nation Alliance invaded Beijing, and the Empress Dowager and the Emperor fled to Xi'an, the Ma family donated many thousand tons of grain and supplied their camels for transport. According to an exaggerated description at the time, the first camel was inside Xi'an while the last one was still in the Ma compound in Liangzhou. White camels were rare treasures, one in a thousand, but the Ma family had three hundred of them. That tells you how many they had altogether.

Everyone said the Ma's fortune grew on the backs of camels.

The farm was strict about taking the weak and skinny male camels away to prevent inferior seed from spreading. Stud camels were naturally those tall, strong, and handsome ones; they didn't work, for they were raised exclusively to breed. Stud camels, like humans, had their own territory and their own females, and any male that wanted to barge in would have to fight the stud camel first.

You're probably thinking I go on too long, but you have to understand how this works before you can appreciate the fight between

Yellow Demon and Brown Lion.

You know, among the camels there is a king, just like a king among wolves, foxes, and lions. Each farm had a king camel, and males often got into fights over the position.

Yellow Demon was the king in the Chinese caravan, and it could mate with any one of the thousand females, while the other males could only watch and swallow dryly. Chinese camels are smaller than their Mongolian counterparts, and they carry smaller loads. Mongolian camels can travel treacherous roads for long distances, so Fourth Master told me to buy a Mongolian stud camel. It was larger than the average males, with long brown hair, like a lion's mane, so the drivers called it Brown Lion. The farm lost its tranquility when it arrived. At first, the other camels picked on it because it was new, and male camels were always attacking it as a group. Though they didn't gain an upper hand, they weren't defeated either, because Brown Lion was such a powerful beast. One day two wolves found a lamb as their target and sneaked up to pounce. Brown Lion stormed up, bit down on one wolf, and tossed it into the air. Then it turned around and kicked the other one at least thirty feet away. From then on, the Chinese camels accepted Brown Lion, no more group attacks on it. He had a few females, but if he had his eyes on one of Yellow Demon's females, then a battle was inevitable. The creed at the farm was survival of the fittest, so the drivers let them do whatever they wanted. A strong one could mate with more females and breed more little ones, while a weak camel could only watch on the sidelines. A failing king camel had to step aside and let someone else take over. Yellow Demon wasn't Brown Lion's match in strength, because Mongolian camels were just so much more powerful. But Yellow Demon, like the Chinese owners, was cunning and sly, and he could compensate for his inferior strength with his intelligence. Neither fared particularly well after a few fights. So, afraid they would suffer terrible injuries, Fourth Master sent Brown Lion back to Mongolia.

Heh—who could have predicted that the two would meet again at Wild Fox Ridge?

2

Sure, on the surface, the camel fight was the origin of the dispute between the Chinese and the Mongolian caravans. But in fact it was only the fuse; the flame would have died out after a few sparks without the blasting cap and gunpowder.

The battle between the two king camels wasn't all that different from two men fighting over a woman. Many men will pay with their lives over a woman, which is why our ancestors coined the phrase, "Affairs breed murder." The same goes for camels.

Can you guess why they both wanted to be the joint caravan king camel?

For food? See how vast the grassland is? A camel can have a belly as big as an oxcart and still can't eat more than a few hundred *jin* of grass. Is that little bit of grass really worth a fight to the bitter end? For attire? Camels have a natural, silky hair, like yellow satin, unlike humans who need to calculate the effect of what they choose to wear. Then what, you ask? I tell you, it's for females.

A camel farm is big enough to accommodate many female camels, but not every male gets a chance to mate. Don't underestimate the privilege of mating. The more offspring one has, the more sacrificial offerings one gets after death. According to our ancestors, the dead can only enjoy offerings from their descendants, unless someone else has been specifically designated.

Naturally, some wandering ghosts harass the living to scrounge up offerings. Usually, the harassed will suffer a headache or run a fever; in other words, whatever symptoms the ghosts have will affect the living. Before my father died, he was weak, completely drained of energy. One day, he "sent me a greeting," and I was suddenly enervated. You have to know I was totally exhausted, so weak I couldn't talk, or open my eyes. I finally understood how it felt to be worn out just before dying. If there'd been a shred of energy left, he wouldn't have died. Liangzhou people call those harassing the living for offerings "demons with cracked heads."

Most of those wandering ghosts had no offspring, while those with offspring don't harass the living, since they want for nothing. Whatever they need is provided by their descendants. As a result, men spread their seed to avoid becoming "demons with cracked heads" after death.

Maybe something similar can be said about camels.

This is only a guess. I could never figure out why the male camels would fight over a female until they kicked up enough yellow sand to blanket the sky. If it was purely to gratify sexual needs, wouldn't one or two females be enough?

The cause of our calamity seems to have been rooted in the battle between the two king camels.

I mentioned earlier that the caravans were stuck at Wild Fox Ridge because pebbles were caught in leather covers that ruined their feet. It was a low-grade mistake.

Later on, another caravan made the same mistake. And it was an even bigger one, with over three thousand camels, escorting the Panchen Lama back to Tibet. To protect the camels' feet, they too covered them with leather pads. In the end, most of the camels perished in the Qinghai-Tibet Plateau, caused by feet ruined by pebbles. Camels with bad feet lay on mountain paths, crying pitifully, loud enough to pierce the sky, before turning into sinister-looking carcasses. It was hopeless; humans are grossly forgetful creatures.

Actually, not all the camels' feet were messed up; I'm sure there had to be some that were not victims of pebbles. Some of the more diligent drivers checked the feet more frequently, sparing some of the camels.

The two king camels fell into that category; the drivers were conscientious and kept the camels' feet unharmed.

You may ask why a caravan had two king camels. Good question. Don't forget that the caravan was formed by merging two caravans, one Mongolian and one Chinese. That's how there were two kings.

Our elders used to say, two tigers can't co-exist on one mountain, and two donkeys can't be tethered to the same trough.

The battle was inevitable.

They were fighting over a young female.

3

From the perspective of eugenics, the two king camels were both superb animals, tall and big, fierce, with magnificent physiques. They were the best, after defeating all comers in their own caravans; they had to have fought many battles to become the king.

Kings were the lead camels, naturally, but the reverse was not necessary so. Each herd had a lead camel, while a king was the most outstanding one in a farm or a caravan.

The king camel in the Chinese caravan, Yellow Demon, was actually white, covered in snowy satiny hair. It derived its moniker from its lightning speed, for it could run like a sandstorm. The king in the Mongolian caravan was Brown Lion, mentioned earlier, a huge animal with reddish dark hair. Mongolian camels are usually larger, with greater strength, capable of carrying heavier loads. It's just the way it is; the Mongolian camels are like the Russians or Westerners, who are by nature bigger than us Chinese. It all has to do with genes.

The two king camels would not have fought if we hadn't needed to stop at Wild Fox Ridge. We traveled only forty or fifty *li* between stops, but it was not an effortless distance to cover, since the camels were carrying a load of over two hundred *jin*. They were drenched in sweat at the end of the daily trek and exhausted when we reached a lodge, where they had no mind for anything but to drink and eat. To be sure, there were a few that had energy for something extra, but they were the exceptions. Most camels would prefer to rest and restore energy for the next day's journey.

But this time, we had a few extra days of rest for the camels' feet to heal, giving the kings time to act up.

Brown Lion had his eye on Pretty Widow, a female in the Chinese caravan. It was a name given by Lu Fuji, who said it reminded him of his lover, a pretty widow back at the farm, so he gave it the nickname to help lessen his longing for her. Pretty Widow was also white, with a nice, neat face, a lithesome figure, and silky hair. She was three years old, a virgin. To a camel she was clearly a beauty, and she appeared to be in heat. Inexperienced as to what was happening to her body, she just ran around in agitation, spreading her rutting odor around. Soon a few males came over, but Yellow Demon cried out aggressively, and they backed off unhappily.

Yellow Demon chewed his foaming lips and inched closer to Pretty Widow, a move the drivers called "on the prowl." A camel on the prowl is somewhat crazed, and we usually stayed clear of one like that if there was no female nearby. A crazed camel can even force itself on a human if it cannot find a female.

"Go on! Do it!" Big Mouth shouted.

Not knowing what was happening, Pretty Widow turned and ran off when she saw Yellow Demon saunter over. But thanks to his longer legs, he quickly caught up with her, bit down on her hind leg, and dragged her down onto the sand.

Brown Lion ran up and thudded against Yellow Demon, knocking him to one side. Outraged, Yellow Demon jumped up, opened his mouth wide, and went after the other camel.

The Mongolian camel made a defensive dodge, but his opponent took a mouthful of his hair, so he hooked his neck over Yellow Demon's neck in an attempt to push him to the ground.

When camels fight, their usual tactics are biting, kicking, pushing, and pressing, biting being lethal enough to cause bloody damage—camels are kind, gentle animals, but can act like mad dogs during mating season. Kicking is also quite effective; their feet are soft, but are powerful from frequent travel on sand. A kick can have such explosive power that it can break ribs, though not strong enough to crack open the chest.

Back at the farm, the Ma family's camels grazed next to the Mongolians. Sometimes, the camels got into fights over grass. Yellow Demon and Brown Lion had tangled a few times, with varying results. Brown Lion was not a mean animal, so he rarely bit during a fight and preferred pushing and pressing until his opponent admitted defeat by making sad cries. When he heard the cries, he would stop fighting. Yellow Demon, however, never conceded by crying; instead he acted his surrender out with bodily movements, relaxing his body and lying flat on the ground, legs spread out like stretching, his struggle gone. It was sort of like a human laying down his weapon, and Brown Lion would stop then. Most of the time, Yellow Demon did not try to match strength with his opponent; he preferred a quick retreat, turning around and kicking out at Brown Lion's ribcage. The tactic often worked.

But this time Yellow Demon decided to bite, which meant he was clearly enraged. When Brown Lion pressed his neck down, he took a chuck of flesh out of Brown Lion, who cried out unhappily, as if to complain to the drivers: Look, he broke the rules.

Mortified, Lu Fuji raised his whip at Yellow Demon. When camels fight with their teeth, they usually do no more than break the skin; biting off a chunk of flesh amounted to a life-and-death battle. Drivers had to intercede. Just think. On warm days, flies will lay their eggs in the wound and, if not treated in time, the camel could die. A caravan is lost if camels start biting each other.

"Right," Cai Wu said. "That ass deserves to be whipped."

"Absolutely," Qi Lu said. Cai Wu and Qi Lu were always in agreement, so in lockstep they could share a pair of pants.

As Yellow Demon dodged the whip, Brown Lion took the opportunity to mount the female, his organ exposed. Pretty Widow shook from fear and tucked in her tail. The Mongolian camel tried several times, but failed to find a way in.

"You're three already, time to have babies." Lu Fuji cursed the female. "Don't act so prim."

She raised her tail reluctantly and Lu Fuji helped the male finish his job.

We suddenly heard a sad cry from Yellow Demon.

4

Lu Fuji never imagined that his meddling move would sow the seeds of calamity.

He'd long had his eye on Brown Lion. Besides being powerful, Mongolian camels have impressive stamina and are hard working. Mating a Mongolian camel with a Chinese one would surely produce great offspring. It cost several bushels of wheat to mate Chinese camels with a Mongolian stud. Besides, even if you pay for the mating, you might not find a camel like Brown Lion.

After the sad cry, Yellow Demon pounced and threw Brown Lion to the ground.

Brown Lion got up with a muffled roar. Knowing this could be bad, Lu Fuji snapped his whip at the camel to keep him away from Yellow Demon. He knew the Chinese camel would definitely suffer if the two males got into a real fight.

We hadn't expected that Yellow Demon's target was Pretty Widow, not Brown Lion; he bit the female's leg and swung his head, biting off a chunk of flesh. Pretty Widow jumped to her feet and ran off, with Yellow Demon in hot pursuit, his mouth wide open, his neck held high.

"Yellow Demon has gone mad," Big Mouth shrieked.

Pretty Widow ran into a sand trough like the wind, blood dripping from her leg onto the sand, sprinkling the ground with dark spots. She was crying in pain, sounding like notes from a *suona* soaring in the wind.

I knew Yellow Demon was incensed by the female raising her tail, which to a male camel amounts to betrayal. A young female surrendering to a Mongolian king in front of her own king, is like a Chinese man betraying his own kind. Besides, she was such a lovely young thing, the Wang Zhaojun of camels. It occurred to me that Emperor Yuan of the Han Dynasty must have had similar feelings when he had to send her to pacify the Huns.

i knew Yellow Demon was capable of anything when he lost his temper, so I took a few camel farmers with me and ran after the camels. Pretty Widow was so frightened she ran around, not knowing where she was going. The male was making odd cries, kicking up sand as he went after her, cutting a scary sight. It looked as if he'd completely lost his head. Camel farmers call a camel in mating season a mad camel, but Yellow Demon looked a hundred times more deranged at that moment.

"Watch out. Don't let him bite you," I shouted.

I went back to the tent, got on my horse, and took off again. Black Clouds over Snow was jet black all over but for four snowy white hooves.

It was the only horse in the caravans. Traveling in the desert is hard for horses, but my horse had been running on sand since it was small; with the leather hoof pads I made specifically for it, the horse had large hooves like a camel's feet, so it could gallop on sand at a high speed. Years later, Liangzhou people would deify my Black Clouds over Snow, claiming it could leap over houses and across rooftops, flying along eaves and walls. That's Liangzhou people for you; they always deify things beyond their comprehension.

I told Lu Fuji to get me a lasso pole, something indispensable in a camel caravan in dealing with intractable camels. They look like lasso poles for horses, but are sturdier and tougher.

The two camels ran into the distance, trailed by a column of sand. I didn't want Yellow Demon to bite the female again, for that could cause infection and spell trouble for us. We were still dealing with the ruined feet, and we'd have to further delay our departure if another kind of injury occurred. Each camel carried a certain weight, and if one was injured, its load had to be shared by others, which might be too much for some camels and tire them out.

Four. Yellow Demon

When he appears, Yellow Demon no longer looks like a camel; he resembles a hunchbacked old man, the image I saw at the Camel Deity Temple. I think he prefers his current appearance, which, after such a long time has passed, has assumed an image.

I think the Camel Deity must have enjoyed the worship and respect of people. Only problem is, camel drivers are a dying breed, and soon there will be no more of them, which will in turn put an end to the temple visits.

On the other hand, Yellow Demon didn't gain the status of a deity from an emperor, but from some reverential camel drivers. They admired him, and so he became a deity; if they stopped, then he'd just be a wandering ghost, called a "mangy deity."

Yellow Demon is a deity with declining fortune and little magical power, but he needs to maintain his posturing, so he has always appeared as a camel deity during my interviews. He looks like an ancient, crooked desert poplar, an odd, freakish sight under the night sky.

The night air moves slowly and quietly, spreading like cold water. Overhead, stars still hang low, but the sliver of moon has grown wider to sprinkle rings of milky white coolness.

As Yellow Demon talks, the other specters fade into the dark. Standing before me is a startling, bizarre looking old man with a hunch back; he has a strong visual impact on me.

His voice has such a texture about it that he sounds like someone poking the night air with a pole; obviously, the status of a deity hasn't helped elevate him to a higher realm in a concrete way.

He still sounds irascible and headstrong.

1

Sure, I was angry. What would you do if your woman was raped by another man? How would you feel if she only put up a half-hearted resistance before undressing herself? So, don't give me a hard time. Don't you know when a female camel raises her tail it's like a woman taking off her pants? If she hadn't, could the brown ass—I never called him Brown Lion. Lion? Hmph, that's laughable—manage to have his way? Besides, did you know that Pretty Widow shut her eyes, with a look to show she was enjoying herself.

It was too much for me to take. How could I not go crazy?

To be sure, there are some men among you humans who willingly deliver their women to other men for their own gain, but that's you. We camels don't care for that; all we want is a daily supply of grass and a bucket of water. We couldn't wear it if we were given an official's cap, spend gold or silver, or live in a mansion. Besides what we need to survive, our only enjoyment is having some fun with a pretty female. If we see one we like, we give chase, letting the wind whip past our ears. We kick up sand with our flying feet, galloping as if riding on wings. How carefree it makes us feel. But you say we've gone mad when we do that. So, you don't go mad then? Look at how your eyes light up when you see a pile of gold or silver, or a beautiful woman.

Sure, I'll admit I was beside myself with rage that day. When I think about it now, I'm aware I shouldn't have gotten so angry over a camel. But at the time I was a hot-blooded, young camel, and, besides, I was the so-called king camel—to me the title now sounds ridiculous. The only benefit it brought me was mating with a few more females, but it feels like a dream now, no matter how hard I try to recall the experience—what kind of king camel would I be if I didn't get angry?

You aren't aware that the brown ass and I were mortal enemies back then. Maybe he'd been a foe of mine in a previous life, for, otherwise, why would I hate even the sight of him? You can surely say I was jealous. Yes, I admit I was a bit "envious" of his physique. For a camel, it's good to have a large frame, be tall, enjoy great strength, no matter how you look at it. But I couldn't stand his arrogance; it was too much for me. Take that incident, for example. He had acted unreasonable first. I never laid my paws on one of their Mongolian camels, no matter what you say. If I had, it would have been so out of line that he could do the same to our Chinese camels. But I didn't. You should know that everyone has his domain of sovereignty. If he stays out of my way, I'll let him alone. But he went against that principle and behaved atrociously in my territory. Sure, he's tall and powerful, and I was a little afraid of him. But I couldn't concede my dignity as a king camel out of fear.

I admit I was mad with anger. I can still recall how the blood rushed to my head and my face burned. I can tell you that my blood doesn't boil often. And I don't fight except when I have to. You know Red Eye was always sneaking around me to pester the females, but I didn't let that bother me. You know, my storehouse of energy has its limits, and I couldn't possibly mate with all the females. Naturally, I turned a blind eye. But that brown ass had all kinds of Mongolian camels waiting to be pleasured, like you humans praying for rain after a long drought. Instead of chasing after them, he decided to fight over mine, like a thief reaching out to pluck a peach from my tree. His action amounted to scooping up shit to fling in my face.

I had to bite him.

I admit I went too far with the bite. But at that moment I would have taken his life if I could have. If I'd known that one day he'd die in the teeth of a wolf while protecting Pretty Widow—that's a story for another day—I might have let him go. To be honest with you, I was quite touched.

I remember I too was stunned after the bite. I sensed something sticky in my mouth, and I didn't know what to do. In past fights, I opened my mouth wide, but mainly to frighten my opponents, and never did take a real bite. This time, however, I used all my strength. I knew it wasn't allowed, but anyone would do that with blood rushing to your head. I heard there were only two kinds of people who never erred, one being the dead—including dead animals, of course—and the other being Buddhas. Why did they make such a big deal over my minor offense?

Back then, besides taking a bite out of that brown ass, I wanted to turn Pretty Widow into a pile of bones. It was just a thought, and whether I could actually do it or not was a different matter. Maybe I couldn't bring myself to continue after a few bites.

But a lasso pole looped over my neck at that moment, and I was outraged. I turned with an angry glare and saw the thickset guy, Lu Fuji, straining to pull me back. He was on a camel, his eyes big as copper bells. Lu Fuji was so strong I sensed that his arms were powerful enough to carry five hundred *jin*. You want to know how I could tell? I'll tell you. I once saw him pick up two litters at the same time; each one weighed two hundred and forty *jin*, and if you add the two together, you'll see what I mean. Once he sent Red Eye down in a sand trough with a single flick of his whip and opened a gash the size of a baby's mouth.

I didn't want him to do the same to my back. Luckily for me, he was carrying a lasso pole, something that didn't scare me. It hurt my neck, but I wasn't afraid of it. We camels were born to have lassos around our necks, anyway. I feared a whip though, especially one with a very soft tip targeting the head. It flew as if riding on the wind and could tear open any hairless spot on the face. But that didn't scare me too much, because they carried whips to use on camels. What frightened me was when a driver's whip missed its aim and the tip hit the corner of an eyes to make it water. You wind up with a blind camel. You do know, I assume, that with one eye blinded, I couldn't be the king camel again, no matter how strong I was. I knew what was good for me.

Fortunately, he only raised the lasso pole, not the whip.

I struggled a few times and failed to get free, so I stopped.

I saw Pretty Widow standing in a sand trough, with her head lowered, obviously still frightened.

She was shaking all over. My heart softened.

2

You know, so many things in the world are easier once you look at them from a different angle. But sometimes changing one's perspective is more easily said than done. Now I've gone through plenty, and I've seen the light, but back then, I really was pretty empty-headed.

I behaved myself for a few days after Lu Fuji dragged me back with the lasso. But that was just for show, because hatred for the brown ass continued to roil inside me. Every time I thought about what the "camel fiend" did on my turf—not geographical turf—I nearly choked on my anger. I kept a close, grim watch on him from a distance. Even at Wild Fox Ridge the Mongolian and Chinese camels did not stay in the same spot. On both sides, tents were thrown up to protect the litters from rain and snow, I knew. It was winter and it was cold, but we hadn't had a snow yet. The wind, on the other, was always howling. Fortunately, we stopped at a sheltered area—a lower spot on the ground surrounded by higher land—so the wind blew right over our heads.

We camels fared pretty well in the wind, since our hair had grown quite long by then. Naked Belly, with less hair, was the sole exception. I heard he had a disease known as "hair heat," which caused him to start molting when the hair was a few inches long. There was enough heat inside that I never saw him shiver, even without long hair to keep him warm. I did wonder, however, if he was struggling to keep up appearances. Two years earlier, another camel that was always molting ended up in a soup pot. Naked Belly saw with his own eyes how several drivers had tied up the camel and plunged a knife into his heart. We were still on the farm at the time. I'm sure Naked Belly never forgot that scene. I think he strained to look fine in the cold wind, so he wouldn't end up in a soup pot.

Cold didn't bother the other camels. I actually don't like heat and feel like I'm in hell in late May and June. Without medicinal water, I'd never make it through the summer.

So, I was squinting at the brown ass; I did that to deceive the drivers. If any of them saw me staring at it wide-eyed, they might take precautions, such as shutting me up behind a crumbling city wall. There were walls like that around here, though they'd been partially buried in the sand until some drivers cleared it away, draped canvas over them, and turned them into chambers. If they put me in one, I wouldn't be able to jump out, not big as I am.

So, I could only keep my eyes half open.

I was looking for an opportunity to punish the damned camel.

It seems ridiculous when I think about it now. Sometimes, time resolves a lot of issues, but back then I got angry when I thought about it, and the more I thought about it, the angrier I got, stuck in a vicious cycle, unable to retreat. All day long I was haunted by the thought of revenge. I found it abominable when I recalled how he'd raped Pretty Widow—even though she'd lifted her tail on her own. I wouldn't have minded so much if it was a rape pure and simple. I noticed how Pretty Widow kept stealing glances at me, and I could tell she was feeling guilty, since she knew how I felt about her. I had favored her, waiting for her to be mine when she passed the threshold age of three. That was because mating time was the key; if not, I wouldn't have been able to do it even if I'd wanted to, like you human males, with your impotence. I'm sure you know how it'd look if I pounced on a female aggressively, bit and pulled her to the ground, and reared up but that organ of mine refused to stand up, if other camels saw it, they'd think I was old and feeble. And that was why I never made a move until that thing of mine was good and ready. Otherwise, how would that brown ass get the chance to perform his evil deed?

I saw him sneaking glances at Pretty Widow. I was sure he was savoring the sensation of mating a young female, and felt great about it. Young females are different from old ones, especially in terms of texture and temperature, but I won't say too much about that. You'll know how it feels if and when you're reborn as a camel. That brown ass looked like a dud to me. He didn't get the full taste; by that I mean he failed to plant his seed, and that must have gnawed at him, just having a taste but not enjoying it to the fullest. The whole thing disgusted me, whether he enjoyed it to the fullest or not.

The fires of revenge raged in my heart, slowly turning into bubbling molten lava, ready to burst if given an outlet.

The drivers herded us out of the sheltered spot a few days later and took us to a distant place to graze. The autumn frost had turned all the grass yellow, but there was at least other vegetation, such as desert thorns, good enough to stave off hunger. My docile behavior over the past days succeeded in deceiving the drivers, who thought I'd changed for the better. They didn't know I hadn't turned truculent, since I've always been that way. Ever since I was little, I had a strong desire to avenge wrongs, and I had a very good memory. I still recall how Qi Lu had tricked me into eating a lizard. Back then he was always winking, with a wicked smile. He caught a lizard, wrapped it in grass, and tricked me into eating it. Sure, he meant well; he wanted me to grow more fat. But he didn't know I hated lizards, truly disgusting things. I knew something wasn't right the moment the grass entered my mouth, because the thing wiggled. Can you imagine a cold-blooded creature struggling and screaming on your tongue—I couldn't hear it, but I could sense its screams, a hundred times louder than a crying earthworm. I was about to spit it out when it jumped down my throat—a living thing jumping down my esophagus. I thought it would create chaos in my stomach, but it disappeared down there, like a mud cow in the ocean. Stomach acid rendered it immobile. I didn't chew my cud that day, for I feared a squishy thing might come up. Eventually, I got my revenge. One day, when he was going downhill on my back, I made a sudden turn while running like the wind, and tossed him way the hell away—don't look at me like that. That happened years ago.

I gave you this example to show you how good a memory I had and how I bear grudges.

The one thing I couldn't forget, even if I wanted to, was that brown ass. Maybe that's what you people mean when you say "mortal enemies cannot avoid meeting." My hatred for him remained even after he fed himself to a wolf to save Pretty Widow—an incident that actually took place after we'd escaped from a sandstorm. I learned about it through omniscient observation, as the scene froze in the depths of Pretty Widow's soul. I can't tell you why, maybe he was destined to be my enemy. No, we were born to be enemies.

We'd often got into fights when we were back at the farm. You probably don't know that the camel farms did not have a clear demarcation, even though we were penned at our own farms. The Chinese and Mongolian farms were separated by a desert that was endless in length but only eighty *li* in width. The two farms were pretty much right next to each other; despite a general agreement on boundaries, it was hard to avoid entering each other's territory. That was why we were always fighting. As I recall, we won some and lost some, but if I count more carefully, the Mongolians got the upper hand more often. They were more powerful, after all. Luckily, there were more Chinese camels and, during rumbles, two Chinese camels sometimes gained an edge by ganging up on one Mongolian opponent. You probably don't know that, despite general similarities in shape, in their states of mind, Chinese and Mongolian camels are quite different and the Mongolians are no match for the Chinese for their cunning. I recall that most of our battles were fights between the two kings, and the outcomes were roughly even. He was stronger, but I was smarter. My cleverness sometimes included tricks or underhanded moves, but there's no honor among enemies.

I wondered if Pretty Widow decided to give itself to the brown ass because of my ignoble approach to fights.

Maybe.

The thought saddened me. Female camels are no good, I said to myself. When the drivers talked about the books they'd read, they were always saying women are the source of calamities, bad enough to cause the downfall of a nation. I had doubted them then, but now I'm a believer. Really, women and female camels may be the same. Just think. The caravans wouldn't have met with such an end if not for Pretty Widow, the tramp.

Don't glare at me. That's my personal opinion. I'm just talking and there's no harm in you just hearing me out.

Stop glaring at me.

3

What happened later occurred when we were out grazing that day.

It wasn't entirely my fault, when you come right down to it. I'd have swallowed the humiliation if that brown ass hadn't poured shit over my head a second time. I did come out ahead the previous time, after all, even if I'd used my teeth and violated rules among camels, which were really just conventions, not actually laws. You can't find any written rules against using teeth during a fight. To be sure, that brown ass didn't use his, but he was free to do whatever he wanted. I wanted to use my teeth, because I couldn't overpower him with my neck or overwhelm him with my strength. Besides, I don't always use my teeth in a fight, and never during the dozens of fights I had with Chinese camels. I was clear about that. I understood what constituted contradictions between us and the enemy, and what were internal conflicts between the people. It was true; the Chinese camels looked at me positively, even though I used my teeth on the brown ass, all but Long Neck Goose, with his perpetual wicked grin. He'd had his eyes on the position of king camel for a long time. I was sure that as I aged, sooner or later we'd have it out. But I was lucky that my sons were growing up—this was the advantage of being a king, mating with lots of females to have many sons. If one of them was stronger than Long Neck Goose before I was too old, Long Neck Goose could think until his head hurt, but he'd never be the king.

I'd made up my mind that day; I'd swallow the insult and forgive the brown ass if he left Pretty Widow alone. I'd let it go, for, no matter what, I was king camel and shouldn't bear grudges like a petty woman. But I'd fight to the death if he got any vile ideas; I wasn't just shooting off my mouth. I'd come up with a plan, I'd surprise him by hitting him during an unguarded moment, and one lethal blow would take care of things once and for all.

You already know what happened. The brown ass was like a dog that can't stop eating shit. Instead of filling his belly, he kept gazing at Pretty Widow from a distance when we reached the grazing ground. Green grass was gone from the area, only desert thorns were left. There must have been an underground waterway, otherwise, desert thorns wouldn't have grown in such abundance. We were lucky camels hadn't been there for years, so we had plenty of desert thorns. Without enough to eat, we'd have perished from starvation before the sand buried us. Heaven always has a way out for all creatures.

I noticed all the Chinese camels were staring daggers at the brown ass. They were grazing, but I could tell they were checking things out of the corners of their eyes. Long Neck Goose, on the other hand, looked at me provocatively. I knew what he was thinking: if you can't protect the female then you'd better step down; don't stay at the hole if you don't want to shit.

It looked to me that a fight with the brown ass was inevitable. Just the look in Long Neck Goose's eyes was enough to set me off.

The brown ass was looking at me too, I realized. I knew he was a little afraid of me now. I wasn't as strong as him, but I always had a surprise move at the critical moment. You do know that Mongolian camels are just like their people, a bit simple-minded and easy to deal with. It's all relative, simple-minded or not.

How would you feel when you saw your rival after he slept with your beloved girl? You'll be able to understand my feelings when you think about it that way. I was jealous, knocking over a vinegar jar, as Liangzhou people say, and a strange emotion raged inside me. I wished my front feet were sharp knives, so I could chop that damned ass to pieces.

Then I saw he was inching closer to Pretty Widow. It was plainly obvious that the brown ass was too lecherous to care about anything else; if not, he'd have been able to tell what was going on in my head. He glanced at me tentatively, to which I responded with an angry glare. You can't imagine that look—it was not friendly. It was absolutely, deadly cold. Even if he was brain-dead, he should have been able to see I was ready to kill. My glare essentially told him he'd better start behaving himself, because his life was on the line.

But he was getting closer. And Pretty Widow actually flicked her tail, which really pissed me off, because that was the same as saying, "Welcome! Come on over!" I was beside myself with rage. How could she forget she was a Chinese camel?

I was dizzy with fury, but managed to calm down to think carefully. I was a Chinese camel; it was who I was. I knew I was no match in strength for the brown ass, so I had to win by outsmarting him. I also knew it was going to be a critical battle. The two caravans had joined to become one, and, as they say, two tigers can't co-exist on one mountain. The alpha camel had to be decided between brown ass and me. If I was defeated, I'd not only lose Pretty Widow, but also the other female camels on the Chinese side. The brown ass would take them all.

He was almost there. I could feel everything between heaven and earth went quiet at that instant, and everyone was watching me. I heard my own heart thumping hard, like a drum; blood continued to surge to my head, but I told myself: calm down; stay cool.

Then I heard Long Neck Goose cry out.

I knew right away what that meant.

It was clear to me that I had to make a move or he would. If he did, he'd be acting as the king, and whether he won or lost, I'd lose at least half my authority.

So, I cried out too, and loudly. I meant to tell Long Neck Goose I was in charge and he should stay out of it, while warning the brown ass that I'd make him sorry if he didn't stop.

I sidled up to Pretty Widow and stationed myself in front of her to watch the approaching brown ass. I'd thought I'd drag Pretty Widow to the ground—she'd be too shy to lie down on her own—and mount her to plant my seed. But I was wary that the brown ass might sneak an attack on me while I was busy with her. You know certain matters require undivided attention; I'd never be able to guard against a lethal attack at a moment like this. I could finish quickly to fight but you know my will to battle wouldn't be as strong. So, I wisely chose to wait in combat readiness.

The brown ass hesitated; obviously he was reminded of his Mongolian identity. I saw a glint of uncertainty in his eyes. But I knew he couldn't stop now, because all the camels knew his intention, and they'd call him a coward if he backed off.

A brief hesitation later, he continued walking toward Pretty Widow—no, toward me, as he was looking at me, not her now. He was aware that pleasure had to come later.

The first round was a staring contest—we looked steadily into each other's eyes. I saw a spark of blurry yellow, and thought it must be my reflection. I couldn't see details, naturally, because I wasn't in the mood for a close examination. If I'd just eaten my fill of water and grass, and was looking at Pretty Widow or another female I liked, I would surely see tiny yellow dots—and someone might ask, "Isn't Yellow Demon a white camel? How could it be a spark of blurry yellow?" Let me tell you. White camels are white only when contrasted with yellow camels, which are considered brown. Despite its moniker, white camels actually are faintly yellow, like off-white, not snowy white. See what I mean?

With a formidable enemy standing before me, I shifted my gaze to his bulging muscles. I had muscles too, was, in fact, the most muscular camel on the Chinese side. But I wasn't as powerfully built as the brown ass. A matter of breeding. My bone structure was clearly inferior, but I won't go on about that, because you might think I'm defending my subsequent actions, even though I'm just feeling sorry for myself.

I realized that, as we continued to stare at each other, the brown ass was looking more and more truculent. We'd had a few close combats before, but they'd been brief, as we usually stopped when a victor was emerging. More often than not, we waged show battles or skirmishes, never used full force. I already knew he was a tough opponent. I never defeated him with strength alone, though it wasn't because he was so much more powerful than me. No. I was the king camel, after all, and I never suffered a crushing defeat. But I have to admit that he was truly the most formidable opponent I'd ever faced.

Our battle started with the staring contest. In the past, quite a few camels had lost the staring contest and given up on challenging me. Camels don't make much noise, but we express ourselves fairly well with our eyes. On that day, we did just that. If you try to convey what we said with our eyes through the technique of stream-of-consciousness, you'd have a terrific essay. For now, all you need to know is we were waging a battle.

I must stress that my anger grew as we continued to stare. At first, I noticed evasiveness in his eyes, like the look an adulterer gives the husband whose wife he's slept with. I was clearly winning at the time. I was experienced enough to know how hard it is on a camel when it feels the urge, and I nearly forgave him. I was saying to myself, "Just let it go. Act magnanimous and forgive his transgression. If he'll stay clear of Pretty Widow and let me keep my pride, I'll stop now." But he gave Pretty Widow another look, and something changed in his eyes. I wondered if she had given him some sort of signal, like an adulteress saying to her lover, "What are you afraid of? You're the one I want." The look in brown ass's eyes changed—no more evasiveness, now replaced by aggressiveness. I can still recall how my anger flared up at that moment, and I felt a tingle spread from my limbs to my heart. It was like nothing I'd experienced before. I'm sure you know that I was most incensed at her betrayal, convinced that she'd encouraged the brown ass with her eyes. I was sure of that, and later developments proved I was right. I didn't know when the change in her began. Maybe she'd always favored the brown ass, even before she raised her tail. Some females among your human race prefer strong men, too. Later, when I thought it over, I saw that a female like Pretty Widow didn't deserve me.

But at that moment I was thinking, "To the bitter end!"

My eyes conveyed my fury to the fullest extent, the flames of anger burning off the last shred of his intimidating effect on me. A strange, powerful current billowed inside me; my blood boiled and surged, sweeping away all rational thought. More than once I had to suppress the urge to pounce and bite, knowing it was not a move known only to me. I had teeth, so did he; I could bite, he could too. I could bite until he was a bloody mess, but the same could happen to me. We'd both be badly hurt, so this was clearly not the best tactic.

The battle left an indelible memory that remains fresh even now.

Hard to say who attacked first. In my recollection, we lunged simultaneously, seeing the intent to attack in each other's eyes. I chose neck wrestling first, but soon realized that was an unwise decision. But you know how, at the height of your anger, you have an inflated sense of self and falsely believe you're invincible. I remember feeling his terrifying power the moment my neck pushed down on his. I had to use nearly all my strength, and barely managed to hold my own. Fortunately, I detected that he too used all his power, for I saw his eyes getting bloodshot. That meant we were about equal in terms of physical prowess. I'd always thought he was stronger than me, but that turned out to be a misconception, which originated in the heavier loads the Mongolian camels carried. I would later learn that they were better than us in terms of stamina.

Our neck wrestling looked very much like camel drivers arm-wrestling, but we were trying to push the other's head to the ground. That was my strength, as I often wrestled with the young camels back at the farm. Sometimes it was for fun, but sometimes it was for real. Just about every young stud wanted to wrestle me when they were old enough. Naturally, they were envious, and they drooled over the pretty young virgins. But you may or may not know that under normal circumstance the pretty young virgins belonged to me; the other young camels had to wait to mate when I was too weak or with a female too ugly for my taste. The drivers at the farm certainly hoped I'd pass down my superior genes, as it was my dominance that terminated the lines of those mangy camels. My neck grew stronger over the semi-serious neck contests. But Brown Lion, I mean brown ass—I almost used the favorable name—had a neck made of steel, which was actually understandable. He must have similarly gone through rounds of sweating neck wrestling. I felt a powerful, otherworldly force pulsing in his neck; it was throbbing, like a slithering python. On the surface we looked to be even, and the necks remained stiff in the air, not tilting to one side, but I knew I had reached the limit of my strength. My legs were getting weak and sweat was pouring out of my pores in tiny beads before merging into rivulets to steam down my neck, drip to the sand, and spread into a pattern.

Can you feel in the thickening silence something akin to roaring waves crashing against the shore?

Several times, when my neck began to tilt under the pressure, I had to hold my breath and strain to force it back straight. I also tried pressing down on his neck; once I even saw a flash of success, but quickly a strong, resisting power surged toward me. At that moment I wondered if he wanted to let me win, though I immediately realized that he'd used everything he had.

I felt I was blacking out. A boom went off in my head. At some point, our necks had stopped twisting against each other and looked to have formed an arched bridge. I was panting, and so was he, though I knew I'd surely be the loser if we kept this up, because I didn't have the stamina. Now I was regretting the choice of neck wrestling, a stupid battle move that requires all one's strength and attention, and intelligence is useless.

I knew I was about to lose. The soreness and exertion on my neck grew more and more intense, and my legs were quaking. My opponent was sweating and panting too, but his legs were dug in deep. Our feet were sinking into sand that was slowly rising up to our knees.

Just as I felt all my energy was about depleted and I was ready to give in, I heard a shout from Ma Zaibo. We both let go when we saw the shadow of the flicking whip.

It was clear that Ma Zaibo had saved me.

I never forgot his kindness, which is why I was willing to sacrifice myself to save his life later, when he was in trouble.

4

The vegetation was growing sparse, which was understandable. With so many camels grazing all at the same time, soon there would be nothing left. So, our grazing ground was moved farther out; when we finished what was nearby, we went looking for more.

I couldn't see Pretty Widow or the brown ass anywhere one afternoon. You know I'd been watching them, as I sensed something might happen between them. I'd hoped not, for if it did, then I'd be a king in name only.

I searched several sand troughs, but they were nowhere to be found. All the grazing camels seemed to be looking at me scornfully, and I heard laughter soaring into the sky from one of the valleys. The loudest came from Long Neck Goose; we'd battled in the past, and he, too, was a worthy opponent, with enough strength to keep the combat going for a while. He lacked stamina, but had the advantage of youth.

I noticed all the young camels were looking at me. Their eyes seemed to mock me. Later, I realized that was a mistaken impression, but at the moment I felt greatly insulted. An urge to tear into something rose up.

A loud crack went off in my head.

Time for a decisive battle, I thought.

I saw that Long Neck Goose had his eyes on me. That was no illusion, it was real.

Many of the camels were looking in the direction of a bend, which told me that was where the brown ass and Pretty Widow were engaged in some sordid act. Kicking up sand along the way, I ran over and had barely turned the corner when I saw brown ass tugging the female's leg, which made me think that Pretty Widow still had feelings for me; otherwise, it wouldn't have taken them so long. All she had to do was lie down when her leg was bitten for the brown ass to have his way.

Pretty Widow cried out when she saw me, in a pleading voice. I'm sure you can comprehend the impulse of a hero wanting to rescue a beauty. The brown ass's massive organ looked domineering, like an angry cobra rearing its head.

To be honest with you, I was really losing my senses. You know, with so many things, people who are right in the midst of them are usually unable to see them clearly. Once it's over and circumstances have changed, one will think differently; what felt like a grave matter was nothing but an illusion. I was like that. When I think back now, it feels as if I'd been possessed; I don't understand why she meant so much to me. Now, Pretty Widow is just a phantom; back then, she was like the sun to me.

I charged at the brown ass, running as fast as my legs would carry me, kicking up sand along the way. I'm sure you've noticed that that is one of my favorite phrases, but it was the way I ran. I preferred digging up sand with my back feet, a move that had actually saved my life once. One day, when I ran into a wolf, that was how I managed to escape; I kicked sand into the wolf's eyes. They called me Yellow Demon because of the sandstorm I trailed behind me. Got that?

I wasn't sure if Pretty Widow's behavior was an optical illusion, including her cries. It was what I'd hoped, but not what was happening. When I got closer, I saw how the brown ass's organ had entered Pretty Widow, and maybe not the first time either, because she clearly looked to be enjoying it. If it had been the first time, it would have hurt, and she'd have looked it. I didn't know at the time—I learned about it after I became a camel deity with mind-reading ability—that Pretty Widow did it first with Long Neck Goose. I don't know when, but he found a moment when I wasn't paying attention to take her.

Long Neck Goose had had a fling with Pretty Widow, but pretended nothing had happened, even putting on upright airs. From this alone you can see how devious he was.

I recall how her moans outraged me.

I have to remind you, however, that I weighed about seven or eight hundred *jin* at the time. When I ran like a wind toward them, I was powerful enough to topple a wall. I was able to fling the brown ass off her. He must have been having such a great time he couldn't stop the pleasurable act even as he saw me charging. I won the first round that day.

5

The brown ass got up. Obviously furious, he was foaming at the mouth as he ran at me. Male camels always foam at the mouths when they're ready to mate. Me for one. It's like you humans drooling, just a physiological reaction.

After the experience of our previous combat, I decided against positional warfare—that is, no neck wrestling. I spun around as he ran at me recklessly, and raised a hind leg. I gave him a vicious kick, with the full force from a foot that had grown immensely powerful after digging in sand for half of my life.

You must know that a camel's kick works as well as a bite. Sometimes, when it hits a vital spot it can kill. To be sure, the foot has to land on the scrotum, for instance; if it lands on the rib cage, it has a similar impact, because the pain will be so great it will take your breath away, and you'll be immediately drained of energy. You see, my kick landed solidly on the brown ass. I thought it was the abdomen, since it felt like it had landed on a bulge. It could have been or might have been somewhere else. You know I was so angry I lost the clarity of mind to figure it out.

The brown ass screamed—it was damned impossible for any camel to make noise that loud. Then he rolled a few times like a bundle of wheat tossed into a sand trough and looked like a tumbling ball of camel hair when he tucked in his limbs. I later learned that the pain had made him shrink into himself. Humans curl up like that after getting the wind knocked out of them.

It thrilled me to see his sad appearance and hear his painful cries.

Then I thought it was odd that, given how big he was, he should not have crumpled so easily from a single kick. I didn't know at the time that the spot I'd bitten before was already festering, which in you humans' term means infected. Too many ant holes can bring down a mile-long levee. It naturally never occurred to me that a small injury would destroy an extraordinary king camel—of course I didn't call him that, not until today, so many years after it happened. Back then I'd never have acknowledged his status as a king. My mind is clear and my head is cool enough to recall the past only now, when all my emotions have vanished like clouds in the sky.

At the time I was still in the grip of fury, my blood was pulsing and burning, like crashing waves. You do know that I couldn't possibly be calm at a moment like that. I'm sure that something else had entered my blood; I mean, my anger wasn't just a mental reaction, but had an additional physical or physiological cause. If you tested my blood when I was calm you'd see its components were different.

Believe me?

I believe it anyway. I'm convinced that many humans, when they're as angry as I was, make wrong moves because that additional component has added fuel to the fire. They can't help it. They have no idea what they're doing at the height of their anger, and if a mistake is made, by the time they finally regain their composure, it's too late for regret. They have to take responsibility for the consequences of their action. But in a way, you can say they're innocent. This was Ma Zaibo's view, which I shared. I'm not defending myself, just showing you that his theory is accurate.

I was mad with anger and couldn't control myself. At the moment, neither my mouth nor my feet belonged to me, as if some current asserted itself to make me act the way I did.

When the brown ass got back to his feet, I thought he'd pounce on me. But, strangely, he didn't. I didn't know at the time he'd been weakened considerably by the infected wound. Like a fish in water, it's the only one that knows the temperature. Only the brown ass knew about his strength; obviously, he was aware that he might lose if he decided to charge and fight me under the circumstance.

He gave me a cold glance and walked off unhappily. To my surprise, Pretty Widow fell in behind him.

I wanted to run up and take a bite out of her. But, strangely, I'd lost the will to fight. Something in the brown ass's eyes had hit me, and it hurt. Seriously, even now when I think back, I sense an invisible rock pummeling my heart.

Yes, I decoded disdain in his eyes, as if he were saying, "I despise you. You're a coward."

Then I realized that the camels were all looking at us, from a distance. No sound came from them, but to me they spoke volumes.

Sanxing is slanting westward.

Sanxing is a term we in Western China use. It's called a cold star in books.

The sand trough is cold as an ice cellar. I try to fight off the chill so my teeth won't clatter, but everyone around me senses how cold I am. It may even be contagious, because I hear shivering sounds. Now I understand; they no longer have their bodies, but they can still read my feelings; they feel my chill and respond in kind.

"Enough, that's enough." Someone speaks up. "No more for today. You don't want to turn into an icicle."

The comment elicits a chorus of agreement.

I plan to go to the next stop, which is about thirty li from where we are. I arrange to meet with them there. To them time and space don't exist. According to our elders, these specters have magical feet that enable them to appear instantaneously thousands of li away. They have all-seeing eyes, can read minds and know fully what others are thinking, they have supernatural hearing that lets them hear anything they want to hear, and they're well versed in transmigration, so they know all about their past and present lifetimes. Of the six supernatural powers, they lack only asravaksaya-jnana, so they're still plagued by worldly concerns.

"Sure, sure." Lu Fuji continues, "We'll be there when you recite the incantation, as long as you're in Wild Fox Ridge."

"In addition to interviewing you, I also want to have a look at the actual geographical locations. Maybe the features will tell me what happened there," I say.

"There's no need to do that," Chain Smoker says. "We all know the story. But it's okay with us if you want to take in the sights."

I get up, stiffly, which is common when it's cold. It's like my bones are frozen.

The coronae begin to disperse. I can see some of them showing faint outlines. Perhaps my interview has helped revive their memories.

The yellow camel gives me an enigmatic look before sneezing violently, when I return to the tent. Something feels different, but I'm unusually exhausted, so I decide not to analyze the changes in the animal.

The white camel still has his serene gaze and yet something seems to be bothering him. It's just a feeling I have, though.

Fifth Session
Ancestral House

I quickly chow down some food when I get up the next day, before hurrying ahead to the next stop by following the trail of caravans of an earlier time. As this part of the trail is a rocky desert, everywhere I look is black rocks. A hundred years have passed, but the trail is still easy to detect, and every once in a while, I see camel carcasses. The harshest sight is the skull, on which the large black holes look unspeakably gruesome. My dog probably feels the same, for it barks constantly. Obviously, the yellow camel fears the skulls, as it keeps tossing its head to struggle out of the reins. I know it doesn't want to enter Wild Fox Ridge. Over the past few days, it has become clear to me that he is lazy and bereft of the common camel traits of generosity and kindness. If the wood ring in its nose doesn't make it tear up each time I tug at it, I'm afraid I won't be able to rein it in.

White camels have the facility to keep their cool under fire. Drivers say they are rare animals, and, it appears, not just because of their color. Their white coat certainly reflects superior genes.

Wild Fox Ridge is also called Dead Camel Valley; hosts of camels have died there over several hundred years, hence the name. I've heard that, before the disappearance of the two caravans in my investigation, many camels had perished there, mostly employed by explorers. Lore about the place mentioned treasure, and in turned attracted droves of explorers, most of whom never made it out, dying of unknown causes. Later a foreign explorer, who was lucky enough to leave, wrote a book and talked about Dead Camel Valley.

From the layout of the land, it's hard to tell that this is a treacherous area. Oddly, however, strange things always happened in there, and stories about the unusual events traveled far and wide, were even recorded in a book about the life of camel drivers. Few people know about the book, for it has only been hand-copied and is yet to be published.

It's almost noon when I get to the second stop. First, I find a spot that's out of the wind, pitch my tent, and wolf down some food before jotting down a summary of the interview from the previous night.

I recite the incantation and light the yellow candle shortly after nightfall.

Soon I hear noise—no, I don't quite hear the noise as much as sense it. It doesn't come from a vocal cord, but a mere manifestation of functional energy. I understand it and know my friends have arrived, as promised. The first I sense is still the sound of a whinnying horse, then the strong smell of tobacco. It's unusual that the aroma remains distinctive after so many years.

The yellow camel is spitting, which is a common reaction when camels see a ghost. I heard that what ghosts fear most is human spit, and likely camel spit as well. The yellow camel spitting sounds are like gunfire, a loud popping noise. Fearful that the noise will affect my interview, I lead him off to a distance. He struggles violently along the way, rearing his neck and crying loudly, as if in protest or as if to tell me: Ghosts! I know they're ghosts, I say silently. I don't need you to tell me that.

I nearly break his nose ring before I manage to tether him to a desert poplar away from my interview spot. On my way back, I hear him spitting like a machine gun.

His hostility toward me is unmistakable but incomprehensible. Could he have been Yellow Demon in his previous life, I wonder. If so, might I have been Brown Lion? It's an outlandish thought, but an amusing one. I won't feel any regret if it turns out that I was Brown Lion in my previous life. And isn't that strange!

Several of them wish to tell their stories on this night, but I want most to hear Wooden Fish Girl's. I'm afraid that too many narratives might mess up the pace of my interview. I must get out of here before the depth of winter, a time when water turns to ice before it hits the ground, I'm told.

I say to Wooden Fish Girl, "Please continue with your story."

One. Wooden Fish Girl

1

My heart is always seized with pain when I think about it, but I'll tell you anyway.

In many people's view, the calamity originated from our ancestral house.

According to Big Mouth, Lü Erye had had his eye on our house for a long time. He had wanted for nothing, except for his son to gain scholarly honors or an official rank. He had two sons, actually, and the one I married was from his second wife. Lü Erye didn't care for the second son, a dimwitted boy, and he didn't look too sad when he died either.

I'd heard that his older son, Ma Zaibo, was a good scholar, but hadn't even passed the provincial exam after several tries. I wonder if he'd found it beneath him or if he just had lousy luck with examinations. Several years later he told me he had no interest in Confucian teaching, which focused on how to enter society, while he wanted only to depart from society, and all those Confucian phrases made him dizzy. He did not want to be in the examination hall, he told me, that he feared passing the exam and, worst of all, detested the idea of being an official. But that changed nothing, because some strive to become officials while others abhor the thought. Ma belonged to the latter group. He loathed the mere mention of the word, "official," let alone be one.

Lü Erye could not have known what was going through his son's head and consulted with some people of superior knowledge—though only heaven knew what was so superior about them. They all said his watch tower was perfect for accumulating wealth, but an impediment to scholarly honors. So, he hired a fengshui master, who then surveyed all around, into ravines and mountain valleys. Surprisingly, the only place he found suitable was our ancestral house, saying it was a spot kissed by the God of Literary Honors.

I didn't believe any of that.

There have been a few scholars on my family tree who left behind samples of writing, some of which may be good enough with enduring importance. But just may be, no guarantee. We have several from previous generations, but they are mostly wooden fish song books. Thanks to the participation of talented scholars among the ancestors, these books were indeed of high literary quality, but they were not the type of material for anyone planning upon passing the examination. And that was the reason why only two individuals among five generations of ancestors had passed an exam, while the others left behind well written books of wooden fish songs and local gazetteers.

But Lü Erye ignored these facts and bought wholeheartedly into the idea that his sons and grandson would gain scholarly honors and official ranks if he could gain possession of our ancestral house and build a memorial hall and a study on the site. With this scheme in mind, he tried to butter Father up. Then one day, when alcohol was involved, he told Pa he wanted to buy the house. Pa adamantly refused.

I'll briefly describe our house. It wasn't very big. Have you seen a typical terraced house? It looks the Chinese character, 非, with a passage way in the center, flanked by rooms on both sides. The rooms are long and narrow, with tiny windows and a single entrance. To thwart thieves, these rooms never have large windows, so it is dark and humid inside. Pa added another story made of wood to protect the wooden fish song books he'd collected. Back then, our village was always flooded during the rainy season, and our house was inundated. Luckily, our ancestral home was well built and remained unscathed from water damage. That was before cement was available in China; since it had to be imported from the West, it was called yellow-hair mud. Pa said our house was as solid as those constructed with yellow-hair mud. Grandpa had built it by mixing cane sugar water, and soupy sticky rice with mud, lime, and seashell powder. It was so sturdy, floodwaters had no effect on it. When we knew a deluge was coming, we'd simply move the most valuable items up to the wooden story and everything would be fine.

I can understand how Papa felt. The house had become the last refuge for his soul, and he wanted to hold on to it. After selling the land, we would have no place to call home in the south if we lost the ancestral house.

Lü Erye was willing to pay a hefty sum and offered to find another location for us to build a better place to live. Papa was on the verge of accepting, and would have if not for Big Mouth, who said something he probably should have kept to himself. He said he'd seen Lü Erya touch Mama's breasts one day. He added that Lü Erye was always calling Mama into his house, and she came out "red faced" each time.

Papa was outraged. To him Lü Erye might as well have poured a ladle of watery shit on his head. A soldier accepts death, but not humiliation. The one thing he could do was vent his anger on Mama; he forbade her from working for Lü Erye and gave her several severe beatings. She never defended herself, just sobbed with her hand over her mouth.

One night a flood came down from the mountains. It was a severe flood, nearly submerged the whole village. Mama had just given birth to my baby sister, who ended up living for only three days. Over those three days, we stayed in the wooden addition. We had nothing to eat. The baby cried at first, but soon went quiet. Pa never showed a shred of sadness over the death of my kid sister, because deep down he had treated her as Lü Erye's.

We were starving after three days. We couldn't get down from the added story. We saw the water had risen high, but none of us could swim. There were seven of us, my three younger brothers, me, Papa, Mama, and the newborn baby sister.

I'll never forget the scene. Despair held me in its grip. Papa and Mama were quiet, as they had become strangers after he'd heard what Big Mouth said. I would relay comments when they had to say something to each other. Feeling hopeless, Papa told me a lot. He hated the prospect of losing the books. "The old texts are the fruits of labor by generations of our ancestors," he said. The new ones were his life's work, and he did not want them to disappear into the water. He wanted me to take them out, saying I was light enough to float out in a wooden bucket.

I left.

But I didn't take the books with me. The bucket was not big enough to take much and, with me inside, it could barely stay afloat. I told him I wouldn't take them because I'd memorized them all. He laughed and called me his Ānanda. I had no idea who Ānanda was back then, but later I learned that Ānanda was the Buddha's attendant, with such a fine memory he remembered everything the Buddha said. From the analogy, I saw Papa's high self-regard; he considered himself a Buddha-like figure.

I paddled slowly, floating the bucket out of the house and into the lane, where our house occupied the lowest spot. It was the spot the fengshui master identified as a treasure bowl, where there was a confluence of supernatural influences.

I believed him, because it was where Papa had written many of his wooden fish lyrics. He'd written as if possessed. It was also at this spot where I'd memorized all the songs he'd collected. I didn't make a special effort to commit them to memory, I mainly did it for fun. I'm convinced that supernatural influences did converge around our house. Therefore, even though we were often stranded by floods, I would not be willing to sell the house to anyone, not even to him with the greatest power, let alone Lü Erye.

There weren't many people out in the alley; our neighbors must have all fled the flood. Quite a few of the houses were no match for the water; some had already collapsed, while the others might fall apart one day soon. But not ours. Papa had said the seashell powder would keep it standing no matter how many years it was inundated by water. That would one day be confirmed. Decades later, a reservoir was built in the neighborhood. Our house—some members of the family renovated it— was as sturdy as ever, after half a century; it was known as the sturdiest house in Lingnan.

After getting out of the bucket, I considered my options and finally decided upon going to the shop. It was erected on a hill, giving it imposing airs. I don't know if the site really did have good fengshui, but it surely was safe from floods. Lü Erye's watchtower sat atop the tall hill. In Papa's view, it was not a spot for human dwellings, that it was fit only for a temple. When people lived there, it amounted to sitting on the Mountain God's head, and sooner or later the family's fortune would decline, if they did not perform enough good deeds. What he said made sense, but the family prospered for five generations, with Lü Erye being the fifth. Their watchtower had first been built in a valley, then been moved up to a hill, and finally soared atop a ridge. But the family had moved away by the time you went to interview them, and all you saw was a dilapidated compound straddling a ridge. Once his family fortunes suffered a decline, no one was brave enough to build a house up there.

I wanted to head over to the shop because I thought of Big Mouth. He was the only one I could think of. To be honest, I hated Big Mouth when Papa beat Mama; I hated him for what he'd said to Papa. I didn't care whether it was true or not; all I saw was the damage it did to my father. Besides, so what if it was true? To be sure I thought, at the time, that Mama had committed an enormous transgression, and I found her somewhat deplorable. What I felt most, however, was how Papa was suffering. I stopped going to see Big Mouth after the incident.

But he was the first person I could think of after I escaped from the flood. And I no longer hated him. Obviously, hatred is not a constant emotion. I knew he was the only one who would be willing to help me.

It was still raining; water filled up the gullies and flowed to lower ground. I knew that at this rate, it would continue to rise in the lowland areas. And it wouldn't take long for our wooden story to be flooded. I shouted the moment I reached the shop, "Big Mouth! Big Mouth!" I didn't know his name, and I'd never called him anything when I talked to him in the past. I didn't how to address him except to call him by his nickname.

He came out and seemed happy to see me. The camel caravan had left without him this time, because of diarrhea, I heard. He was holding a pipe, which was what I disliked most about him. But he'd once told me that he smoked to ward off snakes. He said one night he'd awakened to discover several snakes under his blanket, and that scared him witless. Later, a seasoned camel driver told him to smoke, saying snakes flee when they smell tobacco. That was how he started smoking. He reeked of tobacco, the most pungent type.

He didn't seem to mind when he heard me call him Big Mouth,

except to say it was a nickname someone had given him. "If you like the sound of it, you can call me Brother Big Mouth from now on." So that was what I called him.

Brother Big Mouth saved my family that time. He knew how to swim, so he filled the bucket with food to deliver to our house. I thought Papa would turn down the food because he was always saying that "an upright man doesn't accept charity," but he did.

Concerned that the water would continue to rise, Big Mouth wanted Papa to move to the shop, but Papa told him to take my brothers along. He'd rather die than leave the house, and Mama stayed up with him, at his insistence.

Fortunately, the sky cleared three days later.

2

Later Big Mouth said there was something odd about the flood, because he discovered a path someone had dug on the slope to direct the water to our house, turning it into a small reservoir. Even worse was that someone had also dammed up the mountain pass that could have let water out. A hundred years later, when the reservoir was built, the pass was closed up with reinforced concrete. Papa called the spot "Fairy Blockade." I heard that it was guarded by a fairy water buffalo, and that no one would block it. Obviously, someone managed to do just that when our house was flooded.

I suspected Lü Erye.

Big Mouth said it couldn't be. According to him, Lü Erye was a womanizer, but he wasn't a bad man, and he gave me many examples to prove his assessment. One day, when Big Mouth craved a snack, he stole some beans to exchange for candy in a store, where he ran into Lü Erye. He'd thought he would surely be beaten, so he was surprised to hear the master say;

"The beans are meant to add fat to the camels; take the rice if you want something to eat."

Big Mouth told me some more anecdotes like this. In his eyes, Lü Erye was a good man, though Big Mouth was disgusted by his lecherous look whenever he saw a pretty woman.

"He's a lecher, but he'd never do anything so atrocious," he said.

"The food I took to your house. It was prepared by the kitchen, instructed by Lü Erye. I couldn't have done it without his consent," Big Mouth added.

What he said made me feel bad about wrongly accusing someone who had helped my family.

But Papa was convinced it had to be Lü Erye. "He wanted to drown us all so he could have our house," Papa said.

We couldn't prove he was right.

But later a fire convinced me he was right, after all.

Yet, man proposes, God disposes.

I didn't expect that I would do something unimaginable with Big Mouth. I don't know if it was an unconscionable act. It happened, even though we had no choice.

I feel guilty about it. It didn't matter what reasons we had, but we did cause the death of Lü Erye's son.

I think I'll let Brother Big Mouth continue with the story.

Two. Big Mouth

I can smell tobacco too when Big Mouth talks. I get a feeling that he's very much like Chain Smoker. There appeared to be two separate people in the story of Wild Fox Ridge, but I still feel they're actually one, though they are thirty or forty years apart in age. I think Chain Smoker was Big

Mouth when he was young and Big Mouth would grow older to become Chain Smoker. It was something common among camel drivers, which was even mentioned in a song called "Spring in the North": "My brother is just like my old father."

Big Mouth speaks slowly, like drinking green millet soup. The soup has millet and nothing else, giving the soup a green tint. When I was little, my mother made green millet soup a lot. It has a silky texture and a mild taste. The newly cooked soup is boiling hot, so you have to take a deep breath, very slowly, as a tiny stream of soup will be sucked up and slowly slide into your mouth, onto your taste buds and spread. It's a leisurely, comfortable sensation.

And that's how I feel when I listen to Big Mouth.

1

Meeting Wooden Fish Girl was the first major event in my life.

After all this time, I don't want to keep it a secret any longer.

The way I see it, it absolutely was a major event. What else could be more significant than for a man to see the daylight? In my hometown, we call what a man does with a woman seeing the daylight. Daylight refers to the sun, but it also means a woman's private parts. Just think how important and elevated it is when we compare it to the sun. In my village, a man isn't a man until he sees the daylight; a coffin is too good for him, and he will be taken out and burned at the riverbend when he dies. We called someone like that a big dead baby. A man who dies in his seventies or eighties without seeing the daylight was a big dead baby.

And I saw daylight with Wooden Fish Girl.

To be sure, once you've seen it, you can see it a hundred times and there's not much difference from the first time.

2

I was herding a flock of goats that time we went to Luocha. It was an unusual trip; we took the goats along with the camels. The camels transported cargo and the goats carried camel feed. My flock handled beans, fine salt, highland barley, and other stuff. The goats would later become food for the drivers. After traveling for a certain period of time, they would kill the goats to replenish their energy. They slaughtered several at each stop, and few would be left by the time they reached their destination.

Don't underestimate these goats. They might not look strong enough to carry much, but the ancients had a saying about ants toppling the mighty Taihang Mountains, didn't they? Put the cargo carried by hundreds of goats together, and you can crush several camels to death.

If we were at a spot for a long time, I removed the goats' litters to give them some freedom. Usually, however, we didn't unload the goats. It was their fate. Like our parents, who had toiled all their lives, the goats were born to carry a litter, like your father often said, "An old cow doesn't stop shitting until the day it dies." Normally, after we set out, we don't remove the goats' litters because of time constraints. With a heavy litter pressing down on their backs for a long time, they begin to lose the hair on backs that are rubbed raw and begin to fester and stink. So litter-carrying goats don't taste good, since you can't get rid of the stench even if you cut off the rotting parts.

When we reached Wild Fox Ridge, I removed the goats' litters. Putting them back on is a lot of trouble—just think, I'd have to do that for hundreds of goats—and then tie down the ropes. But I thought I'd let them relax whenever they could, because I could feel their hardship, which was why I called myself "Zhang Yaole"—Be Happy Zhang. My life was like heaven compared to those dumb animals. You may think I also had a hard life, but I could talk, jump, and sing tunes, and I could have all the pleasure of looking at my sweetheart, Wooden Fish Girl. But the goats? They couldn't. So why shouldn't I be happy? A lifetime passes whether you're happy or not, whether you laugh or not. Why shouldn't I laugh?

I was the same as in the story Wooden Fish Girl told. I laughed, and I didn't fake it. I stopped laughing only when I saw Gaqiu. Why? Because he was Wooden Fish Girl's husband, and I wasn't. He was a husband at the age of seven, while I was already eighteen, but no girl would want to be my wife—no, Wooden Fish Girl did, but she belonged to somebody else. I couldn't bring myself to be happy when I thought about this fact, so obviously my happiness was relative.

I want to tell you about Gaqiu, Lü Erye's second son. He wasn't all that bright, was constantly drooling, but sooner or later he'd be the boss. I might be strong and know how to use a club, but I'd forever be his clerk. Lü Erye was so rich he oozed fatty grease. The goats we took with us to Luocha were his, purchased by the caravan. Sometimes a client will acquire a whole team of camels, which was what had happened to our caravan to Luocha that time. Why? Because, I heard, the trek was risky. I didn't know what that meant, and in fact, I didn't feel any danger at all when we first set out. To be sure, "risky" isn't sufficient to describe the situation when the danger cropped up.

Listen to me. I'm digressing. This is how I am. No wonder they called me Big Mouth; I should have a gatekeeper for my mouth.

Shortly after we entered Wild Fox Ridge, I realized that we wouldn't be setting out any time soon, so I took the goats out to graze. There were so many of them it was like a large patch of clouds. Wooden Fish Girl went with me, for the flock was too big for one man to handle. A large flock like that needed at least two people, one in front to keep them in line, and the other in back to move them forward. Otherwise, those in front would run all over while those in back would lag behind. It wouldn't be a flock any more.

Wooden Fish Girl and I had known each other for years already. She was just a little girl who dropped by the bank the first time I went to Lingnan with a caravan. Those who had been to school would say we were "green-plum and hobby-horse," childhood sweethearts. Hell, Feiqing was always reciting the lines in a poem, "You rode over on your hobby-horse and we played with green plums around the bed." Yes, that's how it felt to me.

Back then the clerks at the bank were always giving us nicknames. Mine was similar to the character Black Whirlwind, in the classic novel, *The Water Margins*. When village children gave other kids nicknames, it's usually related to their parents or their names, or it could be associated with a girl. Mine belonged to the latter, as I was called Big Mouth Boy. Some of the clerks would shout when they saw me, "Wooden Fish Girl and Big Mouth Boy, a couple in the ditch, oh such joy." You don't need me to tell you what the couple was doing in the ditch.

It made me mad when they did that, at least at first, because we hadn't done anything. Later, I smiled secretly, because I liked Wooden Fish Girl and how could I still be angry when they linked me with her? Even later, another clerk who was also sweet on her insisted on linking me with another local girl. I knew what he was thinking, so I got angry when he called out his nickname for me. I picked up a dirt clod and aimed at his ass—I didn't want to hit him in the head because I could smash it—and he stopped after a few hits.

She was always stealing glances at me when the clerks used our nicknames. Then she grew up. One day Lü Erye went to see her father, gave him some silver, and brought her over to be the child bride for his seven-year-old son. It wasn't really her father's fault. He had been poor for too long, and they often didn't have enough to eat. Yet he kept searching for wooden fish song books. He had to eat too. I heard she was happy to help him out, and outwardly, she never complained.

I was cutting grass on the hill when I heard about it. My scythe went crazy, flying around and chopping like mad before it bit me on my calf. Hell, it bled like a river.

Enough about that. Those were the days that make me sad when I think back.

3

I'll talk about the first time I saw daylight.

Something like that is most memorable. You once said that many events in life boil down to memory. That's so true. We can never stop things from disappearing, so everything eventually turns into memory. And most of our memories fade into oblivion in the end. That's what life is all about. What you said mirrors the young master's views.

It's true, I realized, that everything in our past turns into memory, no matter how momentous or indelible. Memories don't last forever. I don't believe in any religion, but I believe in this notion. Why should I be unhappy? I'll be happy with my present life, and that's enough. Everything else is beyond my control, beyond anyone's or any deity's control, actually.

I grew up day by day. I didn't know I was growing older at the time; I only noticed the changes in my body. Parts that should be bigger had grown bigger and I had new, unfathomable urges.

I missed her most when I woke up just before dawn. By then she was no longer tending sheep for Lü Erye, who sent a mute old man to go out with me in her stead. People in Lingnan didn't normally raise sheep, but Lü Erye did, because of his fondness for mutton. When she was little, she had grazed sheep for his family and got paid a pot of food three times a day, which helped keep her family alive when life was at the toughest for them. She could sing wooden fish songs too, but the villagers weren't in the habit of hiring her, so she couldn't earn enough to support her family.

She stopping tending the sheep when she became a child bride in Lü Erye's home. I usually took the sheep out to graze on hills with the mute, when it wasn't too busy at the draft bank. He often smiled at me cryptically; I couldn't figure what he was smiling about. He kept the smile until the day he died; one morning many years later someone found him dead, with that smile on his face, and the spot near his heart remained warm to the touch for seven whole days. Ten years after that, when the graves were relocated for some reason and his was dug up, they saw he was still smiling and his body remained intact. It was a bad sign to the villagers, who, afraid he'd turn into a demon, hacked him to pieces with their shovels and spades. I heard there was even blood in the mess.

For a period of time in my life the mute old man was my sole companion. I became a mute myself when I was with him but it felt peaceful to me. At first, I was on edge but later I cheered up, which I attributed to him. I didn't buy Ma Zaibo's idea that the old man was a Mahasiddha. I never saw him reciting sutras or chanting any incantation. He was just happy; sometimes he was happy to look at the sky and at other times at the earth. That was all. I didn't know what he could have attained.

The two of us took the sheep to a hill far away from the village, where grass grew so abundantly the sheep could eat to their hearts' content. They grazed and grazed until they grew up to become pieces of mutton in the bowls held by Lü Erye and his clerks and camel drivers. I grew up too, from a young helper to a camel driver. When I was just a young helper, I often practiced martial arts with the camel drivers delivering goods to us. I got strong enough that in time I found myself old enough to be a camel driver.

One day Wooden Fish Girl brought food to us—I had to add that we never went back for lunch. It was too far, and besides, we wanted the sheep to graze all day. Every morning at first the boss sent a silly girl over with food. Who could have imagined that the silly girl would enter into history one day and have an article written about her in a gazetteer? I'll come back to that later.

Every day around noon the silly girl came up the hill with our lunch, which was boiled sweet potatoes or something else. We ate whatever she brought us, we weren't picky eaters. At the time we ate the same thing the boss had. He didn't have anything cooked specially for him and he wasn't as fiendish as they said in books later. He was a man just like us; he wanted a good reputation and a good screw.

One day the silly girl had a baby and stopped delivering food to us. It was a mystery then and later how she came to have a baby. She wasn't married and she was uglier than a pig and yet she got pregnant. Naturally, it was a mystery.

Lü Erye had started sending Wooden Fish Girl instead when he saw the silly girl suffering from morning sickness.

Which was why I came to see the alluring figure of Wooden Fish Girl appear on my horizon. My Wooden Fish Girl. I can still feel the stirring in my heart when I think about her now. Back then I was as romantic as a poet and would often call out silently, Wooden Fish Girl. My Wooden Fish Girl, my dearest, my precious.

Don't laugh. It wasn't an act.

4

Don't laugh and don't get the wrong idea.

It didn't start on the day she came with food. In those days men and women did it differently from your generation. Now a man can easily make a woman take off her pants if he has money. The same held true in our time too. In those days there was also a Hexi Inn in Liangzhou, where many pretty girls stayed. But I didn't have any money. A high mountain separated a penniless man and a woman he wanted. In fact, there was a mountain between Wooden Fish Girl and me too, maybe a minor barrier like a sheet of paper before she became the second young mistress, but I didn't break it down. The barrier grew thicker until it became a mountain.

We exchanged a few words that day. I recalled she took me aside and said the old animal was getting ideas. I asked her what ideas she was talking about. She said he squeezed her hand when she handed him a bowl of tea.

Later I heard something similar in one of the Liangzhou tunes, "Pawning a Leather Coat," in which a man squeezes the hand of the woman he loves when she offers him tea. It was like Ximen Qing pinching Pan Jinlian's foot in the novel. In Liangzhou it was a blatantly seductive act, like saying, "I'm seducing you. Will you go along?" If she squeezes you back she's saying, "Absolutely. I had my eyes on you already."

Which was why Wooden Fish Girl said the old animal was getting ideas.

"He tried to open my door at night," she said. "I propped it shut with a pole."

I saw the mute smile enigmatically at me. It was odd though; he was nowhere near us, but I could see his smile so clearly. I thought every wrinkle on his face was saying something to me. I didn't know its content, but I knew what it was about. Can you guess?

I got nervous. "Don't say bad things about him. Maybe it was an accident."

"How could something like that be an accident?" She stomped her foot.

Then she walked off.

Sure enough, however, I saw the old ass stealing over to her room and pushing at her door that night. It remained shut, so he slinked back to his room.

But I wondered if it was just a dream.

I stayed at the shop outside the watchtower, so I couldn't see her little house. Lü Erye had several houses. He himself lived in the watchtower. The shop clerks lived together in another building. There was also a guest house, what we Liangzhou people called the carter's quarter, where the drivers stayed. The carter's quarter was separated from the watchtower by a large gate with heavy doors inlaid with rivets. The doors were so sturdy that the outlaws couldn't smash them open even with stone rollers. Like the outer defenses of an ancient walled city, the carter's quarter was such an impediment that it would take outlaws extraordinary efforts to get through, assuming they made it that far.

How do you think I managed to see what went on inside from the carter's quarter?

Well, when Wooden Fish Girl came with food the next day, what she told me was identical to what I'd seen.

I believed her.

In those days, child brides were commonplace. Often it was a young boy marrying a girl around eighteen years old. In those days we even had a doggerel: magpie, magpie, caw all day long/tomorrow an auntie comes along/auntie, auntie, take a seat/let me help you off your feet/my son is the size of an ordinary date/your girl is ten plus seven or eight/I plead with heaven and earth, let me have her." See, that was how the match was made. So Gaqiu, the walnut-sized boy, married Wooden Fish Girl, the girl of ten plus seven or eight.

In those days, some of the boys weren't that much younger than their fathers, so father and son looked more like brothers. Their real fathers were actually their grandfathers. Some said that women were fertile soil, and it didn't matter who sowed the seeds, as long as you reap a harvest. To those who were constantly under the threat of being slaughtered, it wasn't a bad idea to prevent their lines from dying off. Don't you think?—listen to me. I'm actually defending the old thief.

From then on, I was filled with hatred toward Lü Erye, but it wasn't class hatred. It was merely the hatred one man bears against another. Later on, many people characterized it as class hatred. Where would I get the idea of class in those days? He was my boss, and I couldn't be docile enough for him. I hadn't hatred him before then; on the contrary, I had been grateful to him. As I mentioned earlier, I stole some black beans one day—I was too young to know what was right—and traded them for candy. When he found out, I thought he'd beat me up. But no, he just told me to trade rice, because the beans were for the camels. That was all he said. I have to let you know, though; in those days all the beans were reserved for livestock, which, I heard, grew fat only by eating beans. Wheat provided little energy. What I'm trying to say is, Lü Erye wasn't a bad boss, he enjoyed a good reputation among the clerks. He constantly hired workers to repair bridges and pave roads. I only started hating him after he began having designs on Wooden Fish Girl. Lü Erye, I said to myself, Lü Erye, you're an old animal. You're sixty, she's not even twenty. How could you have such thoughts? In fact, I wouldn't have loathed him if I hadn't fallen for Wooden Fish Girl myself. So many lecherous men in the village have slept with their daughters-in-law, I couldn't possibly hate them all.

Despite my hatred, there was nothing I could do. The thought of Lü Erye always reminded me of the old man in the sky; I felt powerless before him. I'd been like that since I was little. Sometimes my heart raced just hearing him cough, even though he'd never laid a hand on me. Maybe the better people treat you, the more you feel like that.

I started hating him because of Wooden Fish Girl, and later, the hatred spread to include everything related to him.

The elders say, once hatred enters the heart, it will sprout and grow.

I'll wait to tell you what happened later.

That was why I treasured happiness that was hard to come by. Whenever I got a chance I'd pull down her pants; we did it everywhere, any spot you could think of, by the river, on the hill, surrounded by goats, which gave us funny looks. Hei, they did it, so we could too, right? I knew they were jealous of me. You probably don't know, but she was such a lovely girl. Her eyes were like the gemstone, cat's-eye. She moaned under my touch, so melodious, endlessly titillating. For her, I'd be happy to be cut a thousand times, let alone lose my head.

Hei, enough of that too. Pleasure never lasts long. Happiness in the human world is like frost on the grass, evaporating as soon as the sun is out.

I could only seize the moment to be happy and enjoy myself whenever I could. Whether I was happy or not, time passed like flowing water. I had to be happy, didn't I? I'd be a gratified ghost if I died on top of Wooden Fish Girl!

5

It was several days after she told me about Lü Erye knocking on her door that I first saw the daylight with her. He often did that at night, scaring the hell out of her. One day when she came to deliver food, she led me over to a rocky cliff, where she said, "We love each other, but we can't be together. So I'm giving myself to you first." I was nervous, but the old mute was nearby. He was always smiling enigmatically; he'd smile and then shake his head, with a mysterious look on his face. I was sure he was laughing at me, for I detected something profound in his eyes that was unique to him. At the time I didn't know he had taken a vow of silence, so I thought he had been born mute. A mute man was no different from mute animals, to the villagers, including Wooden Fish Girl. So, to her there was no one around us at that moment. Still I took her farther off to a secluded spot, an opening made by rushing water, what Liangzhou people call a funnel pond. To the west of the pond was a gentle slope.

Do you know the folk song? "A bright red blouse opens the door/a pair of breasts outward pour/torsos together till we're both so sore /give me what you got, girl/well, help me off with the pants you wore." Heh-heh, the song seemed to be written about me that day.

She undid one button at a time and I was shaking the whole time. I saw her fair skin jump out at me little by little, dazzling my eyes.

Hei-hei. I was clumsy. I hadn't seen the daylight yet. I said, "You do it," I said. "I don't know how. You start."

She blushed and giggled. "I don't know either."

Hei-hei. She was still blushing when she took off her blouse and spread it on the slope, leaving only a stomacher up top. Then she removed her panties. I saw a patch of fuzzy hair on the mound, not much and not too black either, but I was sure it was hair. What I meant was, she wasn't a White Tiger, a woman with no pubic hair. What happened to us later had nothing to do with the White Tiger Star. Later some people called her a white tiger, accusing her of doing me in. But that wasn't true. She wasn't a white tiger. She was normal. She had what could be considered fierce hair down there.

The first time in my memory was hurried. I did think about it a lot later, but at the time I didn't feel much pleasure. I was frightened and I kept seeing the mute's inscrutable smile—I could see it if even when we were down by the funnel pond. Later I realized that his smile had been imprinted on my mind and popped up now and then. And that was why I wasn't getting hard enough; in the meantime, I didn't feel the corresponding dampness in her either. That is, our first time together wasn't driven by burning desire, and we were still clear-headed. It was a rational choice on our part, and we were completing a kind of ritual.

Yes, you were completing a kind of ritual. What you two were doing was a sort of rite too, and with it, you entered a new stage. No matter how close a man and a woman are, without seeing the daylight, they can't poke through a paper-thin barrier, without which they will never be truly close. It is a rite, symbolizing the entry into each other's life to make a life commitment. Naturally, the rite means virtually nothing to those cynics who just want to have a good time when they can, just as the empowerment and conversion of other Buddhist rites have no real meaning to Buddhists who weren't serious.

On many occasions, as a matter of fact, form is content, especially when it comes to what happens between a man and a woman, where form is content. Without form there is no content.

Because of form, you and Wooden Fish Girl could be truly devoted to one another.

6

Please don't interrupt, sir.

I didn't know anything about rites at the time. I just felt she was precious to me; I wanted to swallow her up and she wanted to devour me. That was all. We were like a starving couple seeing well-cooked, tender mutton. To me, it felt more like eating, and that was why our ancestors say it's our nature to desire food and sex.

At the time I realized I couldn't enter her. I had no idea where I was going actually. You'll see that what the elders said about seeing the daylight was quite interesting. It did look like a blind man seeing daylight.

I'd been thinking about what it looked like, where it was located, and what color it was, like a blind man imagining the sun in the sky, pure fantasy. There was once a blind man trying to visualize the sun, and someone told him the sun was round like a gong and hot like a brazier. So when he heard a gong, he'd shout the sun had sounded, and when he touched a brazier, he'd say the sun was getting hot. You wouldn't know what the sun was like if you haven't seen it.

But I finally completed my rite. I thought I was at the right spot but I wasn't sure. Later I did feel a wetness but that was it. An immense joy overtook my mind, however. Looking at Wooden Fish Girl under me, I felt an overwhelming giddiness surge through my heart, and it was more satisfying than any physical sensation. I felt contentment and happiness over truly having her and I completed my own rite amid tremendous joy.

She was blushing when she pulled up her pants, a dazzling glow spreading across her face. The look she gave me was different from before; now it was the expression of a woman who loved her husband deeply. Hei, this may have been the function of the rite you were talking about.

We walked out from under the cliff. The sky was unusually blue and the clouds were oddly white, while the wind gently kissed my face. People can be so despicable, don't you think, pal? These things had been around, but I'd never seen them or felt them before. Everything came alive and became extraordinarily pretty in my mind, after that thing of mine came into contact with the thing of hers. Were they the pretty ones or was it a woman's body? Or had my mind been altered by a woman's body? What do you think? I remember I was truly happy after that. A clerk like me got to sleep with a woman like Wooden Fish Girl. How could I not be happy?

Isn't that true?

I noticed the mute too had a kind of glow on his face. He was still wearing that mysterious smile, but was looking at the clouds in the sky, not at me. Yet I detected something else in his face, a kind of rapture. Clearly, he knew something had happened between Wooden Fish Girl and me.

7

Only later were we truly able to enjoy it. She didn't hurt and I wasn't nervous. When she came with food, she'd always bring a little extra for the mute, something she'd sneaked out of the house. The rules at Lü Erye's household required the young mistress to work as much as anyone else. Having more opportunities was the only difference between her and the others. What kind of opportunity? The opportunity to eat. For instance, she could have some rice after she cooked it, or she could steal a couple of buns when they were steamed. The mute slurped when he ate, with a look of a contentment; as he savored the food, he stopped looking at me. We went to the sand trough farther off to slowly do what we wanted to do.

You get to enjoy it once you're not hurried. One day she suddenly shouted, her face twisted out of shape, Heaven. I'm in heaven. I was scared, I thought she was dying. To my surprise, she wore a sweet, giddy smile as she held me tightly.

"This is worth dying for," she said.

That sounds unlucky, I said to myself. People say that tone is important in a lot of things we say. Say something positive, it could turn out good; say something negative, it could turn out bad. Ma Zaibo said it was karmic connection—don't interrupt, let me finish. To me this was only a theory, and I don't believe our destiny was caused by what she said that day.

What happened later could have developed in different ways, I'll give you that. Maybe there was something we could not understand, something I'll call fate.

Lü Erye eventually stopped knocking on her door. I don't know why, he just stopped, but it did give us our very first time together in bed.

That evening, she told me to go to her room later that night. Of course, I'd go. I wanted to spend all night with her, in bed. When it was late and all was quiet, I put a ladder against the wall, climbed over and down the other side. Now I was in her yard. My nerves were in tatters when I did all this, but with sex on my mind, I was braver than the boldest man around.

I went into her room. It was an ordinary room, but better than a celestial palace in my eyes. It was permeated with a familiar smell, a smell I adored. Ever since our first time together, I smelled it all the time. I don't know why, but I think for writers like yourself it was an important detail, something that couldn't have been made up. When a woman enters your life, so does her smell, until it becomes something you can't live without. At least that was how I felt.

Her room was filled with that smell. The light was dim, but the smell was blindingly bright. Then I saw Gaqiu, her walnut-sized husband. He was forever staring at me wide-eyed. Maybe he sensed something, I said to myself. I didn't like him. He'd grow up one day and would want to do what I had done with her. I couldn't bear to think about that.

At that moment he was fast asleep in a dark corner of the room. I remember it was a bright night, with a lonely white moon outside. It might just have been how I felt. Wooden Fish Girl said there was no moon that night. Was there or wasn't there? I can't tell you now. But I still think there was a moon, because I saw everything in the room. I saw the boy I hated. I saw even more clearly her dark eyes and a fire burning inside, the kind that could bake and melt me. The fire in her eyes seemed to burn brighter ever since she cried out that time about being in heaven.

At the time, that had made me happy, but I felt myself slipping downward instead, to the place unknown to me.

We were in each other's arms. It was the best time we'd had since we began seeing each other. The room was better than the pond, so she was soon moaning loudly. I put my mouth against hers to stifle cries that sounded strange in the dark night. I wished there were a spot where she could cry out as much she wanted; I wished I could hear her cry with abandonment; I wished I could see her twisted face as she cried. So many "wishes," all of them became dreams that could not be fulfilled that night. I blocked her mouth and we expressed our pleasure with our bodies. We had no idea the boy would wake up amid our rocking movements. He opened his startled eyes wide and stared at us. I didn't know how long he'd been staring before he finally shouted:

"Papa—papa—they're doing the donkey thing."

"Papa—"

"Papa—"

He might have seen similar performances with the donkeys in the carter's quarter or overheard someone from his home village calling it a donkey thing. In any case, he knew it was bad. He was so loud we froze in fear. My desire left me; I was worried it might cause impotence after that and it did. I couldn't get it up for many days after that. I remember Wooden Fish Girl telling him to stop shouting, but he wouldn't listen. He kept shouting, making me so nervous I picked up a pillow and placed it over his mouth.

Just like that.

With everything it was just like that.

We stifled the shout and stifled a life.

Oddly, the boy's sudden death didn't cause much of a stir. You have to agree that it was quite unusual. First of all, there were no visible signs of injury on the boy. Secondly, Lü Erye didn't appear to like a boy who was always having epilepsy fits, and thirdly, he didn't seem to notice anything different in Wooden Fish Girl. There could have been other reasons too. In any case, when he saw the dead boy the next morning, he was surprised and sad, and he wailed with the body in his arms. But in the end, he didn't say anything. "When a baby is doomed to die, it lies facing up. Go ahead, burn it." That was all he said. So, they did. I wonder if the murder later had anything to do with the boy's death.

I didn't go see her for a long time after the boy died, because his face kept flashing past my eyes. And my powerful organ stopped following orders. I knew it was impotent. I was scared.

Luckily, it suddenly came back to life one day and saved my soul.

Hei, look at me. I'm worthless, aren't I?

I didn't know so many perilous events awaited me down the road.

Three. Wooden Fish Girl

1

I met up with Big Mouth several times after the incident. We never did it again in the house though. Whenever we found an opportunity, he would take me to "Fairy Blockade." He would just kiss me when we got there; we didn't do anything else. He couldn't get it up for a very long time—hei-hei, don't be shy. You were fine later on, weren't you? Don't be deceived by his appearance. He can be wild too. At some point I discovered that his mouth really was bigger than normal. But he had a good voice. He'd softly sing Liangzhou folk tunes, constantly stopping to explain the lyrics. I was convinced that the tunes and wooden fish songs were the same, but evolved into two different variations.

There was no moon on this night. In the grass were many tiny glowing insects, which I very much liked. They weren't especially bright, but with them around, darkness didn't seem as terrifying. To be sure, I had nothing to fear when I was with Big Mouth. He wasn't very old, and was the best martial fighter among the young drivers. I saw him fight with a pole, and it never took long for the other man to lose his pole or wind up on the ground. Men were always coming to him for a fight, and no one could best him. I always got a heady feeling when I watched him fight. To be honest, for a while I thought he was a young man from a good family who had fallen on hard times. I asked him about his background, he said he was a genuine peasant. His great-great grandfather, great grandfather, grandfather, and father—all peasants. What made them stand out among the peasants was their martial arts skill; they were all experts in pole fighting. They were lethal when wielding a short pole, not a long one, which they called a lash pole. He showed me a few moves once, and all I saw were pole shadows when twirled at the highest speed. He lacked the carefree flair of a young master and the impressive airs of a knight-errant; all he had was a larger than average mouth and a good-natured smile, but I liked him. It was odd, though, that in those days I didn't think his mouth was all that large, in fact, other people's mouths seemed small. Hei-hei. Maybe we were destined to be together.

In those days, he gave me an inexplicable feeling I'd never experienced before. We started meeting at night. After the death of the boy, I didn't want to be in that room, so I went back home to live with my parents. Lü Erye didn't object to my decision, which made it easier for us. I usually sneaked out of the house when everyone was asleep. I bribed one of my younger brothers with rare objects like raisins so he would open the door for me before dawn. Big Mouth did the same with a young clerk at the shop. Whenever we wanted, we could have our tryst at Fairy Blockade.

I liked the spot, for it had a fairly smooth rock, a white one. I thought it could be jade; if not, it had the glossy appearance of jade. We leaned against the rock and talked and talked. I learned about his background, about rules regarding a camel caravan, stories I'd never known existed before, and the Ma family's past. I didn't know until then that Lü Erye had ancestors worthy of unabashed pride.

I must add that what I feared most at the time was getting pregnant. If Papa knew I'd done something to bring shame to our ancestors, he'd surely hang himself again. In his mind, Mama was no longer a virtuous woman—he stopped looking at her after what Big Mouth told him. I was the most important person to him, not just because I was his daughter, but also because I was the carrier of his other life—the wooden fish songs. He had wanted to accomplish something grand, something monumental, at least in his eyes. When I think back now, I realize that he was naïve. How would wooden fish songs lead to something like that, even if he could perfect them? Obviously, our personal likes and dislikes often influence our value judgment.

That was his mistake back then. He was convinced of his ability to do something important, and later of my ability to do the same, something earth-shattering. The reality was, I wouldn't have been the equal of a dust mote in the sky of history if you hadn't written me into your book. Not many people care about wooden fish songs, without which those who muddle through life continue to live and live well.

His idea was so infectious I regarded myself as someone who could bring major changes to the world. I liked Big Mouth, but that's all; I did not plan to marry him. I wasn't sure who I should marry but I knew it wouldn't be a camel driver—I don't mean to disparage you; it was just my thoughts at the time. But I didn't have the will power to control the romantic feelings surging through my heart. When I first met him, I convinced myself that I just wanted to talk, that's all. So, we talked day after day until one day we were in each other's arms and we were kissing. And later it went out of control.

I was frightened by the longing I had for him when we weren't together. Like a rock rolling down a hill, I realized I was losing control. I was afraid I'd do something that would lead to father hanging himself. One day I struggled out of his arms and said, "We have to stop. We can't do this anymore." Big Mouth panicked; he was afraid too, afraid I'd stop seeing him.

Later on, we grew bolder.

It was at Fairy Blockade that I noticed the fire that would change my destiny. The flames were blinding in the dark night.

2

Our house was engulfed in flames when I ran back with Big Mouth.

The fire blocked the front and back doors, both sides alit with piles of kindling. There hadn't been any firewood before, which told me that someone wanted to kill my family in the fire. I ran up, but Big Mouth pulled me back. Then I saw fire erupt inside and I knew it was bad. I bawled and ran up without regard for my life. Many people had come to help put out the fire. They poured water on the flames, but failed to stop it from spreading. It later occurred to me that whoever did this had added something to help the fire burn.

The fire didn't die for a long time.

Just like that, everyone in my family turned to charred sticks. Mama was the only one with a recognizable face. Papa had put his arms around her to block the raging fire from burning her pretty face. He must have forgiven her at that moment, I thought. I was moved by his action for many years after that. She must have felt happy at that moment, for instead of saving his wooden fish song books, he'd put his arms around her. I was pleased and comforted by the thought. Most of the books perished in the fire; only a few survived.

The local government office sent people to investigate after receiving a report. They sifted through the ashes and found a familiar object—a water pipe. It convinced me that Lü Erye had set the fire.

He wanted to wipe out my family so he could take our house, I said to myself. I even thought that he'd known the cause of his idiot son's death, and might have tried to exact revenge.

Big Mouth didn't agree, naturally. He still held to the idea that Lü Erye was a lecher, but not a murderer, not someone who could carry out something so vicious.

Lü Erye, the hypocrite, sent someone over with stuff for me. The man told me that Lü Erye would like to help me repair the house.

I turned him down. I wanted to keep the scene of an evil deed intact.

Besides lodging a complaint with the local government, I searched everywhere for anyone who was related to us, however remotely. I fanned their anger and hatred enough that they secretly prepared weapons. They agreed with me that Lü Erye wanted to kill us off to take our land, which was so obvious even an idiot could figure it out. Just think. If I hadn't sneaked out to meet Big Mouth that night, the site of our ancestral house would be a shambles with no one to claim it, and Lü Erye would get it easily.

Lü Erye's water pipe became an important piece of evidence to me. Other than that, there were no eyewitnesses or other evidence, nothing to show he had committed the atrocity. As for my accusation that he'd harassed Mama, he didn't deny it, in fact, admitted to having something going with her, and that it was consensual. He explained that she had gotten much higher pay than anyone else, which helped keep my family alive.

The water pipe was his. But he had lost it before the fire and had actually gotten some of his clerks to help him look for it. They all supported his claim.

His explanation convinced the government, but I believed he'd bought them off. Lü Erye was filthy rich, and, just like now, nothing was impossible as long as you're willing to spend money.

I decided to keep up with my complaint. I went to the county and then the provincial government; I met with anyone I could find, and filed endless complaints. But the results never varied from the first time. No one wanted to arrest Lü Erye. When social conscience was placed alongside money and power, most people would choose the latter.

It finally convinced me that Lü Erye's money could truly open a channel to the heavenly court.

3

I knew that with what I had, fighting Lü Erye was like a mortal combating the old man in the sky, but I continued to pursue justice without a second thought. I went all over, walking into a yamen when I saw one and kneeling before an official when one showed up. My actions touched many people, and they all wanted to lend a hand, but their help failed to effect any change in reality. There was no eyewitness or sufficient evidence to prove that Lü Erye was the murderer. Our ancestral house turned into a hot potato, no one wanted it now. Even if I were to give it to Lü Erye, he wouldn't feel comfortable accepting it.

Uncle, my father's older brother, was on my side the whole time, and often gave me money for travel expenses. He loathed the Ma family, and hated the Hakka even more, because grandpa had died in a battle between the locals and the Hakka. Uncle was always saying that one could never live under the same sky as the murderer of one's father. He wanted us to remember the enmity while he waited for an opportunity for revenge.

I stayed at Uncle's house every time I returned from lodging complaints. The old house had been turned to a pile of rubble, no longer livable. I was told that someone could be heard crying in the house every night; some said it was a woman, some said it was a man, and yet other claimed it was children. Someone was crying in there, in any case. I heard it myself over those days. It was clear, but I didn't think it was really a ghost; to me it was my heart crying. I burst out wailing whenever I thought about how Papa had lived a tough life. I was reminded of a literary man suffering humiliation because he is helpless in changing his destiny. Many people were moved when I cried, and some of them even held the view that it had led to the later round of battles between the locals and the Hakka.

Anyone who heard my sobs and my story was convinced that Lü Erye had set the fire. To them it was as plain as a louse on a bald man's head, but the government refused to look into it. The county office sent someone to inspect the crime scene but it was perfunctory, for show only. I had once thought about lodging my complaint at the capital, but a young woman like me couldn't make the long trek safely. I wished Big Mouth could help me, but he didn't think Lü Erye was the culprit.

"He could be the one who set the fire and could also benefit from the fire, and his pipe was found at the scene, but I don't believe he could be that vicious," he said.

A good man could be a lecher, so could many charitable men, he reasoned, while some evil-doers might not care for women at all. Lü Erye was somewhat like a lü—an ass—but he was no killer. He didn't take me seriously until I ran into Killer on a ridge.

In my impression, the arrival of Killer happened like the descending dark night. Dressed in inky black clothes from head to toe, he covered his face with black cloth, leaving only his eyes exposed. He said he'd let me go if I promised him one thing—stop lodging complaints all over the place. He told me not to bother Lü Erye again and ruin his reputation. Lü Erye didn't do it, he added. Killer had a true northern accent, very much like Big Mouth's.

Naturally, I refused. I told him I didn't believe that Lü Erye's palm could blot out the sky.

Killer raised his knife.

At that moment Big Mouth raced over with his whip. It turned out that he had been tailing me over the past days. He was afraid I might kill myself or be killed; he was even more worried that some men might harbor evil designs and defile me. He asked for a leave of absence from the bank. Later he told me that Lü Erye had smiled faintly and told him to do what he had to do. It took Big Mouth a while to understand what Lü Erye meant.

Big Mouth and Killer fought. Killer dressed the part, but was no match for Big Mouth's martial skills. After a while, Big Mouth flung him to the ground, with his knife stuck in his own chest. I never figured out whether he killed himself intentionally or by mistake. In any case, he died and before he died, he said,

"Erye, I'm sorry I failed you."

Big Mouth peeled the cloth off the man's face, and we were stunned to see it was a clerk from the bank. Every time I sobbed and exposed Lü Erye, the clerk had always glared at me, as if he wished he could kill me right there. But before he breathed his last, he added, "This really has nothing to do with Erye."

I don't know if by this he meant the fire or his attempt to kill me.

But from that day on, even Big Mouth started to suspect Lü Erye, who, he believed, sent Killer to shut me up.

He was away from the shop for several months, which was lucky for him, because quite a few clerks died in battles later. If he'd been there, his temperament wouldn't allow him to stay back and he'd surely have died at the hands of the rioters if he'd played the tough guy.

4

I went to some more places, with Big Mouth's protection. I continued to kneel when I saw an official and visited every *yamen* in sight, but nothing came of it, as no one wanted to help a young woman like me. I despaired.

But my efforts and complaints had an effect; Lü Erye suffered serious damage to his reputation. He had once been known only as a lecher, but now many people believed he was a murderer as well. He had told his clerks to defend his innocence—he never admitted any wrongdoing—but I did manage to tarnish his name.

My helplessness as a young woman also stoked anger in many people, especially those from our clan and the locals. They started raising a stink, saying everyone chips in to level an uneven road. Uncle played a key role; the hatred and rage that had been building up inside him finally had an outlet.

The locals in the area never took to Lü Erye, because he was an outsider, and yet he'd amassed such impressive wealth for him to rise above everyone else. A lot of the locals found that hard to take. On one hand, they fawned on him for small benefits, but on the other, their jealousy slowly turned into hatred. Envious of his wealth, they'd been looking for an excuse and an opportunity, and what had happened to my family was a good one.

That day, I was asked to go to the clan hall, where an armed crowd gathered. I had no idea they could bring together so many people, nor did I know who organized them. I was touched when I saw all of them outraged for my sake. I wasn't aware at the time that I was only serving as a detonating fuse. I was oblivious to the fact that I'd been swept into a historical event that would take tens of thousands of lives. All I was thinking in those days was, Revenge! I didn't know that hatred was the most heinous seed, that it can sprout and bloom to produce terrifying fruit.

Someone started shouting rallying phrases the moment I walked in. The content of the shout was powerful enough to make people's blood boil. After being ignored by the government for so long, I couldn't help but burst out crying. Like fuel splashing on dry kindling, my tears stoked their anger.

The raging mob stormed out to smash the bank, where they injured some of the clerks, and ransacked the goods. With hatred and fury, they obtained a great deal of rare items normally out of their reach. At the time, it all looked justified.

Then the mob charged Lü Erye's watchtower, where they would obtain even more rare objects.

And that was how a historically prominent battle between the locals and the Hakka took place.

"Keep going."

The drivers are entranced by her story, someone urges her on.

"Enough for today," Feiqing says. "It's easy for you listeners, but look at him, his heart is quivering from the cold." He turned to me, "Actually, you could build a fire, you know. We're not afraid of fire, even though you Liangzhou people believe fire can drive away spirits. The newly dead are afraid of fire out of habit, but to us old ghosts—heh-heh—we're all old ghosts, fire is nothing but a mirage. You can bring your white camel and the dog too. The yellow camel is afraid of us, so he can stay back there by itself."

"You can sleep in a Tartar pit, too. We did that in the old days, when we had enough time. If you build a fire after we leave—actually, leaving is a concept meaningful only to a living person, because we don't really leave or stay; we just appear or disappear—and mix the embers with the hot

sand to spread across the ground. It'll make a warm, toasty bed," he says.

"You can move on to the next stop, if you want," he adds in the end.

Sixth Session
Mad Camel

Drive the camels, up before dawn, head to the fourth stop.
Cross the Great Wall, through the desert, meet up with a windstorm.
Yellow sand swirls, black waves surge, eyes have to remain shut.
You see, this is, the life of a camel driver,
No way to make a living.

——Song of a Camel Driver

A clear day brings a cold night and frost descends. My sleeping bag is slightly damp when I lie down. I've brought a small military tent with me, but I don't feel like putting it up. When I'm in the desert, I prefer sleeping in the open air. The stars are hanging low and twinkling noisily, sounding like flowing water. The yellow camel spat the whole night, chasing off ghosts in his own way. The white one had his wise eyes fixed on the inky sand trough off in the distance, like a meditating sage. The dog lay next to me and licked my face frequently. Dogs truly are man's best friend. It's a smart dog and never barks during my interviewing sessions, sitting as quietly as the virgin Mary in Western oil paintings.

Each time the interview ends, an immense silence presses in, with a visceral texture. I can even feel its sticky, streaky darkness unless I look at the stars, which sparkle noisily when I gaze up at them. It must be the sound of flowing water in the Milky Way. I can shut the world out of my mind only by closing my eyes. But I never want to go to bed too early, for I always want to savor their stories. I keenly feel the vicissitudes of life every time I return, and a great deal of information and feelings rush at me. How many worlds like that have simply disappeared, I wonder, and left not even a shadow behind?

The caravan is the focus of my interview, but now Wooden Fish Girl's story has greatly piqued my interest. How did a girl from the south end up a member of a western caravan? How did she enter Wild Fox Ridge? What kind of spiritual experience has she had? I want answers to all these questions.

My desire to know the answers has surpassed the curiosity about my identity in a previous life.

I wake up early the next morning, likely from the cold. It isn't the low temperature, but a sensation, that rouses me. I feel cold, but it doesn't mean it's cold.

After getting up, I build a fire to boil some water and roast a few potatoes. I love potatoes, but I can't eat too many; I need to conserve, because they're too heavy, and I didn't bring many. I brought mostly instant noodles and hardtack.

I pack after breakfast to head for the next stop. Around me the topography remains the same—black rocky desert, filled with rocks that shine from the baking sun. The white camel carries me, while the yellow one transports my things. He's unhappy and his eyes avoid meeting mine. I know, but I decide to keep quiet about it. You can act up if you like, I say silently, as long as you do your job.

Opening up a hand-made map, I read it carefully to check the route. It was given to me by an old camel driver back home. Obviously, it has been passed down through generations. Made of sheepskin, it is very useful, with marks indicating where to find water and grass, how to keep from getting lost, and the stops. It came alive before I entered Wild Fox Ridge, and I was able to imagine the whole place along with the old driver's narration. I thought I had a fairly clear sense about the area, but once I enter, I still feel like I'm walking in a maze. So many years have passed, after all, and the sand dunes keep moving. The rocky desert, on the other hand, undergoes few changes, making it easy to find the camel trail.

Wild Fox Ridge isn't a commonly traveled trail, and, unlike the Silk Road or the Ancient Tea-Horse Road, won't see a traveler for long stretches, despite its name. It is a short-cut to Luocha, but not many people went there in those days. It leads to the border, for sure. Border towns back then had stalls carrying contraband goods, akin to present day smuggling, coming in through Wild Fox Ridge. But that was just a rumor.

The trail in the rocky part of the desert is relatively flat and low, and, with galloping camel feet kicking up rocks, there are fewer black rocks on the trail than on the surrounding area. There is vegetation like bunch grass, some of which looks burned.

It's wintertime, but in the rocky desert I still feel like I'm traveling under a blistering sun, a false impression from the round, black, baked rocks. The heat must have become their collective memory, if they have one, and they release it the moment they see me. I get dizzy just looking at the endless black, rocky desert; I feel despondent, even though I know there are only a few stops.

The stops along the former camel trail actually mean "places with water." Hence, I only have to locate water sources on the map to find a stop. However, with the major climatic changes in recent years, some of the stops that used to have water have dried up. Luckily, I've brought two large plastic jugs and two sheepskin pouches. Whenever I find water, I'll fill them up and that will last me a few days.

What I find this time is a spring that has long dried up. I don't get to refill, but I have enough water left in the jugs, so I'm not worried. I cut lots of vegetation, and, following Feiqing's suggestion, I light a fire after nightfall. Fire is such a good thing; the sand trough turns lively once the fire gets going.

Feiqing has also said old ghosts aren't afraid of fire, but none show up after I recite the incantation to invite them.

I move away from the fire to a distant spot that's somewhat more secluded, and light the yellow candle to start chanting again.

Gradually, I begin to hear voices that I've been hoping to hear. Later I learn that the fire old ghosts do not fear is in the underworld, while fire in the human world sends uncontrollable fear into them. Even if they did not fear fire in the human world, owing to the existence of a discriminating mind, feel a massive, tsunami-like force pushing them off, like surging waves, when they get closer to me. The giant waves they sense are a bit like the air currents stirred up by the flames, but to me, it's caused by attachments and a discriminating mind.

I've heard only from the Chinese drivers over the past nights, and on this night, I really hope the Mongolian drivers will tell their stories. I'm reminded of Balte, who introduced himself earlier, so I ask, "Is Balte here?" Someone answers me.

I see the man in the quiet of the night.

I ask him to start from where we left off last time.

One. Balte

1

I knew it was bad when I first smelled the odor on Brown Lion's wound. It was the stench of death, which I'd detected one time when I helped carried a dead body. It really reeked. I wondered if it came from the Angel of Death or from the rotting flesh. It was something I can't forget. Later I recognized the same odor in many camel drivers; or, to put it differently, everyone who carried the stench died soon after. There might not be any wound on the person, but the odor seeps out from some unknown spot.

You can say it was a false impression on my part, as long as you don't accuse me of lying. You should know that every liar lies for a purpose. Now—hei-hei, it serves me no purpose to lie to you.

That smell helped me realize that destiny is at play in all matters. Even a small wound like that was a setback in Brown Lion's fate he could not overcome.

This is just how I look at it now. Back then I only felt incensed at the malign camel called Yellow Demon. Brown Lion would have fared differently if Yellow Demon hadn't broken the rules and used his teeth.

I first noticed the changes in Brown Lion the day he had been kicked into a sand trough. He always looked downcast. I really hoped he'd seek revenge, but he didn't. For a few days he wasn't even interested in Pretty Widow. She kept coming closer, but then backed off unhappily once she saw the indifferent look on Brown Lion's face.

In all fairness, Pretty Widow was a loyal camel. Unlike other seasoned, feckless female camels, she kept looking from a distance at the despondent Brown Lion, like an affectionate girl gazing at the man in her heart.

I was even touched by her. I mean it. I've never met a woman who was as tender, devoted, and pretty as her—don't look at me like that. Lhamu, the woman who ran the lodge, was nice to me, but you should know that she had her eyes on the jangling silver coins in my pocket first. If I was reduced to poverty, would she still treat me the same? Hard to say.

Brown Lion was moaning for days after he was kicked into the sand trough. I discovered that, besides the festering wound, his scrotum was badly swollen. I wondered if he'd been somehow neutered by Yellow Demon's foot, a thought that knocked me for a loop. You need to know that many camels in my caravan were sired by Brown Lion, who had passed his superior genes to my camels. Hu Gala, the Daoist priest at Su Wu Temple once said that the destiny of every living creature is determined at the instant a sperm entered the egg. According to him, at that instant, *qi* from both heaven and earth, the essence of the sun and the moon, as well as the father's substance and the mother's blood all enter into the secret code of a life form and eventually settle to create its destiny. He said that all the time, and I never quite believed his outlandish theory, but I was swayed by the concept that good seed is the prerequisite for a good camel. The lead camels in my caravan all inherited Brown Lion's physique, strength, stamina, and other superior qualities. He had sired half the lead camels.

So, I reasoned it would no longer be a mere fight between two camels if Yellow Demon did neuter Brown Lion, for the loss would be impossible to make up.

It's true.

I gave the spot a careful examination and saw it was clearly bruised, looking like a ram after it had been stoned. We did that to rams—using a flat stone and slapping it against the things that bounced between the ram's legs when it ran, that is, forcefully turning the ram's scrotum from its solid state of flesh into the liquid form of blood. Got that? I suspected the kick from Yellow Demon had played the role of the flat stone.

Terrible if true.

2

There was less vegetation around. The spot wasn't a prairie to begin with, and the tender grass, that year's growth, couldn't last long, not with so many camels grazing it. However, we saw plenty of old desert thorns, desert rice, and camel thorns, enough to last awhile. Camel feet marred by pebbles had yet to recover completely; they needed time.

Wild Fox Ridge might have been a real unlucky locale. I discovered that, once we were in there, the two caravans seemed to fall under the spell of a mysterious force. I can't tell what it was, it was just a feeling I had. I got the sense that it would be a terrifying endeavor to get out of this mysterious and extensive canyon.

Don't laugh. I mean it. I got the feeling only after the fact. You can ask Wooden Fish Girl if you don't believe me. I asked her specifically about this particular afternoon. Guess what she said.

"What you're feeling is the end of the world. Know that? The end of the world is right under your eyes." What she meant was the end of the world was near.

I didn't believe her at the time.

Hei-hei. I thought she was blowing smoke, even if I did sense something ominous. I recalled how the village shamans were always talking about the end of the world. They'd said it was coming over dozens of times, and each time the villagers were thrown into a helpless state. Yet they lived through the end of the world intact. I thought heaven had its reasons for creating us, and that it wouldn't destroy the human race so cavalierly. At the most there'd be a few disasters, so I was surprised to see the scale of the calamity later.

I watched Ma Zaibo recite a sutra daily. I heard it was a sutra from ancient India. I also heard that wherever the recitation sound reached, all calamities would be averted and peace would reign. That's what he said.

He also said that he heard countless Dakinis chanting with him when he recited a sutra for good luck. That's what he said too. Because his voice was all I heard. But he had a nice voice, melodious and pleasing, and it carried well. It was soothing, like drinking millet soup, so comforting it could put you to sleep. But Wooden Fish Girl said she did hear the Dakinis singing when she sang along with Ma Zaibo. Later, even Big Mouth learned to sing. He sang it all the time, which was how the song traveled to Liangzhou. Yet it didn't seem to help change the trajectory of his destiny.

I noticed that Wooden Fish Girl's eyes seemed frozen on Ma Zaibo, especially when he was chanting the sutra and she was praying. Strangely, though, she was adamant in her denial when I asked her about it later. I don't know why she'd do that.

Ma's chant started before the sun rose over the sand dunes to the east. He chanted in Chinese. He said it sounded better in Tibetan, but I preferred Chinese, hoping that hearing it might change Han people who heard it. I had a low regard for the Han Chinese, mainly because they were too calculating; their cunning seemed to seep out through their pores, and you noticed it the moment you came into contact with them. We Mongolians abhor duplicity, preferring to be frank and straightforward. The Chinese even infect their camels with their devious nature. See how Brown Lion fell victim to a sneak attack.

More and more things were going in the direction I'd suspected. That is, something was really wrong with Brown Lion. He became a loner, staying away from other camels and looking depressed.

So I asked Ma Zaibo to chant to help the camel recover soon.

Two. Killer

I felt like laughing when I saw Ma Zaibo reciting a sutra. Back then

I didn't believe humming something like that could change one's fate. Naturally, I kept that thought to myself, and sometimes I chanted along to make him happy.

I didn't believe that his guru—the old lama who panted violently when he walked—could change one's fate, since that was the exclusive domain of heaven. I didn't believe it. Hu Gala had already divined Ma's death on this trip, though he didn't figure out how Ma would die. My divination also predicted his demise, so I said to myself that I'd be the one to take his life.

Yes, I also knew the Tibetan and Chinese divination methods. Moreover, I not only knew them, but was an expert in them. Hu Gala, who taught me, said I was better than all his disciples in Kālacakra. I'd made many accurate predictions of solar and lunar eclipses. On the day of the eclipse, Hu Gala would send all his disciples into a meditation room for ascetic practices, which, it was believed, would speed up one's progress. Naturally, that was just what they said, though it did make some sense. Hu Gala said the magnetic field between heaven and field undergoes dramatic shifts during eclipses and positive energy enters a human's central channel more easily; just like the pull from the moon affects the tides in the ocean, eclipses have an impact on the coursing of qi and blood in human bodies. In a way, Hu Gala could be considered my teacher, and I should regard him as my parent. I was grateful to him, but in my view, he was just like all the other scholars who deserve my respect. That's all. I was passionate about the knowledge he passed on to me—you had no idea how marvelous and wonderful his arcane teaching was until you truly got it. When that happened, heaven and earth would merely be lines in your palm. I wasn't that interested in self-cultivation, though, and I was lukewarm about the Kālacakra —a combined method for ascetic practices. But I was enthralled by visualizations of Mandala. I'd once studied the Pure Land Sect, and yet Kālacakra aroused great interest in me once I learned about it.

I waited calmly for the inevitable event after the night I entered the mysterious Kālacakra and figured out the calamity that would arrive on a particular day. I took care of everything that needed to be dealt with—in fact, I didn't have much to do. All I had was a leather sack passed down from my ancestors and the few books it contained, plus a wooden fish and a three-string instrument. I gave away all the worthless odds and ends.

I could see numerous eyes looking at me; they all emitted an unusual vibration, hoping for Ma Zaibo to die by the knife in my hand.

The block of wood wrapped in red cloth pulsated constantly against my vest, like a naked heart that continued to pound spiritedly.

Three. Ma Zaibo

1

I always treated you with the respect due a Dakini, because you knew the Kālacakra. I heard you could recite it forwards and backwards. Hu Gala said you were adept in the visualization of Mandala, which didn't interest me much. I found Kālacakra more attractive because I wanted to become a Mahasiddha, and I'd heard that Kālacakra contained all the secrets for an ordinary human being to become a Buddha through self-cultivation.

I had no idea you weren't interested in Kālacakra.

But it didn't matter whether you were or not. What mattered to me was the fact that you understood it, and I would be happy if you could teach it to me. In ancient India there was once a great scholar who loved to read but did not care for self-cultivation. Later, many of his students turned out to be arhats, because the teaching of Vajrayāna can help people study to become Buddhas. So sometimes I thought about learning about the Kālacakra.

I'd conducted a systematic study of the teaching of Vajrayāna, but what I learned was more about deliverance and less about Kālacakra. I wanted not only personal deliverance, but also to study something that would help me decipher heavenly secrets. I really wanted to know the truth about the world, and wanted to find the fundamental nature behind visible phenomena. Which was why I thought Kālacakra would be a path to lead me there.

I surely didn't expect you would harbor such deep hatred for my family.

If I had known earlier, I'd have stuck my neck out for you to use your knife—you could stab as many times as you want, as long as it erased your hatred and eliminated your grievance. You know grievances are contagious, don't you? Our ancestors said hatred can sprout in one's heart. Oftentimes hatred will enter into the secret code of your life and pass itself down to your offspring or your next life, and grow fruit there. So why wouldn't I be glad to let you plunge your knife into me if it would help dispel your bitter rancor against my family? I'll die eventually anyway. I could die at your hand or in some other way, it doesn't matter, for the outcome is the same.

Besides, you were almost like a Dakini to me at the time.

I was willing to offer my life as sacrifice to a Dakini.

2

That's right, I was always reciting a sutra. Don't laugh. It was a common phrase that might make you laugh, but it had the capacity to bring about many changes. One's thoughts can change everything; your emotions will lead you to a corresponding outcome. A great many people have changed their fate with a positive attitude. The mental state I was in when reciting the sutra would surely have produced tremendous good energy. It failed to change the adverse effects of the caravan's action and help them avoid the subsequent calamity, but it did have positive effects. Some of the drivers experienced mental changes under the influence of the sutra. For instance, back when he was called Zhang Wule—Zhang the Cheerless—Big Mouth was forever complaining about the unfairness of his fate. Later, at the camel farm, he listened to me reciting the sutra and his personality slowly underwent a change. Then he took on a new name, Zhang Yaole—Zhang the Cheerful—and he was happy and worry-free every day, as his heart was transformed. We can at least adjust our attitude toward our own fate even if we can't change it, don't you think?

But I was surprised that the immense wisdom contained in the teaching of Kālacakra did not erase your hatred. Obviously, nothing is harder for a human to deal with than the heart. In fact, what is hatred? Hatred is a stubborn attachment, an attitude that can chill a tender heart. Your heart was water, but the stubbornness turned it to ice, and your heart hardened day by day. And yet the ice will slowly turn back into water if you are able to stop clinging to your hatred.

Do you still hate me as much as you did back then?

Have you realized that all your hatred was in fact meaningless? Except to torment yourself, your hatred changed nothing.

You should know that hatred itself is a kind of evil and all evil eventually begets greater evil.

The world won't change its trajectory because of your hatred, while the flames of your hatred have tortured you for so long and put you under endless pain, that you have become a slave to it.

3

It pains me to think about the battle. The locals and the Hakka were brothers, and yet a bloodbath occurred over personal gains and cultural differences. I'd been through another battle; it was between the Hui and the Han and lasted over a decade, killing and injuring millions. If you'd experienced it yourself, you would tremble in fear and be unable to eat or sleep. Blood stained the ground and turned a river red, and countless bodies lay strewn across a hill; they became bloated and oozed green liquid, attracting swarms of bluebottles, because no one came to bury them. The flies blanketed the sky and covered the ground, where they lay eggs day and night, until fat, white maggots crawled everywhere. Stench spread like an unshakable nightmare. Then came pestilence, from the rancor of all the dead, which, clouded by hatred, could not tell good from bad and tore into all living things.

Many from our Ma family died in this battle.

I can recall the scene even now; it was horrific.

The people caused it, both the Han and the Hui. Who were good and who were evil?

Now there's really no more hatred in my heart. How did I get rid of it? The sutra, along with Vajrayāna, which contains all the good that can eliminate hatred. After the battle was over, I took a few drivers with me and transported our special tea on thirty white camels to Tibet, where I begged an old lama to share the sutra with me. I chanted it every day to deliver the souls of those who had died such a terrible death in revenge killings, I erased their hatred, I cultivated compassion, and I nurtured an altruistic spirit. Finally, I achieved my goal of no longer hating those who had killed generations of my family. My inclination affected many people, who, along with me, attributed the calamity to history and held the corrupt court responsible. We never hoped to seek revenge. To whatever "gifts" brought to us by fate or history we reacted with an attitude that can best be described as "complete acceptance." No longer did any of us consider killing the offspring of our so-called enemies.

So, I'm startled to hear that hatred has become your inheritance.

I'm also surprised that you failed to eradicate your hatred after spending so many years studying Kālacakra. Apparently, knowledge has a limited function. You're better off studying Kālacakra than visualization. Actually, you can erase the hatred in your heart and change your fate if you carry out that kind of wise practice.

Sure, you can divine certain events, but what's the point if you cannot alter the outcome? It doesn't matter whether you cast the divination or not.

What I've pursued all my life is a means of effecting different outcomes.

Four. Balte

1

I had no time for your nonsense back then.

My attention was fully occupied by Brown Lion.

My worries were born out: the kick from Yellow Demon had done irreparable damage to Brown Lion, for I found that he stopped chasing after female camels after that. I brought him some of the pretty ones he'd liked and whistled a special tune to excite him, but he was unmoved. Nothing happened with a menacing organ that would have risen and grown, now become docile as a strip of overused leather.

Nothing could be worse than this. Not another stud camel like Brown Lion could be found among the ten teams of Mongolian caravans. He was in his prime. Under normal circumstances, he could stud several more years to produce a great number of superb camels just like him. Could Yellow Demon have ended all that with a single kick?

I finally gave up after trying more times than I could count. I even did a careful examination of the spot: it was no longer swollen, but something seemed different with the thing that would bounce up and down when it ran. Maybe the testes were injured. If so, the biological foundation for his vitality was lost, just as with those rams whose testes we smashed with flat rocks. It wouldn't matter too much if it was merely caused by a mental block. At the time, I couldn't determine the cause; I just hoped it was the latter and that one day under certain circumstances his former vigor would be revived.

Don't laugh at me.

Right. I had no similar concerns for myself.

You cannot understand the devotion a driver has for his camels. Besides, Brown Lion once saved my life. Without him I wouldn't be here today. He was my father, my son, and my beloved also—don't laugh at me. I never felt the same emotional bond with any women, who, in my view, are the most changeable creatures in the world, not worth the kind of commitment I had toward Brown Lion. I only thought about women when something stirred down there.

You'd be like me if you'd gone through a life-and-death experience with your camel.

2

Brown Lion was a solitary figure in the desert. He barely touched any vegetation over the first few days, and his hump quickly slumped. Later he went back to graze and looked to regain his health, though he still looked downcast.

The vegetation grew scarcer nearby, and even desert thorns were harder and harder to come by. We had to move constantly to a spot with more vegetation. Camel caravans rarely entered Wild Fox Ridge, so it had more plants than elsewhere. We concluded that there was an underground waterway beneath the sand, which had turned the canyon into a twisting green dragon.

Yellow Demon resumed his life of king, chasing female camels like mad and tugging at their hind legs to spread his seed. I loathed that animal, not simply because of the injury he had done to Brown Lion, but also because he had a craftiness I despised. I often noticed the same quality in Han Chinese, who are way too calculating for my taste. The same with Yellow Demon. You could tell how devious he was from the way he tackled Brown Lion. A deceitful camel would surely sire untrustworthy offspring. As I saw it, the Chinese camels might look forthright, but I couldn't shake the suspicion that the appearance covered up their sneakiness as they lacked the directness and generosity typical of a Mongolian camel—no need to argue about that. It was just a feeling on my part. I can't speak for you, and you can have your own feelings. When there are various sentiments there are different worlds. Haven't you said that the world is a reflection of the mind? My world was created by my mind, and in my world Chinese camels are like that. I won't change my tune no matter how much you grumble.

A malicious thought came to my mind when I saw Yellow Demon throwing his weight around. I had to stop myself from kicking him in the scrotum. I can kick a hemp sack filled with highland barley into the air, so I was sure I could smash those two balls between its legs with my foot. Would you stop laughing at me? I wasn't lowering myself to a camel's level; I just couldn't abide his sneaky, despicable tactic. Don't you see? He bit and kicked, nothing but underhanded moves. He wasn't aboveboard at all. A lowlife, just like Lu Fuji.

To be honest with you, I didn't like Lu Fuji either. Yes, you looked crudely expansive on the surface, but I was sure you had plenty of schemes. Later, when a fight broke out between the two caravans, you were second only to Huozi in your performance—don't argue. I know exactly what you were like. You did get a celestial title as Earth God, but I refuse to acknowledge it. Hei-hei. Earth God? It's nothing but someone who knows the area well.

I have a favorable impression of Feiqing, only now, of course. Back then I thought he was just like Lu Fuji. I like Feiqing because of what he did later. I'd only heard about his gallantry, but hearing is not seeing. Besides, I had a feeling he knew how to deal with our camels. Also, Huozi was always badmouthing him. Like people say, groups who spread rumors can confuse right and wrong, and three are enough to make people believe something false. Huozi was always saying Feiqing cheated his brother, slept with his sister-in-law, had eyes only for money, was too rich to be kind, harbored rebellious thoughts, and planned an uprising. How could I have a good opinion of him?

Look at me. I'm still incensed when I talk about Yellow Demon. Can you imagine the hatred in me back then? I think even a mother facing the man who castrated her son would have less anger than me.

I'd sneak angry glances at Yellow Demon whenever I thought about how Brown Lion was suffering. I said "sneak" glances, because that's what Lu Fuji said. Actually, I didn't sneak glances; I glared openly at him. I cursed the camel, and when I did that, my heart overflowed with hatred. As a result, the Chinese drivers thought I was cursing them by berating their camel. They didn't know that my target was really, truly just Yellow Demon. I wasn't railing at them indirectly through the animal. But later I did find out that using those words for Yellow Demon on the Chinese was quite appropriate; so, no wonder they were suspicious. But they shouldn't have acted like their camel. Being devious was pointless.

Our battle started with a verbal argument.

3

I saw Yellow Demon going after Mongolian camels, which was a human trait. Like some Chinese men favor Western prostitutes, Yellow Demon wanted to have a taste of Mongolian female camels.

His behavior meant encroaching upon Brown Lion's domain, but I wasn't upset. I know the best camels come from mixed parentage. In those days, we had to trade a litter of highland barley for our camel to mate once with a Chinese one. I hoped Yellow Demon would mate with more of our camels and give us more, better offspring. Lu Fuji knew my thoughts better than anyone; he was always messing with Yellow Demon, trying to direct his attention back to Chinese camels. He was always lashing at Yellow Demon as he chased our camels. It actually looked quite comical, like Lu Fuji was trying to mate the camels himself—hei-hei, stop laughing.

Compared with nature's primitive force, human interference is often useless. Even under the threat of a whipping lash, Yellow Demon never lost his interest and persisted in chasing the pretty ones to drag them to the ground and stick his organ in to release his life force, to Lu Fuji's great disappointment.

I could even tell what he was thinking from his sigh: Hei. Don't waste the good stuff on someone else.

It was about this time that Long Neck Goose started to usurp Yellow Demon's power. Usually, Long Neck Goose would drag a Chinese camel down at the same time Yellow Demon got himself a Mongolian one. Yellow Demon couldn't divide his attention, so he had to accept the pattern and let Long Neck Goose work his private plot. But I knew there would surely be a fight between the two males once Yellow Demon satisfied his need to mate. They'd be fighting for the position of king camel in the Chinese caravan. I did notice that Long Neck Goose didn't seem to have the strength to challenge the current king, though he was a good enough camel. And he did have one advantage—his age.

I did not know how many Mongolian camels Yellow Demon had mated—impossible to count. If it hadn't been for the calamity, I might have been able to tell from the number of newborns. But it had to be at least ten, which meant he'd sired enough to save us ten liters of highland barley. What a steal that was.

At the time, I often laughed to myself, which reduced the pain I suffered over Brown Lion's injury. Then I saw how Yellow Demon seemed to have lost some of his stamina, likely from over-indulgence. Maybe.

That could be why Lu Fuji stepped in. Hei, a drop of semen equals ten thousand drops of blood, I heard him grumble one day.

4

Brown Lion went crazy when Yellow Demon tried to mate Pretty Widow.

He'd only looked despondent prior to that and tried to ignore Yellow Demon when he could. I knew he was feeling bad, but I never imagined he'd go crazy.

On this day, Yellow Demon went back to Chinese camels, likely because he was tired of Mongolian ones. He and Long Neck Goose had a disagreement, but it ended as soon as it began. I'd thought Long Neck Goose would at least put up a fight, but he ran off when Yellow Demon charged.

Yellow Demon went after Pretty Widow, and she took off running. She didn't run like the average females, who mostly put on a show of rejecting male advances. Pretty Widow was serious about getting away from Yellow Demon. Several times after being dragged down, she rolled, turned, got up, and took off again. As she ran, she kicked Yellow Demon and made a sound that showed her outrage. That flabbergasted Lu Fuji, who roared, "Why are you running like that? You're no virgin, it's time for you have a baby."

"What's the rush?" I said to Lu. "If you're in such a hurry, go do it yourself." That drew riotous laughter from other drivers.

We had little to do over these days, and the drivers were so bored they enjoyed the scene, like watching a peep show. They teased Lu and cheered Yellow Demon on.

Wooden Fish Girl was cheering too. What a clueless girl. Once, as Yellow Demon kept missing his target, she even helped guide the thing to its rightful place, as natural as threading a needle.

When Yellow Demon started chasing Pretty Widow, Brown Lion acted unconcerned at first, but started to react as the female camel's struggle intensified. He coldly sized up the Chinese camel, something he'd never done before. Little by little, his eyes turned and he began to snort.

Yellow Demon caught up with Pretty Widow and bit her hind leg; as if enraged by her resistance, he tugged hard enough to put her flat on the ground. Then before she could struggle to her feet, he pressed down on her.

She cried out helplessly.

Yellow Demon's tool was out and pushing, but she refused to lift her tail. Lu Fuji shouted when he saw it wasn't going too well,

"Don't be in such a damn hurry."

Everyone could see that Yellow Demon would soon being spraying the sticky stuff that was worth a thousand drops of blood at Lu Fuji if Pretty Widow refused to cooperate.

Lu ran up and jerked the female's tail up violently, but before he could help Yellow Demon finish the job, a roar sounded as Brown Lion sprinted over like a whirlwind. His mouth wide open on a twisted face, he no longer resembled a camel. Sand he kicked up swirled into the sky.

"Watch Out, Old Lu!" Feiqing shouted.

Lu Fuji, who had studied martial arts since childhood, was a skilled fighter. He jumped to the side like a monkey and turned his head to see Brown Lion charging, his mouth seemingly ready for him. Lu was fast, but not fast enough to stop the camel from tearing a piece off his jacket.

With a dejected look, Lu ran off. Instead of chasing him, Brown Lion turned his mouth on Yellow Demon and bit off a chunk. Feiqing cried out in dismay. I knew he was afraid the attack would spook Yellow Demon. Sometimes a camel becomes impotent after suffering a surprise like that, sort of like a man having the same reaction under similar circumstances.

Yellow Demon screamed in pain and rolled off the female, but before he could get up, the Mongolian camel returned with his gaping mouth. Yellow Demon did not dodge in time, and a gash opened on his shoulder.

Feiqing picked up his whip and lashed out at Brown Lion, while the other drivers grabbed various makeshift weapons and ran toward the attacking camel. I felt sorry for Brown Lion, before I realized that something was wrong with him. I was afraid he'd lost his mind.

Sure enough. He took a bite out of Pretty Widow too. The whip and other weapons rained down on Brown Lion, who paused momentarily before turning on the drivers.

"He's gone mad, the camel is crazy," the drivers shouted.

By then Lu Fuji had retrieved a firearm from the tent. He appeared to be the first to sense something off with the camel. The caravan convention considered a mad camel a killer, which could be dealt with in only one way, and that was to kill it. If not, it would hurt every creature around.

I hoped it had just lost its mind temporarily, which was not uncommon. A man or an animal, when consumed by sexual desire or anger, can lose reason but will return to normal once the incident passes.

"What are you doing, Lu?" I yelled.

The whip and clubs no longer registered with Brown Lion, as he pounced on one of the drivers, who, brandishing his club like mad, didn't expect the camel would turn to attack him. Before he had a chance to dodge, the camel picked him up with his teeth and tossed him into the air. As soon as the man fell to the ground, the camel charged, picked him up again, and flung him into the air a second time, like tossing noodles. I knew it didn't look good for the driver, whose back would soon be broken.

Lu Fuji took aim, and I was too far away to stop him, so I shouted, "You fucking ass. I'll kill you if you kill my camel."

Knowing it was not an empty threat, Lu turned the muzzle up.

An explosion made the camel freeze. He soon recovered and ran off, trailed by sand he kicked up.

Later it occurred to me that Brown Lion should actually have been called Yellow Demon.

5

That night the driver whose back was broken by Brown Lion died. We gathered some firewood and cremated him. Everyone felt terrible, for, after all, we'd worked and eaten together.

The Chinese drivers now had a reason to kill Brown Lion. But the camel stayed away that night and the next day, and still had not returned on the third day.

He came back on the fourth day, only to bite a chunk off another camel. The man who saw it said he chewed and swallowed the flesh. It had obviously turned into a demon, no longer resembling a camel.

On the sixth day, another driver was attacked, but he ran fast enough to avoid a horrifying consequence. Hei-hei, but what consequence? The

Chinese say, you lose your head and gain a bowl-size scar. I don't believe you can escape your destiny just by escaping the "consequences." No matter how hard we struggle, we all end up as spirits.

Brown Lion launched a dozen or more attacks over a two-week period, mostly biting. I heard he swallowed the chunks he bit off, so he clearly had gone mad. But strangely, he only attacked Chinese drivers and their camels, which let me to believe he might not be crazy. If he was, then he'd attack indiscriminately. A mad camel would never check who was who before attacking.

And that was also why most of the Mongolian drivers felt sorry for Brown Lion and accepted his actions. Huozi even claimed that the camel was doing heaven's work by dispensing justice. He was a Chinese, but precisely because he was Chinese he had to show he hated the Chinese more than anyone else in order to highlight his difference from them.

The Chinese and the Mongolian caravans hadn't gotten along for generations. Starting with the Han dynasty, our ancestors, who had been called something other than Mongolians, had caused the great "Han" people trouble. Since then, disputes cropped up between the two in every generation; you can find records for these in local histories.

The Chinese called us "Northern Tartars." The desert separating the two sides was a barrier only to caravans, not to us. In the past, our ancestors would take their camels through the desert to loot whenever a drought caused a shortage of water and grass. Minor disputes, major conflicts, and large-scale battles formed a history of our relationship. We passed down the incidents by mouth while they recorded every one of the blood debts. In fact, one of their local histories was devoted to these altercations. The officials appointed by their imperial courts always turned the axe sideways in dealing with these clashes. Just think, how could a Chinese official not favor his own people? To be honest, I felt that Brown Lion was venting our anger when I heard about his attack on the Chinese.

I certainly didn't think he was a mad camel.

I thought he was just a killer. Hei-hei, like you, a killer. Don't glare at me. You weren't his equal. Don't think you were nobler because you had more reasons to kill. Let me tell you, even a fly could find plenty of reasons to destroy the human race if a reason was needed. The world is short on nobility, but long on reasons. What are reasons? Cloth used by cheats to cover their shame.

So I wanted very much to sing out: Brown Lion, our national hero!

But for the sake of appearances, I had to look sad and sorry, as if I felt terrible for the victims. I knew I would provoke their wrath if I gloated over the Chinese suffering. I didn't want to, at least not yet, provoke them—hei-hei, I mean you. I don't have to hide anything from you now, so I'll tell you exactly what I was thinking. I certainly look at it differently now. When I entered a different world, I concluded that the division of Mongolians and Chinese made no sense. At some point, many of labels created by humans simply disappear.

So why don't I tell what I was thinking?

I always put on a show of talking with Feiqing and Lu Fuji over strategy to deal with—no, to save—Brown Lion. I was firm in my objection to Lu's idea, which was to kill the so-called killer—no way, brother. I couldn't allow you do that either for rational or emotional reasons.

I suggested vigilance. I only agreed that Brown Lion had lost his bearings, stressing that Yellow Demon had broken the rules and should bear most of the responsibility. "If he hadn't hurt Brown Lion with his underhanded tactic," I said, "Brown Lion wouldn't have acted so rashly. Mating means a lot to a stud camel and Brown Lion would find life meaningless if he couldn't do it anymore. Just think, what does a castrated stud camel have to live for? You don't believe me? Why don't I castrate you? If you can keep calm and let me do that to you, I'll give you permission to kill Brown Lion. I think you'd lose your mind too. And Brown Lion would, since he isn't Sima Qian. Even Sima Qian went crazy for a while, his 'Letter to Ren An' is proof. We should let Brown Lion vent his anger for a while, later, when he's calmed down, I'm sure he'll reconcile with reality. When that happens, he'll be normal again."

"You want to castrate me, you ass?" Lu Fuji fumed.

"If you shoot Brown Lion," I said half seriously, "I'll let your old dick meet my dagger."

"I swear on Tengri I'll do it," I added when I noticed he'd seen through my half serious threat.

He shut up after that.

He knew I meant what I said.

I absolutely would do it.

Even now I can't forgive Yellow Demon for kicking Brown Lion, and I can't stop wondering if things would have turned out differently if he hadn't done that.

Without a detonator, maybe the explosion wouldn't have occurred, I said to myself. On many occasions, a minor scenario, even a tiny detail, can change the course of a major event. I've heard that a loose nail on the shoe of the horse carrying the king brought down a kingdom. The shoe fell because of the loose nail, which caused the horse to fall, and once it fell, the soldiers thought the king was dead and chaos erupted, leading to defeat and the destruction of the kingdom. The same could be said about the two caravans. Yellow Demon broke the rule, resulting in Brown Lion's crazed behavior, which led to a whole series of incidents later. Without the former, there might not have been the subsequent chain and cause of effect.

But you really can't second-guess history.

I often said to myself that there would be some other cause if not for this one. If you pile up dry gunpowder, who knows when a spark might land on it? By gunpowder, I meant the deep-rooted hatred between the two caravans.

To be sure, that insight came to me only now. The old me was a different person.

I'm a wise Zhuge Liang only after the fact.

But to those who come after me, I could be considered a prophet.

Otherwise, what are we doing here, wasting our time?

6

We set a horse-hoof trap in the area frequented by Brown Lion. Heihei, it was called a horse-hoof trap but it certainly could trip and catch a camel. Several drivers were dispatched to lie in wait in a sand furrow. When Brown Lion passed the spot, they would lift the rope buried in the sand to trip the galloping camel. It was commonly used to ambush a cavalry, very effective. In the time of the Three Kingdoms, it caused the downfall of your Master Guan, who was then beheaded by the enemy state. But, luckily for him, his misfortune enabled his loyal spirit to linger, and he was always shouting, "Give me back my head." Later his spirit was pacified by Śramana Zhiyi, the founder of the Tiantai Sect, and he was conferred as a major protector, a Dharmapala. In any case, we realized that Brown Lion always kicked up a small sandstorm and flashed by when he ran, obviously at a very high speed. If his front foot was ensnared by the trap, he'd tumble and be hogtied by the drivers.

I'd originally come up with the idea of a lasso club, but the drivers thought that amounted to a mouse trying to tie a bell around a cat's neck, because no one would dare get close to Brown Lion. Even when he wasn't acting like a man-eating tiger, he was big enough to crush you if he mistook you for Pretty Widow.

You can quash my idea, but at least I was an active participant.

Otherwise you'd have shot the camel.

At the time, I still held out hope for Brown Lion. I felt he'd return to normal once he'd vented his anger. I certainly hoped he'd recover and sire more camels. Over the years he'd worked hard spreading his seed, we had yet to have another like him. His offspring were always larger than the average camel, that's for sure. Superior seed is different, after all.

The drivers laid the trap in the area where Brown Lion was last seen. They took along an oversized blanket to put over his head after he tripped and fell. The hood would render his sharp teeth useless. The drivers also had a pole to press down on the camel once he was down in the sand. Camels are powerful animals, but, if they're lying or have fallen down, you can restrain them by the neck to stop them from getting to their feet. When a camel stands up, it'll first stick up its head, and it can't get up if its neck is held down, no matter how impossibly powerful it is. Hei-hei, you Chinese say to kill a snake, hit its vital spot. Well, the neck is a camel's vital spot. You must have noticed how camels always try to overpower their opponents with their necks when they wrestle. If one camel's neck is tilting but it refuses to surrender, the other one will simply push down hard for its opponent to crumple. I've heard Lu Fuji could wrestle a camel; they all said he had superhuman strength. Hei-hei, what superhuman strength? Sure, he was strong, but more importantly, he had technique, which was actually quite simple. That is, pinch its nostrils to turn its neck around. A camel will have no choice but to fall to the ground. That's what I did with cows; I could always wrestle a large cow to the ground with that technique, and I won loud cheers. The technique was so simple, just pinch at the nostrils and twist the neck. All you have to do is turn its head around and it will fall; it can't help it.

But to our surprise, they waited three days without seeing even a shadow of the camel. Only heaven knew where he'd gone. I wondered if he'd sniffed out something. Camels have a great sense of smell and, if they're downwind, can detect water miles away. He must have smelled something. But then again, if he got wind of the so-called danger, could we still say he was mad? I wondered.

The days dragged on as we waited for him to appear. We hoped he'd show himself from behind some corner in the desert and step into the trap. We watched the area until we nearly went blind. As a matter of fact, we could have searched for him. We'd have found him by following his footprints into the distance. There was enough vegetation in the sand trough to keep him alive. I was concerned, however, that he might end up in a wolf's belly. Everyone said that Wild Fox Ridge was overrun by wolves, but it wasn't until later that we saw them. No one had seen a wolf during the early days after our arrival. Once, when we were moving to a new grazing ground, I saw a pile of wolf scat, but it was dried up by the wind, whitish, with hair and bones. Brown Lion was large enough that one or two wolves were no match for him.

The drivers waited for three days until their eyes glazed over, but Brown Lion was nowhere in sight. I called them back and got a few powerful men out with me on camelback to look for him. The night wind had smoothed out his footprints. We looked all over, but couldn't tell where he was hiding. I got on a soaring sand hill and surveyed the area. The sand ridges rippled out like billowing silk, but no Brown Lion.

"That's fine with me," Lu Fuji said, "as long as he disappeared from the surface of the earth, we don't have to worry and can save some gunpowder."

"Bullshit," I retorted.

He tucked in his neck and cackled like a plagued chicken.

We didn't expect to have another round of fighting between Long Neck Goose and Yellow Demon before we were done with Brown Lion.

Five. Lu Fuji.

1

I saw that Brown Lion was truly crazy.

He later beat off a few wolves, but that didn't change the fact that he was mad.

He launched increasingly frequent attacks, injuring several Chinese camels, one of whom died of tetanus after moaning a few days. I didn't notice that he attacked only the Chinese ones at first, but later, when I spotted the phenomenon, he was doomed.

I had to deal with him or all ten Chinese teams would be lost. You know that the other camels must share the cargo carried by an injured camel, and it would add to their share of burden. Sometimes—when it reaches the breaking point—one more straw is enough to bring down a camel. Imagine if he bit a dozen or more of them. The whole caravan would fall apart.

I had to deal with him.

Balte did swear on the Tengri, saying he'd kill whoever took his camel's life, but I'm going to kill him.

I told Cai Wu and Qi Lu to go with other drivers to set traps in various spots, but to no avail. The desert was vast, and who knew where the mad camel would show up next? I decided on my flintlock, which would not break any rules when used on a mad camel.

I filled it with steel balls, those used to shoot wolves. I did it behind everyone's back, especially Balte. He might try to stop me. Nothing is overboard when tackling a killer camel, like people dealing with murderers, am I right?

I didn't tell Feiqing, either. I was a man who took responsibility for his actions, and I didn't want anyone else to be implicated. I'm not convinced that what I did had anything to do with the series of incidents that occurred later. Someone said a mosquito flapping its wings can cause rain miles away, but I could come up with more than enough reasons to refute that claim. You should be aware that so much had happened back then that it was impossible for anyone to tell cause from effect. Don't blame the heavens when you're knocked down by a wind; there are other reasons.

Over the next few days I went out every day. When asked what I was going out to do, I said shoot wild rabbits. It was a good excuse. Once I actually shot one, though it was like killing a chicken with a hatchet, using steels ball designed for wolves on a rabbit. But the drivers believed me.

I went looking for Brown Lion's resting spot, and to find Yellow Demon in the process. He'd run off after I whipped him. No big deal. He knew how to find food. We used to let the camels loose to graze on their own back when we took them out. Sometimes, weeks or months would go by and we wouldn't go look for them. They never strayed far, usually stayed within our field of vision. You could always find the brown spots you were looking for if you climbed a hill.

I was afraid Brown Lion might harm Yellow Demon. When he was sane, Brown Lion never broke the rules, and they each had their share of victories and defeats. It was hard to say, now that he'd gone mad. When a man's clear-headed, he's just a man, but once he loses his sanity, a dozen men may not be enough to subdue him. To Liangzhou people, an evil spirit or a fierce demon has to enter a man's head to cause insane behavior, and his strength has to come from them. With an additional source of strength, Brown Lion would be more powerful than our Chinese camels.

Listen to me. I'm not very consistent, am I? I just said I wanted to skin Yellow Demon and yank out its tendons, and now I was worried about him. Hopeless. That's how camel farmers are. Our love for our camels is a ball of fire, and our hate for them is a barbed hook that once it goes in, it will pull out a chunk of flesh when you remove it.

For several days in the beginning, I saw no sign of the Mongolian camel nor his Chinese counterpart. I climbed a very tall hill, but neither of them came into view. That was odd. When I wasn't looking for one, it came out to do wreak havoc, but when I wanted to find it, it played a game of hide and seek with me. I suspected he'd gone into a devil's maze, where no one could find him anytime soon.

Later, I wondered if it had to do with the smell of gunpowder. Could that animal sense my desire to take his life?

I followed the prints left in the sand and sometimes came upon footprints left by other camels. I didn't know how to tell them apart, but Feiqing could. He could read the information supplied by the prints and tell whether it was a male or female, whether it was fat or thin, tall or short. But I couldn't. In my eyes camel prints were all the same. I could only see they were large or small, deep or shallow, and nothing more. If I kept looking for him by following the prints, I would surely make a lot of wasted trips.

Then I spotted a pile of wolf scat on a sand hill.

That gave me a very bad feeling, for I knew that wolves are pack animals, and when there's one, there will be more.

The interview is going strong, but the chill forces me to end it for the night.

I can see from a distance that the fire went out long ago. Even the embers must have gone cold. I don't add more firewood because I don't want to interrupt the storytellers.

When Killer is telling the story, I can't actually see anything, but feel a kind of murderous aura. Yes, a murderous aura. He doesn't show his real face. I don't know if he doesn't want to or if there are other reasons. If I want to see his face, there are ways. But since he doesn't want to reveal himself, I have to respect his privacy. As for the others, I can see their faces clearly now. My interviews have awakened distant memories, from which I read and discern their facial features. They have gone through other transmigrations, but I can still see what they looked like as camel drivers. To them, transmigration or existence is nothing but memories.

The coronae dissipate with the conclusion of the interview—not disappear into the distance, but dissipate.

I relight the fire. A warmth bathes my face. Fire is such a wonderful thing. It roars and burns away all the gloom brought by the specters.

Faintly, I hear someone singing; it sounds a bit like Big Mouth's yak voice—

Qi Feiqing stopped Lu Fuji again, and says, Brother Lu, we won't worry, we'll just do what we have to do;

We'll merely break a few ribs if something goes wrong.

Brother Qi, I won't worry if you tell me not to. It's all up to Fourth Master.

I want my name to spread for years to come, and I refuse to let a shitty official bully the people.

I'll flatten out Wanping Township with a kick, and the more it escalates, the easier it is to carry out.

Yang Chengxu has designed a wonderful strategy, and what we want to do will turn out great.

Qi Feiqing, Lu Fuji, two real men from Liangzhou.

Their bones are tough and they are weighty.

Their strategy is superb and their idea fantastic.

Seventh Session
Armed Battle

Drive the camels, up before dawn, head to the fifth stop.
Rocky desert, no end in sight, the farther we travel, the more my heart aches.
My aging mother, my aging father, tears gush when I think of them.
You see, this is, the life of a camel driver.
No way to make a living.

——*Song of a Camel Driver*

The next morning, I continue on the black rocky desert to visit the stop farther down.

My head feels heavy from the sunlight reflecting on the black rocks. The monotonous camel bells make me drowsy. I discover that my sense of reality is getting flimsy. Even in broad daylight, I'm immersed in the atmosphere of my nighttime interviews and constantly feel as if walking in a dream. As I look into the distance, the black rocks are luminescent, as if countless watery bubbles are rising and hovering above them. It's an image common in the summertime, but occurs now in the winter.

It feels like I'm in a dream.

The wind is harsh and cold. Wind in the west is like a knife, and most of the time I prefer walking over riding the camel, for I'm afraid I'll freeze in the wind. I no longer feel cold after walking for a while, but actually start sweating a bit.

I have a sensation of being thrown into a vast emptiness. You can imagine what it looks like with a man walking in an immense rock desert with his dog and two camels. But at some point, I realize that a living black dot has been tailing me. I don't know if it's a wolf or a fox, but it's definitely an animal.

I spot it from the watery mist at high noon. Maybe it's been following me for a while without my detection until now.

It doesn't scare me. The dreamy sensation I can't shake has helped offset lots of feelings and emotions.

I fail to find water. The locale marked as a spot for springs is nothing more than a vestige of its former self. I can see rings of sand that look very much like ripples of water, but it's bone-dry. Luckily, I have plenty of water left in my jugs, and the sheepskin pouches are half full, so I'm not worried. In the expanse of Wild Fox Ridge, I should be able to find a spring, I say to myself.

Somehow, I'm reminded of Wooden Fish Girl. Her face is clear to me now, nice and pleasant, with eyes like bright sparkling stars. Did I actually see her eyes? It must have been a figment of my imagination, I think. But oddly, her eyes keep flashing past me and I even feel a dull ache.

What I want to know more than anything tonight is the rest of her story.

I'm drawn to the fate of her family.

I do see her star-like eyes flashing with tears.

One. Wooden Fish Girl

1

The angry people surrounded Lü Erye's family compound and watchtower.

Most were locals and from my family clan, almost no Hakkas, for they treated Lü Erye as one of their own. At first, they didn't join in because they knew reason was not on their side. Sometimes it's important to have reason and timing. Without the reason supplied by my family, no one would even dare think about meddling with Lü Erye. He had a positive reputation in every respect, except for his lust for women; he'd given aid to many of the poor families in the area, especially those landless Hakkas. Nearly every one of the clerks in his shop was Hakka. It amounted to declaring a war against the Hakkas if a clerk was killed or injured.

Back then the locals and the Hakka harbored deep-seated hatred for each other. For several decades, fights constantly broke out over incidents, major and minor, and blood was often spilled. This time the angry locals only vandalized the shop and attacked Lü Erye, so they should be all right. The problem was, the clerks had to fight back and step in to stop the people from smashing and looting the place. When the clerks were injured, the nature of the incident changed.

At first the angry mob surrounded the watchtower. Have you ever seen one? You've probably only seen those built by the Japanese in movies? Hei-hei, they served pretty much the same functions and looked a bit alike. Ma Siye's was designed by an architect who had studied in Japan. It was impressive. Compared to the average Hakka watchtower, his resembled more a cluster of watchtowers, a large compound encircled by walls that were several meters high, six-story watchtowers on all four corners, and battlements and gun slits atop the walls. The entrance to the compound was a massive mahogany door with brass rivets. Decades later, when the Japanese came and saw it, they were so impressed they turned it into their command center. The Republican forces fired on it, but merely left pockmarks on the walls.

At the time, the compound was more like a small town, and in the end, it saved Lü Erye's family.

The locals, shouting for revenge, surrounded the compound, but they were just farmers with no firearms. They pounded on the door with large rocks —*kuang-kuang*—which shook, but breaking in was a daydream.

The angry mob crowded around the area, but could not get in. They tried a number of solutions, such as putting up a scaling ladder—someone made one by attaching several ladders together—and digging a trench, but neither worked. Lü Erye had marksmen armed with long guns, which stayed silent at first, as they pushed the ladder off the wall. Several locals fell and hurt themselves, which enraged the people even more. They kept up their assault, physically and verbally.

Nothing happened after a siege of several days. The compound had its own well and an abundant storage of food, and the shop's warehouse was inside; they wanted for nothing. Even if the siege lasted six months or a year, Lü Erye would be unfazed. But the farmers had to eat. A rough count told me there were at least a thousand of them. I wanted to give up when I saw the wounded. I went to see Uncle, and asked him to intervene to call the whole thing off. I felt terrible when I saw so many were hurt because of me, and it would be serious if someone died. But he refused; he wanted to use this opportunity to run Lü Erye out of town. Lü Erye owned lots of land here—some of ours had been sold to him—and Uncle said he'd promised those who joined the attack that they would all have a share of Lü Erye's land once they got rid of him. It finally dawned on me that I was but a pawn in the event. Hei-hei, you can call that the earliest example of "beat up the local rich man and divide his land." It was most enticing to the landless villagers.

I finally realized that they would not halt their angry feet even after their anger was spent.

2

When I think back now, I have to say that everything would have been simpler if the organizers hadn't had such a grandiose plan. After the siege lasted a few days, the villagers would disperse along with their anger. The problem was, the head of the clan and other major figures wanted to expand the scale of conflict; they'd been scheming for years, but hadn't found the opportunity. Now finally they had their cause, finally got so many people together, and finally shed all pretenses of cordiality—the head of the clan had been an honored guest at Lü Erye's house. When a bow is stretched to shoot, the arrow never returns. There was no turning back.

The incident taught me why people stage a revolution.

The head of the clan and his cohort began sending missives with chicken feathers, a common communication method in secret societies. A feather was stuck onto a piece of paper and delivered to the recipient's house, telling him to do such and such at such and such place on such and such date, as well as the kind of punishment he'd suffer if he refused to comply. I don't know if all feather-missives are like that, but that's what ours was like. The meeting place was Lü Erye's watchtower, and what every household must do was bring along a certain quantity of firewood. At the appointed hour, a crowd gathered at the spot with bundles of kindling.

I think I need to explain why the villagers had followed the instruction on the missive. It was a conventional rule formed over several decades, and had been used during the countless armed battles of earlier times. If a family decided not to participate, that was all right, except that no one would help out when something happened to his family. You must follow the rules in a group if you want its protection. You see? The same principle was employed in armed battles between locals and Hakkas years earlier, and in your feuds in the West.

They would attack with fire.

They planned to bury the watchtower in the mountains of firewood and burn the people inside alive.

Naturally, it was highly effective, and altogether savage.

But it was also a tactic to tell Lü Erye not to entertain any vain hopes. The result of Lü Erye giving up vain hopes was his order for the marksmen to open fire.

The bloodshed they caused incensed the villagers even further.

Waves of people surged forward, followed by gunfire, shedding enough blood to stain the streams in the mountains.

Over three dozen locals died on the first day of the battle. Pyres were started around the compound, and the attackers flung torches that sent plumes of thick smoke into the watchtower. Intensifying gunfire sounded as a response, along with water splashing down.

Later the marksmen no longer fired only at those bringing firewood to the watchtower, but at anyone within range.

3

The incident escalated.

Hakkas, whose children worked as clerks at the shop, joined in to prevent them from dying in the fire or the melee. Now Lü Erye's watchtower was no longer the sole focus of the conflict.

The flames of anger from the outraged locals spread to other Hakkas, who had no watchtowers or weapons. Willingly or not, they became scapegoats for Lü Erye.

In the eyes of the radical locals, the Hakkas were less than human. In writing that mentioned the outsiders, the locals would attach a reference to a dog to the word Hakka. They did not want to see in their land a group of people who came from who knew where, people who had such a high regard for themselves. Many of the Hakka customs irked them, such as putting ancestors' bones in urns that they laid all over the place. The locals didn't care if the Hakka were ready to move at any given moment, but they fumed whenever they saw the urns. They complained about the unlucky sight of their black urns strewing the hills. It had been a long time since they'd wanted to smash those unsightly objects. Lü Erye, who had a watchtower and firearms, were out of their reach, but not these "Hakka thieves," of that they were sure.

So that was how it went. First to suffer were the clerks' families, after which their ancestral urns became the villagers' targets. Rocks flew at the urns, scattering ancestors' bones all over the place. As they flung the rocks to vent their anger, the locals stomped the bones into muddy ground, effectively turning all the Hakka residences into battlegrounds.

Worst yet, the battle fires continued to spread, thick smoke rose from all over, and rivers were formed from bloodshed. Mountains of locals charged at the outsiders, after which seas of Hakkas swarmed at the villagers. Everywhere there were bodies and people weeping, as the land was turned into a slaughterhouse.

People came up with different means of exacting revenge. Ghastly sights from the Crusades you mentioned also happened in Lingnan. Neither side spared women and babies. The Hakkas speared babies while the locals eviscerated pregnant women; some even fried enemy hearts and ate them. The winners plundered, the losers were eaten. Revenge, revenge, revenge. More deaths deepened the hatred. Later, when the

Japanese came to Nanjing, their behavior was a massive blot on humanity, but the Chinese were equally ruthless killers of each other. Millions died during battles between locals and Hakkas.

An entry in the book *Fenghu Miscellanea* by a scholar name Xu Xu recorded: "A minor dispute broke out in a township near Luobo and Dongguan and escalated into a fight between the locals and the Hakka. It ceased only after intervention by soldiers from the two counties and mediation by local gentry." In fact, the armed battle continued for years and often worsened, forcing the Hakka to settle in the mountains and forests. In those days the Hakkas lived in four-square compounds with portholes for guns in all four buildings; The areas around their houses often turned into battlegrounds. You can see how fierce the battles were.

Think about it. In the eyes of the locals, after they'd lived in a place for generations, "Hakka thieves" came to take their land, seize their hills, and fight over food that hadn't been plentiful to begin with. Do you think they could tolerate it? Of course not. One side wanted something, the other side refused to give it up, and so fighting broke out.

How long did it last? More than a hundred years.

It started out as strife over land and gains between the two sides, but slowly it evolved into hatred. Once hatred entered human hearts, it put down roots and sprouted, so one attacked the other and the other fought back, drawing out armed battles for a hundred years.

You probably aren't aware that to the locals, there were two major "evils" in Lingnan. One of them was the Hakka, who the locals believed to be farmers during the day and outlaws at night. Gangsters of the tongs came in second, thought to "swarm like bees and come and go like ghosts."

Among the Hakka back then, there were some self-styled "paupers" who bullied people of the same trade and monopolized the market, like Niu Er in *The Water Margin*. They plied the trade of kidnapping, demanding ransom, which was called "eat the rich." The locals called Hakka "outlaws," or the savage "Qi" or "Liao," or added a dog reference to "Hakka" to stress their primitive nature.

I was wracked by remorse for serving as the catalyst.

I regretted my action of seeking what I considered justice. Compared with the massive bloodshed, my family's fire was insignificant.

Lü Erye's watchtower turned out to be the safest spot in all of Lingnan. Many Hakkas swarmed to his compound and residence, making him the most popular, charitable man of his time. Whoever he let inside was guaranteed safety. He offered free food to keep the people alive. What happened to my family fell by the wayside, for those people refused to believe that a compassionate man like Lü Erye could possibly have committed murder and arson.

I didn't know whether to cry or laugh over the development of events.

It surely was an unforgettable life experience. I'll tell you more about it later, when you have more time; I'm sure you'll write a wonderous book that could shock the world. But the world has also had too much bloodshed, enough to numb the people, who are dull as calloused heels. I believe it could shock the world, but I'm not sure. You know that just about every living person wants an easier life. They don't want to see bloodshed, hear crying, or think about weighty topics, which is why scoundrels are always the ones who are the loudest in every age. They're as lively as leaves dancing in an autumn wind, and could care less if they leave a mark when the wind ceases.

They'll say, Drink now when there's liquor, and don't worry if it's water tomorrow.

Later the government intervened.

It had no choice.

Rioters raised pandemonium in the county town, smashing the

government office and killing the magistrate. Some even took the opportunity to raise the flag of open rebellion. The government could ignore the trouble caused by a mob, but there was a limit, and that was not to impact "the soil and grain." What is soil and grain? Scholars have given all sorts of explanations, but the common people knew exactly what it was. To be blunt, it simply meant the imperial throne.

Then the government army intervened.

I heard that the Ma family draft bank supplied the provisions, as in earlier years.

Because of the army intervention, some of the locals who sought revenge for me died horrible deaths. It was a bloodbath, even though stone rollers were no longer used to crush the people. Some of the most horrific crimes were committed after the army intervention.

How could I not hate the Ma family?

4

Lü Erye returned to his ancestral home after the bloody incident quieted down. He'd come with the camel caravan and left with it. He arranged for a bookkeeper to take charge of the business in Lingnan, but personally no longer felt safe to stay. No matter how much free food he gave out later, the locals never forgot the blood debt owed them by his marksmen. Some even wanted his life. The watchtower was secure, but he would effectively be a prisoner if he never ventured out.

He went back home after weighing his options.

Lü Erye left under the protection of a large number of marksmen and drivers.

I'll never forget that afternoon. The sun hung above the mountaintop. Lü Erye left with his caravan. They set the obligatory fire to mark a good beginning. The local population had suffered a speedy decline because of revenge killing, so not many people came to watch the lively departure. Big Mouth was going with them. He had told me about Lü Erye's trip home. I knew my chance for revenge would vanish after Lü Erye left for a place that was so far away. I believed I'd have a much greater chance of killing him on the road than in the watchtower.

I fried lots of steamed buns, broke them into pieces to fry in oil, and turned them into fingertip sized hardtack to eat on the road. At the time, I hadn't known how far Lingnan was from Liangzhou—Big Mouth had told me about this strange place. Distance didn't mean anything to me, however; all I cared about was revenge.

My hatred was the catalyst for the armed fight between the locals and the Hakka and had resulted in a massive bloodbath, but at the time hatred still clouded my heart.

Besides the blood debt Lü Erye owed me, I also held him responsible for all the lives lost in the battle. If not for him, I said to myself, all those people would still be alive. Day and night, I heard only one thing in my head, "Revenge!" I was gripped by immense emotions and couldn't shake them off.

In order not to draw unwanted attention, I stopped washing my face and rubbed in coal ashes. Then I gathered rags to turn myself into an old beggar woman. I was disgusted when I looked at my reflection in the water. It was my only way to avoid harassment from hoodlums. Besides food, I had several pairs of spare shoes, plus a canteen for water. Big Mouth had once told me that the caravans traveled at night and rested in the day, usually covering thirty or forty *li* a day. The drivers didn't ride the camels; they walked, he also said. So I thought if they could walk, so could I.

Big Mouth said I was crazy when I told him about my plan.

"You may not know, but it'll take at least two or three months to get there. It's a very hard trip. You may even lose your precious little life on the road if something goes wrong."

He relented when I insisted upon going. He even told me to keep a distance from the caravan, but within range of the bells. In those days, both the lead and the last camel had bells around their necks, the sound loud enough to travel far. He also found me a short-barreled matchlock and gunpowder for self-protection and to sound the alarm if I got into a jam. He'd find a way to come help me when he heard the shot. I was pleased with the weapon. With it, my chance for successful vengeance would increase. I even wondered if he gave me the firearm as a weapon for that purpose. He was unhappy with Lü Erye. We heard that Lü had slept with some pretty girls when the Hakka took refuge in his watchtower. Every time Big Mouth mentioned it, he called Lü Erye an old ass.

"Why don't you kill him then?" I asked. "It'd be easy for you to do."

"I can't," he said. "Have you ever heard of a camel driver killing his own boss? In our eyes, he's the one we depend on for our livelihood. Anyone with a wicked idea would be cutting himself off from the trade, and his life would be over. Besides, my parents still live in Liangzhou, they'd find me easy enough. The temple remains when the monks run off, you know."

He'd made the firearm and fried the gunpowder himself, using saltpeter, sulfur, and charcoal. I didn't know at the time that he'd added loose stool in the frying process, which, according to him, would intensify the explosiveness. He later told me he'd come up with the ingredient on his own. Strangely, it didn't disgust me. Obviously, revenge had become the sole reason for my existence at the time. I'm sure you don't know this, but I used to be very particular about cleanliness, and I'd lose my appetite if I heard filthy words. I was truly an old beggar woman.

He also taught me how to make fuses. After gathering a quantity of mugwort, he rolled it into piles of fuses, which, lucky for me, were light and didn't add much weight to my carrying load. They turned out to be a great help later. For one thing, they drove mosquitoes and bugs away, and for another, they bolstered my courage when I traveled at night. I could quickly set the gunpowder off if I was in trouble. But I used more than half of it before we were even a month into the journey. Every time I saw mugwort, I made sure to pluck some to make more fuses.

To ensure I'd be okay, he brought up the rear with his own team of camels, though he did warn me not to attack Lü Erye on the road. Lü had a team of marksmen who were not to be trifled with; they might not hit their targets from a hundred steps away, but never wasted gunpowder when shooting rabbits and wolves. They could take my life just by raising their arms.

Why would I travel with you if you didn't want me to seek revenge, I said to myself after hearing his admonition. Do you honestly think I've fallen for you and plan to elope to Liangzhou? Hei-hei.

"With all the lush mountains around, there'll be plenty of firewood," he said.

5

Just like that, I tailed their camel caravan and embarked on the longest journey of my life. I'm a bit scared when I think about it now.

You can sense the hardship I went through from "Song of a Camel Driver":

Drive the camels, up before dawn, head to the sixth stop.
So many camels, a long, long row, constantly requiring care.
We walk fast the first half of the night, my back hurts, my legs are sore.
We walk slowly the second half of the night, sleep sneaks up on me.
You see, this is, the life of a camel driver,

No way to make a living.

—*Song of a Camel Driver*

Luckily for me, the caravan followed the convention to stop for the camels to relieve themselves. I was near exhaustion when it was time to let the animals pee, which made it possible for me to keep up with them. Over those days, the bells were the most beautiful sound to my ears—*Kuang-dang, kuang-dang.* It might sound monotonous and dull, but it was truly music for my heart. You have no idea how the bells filled my life for more than six months—ai, your book will be a best-seller if you call it "The Sounds of Camel Bells." You don't believe me? Hei-hei, no need to explain yourself. It's just a suggestion, but I'd sure buy any book with a title like that.

The caravan followed the custom of traveling at night. That came as a great help to me. I wouldn't have been able to escape detection after following them for so long, if it had been daytime.

On those seemingly endless nights, the lanterns were, besides the camel bells, most comforting. The drivers lit lanterns on moonless nights, creating beautiful scenery, even though they weren't very bright. Seen from a distance, they were the hope in my heart. I often thought about Papa and the songs he'd taught me. I sang those songs silently as a diversion. The meaning of some of them still escaped me at the time, but I sang them not because I wanted to understand them, but to keep me company. I also wanted to make sure I remembered all those lovely songs that had filled Papa's head. A majority of his books were burned in the fire, while the remnants turned into bits and pieces. The passing of time and the baking fire had made the pages so brittle that they fell to pieces at the slightest touch, I decided to burn them to keep my poor Papa company. I didn't quite understand their true value, but I knew that Papa had his reason to treasure them, and I did not want his treasures to fall victim to my forgetfulness. On most nights, I recited a few words with every step I took, and time slowly passed like that.

Big Mouth had warned me not to be foolish enough to try to kill Lü Erye on the road, but I kept looking for an opening. I'd never allow him to return to his territory, because I might not be able to get near him once he was back home.

I got close several times, when the caravan stopped to rest. I discovered that the guards were always on high alert. When they set out, the marksmen rode on camels on either side of Lü Erye's sedan. Moreover, I heard that the sedan was made of rattan strips soaked in some kind of oil for reinforcement, so even though it was light, it could withstand attacks from a sword or musket.

I always found an excuse to get near where the caravan stopped to rest, as long as it wasn't out in the desert. When they stayed at an inn at a small market town, I approached them to beg for something. Back then beggars were everywhere, so no one would suspect an old beggar woman. I hadn't washed my face and could hardly recognize myself. Layers of filth covered my face, something hard to accept at first, but I slowly got used to it.

Lü Erye was vigilant. He knew that many of the locals considered him a mortal enemy and wished they could sleep under his skin and eat his flesh. When they first started out, several times he was nearly hit by bamboo arrows. Which was why I seldom saw him on the road. My musket was loaded, and every time I got near their resting spot, I'd light the firing fuse. I was ready and, when the opportunity presented itself, I would ignite the gunpowder and aim the matchlock at my enemy. I even added a steel ball and some buckshot, both given to me by Big Mouth. He told me to use them against wolves and hoodlums, but I chose to think that he knew what I had in mind. I told myself that the marksmen could turn me into a wasps' nest, so long as I could kill Lü Erye.

6

I'll never forget the feeling of walking through those long nights.

Before me was boundless darkness and a road that led to somewhere unknown, with only my footsteps and the distant camel bells to keep me company.

There was also thirst, however.

That, and hunger.

I quickly finished off the hardtack. When the caravan passed through market towns or villages with residents, I usually managed to beg for some food. I didn't eat it all right away; I kept the dried items for the night journey. But most of the time, I didn't get anything solid, because the people along the road were having a tough time, and few families could afford solid food. I usually got leftover soup or rice. I drank the liquid first and kept what was left for later at night. I had diarrhea several times after eating leftovers, clear liquid that seemed never to stop. I got so weak my legs were nearly useless. Over those days, I truly despaired. Eventually, I got some garlic cloves that helped me regain my strength. With the lesson learned, I always begged for garlic when I passed through villages. Once I traded a shawl someone had given me for a lot of garlic, which I roasted when I had nothing else to eat. I don't know if you've ever had roasted garlic. Maybe you'd find it unappetizing, but to me it was delicious. Sometimes, when I couldn't find anything else, roasted garlic made a meal. The only flaw was, eating too much of it stuffed up my nostrils. Hei-hei, that's my personal experience, and I'm happy to share it with you. Even a writer like you can't make up a detail like that.

Garlic was easy to carry, it didn't go bad, it was nutritious, and it was an antitoxin. It helped me through the most difficult period of my life. Once I started eating garlic, I never again had diarrhea from leftover food.

Without it, I don't know if there'd be a continuation to my life story, since I had nothing but leftover food for what seemed like months. I carried a clay jar and a sheepskin pouch in my backpack. I stored whatever I was given in the jar. During the days, when the caravan stopped to rest, I went begging for food and wouldn't stop until I filled the jar. Sometimes the weather was too hot, and the food spoiled quickly. Later, with the raw garlic, even spoiled food looked delicious to my eyes.

The most difficult times were in the desert and rocky gobis, where there was no one to beg food from. Big Mouth came to my aid at those times; he saved food for me when they stopped for the camels to relieve themselves. Either roasted sweet or regular potatoes, or crusty fried cakes. I could find the food easily, because the caravan left a trail when they traveled and stopped. Later, he told me he'd find a more secluded spot to have a smoke and bury the food with a marker when the caravan stopped. When there were rocks, he would lay three rocks at the spot; when there were none, he urinated in the shape of an eight. I never failed to find what I was looking for.

It was tough travelling alone, but sometimes that gave me a chance for pleasurable moments. If Big Mouth's team brought up the rear—he'd have to dawdle when the caravan set out—I could sneak up under the cover of the night to chat with him. I didn't get to do that often, though. He rarely let me come up, saying the lead driver would check around to make sure no team got left behind. I believed him at first, but later I started to suspect that it was an excuse, after I learned that the lead driver didn't have to come around to check on him, after all. The bells alone were enough to tell the lead driver if everything was proceeding normally. I thought Big Mouth didn't want anyone to know about our relationship, afraid that what I planned to do later might implicate him and his family. It wasn't a pleasant thought, and it turned into a seed of discord that slowly sprouted and bloomed to change the nature of our friendship.

7

One night I noticed two green lights behind me. It was amusing at first, but I quickly detected a stink, which put me on alert. In the hazy darkness of night, I saw a dog, a big one, and it bared its teeth and growled at me when it saw me looking at it. My scalp went numb. A wolf? I asked myself. I recalled what Big Mouth had said about the difference between a dog and a wolf—a dog raises its tail, while a wolf tucks it between its legs. It was too dark for me to see the tail and the animal was facing me, but the reeking stink was obviously not coming from your average dog. Wolves' bad breath is overpowering.

After a while, the numbness in my scalp went away and I was no longer afraid. I knew fear was useless. I'd been through a lot and encountered too many deaths over those days. My heart was dazed after witnessing so much bloodshed during the battle between the locals and the Hakka. I wasn't even twenty years old, but I felt I'd lived a thousand years, and there was nothing to fear any longer. Revenge took possession of my heart and left no room for anything else. Just think, how could a young woman make it through the long journey if not for the desire to get revenge?

After growling awhile, the animal started to circle me, and my suspicions were confirmed when I saw its tail in the dark. A dog's tail wags like a flag, but not this one. I can't turn into wolf food, I told myself. I wasn't really afraid at the moment, my only thought was that I couldn't seek revenge if I died. Uncle once told me that my parents and siblings, though dead, continued to exist as ghosts of wrongful deaths. They could be reborn only after I avenged them. He also said that their souls resided in the spirit tablet wrapped in red cloth that I carried with me and would not be delivered until I offered our enemy's blood to the tablet. I believed him, because on occasion I could feel the tablet thumping like a living heart. Sometimes, I even heard my brothers crying when I least expected something like that. Every once in a while, I saw my second younger brother with his string of sparrows, and I often dreamed about Papa, who looked at me with a glum face streaked with murky tears, ugly as snot. He never uttered a word, and yet I felt he'd said a lot. I almost never dreamed about Mama, except once when I saw her back in my dream. I cried out, Ma—Ma. She turned her ghostly white face toward me. I'll avenge you, Mama, I said to her. She looked at me with a sad smile.

When I saw it was really a wolf, my only thought was how difficult it would be for the dead in my family to find deliverance if I were to become wolf food. That mustn't happen. I was also reminded of the ancient songbooks and the songs Papa had written, which I carried in my head. If I died, I thought, they'd be gone from the world forever.

Those two things were what concerned me most.

The wolf growled as it got closer, its stink growing increasingly stronger. It seemed to seep into the depths of my soul; for many years after that, now and then I would smell it. I knew if I fought the wolf, I'd lose, but I didn't want to willingly offer up my neck. I kept striking a flint rock with steel to light some tinder. I'd fire my matchlock if the wolf got any closer. That might draw the attention of the drivers or Lü Erye's guards, but I couldn't worry about that then. They probably wouldn't recognize me now that I looked like an old beggar woman, anyway, I told myself. My hair was as matted as felt and caught lots of hay and twigs. I often rested up by stacks of kindling in villages and market towns along the way, so my hair had collected splinters of wood, and my face had gathered the dust of these places. I looked like a genuine beggar woman, except for the youthful glint in my eyes—but they were often bloodshot from a lack of sleep. Maybe even they showed signs of aging, because I never got enough sleep. I had to be on guard even when I was asleep, so I wouldn't oversleep and lag too far behind to catch up with the caravan.

I still had some mugwort left, but I tried not to use it too often; I only burned a little at spots infested with mosquitos to stop them from swarming all over me. I would burn some whenever I could get near Lü Erye, in preparation for lighting the fire of revenge. I'd burn some mugwort, and I'd shoot if the wolf refused to leave me alone.

The sparks flew off the flint rock, clearly startling the wolf, for it took a few steps back. Ca—ca—the rock made a cracking noise under the night sky. The drivers might find me out but for the camel bells. The light was so bright it momentarily blinded me, and I could not see the wolf. It might pounce, I said to myself. I kept striking the flint rock as I listened for its reaction. Strangely, my mind was so quiet I feared nothing at that moment. Maybe I was simply too exhausted.

You should know that I was really sleepy. When the drivers slept during the day, I had to go out and beg for food, which was sometimes easy and sometimes not. Even if I quickly got enough food, I still didn't have much time to sleep. Besides, even if I did, I could never enjoy deep sleep, and I woke up whenever the camel bells sounded their departure. I might even be startled awake by bells in my head. That was how I learned to doze off as I walked at night.

In many brief instants I thought that the wolf appeared in my dream, probably because I was exhausted.

I ignited the flint and lit the mugwort, and saw that instead of leaving, the wolf had only backed off a few steps. The two lights still shone under the night curtain.

I wouldn't fire if it didn't lunge. I knew the matchlock had a limited range. The wolf would be wary of me if it didn't know where things stood, but if I fired and missed, its teeth would surely be on my throat before I could reload.

I had no time to deal with the wolf. Waving the burning mugwort, I raced to catch up with the caravan, the mugwort a red thread arcing in the air with my movement.

    The wolf gave chase as I ran. I heard its heavy breathing.

    It felt to me that it followed me for a long time. Maybe it was waiting for me to fall. Obviously, my young body was a delicious possibility in its eyes. Just as I could smell its stench, it surely detected me.

    To distract myself from the terror—terror, not fear—I recited wooden fish songs silently as I ran. I recalled when Papa told stories from *Journey to the West*, he said the Tang Monk Tripitaka would always recite the *Heart Sutra* whenever he was in danger. He said that for the best story one listened to the Tang Monk fetching the sutras, and for the best fight scene one watched Wu Song razing a swindling inn. Papa had even turned the Monk's journey into a wooden fish song and later also composed "Guanyin Bodhisattva's Ten Advices." I had yet to memorize the *Heart Sutra*, but did commit the "Guanyin Bodhisattva's Ten Advices" to memory, and since the Bodhisattva appeared in the *Heart Sutra*, it would be similar in places to "Guanyin Bodhisattva's Ten Advices."

    I started chanting, and soon I felt myself drawn into the melody—

First advice is for women to be vegetarians,
The Old Man in the sky above designs his deals.
We all know the good and the bad in this world of ours,
With kindness in the heart, we should do good all the time.
We know the world when we see through human affairs,
Nothing is easy and difficulties we all have our share.
The first husband is addicted to gambling,
You fear he's out on the street playing cards.
Make sure to never marry a merchant.
He'll drink, gamble, smoke opium and wear out his shoes.
He gambles away your clothes and jewelry,

A lifetime seems so long it's hard to get through.
Simple meals can be had anywhere, anytime you want,
if you live in Nature and enjoy the scenery of farm life.

After singing awhile, I saw the wolf was still hanging around, though it didn't pounce. It just followed me at a distance. That was fine with me. You keep your distance and I'll keep mine.

I continued to chant as I pushed on—

Second advice is for a woman not to be greedy,
Being a vegetarian helps with self-cultivation.
Do not back out of your practice and consider marriage;
If you're married with children, you'll fight with your husband.
Marrying the wrong man will lead to a life of hardship,
Once he leaves the house he'll be out for a long time.
You're like a widow if your man doesn't want to return.
Abandoned when young, she has too many worries at home.
Nothing is real when you think about it, and
You think you married the wrong man halfway into your life.
Guanyin Bodhisattva never married,
And she was carefree atop her lotus flower.
Listen to my words, all of you in the world,
Don't be lured by the early morning glow.
Anyone devoted to religious practices will have a good life.
You'll be in Heaven with boundless good blessings.

"Guanyin Bodhisattva's Ten Advices" had unusual power, and I felt my heart soften. I'd always loved listening to the chant as a child and liked singing it as I got older. Its language wasn't elegant, much less refined than "Reunion at the Nunnery," but it never failed to move me when I sang.

Dawn was breaking, bright enough for me to see it was a rotund wolf.

A stirring story developed between the wolf and me later, but I don't want to bring it up casually and ruin a good story. Later, I'll tell you only, and I'm sure you'll turn it into a great novel.

8

I won't talk about the wolf now. I'll tell you another problem I encountered; that is, my shoes were worn through. All the shoes I'd brought along were now in tatters, and my feet were covered in blood blisters. Searing pain shot up with every step I took.

Now I finally understood why the camel drivers all wore heavy shoes. The so-called heavy shoes were made of layer upon layer of donkey skin and cowhide; wherever a spot was worn through it was patched over right away, which, as time went by, made the shoes heavy. The drivers said the shoes helped build up strength in their legs and were sturdy enough for long distances. The pairs I'd made before the trip were in pieces even before we were a third of the way through.

I knew I'd be left far behind the caravan if I didn't find a way to deal with my footwear problem, which was my number one challenge over those days. Whenever the caravan stopped to rest, in addition to begging for food, I'd ask for free shoes. I was able to get my hands on some worn ones, but they never lasted long. Besides, they didn't normally fit well, so blood blisters began to multiply on my feet; luckily for me I kept the sores in check by rubbing garlic on them.

Footwear remained a challenge for a long time. Eventually it was Big Mouth who took care of it for me. When we passed through a market town, he bought ten pairs of hempen shoes and a yard of white cloth. I wrapped my feet in the cloth before putting on the shoes, and that was a great improvement. Have you ever seen shoes like that? They're made of twisted hemp and are much sturdier than regular shoes.

I was so exhausted I couldn't take another step when we were halfway into the trip. Big Mouth came up with the idea for me to hold onto the camel's tail to help myself along. He was in charge of the last team of camels at the time. To avoid complications, if there was any problem, drivers usually preferred being in the middle and not the last spot. The others were happy to let him have it when Big Mouth offered to bring up the rear. I was able to finish the remaining journey of a thousand *li* only with help from the camel's tail. My scalp tingles when I think back now. It's just a sensation. Hei-hei, you do know it was a wild wish to have a scalp in my current state. Ma Zaibo was right when he said once we lose our human bodies, we have no hope of retrieving them.

My plans changed once I started relying on the camel tail for traveling; I decided against killing Lü Erye on the road. First of all, I never saw him and secondly, I didn't want the drivers to find out. Once they did, I'd never be able to continue traveling west. They would only need to tie me up at some spot, and I couldn't catch up with them after they traveled past two stops. I couldn't make the trip all by myself. I made up my mind that I'd reach Liangzhou first and come up with a way to get revenge there.

Many interesting things happened along the way, and I'll tell you all about them later when we have more time. Look at them. They're losing patience with me.

Long story short.

After a long, arduous trek, I finally reached Zhenfan in Liangzhou, where Su Wu was said to have been exiled to tend sheep. It was a real eye-opener. I could hardly imagine such a hellish place, so dry and brown, with very little green. Everywhere I looked was rocky gobi and sand. The locals had a description for it: no vinegar to go with a meal and no tree to provide shade. It really wasn't a place for man or beast.

I had a visceral understanding of the hardships endured by camel drivers after this punishing trip. Those were nightmarish days, each spent on foot over and over again. Most of the time, when they passed through deserted rocky gobi, their footsteps were their only companions. More strenuous work awaited them when the caravan stopped to rest; they had to load and unload dozens of heavy litters each day. But when we got to Liangzhou, I finally understood why they decided to be drivers, which was an enviable profession compared with being villagers stuck in the corner of the desert to scrape out a living.

Big Mouth told me to stay away shortly before we reached our destination. I was able to save energy by holding onto the camel's tail, but still I was beyond exhaustion by then. Pointing at a tiny dot of dim yellow tucked into a corner of the distant desert, he said, that's where I live.

I trailed the caravan from far behind. Reaching my destination after the nightmarish long journey, I was excited and yet somewhat apprehensive. I liked the analogy you gave once, like a leaf being tossed into a strange ocean. It was well put; I really did feel that way. Before me was a brand new, strange world, with different weather, geography, people and many other things.

What I found hardest to face was, Big Mouth's parents had found him a wife while he was away. I went to his house one day, disguised as a beggar, and saw her. Scrawny, like a dehydrated carrot.

I hear the yellow camel's cry at that moment, followed by spitting noise like a machine gun firing. He does that frequently, but somehow it feels different this time.

Racing over, I find a green lamp hidden in the dark. That sends a scare into me; I wonder if it's a fox or a wolf. It must be the latter. Except for the deranged ones, foxes are usually afraid of humans, and will run off quickly if they hear movement. If it's a wolf, then it can get complicated.

I quickly retrieve my musket, loaned to me by the old camel driver before I set out. It belonged to his grandfather, is in very good condition from meticulous care even though it's almost a hundred years old. He oiled the firearm regularly and managed to keep it in top shape, with the help of dry weather in the west.

He also fried the gunpowder for me, mixing sawdust, sulfur, and saltpeter in appropriate portions and frying it in a wok. "This antique isn't very effective, but it'll boost your courage. You can scare off some wild animals when you run into them."

Sure enough, the green lamp recedes before I finish loading.

But the yellow camel continues to snort and spit. Can he actually see the specter? I wonder.

Silence presses down when I return to the site of storytelling. I realize all the stories have become part of the silence. Now that I'm familiar with their faces, they begin to take on concrete texture. Wooden Fish Girl's nice features and unique charm tug at my heart. I always feel my own heartache in someone else's stories.

"How did you think of bringing this?" Wooden Fish Girl points to the musket.

"To reassure myself," I say.

"That makes sense," she says with a laugh. "That's how I felt back then."

"But don't use it," she adds.

"Why not?"

"The wolf will be afraid of you if you don't, but if you do, it'll see the firearm is just a paper tiger, not even as effective as fire."

"Mine looked very much like this one," she adds.

She tilts her head in the direction of the receding green lights and says, "That thing has a karmic connection with you and will continue to follow you. You owed it a debt."

"What debt?"

"A life."

"You didn't know, but it's been following you. You didn't see it until now."

"Will it have its wish fulfilled?"

"That's up to you," she says with an enigmatic laugh.

I know what she means, so I laugh too.

"All right. Let's forget that, and continue with your story," I say as I realize everyone but her is gone.

"Where did they go?" I ask.

"Frightened away by that," she points to the musket. "So it's better if you don't use it. If you do, you'll never see them again."

"But what about you? Aren't you afraid?"

"I'm here to tell my story."

I return the musket to my sack and go back to listen to her story.

Eighth Session
Small Town Junk-collector

Drive the camels, up before dawn, head to the seventh stop.
With a reckless caravan leader, we travel day and night.
Get up early, turn in late, my back hurts and my legs are sore.
My health is ruined. You see,
This is, the life of a camel driver,
No way to make a living.

——*Song of a Camel Driver*

1

I settled down in the small town.

Following Big Mouth's advice, I didn't wash off the dirt on my face right away. I'd be subjected to abuse if I showed my face, he said. I knew what he meant: my disgusting appearance at that moment would not rouse any interest in even the most lecherous man.

That was fine with me.

I hung out with some junk-collector women. Most of them were like me, with rags on their backs. Maybe I looked even worse, with sore-infested feet and a weatherworn face. Luckily, I'd already learned quite a bit of the local patois in my conversation with Big Mouth; it was a stilted, strange language, somewhat outdated, like using "thee" for "you." I also learned about Lü Erye's family background by chatting with the other junk collectors. The wealthy man, I realized, was a very average manager for the Ma family, whom everyone called Second Manager. The locals always wore a respectful look when they mentioned him and called him Ma Erye, Second Master Ma; no one called him Lü Erye. The Ma family passed out free congee all the time; on the first and the fifteenth of every month, starving villagers came from near and far to their congee hut. I'd visited the hut myself. It was Ma Siye, Fourth Master Ma, a man with a kind face, who ran the charitable hut. I heard from the other junk collectors that the Ma family had draft banks all over the country and had been wealthy for over a hundred years. The one in Lingnan was among them, and smaller than the others.

I got a chance to see the Ma compound. It was impressive, almost like a small city, several times more spectacular than the one in Lingnan.

I heard that the city of Zhenfan was sacked during a revenge killing between the Hui and the Han, causing several thousand deaths. The Ma fortress took in hundreds of refugees and remained intact after days of attack from the rioters.

The sight of the fortress made me feel like a tiger trying to swallow the sky.

2

I found that the hatred in my heart was fading, after the long, grueling trek. Along the way I'd gone through so much and found myself on the brink of death many times. Tempered by time and the elements, the hatred lessened, and I thought I'd let go of a great deal.

One night I dreamed of Papa, to my surprise. He still gazed glumly at me, wordlessly. Mama and my younger brothers were by his side; Mama looked at me sadly while the boys wore angry expressions. They said nothing, but I was drenched in sweat when I awoke. I knew they were reminding me of something.

But that something no longer seemed so urgent and important.

How terrible.

Since then, I've done one thing late each night when all is quiet: I take a vow before the ancestral tablet. I eventually wrote down the names and birth dates and time for my parents and brothers on the back of the tablet, after which I pricked a finger with a needle to draw blood and drip it on the tablet. I wrapped it up in the red cloth and carried it on me wherever I went. When I laid eyes on it or touched it, that reminded me to never forget the hatred. The first thing I did every morning upon waking up was recite "revenge" a thousand times. I'd recall the fire while envisioning my loved ones fighting for their lives amid the flames as well as remember those in the clan who had died in armed battles and grit my teeth to recite my "true statement" silently—

Revenge!

Revenge!!

Revenge!!!

Soon my heart was refilled with hate.

In those days, whenever I heard the Ma family mentioned, my hate would spread not only to Lü Erye, but to everyone in the Ma family, and I felt could not live under the same sky as them.

Many of those Ma family charitable acts were pretended righteousness to me.

It was then that I realized that hate had to be practiced too, which I continued to do over the many years after my arrival in Liangzhou. Every month, I chanted silently all the wooden fish songs I'd known so well. From the first to the fourteenth, I recited those from the ancient texts, and from the fifteenth till the end of the month I recalled those written by Papa. The first was called *shuori* and the fifteenth *wangri*, days when the Liangzhou residents offered sacrifice to their deities. Papa and the songs were my deities at the time. Reciting them brought me more joy than hatred, but I always used hate to counteract them. I chanted these songs merely so as not to forget the treasure in Papa's eyes, which in turn was a way for me to remember him. Papa came back alive and smiled quietly at me when I sang them silently. Luckily, these songs would have disappeared from my life if I hadn't insisted on this commemorating rite, and Papa would have truly been dead if forgetfulness had prevailed over memory.

3

Big Mouth came to see me if I was alone. He told me about his parents finding a wife for him. At that instant it dawned on me that I'd fallen a bit in love with him, for I felt an ache in my heart when I heard him say "wife." If I hadn't still harbored hatred, and vengeance hadn't continued to inhabit the time and space of my life, I would surely have shed my beggar's garb, washed the filth off my face, and returned to my true self. The area produced few beauties, because the wind and sand coarsened the women's skin. If I were to appear as a young woman, I thought, I would be considered a beauty around here. It wouldn't be a step down for him to marry me.

I almost did it.

And he wanted me to.

He had no feelings for the girl his parents had found for him, nor did he want to touch her. His parents wanted them to consummate the marriage so the girl could give them a grandchild. Camel hands came home only once a year. Some would leave home when their wives were pregnant and return to see their child running around. Big Mouth told me he didn't give his consent even though he understood what they were thinking. He didn't tell them about me, though; he was worried that they would be frightened, but even more concerned that they might let it slip and ruin my chance of success. In their eyes, the Ma family were good people. Lü Erye was lecherous, for sure, but that wasn't a serious problem, as long as he didn't overdo it. They'd been given shelter at the Ma fortress during a battle between the Han and the Hui, and they'd partaken of the free congee from the Ma family for months. One was expected to repay drops of water with a gushing spring. They would never stand by and watch if they knew someone wanted to kill Lü Erye, an attitude that even affected Big Mouth. He was always trying to talk me out of revenge, saying it was better to resolve enmity than to deepen it. What had passed was in the past. If I could forget my hate, he said, he would marry me, even though he was worried that the harsh life here would be too tough for me.

"What if I still want revenge? Will you help me?"

"I will," he said after a momentary hesitation, adding that he could never forget the bloodshed Lü Erye had caused in Lingnan. At the time, I was unaware that he was a member of the Society of Brothers, a secret organization opposed to the Qing court.

With the information he relayed about the Ma family, I had a general sense of the layout of the fortress. During the first month after my arrival, I went there to beg every day, and each time, I was given something to eat. What people were saying about the family proved to be true. Tales of the Ma family helping others were widespread, and even many among the beggars heaped praise on the family. I would head over there when I couldn't get food anywhere else, and each time, I'd only had to tap my bowl for someone to bring out food, such as cooked rice or boiled potatoes. I heard that the Ma bosses ate with their hired hands and clerks, which meant I was eating the same food as the bosses.

I never saw Lü Erye though. Someone said he had worn himself out on the latest trek and been laid up with poor health; he stayed in to recuperate and rarely left the fortress. I begged the heavens not to let him die. I wanted him to die by my knife so I could offer his blood to the spirit tablet and deliver the souls of the wrongful dead. I wished I could run into him when I was out begging. I carried a sharp knife with me and polished it with a chamois late every night. I polished it over and over until it glinted. If I ran into that old man, I said to myself, I would surely be able to drive the knife through his back and even cut off his head if I had the chance. The scene of blood dripping down his goatee flashed through my mind. Strangely, however, I'd see his eyes darting here and there, an image that frightened me.

Big Mouth told me that the camel and sheep festival was about to take place, and that Lü Erye would surely show his face.

4

Thousands of sheep and camels showed up on the day of festival, so many that Su Wu Mountain looked cramped. Without seeing it yourself, you cannot imagine that the northern desert could be this lively. Devoid of good trees, Su Wu Mountain did have old growth poplars and willows to create extensive shaded areas, while plants like pea shrubs, needle grass, and other vegetation spread and grew into an impressive formation. Sightseers, shepherds, and merchants swarmed like ants, the livestock was keyed up enough to call out in voices they rarely got to use, raising a din and creating excitement on Su Wu Mountain.

The festival was really lively. Listen, someone is singing—

Bowls and cups pile up in a china stall,

> *Goods in a wool shop are a pretty sight,*
> *Where felt hats and sheepskin coats fill the spot.*
> *People pulling bows, shooting arrows,*
> *Bachelors gathering for a smoke.*
> *In Su Wu temple, worshippers drawing lots,*
> *A man by a cauldron cooking intestines,*
> *In eateries people having soup,*
> *In hallways and yards, crowds clamoring,*
> *Carters, cow herds, a circus with a monkey, and oil vendors,*
> *People burning paper, repaying for a wish fulfilled,*
> *An opera singer under the stage,*
> *Awls, shoe soles, a cobbler making shoes in the shop.*
> *Scallion beards, garlic cloves, coins strung up in hemp ropes . . .*

Big Mouth said no one knew the origin of the festival, but it had been around in the late Ming or early Qing, and never promoted by the government. Organized by the people, it took place once a year and lasted seven or as long as eleven days. In addition to townships in Liangzhou, participants also came from Qinghai, Ningxia, and Mongolia in the fur trade. The festival was important to the Ma family, for, besides the chance to do business, it was also a stage for the prominent families to show off their social status.

Big Mouth told me that Lü Erye was the showy type, and any year that he was back home, he was the expected festival director. There was actually more than one director, and each had to put up funds.

"There'll be a huge crowd, with lots going on," he added, "and it will provide a good chance for revenge if Lü Erye shows up."

I'll never forget the festival. I remember camel-racing being the liveliest event. There were two kinds of camel races, walking and running. Camels walking, like horse cantering, was also a competition in speed; though not as fast at running, camels have great stamina, which was why they were used in caravans.

"The Ma family used to pick some of their camels to compete in walking, and they won every year. The prizes were tea from the Ma family, so they ended by awarding Ma tea to Ma camels. Later, the family decided against competing with their own camels, and the other prominent families followed suit. Now only camels raised by the villagers took part; actually, anyone who raised camels could compete, in groups. Some mischief-makers took the opportunity to gamble, vying for liquor and sheep and joining the fun, yelling and shouting, raising the fun level to the highest.

Big Mouth wanted to find a good walking camel at the festival this time. His current one was old and losing its stamina. His camel was different from the average ones. Camel hands usually traveled thirty or forty *li* between stops, while he sometimes was given special jobs by the boss and had to be flexible enough to adjust his schedule. Sometimes he needed to travel several hundred *li* a day on urgent matters, and a camel with less than stellar stamina could easily cause undue delays. He planned to find himself one fine camel.

I carried my knife and waited for my chance.

There were lots of camels, I discovered, but few white ones. Occasionally I'd spot one or two. Leading his camel as if he was joining the festival, Big Mouth followed me from a distance. We'd agreed that, if I succeeded, he would immediately bring his camel over, boost me up, and we'd take off together. Honestly, I'd marry him for that alone. I'd complained about him being a coward with little confidence, but I was eternally touched by the promise he'd made at the festival. One's courage, I realized, was like a skill, and grows after honing. What he did later, hei, made me look at him differently.

Along the mountain path people were selling herbal medicines or furs and pelts, as well as vendors with sundry goods, all hawking their wares at the top of their lungs. Sightseers gravitated toward the racing ground. I saw Lü Erye hollering over there. Later I learned that was one of the duties of a festival director. The so-called director was an honorary title and gave the man no real authority. Anyone who worked at the festival, put up money, or lent a hand could be called a director. Lü Erye, though well known for his lecherous tendency, did not stint on money for public events like this and actually spent more than Ma Siye, which was an obvious effort to show the other man up. It didn't bother Ma Siye, who usually let Lü Erye have the upper hand. Lü Erye was always accompanied by two toughs whose eyes constantly swept the area, I discovered. As long as they were around, I couldn't accomplish my task.

As a whistle sounded, the camels started the walking contest. They were crowded into each other at first, but some quickly pulled away amid yells and shouts erupting all around. Big Mouth saw I was too far from Lü Erye, so he rode his camel up to join the fun. His was a skinny camel and, likely still recovering from the tiring journey, was pushed off the mountain path by a stronger one. Luckily, the path was even and safe, so the camel didn't fall; it just stumbled into a ditch. The crowd burst out laughing. The other camels were far ahead when Big Mouth got back on the path, so he whipped his ride and sent it running. Someone walked over and said, "Hey, you can't do that, it's against the rules." Another man came up to pull the camel over to the side. Big Mouth looked unperturbed, grinning, his white teeth glinting.

The camels stuck out their necks and took big strides at a high speed. One of them, a castrated male, was tall and long-legged; it took even, steady steps, and quickly moved far ahead of the others. Big Mouth tugged at my sleeve stealthily and said, "See that camel, it's a superb animal. I want to buy it." Before I could respond, someone next to me laughed and said, "You want to buy it? You'll have to ask the owner if he wants to sell it first. It was a present from Master Wang Tiao to his nephew." It was a familiar voice, so I turned to look. It was Hu Gala; he lived in Su Wu Temple, where I'd gone begging for food a few times. A generous man, he never disappointed me when I held out my hands. He had a full beard, so it was hard to tell his age, but a lot of people called him Old Mister Hu. Next to him was a hunchbacked cripple, also leading a camel. It was a bit on the skinny side, with bones showing under the hide, and had a minor limp. A cripple with a gimpy camel drew raucous laughter from the crowd.

"Old Brother, you're joining the race?" Big Mouth jested, only to hear the cripple say,

"The running contest. I'll let others compete in walking."

Big Mouth laughed. "Your camel looks like the reincarnation of a hungry ghost released from hell."

"I'll give it a try anyway," the cripple said coolly.

Waves of noise surged amid loud cheers as people rooted. Seen from a hill, the camels were nearing the finish line. The Mongolian camel from the Wang family remained in the lead, several *zhang* ahead of the next closest.

"What a great camel." Big Mouth gushed with praise.

5

Seeing the two toughs sticking close to Lü Erye, I knew I couldn't get near him, so I was in no hurry to act. The festival was eleven days long, sooner or later I'd find my chance. Even a tiger dozes off sometimes, I thought. I prayed silently for help from Papa's spirit, as well as to all the deities I knew for their assistance to fulfill my wish.

The running contest would be held in the afternoon, so the sightseers left after the walking race. Along the path were many eating places offering desert rice snacks, sweet fried cakes, roasted potatoes, noodles, all things to suit one's fancy. Those visitors from faraway pitched tents to spend their nights on the mountain, where food was readily available. But the action was concentrated near the Su Springs. Big Mouth said the spring water added fat to the animals faster to ward off diseases. The same went for people too.

"When a caravan leaves, the drivers get water from the springs," he said. "It used to have much more water, now it's slowly drying up, with only a tiny thread of water seeping out between rocks."

The visitors filled containers with the water, took a few sips, and splashed the rest on the sheep and camels, like Guanyin Bodhisattva sprinkling sacred water, for good luck from Su Wu. I said to myself that Su Wu hadn't managed to change his destiny, so how could he protect the sheep and camels? But according to the locals, one was human when one was alive and a deity after death. Apparently Su Wu had become a deity, and if that was true, then he'd have magical powers. I also prayed to Su Wu for his help. I wonder if my prayer had something to do with what happened to me later at the temple.

Big Mouth told me that Su Wu of the Han dynasty had herded sheep on this mountain for nineteen years. To memorialize him for carrying out his mission, the locals named the festival after him. The gathering of livestock had started when herders came with their animals for the beneficial spring water, which slowly grew into a custom, with the function for trade added later. Residents of neighboring provinces congregated here to barter and trade. Without need of any government promotion, it developed solely from the people's initiative. Besides trade, many festival activities were meant to commemorate Su Wu. For instance, the first nineteen fastest camels were chosen in camel racing, whether walking or running, and they all got the same prize, which was nineteen bricks of tea each to pay tribute to the number of years Su Wu spent herding the sheep. The shadow play and storytelling were mostly about his life here. Some women even embroidered the theme on their pillow cases, head ornaments, insoles, and baby's stomachers.

After picking out several embroidered pieces, Big Mouth went with Hu Gala to a quiet place for a private conversation. Later he told me that Hu was the head of the local branch of the Society of Brothers.

"The county magistrate has gotten into action over the past days. He recruited several hundred young men who have been drilling day and night," he said. "The magistrate also has informers in every township and village. If he's alerted to any movement, he will kill anyone involved. Several days ago, some of the members of the Society set up an altar and held a meeting, but they were careless and the government got wind of it. They were all arrested and tortured. Luckily, the yamen attendant was the only one who knew about the Society, and he refused to give anyone up, even on pain of death. The others had just joined, so even if they wanted to confess, they didn't know anything; they had no answer to any of the questions, so no one else was implicated. Some of the members were upset with the Ma family because of the incident, since the cost for the county's recruiting effort was shouldered by the prominent families, and Ma was the first to respond by offering five thousand taels of silver. Hu Gala said we shouldn't blame Ma Siye. They're a renowned family and had to cooperate with the government, like a tall tree getting the most wind. Several generations of the Ma family have adhered to the convention of not going against the government, and that is why they've prospered for over a hundred years."

Laughter erupted as he talked. Turned out a crowd had gathered around Lü Erye and asked him to sing a tune, with other onlookers joining in, clamoring for fun. A blind storyteller started out with his three-string instrument before Lü Erye opened his mouth and began to sing:

I married a wife with a harelip.
I tell her to turn up the lamp, but she blows it out.
So many poor people in the world, but no one's like me, the shepherd boy.

The crowd laughed lustily. Big Mouth explained that the tune was called "Little Shepherd Boy." I grew to like it. The shepherd boy experienced nearly all the world's misfortunes, but he managed to joke about life, with a joyful attitude. It fit me quite well.

I bought a sheepskin coat; it was infested with bugs and fleas.
I pocketed a black steamed bun and the bugs made it their nest.
So many poor people in the world, but no one's like me, the shepherd boy.

Big Mouth was having so much fun he couldn't stop laughing. I went up and tugged at him, and whispered, "I'm going to do it now. Don't forget what you need to do." He whispered his reply, "No need to hurry. Not yet. It's not every day we have a festival like this, and everyone is having a great time. Wait a while. If you do it today, you'll ruin the festival. Can you wait until it's over? He'll be tired out by then, and it'll be easier for you. I'm sure he'll come to hand out the prizes on the last day."

It made sense to me, so I nodded my agreement. Besides, I also saw that even though I could get near Lü Erye, the two toughs were still protecting him, one in front, one in the back, their eyes constantly sweeping the area.

His eyes half-closed, Lü Erye was more animated the more he sang.

I bought a cow and it had coiled horns.

I took it out to till the land but it broke the plow.

So many poor people in the world, but no one's like me, the shepherd boy.

6

"The camels are ready to go," someone shouted, drawing the crowd over to the racing ground. I was swept along to see over a hundred camels waiting at the starting line. The hunchbacked, crippled old man's gimpy camel was at the rear, cutting a sorry sight. Next to the other tall and powerful, leonine camels, it looked even more comical. "Are you sure you didn't bring the wrong animal, Brother Gimpy," someone shouted. "That's a donkey, not a camel."

"He's right," another one echoed. "This is a festival for camels, not for donkeys."

"It doesn't count even if you win," a third man joined in. "I've never heard of giving prizes to mangy dogs."

Another round of raucous laughter, but the old man wore a cool look, with no hint of embarrassment.

At the sound of the whistle, the camels took off running; dust under their feet exploded into the sky. The gimpy camel was crowded off to the side by the madly running ones. Camels are by nature sedate animals; rarely agitated, they walk one steady step at a time, with a majestic appearance. They retain their impressive air even when they walk fast. Only when they run do they look comical. They dart nervously, a flighty opposite of their usual staid manner. On the other hand, when a hundred camels run at the same time, it's an awesome display, particularly the dirt that sprays into the air noisily under their feet.

After a while they slowly formed a line, no longer crowding into each other, and the difference between the slow and the fast was immediately visible. Then, the old man's gimpy camel suddenly swished its tail and sprang forward; it still looked comical, but the steps it took were disproportionally large, while its body seemed to float in the wind. Before anyone could express their amazement, it shot past the others, like a whirlwind, and made those behind it look foolishly slow.

"Ai-ya, it's a yellow demon reincarnate," someone called out in exaggeration.

I too stuck my tongue out silently. I'd seen my share of camels, but never one that ran like that. Camels are unwieldly animals and never look light-footed no matter how fast they are. This gimpy one was exceptional; it had a camel's gait, but not its awkwardness, with an exaggerated, almost deformed appearance. It was no longer camel-like, resembling more a wing-flapping ostrich running at high speed. In the blink of an eye, it reached the finish line, drawing surprised gasps from a crowd that seemed unhappy with the outcome. Obviously, the skinny camel had won the race in this year's festival, and no one was entirely willing to accept that.

I did, however, sense that the gimpy camel was a cut above the others in the race. It could run as fast as a top-rate steed. I mentioned that to Big Mouth when I recalled his plan to buy a camel at the festival.

The blind storyteller's voice came clearly on the wind—

Delicacies from mountains and seas, why would I want to eat them?
Nothing stuck between my teeth when I slurped millet soup.
Satin and silk clothes, why would I want to wear them?
I can look dashing even dressed in rags.
Beds made of ivory and jade, why would I want to sleep on them?
I can sleep on the floor and never worry about dropping my baby.
Tall buildings and grand mansions, why would I want to live in them?
I lie down in a grass hut and never worry about earthquakes shaking

the tiles.

> *Big powerful horses, why would I want to ride them?*
> *I've got my beggar's club and can travel to thousands of houses.*
> *The dynasties, why would I want to change them?*
> *Chase one turtle away and there comes a tortoise.*

"What he's singing makes sense," Big Mouth reacted with a sigh. "Contentment really does bring happiness, for all time."

I envied the carefree attitude expressed in the song, but I replied, "When the road is uneven, everyone joins in to level it. If no one does anything and the evil-doers continue to plague society, then no one will be able to keep on living."

7

Taking Big Mouth's suggestion to heart, I decided to make my move after the "Selection of the Three Mosts."

It was an important part of the festival.

What was meant by selection was to choose the most immense, the most heavyset, and the most attractive camels from among the contestants. The first two categories were easy and rarely caused any controversy; it was plain to see which ones were the biggest and fattest. The last one was fiercely disputed. What you thought was pretty could be ugly to me, and what was considered unattractive could be the best looking of all to some. There were endless arguments, involving even sightseers, who joined in, shouting and yelling, raising a loud din. In turn, the most contentious category turned out to provide the most fun for the festival.

Finally, the winners of the three mosts were picked and prizes were being given out. Knife shielded, I elbowed my way forward. My filth repelled people, who backed off as I passed. I quickly drew near to the podium, where Ma Siye and Lü Erye were seated, ready to hand out prizes to the winners.

The prizes, supplied by the Ma family, were their world-famous tea bricks imprinted with "Major Merchant Ma Hesheng," the best of the best tea. The winners of the camel races and the three mosts each got nineteen bricks, a number to commemorate the duration Su Wu spent tending sheep here. None of the prize-winners drew any noticeable reactions except for the cripple's scrawny gimpy camel, which had greatly puzzled everyone by winning the running race. Lü Erye asked the old man his secret, but the cripple just responded with a smile.

Prize-giving provided a great opportunity. Lü Erye's toughs let down their guard to watch a rowdy scene and sent secret joy through me. All I had to do was make my way up to Lü Erye, grab his queue, stab him in the back, and it was done.

Just when I was about to act, I heard a gunshot. From out of nowhere, several horse riders had appeared on the high stage, all holding their muskets. I could tell they were home-made fowling pieces loaded with buckshot that had a short firing range, but could reach over a hundred meters if fired individually.

"Outlaws! Desert outlaws!" Someone cried out. The directors rolled off the stage one after another and lay down among the crowd.

The outlaws sure are fearless, I said to myself, robbing a festival. If the crowd came together and joined efforts, their spit alone would drown the outlaws. But there was no chance of that, for chaos broke out at the sound of the gunfire. People panicked and ran all over the place.

Another shot was followed by a shout, "Stop running or I'll smash your heads! Hands on your heads, crouch down."

Most of the people who heard did exactly what they were told, those who didn't kept running. To their surprise, outlaws on horseback with muskets blocked their way. Another shot stunned the fleeing crowd. "Crouch down, hands on your heads," the man shouted again, and pretty much everybody complied, quickly filling up the valley. The shepherds off in the distance ran off at the first shot. I crouched too and looked around me. There were dozens of them, mostly on horseback. Big Mouth, hands on his head, crouched beside me and whispered,

"I think they're Sha Meihu's people."

Sha Meihu roamed the desert at will, mostly targeting powerful families. He had no fixed abode, coming and going without a trace. The county government sent the cavalry to vanquish him, but suffered great losses before they even found the outlaws, for bullets could fly out of a slope or a hollow, from shrubs or grass to take lives, forcing the government to retreat. Sha usually let the people alone and robbed only immoral wealthy families. The county government turned a blind eye to his activities, preferring not to act unless necessary.

One of the outlaws went up and nudged Lü Erye, who was crouched on the ground with his hands on his head. "Are you Second Master Ma?"

Lü Erye looked shamefaced, obviously mortified over his cowering posturing. He stood up and said, "Yes, I am."

"I've been watching for two days," the man said with a smile.

The outlaws must have disguised themselves as festival goers to infiltrate the festivities, and then changed into their own clothes before they got into action.

"Who are you? Sha Meihu?" Lü Erye asked.

"I am," the man said. He was trim and muscular, with an ordinary face.

"Winter is around the corner and we need some traveling expenses," Sha said. "But this time we'll only rob the Tartars."

"Only the Tartars," one of his men shouted, echoed by others, "Only the Tartars."

Clearly, they'd learned all about the merchants' background. Over a dozen of them went over to the Mongolian stalls, and quickly came out with fur, silver, fabric, and tea, which they laid down in separate piles. They began to load the loot.

"I hate the Tartars. You know why? Because they wear the same pants as the Qing court," Sha offered. I caught the reference to Qing and was about to ask him why when Ma Siye went back up to the podium. Big Mouth panicked. I knew he was worried that Ma Siye would be taken as a hostage once the outlaws realized who he was. Before Big Mouth could go up to stop him, Ma Siye revealed his identity,

"I'm the Fourth Master of the Ma family."

"I know who you are," Sha laughed loudly. "I've been to the festival five times, Ma Siye. I know you. Do you know why we haven't robbed you? You're too chummy with the government, and I don't like that, but I know you're in a tough spot. Besides, the Ma family has been doing good and makes its money the righteous way. Your family fortune came from the heavens, and I can't take it away from you."

"Let's put the heavens aside," Ma Siye said with a smile. "But it's true that our family doesn't have any ill-gotten gains." He sighed and continued, "You shouldn't be doing this at the festival. The people have toiled all year and this is a rare opportunity for them to take it easy and enjoy themselves. Now you've ruined it for them."

"You're right, of course." Sha added, "But this year is different. The government has raised an army, and I can't sit around doing nothing. Besides, I have over a hundred people with me and we can't all tie up our throats."

"I'm almost sixty now," Ma Siye said. "I've lived long enough, so it won't matter if I'm killed today. But I'd like to maintain the reputation of the festival. Last year we were raided, but they didn't get anything. If something bad were to happen this year, we won't be able to host another one. Do you know how many people would have to tie up their throats without the festival? Take this fur, for example. You can have a mountain of fur, but the people can't survive if they can't trade the fur for food or money."

"I'm only robbing the Tartars."

"It makes no difference. It's robbery all the same. How about this? I'll give you five thousand taels of silver, and you do me the courtesy of skipping the festival and letting the people keep their livelihood. No one would dare come next year if you rob the Tartars today." Ma Siye handed over several bank drafts.

Sha knit his brow and hesitated when one of the men came up, took the drafts and studied them.

"What are you doing?" Sha yelled at the man. "The Ma family never cheats."

"That's true." The man continued, "Want to let him have it, Boss?"

"I didn't want your money, Siye," Sha said with a sigh. "But my men need to eat. I discovered a gold mine and wanted to grab a few Tartars to carry sand for me. But I'll do you a favor and forget it. Let's go." He mounted his horse, kicked its side, and tore down the mountain. The others weren't in such a hurry, as they slowly pulled out, like a molting snake.

"Those are principled outlaws." Ma Siye said as he wiped his forehead.

I decided against killing Lü Erye at the festival after hearing what Ma Siye had said to the outlaws, even though I'd miss a rare opportunity. The people finally had a chance to enjoy themselves, and I shouldn't ruin their fun.

Big Mouth was happy when I told him my decision. He said I was being sensible.

8

I had to keep going forward.

Like a rock going downhill, the inertia of fate meant I could only continue to move along.

I begged during the days as usual and spent the nights in the Earth God temple, along with many beggar women, who could help me if I needed it. Big Mouth came to see me whenever he was free after working at the Ma family camel farm. Honestly, I might be afflicted with something, for I'd lost interest in the thing between a man and a woman, after suffering the fright and shock that night. When he made an advance, I was reminded of the "husband" who had died at our hands. I'd see his face flicker before my eyes. More than once I tried to convince myself that he had been predestined to die. He'd usually slept like a dead pig, so why had he woken up that night? And when he opened his eyes, why did he know immediately we were doing the "donkey thing?" It had to be fate. Big Mouth and I just wanted to muffle his shouts, we didn't expect him to die like that. Sometimes, when I think of the boy, I wonder if it had something to do with the fire at my house. If Lü Erye did sense something, he might have set the fire as revenge.

These thoughts swirled in my head until it was a mess.

I was still looking for an opportunity to kill Lü Erye.

I often went to the Ma fortress, where begging was easy. I never once returned empty-handed. I heard they cooked more than they could eat at each meal for the beggars who would come for handouts. I didn't believe they'd do that. My feelings about the Ma family were complicated; sometimes I liked them, sometimes I hated them. But later, true to what I'd been told, I saw that every beggar was given food. So I often went too. I was also looking for an opportunity.

Even a tiger dozes off sometimes, I thought. I refused to believe that the old ass wouldn't go down in my hands one day.

In those days, beggars did different things to earn their food. Some sang clapper-songs, some called out for help from grandpa and grandma, some intoned tales. I belonged to the last group. At first, I went out with my wooden fish and sang wooden fish songs—it was originally Big Mouth's amulet, but he let me use it. No one understood the songs, but I enjoyed singing them, which was as much a way to beg for food as review the songs. I might have forgotten many of them if not for singing them over and over. Later, I'd only have to hit the wooden fish and people would bring out food for me. After that, Big Mouth found me a used three-string instrument to accompany my singing, making it even easier.

To carry out my revenge, I also started learning martial arts in secret. By the Earth God Temple was a stand of desert date trees, where Hu Gala often brought over people to practice. I watched his instruction carefully and secretly practiced the moves after they were gone. They did it for fitness, while I had revenge in mind. I practiced all their moves but spent much more time than they did. After a meal, I'd go to a deserted sand trough. Exhausting exercises were hard at first, but I slowly got used to them. Later I asked Big Mouth to teach me some of the moves the drivers practiced. Theirs were different from Hu Gala's, for the camel drivers had simple but practical moves, every one of them lethal. They had to deal with outlaws on the road and, without a real skill, they would not survive. Big Mouth taught me a set of lasso pole moves, very practical. A lasso pole was just a short club, about four *chi* long. The club I used against aggressive dogs during my begging outings was perfect for lasso pole moves. It might be short, but don't be fooled by its appearance; I could easily deal with a few toughs once I got good at it.

Once I could use the lasso pole skillfully, Big Mouth taught me "marching club," something camel drivers did often. It was two people fighting with their lasso poles or a club. It required practiced hands and precise skill, devoid of all tricks. At first my club flew into the air when we practiced, no matter how careful I was. He earned a great deal of respect from me over that. He really was the club master among the drivers; few could last a few rounds with him.

As we practiced, our feelings for each other were rekindled. On one moonlit night we rolled around in the desert in each other's arms, which made it possible for the local gazetteer to write about us. But it was a story the author created, not necessarily mine. Everyone has his own world and his own interpretation of that world.

Big Mouth wanted to reveal our relationship to his parents, but I objected. I was willing to marry him, that wasn't the issue. It was just that I knew if I didn't give up the idea of revenge, this little life of mine would always be like a kite in the sky, and there'd come a time when it didn't belong to me anymore. Whether I succeeded or not, he'd be implicated in what I did, even if we were married, and I didn't want him to suffer on my account.

I wanted revenge, but Lü Erye rarely showed his face. Obviously, he had sniffed out something and stayed in a place he considered safe. On the other hand, was there a truly safe place in the world, be it the Ma fortress or his watchtower in Lingnan? The watchtower was solidly safe, but couldn't keep him alive forever. A hundred years later, when you go there, you'll see it is no longer livable, even though it has become a cultural site. The walls are peeling and the passing of time, along with the humidity unique to the area, has eaten away at the building so much it is dilapidated. The soaring compound walls now parody the notion of sturdiness. It's true that you can build the longest-lasting watchtower, but you can never escape the Grim Reaper.

You'll know stories like this later. I don't want to go into the details now.

I want to move on with my story of revenge.

Wooden Fish Girl lets out a long sigh, sounding like a breeze blowing past the tips of desert poplars.

At some point, the camel hands come over to listen; they are mesmerized by her story. They were together for some time a hundred years ago, but obviously this was the first time they were hearing her story.

This night seems unusually long to me. I wrap the sleeping bag around me and add a sheepskin coat, so I won't feel the chill as badly as the previous nights.

A hint of white appears in the eastern sky, and the camel hands reluctantly disperse.

In my dream that night a pair of wolf eyes stare at me from afar.

Ninth Session
Balte's Story

A prolonged search in the morning still yields no source of water. I can't linger too long. I want to leave the rocky gobi as soon as possible, for I could be trapped and die in Wild Fox Ridge if I dawdle and use up too much water before I find more to replenish my supply.

Strangely, however, I'm not afraid, because I discovered that those who pass away actually don't die, but exist in a different way. What seemed to be frightening in the past is actually nothing to fear.

But the yellow camel looks depressed for no immediately discernible reason. It's as listless as if he had seen through the world of mortals.

The white camel is the same as usual, and I can't tell what goes on in his mind. He constantly looks into the distance with his eyes half-shut, with an indifferent expression on his face. He has the same demeanor whether I'm riding on him or walking beside him. The dog, on the other hand, is acting atypically, for it's unconcerned about the animal tailing us, which has never happened before.

I can see the creature's outline by then. It is a wolf, an old one, big but bony. It looks at me from a distance, with no intention of getting closer, a situation similar to the one related in Wooden Fish Girl's story.

The temperature plummets just before I'm nearly out of the rocky gobi. A northern wind starts blowing and makes me shiver in my sheepskin coat. It looks about to snow. It will get much colder when the snow comes, but I'm nevertheless happy to see snow, water from heaven in a different form.

As the sky darkens, the wind picks up. I have no time to worry about getting to my next stop; I pick a sand trough with vegetation, one relatively sheltered from the wind, and unload the litter.

Without looking at me, the yellow camel lets out a drawn-out sigh.

"Why the long face?" I say.

Silently he goes over to a clump of desert thorns and starts grazing languidly.

You can act up if you want, as long as you can eat and work, I say under my breath.

After tethering the white camel to the clump of thorns, I gather some kindling to light a fire. As the fire burns brightly, the desert turns hazy from snowflakes carried on the wind.

I boil some water to make a bowl of instant noodles and, as I warm up, make a bowl for the dog.

My interview didn't go through on a previous night because of a fire, which prevented the specters from showing, but I want to give it another try tonight. In Liangzhou lore, ghosts enjoy the warmth of embers, which are flameless but still hot and bright.

I decide against lighting the yellow candle, for it doesn't make much sense to have a lit candle by a fire. I chant my incantation to invite them out, but only one comes after a long time. It's Balte.

None of the others appear, I don't know why. Maybe they're wary of the fire.

1

Let's get back to serious matters.

Let's not waste time on the trivial stuff—even though they all think they're profoundly affecting. Sometimes an affair can look as exciting as a battle from a writer's pen, but to me it's meaningless to dwell on these stupid, pissant incidents. A great deal of major events took place at Wild Fox Ridge, and each of them can be turned into a best-selling masterpiece by a decent writer. But not you, heh-heh, because countless terrific stories from your pen have turned out pretty damned insipid. You say you're looking for a breakthrough in literary form, but what is form, actually? Form is like a fur coat, and what it covers is the same old shit. But write whatever and however you want. We'll get on to serious matters. You made it into our world, which means we're somehow connected by karma. People would think we're girly types if we keep harping on about petty matters, right?

For me the important matter was Brown Lion. I knew what went on in Lu Fuji's dog belly—he wanted to use that opportunity for revenge. When fights broke out over grazing grounds in the past, he absolutely hated Brown Lion. In those days we waged a kind of gamble through camel fights, the winner's side getting the ground. Brown Lion gave the Mongolian side a great chance to win, and we often got better grass and water. It was not permanent—there might be other battles later—but nothing lasts forever in the human world, including the emperor's throne. Everything is transient, isn't it? Brown Lion made the Mongolian camels stronger than the Chinese ones, because of water and grass, plus genes, of course. Think about it. Without good water and grass, you'd have a sickly camel, no matter how marvelous the seed.

Maybe the seeds of hatred were planted in Old Lu's heart back then. Certainly, that's what I thought.

I vowed to myself that he would have to answer to me if he actually did in Brown Lion. I'd repay in double measure whatever he did to my camel.

So he brought on himself what I did to him later.

2

I started watching Lu Fuji when I recognized his intent to kill Brown Lion. Whenever I saw him walk out, I followed him myself or sent someone to tail him. And that's how I stumbled upon his secret.

That day I saw him sneaking out of his tent with a musket; he looked like someone out for a tryst. If not for the musket, I would have thought he was meeting a woman. I was tickled by the sight of him, a plain-spoken, carefree man acting as sly as a woman. I'm still amused when I think about it now.

He was heading to a distant sand trough, which had actually been frequented by Brown Lion. The spot was secluded, kind of out of the way, where the ghost of a woman was rumored to linger. People often heard a woman crying over there in the middle of the night, so few would venture out there after nightfall.

Lu's shadow wafted under the night sky, looking like a wandering ghost. I've never been a fearful man, but at that moment my courage was daunted. Soon, however, the fear was driven away by what was happening before my eyes.

I saw a rite.

Then I realized it was a rite by the Society of Brothers.

The sight was plainly clear under a lonely white moon. Feiqing presided over the rite. You probably don't know what their actions entailed. I'd stumbled upon people performing a similar rite in the heart of a desert in Liangzhou. At the time Liu Huzi had often sent my caravan around, because his horses couldn't travel in the desert as easily as camels. One day he got a tip, so we went out together and saw numerous fires set in the famous Dengmaying Lake and a rite being performed under the firelight. Liu Huzi ordered his men to charge. They ran up with their swords and hacked at the heads of their targets, instead of doing something first, like shouting at them.

I will always remember the scene. My nostrils were assaulted by a pungent smell, even though I didn't see blood splashing. It was a repulsive stench that followed me for years. The odor sprang to my mind and brought back many memories, when I least expected it.

In each of my recollections, there were always the rolling heads. It was odd however, because only two or three were beheaded during the night-time massacre. Most of the others died with their heads still on. You should know that not many people can lop off a head with one swipe of the sword; it requires a powerful arm and speed, as well as perfect aim and skill. But, strangely. there were so many flying heads in my memory, while I don't remember much about blood. What we saw the next day under the sun was the dark brown crust of dry sand that had soaked up all the blood.

In my memory, those who had died under the frenzied butchering swords seemed to scream, which was actually drowned out by the whooping shouts of the cavalry at the time. The police had used their shouts to overwhelm their targets and many fell into pools of blood before they could react.

Their deaths earned the police merits in service, for the victims were called rebels.

3

I backed away quietly. I didn't know what they would do to me if they found out that I had happened upon their secret. They would kill me to silence me. Sure, there could be another possibility; they could force me to join them, the way Lu Junyi was treated by those on Liangshan in *The Water Margin*. I wouldn't. We were different.

My face was a ghostly white when I returned to the tent, according to Huozi.

"Look at you. Why is your face so white, you look like you're about to collapse?" he said to me. I did feel like collapsing, or like seeing a ghost in broad daylight—they were too damned audacious. There had to be running dogs of the Qing court in the caravan. I should have waited quietly and recovered, but instead I told Huozi about it. You couldn't know that there were no secrets between Huozi and me. Besides, the survival of the caravan was on the line here. They could ruin things, like a single rat dropping spoiling a pot of porridge; I didn't want them to take everything away from us for their own special interest. Sometimes, when a wall is toppling, you can't tell the good people from the bad.

So I told Huozi what I saw. Of course, it was wrong; Huozi was part of the team, and he didn't join the Society, but he was the cashier, actually also an advisor. It seemed inexcusable to keep something so important from him. He mulled over the news for a long time before saying not to alert them yet. I hadn't expected him to snitch later, not to mention the bloodbath it would then cause. Someone thought Huozi had dug Feiqing's grave, but in fact I was the one. Everything that happened later would have turned out different if I'd kept my mouth shut.

I did feel guilty when Feiqing died such a tragic, horrible death, which I sensed in a different time and space, in the form that you could probably call "the soul and spirit of the deceased." Ma Zaibo wanted me to repent, saying it was my only hope for salvation. Repentance, according to him, can save fallen souls, but I found that hard to do. I couldn't help it. You're right when you say repentance is a form of wisdom, not something anyone can have just because he wants it. See all the evil-doers in the world? They're just like me; they find all kinds of excuses to absolve themselves, but refuse to repent.

I thought I'd come to a terrible end, as retribution, and I did. Even now I can feel myself roasting in the poisonous flames of hatred and anger. I am called Feitian, sometimes Asura. You cannot imagine how bad it feels to be roasted like that. I long for a hint of coolness. Sometimes I do feel something cool when I listen to sutra-recitations, but it's a sprinkle of rain that quickly evaporates when it reaches the sky above the hill of flaming hatred.

Hate has seeped deeply into my soul. I heard that hatred will sprout once it's in the heart. That's so true. The more I hate, the angrier I get, the angrier I am, the more deeply the hate goes; it's now a vicious cycle.

Huozi told me at the time that I must let him in on something like that. I wasn't aware that he'd been in frequent contact with Liu Huzi and Li Tesheng.

It makes me retch just thinking about Huozi later. It would be a wonder if he didn't fall to hell. I don't want to ever see him again. Now I even loathe myself for being friends with him for so long. I disgust myself.

But back then our karmic connection lasted fairly long; it was beyond my control. There's nothing one can do to break off a relationship when the connection remains.

There's a fly like that in everyone's life.

4

When I saw them the day after the rite, they looked perfectly normal, apparently oblivious to the fact that I now knew their secret. Feiqing gave me his usual gracious and polite smile, which was how he interacted with others; but I knew he was ambitious and proud, and what others saw on the surface was a façade. That was how he was. Well read, he was good at composing poetry and painting, and was an expert martial artist, so in his eyes, he was virtually peerless. Yet he was always modest and courteous, which was why he became the head of the Liangzhou branch of the Society of Brothers. As he presided over the rite, I saw that he proceeded leisurely in the same manner that he took charge of the caravan, as if he had no idea that what he was doing could cost him his head. He was later called a national hero, but to me that was far-fetched. What kind of hero was he if he only competed with Mongolians? Taking it a bit further, if he went up against the Qing court, he still would be no hero, since we all count as Chinese people. To be a true national hero he would have had to fight the soldiers from the Eight Nation Alliance, isn't that right? It's been my belief that the Boxers were the real national heroes. Sure, they caused lots of trouble, but heroes are still herocs, even when they stir up trouble, and cowards remain cowards, even if they do not disturb the peace. Hehheh, I can fit anything into that sentence pattern of yours.

I came upon another secret. I noticed Wooden Fish Girl constantly sneaking glances at Feiqing. At the time I thought she was in love with him; I didn't know she had something more serious in mind when she looked at him.

It could add excitement to the trip, I said to myself at the time. Huozi saw what I saw and he was happy, looking as if he'd found gold ingots when he told me about it. He'd been looking for an excuse to scandalize Feiqing. National and righteous causes meant less to him than a rag; to him an enemy was an enemy, and whoever got on his wrong side was an enemy. In fact, that should be the standard of a natural man; why must humans add all sorts of external factors, such as nation, class, party, religious sect, and so on? That only complicates simple matters. In fact, it was better the way Huozi was. Feiqing bullied him, so he hated Feiqing;

our Mongolian caravan paid him more, and he helped us out. Whoever has milk is the mother. In fact, there's nothing wrong with that. He had to eat too.

Huozi kept a close watch on Feiqing. If he had anything on him, meaning Feiqing getting it on with the girl, when they had their pants down, Huozi would take some of the men and storm over, and hei, Feiqing would stink to high heaven. In our profession, rule-breakers are never to be hired again, as their reeking reputation spreads quickly.

Huozi hated Feiqing viscerally. It was a hatred that bored into his bones. Some thought Feiqing went too far and should not have made fun of someone's biological defect, but Huozi hated him for something else. Liangzhou people are like that. They were both from the Qi clan in Danghu, so why was Feiqing so wealthy and well known and respected? Why? It wasn't fair, that made Huozi resentful, and once the resentment built up, it turned into hate.

Huozi had been looking for ways to bring down Feiqing. He never expected to wind up cementing Feiqing's place in history, like randomly planting a willow branch only to see it grow into a shade tree. If Huozi hadn't done what he did, Feiqing would have just grown old, turning from a strapping young man into a shriveled old man who would eventually be put in a coffin and laid into a hole in the ground. But thanks to Huozi's scheming, Feiqing became a martyr. When someone wrote the history, he saw Feiqing and said, hei, this young man was something, I should keep his name. Feiqing got his place in history.

Your enemy is actually your helper, and it makes sense when you call it "the adversarial Buddha."

On this day, Huozi sidled up to me and said Feiqing went to the other side of the mountain, followed by the girl. He asked me to go catch them in the act. I could care less about stupid things like that, so I told him I wouldn't go. You do know it was against my nature to be involved in matters like this, though you could, if you wanted, make it up about me. In fact, I was sometimes given to doing things against my nature. I did want to see if Feiqing was still his sanctimonious self. It was important to me, because you have to know his dignified demeanor put pressure on me. I wanted to bring him down in my heart. I tell you, something like that is quite enjoyable. It has to be something in competition with you.

In the end I went with Huozi. It wasn't completely dark out, there was a sliver of a moon. He pointed at a distant sand hill that looked like an ink painting, with a beautiful outline. It reminded me of Feiqing's paintings, which were all very nice. There weren't auctions back then, but his paintings fetched a good price, sometimes high enough to trade just one for several camels. To us back then it was nice sum.

Huozi and I were the only two following them. I told him not to get any more people because I didn't want them to think I was despicable. I wasn't riffraff, though every once in a while, I didn't mind acting like a lowlife. Aren't we all like that? But still, I didn't want anyone to know I'd done something that low.

We didn't see him after reaching the other side of the hill. I wondered if Huozi had mistaken Ma Zaibo to be Feiqing or if Feiqing had gone elsewhere.

I saw Ma Zaibo. He had come to a quiet spot to meditate. I knew he was practicing something, but exactly what I didn't know. With his eyes open wide, he was staring at the night sky, which ought to be an impossible detail for you, since you can't actually see eyes in the dark. But strangely I did. I saw light in his eyes, like a glint from an animal's eyes at night. An animal's gathered light in the day shines in the dark at night. I was surprised to see the same thing happening with Ma's eyes. Later, someone said it was a magical power known as Siddhi, derived during meditative practice. According to lore, it could help him see underground treasure.

Ma Zaibo's eyes emitted an eerie green glint that floated in the air like tadpoles, and expanded and shrank at will. I thought he was gathering light. Stories like this abounded in those days; I'd heard about people gathering light, *qi*, or vital essence. Some young men were always being sapped of their vital essence by fox fairies. That was what convinced me that Ma Zaibo was gathering light, and that the pure essence of heaven and earth had entered into his life in the form of light. Naturally, I believed that all his later accomplishments had benefited from these practices. Without a comprehensive transformation from genetic mutation, mangy dogs will never produce a Tibetan mastiff, am I right? But this would come later.

Wooden Fish Girl appeared, sticking her head out from behind a hill like a fox. An impish expression could not hide the sweet halo on her face, a look exclusive to those who are deeply in love. The girl has fallen for Ma Zaibo, I said to myself. It was only a guess.

She stuck her tongue out constantly as she looked at Ma in meditation.

5

When he finished, Ma Zaibo got up and said,
"Come out here, girl."
She walked out, without a hint of embarrassment over her spying act. Ma stared at her for a while before asking, "Are you watching a circus monkey?"
"Of course not. I was looking at you," she said.
"Do you want to practice meditation? I can teach you."
"Are you trying to deliver my soul?" she said. "I don't like people doing that. Besides, sitting motionlessly like that is boring. I don't care for it."

"Foolish girl. We in the Ma family paid for it with gold. A lot of people want to learn, but I don't want to teach them. You don't know, but this could put an end to life and death."

"When you're alive, you're alive, and when you're dead, you're dead," she said with a laugh. "What's the point of ending it? Shakyamuni Buddha practiced for decades, but he didn't manage to escape death, did he?"

"That's not death. He reached nirvana," Ma replied.

"It's death whatever it's called. He's not alive now, and that's all I know." She continued, "Even if he could live till now, he can't really live far into the future, can he?"

Wooden Fish Girl looked young and guileless. I was surprised to hear the strangely profound meaning in what she said.

"Stop spouting nonsense," Ma chided her.

"I saw Hu Gala sitting motionless like you." She changed the subject. "Are you two doing the same thing?"

"Not the same. Sometimes I teach him, and sometimes he teaches me. We're teacher and disciple to each other," Ma replied.

"That's weird," she said. "But if sometimes I could be your teacher and we could teach each other, I wouldn't mind being your disciple."

"What could you teach me?" Ma burst out laughing. "Embroidery?"

"As Confucius said, you can always learn something from someone. How do you know I have nothing to teach you? Let's put everything else aside and focus on the 'end' in what you said about ending life and death. For me, the best way to end is not to end at all. You want to end life and death, and that seems exhausting to me. I don't want to end anything, but everything ends."

Ma fell silent as he stared at her in surprise, but an impish look returned to her face.

"What are you looking at?" she said. "Did I say something wrong?

Actually, the result is the same whether you try to end it or not. I have yet to see anyone who truly manages to end it, but there isn't anyone who hasn't ended it either. So many things that can't be ended will end when the time comes."

Ma looked stunned. In fact, I was too, but I was also confused by what she just said. I didn't know what it meant to "end" at the time.

"Are you a Dakini?" Ma asked.

"What's a Dakini?"

"Then you're not. If you don't even know what a Dakini is, you surely can't be one."

"Not necessarily so." She added, "So many people have no idea what it means to be human, but they continue to live as humans. It's just a name, isn't it? Dukini, Dokini, they're just names. If you say I am, then that's what I am, even if I'm not. If you say I'm not, then I can't be even if I am."

"Ha-ha, but enough of that." She made a face and walked off, leaving Ma Zaibo dumbstruck.

Honestly, I was too.

I had no idea what a Dakini was; it was the first time I'd heard the term.

Balte yawns—not like a living person yawning; it's more like an inclination. He feels like yawning and I feel it too, so he yawns.

He looks staid, probably because no one else is in the audience. It's cold and it's still snowing. I can hear the faint sizzles of snow falling on fire.

"It's snowing. You should go to bed early," Balte says. "I'm not much of a talker, never was, never will be, so you must be disappointed." He vanishes like a puff of dissipating air before I can respond.

Balte wasn't a positive character in the Chinese camel drivers' stories, but deep down I feel a sense of respect for him. I can't say why; it's just a feeling. I even wonder if I might have been him in my previous life, which wouldn't be a shame either.

I find a thicker piece of kindling to stir and mix the embers with the sand. I should have pitched a tent, but I was worried that the tent would be crushed if the snow got heavy. I decided against it. The sand quickly turns hot after mingling with the embers. All around me is a blanket of white, except for the spot where the fire was lit. I check on the plants where the camels were tethered; they seem sturdy enough to me. Then I spread my dog skin bedding on the hot sand and crawl into my sleeping bag before adding the fur coat on top. I quickly fall asleep.

The drivers gather around me in my dream to tell me their stories, stunning and surprising me. I feel they have given me lots of material, but I can't recall a thing when I wake up.

The snow stops after a while. The wind howls all night, however. I'm lucky to have a Tartar kang to spend a warm night.

Tenth Session
Assassin

The wind is still howling when I wake up the next morning. There are snowflakes here and there in the sand trough, but most of the snow has been blown off somewhere. My hope to replenish my water supply with melting snow is dashed.

I stop washing my face now that the water level in the jug is getting lower by the day. The camels should get some water. The yellow camel cries out constantly, which, I know, is a reminder. But I'm also aware that even the remaining water in the jug isn't enough for one big camel mouthful. Conservation is the order of the day.

Searching for water means I have to put aside working on my interview from the night before. I quickly jot down some notes before following the markers on the map to a few spots. There are clearly signs of moisture, but most have dried up, all but a place called drip cliff—that's how it's marked on the map, it's where water drips from a cliff. I spend hours catching it and only manage to fill half a bowl, though I'm ecstatic.

I make up my mind to spend more time here to collect water before moving on. After tethering the camels, I'll take a basin to catch the dripping water.

It's an unusual spot, relatively warmer than elsewhere. There should *be ice at this time of year, but the water continues to drip. The cliff also feels much warmer.*

After carrying my basin over to catch water, I light the candle.

I can see the old wolf in the distance. Wooden Fish Girl has said it was my karmic enemy from a previous life, but to me it's something else altogether. I'm wary that it may decide to pounce on me at some point.

I decide not to light a fire that night.

And no protective shield either. Come listen if you want, I say silently. Even with that setup, not too many show up. Maybe they're tired too.

Some who had nothing to do with the caravan turn up to listen, however.

Maybe they're drawn by Wooden Fish Girl's story.

1

What I said to Ma Zaibo sounded profound, but in reality, was superficial wisdom. I could talk about ending it, but couldn't do it. Put everything else aside, just the hatred alone was impossible to end. I'd learned a lot from the wooden fish songs, but it was more like parroting, with little effect on me.

So let me say more about my revenge.

I entered the Ma fortress one night by crawling in through a drainage hole. The fortress was impregnable, but had the spot no one knew about, the drainage ditch. It was small, for draining waste water only, and difficult to see, as it was hidden beneath a stump of bunchgrass. But no one would go in from there even if they found out about it. The locals believed that contact with the filthy water brought terrible bad luck.

I crawled through the space and went into the fortress.

It was massive, almost a castle.

Big Mouth had told me about the layout inside, but I still had trouble orienting myself. The structures all gave me a vague impression of splendor and wealth.

In the Ma fortress, the bosses and drivers had separate living spaces. The drivers were put up in spacious carter's quarters, and there were many of them, while the bosses' compound had far fewer residents, making it a kind of forbidden city. Ordinary servants could not easily gain access to a complex that was protected by patrolling guards.

The guards spotted me before I located Lü Erye's room. They swarmed over and pushed me to the ground. Fists and feet landed like pelting rain. Except for a few times when a heavy kick sent searing pain into my chest, I felt little from their beating, probably because the layers of rags blunted the force. Their racket roused the bosses. I was dragged into a large room and questioned. I told them I was so hungry I planned to steal food from their kitchen.

I had my knife, but surprisingly, they didn't search me, likely because I was a familiar sight. I came to their door to beg nearly every day, and they all knew me. They believed me when I confessed about my intention to steal food.

"Let her go. Don't make it hard on her," Ma Siye added, "Go get some steamed buns."

"Give her enough and let her go," Lü Erye said. "Come ask for food in the future when you're hungry. Don't do this again. If you act like a thief, you're bound to suffer."

They let me go.

The failed attempt made me aware that, given my skill set, I could not hope to achieve vengeance. Assuming I could even get near Lü Erye, I might not be able to kill him. I'd heard he was a renowned martial artist who'd practiced fighting with the drivers as a young man. He might be known as a lecherous man, but he was quite fit. In fact, many people believed his sexual appetite was the manifestation of fitness. The drivers were always saying that a stiff dick meant a man never got sick. I figured that a girl like me would have to take up martial arts if I was ever going to kill Lü Erye.

Big Mouth was upset when he learned of my attempt.

"You can't get near him, girl. Even if you could, you can't touch a single hair on him, not with what you've got. He may look old, but he can still carry a litter weighing two, three hundred *jin*. Besides, he also has a personal maid who is a terrific martial artist. She can shoot an embroidering needle through a glass pane to hit someone outside the room. I consider myself quite good at lasso pole fighting, but I'm no match for her.

"You have to have polished skills if you want to seek revenge, girl. Be patient and take it slow. Once you're skillful enough you'll succeed; otherwise it's just a waste of mental energy."

That was when I started a program of arduous training.

And I discovered that what I'd been doing was only good enough to deceive myself.

2

After a year, I was pretty much Big Mouth's equal in lasso pole fighting. That meant that the other drivers wouldn't last long in a fight with me.

Big Mouth said it was pretty much miraculous. He didn't know that I'd put in more than ten times the training effort of most people. It takes a year to be good with swords, but only months for clubs, and a lifetime for muskets. Lasso poles are in the same category as clubs, so it would take anyone willing to put in the effort mere months to hone the skill. Compared to Big Mouth, I was nimbler with the pole. I wasn't as strong, but I developed techniques to fend him off, using light force to direct a blow away from me. Sometimes I even got the upper hand when we sparred.

The fighting technique known as Wooden Fish Club became legendary in the martial arts world of Liangzhou. One of my trainees was even hired as an instructor for the Ma mounted troops. He combined the techniques of lasso pole with sword fighting, which was so effective a couple of moves was enough to take an opponent's life. They killed countless members of the Red Army and lopped off many Japanese' heads in the Resistance War. How do you think I should react? Should I laugh or cry?

In Big Mouth's view, I'd entered the ranks of martial arts masters, though I thought he was joking or cheering me on. Later, when I had a chance to see all the club fighters, I saw they were unseasoned, with countless flaws in their every move.

My horizon kept expanding until I could even detect flaws in Big Mouth's moves, probably because I was so focused. The long-distance trek had not only built up stamina and strength in my legs, but also shored up my willpower. In my eyes there was nothing to fear. Except for eating and sleeping, I spent most of my time practicing in a quiet spot in the desert. At first, I focused on the same routine until I knew the Wooden Fish Liuhe Lasso back and forth. Then I no longer needed to follow a routine; instead I had a free run with the steps, and developed numerous routines, until I didn't even have a routine any longer. In my mind were imagined opponents—I defeated every one of them. Don't underestimate my imagination, for it was precisely during my imagined training that I heightened the speed of my reactions. I was constantly on high alert, but I looked calm and unhurried. Even Big Mouth was amazed. You should know that I'd braved too many storms, influenced by wooden fish songs, and experienced deaths in the family, assassination attempts of a killer, a protracted trek of life and death, and slights from people around me. I'd gone through what I had to as well as what I should have. Besides, what important matter could better occupy my mind than honing my skill for revenge?

I spent my first three years in Liangzhou chanting the wooden fish songs silently and training hard on the lasso pole skill.

When I was truly adept at the pole, I started looking beyond techniques and skill. I knew I could not enter the fortress with a knife. The locals agreed that anyone could beat and stab an intruder to death with no repercussions. I could turn my club into a begging aid. Instead, I began training for strength and accuracy. I asked Big Mouth to find a camel pelt on which I drew small circles and hung it on a date tree as targets for my club. I missed a lot at first, but then I could hit eight out of ten, until my aim was nearly perfect.

After that came strength training, which had been what set Big Mouth apart from me. I could easily defeat him in a club fight, but would be powerless if he grabbed me. There is a saying that goes, "A superb club fighter is no match for powerful hands." Sometimes force alone can overtake great talent. I had to strengthen myself.

I thought I should work on my *qi* to get stronger, but Big Mouth didn't know *qigong*.

Hu Gala did, he told me.

And that was how I became Hu Gala's disciple in breathing exercises. The type I studied with him was called "Yijin jing," on internal energy, said to have been passed down by Bodhidharma. It develops strength by working on one's *qi*, and can lead to massive power if one keeps at it. That was why I decided to work with Hu Gala. In those days, people were always calling him Old Master Hu. Years later, they realized that he hadn't been that old; they had been fooled by his full beard.

Big Mouth wanted me to join the Society of Brothers soon after I became Hu's disciple.

I turned him down. All I wanted was revenge; I had no interest in rebellion. I didn't want to give the government a reason to lop off my head before accomplishing my goal.

Every day I went to a deserted sand trough to practice lasso pole and *qigong*. The Yijin jing was truly marvelous, for my strength greatly improved within only months. Later I could easily punch through cow hide with my club.

The time for revenge had come, I sensed.

3

I walked out of the Earth God Temple one moonlit night.

The moon was out but not bright, though enough for me to see the road. I planned to get in through the ditch, the weakest point of the fortress; they had no choice unless they stopped using water. I heard that outlaws went through the same route years later and brought on a different kind of bloodbath. But that happened later, something for you to write about.

I didn't make it this time. I went in through the ditch and reached the other side of the wall. When I was about to stick my head out, something occurred to me, and I got wary. I thought I saw someone standing against the wall holding a shiny steel chopper. Instead of sticking my head out rashly, I raised my club tipped with my tattered headscarf and was immediately rewarded with a knife slicing off the tip of the club.

I pulled back and returned the same way, drenched in a cold sweat. If I'd stuck my head out, I said to myself, where would I be now?

The sweat hadn't dried yet when I returned to the temple. My mind was a blank. I found that I was like a water bubble that had burst from a minor accident. Li Tieguai, one of the eight immortals, was said to have achieved enlightenment after the gourd on his crutch was lopped off by a sword. I had a sense of disillusionment, but no enlightenment, for the hate in me had crushed everything, as if by a mountain.

I told Big Mouth about it the next day, and he glared angrily before telling me that all the drainage points in the fortress had been fitted with booby traps after my entry the last time. When an intruder goes in, it triggers the chopper. He also said I should never think about doing anything inside the fortress, for marksmen stood guard, especially at night. The bullets could come from any angle, and the fortress had no blind spots.

"Don't be a hero," he warned. "Do you have any idea how many master Boxers died from their bullets?"

I realized at that instant that the martial art skills I'd practiced with such diligence were unreliable. I was disheartened and demoralized.

"It won't be easy killing Lü Erye, but in fact it won't be hard either. It will just be a matter of finding the right moment." He added, "That will be the time for him to die. No one can kill him if it's not his time, but if heaven wants him dead, he won't be able to do a thing to stay alive."

What he said annoyed me. "He should have died long ago. What is heaven? According to what you all say, heaven is a blind ass-kisser."

I continued to practice as before, even after realizing that martial skills weren't all that useful. It had just become a goal. I knew I was vulnerable to bullets, but Lü Erye couldn't stay inside like a rat in its nest forever, I told myself. He had to go out sometime, and once he did, my opportunity would come.

So I asked a blacksmith to forge sixteen darts, which I practiced throwing to complement my lasso pole skill. On the city wall in the desert I drew a human head as a target. I saw the head as Lü Erye. I never did get good at throwing darts, however, because I had no one to teach me. The darts refused to do my bidding. I couldn't even make the tip face forward when it flew through the air; more often than not, it was the dart barrel that hit the target. Later, I decided to use rocks. There were so many rocks around I could pick one up and turn it into a weapon.

And little by little the rocks began to obey me.

But a different kind of trouble found me; my belly was getting bigger. I was pregnant, the result of one of my trysts with Big Mouth. Ma Zaibo had read about what happened later in a gazette, so I'll let him tell you. What he'd say is pretty much what happened between us, except for a secret that was unknown to him. As for his claim that I was a Dakini, that's only what he said. We're allowed to say what we want. In fact, I have different views about myself. Sometimes I think I'm like this, but at other times I think I'm like that. My self-image changes according to how I feel at the moment, and I don't know my own true nature.

4

Over a year after the baby was born—it was girl—I left her at Hu Gala's house and asked him to be the child's *gandie*, a sort of foster father. He lived in a temple, but he was married, and his wife adored children. Hu was my martial arts teacher, so by rights he should be the child's grandpa, but he always wanted a daughter, and I didn't care what he was called. He could be anything to the baby he wanted. I wanted the girl to have someone to rely on. I did not know when I might die at my enemy's hand, so it seemed best for her to have a foster father. Except I never expected it would turn out that way for him. It's so true that life is impermanent.

Finally, my opportunity came.

It was the first day of the lunar New Year. The local custom required everyone to leave their houses to welcome the Deity of Happiness, an observance that had been in practice for a thousand years. Early that morning, the villagers herded their animals and headed east, where the

Deity of Happiness was to be that year. Camels, horses, cattle, and sheep swarmed toward the deity. Lü Erye had missed it several years in a row for reasons unknown to me, and I'd waited in vain each year. This year, however, Big Mouth had asked around to confirm that Lü Erye would surely be there, because he would be the "rite master," invited to serve for the New Year's celebration in the village. It was a special honor, reserved for those of good moral standing and reputation. Ma Siye who had served in the past, was in poor health this year, so Lü Erye took over for him. The rite master had to be out on the first day of the new year and, as the village welcomed the Deity of Happiness, burning incense and yellow sacrificial paper and saying something auspicious.

I was elated when I heard the news.

I went to bed early the night before. The small town was immersed in a festive air, but all I could think of was revenge. I dreamed about my family all the time. Papa always wore a glum look, so did Mama, while my younger brothers were lively, though they were just trying to mess with me, grinning, impish, being a nuisance. Something unpleasant always happened to me after I dreamed about them, and I wondered if they were complaining about my failure to avenge them. I wanted to speak with Papa in my dream, but he ignored me, which caused me great heartache.

Following the people and animals, I reached the desert to the east. Children were setting off firecrackers. I felt numb inside. Villagers were constantly offering me food, a special pastry for the new year called "stove buttons." Resembling Chinese knots that became popular later, they were fried in a griddle and smelled wonderful. The locals were friendly to beggars. They didn't give away anything over the first lunar month, according to local custom, and yet there were kind-hearted people offering us food. I was touched, and unsure if I wanted to ruin their festive celebration. If I did manage to kill Lü Erye on New Year's day, it would surely come across as unlucky to the locals, who called incidents like this fatal disasters, the worst among all calamities.

I spotted Lü Erye in the crowd. I'd had chances to kill him, such as at the camel race, where I didn't act for fear of spoiling the festivity. Similar occasions presented themselves later, but I was always afraid of involving innocent people. Finally, I understood the principle that an avenger must be hard-hearted or she'll never succeed. I'd been paying attention to the evil side of Lü Erye, though I often heard high praise from the locals—he had indeed done a great deal of good. To them, being the ass, for Lü Erye was literally Second Master Ass, wasn't terrible; the outcome of his lecherous behavior was a lack of the wide respect Ma Siye enjoyed. Lü Erye was still the philanthropist to many, and those who had received assistance from him even considered him a living Bodhisattva.

Lü Erye walked to the eastern desert, surrounded by tough-looking men, which made me wonder if he knew I planned to kill him. Why else he would have such an entourage? Later Big Mouth told me that he had indeed be alerted to an assassination attempt. Someone who knew *xiao liuren*, a kind of divination, made the prediction and told Lü Erye not to leave the fortress unless necessary to avoid a fatal disaster.

I headed to a sand trough with the villagers, where a large crowd had gathered. They had brought wheat grass, corn stalks, and other kindling to build a fire dragon extending a hundred paces in distance. Flames shot into the sky, creating a splendid spectacle. The locals believed that the fire would open the door to wealth and riches; fire was the most auspicious object for the first day of the year, the best gift to welcome the Deity of Happiness. Next to the fire dragon was a long row of food, liquor vessels, incense and other sacrificial offerings. I wondered why they welcomed the Deity of Happiness, not the Deity of Fortune. Perhaps happiness was most important to the residents of Liangzhou.

Lü Erye took up his position by the fire dragon's mid-section, the pivotal spot, and offered his prayer. He was loud, obviously intending to show-off and call attention to himself, which was the most marked difference between him and Ma Siye, who exuded virtue. But not Lü Erye, who seemed to be on stage all the time or showing off. I found it off-putting. There was nothing new in his prayer either, just clichés like "make a thief lose his way, seal the mouth of a wolf when it comes, great fortune, stupendous prosperity," and so on. I was very close now; all around me people held their palms together, absorbed in the prayer. It would have been easy if I'd acted at that instant, but I hated to ruin the auspicious moment. The locals cared a great deal about the beginning of everything, and would suffer a year of unhappiness if the first day of the year did not go well.

I waited quietly for the rite to finish.

After the prayer came drinking games, also a local custom. The festivity was meant to thin out all things negative. Lü Erye looked animated as he greeted the villagers, joking and mocking whomever he saw, a display of amity. Yet I could sniff out the blood in him.

As I had no plan to foul up the festive air, I slowly made my way out of the crowd and headed toward the Ma fortress. I wanted Lü Erye's blood to splash on the street before he walked through the gate, which would let me carry out my revenge without destroying the villagers' celebratory mood.

I ducked behind one of the stone lions when I reached the fortress.

I later learned that I'd missed another great opportunity, which was at the festival; Lü Erye might have let down his guard in the chaos at the celebration.

5

Lü Erye came up, trailed by members of his family and several "big men," which was the locals' term for long-term hired hands. They were mostly bachelors, with no family, who lived in the Ma's carters' compound. Those with families had gone home for New Year's.

When Lü Erye reached the gate, I charged with my beggar's club. It was made of a branch of a desert shrub and very solid; used as a lasso pole, it could penetrate the first layer of cow hide. My strength and speed would be enough to take his life.

Naturally, I never imagined he would have such a highly accomplished warrior by him. As the tip of my club whizzed at his throat like the wind, a young woman who looked to be a maidservant took away my club with a flick of her hand. The move was smooth and effortless, using my strength against me; it was incredibly well done.

With my club in her hand, she turned it back on me, striking my ankle with another flick of her hand. I fell to the ground the moment I felt the pain. It was impossible to believe that what I'd practiced so hard at could be so useless. Maybe I was too nervous; maybe I just needed real-life combat experience. I had trained hard, but it had yet to become second nature. With no training in real-life combat, what I'd learned was just a bunch of moves, you know, like Mount Tai weighs tons, but is incapable of crushing an ant. It was like people who study a foreign language for years and yet cannot communicate with a native speaker.

I couldn't flee, not with the pain in my ankle. I could only let them capture me. The big men ran up and held me down while one went for some rope from inside the fortress to hogtie me.

That's how the first day of the year went for me.

As I said before, local custom emphasized the importance of the beginning of the year. They refrained from anger, made sure not to break anything, or act in ways that brought bad luck. Which might be why they merely tossed me into a small room like a jail cell, with no regular window, just a tiny opening large enough to push food through. The door was made of heavy elm wood, possibly from a former prison.

They didn't question me for days. I knew they couldn't spare the time, as they had to entertain guests coming to wish them Happy New Year, while they continued to participate in the festivities. Besides, they wanted to steer clear of anything unpleasant around this time of year. Food and water were delivered with no delay. Those were good days for me, since I hadn't had such good food for a while.

Except I didn't know what kind of fate awaited me.

On the other hand, I wasn't afraid, come what may. I was exhausted from all that I'd been through, and to me real rest would begin with my death.

You might be able to understand the kind of fatigue I was experiencing. It was a rootless, pessimistic drifting, a dark night without a spark of light, waiting with no hope in sight. I dreamed about my dead family at first; they were crying, calling out, and talking to me. Sometimes I'd see the fire and my family members screaming in it. But later, they disappeared and I stopped dreaming. Just think how lonely it is when there are no more dreams.

Meeting Big Mouth was the only thing I could look forward to, but even that thought faded. Perhaps his father sensed something, or his wife found out about it. There had been gossip, though I never heard any of it. You should know that no one would share gossip with a beggar in that place.

I spent over a dozen days in that small room. The *kang* was filled to supply heat shortly after I was locked up, so it was warm inside. Those were peaceful days, almost like heaven when compared with life in the Earth God Temple. I did not want for food or clothes, and I was out of the wind and snow. It was a rare period of stability, as long as I didn't think about the future—such as what they'd to do with me after the festivities were over. I even put on some weight, I discovered to my surprise.

Sometimes I mulled the rationality of my revenge, which was to say I thought about giving it up. If Big Mouth could have married me, it might not take long for the flames of my desire for revenge to go out. Humans get lazy all too easily. I had to constantly spur myself on to keep the fire burning. I even wondered if my family wanted me to give up; otherwise, why wouldn't they come into my dreams anymore?

I started to have thoughts like that after only a dozen days of a comfortable life. How true it is when people say "a life of ease can make one decease."

6

I was brought out by the big men when the festivities ended on the fifteenth day after Lü Erye had successfully served as rite master. I finally saw him up close. There were red lanterns in his room, lending it a celebratory air.

He told the big men to leave, keeping only the maid by him. She was the one I'd encountered on the first. Slender and ordinary looking, she didn't look like a master martial artist.

Lü Erye looked at me for a long time without saying a word. I knew he recognized me. He let out a long sigh and said,

"I know who you are. I've known for a long time already, but I never wanted to kill you. I'm your karmic enemy but you're not mine. You're convinced that I murdered your family, but that is just what you think. I don't want to defend myself. I knew how it all happened, but I can't share it with you. All I want to say is, I didn't do it. I would never do anything that horrendous. Go home if you believe me; if not, you can come back to kill me. But you won't succeed no matter how hard you practice. Go a few rounds with my maid if you doubt me." He tossed me a lasso pole, one with a great feel, slick and smooth.

"Go hit her," Lü Erye said.

She smiled sweetly at me.

"Go ahead. Don't hold back," he said before puffing on his water pipe.

I was tempted. I recalled the praise Big Mouth had heaped on her. Tossing the pole to her, I picked one by the side for myself. The pole buzzed from the force in my hand. She stayed put, still smiling. I couldn't see how, but I missed, and the same happened with the next few moves. It felt as if I were hitting the air. Really odd.

"Why won't you fight me?" I was getting upset.

She laughed out loud this time, and my pole fell into her hand amid the laughter.

She tossed it back to me, but it disappeared as soon as I moved. The pole turned into a slippery fish, gliding out of my hand despite my grip.

I tried a few aggressive moves, but all with the same outcome. I couldn't keep the pole in my hand. Now I saw what Big Mouth meant.

"I wasn't lying, was I, girl?" Lü Erye smiled before continuing, "Go. It's better to end enmity than deepen it. Our Ma family isn't as nice as people say, but we aren't as bad as you think either. It's now the new year, and I don't want to hurt you. I actually made sure you had an enjoyable holiday over the last couple of weeks.

"You should go now. You can decide what you want to do after this. You can continue your attempt to kill me or go on with your life as a beggar, but you can also think of something else. I'm getting old, and it could be my good fortune to die at your hands."

That was it.

That was how my assassination attempt went.

7

An icy wind came at me as I walked through the Ma's gate. The snow on the street was covered with footprints, but not many people were out at the moment, just a few kids setting off firecrackers. I was in a funk. All the preparations over the years hadn't worked. I knew I probably had to stop begging on the street now. The Mas were the most powerful family in this small city, and no one would dare give me food if they knew I was an assassin. Strangely, however, they treated me as before, and I was given some local pastries. Maybe they didn't know I wanted to kill Lü Erye.

The Temple was deserted when I got there. The other beggars had gone home for New Year's, since they had families. My heart ached at the thought of family. My confidence had vanished when I walked out of the Ma gate, for it felt like I was challenging heaven; I didn't think I could be an assassin again. But hate rose up again when I thought about my family. As tears streamed down my face, I laid out the pastries in the temple as offerings.

"Come have some food, Papa, Mama," I cried out and began to wail. With no one around, I cried to my heart's content until I choked on my tears. When I was exhausted from so much crying, I fell asleep.

Big Mouth was sitting by me when I woke up. He brought me some fried pork and vegetables, but it had gone cold. He'd heard about the Ma family letting me go. He said he'd planned to rescue me.

"If I'd managed to rescue you, we'd have fled into the desert, and I'd never be a camel hand again," he said.

I was touched. "That sounds like a good idea," I said. I'd like that. After the celebration is over, the whole town will know my identity. It won't be easy begging."

"The bosses told the big men to keep it a secret," he said.

I wasn't sure why they did that. Was it because they worried about losing face or they didn't want anyone to harm me? Naturally, I hoped the incident would blow over like a pebble making a few splashes after skipping across the surface.

"Did the maidservant make you lose confidence?" he asked.

"Is she even human?"

He laughed. "I asked someone the same question. I think she has to be human."

"How does she move like a shadow?" I asked again.

"She knows *qinggong*, the skill of moving without leaving footprints. I never looked into her background, so I don't know where she came from or where she learned her skills. Everything about her is a mystery. I fought with her once, and it ended the same as you. I don't know if she has any other special skills. She keeps everything to herself, and that alone reveals quite a bit."

"I wasted all that time and energy training. All the hard work amounted to nothing," I said with a sigh.

"Don't look at it that way." He smiled. "You're a superb martial artist, and few can beat you now. Don't compete with that girl; no one does that. She's reached perfection. I hear she has her weakness too, but no one knows how to find it."

After I ate some of the pork, he took me to see Hu Gala at the Su Wu Temple. Some men were drinking there, raising a din. In the first month of the new year, it seemed like everybody drank. Every family offered drinks to guests, as a way to foster happiness and good luck. Spring was when people made plans and, with a festive spring came a happy year.

The cripple whose camel won the running race was there, but he wasn't drinking. He wore a grim look as he polished his cane with a piece of cooked mutton, making the dark wood glisten.

They did not treat me like an outsider. I was very much taken by the atmosphere of a group drinking from large bowls and taking huge bites of mutton; it was noisy and yet homey.

"We were just talking about rescuing you," Hu Gala said when he saw me. "I knew they wouldn't harm you until after the fifteenth. No one wants to be tainted by bad luck. That's like an unwritten rule in Liangzhou. Even thieves take the first month off. So, we were thinking we'd try rescuing you after the fifteenth."

No one expected Lü Erye to let me go, and they agreed that it was highly unusual.

"It's the first month of the year, they didn't want to bring up anything unpleasant," one of them attempted an analysis. "Not many people knew about your attempt, but I think it won't take long for the news to spread. Like a body emerging after the snow melts. By then, if the Ma family does nothing, someone will act for them.

"Maybe Lü Erye didn't want to get the government involved, because you'd explain what lay behind your attempt, and once you did, a lot of things unknown to people would be exposed. Naturally, he didn't want you to disappear in their house either. It'd be a lot of trouble for them if you died there. Everyone has enemies. Take Master Wang Tiao, for example. He's been watching the Ma family.

"But I don't think it will end so easily," the man said. "So be careful."

Hu Gala told me the man's name.

It was a name that scared the locals witless: Sha Meihu.

When I heard Wooden Fish Girl say those words—Sha Meihu—I felt a commotion. The crowd obviously knows who he is, to which their silent noise attests. The name is like a stone tossed into a pond, sending ripples in all directions.

I ask her what happened next, but she just smiles. I don't know why. I can't tell you what kind of relationship she and Sha Meihu had after their first encounter. I know about what she says next, but she doesn't say anything about the two of them. She remains silent every time I press her, and only after I ask too many times does she say, "I'll tell you later."

"Your novel will be boring if you reveal too much," she adds.

That makes sense.

Sha Meihu makes only a few appearances in the scenes related to my interview, but he leaves a deep impression on me. Subconsciously, I even hope he was me in a previous life—it's not normal, I know, but I can't help it, though it does help illustrate an innate outlaw tendency in me—but like Feiqing, he's not someone I could be just because I want to.

When the interview ends that night, I see there's not much water in the basin under the dripping cliff, just barely enough to cover the bottom. But I can't complain. The problem is, I have two camels and a dog, and they need water. Camels are good at going without water, but not forever, and the dog has to have water every day. When it snowed, I saw the dog sticking its long tongue out to catch snowflakes. Obviously, thirst is driving the dog crazy.

No matter what, I have to reach the next stop to find water. On the map there are several water sources at that stop. The dripping cliff still has water, so there must be some sources that haven't dried out completely.

It's not entirely risk-free. At least I'm now at the dripping cliff; there isn't much water, but it's water. It would be great if I moved on and found water, but if I didn't, I'd be in serious trouble.

On the other hand, I didn't come out here hoping for an easy life. Besides the interviews, I'd like even more to travel down the route taken by the camel caravans. That desire alone means I must keep moving forward.

Eleventh Session
Gimpy Camel

I leave dripping cliff with determination despite my apprehension that the road ahead is unpredictable. I got up earlier than usual, intending to give myself time to look for water.

First, I pour some water for the dog, though it's just enough for it to wet its tongue. The camels need water, too, but they're more resistant to dehydration, so they'll have to wait until I find a water source.

Continuing along the camel path in Wild Fox Ridge, I walk out of the rocky gobi and into the sandy desert. Here the desert is vast and towering, with plants everywhere; it is likely the spot where the camels had their fights, as relayed by the drivers. Their camels' feet were apparently ruined in the rocky gobi.

The old wolf continues to trail me. I know it's waiting for me to fall to the ground on my own, for it surely doesn't want to risk it. I load the short matchlock with gunpowder plus a steel ball. I'll fire if it dares run at me. Wolves have a keen sense of smell, and I'm sure it can detect the gunpowder.

On the map from the older drivers there are several spots marked as water sources. One of them is a desert lake, with fresh water. Many deserts have lakes like this, reminiscent of Dunhuang's Crescent Lake, some with *fresh water and some with salt water. Camel caravans of days past used to stop at fresh water lakes.*

I found the lake marked on the map, almost like a valley, probably created by gathering snow melt from the mountains, but now it's a lake in shape only. There is no water, and gaping cracks open here and there, exposing layers of dirt crust.

I follow the map and check out the marked spots, but they're pretty much all the same. The yellow camel is crying weakly, and I can sense the unease in the white camel, though he's silent as a sage.

Luckily there are several more spots at the next destination, and I hope I can find them.

But the interview goes well that night.

One. Feiqing

1

I didn't consider Wooden Fish Girl a Dakini or anything like that; to me she was just a woman in need of help.

Later, when I learned her story, I decided to help. I agreed to take her along on the trek mainly because I didn't want something to happen to her in Liangzhou. Even a tiger dozes off sometimes. Staying in the small city would be dangerous for a woman, an outsider at that city, who planned to assassinate someone from a powerful family, no matter how good she was at martial arts. So I let her come with us. I never expected she had her own design.

Another major event occurred soon after—that's right, the one caused by the gimpy camel. I don't know if it was the same one Wooden Fish Girl saw at the camel festival.

It arrived at noon.

Camel drivers were all napping, and the camel ground was hushed, not even a sound from the camels and horses. The animals were used to sleeping in the day and traveling at night, so they lay down on the grass to sleep after lunch. Like humans, camels sleep on their side, stretching out the legs to give this worn-out part of their body plenty of rest. Under the caress of the lazy warm sun, some camels were even snoring, though softly, almost indistinct, like the sounds made by Chain Smoker's pipe, so as not to rouse their masters.

Wooden Fish Girl skipped her noontime nap that day. She obviously had gotten plenty of sleep the night before, and now she found the daytime hard to get through. She alternated between lying in Ma Zaibo's camel sedan and sticking her head out to look around. The sedan wasn't spacious, but if she lay diagonally she could more or less stretch out. Cotton wadding was spread inside, making the sedan a comfortable place to rest.

Then she got out and headed toward a sand hill nearby.

I was lying on a dog skin blanket spread out in a sand trough. A wind blew over my face, pleasantly ticklish. The sky, blue as if freshly washed, came into view when I opened my eyes, along with the ocean of sand that rippled out into the unknown. The dog skin felt itchy that day, which, according to the ancients, was a warning from a blanket that had acquired supernatural ability, alerting me to thieves lurking around. I wanted to stay awake, so I kept my eyes half open.

Then I spotted the gimpy camel waddling down from a sand peak. It looked like an old rooster pecking at food, quite comical.

"Hei-hei . . ." Wooden Fish Girl shouted, "Look at that. A gimpy camel."

It was gimpy, but moved at a high speed and soon drew closer. Someone jumped off, a hunchbacked old man. He limped his way over, a cripple himself.

She burst out laughing, earning a vicious glare from the old man.

"Are you laughing at me or my camel? I'm a cripple and it's gimpy, so we're both lame on the outside, but not the inside. It's been with me for years. If I don't ride it, do you mean for it to be skinned for meat?"

"Bring me some water, boss," the old man shouted while patting his camel, "My gimpy brother, you're going to get some bean water, so make sure to drink your fill." The camel farted loudly, as if in response. Wooden Fish Girl laughed herself silly, her hands over her belly.

The old man tossed over a cloth sack, to pay for the water. Lu Fuji picked it up and gave it a few squeezes. "Hey, beans," he shouted, "bring over the water trough, Big Mouth."

Camel drivers like silver, but prefer grain when they are on the road. In places like this, they couldn't find ways to spend money even if they had it.

I checked out the gimpy camel. It was large and had erect humps, despite its scrawny appearance. Obviously, the crippled old man treated it well. Wooden Fish Girl sized up the man, who returned the favor with an insolent look.

"Your family runs a desert lodge, girl. I can tell just by looking at you."

She wasn't pleased, but the man continued,

"You don't want to say yes? Hei, I can see you grew up in a lodge."

"What nonsense." She spat. "I'm going to Luocha."

"What's Luocha?"

"I'm not telling you."

"Where are you from?"

"From where I'm from."

"Where are you going?"

"To where I'm going."

A bright light shone in the man's eyes as they bantered. Lu Fuji came and shouted at her, "Get over here. He's an outlaw." Several drivers came running over with their weapons.

We didn't see the man move much, but Wooden Fish Girl was on the camel's back in the blink of an eye, as if riding on a cloud.

"Put me down. Let me off." She struggled to get free. The man growled at her with a sinister look, "Be quiet, or I'll break your spine and paralyze you."

She stopped, fear written on her face.

The gimpy camel jumped up and ran off like the wind. Strangely, it didn't look gimpy when it ran. Lu Fuji and the other drivers all gave chase.

2

I shot out of the lodge on my horse, but the camel was so far off it was just a brown dot. The drivers kept up the pursuit, but clearly, they couldn't catch up. I cursed as I spurred my horse on. If something were to happen to her, the reputation of the Ma family caravan would suffer greatly. Caravan transport was how the family made its fortune. It didn't bring in as much profit as the tea shops, but one loss could lead to more, and the negative effect could never be washed off by water or carved out by a knife.

The horse hooves, fortunately, were wrapped in camel foot pads, so they didn't sink too deeply as we raced along on the sand. I quickly caught up with the drivers. "Be careful. That outlaw is good," Lu Fuji was panting as he said to me.

I made a noise to show I heard him while spurring the horse to fly up a sand dune.

I was getting close. The camel was fast, faster than any working camel, but it was still a camel, and no match for my horse. The danger for a horse traveling on sand was sinking hooves, but now that the contact surface had been enlarged, it outpaced the camel, though galloping in the desert was still taxing, and we might fail to catch up if the distance was too great.

"Feiqing!" Wooden Fish Girl shouted at me. "Feiqing."

"Dai! Don't you know the rules?" I yelled at the cripple. "A true hero takes property, but never a beauty."

"I'm an anti-hero. I take only beauties." He yelled back and tossed something at me. I caught it. It was a hemp shoe sole with two lines inscribed,

"I'm borrowing the girl. She'll be returned one moonlit night."

"Go to your Lü Erye and remind him of the hundred thousand taels of silver for the troops when Commander Zuo slaughtered the Hui. He was an accomplice."

"What does that have to do with you?"

"The Qing court killed our big boss' family."

I'd heard that Sha Meihu's family died a horrible death; some blamed it on the Qing court, while other said it was caused by revenge killings between Hui and Han, or between the locals and the Hakka. I wanted to say,

"In revenge killing, it's always one killing the other, back and forth. Everyone kills and everyone suffers the death of a family, babies included. When people get into that kind of killing, blood sheds too easily and hundreds of thousands could die or be wounded. It's hard to say who's the real culprit."

But I knew this was no time for debate, and I didn't feel like arguing with him. I tightened my legs on the horse's sides and shortened the distance between us.

"Hurry, Feiqing." Wooden Fish Girl cried out tearfully.

The man whipped his camel.

"You're quite a man, and I respect you," he said, "that's why I'll spare your life. But I won't be nice forever, if you keep pressing me."

I took out my club, but I'd barely untied the knot when I heard the man's slingshot whirl. I cursed under my breath. I'd been a slingshot expert too. As a young boy herding goats, I'd practiced until I was almost magical with it. It was made of two lengths of rope attached to a leather sack, to which a rock was added; you swung it round and round and let go of the rock. It looked simple, but was highly effective. The rock could fly as far as a hundred meters. When you were really good at it, you could hit any spot you aimed at. It was a common tool when we grazed camels. Before letting go of the rock, the slingshot must make a tangible arc, which was a telltale sign for the target to dodge.

I flattened myself when I saw the rock flying at me. It whizzed past.

"You can dodge, but your horse can't," the cripple said. The words were still in the air when a rock flew over, knocking my horse to the ground. I was lucky he'd alerted me or I'd have been crushed by my own horse.

"Stop chasing me, or I'll go for your horse's eye next time," he shouted.

Back on our feet, I had to stay back to avoid flying rocks and follow from a distance. A short time later, Chain Smoker and two other drivers caught up. I was worried about a diversion tactic by outlaws, so I yelled at Chain Smoker, "Go back and guard the campsite."

Heeding my warning, the three of them turned and headed back.

The gimpy camel was fast, but my horse was faster. I was incensed from being intimidated by little rocks. I couldn't take it. I wanted to storm ahead, but I was afraid he might actually injure the horse's eye. It was evident that the old cripple was a slingshot master. Following at a distance like this would surely get under his skin, and he would not go straight back to his lair.

The sand hill rose higher and higher, its slope nearly perpendicular to the ground, a majestic background that turned the gimpy camel into a tiny black dot. Wooden Fish Girl continued to shriek, but I could tell she no longer sounded afraid; it was more like a show.

Even with padding on the hooves, the horse was still breathing hard, as it wasn't used to climbing sand hills. It would soon be exhausted if we kept going like this. Horses are no match for camels when traveling on sand. I got off the horse, hooked the club on my belt, and gave chase with my four-chi-long lasso pole.

It had to be strenuous for a gimpy camel to carry two people. I was getting close.

"You're a hell of a pest. Don't blame me when you get hurt," the cripple said while flinging another rock in my direction. I dodged without slowing down; the horse was smart enough to stay beyond his shooting range.

More rocks came at me, but they all missed. The cripple struck his camel's rump with his cane, but it didn't pick up speed, obviously tiring. With increased effort in my pursuit, I was soon right behind them. Wooden Fish Girl struggled and screamed for my help.

"What's your hurry?" the cripple sneered and took out a rope with which he deftly tied her to the camel.

She kept struggling and spitting, a taboo to camel hands, who believed a woman's spit brought disaster. But the cripple ignored her. He let go of the reins and came after me with his cane, which I blocked with my pole. The first contact sent a shock through me, for the cane felt as weighty as Mount Tai, as if made of steel. I twisted and leaped to the side. Drivers were always practicing club fights, an indispensable exercise for us, like loading a litter. Among the drivers in our caravan, Chain Smoker was the only who could beat me in club fights. No longer a young man, he nevertheless had magnificent skill that took the club to wherever he wanted and found gaps in the opponent's moves to strike him in the chest. The rest of the drivers weren't my equal; fewer than five could last three rounds with me. But when confronted with the cripple's cane, I seemed to have lost my power, and he was not intimidated by arm strength that I'd honed over years of loading and unloading litters. He dodged my every move effortlessly, while I couldn't hold my own against his cane. He had powerful arms, too much for my lasso pole, which would snap if I tried to block the blows. I had to employ the nimble moves I'd learned from Chain Smoker, dodging and fending him off at the same time. I managed to break even, but it wasn't easy; Wooden Fish Girl could see the danger I was in and shrieked.

The cripple was quiet, but the cane in his hand moved faster and faster. It had an edge in weight, but it was clumsy. Although my lasso pole was short, it was quick and nimble. Several times it scraped his clothes, but always inches short of hitting him.

Suddenly he kicked sand in my direction. It was a vicious move. I'd be in real trouble if I was temporarily blinded. As I dodged, the cripple jumped back onto the camel, flicking his wrist to send a rock my way. It hit me in the foot. It hurt, but I felt he'd spared me.

The camel flew off the instant I fell to the ground, and soon it shrank into a tiny brown dot. I stomped my foot and cursed when I noticed blood on the horse's knee. It wouldn't help matters if I continued my pursuit, and I could end up with a blind horse. I never imagined a common slingshot could render me helpless. I couldn't stomach the defeat.

I was thinking about following their tracks, but was worried it might be a diversion for them to rob the caravan, so I returned to the campsite. After giving instructions to Cai Wu and other drivers, I picked up a musket, a slingshot, and several sacks of round stones to hang on the saddle, then I packed enough food and water before setting out with Lu Fuji and other drivers to follow their tracks.

Soon it was dark. We lit a lantern and continued our chase. After traveling for some time, we heard someone shouting behind us. Ma Zaibo quickly caught up. I was concerned that instead of helping us, Ma would become a burden and would cause us serious trouble if he were captured by the outlaws. As I hesitated, he said, "I was at Xiongwogou in my search for the Hu Family Mill, and saw people there. It may be the outlaws' den."

Before I could respond, he lashed the camel with his whip and shot out ahead of us.

We saw a row of prints as we rode up a slope; they destroyed the fine grains of rippling sand and disappeared into the night. Luckily for us it was a windless night, so we could follow the tracks; I decided not to stop, because I didn't want the tracks to fade if the wind started up.

It was pitch black out, but with the help of the lantern, we could see the camel tracks. If a windstorm were to start up, we wouldn't know what to do even with an army; it would be like a tiger trying to swallow the sky, not knowing where to start. The lantern lit up only a few feet ahead of us, but the gimpy camel had left a sizable track, easily spotted even at night. Yet I felt weighted down. Most outlaws wouldn't dare raid the Ma family caravan, as the official titles given by the government, such as "Major Merchant," or "Guardian Official of the Nation," would scare off petty thieves. Sha Meihu, by contrast, feared no one; he didn't have a large group of followers, but they were ruthless. They would surely demand a lot for the ransom. We had to find out where she was before we acted. It pained me to think about a pretty girl in the hands of the outlaws. I'd heard that Sha Meihu was a profligate man who came to grab village women. They were strong and healthy when they were taken, but weak and sickly when they were returned. But then I also heard that some petty outlaws had impersonated Sha when they carried out these unsavory acts, because Sha was said to be a woman in other stories. There were so many tales about Sha Meihu. Some said he was a Hui from the West; some said he was a Lingnan local; some said he was a man, others said a woman. Sha was a legend. No one knew which version of the story was accurate.

The tracks vanished around midnight. We searched all over, but failed to pick up the trail. I was puzzled. The cripple couldn't have sprouted wings and flown off.

Suddenly the horse's ears pricked up, and it began to snort. I looked around. There were green lights everywhere, wolves, obviously. Without a word, Ma Zaibo lit a fire and tossed in some kindling. As firelight burst into the night, the green lights backed off. I removed a rock from the saddle bag, put it in the sling, and sent it whizzing into the air. A green light went out, followed by a screech. I looked into the distance and shot several more, pushing the green lights into the dark night.

We were quiet when the sound of horse hooves came into earshot. Before I could react, Lu Fuji quickly shoved sand over to douse the fire. Darkness fell all around as we crawled behind a sand trough. Some time passed before we saw spots of light slowly rounding a bend in the sand. "It's mounted troops," Lu Fuji whispered.

The horses all had brass bells around their necks, and when bells from a hundred galloping horses jingle all at the same time, that can be fearful.

"Who are they?" Big Mouth asked. "Sounds like some of the horses are carrying hostages."

As the East gradually lightened up, the mounted force roared past like a whirlwind; they stopped at one spot for a long moment before storming off. We finally started breathing again as the sounds of the hooves blended into the fog.

Chain Smoker ran to the spot where the horses had stopped and shouted to us. We ran over. Three men were buried in the sand, eyes popped out of their sockets. They were dead.

I sucked in cold air.

It grew light enough for us to see piles of bleached bones beside the newly buried-dead. I shuddered and said, "Come on, let's do some good and bury them whole."

"No use," Lu Fuji said. "You can bury them but the wolves will come to dig them out for food." He went up, jerked one of them up by the neck, pulled it out of the pit and tossed it into a sand trough. He did the same with the remaining two. All three were a bloody mess, covered in sand, as if they'd been beaten or their skin had been scraped raw by sand. Lu lined them up, went up the slope side, and kicked his feet like treading water. Sand slid down and quickly swallowed up the bodies.

We were quiet for a long time, each feeling oppressive silence. After looking around, we saw hoof prints in the sand and a row of wolf prints, but nothing else. The cripple and his gimpy camel seemed to have soared into the air. The relentless stench of blood assailed our nostrils.

We turned back in low spirits after some more searching. I felt a tightness in my chest, as I knew something terrible would follow.

I'd heard that Sha Meihu had informers in every shop in the Northwest, so it appeared that he knew details about every caravan: the cargo it was carrying, the route it would take, and the number of camel teams.

Who were Sha Meihu's informers?

3

Soon a red sun jumped up over the ocean of sand, its red rays painting the desert. Any spot they touched was brilliantly rosy, as if rouged, while other areas were as dark as an ink painting. We saw mounds of bones along the way, a frightening, eerie sight. Some were from camels, but most were human. Every so often we came upon a skull with two black holes staring into the sky; it made me shiver, despite the weather. What had happened the night before now felt like a dream.

It was close to noon when we rode out and looked around. The sun was screaming above our heads, so we dismounted and found a grassy spot to graze the horses. We took out food and water and chatted as we ate. Then we heard someone crying. We looked in the direction, but saw no one. Lu Fuji put down his steamed bun and went up a sand dune, where he shouted,

"What are you doing, Young Master?"

I went up to see Ma Zaibo picking up bones and sobbing as he went. The bones in a sand trough rose like a small hill. We called out to him, but he ignored us. He was crying Mama, Papa, and it didn't sound like he was faking it.

"Why are you picking up those bones?" Lu went up to tug at his sleeve.

"What bones? These are my parents," Ma wiped his tears.

"Your parents couldn't have so many bones," Lu said.

"Here . . . and there . . ." Ma replied and made a sweep with his hands. "My parents' bones are everywhere." He began to wail again, "Papa, Mama." He picked up more of the strewn bones and tossed them into a pile. I noticed a clump of desert thorns under the bones, which told me he planned to set them on fire.

"All Buddhist teaching is nothingness. Cremation or not, there will be nothing. Why go through all the trouble?" I said in jest. To my surprise, he grabbed my hands and asked, "Why are you looking for her if you know it's nothingness?"

I was dazed. "And so what if I find her?" I muttered to myself. "She'll be a pile of bones after a few decades. And the Ming or the Qing would also be nothing, so why are we trying to restore one and fight against the other? Even the universe has a life span. When the time comes, no one can escape the grip of death, so what's the true meaning of everything?"

"Listen to you. You're sounding a lot like Ma Zaibo." Lu Fuji added, "What's the point of searching for meaning? Just keep on living and that's enough."

"You're right," I said with a sigh. "Heaven can do what it wants and we humans must maintain our dignity."

4

When we got to Xiongwogou, we spotted a beacon fire mound in the distance. Someone was on it, but he ran off upon seeing us; I knew he went to alert the others. "Be cordial," I said to Lu Fuji.

"What do you want?" a man came over to ask.

"Looking for someone."

"Who?"

"Sha Meihu."

The man disappeared, but came right back,

"The big boss said you should go elsewhere if you're looking for the girl," he said, "and don't bother us."

"That's weird. How did he know we're looking for a woman?"

"We're not looking for anyone. We just want to meet Sha Meihu," I said to the man.

"There's no Sha Meihu here, just a few camel grazers. Come take a look if you want."

I tossed my reins to Lu Fuji and went in unarmed. There was no fort, as I'd imagined, nor any weapon; it actually did look like a normal camel herding spot. In the center of the sand trough were a few houses whose appearance meant they were made of packed sheep droppings. A few camels looked up at me.

I went into one of the rooms with the man. Sure enough, I was immediately greeted by a heavy odor of sheep droppings. Sitting on the *kang* was a lean-looking man, with somewhat feminine features, dressed in a wool waistcoat, slicing mutton with a knife. He didn't move when he saw me, just tossed me a knife and said,

"Come, have some mutton."

He was an ordinary man, lean and neat, like a real shepherd, except for the fur lined blanket that caught my eye. No ordinary shepherd could afford a blanket like that. On the wall were also two firearms, one long barreled and the other one short. "Help yourself and have some mutton," the man said again.

I picked up the knife to slice some mutton when I realized he wasn't Han. They usually ate well-cooked meat, but the meat before me was tough and hard, and cold. I cut off a few pieces, each going down like swallowing medicine.

"Looks like you're Han, you can't eat meat this tough," the man said with a laugh. "Tough mutton toughens you up."

"Cows eat spinach and what a pig likes isn't for the dogs," I replied with a laugh of my own. "To each his own."

Tibetans like undercooked meat. Living on the high plateau means they don't get to eat fresh vegetables often and are used to meat like this—sometimes it still dripped blood—to supplement nutrients like vitamins. That was why outlaws and shepherds who were in the desert year-round were used to undercooked meat. But not me. I couldn't force myself, so I made up the deficiency in different ways.

"You want to see Sha Meihu about the woman? I can tell you he never saw her," the man said.

"You sound like you're defending something obviously opposite to what you claim." I replied.

"Sha Meihu would have done it, but this time it wasn't him." He was upset.

"Then who was it?" I asked.

Yawning lazily, he wiped his hands on a piece of paper and got down off the *kang*. He looked feeble. "Go now. Go look for her somewhere else. Don't delay, you'll be too late if they cook and eat her."

"Are you Sha Meihu?"

"I don't know who I am. I've been asking the question for decades, but no one can tell me. I only know it wasn't Sha Meihu. Go tell your friends not to accuse him for what he didn't do. But you can if you want. Sha Meihu is a man with backbone, and he can take responsibility for countless actions."

He was yawning again, so I walked out. Another man had appeared on the beacon fire mound. Sha Meihu was so famous that the government had been looking for a chance to skin him alive. Could he be living in crude houses like these? I wondered.

I sighed long and hard, my heart feeling heavy. Instinctively, I knew the man was telling the truth. There were two kinds of desert outlaws: one settled down somewhere with a base, where they recruited men and amassed weapons for open battles with government troops. The other spread out to carry on individually, and joined together only when necessary. Which was Sha Meihu's style? I'd like to know.

As I pondered these questions, a young man came up to hand me a snuff bottle and writing instrument. I knew it meant the man knew who I was. I smiled. The brush was too thick, so I plucked a stalk of slender needle grass and wrapped it in a strand of horse hair before dipping it in ink. A few strokes from the brush added to the snuff bottle a grasshopper atop an orchid, its wings spread as it chirped.

The young man took the bottle and handed me a tael of loose sliver pieces before running off. I had to laugh. Not only did he know who I was, but he also knew my fee for painting a snuff bottle. Where did they get ink and brush around here? I found that odd.

"Ai-yo. You make money wherever you go," Lu Fuji said with a laugh.

I laughed too as I tossed him the silver pieces.

"Now we have a problem. If that's not Sha Meihu, who could he be?" He continued, "I don't think that was a man."

"How so?"

"No Adam's apple."

Two. Killer

1

The Mongolian caravan set out a few days later. They moved to a grazing ground off to a distance. The marksmen wanted to go along, and Feiqing had to be let them go.

I discovered that Balte was plotting something.

It surely wasn't just my imagination. I was the pair of eyes hidden in the dark, while they were all out in the open, so I could see what they couldn't see clearly.

Balte was first to suggest the move, with water and grass as the reason. Indeed, it wouldn't take long to exhaust all the vegetation, with two out-sized caravans together; the situation would improve greatly if the two were apart.

But I knew the separation, though likely to reduce friction, meant the possibility for reconciliation was lost. Balte would not have been unreasonable if Huozi hadn't stirred up trouble. To Mongolians, no matter how serious the trouble, everything blows over as long as they can have a hearty drink together. Now with the two caravans living separately, Huozi's mouth would block out Balte's sky. Feiqing didn't see the potential problem, so he agreed with only one request—that they stay close by, not beyond one stop apart. If something happened, the Han and the Mongolians could help each other out.

The Mongolian caravan left despite the absence of Brown Lion. Obviously, the world kept turning even if someone was missing.

But I sensed the Mongolian camel now and then. He hadn't run away, for that was his nature, so deep-rooted it was part of his soul. I didn't know how far he had followed them though.

In those days, I saw a different monster following us. I was always seeing a wooden fish flying around in the air. It came and went without warning. On the surface, it seemed to come and go, but I often detected changes. It looked very much like a wooden fish at first, but Chain Smoker insisted it was a millstone. Then it did take on the shape of a millstone, day by day.

It also slowly got bigger. I'm sure you wouldn't know the significance of a millstone's size. I once read a magical book about a millstone that would start out as a wooden fish and slowly change into a real millstone, as its shadow spread like water on the ground. Then disaster would strike. By that time, according to the book, oceans of human blood would flow out of the opening, along with bones, flesh, fingernails, and hair. Among all the waste produced by a human body, hair was a reusable resource that could be turned into a blanket or something like that.

You're right. I heard the Germans used Jews' hair to make military blankets in World War II. In a concentration camp called Auschwitz, where over twenty tons of human hair was found later. Human bodies have other uses too, like provisions for the troops applied by Zhang Xianzhong.

That has nothing to do with us, so let's not talk about it.

I saw how the millstone continued to grow daily though almost imperceptibly. I only detected the change in its shadow when it flitted over my head—what? You say the millstone was a mere illusion? No, that's not how I see it. An illusion has no shadow. Besides, Chain Smoker saw it too. Do you mean to say we shared the same illusion? He started out claiming it was a millstone and changed it to a wooden fish; I was the opposite, wooden fish first and then millstone. Human hearts are different, so their perceptions of the world aren't the same. It did resemble a wooden fish, but a millstone is still a millstone, no matter what shape it takes, am I right?

In the shadow of the ever-enlarging millstone, I realized that the calamity was pressing down on us. I waited with anticipation. Though somewhat fearful, I knew the fear itself had no real meaning to us, because it would not stay away just because we were afraid. Of course not. Whatever was going to happen would happen whether we were afraid or not.

I also knew we couldn't escape our fate in Wild Fox Ridge, no matter what move we made next. Perhaps a lucky few would leave alive, but they could not dodge their fate; they would never be able to elude the Wild Fox Ridge in their destiny.

For several days, I saw the millstone at dusk; it spun as it whipped its way over like a fast wind. I yelled out when I first saw it,

"Look. A millstone."

Everyone roared laughing, saying I'd lost my mind. Chain Smoker, the exception, said he saw a twirling wooden fish. They still laughed when I yelled out the second time, though Chain Smoker said he didn't see anything. After that, I saw it almost every day and could even hear the sound of whipping wind, like crows flapping their wings. I used to say the crows' fluttering wings sent down the curtain of night. Yes, that's right. I even wondered if the descending darkness might be the millstone's shadow. It was possible. Scientists were always proposing this theory and that hypothesis, but none of them could convince me, because I learned that scientists from a later time could always negate their predecessors. So current scientists would have their ideas refuted by those who came later. They could all end up invalidated. How could I believe any of them?

The Kālacakra mentions a heavenly body called Rahula; it has no color or shape, but it takes part in the movements of celestial bodies. I heard it was involved in many astronomical phenomena. The same with the millstone; it existed whether you could see it or not.

Its shadow kept growing each day.

I knew disaster was near.

2

I was looking for an opportunity to kill Ma Zaibo. To be sure, I could kill him with brute force like a butcher slaughtering a cow, but I didn't want to. I wanted to make the process more imaginative; or put differently, I'd like it to be a kind of behavioral art—heh-heh, I didn't know the term back then, that's for sure.

Like Feiqing, Ma Zaibo was calm and composed, both practitioners of meditation, at which they were very accomplished, said to have seen through the world of mortals. Ma wanted to be a monk after he'd reached this stage, for he was no longer interested in meaningless endeavors. Feiqing was different; he wanted to join an anti-Qing movement. I wasn't sure which one deserved our respect more.

Once I asked Feiqing,

"Why don't you give up now that you've seen through worldly affairs?"

This was his response:

"It's true. I've seen through it all, and I know none of us can escape what's coming. What I can do is change my attitude. A real man undertakes challenging tasks when he knows they are nearly impossible to accomplish."

To be honest with you, I admired his character a great deal, and yet I couldn't agree with him. I didn't believe he could change what was predestined.

I honestly didn't.

On my part, I thought the two caravans split for more than just limited resources for the camels.

I had a powerful premonition; I could tell something else was in the air.

Ma walked around with an enigmatic smile, I saw. He kept chanting his sutra, to the delight of some of the drivers. I knew he wanted to erase the murderous air permeating the caravans; it would have worked if the aura of death hadn't been so powerful. The problem was, it was everywhere, like a raging fire feeding on dry kindling, while his chant was a cup of water. That tiny bit of coolness wasn't likely the salvation needed by human hearts.

What I'm saying goes somewhat against my nature, which goes to show that I'm a complex person too. Despite my understanding of Buddhist doctrine, I wouldn't give up my mission. As I said before, I wanted to offer blood from a Ma family member to the ghosts of wrongful death.

"Hey, can't you stop chanting?" I recalled saying to Ma Zaibo not so long ago. "You can't save the world, you know." And guess what he said in response.

"I've never wanted to save the world. I just want to save myself." He added, "I want to save those connected to me by fate."

"Actually, what's going to come will come whether you chant or not," I told him. "Don't you know the giant millstone is flying at us? It could crush everything in this mortal world of ours."

"It's a millstone to you, of course." He laughed. "But it's a wooden fish to Chain Smoker. Guess what it is in my eyes?"

"What?"

"A boat. Can't you see it's actually a boat?"

"What kind of boat?"

"A boat to help rescue the human heart. What I'm reciting is the boatmen's work chant, and everyone who likes to hear it will gain salvation."

I just smiled, for I'd heard it countless times. So many sages or frauds had said similar things, and I had yet to see anyone receive salvation, including Jesus. He was called a savior, but in fact he couldn't even save himself from the cross, let alone other so-called sages who have proclaimed to be the saviors of the world. I failed to see the actual meaning of the salvation they proposed.

But I just smiled.

When I interview Killer—he rarely makes an appearance, I see a murderous aura. He's a black corona oozing death. He never shows up in human form. I could observe him in meditation, but I know I shouldn't force the issue, since he doesn't want to let me see his real face. Sometimes following someone's wishes is a form of respect.

But I noticed something unusual: I haven't heard any of the drivers describing Killer in their stories, as if he were invisible. It's odd, but I don't want to pursue the subject. It's my principle in interviews that I let their souls flow whichever way they want after I revive their memories. More often than not I get more than I expected that way, such as Wooden Fish Girl's story, which came as a surprise to me.

The sand trough is quiet. The camels and the dog have been well behaved in recent days. They rarely make a noise during my interviews. The moon has rounded itself into a platter, sprinkling enough chill to seep through my body and my heart. I didn't build a fire, because I'm already dehydrated, and a fire may well bake away the remaining fluid in me.

I spread the dog skin, wrap the sleeping bag around me, and pile on the fur coat. Dog skin is just wonderful; it takes no time at all to warm up my backside. With that and the Kundalini I practice, the cold is within the limits of my endurance.

I go up a slope to look around; there's no green light from a wolf's eyes, but I know it's still following me. It will not easily leave me alone.

Twelfth Session
Fighting the Police

I reach the next stop the following day. It's been an arduous journey, mostly because of thirst. The water in the jug is gone. There's still some in my pouch, but I try not to drink too much from it and only take a sip when thirst gets the better of me. Despite my conservation effort, we'll surely die in the desert if I can't find water, I know. I'll never make it out with this little bit of water.

A terror I hadn't anticipated occurred to me: due to climate change, all the water sources on the map have dried up. This map was a treasure map for the camel trail of yore; with it, the drivers could ensure the survival of their camels, and the outlaws would know where the caravan stopped to rest. Control of the water source had allowed Ja Lama, a famous figure in history, to maintain a chokehold on the Hexi Corridor, which then enabled him to accumulate massive wealth and build a fort on a hill. But a parchment that had been regarded as a treasure at one point was more or less trash, now that the water sources had all dried up.

His confidence clearly sapped, the yellow camel goes on a strike as he lies down and refuses to get up. With an ugly look on my face, I whip him more than a dozen times before he reluctantly gets to his feet. His shameless behavior makes me feel that once believing he might be the reincarnation of Yellow Demon was a profane thought.

In contrast, the dog tries to keep its spirits up and wags its tail at me. The white camel is quiet, staring ahead and not at me, with an indifferent expression. He makes me keenly aware of what a Buddhist calls mana, for the camel remains indifferent whether he's favored or humiliated.

I look around for four hours after reaching my destination of the day. I don't feel like searching any more when I find two spots whose water source had long dried up. I know it's nearly impossible to locate any water, and an oppressive sense of worry comes at me. With that little bit of water, I will never make it out alive.

Surprisingly, I find to my delight, large trees with parasitic cistanches, a juicy desert plant that is good for a person's yang, among other medicinal benefits. In my eyes at this moment, they're just water and food.

A careful study of the topography leads me to conclude that this was pretty much where the drivers said the event took place. I don't feel like going any farther. If nothing else, the cistanches alone are reason enough to stay. I plan to use this spot as the central point and draw a circle around me.

After locating a sand trough more or less leeward, I pitch the tent, a small canvas tent I hadn't put it up in the past because it's too much trouble. But now I have to make the effort, since I plan to stay here awhile.

I gather some cistanches. They're best in the spring, but I'm too thirsty to care. I toss a few at the camels for them to chomp on happily, with juice dripping down their chins. It's called desert ginseng, and the way they eat them, they're good for camels. Then I break a stalk into pieces for the dog; it refuses with a shake of its head.

"Don't blame me if you die of thirst," I say to the dog before biting down on mine. A soothing sweetness spreads in my mouth.

I hope to complete the interviews as soon as possible, for I'm worried that the cistanches won't last long. But it's just a thought; I don't want it to *influence my interviewees. It concerns me most that they may finish in a hurry so as not to make my situation worse. If that happens, many of the wonderful sections will be left out.*

Sure enough, Wooden Fish Girl points that out to me later at night.

One. Wooden Fish Girl

Don't be in such a hurry. We'll feel bad if you are. Storytelling should be like drinking hot millet soup; you need to take it slow and drag it out as long as possible, or you won't get its full flavor.

I know you really want to learn about the caravan, but it won't be the same without my story. What happened to me caused the caravan to suffer the consequences. You see? There's no effect without a cause.

So let me continue with my story.

The riot that rocked Liangzhou later took place in the first month of that year. A tune spread throughout the city overnight: The twenty-fifth day of the year's first month/Flames spread through Liangzhou far and near/Horses galloped into the ancient city/Attacked Zhangyi Fortress while they were at it."

Big Mouth took several men with him the night before to deliver chicken feather missives calling for a meeting. Added to the missive was a threat that whoever refused to show would have his house burned down.

The missives were on such a large scale that just about every family in Liangzhou got one.

As mentioned before, chicken feather missives were a means of communication in those days. A chicken feather was attached to each message to imply urgency and importance. The contents spelled out what its recipient must do. It was a common practice among secret societies, with speed as its major advantage. If well organized, everyone who needed to know would receive corresponding information overnight. It also had the characteristic of secrecy, providing protection for whoever started the action. Just think. With all the people showing up at the preset time at the appointed place to carry out a mission whose ringleader could not be identified whether they succeeded or not. The law does not punish the masses. Heh-heh, it was a naïve concept, to be sure. In Big Mouth's words, it was like pulling down your pants to fart. No wall is airtight, and there are always traces in whatever you do. Feiqing got his head lopped off later, didn't he?

You've said enough about Feiqing, so I won't talk about him now. All I'll say is, the Feiqing you saw was the one you closely observed, but not the same as the one in my eyes. In Liangzhou's tune, "Story of the Lasso Pole," he was portrayed in yet another way, "Take another look/the Qi Feiqing/with crimson face/a towering heroic figure/standing tall between heaven and earth."

Heh-heh, just listen to what they sang about you, Feiqing.

It's hard to say which version was right. Everyone is different inside, which makes the world they see different. Feiqing was like that. He wasn't as attractive as Big Mouth to me at the time. I couldn't help it. He had money and the charisma to rally supporters, but to be attractive to a woman—tee-hee, am I still a woman?—has different criteria. Don't look so crestfallen, Feiqing. Such a long time has gone by, whatever you can remember is but a dim yellow spot, isn't it?

No more chitchat. At the time, I found the chicken feather missive amusing. As one of the messengers, I walked through one village after another in the moonlight. In those days, there weren't many grand-looking houses in Liangzhou's villages, and trees were scarce. It looked sad when I compared it with the lush mountains and emerald rivers. Big Mouth and I were in charge of Bali, which, in Liangzhou dialect, meant plains. Residents were grouped as Bali—those in the plains—Shanli—those in the mountains—and Huli—those by the lakes. The term bali originated from the ponds they dug for irrigation purposes. Back then, they used water from Qilian Mountains for their fields; along its waterway, each village built a dam to create a pond, giving rise to names such Touba—first pond, Erba—second pond, or Liuba—sixth pond.

I felt increasingly terrible as Big Mouth and I walked through Bali that night. For the longest time, I'd had my eyes on the Ma family, and I saw nothing but signs of their incredible wealth. But that night what I saw was squat, crude houses, a sight that made me feel worse as I walked on. Every village exuded the air of poverty, and the houses seemed to cower under the moon. I got emotional and thought I really ought to do something for them. I'd been fooled by what Feiqing and others said, mistakenly believing that we were really trying to get rid of Mei Jiangzi and replace him with an upright official or we would overthrow the Qing government to bring a good life to the people. Maybe the kind thoughts of mine helped create all the stories about me in Bali. The locals built a temple to honor me and called it "Shuimu Sanniang." Their offerings enabled me to watch over Liangzhou in a different manner after my death. Looking through the eyes of Shuimu Sanniang, I witnessed the downfall of the Qing court, the founding of the Republic before the Japanese came and caused many deaths. Then came the battle between two brothers, leading to more deaths. One of the brothers won, not long after which a major famine occurred and many died of starvation, followed by never-ending armed battles and more deaths again. I keep asking myself if what we did back then was meaningful at all.

My question to myself led me to weep sometimes late at night, prompting the villagers to say, Listen, Shuimu Sanniang is crying again. A story emerged in Liangzhou to spread the idea that killings would occur whenever Shuimu Sanniang cried. But the truth was, I only wailed when I saw or thought of bloodbaths.

I digress. What happened to me later all started with the sorrow I'd felt on the night I went out to deliver the messages. I thought I should mention that first.

I did digress. Weighty thoughts like this must have often been present in your novels. I haven't read any of your work, but I can read that in your heart. Life can't always be weighed down like that, even though it can be unbearably light. You don't have to shoulder the cost of human suffering; there's no need for you to do that at all. So why don't you take it easy and gaze up at the stars and the moon with the woman you love? It's useless for you to feel this way; humans have their own trajectory of destiny, no matter how they feel, weighty or not. You can light as many torches as you want at night, but the eternal darkness will overpower everything. No matter how bright the torches, sooner or later they'll go out, while darkness will last forever. Everything has its own fate.

These thoughts didn't occur to me until later, however. I hadn't reached this realm on that night. I wouldn't have been as nonchalant as those who have seen through it all, if my sleepless soul hadn't experienced so much over the past hundred years. We all need experience, without which no one can truly grow up. My experience gives me another pair of eyes. You can treat what I'm saying as a different kind of weeping by a hundred-year-old lonely soul. Liangzhou residents gave me the respectful title of Shuimu Sanniang, but you can consider me a yaksha, or anything you want. It's just a name.

Let's go back to that night then.

I was swathed in noble sentiments that night. Feiqing was a good speaker. I had yet to learn that he'd actually memorized the rules and regulations of a secret organization called the Longhua Society, starting with Yue Fei and touching upon the humiliation inflicted upon China's Song dynasty by the Mongol's Jin dynasty, the precursor of the Qing. He said we must "drive out the Manchus and revive China." In modern lingo, he'd stirred up nationalistic sentiments in me. It was a different kind of sentiment that sometimes even surpassed my hatred for Lü Erye. I added my hate for him to the nationalistic fervor, because the Qing court had helped build up the Ma family and bestowed upon it over a hundred years of wealth and power. If it hadn't been for the Qing, Lü Erye wouldn't have had that kind of influence, a viewpoint that had taken over my mind for a long time. You'll understand how I felt that night if you see where I was coming from.

I was really fired up that night.

My steps were powerful and spry. There were at least a thousand pairs of feet just like mine on that night transmitting the arrangement of conviction and violence. I didn't know there would be so many fired up people in Liangzhou. I thought people were always saying that Liangzhou residents were like loose sand. It came as a surprise that they were clumping. I didn't know until later that loose sand can only form a loose clump, no matter the size. Clumps of loose sand can never become rocks. Some water would bring all the grains of sand together to form clumps, but they fall apart once the water dries.

I won't go on and on about it, since you all know the story.

I learn that many events are quite interesting: you think you're changing the world when you carry on, but when you reflect upon your actions, you realize they're of no great significance. When you look at it this way, you have to agree that the world is truly a reflection of the mind.

We inserted the chicken feather missives in every farmer's door for them to drop to the ground in front of them when they opened it in the morning. They might not all know how to read, but they could see the feather and knew enough about them. They knew that people who failed to show had their houses burned down. Houses that might be run down, but were still good enough to provide shelter from rain and wind; with a house comes the sense of home. I'm sure you understand what a house means to a family. The Earth God Temple helped protect me from the elements, but gave me no sense of home. Why? Because anyone could go there. If you get in a bit late, your usual spot on the floor would be taken by another food-scraper. That was what Liangzhou people called a beggar. Heh-heh—I was a food-scraper in many people's eyes. When I got into an argument with Big Mouth, he'd try to insult me by calling me a food-scraper, but it would only make me laugh.

We were out until past midnight and Orion's Belt was settling in the west before we finished delivering to the houses assigned to us. We ran into no people, only dogs. People here rose when the sun was up and rested when the sun set. Once the night fell, the whole village was deadly quiet.

What we did was mentioned in *Story of a Lasso Pole*, a well-known Liangzhou tale. Why don't I sing a passage for you—

> *Quickly scribbled on chicken feather missives*
> *Sent to four townships and six villages.*
> *From Jinqu to Daqu, from Daqu to Zaqu,*
> *From Zaqu to Huangqu, from Huangqu to Huaiqu,*
> *From Huaiqu to Yongqu. From here to there, from this village to the next.*
> *It reached Qingzui Lama Bend, it reached Zhangyi Fortress in the far end.*
> *People in the four townships and six villages sent it around.*
> *Let's put aside the number of villagers who came,*
> *And just count the headmen, seven thousand eight hundred and ninety-three.*
> *They arrived at the Guangong Temple, made a list, and reached an agreement.*
> *Lu Fuji, Qi Feiqing, and Yang Chengxu would be the ringleaders.*
> *Listen up, everyone, today we're going to storm the yamen,*

We'll catch the two damned officials, Wang Zhiqing and Li Tesheng.
You're all headmen here, and you must have a clear record of the households.
When the time comes, tell the children and the old to stay inside.
Bring out the hot-blooded, the strong, and the rash young men.
Bring them over to surround Li Tesheng and seize Wang Zhiqing.
Then we'll attack the police station and storm the yamen.
This time we'll fight with our lives.
We'll all benefit if we succeed, but I'll take full responsibility if we fail.

The headmen looked up with wide-open eyes when they heard:
Black beard, a big fat guy, a brawny tall man.
It was sure enough Lu Fuji whose words stirred the people.
Then they glanced at Qi Feiqing, a man with a ruddy face.
He was tall and valiant, standing tall between heaven and earth.
The people shouted in unison:
"Brother Qi, Brother Lu, we'll follow you in whatever you do.
Death doesn't scare you and we'll fight with our lives."
"Everyone, listen up. Go back to your village now,
Quickly get ready to set out.
We'll take Li Tesheng on the thirteenth of the eighth month and
Capture Wang Zhiqing. On the fourteenth we'll lay siege to Liangzhou."
Strong as nails hammered on a steel plate,
Orders were given to the headmen crisp and clear.

Now the headmen returned to their villages,
With enough people nothing is impossible.
The command to start was spread quickly,
And every household got its notice.

Life was so hard for the people they could barely survive,
Heads in hands, they were ready to storm the Liangzhou government office.

2

Back to my story.

Heh-heh, I can only give you my impression. You do know that so many years have gone by, and memory, after all, is only memory.

The Liangzhou story was wonderful; it says "In whatever they did, the Liangzhou people never balked and were always 'screwing someone's mother' when they talked." It's so true. Oceans of people showed up on the prearranged morning and gathered at a spot; it was very much like now, with explosives building up until a single spark would set them off.

I realized that despite the difficulty in grouping Liangzhou residents, they actually liked to be clumped sand—they called joining an organization grouping. Why? It was hard because they usually didn't have a leader, whom they called the tall man. If there was a tall man, they were happy to vent their anger and indignation. What was there to fear? The tall man would prop up the sky if it fell. That is, the ringleader would take responsibility for possible adverse outcomes, and the rest would be unscathed. On that morning I was greeted by many with reddened faces, once wan but now tinted red by their outrage. Every single cowardly resident had turned into a red-faced man.

They ran first to Wang Zhiqing's house, which was in Yongchang Prefecture, north of the City of Liangzhou. He was obese, which earned him a nickname, "Puffy, rotten coffin."

Actually, what I wanted most was to torch Lü Erye's house, but Feiqing wouldn't let me. I didn't know why. Many of the members of the Society of Brothers didn't want to either; they'd benefited from the

Ma family one way or the other. I was convinced that the Mas were hypocrites, so I demanded angrily,

"Why can't you see their true faces?"

They told me that the Ma family was so large and so rich that it was unavoidable that there were one or two bad seeds, but most of them were good people.

"Puffy, rotten coffin" was an interesting nickname, entailing a kind of wisdom unique to Liangzhou. His status was hard to pin down; some said he was a member of the local gentry, while others called him the police chief. In any case, he was an important figure. Actually, it didn't matter whether he was important or not; being so obese was a crime. In the views of the locals, a wealthy man was evil and a righteous man was never rich. It was unforgivable for a fat man like a puffy rotten coffin to rise among the countless rail-thin Liangzhou residents. Yet I can't find evidence of his evil deeds even now; everyone said he got rich from ill-gotten gains, but no concrete example was ever offered to explain how he did it. Years later, after I calmed down and was thinking clearly, I figured it out: to the locals, obesity alone was reason enough to torch his house. Other than that, no more reason was called for, like the revolution years later, during which one's wealth was reason enough to be struggled against.

For a while I didn't trust Lu Fuji, also from a Yongchang wealthy family. He wasn't rich enough to be called a puffy, rotten coffin, but still a fat enough donkey. Generally speaking, two fat donkeys couldn't be tied to the same trough. As one of the planners for the chicken feather missive, could he be doing it entirely without any ulterior motive?

. . . Heh-heh, don't try to defend yourself. That's just what I was thinking, and no one took it seriously. You're now part of history. Once being part of history, you shouldn't be so hung up on doubts, which were nothing but a vasana, almost a habit that was outside history. What is history? History is written by victors to explain their actions. It doesn't matter what really happened; what's important is how you present it.

The outraged villagers torched as they went along. Our original targets were Li Tesheng and Wang Zhiqing's residences—

> Pick up a three-string zither and tune it right,
> We'll talk about nothing else,
> But Li Tesheng, who had plenty of evil relatives.
> The secret order to rise up spread quickly, his relatives tipped him off.
> Li Tesheng flew into a rage when he heard; he cursed Lu Fuji, Qi Feiqing,
> What can you accomplish with a bunch of poor villagers?
> Li was not easily intimidated, but a second thought told him it was no good.
> He fled with his wives and children.
> And that was how Li got away, and the villagers stormed an empty house.
> Now on to the other plunderer, Wang Zhiqing, also tipped off by his relatives.
> Surprisingly he didn't flee.
> The walls around his estate were treacherous,
> Traps were set up in the gulch outside the walls.
> His running dogs guarded atop the walls with fast-loading rifles,
> And rocks the size of donkey droppings piled up like a stockade.
> The gate was sealed tight, he thought it would keep him safe.
>
> I won't talk about the fleeing Li Tesheng or Wang Zhiqing sealing his gate.
> I'll talk about the early morning of the thirteenth day of the eighth month,
> When the villagers thudded down the streets.

From afar and from nearby, with a hoot they gathered together.
The sun rose atop Li's estate, but it was empty, no one inside.
Puzzled, with a hoot they stormed in,
The green bamboo doors and target practicing walls,
Windows like tiger heads, all so pretty.
Bang, bang, bang, they smashed everything, wrecked the furniture.
They found his grain storage; bang, bang, bang, they filled up sacks.
When nothing was left in the grain storage,
They tied reins to poles, and pulled down all the houses in the compound.

Qi Feiqing, his anger rising, took the people out,
Quickly arrived at Wang Zhiqing's gate.
But Wang's gate was sealed airtight,
And his running dogs were watching from atop the walls.
They threw down rocks the size of donkey droppings,
They fired their rifles and home-made cannons nonstop.
The villagers were blocked by the firepower,
They could not rush into Wang's estate.
Liangzhou residents are known not to balk,
They're fucking someone's mother when they talk.
Wang Zhiqing, a big lump, I'll fuck your goddamned mother,
I'll screw all your goddamned ancestors.
We're not real men if we can't break down your gate today.
Some of the young men were clever,
They brought a big cart,
Piled high with wheat stalks, tied down with pine slats.
With a shout they raised it up to block their heads.
Some brought hemp stalks; shouting and roaring as they ran.
The rocks hit the cart and dropped weakly onto the wheat stalks.

Soon they were right outside the gate.
Lu Fuji yelled out to attack with fire.
The villagers bundled up hemp stalks to torch the gate.
"Whoosh!" They caught fire and a wind blew over.
The hemp stalks burned brightly
And the gate crackled as it burned.
When the fire roared, the crowd shouted,
Let's go, and they set upon the estate.

Inside Wang Zhiqing was panicking,
He failed to stop the villagers at the gate.
Quickly he strung up his wives and children,
Each one was quickly sent on the road.
Tying a rope to bring them down, young girls, women, wives.
The young men were bold; they all wanted to cop a feel.
Touching the hand, grabbing the feet, tucking at the braids.
The womenfolk were too scared to say a word,
If they did they would get a taste of the man's hands.
Lu Fuji was outraged when he saw. These young men were all rascals.
What are we here for today? How dare you abuse the women?
You're so shameless you disgust me. Set them free and let them go.
Let's go home too, he shouted. Everyone go home and get ready.
Be ready to lay siege to the city office tonight.
With a single shout, they left, going home to get ready.
Bake flatbreads, gather provisions,
They must take along lunch for the next day.
Some baked potatoes, for they needed to have food at the ready.
After dinner they set out, the villagers blotting out the sky.
Wah-la-la they leapt and jumped to lay siege to Liangzhou city office.

Something else happened on the way to the Liangzhou city office. The villagers were so keyed up they burned any good-looking house they saw. They didn't care who lived there; a nice house was an eyesore to them and an eyesore deserved to be torched. Many cheered when black smoke rose up, so loud they drowned out the crying owners. Their wails never disappeared from my mind and thinned out the sense of moral high ground I'd experienced the night before. My heart had hardened after the punishing trek, but I still had feelings. Reminded of the fire that destroyed my family, I quickly teared up and ran up to stop those men with torches in their hands.

"Get lost. You food-scraper. We'll torch you if you don't." They screamed at me. Big Mouth came to drag me away. One of the owners had tried to stop them, and they'd doused him with fuel and set him on fire. He, or the ball of fire, screeched in pain as he dashed here and there like mad until he was turned into a charred stick.

I had never imagined that, once ignited, the cowardly Liangzhou residents could act like that, a winning cat happy as a tiger, as the local saying goes.

3

In the darkness of the night the villagers came to the base of the city wall,

They walked along and circled the wall.

Then they hid in the quiet potter's field, waiting for dawn to enter the city.

They waited until early morning when the sun was about to rise.

From far and near, everyone came from everywhere.

People in four townships and six districts all came out.

The time came and the city gate opened.

With a shout, the people blotted out the sun,
Clamored into the inner city.

Torches lit up the road that filled with crying. The rioting mob of Liangzhou, made famous in the local gazette, finally made its way through the city gate. The small city had a well-known history of wealth. As the saying goes, "One can never empty out Ganzhou or fill up Liangzhou." It meant Ganzhou produced bountiful resources and Liangzhou had strong consuming power. Goods were everywhere; wares that made the villagers' eyes glow red with envy.

Based on an arrangement made early on, the target of the uprising was the township yamen. So the villagers charged the yamen, but failed to find the magistrate, Mei Jiangzi, who was rumored to have fled. They turned to smash the *yamen*, which they did with zeal. I found they had a natural hatred for anything good. I wondered why they didn't simply take the things home. Later, I realized that no one dared take anything. Whoever picked up an item was immediately set upon by his fellow rioters. So, trash it they did. It was better that way and no one objected. They'd been stewing in silent anger for years and, finally given an opportunity to vent their wrath, they wrecked the place to their hearts' content.

I found a cane amid the chaos. It might have been made of rosewood, for it felt good in my hand. Suspecting it had belonged to the county magistrate, I quickly twisted off the knob and threw it away. No one could tell what it was now. then I slid it along my nape down to my back, and heh-heh, that was how I got the beggar's stick that later made a name for itself. It became my lasso pole, a handy tool, and the most memorable gain from my participation in that incident.

Mei Jiangzi's flight intensified the people's anger. The township office was not big enough for the destruction to last long and soon the rioters stormed out onto the streets.

They started on the police station, an easy target and necessary channel to vent their rage. When outraged, people naturally want to smash what they can see. We wouldn't spare the police if they hadn't tried to stop us, for they had a hard life too. But they tried, and someone shouted, Beat them, beat these motherfuckers. Thousands of people charged and laid the station to waste.

I have to agree with what you say, now that I'm at this part of my story. You're always saying that no matter how significant an event may be, it's just a memory. That's true. In my recollection it was an impressive spectacle, on a scale comparable to the revenge killings between the locals and the Hakkas I'd witnessed. But what I can recall now are just a few scenes, which, besides beating the police, were torching houses and wrecking the magistrate's office. Not much more after that. I heard that the magistrate, Mei Jiangzi, had fled. Why was he nicknamed Jiangzi-pulp? Because he was a terrible official, so the Liangzhou people called him that since it fit his surname—Mei, plum.

See, a significant incident in the local gazetteer was actually that simple.

I heard it was the biggest event in Liangzhou in a thousand years. Liangzhou people were cowardly but, as they say, even a rabbit will bite if cornered.

4

What happened next bothered me for a long time.

The villagers were hungry after smashing the police station. At first, they bought snacks from street vendors, things like cold noodles and fried cakes. But in those days, not many farmers had ready cash for snacks, so those who had it paid for their food, while those didn't could only watch and drool. Then someone made a comment, "We rose up for you people, so why do we have to pay for something like this?" It alerted the starving villagers, who began clamoring, "Righto, righto. We're willing to lose our lives, so why should we have to pay for a little something to eat?" Righto is "that's right" in the Liangzhou dialect, which now filled the streets strewn with rubble.

The looting happened amid a din of "righto," "righto."

The mob stormed the vendors' stands before ransacking the shops. Everything edible was a target of the shouting, cheering crowd, which exuded a degree of glee comparable only to the mood of the heroes on Mount Liang after they took Zhu Family Village.

The Hui suffered most from the looting at first. It was a time when disputes constantly broke out between Hui and the Han, so the mob ran at those in white skullcaps. In those days, most merchants on the street wore white skullcaps. Liangzhou residents generally believed that farming was an honorable profession, running a business wasn't. Chinese looked down on the Hui merchants and, with the memory of revenge killing by the Hui still fresh, they quickly forgot the mission indicated on the chicken feather missives. They now trained their hateful gazes on the Hui merchants on the streets of Liangzhou.

Naturally, they met with resistance.

It was a feeble attempt, but enough to arouse more ire. As a result, one Hui shop after another was rendered a pile of a rubble, like the police station. Fights broke out all over the city. Shop owners and angry villagers got into physical combat; sounds of club against club, screams, shouts, things breaking, and crying filled the air above the streets.

I was suddenly reminded of the killing between the locals and Hakka. With tears streaming down my face, I ran at fighting people and tried to stop them, but each time the irate villagers tossed me aside. Luckily for me, I stood out because of my appearance as a food-scraper, so they didn't mistake me as a Hui and beat me to death.

Over and over I was thrown to the ground, until I saw stars. Big Mouth helped me up.

"Want them to kill you?" He was apparently frightened by the chaotic scene, for he stomped his foot and muttered, "How can this be? How?"

I knew I was just a cup of water that could not put out the raging fire.

I also knew that only very few among the villagers were looting, beating and killing. They could be rascals, hooligans or local bullies. Their numbers were few, but they were tinder and, once they started, could ignite the innate evil in others. The desire for destruction might not have been present in every individual, but it did emerge when there was a mob. Like an avalanche, once the line was crossed, once someone lit the detonator and the fuse, it would cause staggering explosions. I noticed the faces reddening on those who were usually kind, simple, and law-abiding; like cattle in mating season, they were breathing hard as they ran at the weak Hui. They were probably reminded of ancestors who had been killed by the Hui, and now every Hui became the enemy. Revenge was high on their minds, turning their earlier acts of common looting to murder. In the magnetic field of mob violence, Liangzhou people who were averse to killing were transformed into bloodthirsty butchers.

Dead bodies appeared on the streets of Liangzhou, mostly from the Hui, but some were Han slain by the Hui. Bloodshed, once on the scene, bred more bloodshed.

Heads were strewn on the streets. "Kill them! Kill them!" Someone was shouting. "Kill the Manchus and take back the Chinese nation."

Yet no one even asked, "Are the Hui Manchus?"

On many occasions people have a need for slogans, even if the slogans run counter to their actions.

I later discovered that the Hui people actually had a blood feud with the Qing Manchus, and yet they suffered most in the riot.

Many shops were set on fire, and thick smoke shrouded the streets. The smell of blood was mixed with smoke, as well as the stench of burning flesh.

Tears wetted my face. "How could they be like that?" I asked myself.

In the arms of the rioters was loot that included food, fabrics, tea and other items.

Then I heard Feiqing's angry shouts as he rode over on his famed black horse. Whip in hand, he lashed at the looters and attackers.

I thought I heard in the chaos several big men belting out something, which could have been from the *Story of a Lasso Pole* that I would hear decades later:

> Brother Qi, Brother Qi, as long as you take the lead,
> We'll follow you wherever you go.
> As long as you're not afraid to die,
> We'll give our lives to whatever you want to do.

His face dark with anger, Feiqing snapped his whip, landing solidly on the rioters. Those who were hit screamed in pain, those who hadn't continued their frenzied pillaging.

"Dai, Mengzi. I'm fighting for you with my life, so why are you hitting me?" One of them complained. He was talking to Feiqing, whose nickname was Mengzi.

"Go kill Liu Huzi, if you're that good," Feiqing yelled back. "A real man doesn't pick on the poor."

"What do you mean poor? They're so rich they ooze money." The man looked wronged.

"They're rich because they worked hard for it. It's not ill-gotten gains." Feiqing urged his horse forward as he continued to lash out.

The rioters quieted down and stopped looting when he got to them.

Want me to go on?
All right, I will.

Thirteenth Session
Flying Lasso Poles

The villagers went through the city gate,
Grabbed pine poles from every street.
The villagers were fierce, old hemp rope around their waists.
And rocks filled their pockets,
Beat, beat, beat, and fight, fight, fight.
Ping-pang, ping-pang, raising a racket.
Up thoroughfares and down alleys,
Smashing the police station and evening the score,
They turned around and headed to the yamen.
The township office door was shut early on,
With guards and soldiers standing atop the city walls.

1

In *Story of the Lasso Pole*, there was a passage that sounded like a debate. Without it, a great deal would be missing in the historically well-known uprising.

Liangzhou residents offered their explanation in the argument at the township office:

> Liangzhou people in whatever they do never balk,
> They like to screw someone's mother when they talk.
> Magistrate Mei, a turtle spawn, I'll screw your whore of a mother,
> I'll fuck your thieving ancestors. So you'd better get out of here.
> Tell us everything about the wheat chaff and animal feed,
> Explain to us what the fees are all about.
> The villagers are about to enter the yamen office,
> His running dogs are so scared they don't know what to do.
> They run to the back and give a trembling report,
> "It looks bad, Old Master. The people are rebelling.
> They're coming through the gate now."

> The news stunned Magistrate Mei; he was scared witless.
> He wished he'd known the people were so hard to control;
> He regretted coming to Liangzhou to assume the post.
> And now he called heaven for help, but heaven didn't reply.
> He called earth, but earth had nothing to offer.
> He cursed Wang Zhiqing the blind dog,
> And screamed at Li Tesheng, the fucking dog.
> You already knew what was happening,
> So why didn't either of you alert me?
> You sent a message late last night,
> Saying the people were stirring up trouble.
> But you didn't say what it was about, or when it would happen.
> And now early in the morning the people have surrounded the yamen.
> They are out of control.
> Ai, tell the advisor I need him now.

You go talk the people around and I'll stay inside.
Pulpy Plum, what a sneaky man,
He's found a way to flee for his life.
He sent an advisor who had no real power
To the gate to sweet talk the people.
He himself got onto the roof, over the wall and into the outhouse.
In the pit was a large yellow dog, a vicious, scary dog.
"Ou!" it leaped up and caught Pulpy Plum by surprise,
It tore the Magistrate's Achilles heel to shreds,
And turned into a sorry, bloody mess.

Let's skip the yellow dog tearing into the Magistrate,
And move on to talk about the advisor at the Yamen gate.
He was trembling so badly it was beyond words,
His face was more pallid than yellow spirit paper.
"Grandpas, Papas, please stop shouting and fighting.
In broad daylight under a red sun,
Why are you surrounding the yamen?
Who's the leader? Come out here and explain yourself."
Qi Feiqing, a courageous man, and Lu Fuji, the fearless one,
Thumped their chests and said,
"We'll screw your whore of a mother,
Why do you want to see our leader?
We two are the leaders. You asked why we're surrounding the yamen?
There's a fee for celebration and there's a fee for funerals,
Harsh taxes and levies in four seasons, all year round.
The cost for chaff and animal feed grows higher by the year,
We'll show you if you don't believe us.
Think about the amount of grain we used to send up,
Compare that with what we have to give now.

You really don't know when to stop, do you?
You don't follow the rules, you do what you please.
You want to know why we surrounded the yamen?
This is why. All these shitty things you're doing to us.
Today we're going to break down the yamen gate,
So we can get the thieving Plum out to explain himself."

The advisor formed an evil scheme after hearing them out:
"My fellow villagers, listen carefully.
Magistrate Mei is away from the Yamen today.
Please don't be angry, go back home.
I'll take care of all your problems.
You'll receive good news in less than three days."
Liangzhou residents never balked,
Some of the rash young men feared nothing at all.
"Forget it and get the old thief out here.
Or I'll screw your whore of a mother.
Standing in the toilet, your back doesn't hurt.
In the four seasons all year round,
What do you eat, where do you live, what do you wear and put on?
You live in cool houses,
You eat enough rich food to smear your lips in grease.
You dress in silk, satin, and brocade,
You sleep under felt and fur.
But the poor people like us are suffering,
We have nothing but soupy millet with potatoes.
We live in rammed-earth houses and tattered grass huts,
Earth is our bed sheet and heaven our blanket,
We suffer all our lives, every day bringing more hardships.
You want us to wait for three days?

Don't even dream about one moment of delay."

The advisor panicked,
Afraid the young men would slap him around,
He quickly softened his tone,
"Grandpas, Papas, I'm just an errand-runner,
Please don't be mad and wait a while,
I'll deliver your message and give you an answer."
He ran off like the wind; the advisor was a cunning thief.
He found Pulpy Plum and they whispered to each other
To form an evil scheme to do in the Liangzhou residents here and now.

It's hard to say whether what was written in the story truly reflected what had happened at the time. But I think it did happen or at least it might have happened. The truth notwithstanding, the defense added a hint of rationality to the famous uprising.

Don't you agree?

2

The villagers who stayed behind started looting again, once Feiqing went with some men to the county office. The situation was hopeless, and the sight plunged me into despair.

"Look out! Liu Huzi's cavalry is coming," someone yelled.

Brought to a sudden stop by the shout, the looters looked around anxiously.

Sure enough, loud, heavy sounds of horse hooves were coming from the gate. I jumped onto a flagpole stand and saw the military police charging with their swords.

"Get out of here! Let's go! Liu Huzi's cavalry is here," they shouted amid the chaos.

At the shout, the villagers scattered.

I remember there was no combat during the uprising between the police and the villagers, who started with torching, followed by looting, and ended with flight.

It was just as you said, "It rose with a roar, and dispersed in confusion."

"Get Qi Feiqing!" A bearded man shouted.

Liu Huzi's cavalrymen raised their swords and hacked at the fleeing villagers. Some screamed in pain, hands on their wounds, strewing the streets with loot. Some of the Hui merchants who ventured out to pick the stuff up were mowed down by the police.

I knew this was no time to run, so I sat down at the base of the wall. In those days, beggars swarmed the streets of Liangzhou, so one more woman wouldn't catch anyone's eye. I could hear agonized cries up and down the streets. Some were moaning and cursing, "Screw Mengzi's mother. He did me in this time." He was clearly angry with Feiqing.

Actually, I did a rough count and came up with slightly over a hundred policemen in Liu's force. There were several thousand villagers, in contrast. If they had been organized, and everyone fought hard with their clubs, they wouldn't have failed. Besides, there were many good martial artists among members of the Society of Brothers, and they often practiced with their clubs and cudgels, so it wouldn't have been hard for them to fight one on one with the police. But the flight following the melee meant putting down weapons. It truly was, as the saying goes, troops in defeat are like a toppled mountain. It resembled an avalanche, with snow crashing down at the slightest tremor.

Many of the villagers looked frightened and lost. They stood still at first; then they panicked and fled like bees from a disturbed hive when they saw more and more running. Then came the cries of pain, shouts of surprise, and manic laughter.

Cries of pain rose and fell all over the place. The dim autumn sun provided a backdrop for the scenes before me: splattered blood, dancing swords, villagers in pools of blood letting out blood-curdling screeches . .

The police followed Li Tesheng as they cut a killing swath through the crowd, their humanity erased and replaced by murderous intent that turned them into beasts. Their black batons were stained red; each time one fell, blood and screams followed.

Just like that, the famous uprising in Liangzhou history rose with a roar and receded the same way.

Pulpy Plum took the opportunity to escape.

And left with no choice, so did Lu Fuji and Qi Feiqing.

I heard Feiqing and the others had spent several years planning an uprising that ended up like a joke.

Story of the Lasso Pole had the following description for the uprising:

Magistrate Mei devised an evil scheme,
A report was sent to the prefecture magistrate and the circuit chief,
Eventually it reached the provincial office and the governor spoke up,
"Since the people in Liangzhou are so audacious, we'll put them down.
They have no respect for the laws of the land, so I'll see how bold they are."
A hundred teams were sent out, a fearful sight;
Shouting, "Kill them!" They charged forward.
The commanding official said to the soldiers to
Quickly kill these Liangzhou people and turn them into ghosts.
Rounds of shots were fired, so terrifying to hear,
Raising dust to swirl on the streets.

The dead lay bleeding on the street,
The injured crying in pain for their Papas and Mamas.
Finally, the people were scared witless,
They ran off, their feet thuddering along.
Qi Feiqing and Lu Fuji shouted for them to stop, to no avail.

Troops in defeat are like toppled mountains.
The villagers ran and ran in all directions.
Some had broken arms, some had crushed heads.
Some were trampled to death by the fleeing crowd,
Some managed to run all the way home.
They were quickly surrounded.
The soldiers were many and powerful,
And their commander was from the military camp.
Charging forward on horses, with muskets and swords,
The soldiers surrounded the people, most of them young,
They felt sorry when the muskets were fired, regretting their actions,
Saying if they had known the uprising would lead to death,
They'd rather have stayed home and not gone anywhere.
Now we're arrested, but we didn't do anything.
At that moment the commander shouted,
"Get in, get into the camp. You all get in there."
They were herded into the camp;
All four gates were locked and sealed airtight.

Now look at these villagers; they were thirsty and hungry,
Afraid to get into more trouble.
Every one of them was wiping tears.
The commander had something else in his scheme.
He had sweet, sticky rice soup cooked and ready,

For all the villagers to eat without delay.
That made them wonder why the commander arrested them.
They were even given something to eat, so eat they did.
They could do whatever they wanted; so, we will cast our lot with fate.
As they started on the food, the commander came to lecture them:
"Listen up, you people. You all look like you're barely into adulthood.
I brought you into the camp today because there's something I need to say.
You are villagers and ought to live peacefully in your village,
So why did you follow the rebels to stage an uprising?
Why did you smash the police station?
Why did you lay siege to the county yamen?
I know your two ringleaders; they're Lu Fuji and Qi Feiqing.
Those are two bad seeds from Wuwei,
And you should never listen to their heresy.
Why did you follow them to beat the police?
Why did you follow them to attack the yamen?
The imperial court has the right to demand taxes and fees,
And you have to turn over the chaff and feed, all of it.
You people must be obedient and do what you're told.
Why did you follow heretical ideas and rise up against the court?
If I didn't bring you all into the camp and talk some sense into you,
You all would have lost your lives, no one would be spared.
You would leave behind your wives and children, and your parents.
Who would take care of the orphans, the widows, and your old folks?"

The commander was such a cunning man,
Sweet talking one moment and threatening the next, on and on.
The young men began to cry and their tears dripped onto their chests.
Elated by the sight, the commander changed his tune once again,

"I've told you how I feel.
Now you should all go home.
Farmers back to your field and till your land.
Be a good farmer, but if you try to rise up again,
My bullets have no eyes.
You are just common folks; what do you know,
And what feat can you accomplish?"
The four gates were open as he talked.

Ai! The people, fleeing for the lives, quickly ran off, back to their homes.
One ran faster than the next and in the blink of an eye no one was left.
Ai! These officials, they really know how to sow discord.
With a scheme so devious, the people were convinced and talked around.
Ai! These Liangzhou residents, they are bold when they have guts,
But are cowardly when their nerve leaves them, scared witless.

Qi Feiqing, Lu Fuji, by this time they were both fuming.
They'd thought the Liangzhou people had backbone, guts, and brains.
Turned out it wasn't true, they were useless and frightened by flying bullets.
Everyone ran off and no one was left. They knew it didn't look good,
So they took off and ran out of the city, all the way back to their homes.
They went over what had happened on this day:
"We did good today; we smashed the police station.
It went well today, but looks to have been a total waste of energy.
First, we failed to capture Li Tesheng; Second, Wang Zhiqing got away.

Third, Magistrate Mei went unharmed.
We fought a tiger and got bitten in return.
More will come after today so we must be careful."
"What are you talking about, Brother Lu?
We decided to do something and shouldn't be afraid.
Affairs in the world change all the time,
And the good and bad come in turns.
Everyone gets to share the glory if we succeed,
But we'll take full responsibility if we fail."

3

Later I learned that similar, laughable incidents happened in many places. Uprisings like this were being staged everywhere, but by confronting the Qing court, they were like a child against a mighty man, who could knock the child down with a single punch; but the child got up again and again, tangling with the man, throwing snot and spitting at him, attacking in any way the child could think of. When one died, countless others came to take his place. At first, the man was unaffected, but little by little, he tired and fell into a nightmarish state. He began to stagger and finally went down in a movement called the Wuchang Uprising.

The uprising started by Feiqing was but one of countless acts that had seemed laughable. But it was a well-known event in Liangzhou history, where nothing like it had ever happened before.

No one told me how many died during the uprising, since no count was taken. Years later, an old man said he had been going from a cave to the back of the mountain one day when he heard horse hooves. Too scared to show his face, he hid for a long time until the hooves receded into the distance. When he came out he saw many dead bodies in the valley. Wolves were already closing in. No one was alive to hear about the bones when the night was over.

Bones like those were buried in mountains all over Liangzhou, and similarly, countless bones were later enfolded in the fields all over the city.

Big Mouth and I fled into the desert, for we had nowhere else to go. Members of the Society of Brothers also dispersed into the desert. We eked out a stubborn existence in a place called Dengmaying. Back then water and vegetation could still be found there, unlike now, when only a dry lake remains. Over there, the water was sweet, the plants lush, the sky big, and the land vast, with numerous hiding spots to make survival easy. When I say easy, however, it was only compared to those who perished. Life was hard, even when I think about it now.

I had no idea how many had died but only about a hundred managed to escape alive. People can talk about our courage all they want, but we were seriously overwhelmed. You can imagine how it would go when rising up against a government; you could have tens of thousands of comrades but it would still be like hitting a rock with eggs. That was what happened with us. As the saying goes, a centipede dies but never falls down. Later, when people talked about Zeng Guofan, they would say he could have overthrown the Qing court had he fought all the way to Beijing after quelling the Boxers. I doubt that would have happened, however. You have to understand that on many occasions, a legitimate status commands respect and obedience, which was what the Qing court had given Zeng. Without it, he would have been a mere rebel, and no one could predict the outcome. In China, it's often the case that monkeys run off when their tree falls. When "grouping" starts, everyone clamors into action under the effect of mob mentality, but if it is something major, especially when they realize they could die, they will disperse in confusion. You won't understand Liangzhou if you fail to see this.

I even wonder if those who fled had followed us out because they feared the punishments from the Qing government. I don't know how many among them were true die-hard revolutionaries.

In Liangzhou lore, Feiqing fled to Mongolia. There are many versions about his flight. One had him being chased by Liu Huzi's cavalry as he ran out of Liangzhou city on horseback. They chased him all the way to Sancha Sheep Temple. What's a sheep temple? It's a place for offering sacrifices to the Sheep Deity, which was a common practice among shepherds at the time. You could call it the shepherd deity too, if you want. Don't poets write something like this, "Ah, the almighty shepherd deity?" Right, that's him. We call it a Sheep Deity. In the local lore, Feiqing and his horse were exhausted by the time they reached the temple, so he prayed to the Deity for protection to help him escape death. He offered to rebuild the temple and gild the statue later if he was saved. It was a common plot line in Liangzhou storytelling and wooden fish song tradition. The Sheep Deity showed its magic. Gusty winds greeted the police when they got to the temple, blanketing the sky with dust. The temple disappeared, Feiqing escaped death, and ran off to Mongolia.

It was a popular version and I believe it was true. Not long after that, Feiqing sent a message for us to build a temple at the spot called Sancha. We did. It was a magnificent temple. No one outside our group knew that under the temple we dug secret tunnels and rooms, where we buried a large amount of silver. Then we sent a message to him, telling him to come get the silver if he ran into trouble. Unfortunately, man proposes, God disposes. We had the opportunity to leave silver for Feiqing, but he did not have the good fortune to enjoy it. One day over a decade later, the temple collapsed during an earthquake. Half a century later, a shepherd boy spotted an opening in the ruins and went inside to find piles of silver ingots.

Is my story getting too long and boring again?

You don't have to pretend you're listening. Listen if you want; if not, let your souls doze off. I won't mind. You should know that by now I don't care how many are listening to my story-telling. I reach my goal by telling. I've kept it inside for so long, almost a hundred years, and I've been trying to find an outlet. I couldn't, because no one could understand me. Finally, here you are, so let me prattle on. You can treat it as a lonely old woman's pathetic mutterings.

Without knowing it, the purpose of my revenge began to change. I'd had an ulterior motive when I joined the Society of Brothers. I couldn't get near Lü Erye through my own effort, but a crowd can bring down a wall. With the help of dozens, hundreds, thousands of brothers, I would be able to level the Ma family. There are stories like this in wooden fish songs. It happened to Hongniangzi, the woman who saved Young Master Li. On her own, she would never have been able to break into the jail. I'd wanted to be like her. The idea of overthrowing the Qing and restoring the Ming never occurred to me. I wasn't interested in rising up against the imperial government, for the court and Qing dynasty meant nothing to me. Lü Erye of the Ma family was my enemy. To be sure, my revenge could be extended to the whole family, for, as they say, a fire at the city gate is also a calamity to the fish in the moat. I just never imagined that the wheel of fate would take me to the lake at Dengmaying, where I mixed with a bunch of men in disarray from government pursuit.

We cut down many trees to plant in the sand and dug up mud from the lake to smear over the tree to throw up makeshift shelters. Those were crude houses that could not withstand gusty winds, but we didn't think of building sturdy structures. On the highest point of a nearby sand hill, we planted a tree as a kind of messenger that would send us fleeing if it fell. We were ready to be on the run at any moment; our heads were tied to our waists on belts made of camel hair, and could be lopped off at any time.

Food was abundant, however. We dug into many yellow rats' nests. There was no grain in there, but the rats were a great food source. We could survive on them, either roasting or boiling. In addition, there was desert rice, Artemisia seeds, Suoyang roots, and cistanches, all of which we could live on. Once in a while, at night we "borrowed" food from houses we'd picked out beforehand. To tell friends from enemies in the dark, we painted our brows white, and as time went by, people started calling us Shamei hu, tigers with sandy brows.

Heh-heh, don't ask me if we were the same as the legendary Sha Meihu. I don't know. I don't know who he is either. We were looking for him too. We knew there was a Sha Meihu in the desert, but we knew nothing about his identity. On the other hand, we never denied it when we were called Shamei hu.

4

I got a different notion when I learned about the nature of the Society. Hu Gala and his friends planned to overthrow the Qing and restore the Ming, which didn't mean much to me. Qing or Ming, it was nothing but a shadow, while Lü Erye was the real enemy. Day and night, I dreamed of killing him. Later my notion changed, however, as I realized that killing him wouldn't erase the hate in my heart.

Why?

Because he was getting old. I heard that he took a fall one morning when he got out of bed; his mouth twisted to one side and he lost control of half of his body. To a lecherous man, it had to be worth than death. The servants heard him scream constantly, "I want to die. Let me die." I was dazed when an informant relayed the news to me. Lü Erye did want to die, I knew, and death would come as a relief to him.

I could not let him die so easily. I wanted him to live a life worse than death.

I began to ask around to learn what he treasured most. Whatever it was, I would take it away from him.

"His son, of course. He loves his oldest son the most," the informant said.

I mentioned that Lü Erye had two sons. The younger one died of epilepsy, the other was Ma Zaibo. When Ma Zaibo was little, his father had treated him like a fragile treasure, and not much had changed after he got older. Ma Zaibo didn't follow his wishes to become a merchant, but Lü Erye said, "Shit, he's my son and I'll let him be. The money from our ancestors is enough for more than one of his lifetimes. He can do what he wants."

All Lü Erye wanted from his son was to marry early and give him a grandson, which was the last thing Ma Zaibo had in mind. He was obsessed with self-cultivation. Now you see? Right. That's why Ma Zaibo became my target.

What I wanted to do was not kill Ma Zaibo, but get him to join the Society of Brothers and become a revolutionary, so that his whole family would be executed by the Qing court. What revenge could be sweeter than this? That's what I wanted to do in those days.

I didn't realize it was also what Feiqing wanted.

Several people also had that in mind; we had different goals but shared a method.

We joined forces to reach the same revolutionary goal. Heh-heh, I can recite that too.

I return to the tent when the nightly interview is over. I build a fire to boil water and make instant noodles. I have about half of pouch of water left, around five jin. It isn't a lot, but cistanches help solve the water shortage problem for the camels. Even my dog starts eating the plants. Now the water will last a few more days. The only problem is, I don't have a lot of cistanches either. I have to tether the camels so they won't eat too much. Otherwise, it wouldn't take them long to finish them off if I let them eat to their hearts' content.

It's getting colder still. I could sleep out on the sand when i first entered the desert. But now I feel cold even inside the tent and I often wake up freezing at night. It would be better if I could sleep in a Tartar's *kang*—mix hot and cold sand and spread out a dog skin blanket. But I discovered that the drivers' storytelling was often disrupted by the flame whenever I lit a fire. Some of the specters didn't dare get closer and stayed off to the side to look. Obviously, the folklore about fire dispelling demons isn't entirely without merit. At least some of the specters are afraid of fire. To be sure, it's the working of their discriminating mind; they're afraid because of the notion they hold about "ghosts fearing fire."

Fourteenth Session
What a Charming Girl

Drive the camels, up before dawn, head to the eighth stop.
We travel in the wind and trek in the rain, catching a cold and falling ill.
The boss complains about me, saying I'm not a good worker, still.
You see, this is, the life of a camel driver,
No way to make a living.

——*Song of a Camel Driver*

After getting up in the morning, I have some cistanches and break off a few pieces for the camels. Not too much, though. When they are on the trees, they hold their moisture and offer sweet juice, but once they leave their hosts, they dry up quickly. Cistanches are wonderfully refreshing. The camels look different already, after eating only a few of them. The yellow camel is no longer lethargic and even expels a drawn-out cry sometimes, as if he's ready to mate.

I find myself energized after eating the cistanches. There was even some stirring down here when I woke up just before dawn.

A quick inventory of the cistanches tells me that there should be enough for three or four days.

I walk around after breakfast, hoping for other pleasant surprises. Among a copse of trees in the distance I find several with cistanches, not a lot, but enough to cheer me up.

Then I spot the black wolf lying under a large tree, watching me with an unfriendly look. I say loudly, "Follow me if you want, I'm not afraid of you." On second thought, my declaration means precisely that I am afraid. I wouldn't need to say anything if I wasn't. Luckily, I have the dog with me, I say to myself. Or the wolf might sneak up on me at night to bite into my throat.

As dusk falls, I find myself eagerly awaiting the nightly interview.

Wooden Fish Girl's story has me enthralled. It's truly an unexpected find.

She's looking increasingly lively, because the drivers' memories are becoming more vivid. She still looks vibrant in their distant memories. A girl with fine, delicate features, she's slender but muscular, a beauty in the West back then, I'm sure. In the drivers' recollection, she never appears with her beggar's look; what remains deeply entrenched in their minds is still her lovely face. Maybe our memories are selective to a certain extent and we like to hold on to the beautiful segments that once delighted us.

I can see the drivers in her recollection also. Their memories of each other form a treasure trove, supplying me with information of their time. Hence, they appear vivid in my mind too.

There are still unsolved puzzles regarding Wooden Fish Girl. For instance, I want to know what she went through after she was kidnapped by the outlaws, but she hasn't said a word about it. Perhaps it involves some personal privacy—such as whether she was raped after the kidnapping—and I can't bring it up to expose her sore spot in front of all these people. And there's also her return to the caravan. It remains hazy how she made it back. She seemed to have returned after one of Ma Zaibo's "awakenings."

I wonder if a complicated story might have developed between her and Sha Meihu. I asked her during one of the interviews, but she just smiled without answering.

I'll let everything remain a puzzle.

Besides her, Ma Zaibo gives me the most vivid impression. In the drivers' memories, he was always like a splendid tree standing tall in the wind.

What I want most in my previous life is to have been Ma Zaibo.

But the more the story unfolds, the more I realize that I seemed to have experienced what they relayed in their stories, and they all ring true. I'm downcast from the discovery.

In the drivers' stories, Ma appears to have the halo of a sage around him, but he fails to display any unique quality of a sagely person in his own narrative. He had desire, love, and a wish to escape the mundane world, which is in conflict with his love. His heart is the only manifestation that makes him different from the others. For instance, I discern a higher realm in his understanding of Wooden Fish Girl: in her own narrative, she appears as an avenger and a lovely girl in Big Mouth's eyes, while in Ma's view she is a Dakini. The world in Ma's eyes is always bathed in a holy light, so perhaps that is how he manifests his holy heart?

I want to talk to him some more.

Circumstances change with one's mind. Ma shows up at nightfall before I begin chanting. The drivers come with him.

What he says about Wooden Fish Girl is so different from her own story that they might as well be two different persons.

I can't tell which one is the real Wooden Fish Girl.

One. Ma Zaibo

1

I left the caravan when the crazy camel stirred up so much trouble for you.

It was too noisy, I wanted some peace and quiet.

Feiqing gave me a gun to protect myself against wild animals a few days before I left. I suspected he knew what I had in mind, but maybe he didn't.

I told him privately that if he needed me, he could go to the Hu Family Mill. I'd leave instructions there.

Then I got on the road for my search. I knew none of you would agree to let me go if I told you about my trip. That was why I had to sneak away.

It felt a bit like Wang Chongyang.

Ages ago, when Wang received a secret incantation for self-cultivation, he wanted a quiet place to practice, but couldn't get away from his family obligations. In the end he had to fake insanity, biting anyone in sight, forcing his wife to lock him in a small room, where every day someone brought him food. Twelve years later, he had reached his goal.

Naturally, I couldn't fake insanity. It would have been impossible for me to leave if I had.

I wasn't like Wang, who had already been given his secret incantation. I'd had my initiation rites and been accepted by a teacher, but I had yet to obtain the incantation I really needed. I knew my mission from the day I understood what was going on; I had to find the Hu Family Mill and Wooden Fish Incantation.

I had to leave the caravan amid the mayhem. Another reason for my departure was, I'd sensed something ominous stealing up on us. I didn't know what it was exactly, but I definitely felt the danger.

The danger wasn't just the flying millstone or wooden fish you were talking about. Those posed a danger, for sure, but not the one I had in mind. You referred to it as fate, but to me it was a murderous aura, which came at me constantly. It was sinister and chilling, cold enough to wake me up from sleep.

I wasn't afraid to die. What I feared was not finding what I was looking before I died.

I had to find it. And I would willingly die once I found it. The ancients said, "When one learns Tao in the morning, one could die the same evening." That was the case for me.

I couldn't die before I found what I must find.

Please forgive me for all the trouble I caused you.

Now, let me tell you my earliest impression of Wooden Fish Girl.

2

Even now, the local gazetteers got it wrong, just like you. Their eyes were similarly blinded; when she was mentioned, she was called a foolish woman. They thought she was dimwitted.

But she was a Dakini, in my earliest view of her.

Naturally, you don't know what a Dakini is, but you can understand it as a goddess. Even so, Dakini is a goddess above and beyond our world. She has broken away from clinging and attachment, and has erased dichotomy. What is a dichotomy? It is like good and bad, kindness and evil, success and failure, and so on. It is a narrow confine that leaves corresponding imprints on the phenomena of mind and matter in the world. Which is how we humans have a discriminating mind, clinging and attachment, greed, hatred, foolishness.

Women we call Dakinis are not burdened with this clinging and attachment; they transcend those standards. To them "gold is the same as cow dung," "palms are no different from a void." Clean or dirty, it makes no difference to them, they want no attachments and give up none. Whether coming or going, sitting or lying down, they always embrace clarity and emptiness. Petty arguments with ordinary humans are beneath them, which is why they are called foolish women. These people are unaware that true sages always seem foolish, and the most foolish types tend to be the wisest. One of Buddha's five kinds of wisdom is the wisdom of the Dharma realm. Its practitioners appear as the most foolish.

To me Wooden Fish Girl was a Dakini who had obtained the greatest wisdom of foolishness.

I saw her out roaming the streets carrying bundles of tattered clothes, rags, and other worn objects. Her face was filthy and she reeked a pungent odor. Vagrants steered clear of her. But to me the smell was her protection. Just think, how would she have time to do what she wanted to do if she showed her pretty face and looked clean, someone people wanted to be with?

You probably don't know about a woman named Sun Bu'er in the Ming dynasty. Her beauty was well known near and far. Later, when she met Wang Chongyang, who taught her the formula of dangong—women's internal qi—she wanted to travel far from home to practice in Luoyang. Naturally, she could stay at home to practice, for she was married to Ma Yu, a wealthy man who could easily support an idling wife. What I meant was, she could have stayed at home. But she could only obtain her enlightenment in a distant place, not close to home. Just think, socializing and entertaining guests alone would consume much of her energy if she stayed. Life is too short and will be over soon if you spend it on this and that trivial pursuit.

She came up with an idea.

One day she poured oil into a pot and waited until it was boiling hot before closing her eyes and leaning over while splashing cold water into the pot. A loud pop later her beauty vanished along with the thick smoke. She was now an ugly woman, and begged for food as she made the long trek to her destination. With an abandoned kiln as her residence, she practiced breathing exercises in the morning and worked on her energy center at night. With bundles of trash over her shoulder and a sooty face, she was dressed in rags, like a real beggar. No one bothered her. Twelve years later, she reached her goal. One day, when someone found her in the kiln, she was mistaken as a demon, so people piled firewood at the kiln entrance with the intention of burning her alive. When they lit the fire, they saw instead a puff of red clouds atop which was a fairy with otherworldly beauty. Now the people realized that she had become an immortal through her self-cultivation. She then went home, where she saw her husband still mired in worldly affairs and unenlightened. She convinced him to disperse their family wealth and devote himself to self-cultivation, which is how he eventually became the Daoist True Master, Ma Danyang.

I'm telling you this story to show you that Wooden Fish Girl was like Sun Bu'er to me in those days.

3

I first saw her in Zhenfan.

They called her Wooden Fish Woman.

Dressed in rags, she acted like a mad woman, banging on her wooden fish and humming a song. No one knew it was a wooden fish song. People usually treat a wise person's chanting as the muttering of the insane.

The wooden fish in her hand earned her the nickname, Wooden Fish Woman. She roamed the streets daily, scratching for food like a hen and lying down to rest like a pig, with no set schedule. No one understood what she was singing, nor did they like it. She could sing with all her heart in the prettiest voice, but all she got in return was some left-over food. She was called a foolish woman in one of the history books.

I often saw vicious women scream at her. I didn't know why, because she never did anything to provoke them. All she did was sing and, when at the height of her songs, did a few dancing moves.

In those days, I thought she had to be doing a kind of impenetrable Vajra Dance, which must have come from sacred India.

You should know that our world doesn't need real images. As the ancients often said, "a load of copper and a load of gold/to test the human hearts in the world/the copper is sold out but the gold remains/people like the fake and shun the real." It's so true. When the fake is in fashion, the real is crowded out. You're right when you say one could wrap copper over gold when the world wants fake copper.

One day Wooden Fish Woman lay on a snowy street moaning, as if afflicted by a serious illness. People crowded around her, and then fled holding their noses. No one was bothered by the pained cries of a beggar woman freezing to death in the snow.

My uncle, Ma Siye, showed up.

He took the howling woman home, where he discovered a round, protruding belly under her tattered clothes. He realized then that she was pregnant.

It truly was extraordinary news in Zhenfan at the time. No one knew who got her pregnant. I was the only one who had sensed something unusual. One night I saw a bright light emanating from the Earth God Temple. I was practicing Cankramati, a kind of walking meditation, that day, though I had yet to learn the real meaning of self-cultivation.

I headed toward the Temple, where I saw the brilliance was coming from Wooden Fish Woman, except that she didn't look the same. I found, on this day, that she was actually quite young and pretty. The supreme bright light was rippling out of her body in waves, but it wasn't until later that I learned she was silently chanting wooden fish songs.

I was curious, so I told my grandma about it. She just laughed and said I slept without covering my butt and had had a dream.

Ma Siye got the best doctor in town to check on Wooden Fish Woman. The doctor cried out in surprise after the examination, "Hei, the foolish woman is indeed pregnant." He continued, "What kind of disgusting man got a mad woman pregnant?" I felt like saying to them,

"You don't know it, but she's actually very pretty."

People's gazes were blocked by the filth she'd intentionally covered her face with.

That was how the baby was born.

When dawn light had barely whitened the eastern sky the next morning, the sound of a crying baby spread throughout the compound. People said she'd given birth to a fleshy ball, but in fact it was the placenta. The midwife was experienced enough to tear it apart, and a white liquid like milk flowed out. I didn't see it with my own eyes, but Grandma later told me that it was milk-like, not blood.

Hu Gala later said it was sweet dew from the land of Buddha, of which a single sip would add a hundred years to one's life. But the midwife poured it all into the drainage ditch outside the village, for it ended up at a spot called Zhuyeze. Decades went by, giving rise to a great many turtles that grew old but did not die. If people hadn't killed them, they might have the longevity of the sun and the moon, I heard.

I was happy to hear the lore despite my awareness that nothing lasts forever. Even if one can enjoy the longevity of the sun and the moon, the earth will reach the end of its life span one day. Sure enough, it didn't take long for Zhuyeze to turn dry. The sweet dew from the land of Buddha failed to nurture the human heart and temper its greed.

No one expected the Wooden Fish Woman to give birth to a plump baby girl with the appearance of good fortune. A fortuneteller said she surely did have a lucky look: broad forehead, with earlobes reaching her shoulders, and infused with signs of wealth. I heard she had the look of Guanyin Bodhisattva.

. . . Don't look so smug, girl. I'm just repeating what they were saying back then. You actually looked quite ordinary to me, average eyes and an unremarkable figure, plus a common mind. But it was the common mind that let you become who you were later.

Sometimes I can see the surface and not the inside, that's for sure. It never occurred to me that someone with the face of a Buddha could harbor a killer's intent.

I often saw Wooden Fish Woman out with her daughter, like a sow with her piglet. The baby rolled in dirt, as a wind blew, doused by the rain and baked by the sun. Her mother was always humming a wooden fish song; she listened and soon she could hum along too.

Wooden Fish Woman remained dimwitted even as her daughter grew up. Naturally, her dim look might have been the result of an indiscriminating mind, right, Mr. Xue Mo?

In the eyes of others, she was a foolish woman. People would often tease her, pretending to take her baby away from her or hiding the baby somewhere. But she seemed unaware, as if nothing had happened. She'd sing her songs idiotically, as though her baby came from a sow. She seemed to think of her child only when her breasts were full and milk oozed out. Sometimes someone would hand a puppy or a piglet to her and she'd nurse it like her daughter. But a new lore was created later about the puppies and piglets she had nursed and how they shunned the evil planes. That's how folklore develops.

The girl grew day by day like that. She was clearly a beauty, even though she had a filthy face just like her mother.

What happened later took place fast and unexpectedly. One day a famous childless salt merchant, hatched an evil scheme. When Wooden Fish Woman was asleep in the Temple, he sent people over to stuff a pillow in her arms and take her daughter away. She didn't notice anything different, and blithely roamed the city with the pillow, singing her wooden fish songs.

Sometime later, the owner of the Hexi Inn offered the salt merchant a large sum to buy the girl. It was an incredible amount, I heard. As the two men were negotiating, they heard someone scream outside. Heaven and earth seemed to be quaking, while the house appeared to be under the assault of a storm, its rafters about to break and the whole structure seemingly in danger of falling apart. The salt merchant went out to check and saw Wooden Fish Woman, her arms around a post in the yard, hitting and kicking at it. When she saw him, she banged her head against the pole, loud as rumbling thunderclaps. Afraid she might die and cause him big trouble, he quickly handed her the girl. But instead of smiling, she burst into tears when she got her daughter back.

She had been banging against a post, but at some point, the salt merchant's face swelled up; it was bruised in blue and red, puffy as a pumpkin about to crack open.

This was another story about Wooden Fish Woman that circulated in Liangzhou.

No one was sure if she and Wooden Fish Girl were one and the same.

Likewise, no one knew if the Ma Zaibo in the gazetteer and I were the same person either.

And don't ask me, because I don't know myself. All I know is there's a Ma Zaibo inside everyone. So just listen and stop questioning whether the story about Wooden Fish Woman is true.

4

I went into Wild Fox Ridge with you also because of a story, one that had been around Liangzhou for a thousand years. It claimed that you could enter a secret realm when you were in Wild Fox Ridge. The key to the realm, Wooden Fish Incantation, could be found in the Hu Family Mill.

You thought I was just like the rest of you making the trip. You didn't know I had been searching.

I grew up searching, searching for my destiny, the reason for my existence.

During those days in Wild Fox Ridge I went out every day to search, looking for the Hu Family Mill. I'd thought it had to be in a grove of desert poplars, but later I discovered it wasn't the spot.

If I could do it my way, I'd have shut myself up to meditate in seclusion and stay until the real Hu Family Mill appeared. According to the ancients, the wooden fish incantation would only show itself when a practitioner had erased all karmic obstacles that stood in the way of enlightenment.

Which was why I kept on searching while continuing to eliminate my karmic obstacles. But don't ask if my search took place in real life or in dreams, for they were the same to me. All you need to know is my continued search.

Nothing in my life was real, only my search. Yes, I was looking for the Hu Family Mill and the wooden fish incantation.

In my life it was like a woman or a song, or more like a secret realm or secret symbol.

I started searching once we were in Wild Fox Ridge. To you it was a desolate place, but to me it was a plentiful, colorful world. Sure, you can say I saw a secret realm; sure, you can call it dark matter or a negative universe. Names and appearances were unimportant; what mattered was my relationship to that world.

I wasn't tired because of the excitement I felt. I walked on and saw a riverbend overgrown with trees. Their leaves were withered, their branches twisted, presenting a scene of passing time. The Hu Family Mill in the lore was in there, where a few isolated houses were said to have been made of desert poplars. They fit in with each other harmoniously to form a whole. Except that one could hear the mill turning late on moonless nights even when no one was in the millhouse. Camel drivers blanched when it was mentioned, and regular drivers wouldn't dare get closer.

Ghosts didn't scare me. To me they were mothers too. Every night, I'd summon tens of thousands of ghosts, thinking about killing myself as an offering to them.

I laid down my things, including food and water once I was in the mill house. The mill employed animal power, for in it was a rope harness for a camel. The rope was made of camel hair, twisted and rolled into a sturdy cord.

First, I cleared my mind and expelled all concerns. I prayed. I prayed for all the Dakinis and Dharmapalas.

For three nights I didn't hear the millstone turn; instead, I heard a woman crying, sad and bleak, filling the trees with sorrow.

Then I saw a camel pulling the millstone; it looked like Brown Lion.

At the time it felt strange to me. I thought Brown Lion had lost his mind.

At the time, I didn't know a pair of a killer's eyes had been following me.

Well, why don't we ask Wooden Fish Girl to continue her story?

You don't have to wait. She'll start when she wants to.

Her story is enthralling, so of course you'll all like it.

Two. Wooden Fish Girl

1

Let me continue with the attack on the police.

As I mentioned before, those who managed to escape fled to Dengmaying Lake, a naturally formed lake in the heart of the desert; snowmelt from the Qilian Mountains traveled through Liangzhou, with some of the water flowing to this spot. Before it dried up, reeds grew on the shore, which was visited by many other animals. It was created by Nature to support living creatures. It had dried up long ago, for when a reservoir was built upstream, no more water flowed downstream.

We practiced our martial arts every morning when we were there.

Dengmaying Lake was a wonderful place. In those days, everywhere we looked we saw water, reeds, and birds. It was a large spot that could accommodate many thousands of people, like sprinkling a handful of sesame seeds in the rocky gobi desert. Sometimes Liu Huzi's mounted troops would come to put on a show of searching for us, but everyone could see they weren't in the mood to crush and kill us all. It wasn't a matter of whether they could do it or not, they simply didn't want to. If we were gone, what excuse would they have to ask for money from the local gentry? I realized that, without knowing it, we were turned into frauds and became an important reason behind the riches accumulated by Hu and his cohort. It might appear as if they'd cooked up a scheme with us to put on a show, in which we were the outlaws and they were the police, and by joining forces that way, we defrauded the gentry and the villagers.

We were successful in our "cooperation." To survive, we often had to ransack the village, forcing them to come and crack down on us now and then. We ran into each other several times and lost one of our own, shot by one of their muskets. But we didn't avenge the death, since we were no match for them. I didn't realize until attacking the police in Liangzhou that we weren't their equals. I don't know why, but all our well-trained men did not know how to fight when confronted by the police. Liangzhou residents did have an inborn fear of officials, like a mouse instinctively frightened of a cat, no matter how big it had grown. Those good fighters who could normally take down a formidable opponent often recalled a lethal move they should have used only after the fight was over.

At the time we all thought we weren't skilled enough. We often practiced club fighting in Dengmaying Lake, something Liangzhou fighters did all the time. Following a set of moves, two men fought back and forth with their clubs, like going through rounds portrayed in ancient books. They walked toward each other to engage in hand-to-hand combat once they were face to face, but if one of them jumped out of a pre-drawn circle, the other one must stop.

When we encountered the police, I found that we were victims of our training. Instead of following rules, they hacked with their swords, fast as the wind, fired at will, and jabbed with their spears. Courage and trained skills were their strong suits. I was convinced that none of them would be our equal if the protocols of club fights were followed. But they weren't, and they were intent on killing us.

We did not know that at the time, and practiced daily at the lake. It was a good way to improve our skills, but virtually useless in real combat.

Later Feiqing returned from Mongolia, bringing with him things we could use. Several Mongolian drivers came with him. No matter what had happened between the Chinese and the Mongolian drivers, they were the only ones who could help us at a critical moment like this. To them there were only friends and foes; they could care less about the Qing court and its officials.

Over the years we spent at Dengmaying, they supplied us with a great deal of food.

We started our training once Feiqing was back with us. In addition to the routine club fights, we also tied sand bags to our legs and ran along a sand ridge. He was good at lifting our morale, enough to drive away the dejection caused by the bloodshed in Liangzhou. We were bathed in loftiness. Besides the regular, physical training, we had spiritual practice, which, like its religious counterpart, was meant to bolster our confidence. Despite the awareness that our opponent was a behemoth, we were not afraid, because we were doing good things for future generations. No one asked what happened after we restored the Ming Dynasty or knew how the Ming was better than the Qing; no one questioned the misdeeds committed by the first emperor of Ming, Zhu Yuanzhang, and his offspring, nor did anyone mention the prosperity of the Kangxi and Qianlong reigns of the Qing. All we talked about were events such as the Yangzhou Massacre, with Qing soldiers slaughtering the Chinese, and vowed to avenge our ancestors. We also frequently offered sacrifices to Yue Fei, because he had fought the Jin, the ancestors of our enemy, the Qing.

A fervent zeal overtook us.

Those were truly passionate days.

2

I returned to Zhenfan.

Ma Zaibo, who was meditating in Su Wu Temple, needed a cook, so Feiqing sent me back there. He wanted Ma to join the Society of Brothers, a goal I shared.

Naturally, I changed back into being a woman. I surprised everyone after washing my dirty face and putting on clothes Feiqing had taken pains to pick out for me. They said they hadn't realized that the beggar woman with a filthy face and piles of rag and junk on her back was actually a pretty girl.

To be honest, I was no beauty. I was only better looking than the average girls back in Lingnan. In the place where sand was all one saw, I did stand out, however. Usually, I wore a head scarf like the local women, which helped shield my original features and block elements harmful to the skin, like the sun and the sandy wind. Women in this area didn't care, so their skin looked like cow dung.

Do you remember the story of Sun Bu'er? I was like her, but not entirely. She ruined her looks by pouring water into hot oil, while I covered my original features with dirt. I usually carried a bundle of rags and tattered cotton. One purpose was to keep warm, but it also served as a prop. Small towns in the West in those days saw many junk-collecting women; the pungent odor emitting from their bodies was their best protection.

For me too.

My brothers-in-arms were naturally stunned when I shed my prop, washed off the dirt, and put on a young woman's clothes. I wasn't Hua Mulan, and I hadn't dressed like a man, but to them I'd always been sexless. Except for Big Mouth, everyone called me Wooden Fish Woman, a term that gave them the wrong impression about me.

So they cried out, "Oh, what a charming girl. Ma Zaibo has no choice but to fall for her now."

I just smiled. I'd been used to their raucous laughter, but now the girl in me came alive. Everything about my earlier self was awakened. I saw my long-concealed self in Feiqing's bronze mirror—he used its reflected light in seal carving. Tears ran down my face as I was reminded of Papa's laugh. When I was little, he used to hold me over his head and toss me into the air, calling out "Wooden Fish Girl." He continued to use the nickname after I grew up, as if it was his incantation of happiness. Warm currents flowed through my heart and I couldn't stop sobbing.

Feiqing misunderstood the reason behind my tears.

"I know it's hard on you, so you don't have to go if you don't want to."

"He's right. We don't want to force you," Big Mouth said.

He'd been in a funk since we'd decided for me to go, and wore a long face all the time. Before we came out here, his father got wind of us and his wife's brothers went to raise a racket at his parents' house. They told him to behave by threatening to trade a lamb's pelt for an old sheepskin. That was a local saying that meant a young life for an old one. He told me he'd gotten lashed by his father's whip. He hadn't gone back once since coming to Dengmaying Lake. He was always saying he'd marry me after we overthrew the Qing government. He didn't want me to go care for Ma Zaibo.

"My tears have nothing to do with this. I was just reminded of my Papa," I said as I dried my tears.

Feiqing knew all about my family, so he let out a long sigh without saying anything.

Papa must have been reduced to a pile of bones by now, I said to myself. Did he know how much his daughter suffered in seeking revenge? Maybe it was better he didn't. He'd feel terrible if he was able to see what was happening. On second thought, I knew he'd be pleased that I remembered them and never gave up on avenging their deaths.

"I'm off now," I said.

Big Mouth walked me out of Dengmaying Lake.

3

Mount Su Wu couldn't be considered a real mountain. After seeing so many mountain ranges, I saw it as an ordinary hill.

Su Wu, in the Han Dynasty story, had herded sheep here. To preserve his "integrity," he carried a staff, its fur worn off, as the symbol for his status of emissary of the Han court. He had tended sheep for over a decade, so touching the locals that they built a temple for him. It was not big, with only a few Daoist monks. A Daoist nun had cooked for them before she left for Mount Wudang, which was why Hu Gala wanted another cook. Feiqing thought it was a great opportunity and sent me over. Later I learned that Hu was also a member.

Tall and rotund, Hu wore a Daoist cap and a Confucian gown—a common garb for a Confucian scholar in the area—and a Buddhist monk's shoes. He was always reading books on divination. He told me he felt a skylight open in someone's fate when he read the person's fortune. From the skylight, he could see everything about the person. He told me about this later, though; when I first got there, he only wanted me to cook. I didn't know much about local cuisine so I made a few Hakka dishes, which, to my delight, pleased him enormously. Later, even Ma Zaibo and others praised my cooking. Local food wasn't refined, for they cooked everything in one big pot. Hakka dishes were delicious, but hard to cook well. Before I came, Feiqing told me the best way to win a man's heart was through his stomach. That I believed. Papa had married Mama because he was taken by her cooking, and I had learned most of her dishes.

Ma Zaibo was chanting in a small house. I had no idea what he was reciting, but his chants often buzzed through the latticed window. It was pleasing to my ears. I asked Hu Gala about it but Hu didn't know either. Later I learned that it wasn't a sutra, but a kind of tantric ritual practice.

Hu told me that Ma was a lama incarnate, which had been confirmed by several Mongolian lamas. They had gone looking for him when he was a little boy and immediately identified him as the incarnate of a Living Buddha from their temple. Many people believed the lamas, but not Lü Erye, who was skeptical about deities and Buddhas, as he believed in things he could see and touch. He was adamant about not letting the lamas leave with his son, to the extent that he'd appealed to government's help. He offered sufficient reasons by claiming that the Mongolian lamas had revenge in mind. Over the years of conflict between the Chinese and the Mongolians, the Ma family had made more contributions than anyone, with either manpower or financial assistance. He asserted that the Mongolians wanted to take his son away and find a way to kill him. Lü Erye sounded so convincing that the government sent soldiers to drive the lamas back to Mongolia.

From here, Mongolia can be reached by following the yellow sand and going east for about eighty *li*. In the Ming dynasty, Mongolian cavalry swept down and took off with their loot, including Chinese and their sheep. The Chinese were sent to work or tend sheep and the sheep were turned into food. Sometimes the Ma family raised an army to pillage the Mongolian's salt lakes and engaged in a major battle if they encountered each other. When their heads were injured, they wrapped straw around them and continued to fight, as the saying goes. That's been going on for over a hundred years.

Ma Zaibo did not become a Living Buddha in a Mongolian temple, but he had a natural preference for peace and quiet and a plan to become a monk. Lü Erye later agreed to let him practice meditation, with the condition that he remain a secular monk. To ensure that his son would not change his mind, Lü Erye went to Labrang Monastery in southern Gansu and invited a Living Buddha to initiate Ma Zaibo, so he could be a secular monk at home. The Living Buddha told Ma that he had to take a consort when he reached a certain level of realization; since once he became a monk, he could not have actual contact with women. But the Living Buddha said that Ma's karma determined that he must have a physical consort or he would not reach the desired state. In Tantric Buddhism, the

Guru reigned supreme, so Ma had to give up being a monk in a temple. To maintain peace and quiet, he'd asked Hu Gala to find him a house. The Ma family was one of the principle donors to the Su Wu Temple, and they also paid the temple's yearly expenses. Naturally, a small favor like that was carried out swiftly and diligently.

Hu Gala had told me all about this. He seemed lonely, maybe because there weren't enough worshippers at the Temple. When I arrived, he couldn't stop talking, like pouring walnuts out of a clay jar. He wanted to also teach me the kālacakra calendar, saying it was difficult to learn, but oddly it took me no time to get into it. Hu said I must have learned it in my previous life. I didn't care about previous life though; I was attracted to the kālacakra. Once I started, I felt a hole open up between heaven and earth, and I could see many of Nature's secrets through it.

4

I saw Ma Zaibo only at lunchtime.

He was tall, with a slender build, giving the impression of a graceful tree in the wind. A reticent man, he rarely looked people in the eye, but always wore a tranquil or indifferent expression. I believed the Mongolian lamas when I laid eyes on him; he had to be an incarnate. Something hard to describe oozed from him inside, which softened my heart. I had to tell myself again and again, He's an enemy. My enemy. He's Lü Erye's favorite son. I felt my hatred grow a little after repeatedly reminding myself. It was motivated hatred; that is, I thought I had to hate, so I did.

Ma didn't look at me or Hu Gala. In fact, I never saw him look at anyone. Sometimes I thought he was looking at me, but when I examined his eyes, I'd see he was still in his own world. His eyes were two deep lakes, unfathomable, showing no ripples. I felt I shouldn't be scheming against him when I saw those eyes.

I used to recite something I made up every morning when I got out of bed. I'd recorded the fire in the format of a wooden fish song and said the same thing to each one in my family, naturally all about revenge. I imagined the fire that had killed them as I recited. I did it at least twenty-one times a day, which enabled me to remind myself of the reason for my existence at my earliest waking moment. After coming to the Su Wu Temple, I increased the reciting time to make it a hundred and eight times daily, which took an hour. Besides cooking the meals, I spent the rest of the day practicing at an empty spot behind the temple. I was a superb club fighter by then, and I could hit any fly or bee I chose, but I never cut corners on practice. Back in Liangzhou, when we fought the police, I realized that I'd forgotten my martial skills and couldn't muster a shred of will to fight as the mounted troops ran at me like a whirlwind. I might have been a highly accomplished martial artist, but inside me was the heart of frail girl that pounded when I saw those ruthless men. I couldn't bring myself to fight them, even though I knew I only had to raise my club to douse their "lights"—the term for eyes among the brothers in the Society.

What I worked on at Mount Su Wu was the will to fight. I wanted to breed evil thoughts to make myself as ruthless as the evil ones, but the kindness in wooden fish songs rubbed off on me and constantly lifted me out of the vile realm. Think about it. I knew very well that everything was over and that the dead were long gone. They suffered but just briefly before they died and entered into oblivion. I even believed that my parents were truly no longer aware of anything because Papa would have appeared in my dream if he could really see me. He hadn't made an appearance since I came to Liangzhou. There were times when I didn't believe in any gods or deities. I often placed them before the fire that killed my family and interrogated them, which many people had done before. For instance, why didn't they save my family when the evil ones were burning them alive? If they could have but didn't, then the deity was evil too and not worth my belief in him. If they'd wanted but couldn't, then they were powerless and not worth my belief either. If they didn't know about what was happening to my family, then they were ignorant and less deserving of my belief. I found it hard to believe in them wholeheartedly, after forming such questions.

Papa had believed in deities, but his belief did not change his fate of burning death.

I wanted to be wicked beyond redemption myself, and I didn't think it would be that hard, if not for the influence of the wooden fish songs over recent decades. The songs that had been etched on my heart fought me all the time. A lot of them contained Daoist ideas such as "Han Xiangzi Learning the Dao," "Lin Yingnü Burning Incense," some with Buddhist teachings such as "Guanyin's Ten Advices," some with traditional culture, such as "Flower Notes." They had long been a part of me and no matter how much I chanted about revenge, the compassion planted years ago could not be wiped out.

At the moment I first saw Ma Zaibo, I found welling up inside me a tenderness and warmth I hadn't known for a very long time. His solitude from living alone pierced my heart. And that night what appeared in my mind was his face, one that brimmed with an indescribable loneliness.

What puzzled me most was his face entering my dream.

He was looking at me with eyes, bright, gentle, and full of compassion, as if he had a lot to say to me, but he didn't say a word. His gaze poured into my heart like moonlight, giving me a totally new sensation.

I slowly realized that those eyes were actually on my Papa's face.

I awoke to find my face wet with tears.

5

I woke up early the next morning. The wind howled, but I was still immersed in my dream world. I did not want to go back to sleep, but didn't feel like getting up either. I found no desire to recite the words of revenge. At a moment like that, any other action would destroy the tender beauty. I'd turned coarse since my arrival in Liangzhou. I used to be tender and delicate. I could feel the character's heart when I sang wooden fish songs, and their happiness or sorrow could make me sing or weep. My audience would cry or laugh, feel happy or sad, from the way I felt myself. Gentle feelings constantly billowed in my heart, which was perhaps why I could understand the pain deep inside Papa's soul.

Later I carried a big load on my back and my heart was shrouded in layers. I rarely thought of anything but revenge and, as time went on, my heart grew numb. Maybe a lot was tossed out of my heart when I shed the bundle of rags, and maybe a great deal was cleansed inside when I washed off the dirt. The tender heart of a young woman was bare.

Now I had trouble telling whether it was Ma Zaibo or Papa who had appeared in my dream.

I felt uneasy when I recalled my idea of getting Ma Zaibo to rebel so his family could be executed. I repulsed myself, but soon the scene of the fire made an appearance in my head, and my apprehension vanished, like frost evaporating in a fire.

It was still dark, but I got up without lighting the mutton tallow lamp as I walked out. The room, still well lit, came into view, and I faintly heard his resonant baritone voice. Everything else was still dark. The wind was harsh, the stars many. But the wind was too chilly and left a pinpricking sensation on my face. The darkness that pressed in on me had a noticeable texture, and I felt myself shrinking to a non-existence from the pressure. The fear of being extinguished surged up, something I'd never felt before. I discovered that freedom in the heart was more often than not determined by freedom of the body. You cannot feel free if your body is wrapped in layers of garbage. My heart felt full in the past, whether I was lodging at the Earth God Temple or at Dengmaying Lake. Darkness never felt oppressive, and I was neither afraid nor sensed my own annihilation. The new sensation made me anxious.

Light was spreading out of the window in rings—soft, sweet, somewhat dizzying. It was odd. The pressure was still there, but now I felt as if I'd taken a painkiller and the pain was slowly dissipating. Something else was rising to drown out the pressure and the fear of annihilation.

I stood by the door for a long time to let my heart soar in the peacefulness created by the light. For a while I didn't even hear the wind.

I didn't practice my martial moves that morning, I had no desire to. It had been a necessity every morning to keep me from feeling I'd let Papa down if I missed even one day. I could not bear the thought that our enemy was still alive and well; I could not abide knowing we were living in the same universe. But on my first morning at the Su Wu Temple, I skipped my practice and my revenge mantra. I sensed a strange transformation taking place, and that frightened me.

I made breakfast, a simple meal around here, usually potato millet soup. I could make it in an hour by filling a pot half full with water, millet, and several potatoes, then letting it boil before adding flour slurry. Soaking steamed bread in it constituted breakfast for the people at the Temple.

Ma did not show. Hu Gala said he hadn't eaten breakfast or dinner. Lunch was Ma's only meal for the day.

No wonder he's so slender, I said to myself. A tender feeling rose up inside me.

Then I was abruptly reminded that he was Lü Erye's flesh and blood. How could someone like Lü Erye give birth to a son like Ma Zaibo? A true mystery.

The tender feeling in my heart disappeared when I was reminded of his father.

6

I continued practicing my revenge ritual as before. Every morning, I gnashed my teeth as I chanted the mantra I'd kept at all these years. Ma Zaibo and I got up at about the same time. Light came up in his room around the fourth watch. Oddly, that's around the time I woke up too. I'd never gotten up that early before. Since coming to Mount Su Wu I'd experienced an unusual lightness. I was taken by the place, because it was away from the noisy Dengmaying Lake, and also because I bathed before I arrived.

But my teeth-gnashing recitation brought me fewer feelings of hatred than before. In earlier times, I'd wept till my face was wet from tears when I recited; now the visceral hate was fading. I did not want that to happen; I wanted the hate to remain in my heart. Once it was gone, I would lose any reason to stay in this bleak, desolate place and as a result, any reason to live. But I couldn't help it. Su Wu Temple had an unusual magnetic field that had an almost corrupting influence.

The most obvious change took place at noon the day I awoke up from my dream. Ma Zaibo walked out of his little room, languidly, and came to the guest hall with an indifferent expression. Still not looking at anyone, he quietly finished the food I offered him. He ate slowly, somewhat absent-mindedly and yet seemingly savoring the food. I'd made a point of cooking several Hakka dishes that day. I watched him and his reactions; he did not seem to have noticed anything different. Hu Gala was the one who heaped praise on my cooking, after which Ma finally tasted the food with care. He looked at me, smiled faintly, and nodded.

"Newly arrived?" he asked.

"Yes. The Daoist nun went to Mount Wudang," Hu Gala offered. "Try her food. We'll keep her if you like it."

"It's good. Very good," Ma said. Then he nodded at me with another smile before walking out.

His smile was penetrating, I found, and my heart softened at once. I quickly cleared the table, quickly did the dishes, quickly put things away, and hurried back to my little room.

I fell onto the *kang*, my hand over my chest, and took deep breaths to drive away the weakening sensation. But I had trouble doing what I wanted, which for me was a first. A gale was howling outside the window. This being a windy area, the wind blew from spring to winter. Sitting high and unprotected, Mount Su Wu rarely saw a windless day.

Ma Zaibo had a strange power; I couldn't say what it was, but I could feel it. Your heart softened despite itself when you were near him. That was it.

Over the next month I only saw him at noon. He arrived in his usual languid manner, finished his lunch quietly, and returned to his little room unhurriedly. Sometimes I heard him chanting in his sonorous voice, but mostly there was only silence. Yet I felt a power to soften my heart in that silence.

Hu Gala told me a few things about the Ma family. He said Ma Zaibo's religious practice frightened Lü Erye most—he called him Ma Erye, of course. He was afraid that his son would leave for Mongolia to be a Living Buddha in that temple without telling him. Lü Erye hoped Hu would come up with something to distract his son; train him in martial arts, teach him divination, instruct him in the kālacakra or make him fall in love. Anything, as long as Hu could take his son out of the religious frame of mind. Lü Erye said being in that frame was like smoking opium, and he would become more addicted as he went along. Lü Erye even wished his son would go to brothels and have some experience with women; he would find his son a wife to produce offspring. But Ma Zaibo wasn't interested in any of these.

He did show some interest in martial arts at first and learned how to use a lasso pole and some floor boxing moves. Soon he was pretty good at both. Then he was taken by divination and studied diligently for a while. Being exceptionally smart, soon he was able to predict someone's lifespan and fortune. But then he realized that certain things remained the same whether he could divine them or not; what was important, he learned, was change. He lost interest in divination, for he wanted to learn how to change fate, not divine it.

According to Hu Gala, Lü Erye would rather his son whore his life away than become a monk. At least the former would give him sons and grandsons; Lü Erye's family line would be severed if his son became a monk. "Can you imagine a father like that?" Hu asked. "As if religious practitioners like us are worse than whoring men."

The drivers all laughed, their laughter spreading out like waves.

Suddenly I spot several new faces, and it dawns on me that I've forgotten to create a barrier. Only those I invited could come in if I'd set up a barrier with the traditional ritual. But I don't mind them coming to listen so long as they don't interrupt the narration. I do feel, however, denser yin around me. My bones seem frozen, whether because there are too many specters or because it's simply too cold.

I build a fire once the interview is over. Flames from the fire lick the night sky, and I'm no longer so cold. One depends on fire when spending time alone in the desert, not merely for physical needs, but also for psychological reasons. I've brought a dog as a companion. But during the interviews, the specters are wary of something about the dog. I'm not sure if it's a murderous aura or just its smell. Something about the biological field changes when the dog is present—ah, yes, the interview site seems like a strange field, where all sorts of information flow and interflow in it. It feels different when the dog comes, which is why I don't bring it with me. When I'm done and go back to the camp site, the dog wags its tail and runs up to me happily, warming my heart.

Without knowing it, I also begin to change after conducting enough interviews. I don't know where it happens, but I can sense the change. I have a friend who's a policeman. He kept a little demon, and it helped him solve cases, but as time went by people started to notice a strong yin on his face. It could happen to me too, with the kind of interviews I'm conducting. Both what I think about in the day and hear at night are other-worldly, which may permeate me with the aura of yin after I'm around too long. Sometimes when I get near the yellow camel, he spits at me the way he did when he sensed a ghost. To camel drivers, the animal is being provocative. According to Liangzhou custom, spitting at someone is the greatest insult, but I decide to ignore the yellow camel. He's just an animal, and I can't let his attitude bother me, though I do feel a hint of annoyance wafting inside me like strands of hair.

Another change lies in my ability to see their faces clearly—except for Killer, that is. My religious practice has enabled me to see things invisible to others ever since I was little. Now that I'm older I can, whenever I want, enter a meditative state and see what I want to see. During this evening's interview, I see a lot from the narrator's memory, but then the narrator slowly appears before me. I can see him not from others' recollection; I do see him clearly.

Do you think it's just an illusion?

One thing is sure, though. I see a wolf and it's real. When I'm downwind, I can detect its smell, a stench unique to carnivores.

I have a dog, so I'm not afraid the wolf will sneak up on me. My dog is a Tibetan mastiff, raised by the Tibetan elder Aka. It killed several wolves *back in the mountains, so the wolf won't dare make a move with the dog around. I can see the wolf, but the dog is indifferent to its presence, which is strange. Maybe the dog doesn't consider the wolf a worthy opponent. It has not barked at the wolf, not once.*

Fifteenth Session
Wooden Fish Girl Relates Her Affair

1

A month went by before Ma Zaibo noticed me. It was the fifteenth of the month, when many visitors came to burn incense. A blind storyteller played his three-string zither and sang a segment of a Liangzhou tale. I saw Ma Zaibo come out of his room, a rare occurrence. He never came out except to eat or relieve himself.

Worshippers crowded around the storyteller to hear him sing "Lü Dongbin Buying Medicine," an interesting piece. I'd heard it before, but there were far more interesting tales in wooden fish songs. The sound of the zither rekindled a myriad of emotions, so when the storyteller took a break, I picked up his instrument and sang a wooden fish song.

I remembered being filled with artistic emotions that day, and my voice was unusually good, after being well-rested in the Temple. I sang, in Liangzhou dialect, "Looking for Luan in the Nunnery," a highly literary piece in the wooden fish song repertoire. The story was about Scholar Li from Baima Township who had a loving relationship with his new wife, Luan. Concerned that he wouldn't do well in the exam for officialdom, his parents forced him to study away from home. After his departure, his mother bullied his wife to the point that Luan left home to become a nun. When he returned after failing the exam, he was greeted by an empty room. He was heartbroken. His parents forced him to remarry, but he missed his wife so much he went looking for her. Finally, he found the nunnery and visited her at night. They poured their hearts out when they met:

> *The clouds are like gauzy silk, the evening rain has stopped.*
> *Like Brahmā's palace, the moon spreads its soft light.*
> *In the clear blue sky, a wild goose cries out,*
> *And the Big Dipper shines brightly above.*
> *Dew sprinkled on the meditation room wetting the flowers inside.*
> *A wind blows over the temple yard, gently rustling the bamboo.*
> *We hear crickets chirping beneath the tree.*
> *While above a monkey hangs from a high branch.*
> *Flowers in full bloom, their petals seem to be everywhere.*
> *The crisp sound of a sutra bell rings loud and clear.*
> *Strolling through the pine gate under the moon, we see a crane's shadow.*
> *At the pond we stop to listen to sutra chanting as fish swim in the water.*

The song should have been sung in the Lingnan dialect, but it flowed off my tongue in the local dialect. Odd but somehow natural. There were few women storytellers in Liangzhou, so temple visitors swarmed over the moment they heard my voice. I was sure no one would know I was the same beggar woman who had roamed their streets for several years.

> *Silently chanting lines from a sutra, I saw flowers smile.*
> *When the Dharma was fully explained, even rocks nodded.*

People say that Buddhist allegories can free one from suffering,
Why could they not help me shed the sorrow in my heart?
I recall the very day we got married,
There was an autumn moon in Yangcheng.
I planted yellow flowers in a secret spot to bring us laughter,
But drank a pot of green tea to forget my worries.

I noticed a strange glint in Ma Zaibo's eyes, which convinced me that he understood my song. His expression changed as the words flowed. I was in character as I sang until my face was tear-streaked. I often cried over other people's stories. Then again, the story seemed to be about me too. I hadn't fared any better than the wife in the song. She at least had a nunnery for her meditation. What did I have? Only hatred. And it was hatred that gave me a reason to live, though now I felt that even it was leaving me. My heart felt empty. Suddenly I understood the wife completely.

I saw tears on Ma Zaibo's face too, though he did not seem to realize it. Still not looking at me, he just wept quietly. Several local women were also crying, and I knew that their fate was far worse than Luan's. She could retreat to a nunnery, where could they go?

Total silence greeted the end of my wooden fish song. Ma Zaibo dried his tears and looked at me. He was obviously moved. So was Hu Gala, who said, "That's an odd piece. I never heard it before."

I smiled and said, "It's not a Liangzhou story. It's a wooden fish song."

"What's a wooden fish song?" he asked. After I explained it to him, he asked me how many I knew.

"A short one like this, several hundred. And a few dozen longer pieces." He then asked if I could sing at temple fairs in the future.

That was how I came to sing wooden fish songs at the Su Wu Temple.

According to local custom, the residents came to offer incense on the first and fifteenth of every month, and on important dates such as the eighth day of the fourth month, the day Guanyin obtained enlightenment. These were days devoted to deities. Hoping to attract more worshippers with my singing, Hu Gala was so enthusiastic he offered to pay me handsomely. I did not turn him down, since the society of brothers at Dengmaying Lake could use some money.

I sang twice a month and drew a large crowd each time. The temple was packed when I did, and I was rumored to be a beauty. As I said earlier, there were not many women storytellers in Liangzhou, and those few were mostly blind. Having a young woman with nice features sing and play a zither was irresistible. Liangzhou had a well-established storytelling tradition, so many people thought I was singing their local tales when I performed wooden fish songs in their dialect. There were differences, to be sure. I soon learned to sing their tales, which further reinforced their impression that wooden fish songs were the same as their own.

I could not sing many songs in a day, and the longer songs required several days to sing from start to finish. Someone suggested to Hu Gala that they ask the worshippers to chip in and raise my pay for me to sing longer songs, if my voice permitted. And that was how I came to perform many songs over the next few months.

Ma Zaibo would bring over a small stool to sit near me when I sang. He did not look at me at first, but later he gazed at my mouth. His eyes appeared calm, but I could see his emotions, noticing how they varied from song to song.

"These are good. Are they written down?" he asked one day when I laid down the zither.

"They used to be. But they were burned in a fire," I said.

"What a shame." He sighed and frowned a long time before asking,

"Can you help me write down the lyrics?"

"There are so many, like filling an ocean. Not just a few lines, you know." I laughed.

"I can write them down as long as I set my mind to it, no matter how many there are," he said. "It would be a shame if they're forgotten. They are a treasure."

"Sure, Young Master." Hu Gala smiled. "You can do it if you're interested. I heard that wooden fish songs teach people to do good, so you'll be doing a good deed by writing them down."

"You're not her. You want to do it, but we're not sure if she'll agree." Ma was smiling.

"You're right, of course. A lot of people would rather their candles grow moldy than let others light them." Hu added, "But Wooden Fish Girl isn't like that."

People started calling me Wooden Fish Girl once I started singing at the Temple. Fate is fascinating. No one had called me that for several years, and now, without meaning to, I got it back.

When I arrived at Zhenfan, I did not have a zither, so I banged a wooden fish to the beat of the songs, which earned me the moniker, Wooden Fish Woman. What a fluke.

Big Mouth found me a used zither, but people continued to call me Wooden Fish Woman.

They didn't know, however, that the "Girl" and the "Woman" were one.

"I have the time, so you can write them down while I can sing for you, if neither of you minds the trouble."

"I don't have time for that," Hu said with a laugh.

"I do," Ma said.

2

Finally, I understood the dream and why Ma Zaibo turned into Papa in it. It was no ordinary dream, I told myself. There had to be something unusual about it.

I went into his room the next day. It was neat and clean, with piles of thread-bound books. A piece of felt was laid atop a large desk by the window, which I surmised was where he practiced his calligraphy. On the desk were some sutras he'd copied. A whiff of ink rushed to my nose, an odor I hadn't smelled for a long time and which brought back memories. A warm current rose up inside as I thought of Papa. He would never have imagined his daughter in such a state. I recalled back then that a lifetime of happiness could be had by owning a study like this, to be next to Papa, living quietly in my own world. It was a modest desire, but the club of fate struck down and smashed it all for me.

The warm current rushed up uncontrollably and turned into tears. Ma Zaibo panicked when he saw me crying. "It's all right if you don't want to do it. I won't force you," he said.

"I'm happy to do it. I was thinking about my Papa. He loved books, just like you." I dried my tears and said with a smile.

"Can you tell me about him?"

I took a deep breath. *I'll tell you one day*, I replied silently. *I'll tell you how your family has my family's blood on your hands.* The warm current disappeared and my heart turned cold.

I recited the song lyrics mechanically for him to copy in neat, printed characters. The people around here enjoyed writing with a brush. It was customary in Liangzhou. Many families had installed on the gate a saying molded in clay, "A Farming and Learning Family," and a lot of their youngsters practiced writing on square bricks in red clay. Ma was a superb calligrapher, though; he wrote well and fast, and rarely had to ask for clarification. He had no trouble understanding the highly literary songs, except to confirm some of the local expressions from the south. I thought he might have known these songs in his previous life. For a brief instant some time later, I even thought that Papa's soul had taken up residence in Ma's body.

He did his meditative work in the morning and copied the songs in the afternoon. When he was meditating, I went out back to work on my martial skills for at least two hours a day. I'd lost my earlier fervor and passion with the practice. I tried my best to stay focused, and yet something was gone from my heart. It was like a lit candle burning without a flame.

Ma took a short break after lunch before we started transcribing. I discovered that I'd been eagerly awaiting two moments daily: one at noon when we had lunch and two, the afternoon when I came to his house to recite the wooden fish songs for him. The anticipation later turned into longing and terrified me.

It took us more than a month to finish "Story of the Flower Missive" and "History of the Two Lotus Flowers," two of the most representative songs in the tradition and Papa's favorites. What I memorized was no longer the traditional versions, for they were infused with Papa's body and soul; you could even call them his re-creations. Ma could not stop praising them when I read him the pearls of beauty. "This is truly great poetry," he said. He did not know that a German poet name Goethe had once said the same thing.

We followed up with more songs. I recited those considered the best by Papa; I was in no hurry to narrate others that might have been preserved in book form. On the other hand, I wondered if those books I'd seen in Lingnan had survived the wars. I wanted to do my best to help Ma Zaibo write down the lyrics. Luckily, I'd been reciting them silently to distract myself from loneliness when I was staying at the Earth

God Temple, and before that in the desert. It took more than a month to chant them all. At first, I did it every three months and then switched to once every six months. When I recited them this time, I noticed that I'd committed every word to memory, and that I finally understood what had motivated Papa to ask me to memorize them all. I'd wondered why I needed to remember the words when there were books, but now I could see that he might have had a premonition about the books meeting a terrible end.

It was a delight to recite, so that he could write them down. Ma Zaibo had an airy quality, a noticeable trait that set him apart from the locals. His pen moved effortlessly and smoothly. At first, he had to stop now and then to ask about an expression, but later he wrote everything down with no further need for my explanation. The only sounds in the room were my voice and the rustling sound of his paper. On more than one occasion I forgot where I was, even who I was and what I'd gone through in life. Until one day someone brought a message from Big Mouth, who asked me to meet him at a certain place in the city. I was annoyed by the message and sensed that Big Mouth almost felt like a stranger to me. For the first time since we met, I failed to make the appointment. Moreover, I had a strange feeling about my relationship with Big Mouth, which now seemed wrong, and that it had soiled my body.

I didn't know what was happening to me.

I even wished I hadn't met Big Mouth.

But then it occurred to me that I wouldn't have come here if I hadn't met him; nor would I have come to this small room to recite the songs—don't laugh. At a time like this, I don't feel the need to lie. I have to say what I think needs to be said; if I don't, so much would disappear and what we did would vanish like dissipating smoke.

I am lucky to have met you, so I have to tell you everything. It's what I experienced during a period of my life. I want to bring it up even though

I know that some will be hurt and some will criticize me.
I don't even want to be called a Dakini anymore.
I just want to be a woman.
What are you laughing at?

3

Don't ask me if we had a relationship.
We did.
You want to know what kind?
All kinds.

Concrete changes occurred shortly after a talk Hu Gala had with Ma Zaibo. I didn't know what Hu said to Ma, but I wondered if Hu had deified me by calling me a Dakini. It must be. Hu turning me into a deity had led later generations to share the same idea.

Hu, adept in the kālacakra, was always reading books about it. When I first went to the Temple, I had nothing to read, so I flipped through his books. I actually understood a little after a while, which greatly surprised Hu. He then gave me some pointers now and then.

He enjoyed respect and prestige in the area, a kind of religious authority. When he said I was a Dakini, I became one in many people's eyes. I had a great voice, and I knew so many wooden fish songs that were filled with exhortations to do good. Naturally, they believed Hu Gala when he called me a Dakini.

Including Ma Zaibo. He looked at me with awe.

But I was sure that Hu Gala had said something else, probably about yuganaddha, the dual cultivation of Tibetan Buddhism. One day Ma Zaibo brought it up.

"Would it speed up the attainment by being close to a Dakini?"

"What's a Dakini? And what do you mean by attainment?"

I honestly didn't know what they were, for I had yet to know about Tantric Buddhism at the time. I'd acquired some ideas about Buddhism from the wooden fish songs, but those were just ideas. I was unaware of the contents privy only to those who were at the core of Tantric Buddhism. I wanted to ask Hu Gala, but couldn't bring myself to do it.

Hu Gala talked about it on his own. Once when he was explaining the kālacakra to me, he mentioned the Dharma of Kālacakra, which touched upon dual cultivation.

"The time has come," he said. "You haven't forgotten what Feiqing wanted you to do, have you?"

I was startled. I felt the same thing as when I was told about Big Mouth's request to meet.

All of a sudden, I didn't want to do anything. I just wanted to stay in one place and live peacefully. It would be best if he was there with me. We'd copy the lyrics together and I'd sing for him alone. I'd cry if I felt like it and laugh at will.

I was stunned to realize that I'd fallen in love with him.

How terrifying.

I was preoccupied even when I was cooking. I was wracked by regret over what I'd done with Big Mouth. I'd have pursued Ma if I didn't feel unworthy because of what had happened between Big Mouth and me. Yes. That was terrifying.

But my heart had a mind of its own despite my fears; it was always thinking about him. My ears strayed from me as well, always listening for movement in his room. Every dish I made was meant to earn a smile and praise from him. Hu Gala and Ma Zaibo enjoyed the Hakka dishes that the locals considered strange. Sometimes Hu invited members of the local gentry to try them out. I was worried that Lü Erye would join them, but I heard he hadn't recovered from his stroke and still had no use of half of his body.

You may sense changes in me from what I just said: I used to long to be near Lü Erye, so I could deal him the fatal blow. I'd tried everything, but never found a way. Now I was actually concerned that he might show up. Why? I didn't want him to recognize me. Why would that be a problem? Because I didn't want him to disrupt my current life.

My heart betrayed me completely.

It was truly terrifying.

One day, when I went to his room, Ma Zaibo had just washed his hair. His robe was only partly buttoned when he opened the door. I saw his bare chest. As my eyes glanced at the fair skin, I had a sudden desire to kiss his chest. My face burned, I was sure it was bright red. He noticed my awkward reactions and quickly buttoned his robe. We were both flustered, as if we'd done something already. I'd never felt this way before; Big Mouth and I had done it many times, but each time it felt like going through a process. We did it because we thought we ought to, and it felt insipid. I could see Big Mouth's naked body without feeling the sensation I had when I glanced at Ma's chest—don't be upset with me about what I just revealed. It's the truth. This could be what people called predestined connection.

Nothing really happened until later that night. Hu Gala, who was invariably asked by local families to conduct funeral rites, went out and left the two of us at the temple alone. Ma was in high spirits and wanted to copy more, so I went to his room in the evening. We were writing down affairs between a young man and woman, with charming lyrics that were hard to read out loud.

"Let's not write these down," I said to him.

"Don't leave or keep anything based on your personal taste. If you cut out what you don't like, and then someone else does the same, nothing good will be left a few generations later."

"Fine," I said and began to read the words to him. We were acting prim and proper at first as we went along, but slowly the ambience in the room changed.

Don't ask me who broke the deadlock. I tell you, there was no deadlock. How could there be? We were like two boiling pots. For some reason our hands touched and the two sweaty palms grabbed at each other eagerly, followed by our eager lips searching for each other.

We rolled onto the *kang*. I remember it was heated that day and the room was cozy and warm. The wind howled outside. It was always windy at night back then. We rolled into each other's arms, our clothes gone. I don't know who took off whose clothes, but quickly our naked bodies were intertwined.

He didn't know what to do next. I had to guide him. I felt myself falling into the lava of happiness; it surged and roiled and my heart felt like a fallen leaf. I cried out despite myself when he finally entered me.

Don't laugh.

Seriously, it was one of the most indelible memories of my life. I'd never had such incredible, amazing sex before. It didn't last long though, because he was a virgin and he was done quickly. But the sublime instant surpassed countless others because of love.

"Are you really a Dakini?" he whispered as he slid off me.

"More than a Dakini," I said with a smile.

4

After that, we put on the same show frequently.

We were in each other's arms when I walked in every afternoon; we'd finish the reserved show before moving onto the songs.

In the beginning he tried to explain away our action through dual cultivation. He followed the kind of meditation mentioned in a book that taught how to delay ejaculation, which gave us enough time to try different methods. We imitated the bodies depicted in thangkas and added moves to the simple process. He improved his skill and was often successful in holding back. What I meant by successful was based on when I had my orgasm. When Hu Gala went out for funeral rites and no one came to the Temple, we'd spend all afternoon on the dual cultivation he mentioned. Even when he wasn't careful enough and failed, he would follow the instruction to lick the "bindu." He looked at ease illustrating our love in this quasi-religious fashion.

But soon everything started to change in my eyes. He was enthralled by reaching the apogee of happiness with me. He was captivated by my cries and I was by his. We became one, incomparably blissful, when we were both intoxicated by our union at that moment.

I often rued what I had done with Big Mouth. In those days, I'd thought he was the one for me, but now I realized he wasn't. I was unhappy about that and sometimes even in agony. Ma didn't know my past but I knew it would come, like a body exposed after a snow melt. Too many people knew about me and Big Mouth, including Hu Gala; they even knew I'd had a baby girl by him. The reality was an unpassable iron threshold before Ma and me. I'd like to marry him, if I hadn't had a relationship with Big Mouth, and if he weren't Lü Erye's son.

What a terrible turn of events, that Lü Erye could have raised a son like that. Ma Zaibo was kindest person ever; he was also simple, without a shred of bad intentions and a heart as clear as crystal. I couldn't have a single bad thought when I was with him. Even if I intentionally called up the bad thoughts I should have, they disappeared as quickly as fleeting dark clouds.

I didn't know how long we could stay that way. I started wishing for eternity, as I felt I couldn't live without him. If he were gone from my life, everything would lose meaning for me. See how terrible I was. Revenge had been the reason for my existence, and now it was love. I was often remorseful, reproaching myself for falling in love with my enemy's son. I knew it would hurt Papa a great deal if he could see me, and yet I would still fall for Ma if I had to choose.

During breaks from copying the songs, I'd tell him about the need for revolution that I'd learned from Feiqing. Skillfully, I linked it with the Buddhist notion of delivering the masses—I was aided by the Buddhist knowledge I garnered from the songs. It was a tactic used by several historical rebels who were considered Buddhists. I knew what he needed. Just as he used dual cultivation to explain his relationship with me, I was happy to tell him about the revolutionary party in ways he could accept, by talking about saving those who were suffering, about rescuing the people from fires and floods, about overthrowing the Qing and restoring the Ming. The goal of my action seemed to be different now. I had wanted him to rebel so Lü Erye's family would be executed; now I wanted him to do the same thing so I could be with him. I'd live or die with him by my side.

I couldn't stand any revolution or rebellion without him. I wanted him to be with me.

And he obviously couldn't live without me either.

Fate is hilarious, when I think about it now.

5

Three months passed before a major change occurred. We'd written down a great many lyrics, all those treasured by Papa. After we were done, Ma Zaibo paid for someone to transcribe and make several copies. He'd also contacted a print shop in Lanzhou, with the plan of printing a thousand sets. Only by printing, he said, could the songs truly be preserved and passed down to future generations. Visitors to the Temple were happy to help spread the books; they made generous donations, as they thought it was an endeavor of merit.

One day someone from the Ma family showed up. He came to Ma Zaibo's room and acted strange when he saw me. I could tell from his face that he knew who I was. It couldn't be avoided. Actually, Lü Erye would have known long ago if he weren't incapacitated by his stroke.

Ma called me inside when the man left. He was seated, lost in thought. He pointed at the bed for me to sit. We were both quiet for a long time.

"I know who you are," he said finally.

I smiled.

I just smiled. I knew it would pain him if I told him what had happened. I didn't feel like explaining.

"But I know you're not a killer," he smiled sadly. "I would have died a thousand times if you were."

That was true. But I had wanted to kill him at first. Then I thought I'd wait until we finished the songs. My intention to kill him eventually died out.

"I know you're doing this for the songs. They're real treasures. If you do want to kill me, wait until we're done," he said.

I smiled again, not knowing what to say.

Neither of us said anything after that. It was better to keep quiet if nothing we said would make much sense. The setting sun slanted in through the latticed paper window and cast white strips in the room. I felt as if I'd just awakened from a long dream, maybe I could even still be asleep. Now that he knew about it, I decided to not to hide it any longer, and told him my story. I started out calmly, as if talking about someone else's life. Then I told him about the songs and the Society of Brothers, but I didn't name names, except to say that I was a member. I told him he could report me to the government. I actually wanted him to. I was tired. I didn't know how I should act in this drama anymore, and would like to be beheaded by the government.

I wouldn't run if he did report me, I said to myself. I felt I'd walked for a very long time, and that fatigue was boring into my bones. I did not want to walk any longer.

I went quiet.

"My father couldn't have done that. He chases women, but he has a good heart. You have to believe me," he said.

I didn't reply.

"I won't report you. I joined the Society too, because of you and because I believe in what you told me." He added, "I could continue to meditate for thousands of hours, but that would be worth less than actual deeds. I read many books before I met you, and I agreed with what I read in them."

What he said did not lighten my mood. It was odd, I know. I was feeling so exhausted that day that nothing interested me, including my feelings for him.

I wanted to quickly go hide some place, away from everyone, and stay there forever.

"Maybe my father will tell Hu Gala to expel you, so you should be prepared. I'll go with you if you have to leave," he said.

6

I didn't go see him over the next couple of weeks. Except for cooking meals, I slept all the time, I slept the sleep of the dead. Whatever others did, even lop off my head, I didn't care. I wasn't about to hide. I even lost interest in the songs; without them people managed to live and live well, I thought. So many of them had never heard a single wooden fish song, never even heard of them, and they weren't missing a thing. The songs' importance or value was conferred on them by people; they were valuable if you thought they were. When you didn't, they were nothing special, just songs that did not exist until you sang them, and that disappeared with the voice when you finished.

I just wanted to sleep and empty my mind. I wanted to sleep forever. Hu Gala acted pretty much the same, but for the questioning look he gave me when we met. Maybe he didn't know about me and Ma; or maybe he did, but pretended he didn't.

I wasn't in the mood to sing when the first and the fifteenth of months arrived—I said I wasn't feeling well—I couldn't muster a shred of interest in it. I stopped my martial arts training, since I couldn't find any meaning in it. I had enough skill to take care of Ma Zaibo if I want to carry out my revenge. All I needed was to pick up a pillow and press it down on his face to make Lü Erye suffer for the rest of his life. I didn't even want to be part of the revolution. Those people who were living in the abyss of suffering had nothing to do with me, so why should I try to save them? Why should I overthrow the Qing and restore the Ming? Why should I help restore a dynasty whose first emperor had eliminated many who helped him established the empire? When I thought about Papa, he felt like a hazy reflection of the moon in water. The heartache was gone.

I failed to locate a reason why I felt that way. Was it because someone had destroyed the perfect image of me in Ma Zaibo's mind? I wondered. Did I feel like giving it all up? Maybe, but not entirely.

Back when I traveled the long distance at night with the caravan, I hadn't felt the kind of fatigue that bored into my soul now.

I slept day and night for over ten days, getting up only to cook. I'd been waiting for Hu Gala to send me away, but he didn't, and was actually concerned about me.

I thought I was truly ill after sleeping away all those days. My body felt heavy and I was nauseous. I had no appetite for anything but the pickled vegetables offered at the Temple. Hu knew some medicine and offered to feel my pulse. After he did, he looked at me with a somber expression for a while, but stopped short of prescribing anything. "It's nothing. You'll feel better in a few days," was all he said.

Ma Zaibo looked drawn when he came for lunch. Lovesickness is terrible, I realized, for he'd lost his charming languid airs and gained a look of yearning. He didn't look at me and I ignored him; we were polite, like people passing on the street. He was the Young Master and I was a mere temple cook, as if nothing had ever happened between us.

On this day, out of the blue, Hu Gala asked about the time and date of my birth and offered to tell my fortune. I didn't believe him, but didn't want to turn down his kindness. I gave him the information, but after he finished he didn't say anything.

Big Mouth came to see me, disguised as a temple visitor. It was the fifteenth and the place was crowded. He wanted to talk to me, and repeatedly signaled me to meet him in a quiet, secluded spot. I didn't want to see him. I was startled to find he really did have a damned big mouth; it was unbearable. I nearly threw up when I recalled how that big mouth had pressed down on my lips.

In that mood, my days went by like a millstone crushing wheat with a monotonous rumble and a parched flavor like wheat ash.

7

My mood changed one night a month later. Hu Gala went out to help with a funeral, something he seemed to enjoy, for he left in high spirits and returned similarly keyed up. We were treated to steamed buns when he came back, though he called them alms eggs. Each time he returned, he brought with him a headless chicken and twelve alms eggs. Ma Zaibo didn't eat chicken, but the alms eggs were his favorite.

This time it was a large funeral that required three days of rites and many helpers. Hu had engaged several Daoists. A few idlers used to stay at the Temple to help out with sweeping the leaves and other chores, but he sent them away after I came.

When he left and shut the temple door, the place was as quiet as death.

By then Ma had stopped reciting sutras. He didn't send for me and I didn't go over. On the first day of Hu's absence, I made his favorite—hand-pinched noodles. He had two bowlfuls. I didn't eat much, for if I wasn't careful, I might throw up.

"Are you not feeling well?" he asked me. "Go see a doctor."

"Hu Gala checked me out. He said it wasn't serious. I'll feel better in a few days."

He exhaled. He wanted to say something, but nothing came out. Then he went back to his room, looking like a shadow from behind.

I felt sorry for him, but couldn't say what for.

It was windless night with a solitary white moon shining down on the yard. I sat on my door sill. I thought I'd lost weight from my irregular diet. After a while, I was bored just sitting there, so I opened the temple gate and went out onto a desolate floodplain, with no trees or grass. Standing at the gate, I could see far into the distance. The temple was built on Mount Su Wu, a mountain that didn't look like one. Everywhere I looked was a dreary sight, except for a few trees. There could have been a lake and grassland here a thousand years ago. If not, what would Su Wu's sheep have eaten?

Everything looked hazy in the moonlight. It was so quiet I could even hear the sound of the moonbeams hitting the ground, like water. There was no wind, but an air current caressed my face, feeling like water. Moonlit nights were perfect for thinking private thoughts, but I didn't feel like doing that. "Humans are clever and always scheming, while Heaven takes its time to carry out its plans." I was reminded of the lines from a wooden fish song. Perfect. So many things in the world are truly beyond our comprehension.

I wished I could spend a night out under the moon. After so many busy, noisy days, it was tempting to want to be alone on such a quiet night. Then I thought about the brothers huffing and puffing as they practiced their martial skills back at Dengmaying Lake. How boring. They usually practiced on moonlit nights. Everyone had the expansive passion of changing the world, but I found nothing interesting in that at this moment. How had that happened? Could I have been polluted by the air in Ma Zaibo's room? Maybe, hard to say.

What Feiqing had asked me to do came to mind; it was equally banal. Why had I treated it as the most important matter in the world? At this moment, everything, no matter how big, looked like a wan moon.

I sensed Ma walk out and come up to me from behind, like a breath of air.

He didn't say anything, just stood quietly. I heard insects chirping, more than I could count, singing a wondrous song. The airiness of the man behind me slowly billowed out, adding something to my heart and taking something away. He sat down beside me. My heart raced each time his lapel brushed against my arm.

A heart that had died over those days came back alive.

I leaned over and rested my head on his shoulder.

I listened to him breathe, heard his heart beating. It could have been my heart, pounding loudly enough to wake up heaven and earth.

He exhaled long and deep.

"I don't care if it's true or not. And I don't care who you are, as long as you are you."

He spoke my mind.

I knew I was beyond help. He could think that way, I said to myself, but I couldn't. I would let Papa and everyone else down if I did, but my heart was enraptured by the resonance of what he'd said. I leaned over to kiss his earlobe.

We were soon in each other's arms again after days of stalemate.

8

We threw ourselves into frenzied lovemaking after returning to his room, as if to make up for the days of absence. He was no longer cautious, nor did he care about poses of dual cultivation or holding back. We reached the highest point again and again as we drank each other in and nearly died from ecstasy.

With no one else around, I let myself go and cried out like a cat in heat, while he turned into a crazed camel. You wouldn't believe he had been quiet and serene when you listened to him now. For a brief moment I even thought that Lü Eryc's genes, latent in him, had been revived. It was a disgusting association, but it didn't dampen my spirit. All I wanted was to cry out wantonly and enjoy every moment of it. I even had the urge to let all of Liangzhou hear my lustful moans.

We carried on late into the night. I didn't go back to my own room, as I had before. On this night, we were alone and I could steep there with him. I loved the expression, steep, as I was really steeping in his world, in his body and in his soul. Like an injured fawn, I curled up in his arms, surrounded by his smell. His serene, peaceful air that had so attracted me returned that night.

After we'd settled down I asked him,

"When were you first attracted to me?"

"When I listened to you sing the wooden fish songs."

"So which did you like, the songs or me?"

"They're the same. You're the songs and the songs are you."

I didn't know how to react to his response, be happy or feel sad.

He cradled my head and said with a smile,

"No more questions. No one can explain things like this. My father found me lots of pretty girls, but I always felt numb when I saw them. I felt numb with each one, without fail. They were fine, but I was numb. I felt I was inside a glass case. I could see the outside world, but the world could not come in. Then when I heard you sing, a crack developed on the case and let in human breath. The crack grew larger and larger, and here we are."

"You ought to know that I was a beggar," I said, half in jest. "You'd lose your respectability if people knew you're with me. As we say in Liangzhou, your ancestors would be so ashamed they'd jump off the sacrificial table."

"I don't care, let them jump." he smiled. "Beggar woman? You're a natural beauty. No one could tell a sweet girl like you could be more ferocious than a wolf when she lets herself go. Besides, what's respectability? I don't care about stuff like that. It's enough to be alive. Why worry about something like status?"

"We met before. I saw you when I was out begging for food. Once you gave me some loose change, but you didn't even look at me," I said.

"Only when you sing the songs does your special quality shine through. It's really strange, but there's something about you that's familiar to me. I can't say exactly what it is. When you're not singing, it's a fire without a flame, but the flame roars when you sing."

"Maybe it's the disposition that scholars talk about," I offered.

"There was once a literary figure who called it 'manners.' I didn't understand what he meant. What's strange is this: your features remain the same, but once you start singing, you look irresistibly attractive."

We flirted and bantered back and forth.

Then we fell asleep, exhausted.

9

I didn't know how they got in, but several men were inside the room when I sensed something wrong. Ma Zaibo was so tired he was still snoring airily. I nudged him and he woke up with a shout, Oh, no. He sat up. I tossed his clothes over to cover his bare lower body.

"Did you see? How dare they do the donkey thing in a temple."

I knew the voice, a county official who visited the Temple often. I heard he was tight with Master Wang Tiao, another prominent family in town and the Mas' rivals. Later it occurred to me that Wang had wanted to use this incident to humiliate the Ma family.

With matters like this, no tip, no government probe. Someone must have reported us. Maybe we'd been seen in an intimate pose when we were outside the Temple. It was possible. We'd been careless. I was worried. Ma Zaibo's reputation would be ruined if the news spread. It wouldn't affect me much, however, since I was a food-scraper who didn't worry about her name being tarnished. He was the young master, and his family would suffer a great loss of face if his character came under question.

I had been through so much that nothing mattered to me, so I wasn't too concerned. The worse they could do was lop off my head. But losing a head just means gaining a bowl-sized scar. It wasn't all that scary if you thought about it. Ma Zaibo, on the other hand, wasn't experienced; he was so scared his face was ghostly white. My mood plunged when I thought I had put him in this situation.

The intruders turned around for us to get dressed. Ma regained his indifferent air when he was no longer naked; he hadn't completely recovered from the shock, but his air of tranquility was clearly visible. I recalled the couplet in his study: "Be tranquil when confronted with major events/There must be sages in today's world." I was reassured by his demeanor. Don't look for trouble when everything is going well, but stay calm when something happens. We did it and we'd take the responsibility. That's all.

They cursed us viciously. I understood how they felt. To them the temple was sacred ground, and we shouldn't have done it here, for that was blasphemy and would incur calamity. I heard that on the first and the fifteenth of each month, red dew would flow down from the statue of Vajravārāhi. One day an imperial consort blocked the statue's lower body with a vajra pestle and soon a fight broke out in Liangzhou. The incident could be found in a local history book. Su Wu was a shepherd deity. On the first day of every year the people herded their livestock here for the "Welcoming Deity of Happiness." A departure caravan would always make sure to take along some water from Mount Su Wu as a kind of lucky charm. The people were obviously afraid that the deity would be offended by what we did and strike down on them.

They were coarse and their curses vulgar, typical of the language farmers used on their wives. It was a strange custom around here: the men used the worst language on their own wives, calling them a whore, a slut, a cunt. Now they were using those words on me, for they were apparently convinced that I'd seduced the Young Master of the Ma family. For months I'd been singing the wooden fish songs, attracting the attention of many men, and the village women had been calling me a fox fairy. And now the moniker was going to stick, whether I liked it or not.

Would they still call me a fox fairy if they knew I was the old beggar woman?

I didn't care what happened to me, but I worried about Ma Zaibo. I'd had my share of insults when I was out begging for food, so "my skin was thicker than the city wall," to borrow the curse words Big Mouth used on me later. I knew why the Mahasiddhas would always send their king-students to a brothel to test his self-control and why the Buddha told his disciples to beg for alms. With those kinds of experience, they could remain calm and resist temptation when opportunities presented themselves.

To be sure, I hoped they wouldn't let the incident escalate. The Ma family was highly influential, and once it was made public, it would be like dumping excrement on their ancestral shrine—see how I was actually concerned about their family, when earlier I'd wanted the whole family executed by the imperial court? Later I learned that some in their own Ma clan were gloating over the incident.

We were taken into Su Wu Hall. The Temple was named after Su Wu, but he hadn't been vested a celestial title by the emperor, so he could not be installed in the main hall. Only figures such as the Supreme Deity and the Founding Deity of the Daoist doctrine could enjoy offerings in the main hall, so obviously a celestial title was important. Su Wu wasn't, so he had to stay in a side hall, despite his fame. It was a small hall, somewhat deserted, for not many worshippers came here to offer incense. During my stay, I had come often to burn a stick of incense; I didn't believe in deities, but I respected his integrity.

I prayed to Su Wu when we came in, like a dying person seeing any doctor she could find. I prayed for the incident to blow over and keep Ma Zaibo's reputation untarnished. I only prayed; I didn't offer a vow to pay back for the favor. Usually, when people prayed to a deity, they would offer "to rebuild the temple and re-gild the statues," but it was beyond my ability. I didn't want to deceive Su Wu. If he could, he'd help me get through the trouble.

More people showed up. Now I knew they wanted to blow the incident up. It was dark out and many were still asleep. Without the busy work of the "public minded" no one would be bothered by such trivial matters. My mind was put at ease when I saw that. I could not avoid predestined calamity, so I'd just have to deal with whatever was going to happen.

No one came to interrogate us, as we'd been caught in the act. Instead they cursed, screaming at me for blasphemy, calling me a demon, telling me that I'd ruined Ma Zaibo's life . . . In any case, they heaved whatever they could think of on me. I felt like a dead pig, unconcerned when it was dunked into boiling water. Sitting on a cushion for worshippers, I had little fear, for my mind was a blank.

Gawkers gathered after breakfast, including many women, who added diversity to the contents and the methods of cursing. Spit fell on my head like rain. I didn't bother to wipe it off. I felt numb and sluggish, as if something sticky had gelled in my brain.

Suddenly an old woman ran up, cursing and smacking a shoe on my face. I was quickly knocked dizzy and my face burned.

"It's not her fault, Mother." I heard Ma Zaibo say, "You can hit me if you want."

"All right, let's stop here for tonight. I'm tired," Wooden Fish Girl says.

I can tell she really is worn out. It isn't always easy to revisit the past. Anyone would be exhausted after going through what has happened to her.

All of a sudden, she looks so much older.

—wait a minute, she is old.

Sixteenth Session
Killer's Pursuit

I see that the yellow camel is missing as soon as I open my eyes in the morning. I'm astounded. I remember tethering him, tightly, to a tree.

I walk up to examine the tree; it's rotten, been dead for a long time and its roots are crumpling, too weak to withstand the effort from the camel as he freed himself.

After wolfing down some food, I go searching for him.

I spot the animal as I round a ridge. He hadn't run away, after all. He's by an Artemisia shrub loaded with cinstaches, in an eating frenzy. Whip in hand, I run up to chase him away, but he's finished most of the cistanches. His belly looks flat, a sign that he has eaten his fill. What a shame. But I can't bring myself to hit the camel, for he may feel guilty and truly run away. Instead, I tether him securely to another tree.

Too bad. He nearly ruined all the cistanches. I check the others in a sand trough off to a distance, but none is left. The camel clearly went at those first, finishing them before moving back for the closer ones, apparently afraid his chewing sound would alert me. What a sneaky animal.

A quick inventory shows three whole ones and some bits and pieces. The camel must have had some before. He's experienced enough to not only devour the exposed ones, but also dig into those buried in the sand. He has used his feet as shovels to clear the sand so he can eat—no, ruin—the parts under the surface. He can't digest this much food so quickly, so most of the plants he has eaten will simply turn into waste that he will later expel. What a sneak. If we were careful, we could have survived several days on these plants, but his rampage has ended that.

I don't have time to punish the camel. Instead I gather the leftover pieces for the other camel and the dog. The dog has learned to like the plant. Then I wrap the three whole pieces that have escaped the camel's maw, and finish a half-eaten one. I know it has the animal's saliva on it. That's gross. After quickly peeling it, I swallow it in a few mouthfuls.

The yellow camel's antics have complicated my situation.

I lie down on the sand, my mind a blank. The water in the sack will last us one day at most.

It feels like a staggering blow. Before coming out here, I made plans for all the possible scenarios I could think of. Mostly I thought about what I'd do if I were lost, or if I ran into a wolf, or the jug sprang a leak, and so on. I had a plan for every situation, but never imagined that the water sources marked on the map could have all dried up.

I'm despairing. What's the point now, even if I could interview them all? If I can't make it out of Wild Fox Ridge alive, my interviews, no matter how great they are, will be buried in the dust of time. I wonder if anyone else might have the same chance to conduct another successful round.

But my dejection notwithstanding, I go for the interview once nighttime arrives. I'll do what I need to do and leave the rest to the gods.

A green light follows me from a distance, its hulking body obscured by the darkness of the night.

One. Killer

1

I started looking for you, Young Master, the day after you left the caravan and went to the Hu Family Mill.

But a gale smoothed out all the traces you left behind, leaving me nothing to follow.

To me, you weren't some kind of holy man; you were just a man.

During those days of my search, I failed to see anything that you talked about. All I saw was the desert and the rocky gobi, plus some desert poplars and wild camels. None of the wonders you mentioned.

Don't be upset. I know you had enough religious attainment not to be angry with me. You're free of anger and hatred, aren't you? I've seen enough people who claim to be rid of obstinacy and yet get more obstinate when someone insults their beliefs.

Don't be like them, Young Master.

Everyone called you a holy man. But you should know that to a killer, no one is holy. In his eyes, there are only the killers and those who get killed. Yes, sometimes I worship the Buddha, but it does nothing to my intent to kill you. Haven't you heard that during the Crusades, the crusaders praised the lord as they thrust their spears into the heads of pagan babies? They called it a holy war.

Even now, there are plenty of people who shout fanatic religious slogans as they turn themselves into human bombs.

I'm one of them.

2

I watched you on countless occasions when you weren't paying attention.

I was a pair of eyes spying on you. There was another pair you could not dodge, those of the Grim Reaper. I was the only other one who paid such close attention to you, and I failed to see what made you holy.

Nothing.

I did see you relieving yourself, sneezing, farting, snoring, and doing other things. I heard you'd stolen someone's radish as a kid. I couldn't associate you with the holy men of legends. But I knew you were a good man. So was Emperor Chongzhen, but he had to be responsible for the evil deeds committed by his ancestors.

I knew you were a good person, but I still had to kill you. I needed your blood for the souls of wrongful deaths.

You were just a good man to me, not a holy person, but I never said anything bad about you to the drivers. I found those who believed you were holy indeed enjoyed a happy life later. They were smiling before and after they died, and that was enough for me. They weren't my enemies and I didn't want to sever their positive energy. All I wanted was to kill you.

It didn't matter to me even if you weren't really a holy person.

3

I'd looked for you over several days. But you left no trace, as if you'd evaporated from the human world.

Yet, I had a feeling that I could find you once I located the Hu Family Mill. Trouble was, I didn't know where it was either.

Some people claimed the Mill was an entrance to another time and space. Or you could call it a transition point into dark energy and dark matters.

I finally saw a mill one night after a long search. I didn't know if it was the Mill, because no one told me. On the other hand, I'd never heard of another mill in Wild Fox Ridge, so I assumed this was the one.

The moon was out that night, but wasn't very bright. A lonely pale orb in the sky. I had what I'd need on me. I wasn't planning to just kill you with a knife. Among ways to take someone's life, a knife was the least imaginative method. It was actually easy, almost too easy, to stab you once or many times. I'd been thinking about the most innovative way, as long as I could spill your blood in the end, of course.

I was aware that revenge would be my last performance in life, or the last encore of my lifetime. I wanted it to be spectacular.

Waves of pungent air swirled in the sand trough. Over those days I kept seeing the ever-growing millstone circling in the air, blood splattering to turn into rosy clouds as it bled. The heavy smell of blood kept assailing my nose.

The Mill was the lone structure on a hill, which must have been tall, but was more like a mound in the desert after sand and dust buried it over the years. I heard that the Hu Family Mill derived its name from its building material, the poplar tree, *huyang*, but no one was certain of that. There were lots of stories about the Hu family, one of which had it in a little ditty: "The Bao family produced a monarch, the Li family a minister, and the Hu family an empress." Local lore had it that Liangzhou was supposed to produce an emperor, and if that happened, the empress would come from the Hu family. But they produced nothing, only left behind the mill, along with the fable of the "wooden fish incantation."

I could see the mill suspended in midair through the hazy moonlight. Half was on the hill and the other half over a cliff. I didn't expect to see such a structure in Wild Fox Ridge. Under the moon, the smallish mill house had an odd-shaped silhouette, like it was scaling the cliff. Later, I saw that more than a dozen beams had been drilled into the cliffside to support the mill house, so it hung in the air, presenting an eerie image at night. I wondered why the owner had built it that way. Was it to prevent the wind-blown sand from burying it?

I heard that people normal shunned the place, that it was haunted by strange sounds or images, that the ghosts of camel drivers gathered there. Some even said it was connected to a secret realm, but guarded by evil spirits and non-human creatures.

I didn't believe any of that.

What was so desirable about a place guarded by evil spirits?

I walked on a path laid with limestone pavers, with worn, dimpled spots. Who knew how many camels and their drivers had traveled through the area?

The mill was unlit, as I discovered upon opening the door.

But I was seized by genuine fear. Our ancestors had said a killer carried enough murderous aura to frighten off ghosts, but I was afraid. Because I heard a noise.

Have any of you ever walked under a bronze bell when it was ringing? If you stayed under a giant bell that had just struck, you'd hear a sound echoing into the distance. The sound waves had a texture, rising slowly into the air, to the end of the sky, like gossamer.

That was what I heard when I walked in.

It didn't feel like going into a millhouse to me, but more like entering a different space.

In the haze of moonlight, I saw a colossal millstone, with an outsized eye. I hadn't seen one this big before. An average donkey could only turn a small mill. Later, I learned that a mill this size had to be turned by a camel.

I saw many tools related to the mill, a leather rope, a pole, a leather harness for a camel's neck. I knew them all. They were useful tools that would get the mill moving once they placed were on a camel.

A sieve for sifting flour came into view when I went into a smaller room.

The floor was smooth and signs of human habitation were on the polished floor.

I noticed things that Ma Zaibo had used.

A great joy floored me to drive away all my fear.

You have nowhere to hide now, Ma Zaibo! I cried out silently.

4

Sure enough, Ma Zaibo appeared, like a spot of ink spreading on rice paper.

A slender man, he wore an aloof expression. A moonbeam shone down on his pale face and an aura of yin billowed around him. Yes, it was a yin aura. I didn't see any holy halo on him. It was yin. I got the sense he was feeling glum, as if he was about to die, for there was nothing bright, no yang, about him. He reminded me of a man I'd seen, someone who'd kept a demonic imp. He had dug up a newly dead boy and buried the body in a place away from human traffic. Then he'd chanted incantations and offered daily sacrifice. Forty-nine days later, the little demonic imp followed his order to do his bidding. Keeping a demonic imp was similar to raising a demonic insect; both could be of use to him, but they could attract unclean things. The man had a sinister look. It was just a feeling, of course. The yin aura was a kind of atmosphere you could feel but not tell. That was how I felt about Ma Zaibo. Hei-hei, he was no holy person in my eyes, not then, not now, and not in the future. You could offer him any sacrifice you want and he could be endowed with supernatural powers, but to me he was still not holy.

It seemed to me that he was also keeping a demonic imp. He often offered water and food to hungry ghosts, which could be considered a charitable act if you want to be kind, but could also be for keeping a demon, to be less charitable. On several nights, I'd seen him offer food to the ghosts, and he was always surrounded by countless little demonic imps. I'm not making this up; I really did see those strange figures. I also saw my ancestors, who were sobbing and covered in blood, of course. They were always roaring at me, "Revenge! Revenge!" Their rumbling voices could almost shatter heaven and earth, so very moving.

Ma Zaibo started out chanting an incantation. I saw eerie blue lights swim in all directions, like tadpoles. To ghosts these were invitation cards. Then I saw numerous ghosts arriving in high spirits; they were actually more like currents of air. Those with serious karmic hindrance had thick, gray airs and those with less serious setbacks had a lighter shade. Some air currents took up human forms, while others appeared in various, odd shapes. They had energy. You were right; they were a kind of functional existence. You can also call it "bio-info," of course.

Ma had summoned pervasive, gray air currents. Like a pack of crazed fighting dogs, they were growling, snarling, and biting, their noise a blaring din.

He started a different incantation to draw coronae of light seeping into the gray air currents to quell the noise of imps fighting. Those were peaceful magnetic waves, and the ghosts quieted down. Later, I realized that he was ridding them of their karmic hindrance and dissolving entanglements of animosity, before he produced food to offer them.

His face looked greenish pale under the moon. Deeply immersed in his own world, he was oblivious to the threat of death pressing down on him. He'd been like that for days. You could say he'd transcended the boundary of life and death, but to me it was more like a numbness. A mental patient can dance on a cliff's edge, but that isn't being smart, it's foolishness. Which was why I never thought he was a holy person.

Like a cat stealthily eyeing a mouse, I watched in the dark, my staring eyes brimming with the desire to kill. I gritted my teeth and cursed under my breath.

I thought of the many ways to take his life. But as I mentioned earlier, I didn't want to use a knife. Only a stupid man would kill with a knife. My dead family members were high in my thoughts as they shouted in the silence,

"Right. Don't act like a fool. Be creative."

They wrapped around me like a dense fog and turned me into the carrier of their hatred. You could understand it as a kind of atmosphere, and its existence was real, for you'd become evil once you were part of it. If you don't believe me, just think about those pretty Cultural Revolution Red Guard girls wielding a belt and you'd know what I meant.

I found myself swept along in the atmosphere.

So I said to myself, "Yes, my revenge must be creative. It has to be earth-shattering and rousing for both ghosts and deities."

My heart was pounding like mad. It wasn't from fear, but from wild joy. The quiet, secluded mill house was the perfect locale for my revenge. Ma Zaibo was now a rock and I was a sculptor. I could carve him in whatever way I wanted. I wanted to slice him three thousand three hundred and fifty-seven times, mince him into fly-size bits and sprinkle them into the air like rain. I could start with the big toe on his left foot, removing the nail and slowly picking off the flesh. It was the "white bone" doctrine of visualizing oneself as a pile of white bones, which I heard he'd done before taking up Tantric Buddhism. I'd help him out. I'd carve out all the flesh and tendons on the foot, yes, all the flesh and tendons, leaving only the white bones. I was convinced at the time that his bones were greenish white, with an air of yin.

Following his calf, I'd keep skinning and whittling, little by little, bit by bit, as I savored the pleasure of revenge. It would be roaring ecstasy surging to the horizon and into eternity. I was in ecstasy, so were my ancestors. They were reveling, enjoying the pleasure brought to them by the flesh on the tip of my knife. They loved blood, like many of the ghosts and deities in the world. Which was why people kill a chicken as an offering to the Earth God, along with a pig's head or even a cow or goat. All because the Earth God is addicted to blood. Just think how fertile the land can be when it is infused with fresh blood. Could war disappear from the world if the God of the Land loved blood?

I'd carve off the flesh, and Young Master Ma's handsome calf would look like a dried-out claw on a corpse, ugly beyond words. If I needed a weapon, I'd pick a dead man's claw; one made of tempered steel, of course. I would use it to grab at my opponent and dig in to rip off chunks of flesh. It would feel just wonderful.

Then why wouldn't I just give up on a knife and use a steel claw on his chest? A single strike would open him up for me to see the lump of crimson flesh throbbing, alternating between larger and smaller sizes. But I would leave the lump alone for now; I couldn't make it too easy on him. Don't let your enemy die too easily. There's nothing simpler than taking someone's life. I wouldn't want him to die yet, I want it to be a horrible death—hei-hei, that didn't sound very much like me.

Don't curse me. You may not know that cruelty and violence are part of human nature. When a man enters a vicious realm, evil will grow in him. If it were you, you would comment on how enjoyable it is to battle heaven, how delightful to combat earth, and how satisfying to fight another man. You're a murderer if you kill one person, a cold-blooded killer if you kill a hundred, but you may be a hero if you take ten or a hundred thousand lives. With tens of thousands, you could be installed in some hall to enjoy worship and offerings for generations to come. You don't believe me? Go read your history and see if there's one dynasty that didn't do that.

I would claw off the flesh on his body, as well as the tendons and membranes, reducing Young Master Ma to a carcass, very much like

Sitavana, which I heard was actually two deities combined, but that's just what people said. I also heard they'd been delivering souls, countless of them who were meant to be saved. But again, that's just what I heard—yes, the two intertwined skeletons. But Ma Zaibo would not be the same as them, since his heart would still be beating. Think about it. A skeleton with a beating heart. Wouldn't that be an amusing sight? Hei-hei, you can call me psychotic, of course. But you might not be any different from me if your own family suffered that kind of bloodbath, am I right? You should know that a forgetful people can't be considered human; they're pigs, at best.

In this world, certain things should always be remembered, hatred among them. If you kill someone, but others keep forgetting it, then you'll keep on killing, won't you? You should know that cause and effect is a universal law, that good has its rewards and evil its retribution. If none of us remembers, the evil-doers will carry out more terrible deeds without concern. Seen from such an angle of significance, a killer like me is actually the guardian deity of the universal law of cause and effect. I want to make it clear to people of the world that blood for blood and an eye for an eye is just. A blood debt must be repaid with blood. You have to know that you're digging your grave when you're doing something terrible.

I could see Young Master Ma's skeleton dancing. It might look like he was reveling, but I was convinced it was caused by pain. What was the point of revenge, if he wasn't suffering? I could see numerous bloodthirsty deities in the air; they were also reveling, their nostrils flaring as they sucked up the blood flooding the land. I see a line of poetry popping up in your head, "Blood enriches the Middle Kingdom and the grass grows lush and green." Heh-heh, what a great line. So, you see, there are also bloodthirsty poets in the world.

After dancing madly for a while, Young Master Ma turned and fled, as if he'd sensed something. He ran like a rabbit. I gave chase. I saw he was running to the backyard of the Hu Family Mill.

I knew you cannot run away from your destiny no matter where you flee to.

Two. Ma Zaibo

1

I hid the matchlock Feiqing had given me in the Hu Family Mill. He'd meant for me to protect myself from wild animals, but to me nothing was more terrifying than one's own desires.

For me, the wild animal was always myself. The weapon would not shatter my obstinacy, so I had no use for it. I spent quite a bit of time trying to hide it, for a lethal weapon like that needed to be hidden somewhere deep.

There was a small path in the millhouse backyard leading to a deep ravine, where clouds and fogs swirled. Through the misty screen I saw three streams down the ravine, one murky yellow, one inky green, and one crystal clear. The three had come from different sources before merging in the ravine—no, please don't say they're symbols, representing the three evil paths. No, they were just streams. There are no symbols in my story. Sure, you might detect countless symbols, but to me they're not symbols. Symbols are the most ineffective words in any discourse system.

At the time I was wondering if the water was real. If there could indeed be that much water in the desert, then the ocean of sand would have been an oasis long ago. Then it occurred to me that the ravine was too deep for the water, if real, to flow up onto the desert.

To be honest, this was different from the Wild Fox Ridge that I'd imagined. When I was young, I'd often heard people call Wild Fox Ridge a mysterious gorge in the desert. Back then I said to myself that since it was in the desert, there must be sand and nothing else, with some poplars, at most. When I got here, I realized that there were lots of unusual things, such as the Hu Family Mill, an oddity for sure. I'll tell you another time why it was odd.

I surmised that the other end of the ravine had to be a peculiar spot also. Maybe what I was looking for would be there.

So how do I get there from here? I wondered.

As I pondered, an overhead rope appeared.

Do you know anything about ropes? See, an overhead rope stretched from one end of the hill to the other. On the rope was a sliding tube made of hardwood. As you attach yourself to the tube, you kick off to let yourself slide from one end of the ravine to the other, as if riding in the clouds. See, like this.

I'd done it before, so I knew how. I secured myself with a length of twisted cow hair so I wouldn't slide off if my arms grew weak. Then I saw a bloody red sun in the sky.

That's right. I saw a red sun. It was unusual, because in the past I'd only seen a pale white disc in the desert. The crimson red left a deep impression on my soul and would seep out even now if I shut my eyes.

I kicked with all I had and the tube slid to the far side. I smoothed the rope ahead of me with a wet towel. It was like riding in the clouds, with wind screaming past my ear. I felt a kind of expansiveness, yes, the feeling that you get when all the mountains before you seem small. The distant mountains were now mere creases on a linen towel, the paths among them a slithering snake.

Despite my effort not to be afraid, fear set upon me like thick fog. I was in its throes; I was fearful I might fall into that terrifying abyss. The water in the three streams sent up frightening sprays, while crocodiles leaped up, barely missing my feet. I quickly shut my eyes, though I knew that would not change the world around me. But it was all I could do. I could only shut my eyes when I was powerless to change the world or my mind.

Suddenly the harsh sound of the rope grated on my ears and felt like I was gnashing my teeth, like I was chewing sand. I opened my eyes and discovered that the tube had developed a crack, probably from being exposed to the weather for so long. By then I was already attached to it, so if it fell off the rope, it would take me into the abyss. At that moment it became clear that the thing I was dependent upon was itself unreliable. Despair set in. The situation was the same as learning that a guru I'd equated with the Buddha was in reality a common narrow-minded man. The sky turned gray just then.

While I'm at it, I'll tell you all that I am not a holy individual, that I too know fear. But beyond the fear, there is something that I know I fear, and that something is not fearful. And so, I find solace in that unfearful thing. Then in my eyes, fear is illusory. But when I attached myself to the rope, what I'm talking about here is only something to think about, not any sort of wisdom. I was well aware that the essence of the world is an illusion, and yet, I could not control my heart. I often confuse the false from the true, regarding such an illusion as real, and become uncontrollably agitated.

I heard the worn tube cracking like thousands of snakes gnawing at my nerves. I was in the middle. Below me the flowing water thundered away. Strangely, however, the sound of the slide was drowning out the rumbling water. The crocodiles leaped up, my feet their target. Rationally, I knew they could not reach me, but I could somehow feel them nipping at my soles. Each contact prickled unbearably. I was terrified. I smelled a horrible stench and could tell it came from the rotting meat between their teeth.

What was catastrophic was the slide slowing down as if to settle in the middle of the rope. Only two possible outcomes awaited me if that happened, turning into dry meat on the rope like the jerky the Tibetans make, or falling into the water to be devoured by the crocodiles. At that instant, I understood why Tangdong Lama vowed to devote a lifetime of effort to build a bridge over dangerous water when he witnessed someone fall off a rope into a river. So I made a vow; I promised to build a steel bridge over the ravine behind the Hu Family Mill if I came out of here alive. I was obviously copying someone's vow, but it gave me enough power to drive away my fear.

Later I wondered if my vow brought out Dharmapalas to help me reach the far end.

The sun was gone, maybe setting behind the western mountain, but was blocked by misty clouds. A greenish hue showed on the pale white sky.

The slide glided to the edge of the ravine, overgrown with trees, all very unusual. I didn't know any of their names. It was truly a strange sight, for the other side of the ravine was nothing but dry sand, while on this side was a canopy of trees.

With great difficulty, I landed on solid ground. The tube shattered the moment my feet touched the ground and drifted with the wind like catkins into the unknown.

Three. Lu Fuji

1

I'd always thought the Young Master was delusional.

Later, I understood him, even believed he was a holy person. I saw him at the moment my head was chopped off; there was a halo over his head, which convinced me that he was truly a holy man.

The real holy man lived away from the mortal world; he was an eminent existence far beyond the differentiations of space and time.

And I was finally grateful for his search; without his search in Wild Fox Ridge, there would be no transcendence later, nor my salvation.

But at the time, I did believe you went to the Hu Family Mill for meditation in seclusion. You had done that often in the past, so we weren't worried about you. We didn't expect you to experience something like that.

If something were to happen to you, what would we have said to Ma Erye?—only Wooden Fish Girl called him Lü Erye. To us, he was Ma Erye.

I never doubted the magical and strange things you said about Wild Fox Ridge, though. I myself had seen some uncommon topography there too. But others had said there were no signs of human existence in Wild Fox Ridge, where everywhere you looked there was only wilderness and desolation.

I didn't want to doubt your wondrous encounters.

I remembered what you once said: we all have our own Wild Fox Ridge.

I wonder whose was the real one.

Don't be angry with me, Young Master.

You should know there was no holy man in the eyes of an attendant. I wasn't your attendant, but I'd watched you grow up. I was there when you relieved yourself, sneezed, and farted. I never forgot you'd stolen a radish as a kid, and I couldn't associate you with the holy men I'd heard about in stories. I do know, however, that you were a good man.

It doesn't matter even if you're not a holy man, I said to myself.

It doesn't matter who you are; you are what people think you are.

Likewise, Feiqing wasn't a national hero to me either. He was cowardly and lecherous. He and I had gone to the Hexi Inn once, and he was all smiles when he saw those coquettes. All I knew about him was far from the image of what I consider to be a national hero. But you said he was one, so he was.

2

What I wanted to do most in Wild Fox Ridge was kill that mad camel. He had injured two camels from our caravan. Like a shadow, he drifted over whenever he wanted, impossible to guard against. Worse yet, the two injured camels were looking somewhat deranged, often foaming at the mouth, as they looked at us with blood-red eyes. They didn't bite anyone, but they could at any time. I didn't know if Brown Lion's madness was contagious; if it was, then those two would become just like him. They'd bite other camels, and the other camels would do the same, and it wouldn't take long for the whole caravan to be destroyed. You must have heard how people say that a bad horse in a herd will turn every other horse. The same is true in a camel caravan. What worried me most was the possibility of Brown Lion's injury turning into an epidemic, because every bite would then be a fatal curse.

I made up my mind to take out the mad camel.

I knew Balte would object. He never believed anything we said about Brown Lion, and insisted that his camel would never bite us. He explained that the camel had been nursing his injury in their camel grounds and had never been out. That was a lie.

I didn't care anyway. I walked around daily looking for the mad camel with a matchlock loaded with steel balls used to kill wolves, standing in combat readiness. But, strangely, I searched all the sand troughs, and couldn't find him. Later, when I went to the Mongolian ground, I saw he was there nursing his own wounds, just as Balte had said. He lay in a sand trough, eyes half shut, chewing his cud, looking calm and tamed, an old camel on the mend. But I knew he was faking it. You can fake for now, but not forever, I said silently. If you act up again, I'll kill you on the spot.

Feiqing was extremely anxious over those days, eager to reach our destination, to get the firearms, and do what he planned to do. I could hardly agree with his idea. I'd learned from Liangzhou stories that no matter what revolution the people stage, it will be like getting rid of a turtle and getting a tortoise in its place. Revolutionaries usually turn into dictators, and sometimes the new despot is worse than the previous one. We don't have to look far into the past and just focus on the Yuan and the Ming dynasties. The Mongolians of the Yuan would never have carried out the kind of bloodbath waged by the first emperor of the Ming, who killed off all those who had helped him. Every time I heard a storyteller sing "Heroes of the Ming," I wondered if Xu Da, Chang Yuchun, and Lan Yu would have joined the rebellion if they'd known they were propping up a bloodthirsty butcher. Don't laugh. We have to ask the question. If not, benevolent and righteous men would have shed their blood in vain over the millennia. I could be considered a martyr, but I didn't follow blindly.

Which was why I had an enemy at many different stages.

And now it was the mad camel, and I really wanted to kill him.

Strangely, another camel in our caravan was attacked when I returned from the grazing ground. A chunk had been torn off the camel's leg, and it cried incessantly.

Have you ever heard the pitiful cry of a camel? It is a monotonous, hoarse sound, the worst in the world. Even thinking about it now makes me shudder.

"Brown Lion!" Qi Lu shouted when he saw me. "It's still Brown Lion. Hei, a real yellow demon, that one."

What was he saying? I knew he had to be talking about the evil deity in folktales, not our Han caravan king camel.

"Are you sure?" I was puzzled. "I saw Brown Lion lying in the desert recuperating."

"Impossible." Qi Lu nearly screamed at me. "It was clearly Brown Lion. He tore over like a whirlwind and sent some of camels running like crazy. He tore a chunk off one that wasn't fast enough."

"I saw him chomping on the piece, smacking his lips like he was really enjoying it." Cai Wu joined in.

"It really was him." Qi Lu insisted. "I even saw his bloody crotch."

"Nonsense." I laughed. "It's been so long the wound has healed. Where would you have seen blood."

"There was blood. We all saw it," Cai Wu said.

"Could it have been another mad camel?" I asked.

"Impossible. It was Brown Lion. I'd recognize him even if he were burned to ashes."

"Keep your eyes out then. Kill him when he comes again."

"He comes like the wind, too fast for anyone to react. He takes a bite and runs off like a whirlwind. We wouldn't have time to kill him," Cai Wu said.

I had to believe them. The mad camel had pretended to be recovering in the sand trough to deceive me. He took a detour and stormed over to commit another crime as I was on my way back. It had to be. When a camel runs it's fast enough to catch the sun, so naturally he had the time.

No matter what, I had to kill Brown Lion, I told myself. I couldn't wait until it was too late, when the damage got out of hand.

On a moonlit night I got closer to him.

3

I raised my weapon and aimed. I was carrying two kinds of

ammunition, a handful of buckshot and a single steel ball. I wanted to take his life quickly.

The Mongolian drivers appeared to be asleep. The sand trough was so quiet I could hear my heart pounding.

Brown Lion was lying in a sand trough. I supposed he knew his end was near, for I noticed a bright glint in his eyes. I thought he might be crying. The scene would appear again and again over many years in my life; now and then I felt a needle pricking my heart.

I hesitated momentarily before pulling the trigger. I was killing a camel, after all. For a driver to kill a camel, it had to be a last resort. I'd never have thought of killing Brown Lion if he hadn't been a killer camel; if he hadn't attacked our camels. I prayed silently for the understanding from the Camel God and said silently to Brown Lion, "Don't blame heaven or earth; blame yourself. You're ruined, so it's better to sever your karmic connections and leave to be reborn."

Then I pulled the trigger.

A fire dragon leapt at Brown Lion, followed by an explosion that made me jump. It wasn't a shot I'd heard before. I felt as if I'd been blown to pieces myself. My ears rang for a long time after that.

The dragon took off a big chunk of Brown Lion's head. I saw his blood splatter. Logically, I shouldn't have been able to see that under the moon, but I did. How odd. His blood quickly turned half the sky red. It would not be until later that I learned the image represented another terrifying situation.

He let out a blood-curdling scream. I'd also never heard a camel emit such a scary cry. His voice unfurled, like a hurricane, or the descending dark night, and spread all around me.

Mongolian drivers rushed out of their tents, shouting as they ran to Brown Lion.

I knew that no amount of explanation would be enough to stop them from tearing me to pieces.

I ran—the best strategy of all.

I heard Balte howling amid Brown Lion's scream.

4

Balte stormed our tent site with his drivers, all carrying their favorite weapons. They started smashing things the moment they entered. A chest broke and everything spilled onto the ground. Some of my friends who went up to stop them were knocked to the ground, where they moaned in pain.

He started howling again after ransacking our tent. I heard that Brown Lion had saved his life once, but there was no need to wail like that even if it was true. I'd never seen him cry before, so I was unnerved by the sight. Maybe I was wrong to do that. But if I hadn't, how many of the hundreds of our camels would be damaged by Brown Lion?

That was how I explained it to the Mongolian drivers.

"Horse shit!" Balte screamed and charged at me. Feiqing went up to stop him and said, "Let's talk it over, Brother. Let's not fight."

Balte sounded different when he said, "I didn't see him leave the sand trough once over these past days. How can a man spew that kind of nonsense?"

"He's right. It didn't move an inch," one of the Mongolian drivers said.

"You must have seen it in a dream," another joined in.

Balte dried his tears and pointed a finger at me as he seethed and said,

"I know you're dirty inside. You were thinking about revenge when it got the better of you last time. Listen to me. I'm done with you. My old sheepskin for your lamb's pelt!"

He meant that sooner or later he'd fight it out with me.

My drivers spoke up for me, "We also saw Brown Lion injure our camels. Come with us if you don't believe us." Cai Wu took the drivers out to check on those injured camels. They returned shortly.

"They look like real bites," one of them said weakly.

"Anything with a mouth can bite. How can you prove it was Brown Lion?" Balte said.

That was critical question, and we all went quiet, before someone said,

"I can prove it." It was Chain Smoker.

"I'm sixty now and I never lied, except to make empty promises to a few women. You will believe me, won't you? I saw it with my own eyes. It was Brown Lion."

"I've never lied either, and I can be a witness too." It was Wooden Fish Girl. "The one that caused the trouble earlier this afternoon was Brown Lion." Then she added something odd, "But a different Brown Lion."

I was the only one who heard her clearly, but it would take me a while to understand what she meant.

"We can prove that Brown Lion never left the sand trough all day," Huozi countered.

And that restarted an argument between the two sides.

Later, I realized that a tiny fissure can actually destroy a mile-long dam.

5

Several days later I saw Brown Lion; part of his head had been blown off, but he hadn't died. He roamed the area with his ripped head, constantly crying in a long, drawn-out voice. I shuddered every time

I heard it. It was a sad and horrific sight; with half of his cheeks gone, blood dripping from the exposed side when he chewed.

I sent Big Mouth over with a message for them to kill the camel. Stop torturing the animal and give it an easy death.

Balte slapped him before he finished, Big Mouth came back to tell us.

"Go tell that old ass. I keep Brown Lion to remind myself to never forget revenge." Balte had told him.

"He meant it. You need to be careful," Big Mouth said, holding his hand on his red cheek. "One of their drivers said Brown Lion is the guardian camel of Balte's life. He'll die if the camel is gone."

"What nonsense is that? I've heard of sacred guardian rocks, but never a camel guarding someone's life." I replied.

"That's what they all said. They said Balte had his fortune told when he was little. He wouldn't live long without help from a guardian camel to dodge the trouble in his life."

"That's ridiculous," I said with an unhappy smile.

"I can see that Huozi is a trouble-making piece of shit. He's stirred up a lot of trouble. And our marksmen have changed too. They're tight with Balte, calling him brother. His drivers are learning how to fire from our marksmen. It all feels strange and frightening."

What was most unusual was that people still saw Brown Lion, even with his shattered cheek, pouncing on Chinese camels. Chain Smoker said he saw it with his own eyes, that he was incomparably ferocious and not injured. The mere sight of him threw the Chinese camels into a panic, but he didn't harm any of them.

To be honest, I sensed something strange too. I was wary of Huozi. Many problems in the world are caused by people like him. In the Liangzhou storytelling tradition, the Huns waged wars against the Han court mostly because of a Chinese eunuch named Zhong Hangyue. People in Liangzhou call someone like him a maggot.

Don't get angry, Huozi. I'm just saying what comes to my mind.

Four. Huozi

1

I have something to say.

If I don't speak up, a lot of truth in the world would be covered up by lies.

There are so many lies in the world. Even now many Liangzhou people believe I caused Feiqing's death. They all say he wouldn't have died if I hadn't betrayed him. That's horse shit. Everyone dies. Let's put everything else aside and let me ask you something. Those founding members of the Ming dynasty Lu Fuji just mentioned. Did I cause their deaths? Did I betray any of them from a later dynasty? But did they all live to a ripe old age?

So, you see, everyone's fate has its own rhythm.

More often than not, people dig their own graves. In Buddhism there's the idea of cause and effect and retribution. You use a different expression, like "you reap what you sow," and I agree with you.

You only saw me tipping off the township's mounted troops later, but you forgot Feiqing's shortcomings. I'm telling you. He slit a dog's upper lip and called it Huozi, comparing me with a dog and turning my physiological defect into a joke. That should be enough for you; you just focus on this detail and nothing else, and you'll know what kind of person he is. How could he be a national hero? He's a nuisance. Let me ask you. Would you like someone like that if you were the emperor?

I have to admit I did really hate him, and I did really want to accomplish one thing when we were in Wild Fox Ridge. What was it? I wanted the place to be the turning point in his life. I wanted him to suffer a decline in fortune. At the time, I just wanted him to lose money, yes, money. I intended for them not to reach their destination. I was thinking that the reimbursement was such a large sum that he wouldn't be able to pay it back in his lifetime. Guess what he'd be like if he did make it? He'd host a banquet at his house for his friends, who would raise a racket from merrymaking. He'd swagger and act unbearably smug. We're brothers—I mentioned that we were cousins, so how come he got to act so arrogant and I could walk like a dog with its tail between its legs?

I wanted to stab him whenever I recalled his bluster—I still feel the urge even now. Maybe we were karmic enemies from a previous life.

I'm getting off track, so let me go back to Wild Fox Ridge.

You always blamed me for stirring up trouble, causing discord between the two caravans, which led to an armed conflict. I admit that I did "fan the flames." But let me ask you this. The Chinese and the Mongolians were already having trouble with each other before I was born. Should I be blamed for that too? Why can't you see all the historical issues instead of treating trivial matters as the motivational force behind historical developments? Let me tell you this. Even without me along, you'd still have lots of strange trouble in Wild Fox Ridge. As long as there are people, and as long as they have different minds, there will always be problems in the world. Agree?

But I have to admit that I did play a bit of role in what happened there. What role did I play? I was the one who pushed a rock off the mountain, as they say. I did so at a critical moment, and the rock followed the slope, rumbling down. But I have to add, I did that merely to get back at Feiqing, at first. Once the rock I'd set in motion reached the slope, I couldn't have stopped it even if I'd wanted to.

I did feel terrible about Brown Lion. Of course, I did. You can even say he saved my life too. More than once when we were stuck in the desert, he covered me with its chin hair. Think about it. On the icy cold, snowy desert, I'd have frozen to death without its chin hair. I can't be ungrateful. I bear grudges, but I never forget a favor.

Brown Lion was screaming in pain all night long. Just hit yourself in the crotch if you want to know how it feels—you don't even have to break your balls to understand what agony Brown Lion was going through. I'd thought of maiming Yellow Demon to avenge Brown Lion. I did something later, but I don't want to talk about it now.

It was better in the daytime, because there were enough odd jobs to occupy my mind. Once night arrived, I heard Brown Lion's screams. It must have been the same for Balte. I noticed his forehead bathed in sweat whenever the camel howled. He felt terrible. How could I not hate the bastard who blew away half of the camel's head?

The kick from Yellow Demon was a low-blow, but it was between the two camels. On the other hand, there was absolutely no reason for Lu Fuji to fire that shot. They called him a killer camel, but we never saw him kill anyone. We refused to accept the many incidents you claimed were caused by Brown Lion. The reason was simple. He was resting in a spot where we could see him each time Cai Wu and others said he launched an attack. In other words, we had an alibi for the camel.

To be sure, that was just how we looked at it back then.

We even thought you were merely looking for an excuse to kill the camel, no matter what you said.

Think about it. How were we supposed to abide the shot Lu Fuji fired?

2

I realized it was a bad sign that they shot Brown Lion. I told that to Balte.

"What sign?" he asked.

"I think they changed their destination."

"Why is that?"

"They may have changed from reaching Luocha to staying to become outlaws."

"I doubt it."

"Why? Think about all the treasure. Even Sha Meihu can't be that rich. At a chaotic time like this, being a Sha Meihu isn't so bad." I replied.

"Do you mean Feiqing and his men want to be desert outlaws?"

"They don't want to, because they already are. The Society of Brothers is an anti-Qing court organization."

"In fact, I knew all along that Feiqing had lots of visitors and that they were always setting up an altar. Unsavory characters often showed up at his door. He probably wouldn't have become an outlaw under normal circumstances, but he surely would in order to survive if someone put a knife to his head. You probably are unaware that the government has found out about the Society of Brothers, and they already gave up Feiqing."

"How did you know?"

"A message brought by a homing pigeon. Think about it. He'd surely die if he went back. We'd be his greatest obstacle if he planned to settle here," I explained.

"Will he kill us?"

"Of course, he will."

"I've been puzzled too," Balte said. "I never believed Brown Lion could hurt so many Chinese camels. And I saw him recovering in the sand trough. So, they were just trying to come up with a reason. But does he need a reason if he wants to kill us?"

"No, he doesn't, but his drivers do." I continued, "Understand? Drivers who don't know his identity wouldn't follow his lead without a good reason. Fanning the flames of the conflict is the best way to create a reason. Shooting Brown Lion was a fuse; they will have a reason if we take it seriously."

"But we do take it seriously," Balte said.

"Then they have a reason now, so we have to be prepared." I cautioned him.

Yes, I admit that all the preparations we did later originated from the talk I had with him that night.

The next day, I relayed the conversation to the Mongolian drivers, who then decided to set out without delay, even if some of the injured camels hadn't completely recovered. We'd keep heading toward our destination. Some even believed that it would save the Mongolian caravan.

Hei-hei, but what others said made sense too—what we did actually destroyed the whole caravan. But when we think about it a hundred years later, how many could have made it out alive even without my scheming?

Yes, you're right.

I hear many sighs; they fade away like the wind.

Everything will be over sooner or later, no matter how hair-raising when it's happening. Once it's over, it's nothing but memory.

I'm still mired in the gloomy mood caused by what the yellow camel has done when the interview is over. He stares at me glumly, obviously aware that I will punish him. He knows I'll whip him, so now he appears resigned, ready to let things come to a head. He will even return my gaze with provocation in his eyes, filled with hate and viciousness. He would surely be whipped if he had an ill-tempered driver. But I ignore him. He's waiting for my retaliation, so I won't do anything to punish him. I won't forgive him either. Sometimes forgiveness must not be given easily, and he has to suffer what he deserves, for one shouldn't do away with cause and effect too lightly. But I replace the whip with silence; I believe that to the yellow camel, my silence is like a sword hanging over his hand, ready to fall at any moment.

Thirst is indeed awful. It has lain dormant after I found the cistanches, and seems less overpowering. Once the plants are gone, however, thirst will become a ferocious beast and pounce on me. My throat is so dry it feels like leather, as if baked. I take a few sips of water, but the thirst remains. I have to stop myself from drinking it all down, though I know no amount of water will slake the thirst in my soul. My confidence is suffering greatly because of a disaster that has yet to happen.

I'm exhausted, fatigued inside and out. Finally, I fall asleep, only to be plagued by bad dreams. I dream about a lot of things, but can't remember any details. I am often startled awake from the dreams. My heart beats wildly whenever I think of what I may have to confront later. I can go back to sleep only when I put myself in a realm where my heart doesn't race. So, I repeatedly use Dharma's "adversity from retribution" to convince myself until I finally forgive the yellow camel.

No matter how exasperated I'm with the yellow camel, he's still better than the wolf following me. If I can stand a wolf trailing me, why can't I tolerate my own camel? The thought immediately brings me peace.

Seventeenth Session
Stoning

Drive the camels, up before dawn, head to the ninth spot.
A seriously ill man, has trouble getting up to leave, who's there to care for him?
Looks like, he's ready to depart for the underworld, quickly take him to back home.
The whole family, cries so sadly, shedding enough tears to drown people.
You see, this is, the life of a camel driver,
No way to make a living.

——*Song of a Camel Driver*

The water is low.

I used less water when I had the cistanches, which I also fed to the camels and dog. The abundant juice from the plants supplied us with plenty of the fluids we needed. But it's really tough now that I don't have any more of them.

I'm parched when I get up in the morning, so I have several more sips.

After breakfast I go out to look for water, after quickly jotting down the major ideas from the previous night's interview. I know it's pointless to search, but I can't sit and wait to die, can I? Besides water, I actually hope to find some cistanches and suoyang, which is not impossible. They grow in the desert as long as the conditions are right, and they're now the lifesaving straw. Experience tells me that my chances of finding water are slim, but there may very well be succulent desert plants. I found some earlier, so I should be able to find something. I focus mainly on areas with both sand and soil, where suoyang tends to grow. It needs more than just dirt for suitable growing conditions, to be sure. Besides, they'll be underground, if there are indeed any, and I'm too weak to dig a large area to search—the surface of the earth cracks only when they're in season. When they're not in season, I can't tell where they may be—so I have to pin my hopes on cistanches. I spend over half a day checking lots of plants, but to my disappointment, I not only can't find what I'm looking for, but I end up drinking most of the water in the sack.

Thirst never relents in its assault on me.

I collapse when I return to the camp site. I lie down on the sand and rest for a long time to recover. Because of the walk, I'm not too cold, even on a winter day like this. Actually, I was sweating from the fast walk, and now the rest cools my body.

I know I won't last long like this.

The green light is inching closer. I wish the dog would make a noise to scare it off, but the dog remains silent.

When I've rested enough and feel better, I wrap the fur coat around me and start the incantation to summon the specters.

One. Ma Zaibo

1

Being discovered with Wooden Fish Girl at Su Wu Temple was a staggering blow that knocked me for a loop.

I lost my "serenity;" I felt shaky.

I wasn't a holy person. I'd never been one, nor would I ever be. I wish you'd stop treating me like a holy man. I was just trying to be one. I hoped I could be holy and so I worked hard toward my goal, earnest and honest with myself as I did.

I thought about women. I thought about the type of women I liked, not those from my hometown. They were fine, except for their additional demands. I was the young master to them. When I was with them, I could often hear what they were saying to themselves, most of which was pragmatic and could be turned into something materialistic. I never fell for any of them.

I valued my life too much to waste it on women like that.

The woman I wanted lived in my heart, and I longed for her. She wasn't a goddess, but was nobler, lovelier, and livelier than any goddess. . . In any case, I had many vague but clear demands. I'd been looking for her. My condition was quite simple: I'd know her when I found her. "Yes, that's her."

I had that feeling when I listened to Wooden Fish Girl sing that day. I saw something familiar in her face; it could have been a light, a kind of holy purity, or a beauty unique to a woman. To be honest, I wouldn't have been able to see how remarkable she was if she hadn't sung. No matter how pretty a woman is, she has the same features as everyone else. Could a beautiful woman be prettier than a flower? Heh-heh, listen to me. Back then I did prefer flowers to those women in my hometown, because I felt something when I saw flowers, but nothing when facing one of those women. When she sang, Wooden Fish Girl brought alive something deep in my soul. You want to call it a poetic flavor? I say yes and no. More like the passion innate in life. Yes, innate. It had been asleep for years and awoke on that day. I opened my bleary eyes to a hallucinatory, extraordinary world.

In the beginning, I was rational enough to suppress my impulse and curiosity, which I tried to counteract with something I'd learned, including the "white bone" doctrine. Sometimes it worked, but it had very limited power. I could only supersede it by redoubling my effort in self-cultivation, and that worked too, but still with limited power. Worse yet, when I practiced by imagining myself at the yidam, her expression when she sang crashed into my mind and took the yidam's place. At the time, I was studying Vajravārāhi, but with the invasion of her vivid image, I could no longer imagine Vajravarahi's features, and later she even became Vajravārāhi. I saw her everywhere, whether I was sitting, lying down, or walking. She always wore a charming smile, singing the strange and yet familiar songs.

To be sure, I was also interested in wooden fish songs, as I was in Liangzhou's stories. I didn't think hers were necessarily better, as I knew hers was a variation of Liangzhou's songs. To be sure, you can say the Liangzhou tunes were a variation of the wooden fish songs. They came from the same source: classical fiction or Dunhuang vernacular stories. I had to admit that I was drawn to these songs, but it was the singing girl who had me in her thrall.

I didn't care if she'd been a beggar, I really didn't care. I didn't even care if she was an assassin or a killer, for it had nothing to do with me. To me at the time, she was just a lovely girl, though I did treat her as a Dakini. Seen from a certain level, she was the Dakini of my life, because she ignited my passion as a man. Over the past two decades or so, I'd met enough women, some of whom could be considered beauties. But they were them and I was me. They couldn't obliterate my feeling of being inside a glass cocoon. Only she could do that and let me feel fresh human air.

Do you think she's my Dakini?

Hu Gala also said she was a Dakini. I'd observed her based on the prerequisites laid out in copies of Buddhist classics and saw she did have characteristics of a Padmadakini, the lotus Dakini, which formed one of the most important conditions for me to let her into my life. Without it, the single act of singing alone could not have shaken my beliefs.

You clearly haven't witnessed the sacred purity on her face when she sings. There seems to be a sacred glow. And that voice, it has magnetic qualities. Sometimes I even ignored the content and focused on the voice itself, which was enough to take me into a realm where I'd never been before. I felt something in my life had been awakened.

I welcomed the awakening with amazement and joy.

I regretted it after our first physical contact. I wanted to distance myself from a temptation that was greater than any power. I noticed she had the same feeling, so we ignored each other. Over those days, I prolonged my meditative practice, forcing myself not to think about her, but I found myself incapable of sleeping peacefully. I felt suddenly weightless when I imagined not being with her; I couldn't regain my former tranquility.

When we were discovered that night, I was like a moth flying into a fire. I wanted to burn in the fire of passion.

I hadn't thought someone would be watching us. I asked myself later if I would have been involved with her had I known earlier about what would happen that day? My answer would be, "No."

The price was too high for my life. I lost more than just the worldly part, but also the means of transcending this world.

It became a stain I could not wash off, not until I carried another sublimation, that is.

2

I regained my composure after a brief panic. I comforted myself: you did it, so you must accept the outcome.

It was probably another manifestation of the law of cause and effect.

Whatever I do in my life, I must accept the consequences.

But I was also aware that my life could be ruined after something like this. No one in this small city would respect anyone who had sex in a temple, not to mention the fact that the man was known as a religious meditator who had sex with a beggar woman.

Just like that, I fell from heaven to hell. The spit aimed at her face landed on mine too.

I don't feel like describing the scene. You can imagine how it was.

Just think how some men and women who had always smiled solicitously and deferentially to you now played the role of moral judges and spit on you. All kinds of weird things came out of their mouths. They may have just come from doing something terrible, but now they assumed the attitude of honorable people. You might wonder what gave them the right to judge you. They were like clusters of will-o'-the-wisps roaming a graveyard, but who dared to put the sun on trial.

Yes, Wooden Fish Girl in my mind was still the sun at that moment, even though I might have chosen differently had I known we'd be found out. Deep down, I still loved her. It was hopeless. Love is a frightening disease. No wonder our ancestors called it the demon of emotion.

Hu Gala looked outraged, but to me most of his anger seemed to be for show only, as if he knew he should be incensed, but he really wasn't.

He suggested that they give Wooden Fish Girl a beating before driving her out of town. I knew he wanted to protect her, but the elders refused by trooping out many rules in our clan order. I was aware that something like this could end easily, but could also be blown out of proportion. They could quietly deal with it and everything would be fine. But some wanted to escalate the situation, and Hu Gala could find no excuse to keep it down.

We were taken to Su Wu Hall, then to my family hall. I knew someone was behind it when I saw they wanted to make it a big incident. Naturally, I didn't know who he was, but the first one who came to mind was anyone who would benefit from ruining my reputation. There were quite a few of those. It couldn't be helped. A young master of a powerful family was sometimes a target. We were a big clan with several branches, each with people who envied me. I didn't want to examine every one of them. All I could think was, I did it, and I had to deal with the consequences. It remains an iron-clad convention that you reap what you sow.

The serenity that Wooden Fish Girl saw was the product of such mentality.

To be sure, I also knew it would blow over quickly, no matter how it escalated. My continued practice of visualization led me to discover that everything, including my own life, rushes away like water unleashed from a floodgate. I was never sure before I fell asleep if I would wake up the next morning, so I knew nothing stayed the same no matter how big a deal it was.

But I knew my life was over, despite my wise thoughts. To fall like that over a woman was absolutely not worth it, for it left a lifelong stain.

At the time, I had planned to spread the Dharma. No one would believe a word from a man who had sex with a beggar in a temple now, I knew.

They would instead call me a hypocrite or a liar, a fact I rued the most.

Once during his illumination, the Guru focused on this aspect, and said, "You will be fine in many respects. You come from a rich family, so you'll have no money problems. If something were to happen to you, it would have to do with women, so you must follow our proscriptions steadfastly."

I'd followed his instructions for years, but unfortunately, sex was my undoing.

The family hall was jam-packed, with the lively airs of a New Year's celebration. My father had the reputation of being a lecher, so I was just continuing the family tradition. Hear that—someone was saying: "A dragon begets a dragon, a phoenix sires a phoenix, and a rat's son is good at boring through a wall." He-he-he, ha-ha-ha. It was so festive.

I felt terrible for my mother. Her sky had fallen and she looked old. She had never been happy because of Father's affairs, but instead of raising a stink, she just looked glum. She retched every time she learned about another affair, throwing up liquid like cow's saliva, and that often led to chest pains. I felt wretched when I thought about the blow on her.

But I knew a bigger blow was coming. Someone had enlarged the scale of the incident, and now it could not be settled quietly. I did not know how the clan would deal with it. Even with the best possible outcome, she would still suffer immensely over the process alone.

I did not try to soothe Mother, I didn't know what to say. All I could do was calmly accept what was happening. I'd take whatever was coming at me, whether it was from someone in the clan or not. I did it and I'd own up to it.

I worried more about Wooden Fish Girl. Her long hair was so rumpled I couldn't see her face, though I did know something horrific awaited her. The clan had once dealt with an adulteress by making her ride a wooden donkey; she was stripped naked and paraded through the streets atop a wooden donkey. I knew the people enjoyed the spectacle, and that she would suffer if the elders in the clan insisted upon the same punishment.

At a moment like this, I could do nothing but let heaven decide.

I did not see Father, though I could imagine how the news affected him. He'd sought the help of many matchmakers to find a number of pretty girls. He would likely wonder why I hadn't liked any of them and instead fell for a beggar. He can wonder if he wants, I said to myself. I didn't feel guilty where he was concerned, since he had gone through enough himself to make it through this time.

The elders all wore serious expressions as they discussed how to deal with us. This had to be the most important event requiring their attention in recent years. Father had been among them in the past as they meted out punishment to some of the bad seeds. They had the guilty ones brought over, stripped them naked, and lashed them on the backs with a willow switch, before making them put on a banquet to promise the elders they would never transgress again. I was hoping to see Ma Siye, whose participation could mean leniency for Wooden Fish Girl. But he was nowhere in sight, and I didn't see any elders from my branch of the clan either. Maybe they were too ashamed to come.

Do whatever you want then, I closed my eyes and said silently.

3

The judgement was made.

The clan's decision was: stone the whore to death for seducing a young man from a respectable family.

It was a practice popular in many places, mostly used on adulteresses, and for thousands of years. One of its advantages was, everyone could be the executioner. Anyone could throw a stone. I'd seen it done once, when a group of young men waged a contest to see who had the best aim. The loser had to pay with liquor and food.

As for me, I was to be locked up in the family hall for three days, with no food, before I was sent home for further discipline by my family.

I told everyone I saw not to subject her to that punishment. I repeated myself, "She did not do anything wrong. It was all my fault; I forced her into it. You can punish me for raping her. She's a victim." No one listened to me, except for one, who laughed and said, "Enough, Young Master. They listened outside your window long enough to hear all the dirty talk from the slut. Everyone in the city knows about it. It was not rape."

On the day of the punishment, gawkers crowded onto Mount Su Wu like ants moving house. I supposed the whole township had turned up. It was a rare event, not something one could see whenever one wanted. I was locked up in the family hall. I should have been in attendance to watch, but they locked me inside because I was a member of the Ma family and they wanted to preserve the family reputation.

It was the longest day of my life.

I came up with many ideas, but none of them worked. For one thing, everyone ignored me, including those guarding the room. I shouted and raised hell, but they were impassive, as if I were facing a gaseous ball. I ran out of options after shouting and yelling for a while.

A scene kept appearing before my eyes:

The excited—not angry—people hogtied Wooden Fish Girl. It was the locals' favorite way of constraining a person, using a long rope to tie the arms and twisting them around to the back. Yes, that's right. They'd already cut her hair short for the gawkers to see her face more easily. The keyed-up crowd was eager to see the feminine face. Her eyes were partly shut, the hint of a smile danced around the corners of her mouth. I believed she would be smiling, the same as when she was singing, as if entranced. They'd beaten her repeatedly, but I saw no marks, because I didn't want her to be hurt. When a stoning death had been executed in the past, the target would have her head covered, but not this time. They were more interested in seeing the pain written on a woman's face. There wouldn't be any excitement if her head was covered.

Several young men from the clan pushed and shoved her toward a pole on Mount Su Wu. It had been erected specifically for a stoning, which had always been carried out at the same spot. As far I could recall, eleven women had been stoned to death here; Wooden Fish Girl would make number twelve. It was a familiar number, reminding me of the twelve disciples. Then the crowd's cheers sounded in my ears. Stone her. Stone her. Stone the whore's spawn to death. These were common curses in the countryside back then. Sometime even a father would scream those words at his own daughter.

I shuddered.

I saw a wind from the north of the desert raise thick columns of dust toward the crowd. I wished the wind would grow strong enough to blind those gloating onlookers. They weren't angry, I could see; they were roused, as if watching a stage play. I didn't think anyone was upset over what had happened at the Temple. I did not believe that. Would you? If Su Wu himself showed up, the people would have dealt with him the same way they treated me. They didn't care about things that did not concern them; whatever happened to others, major or minor, had nothing to do with them. They cared only about an opportunity like this. So many were hoping she'd be made to ride the wooden donkey or turned into a hanging lantern. On the wooden donkey, they'd get to see her naked. Even though they'd stick a wooden plug up her, they'd still get to see her breasts sway with the rocking donkey. Compared to riding a wooden donkey, a hanging lantern was more pleasing to the eye. They'd see a woman scream as they set her on fire and strung her high up on a swing set. Lengths of cotton doused in cooking oil would be wrapped all around her body and, when it was lit, it would pop and crackle. Her screams would sound watery, the roaring cotton would be fiery, creating the sensation of water working in concert with fire, when the two were put together. Lonely people could relish the event for a long time, sometimes it was enough for several generations to savor. I often recalled what Grandpa had said about a woman being turned into a hanging lantern. When he retold the story, he clearly wanted to show off, though he also wished there were more to say.

"It was a sight you'd remember for the rest of your life, my boy."

The only flaw was the cotton wrapping that obscured the woman's body, so they couldn't see more. When put side by side, riding a wooden donkey was clearly a better show. That was why a lot of people wanted to see Wooden Fish Girl ride one. I was curious why the elders opted for a stoning death; maybe they wanted everyone to take part in the punishment. In those days it was a highly effective educational method.

I was out of my mind at that moment. You can hear it still in my narration, can't you?

As the crowd hollered, Wooden Fish Girl passed through a net crisscrossed with countless gazes, slowly and sluggish like a fish swimming in glue. Naturally, I hoped she would take it slow; I didn't want her to move too fast to become a meat patty. A few women were turned to pulp in the past, because some who needed to vent their spleen smashed the women with big rocks after she stopped screaming. Not to leave an intact body was considered a horrible death. In ancient times, people's greatest hope was to have an unbroken body when they died, the last sign of dignity. More often than not, they were deprived of the dignity.

I detected in their cheers a long-awaited anticipation; clearly, they'd been waiting for this opportunity, yearning for an excuse to strip the life of another person. Finally, their chance had come. They covered their excitement with feigned anger; they smacked their lips noisily, a rowdy crowd at a carnival, like a hungry wolf seeing a tender new baby.

Wooden Fish Girl was doomed, I knew.

4

She would be bound to the pole amid loud cheers. Tied to it would be a blood red streamer that flapped in the wind, an amulet to ward off evil spirits. When it was over, the streamer would be shredded and the stoners would each get a piece to tie to one of their buttons or hang on the lock at their doors. It would prevent the ghost of the one they stoned to death from seeking revenge.

On the morning of the execution, the people would gather a huge load of stones of various sizes, shapes, colors, and patterns from the desolate riverbank. The stones would be piled not too far from the pole, so anyone interested in participating could pick them up. After the execution, the stones would be placed directly on the body to form a kind of grave mound. In Liangzhou's local lore, these stones had the evilest power; with them on the body, the soul and spirits of the dead women would be frightened off, and they would never be able to free themselves. If something wasn't going right in your family, you could pick a sturdy small stone, kneel and bang your head on the ground with your prayer, then take the stone home to heat over a fire until it was bright red. You put it in a metal ladle that had hair in it and ran around your house like a cat or dog leaping and jumping, while sprinkling vinegar on the stone for sour steam to rise and drive away evil spirits. It smelled rancid, burned, and something else—right, that stone was the deity of a vinegar bomb. Among the stones that could be used for this purpose, those that had killed a woman had the most demonic power.

An elder representing the clan would begin his speech, bold and assured, for he'd often spoken like that. His role in the clan was the equivalent of the monk in Tibetan temples in charge of discipline. He was born with a grim, steely face, so when he said all those things, he would definitely sound and look filled with indignation. It wasn't every day that he could get to scowl, so he has to exert his power and authority to the fullest.

It would be a long speech but the gist of it would be as follows:

"You're a donkey's ass, a horse's spawn, a food-scraper from the grass lake. How dare you seduce a young man from a respectable family and do it in a temple? You're utterly shameless. How could you do something like that? Use a rock if you feel an itch down there; a fire tong would work too. Why must you seduce a young man from a respectable family? You've ruined his life. You whore. How is the young man going to face the world? Why didn't you take a piss to look at yourself? He's too good for you. See, and you're still smiling?"

Then he would go up and give her a vicious slap.

I'd seen him do that often enough to know.

I could see her face now, and she looked just like when she was singing. Despite a splotch of blood at the corner of her mouth, she was still beautiful. That was weird. How did I think she was pretty? I admit that I'd fallen in love with her. We got ourselves into serious trouble, but if we could turn back time, I wouldn't be certain if I could resist the temptation. I had thought about consequences, don't get me wrong, for there is no airtight wall. But I couldn't help it. My heart had a mind of its own. I'd thought I had practiced meditation long enough and had reached a certain level. I hadn't expected to lose control when I met her.

The people would be picking up stones now, almost feverishly choosing ones they liked. They'd be jovial, caught up in holiday spirits. I longed to see reluctance and compassion on their faces, but there was none, only exhilaration. Why were they so excited? I wondered. What would they get after turning her body into pulp? I wanted to ask them, but was quickly drowned out by their laughter. It is human nature to thirst for blood, I understood that.

The pile of stones quickly disappeared. Those who managed to grab one cheered, holding it high, while others continued to search the ground. Some even went over to pick one from a previous execution site, which was against the rules, but was ignored.

That was how the pile of stones at another pole vanished and exposed a jumble of bones underneath it. The bones had fallen apart until they no longer looked like they came from a human body, more like from a dog or a pig. But not human any more. I detected the stench of a corpse, the only proof that it had belonged to a human body. I heard that human bones smell the worst. The pile proved it had buried a woman through its unique stench.

Now I recalled it had been a pretty woman too. She had been married to a camel driver, who had been gone for three years without a word. She'd had an affair with a village butcher. Unexpectedly her husband returned one day in the middle of the night. He hadn't wanted her to die by stoning, but the other camel drivers egged him on, for they feared that their own women would do the same while they were away. They insisted upon a stoning death. So, a group of angry—truly angry this time—camel drivers swarmed to the site and turned the wife into pulp.

"Don't pick those! Stop picking those stones, you jackass!" The district leader yelled.

Those who wanted to take stones from another pile of bones smiled sheepishly.

"Enough, enough. These will do. Do you want to turn her into meaty paste?"

5

They cleared a space. Those with stones stood to one side, while the larger side was left unoccupied so the onlookers wouldn't be hurt in case the stones missed the target. Many of the clan youths raised a spear to stop the crowd from rushing forward. I even saw a few scoundrels waging a bet to see who would hit her head first. It had happened often. There was a group betting on how long she'd hold out, and even some people having steamed buns ready to dip in her blood and brains. A man was pointing at Wooden Fish Girl as he "showered water" to a few women. To locals, "shower water" meant to educate and instruct. I knew he was instructing his own wife, though I also knew he himself had several mistresses. There were all sorts of people with all sorts of ideas. Strangely, however, I knew all of them. Don't ask if I'd attained enough magic power at that moment. I didn't know. But I did know about these people.

They were all holding their stones, waiting for the executing elder to give his order, which would come from the stone in his hand. When he flung his, many, many more would fly at her. The smaller ones would go for her head and raise lumps on Wooden Fish Girl's face. If they threw it hard enough, it would open a hole that oozed blood first and then squirted it. As for the large stones, it would be hard to predict. I'd once seen a rock slice off a woman's scalp. It was like a horse hoof, with the force of a galloping horse. You know how powerful those hooves could be. If a horse kicked with all its might and hit you on the head, a piece of your bone would fly off. Believe me? Back then, the people were nicer and weren't allowed to use big rocks; otherwise, someone with great power could throw a large rock and take half of a woman with it. Using only small stones ensured that the execution would last longer, like a prolonged battle, not a blitz, so the many women would receive the education they needed.

I saw that most of those holding rocks were men, almost no women. The same held true for earlier executions. Were the women not allowed to participate? No, there was no rule against it, but they did not take part. Does that mean the women were compassionate? No, definitely not. When they watched the men throw stones, some of the women blanched, while others laughed as if enjoying a circus show. That was how it was and there was nothing to do about it. I was like them when I was little, as I watched the screaming woman as if it had been a circus. At the time I couldn't possibly have imagined that I'd be associated with such a horrendous execution. Yesterday I watched them, today they're watching me. That's how things are, aren't they?

I'd thought Mother would be among the stoners, but no, she wasn't there. I hadn't seen her since the day I told her I was to blame. I knew she was suffering. She couldn't face the world, I could not face her. I wished I could turn into a bubble and disappear from the world, no, not a bubble, wispy smoke. I wanted to vanish like a wisp of smoke.

Someone brought over lime to sprinkle on her after she was turned to a pulp. I was told it could stop a stench from rising in the future and prevent pestilence, something that had happened years ago during an execution. Many of the village men, mostly the stoners, died. Some said it was caused by a pestilence, but others claimed it was revenge by the dead woman's ghost. From then on, lime was spread over the bloody mess after each execution.

I smelled the unique odor of lime, which, I believed, Wooden Fish Girl detected also. She probably should be wailing. In the past all the women wailed, cursed in tears or struggled, just not acting impassively or indomitable, as she was now. The spectators need your cooperation, and the best thing you can do for them is show them you're afraid. They won't enjoy themselves if you grit your teeth, not crying or screaming. I wanted to tell her this, but then on second thought, I decided to let her be.

I hope you don't cry or scream and smile instead, as you watch the stones flying at you, and let your smile freeze in their hearts.

I could see the first stone, a kind of firing shot, fly out and crash against your forehead. Not a powerful hit, just enough to bruise the skin, but it's soon followed by a much larger one whizzing at you. Its aim is too high and so it hits the pole to make it sway. Fear begins to appear on your face, I can see; you must have been frightened by the sound. I can't see any stones after that; all I see are flocks of flying crows screeching as they swarm toward you to peck off your flesh and suck on your blood. They are all over you now. I can't see you any longer. You hang your head, your hair that had been snipped and cut haphazardly draped over your face. You are no longer pretty.

Stop! Stop! I hear someone shout. He goes up and, with a flick of his hands, braids your hair into a rope and weaves it into the rope binding you. I know they all want to see your face, to enjoy the horrific sight on it after the stoning. They did not aim for your face at first, because they wanted to gaze into it as they cast their stones. The mentality is similar to why a man stares at his victim as he rapes her. Rapists like to carry out their violence in a well-lit place so they can look at their victims, getting more excited the more the women scream. These men are the same; they would be deprived of pleasure if your head is covered.

The rocks land on your feet and legs first, but mostly they hit the air around you.

It would go on for about an hour.

Like a cat toying with a mouse, they hit and miss you, so that you won't die too easily or quickly.

Later, when they've had their fun, the betting scoundrels will aim their bowl-sized rocks at your head.

A perfect hit draws a loud cheer. He'll win a bowl of cow guts.

More perfect hits follow. Your body slowly weakens, slumped against the pole like a strip of leather. Then the elder comes up to cut the rope tying you with a knife, for more rocks to come and smash you into pulp.

The lime will come to cover what has just happened.

I saw the same thing eleven times and I know all the details.

Two. Big Mouth

I heard about what had happened as soon as I got in town. It was like a lightning bolt. "You can have had any woman you wanted, Young Master Ma. Why did you have to pick her?" I lamented silently. "A great loss of face. It's something I can do, but not you. It's beneath you."

My first reaction was to stab everyone, but then I said to myself,

"Who do you think you are? She's not your woman or your mother. What right do you have to use a knife on her?" The thought lessened my anger.

I knew they wouldn't let Wooden Fish Girl off the hook easily. There were rules for matters like this.

I didn't know who to talk to. I was aware that Feiqing should know, but I didn't have time. You know the Lake was too far, there and back would cause an unacceptable delay.

No solution came to me when the execution day arrived, but I got a few brothers together anyway. If there was no other option, we'd raid the execution site and rescue her that way. But they lost their nerve when we got there and saw the huge crowd. I couldn't blame them. We'd all be turned into meat patties if the stoners turned the rocks on us. Raiding the execution site was out of the question.

I was afraid too. To be frank, I was good at club fighting, but I wasn't brave. When we attacked the police that time, I'd lacked the will to fight, just as Wooden Fish Girl told you. I couldn't help it. I crumpled at the sight of anyone in official garb. It's an incurable affliction.

My parents came to watch that day, but I was wearing a straw hat and they didn't see me. They had clearly aged. I'd brought disgrace to them, in their eyes. They fear the government too and wanted least for me to get on the wrong side of the law. Me, too, actually. But sometimes it can't be helped; you obey the law but the law doesn't always leave you alone. You have to fight when their hands grab hold of your throat. Over those years, I'd seen too much injustice and I hoped to change it. I'd wanted to overthrow the Qing court, but I hadn't expected life to be even tougher after we did it. Be it the Republic or what came after that, I failed to see the world I'd hoped to see. It was hopeless. I open my eyes wide, now as a wandering ghost, but still fail to see any light after a hundred years.

The first rock flew at her and great numbers would follow. She knew some *qigong*, but I doubted she could hold out long. I was keenly aware of my own powerlessness in reversing the dire situation. She would surely die now. Even women with a powerful maternal family had died by stoning, let alone her, a food-scraper to the villagers, who seduced the young master of the Ma family. What a wonderful young man he was, so graceful, like a jade tree in the wind, the man of many young girls' dream. Many families would have loved to have him as a son-in-law. What else could happen, but death after what she did?

See, the people had their rocks ready, waiting for action.

Another rock flew at her, then several more, then over a dozen. I knew countless rocks were about to fall on her turning her into bloody pulp. I was so worried my forehead was beaded. I should go out there, yes. I will. I was about to leap out when I heard a voice:

"Put down your knives!" It was Hu Gala on a camel, waving a whip and shouting.

It was clearly inappropriate to say "put down your knives," since no one was using a knife. But everyone stopped when they heard his shout. In Liangzhou's storytelling tradition, if someone shouted "put down your knife" when a loyal minister was about to be killed, the subsequent development of the story would be very satisfying to the listeners.

Hu Gala reached the site, got off his camel, and said, "My god, you nearly committed a terrible offense. Do you know the girl is carrying the flesh and blood of the Ma family? She's pregnant with Ma Zaibo's baby."

"Is that true? Is it really?" A commotion broke out among the crowd.

"Of course, it is. Would I lie to you in broad daylight? She's guilty, but the baby isn't. Can you wait to stone her after she has the baby?"

"Can it really be true?" The elder's eyes bulged. "Don't you dare tell dirty lies."

"Of course, it's true." Hu Gala added, "I never lie. I felt her pulse, and I'm sure of it. It's a classic rolling bead pulse. I can feel a hundred pulses and get it right a hundred and one times."

"Does Ma Erye know?" someone out there shouted.

"Of course, he knows. I was just at his house. Ma Erye said he'd accept it if she's pregnant. He'd accept her and the baby. If he has no problem with it, then there's nothing wrong. A young man got himself a woman, and it's no concern of ours. Heh-heh."

"Why did you wait so damned long to tell us?" The elder flew into a rage.

"He's right." Those who had found a rock to their liking put it down unhappily, their fun spoiled.

"I had to tell Ma Erye first." Hu Gala smiled. "I wouldn't dare say a word if he didn't want to have anything to do with it."

Three. Ma Zaibo

You have no idea how everything was in turmoil after that.

Mother cried all day long, dead set against her treasure of a son marrying a food-scraper; I'd brought shame to her and broken her heart.

She made it clear to me that she would hang herself if I married her. Father was in a foul mood, like an ill-tempered thunder god flaring up. He was angry that I'd brought shame to the family. But I wondered if he had been more upset with my choice. I'd turned down so many young ladies from good families, and what I had done turned them into laughingstocks. Many were stunned and said a great deal of terrible things.

But Father had been around long enough and his anger soon died down, at least on the surface. He realized that what had been worrying him had resolved on its own. He'd been worried I might become a monk, which I'd wanted to do all along, and had used that to turn down all the proposals from matchmakers. Now, after what I had done, he could breathe a sigh of relief. He didn't let on, but I sensed it. Hu Gala later revealed to me in private that Father had looked faintly pleased when he told him about Wooden Fish Girl's pregnancy. Obviously, my plan to become a monk had been a serious concern of his.

It was possible that Father said "he'd accept" her to save a person's life. For years, he'd had the reputation of a lecher, but he'd also been kind to others, done many good deeds, and helped many out. You shouldn't believe that a lecherous man is necessarily evil. Many good men like women. What normal man wouldn't?

I found that Father was serious about "accepting it." He wanted to bring Wooden Fish Girl home to give birth, but Mother objected, so did my uncles and cousins. We lived in a hundred-year-old compound, and they did not want to be laughed at because of a food-scraper. They were what Father was up against in the end.

The critical question was, "How do you know she's carrying Zaibo's child, not someone else's?"

It was naturally a sobering question. The Ma family could never bring in another man's baby.

I gave him the affirmative answer when Father asked me.

With that resolved, Father displayed his extraordinary talent. First, he said to me, "You did whatever you wanted to do in the past, son. Now you must act like a man. I don't care who she is, food-scraper or not, she's human. She's a woman, and you were involved with her, so you have to marry her. And from now on you have to stop your nonsense about being a monk."

"You old fart, how could you say that?" Mother screamed at him. "How can my son marry a beggar? It makes me want to throw up just thinking about it. Stop the nonsense."

"Why don't you ask your treasure of a son? Why did he do that? If he doesn't take responsibility for what he's done, who will?"

Arguments like that erupted in the house frequently over those days. Heh-heh, sounds familiar, doesn't it?

I obeyed Father's order. Honestly, I was out of sorts for a while at first. The incident brought on many changes in my life. I'd never had to worry about mundane matters, as I indulged myself in my world. Now I had to confront many things that I hadn't wanted to face.

I was wracked by a kind of regret I'd never felt before. But at the time, I thought I finally understood Father; I saw something I hadn't noticed in him.

The argument continued, so did visits paid by many, who brought more rancor.

Someone even came up with the idea of doing away with Wooden Fish Girl. Father laughed when he heard. "If I had that in mind, why didn't I let her die under the stones? Why did I stop them?" Father continued, "No matter what, it's a human life, for me to save if I could. Besides, she is carrying our flesh and blood."

Later Mother relented. "Let heaven be the judge then. I'll accept the baby if it's a boy, but I won't if it's girl."

Many people accepted Mother's idea of leaving it to heaven.

"Let heaven decide then," they said.

Eighteenth Session
Hu Family Mill

And I, too, have to leave it to heaven.

I have virtually no water left, and the roasted potatoes are long gone. I have no way to make the instant noodles go down; each time I eat some it feels like chewing dry twigs.

But I have to keep looking. Besides cistanches and water, I'm also looking for the hope to survive. This time I leave with the camels and the dog, as well as the other stuff, because I'm afraid I won't have the strength to return. Like letting a horse lead the way, I say to myself. Where we go is where we'll be. If heaven really wants to take my life, then there's nothing I can do to stop it.

I don't even care what direction I take; I just follow a feeling. Let me die in the desert if heaven refuses to help me out. That's what I'm thinking, when it suddenly dawns on me why my interview subjects never express any concern over my situation. Could they not know? Or is there some other reason? Should I have asked them where to find water and how I can survive?

I'll definitely ask them tonight, I tell myself.

I still can't find what I'm looking for after walking nearly all day. I continue to wander aimlessly amid the same foliage. I get my compass out and check the direction before taking out the map. What I'm looking for this time isn't a water source, but a landmark structure: the Hu Family Mill. It isn't marked on the map, but there's a sign for a house. I'll go look for it whether it's the Mill or not. Actually, I'm hoping to find water or cistanches along the way. I must be proactive; I can't stay passively in the sand trough and wait to die.

I have no food with liquid after I finish the last half of a raw potato. It's truly scary. Unbearable thirst continues to assail me. It's probably worse for the dog, for it hasn't had any water for several days. It hasn't made a noise for a long time and only follows out of habitual loyalty. The yellow camel looks about the same, with the nourishment and juice from the cistanches. He continues to look at me provocatively; clearly his hostility toward me has not abated.

My eyes feel dry and turn with great difficulty. The white camel has knelt down, letting me know I can ride on his back. My heart warms as I climb up. I pull the dog up to rest in my arms. Now I'm facing a dilemma—I may freeze to death riding a camel—the cold wind never stops blowing, but if I don't, I'll die of exhaustion or of thirst. Those are the odds.

Turning my dry eyes, I look around me, but there's nothing except sand. The compass points the direction to me, but how can I know it's right, since there are no visible landmarks? There are plenty of sand dunes, but they move around a lot. At least there are poplars, the sole stationary landmarks on the map. There's an ancient tree, which I heard is over a thousand years old. There are what look to be city walls—there must have been a city a thousand years ago—other than that, there's nothing. I can't be sure, but I have my compass, which tells me the way to go.

I feel I'm about to pass out. My eyes are dry and my mind is losing focus. My blood must be at its thickest, something I've experienced in the past. I also feel bone chillingly cold; I have the fur coat around me, but the relentless wind bores into me. I can almost see the end: dying of thirst or cold.

I hold tightly onto the dog—in this circumstance it and the camel give me warmth and a great deal of comfort. I'm not alone, after all.

Suddenly the yellow camel stops and refuses to move even when I jerk the reins.

He needs to pee.

The dog tears out of my arms and jumps off. I can hear him lapping up the camel's urine.

It's a signal to me. I get off the white camel, bring over the jug and put it under where the urine is coming out. I see yellow liquid and detect its odor—it even has the smell of the cistanches—but I can't let that worry me now. This is the only liquid I can see at this moment. I even wonder if it contains the nutrients the yellow camel has wasted.

He stops quickly, probably because he doesn't want me to have too much liquid, or because it's a habit. Camels never release too much at a time.

For the first time in my life I drink camel urine; it doesn't have a terrible taste. I've been drinking my own for some time. I drink whatever I relieve the first time every morning, which is my intention to deal with my differentiating mind. Camel urine doesn't go down as nicely as its human counterpart, but it's urine, nevertheless. I don't want to finish it off, but I know I shouldn't keep it long or germs will grow. I let the dog have the rest. It wags its tail gratefully.

I feel much better now, even though I know that little bit of urine won't make much difference—I've managed to resupply my body with some liquid.

After that I make sure to catch the urine whenever the camel relieves himself. But the intervals between stops are taking longer and longer, and in the end, it nearly stops—he needs water too.

I have to admire the old wolf tailing me when I think about camels *getting thirsty. I have no idea what it eats and drinks. The desert is overrun with rats, and it can find a feeding ground by large plants. I wonder when it hunts—I nearly forget that I can roast and eat rats too. But the thought of the awful creature makes me retch. I'll only eat them when absolutely necessary.*

By dusk I feel I'm delirious. I see countless suns in the sky and boundless bright light, in which there seems to be a house, from which rings of light emerge.

What Ma Zaibo told me the other night seemed to have happened in a house. I wonder if it's the Hu Family Mill. The place sounds different each time he talks about it, which was why Lu Fuji said he was delusional. But I tell myself not to jump to conclusion about lots of things. Certain matters are hard to explain in a few words.

1

I am startled awake that night.

I open my eyes to see myself in a dilapidated house that has been abandoned for who knows how long. There's no light, but a moon slants its rays inside.

The house is infused in an eerie blue.

It looks very much like a house I lived in as a child, I discovered. But then again, I recall clearly it was razed to the ground long ago. I touch the eerie blue, as I walk into my childhood bedroom; my bed remains and I'm greeted by a familiar smell. The bed and everything else in the room are covered in a thick layer of dust that has hardened and turned black. On the floor and everywhere my hand touches is the same hard, black stuff. I have no idea how thick it is. Oddly, however, the vague shape of a person can be seen on the bed covered thickly in spider webs and dust. The blanket seems to have been tossed hastily to the side, as if someone were just lying there.

Who could it be? The thought carries a murderous intent and makes me shudder.

I look out through the window; it's even gloomier and I can see the area is completely deserted.

Killer appears at that moment. I happen to glance out of the corner of my eye at a flickering shadow in a spot by the wall—a closer look shows a hanging "man," or more precisely a monster. He is green with a hideous face that is twisted out of shape, a large mouth with exposed fangs, and exceptionally well-developed green muscles. He looks huge on top while his lower body is obscured in darkness. The monster isn't too tall. He's strung up by a chain in his hands. It appears he has hung there for too many years to count.

Despite his hanging position, he carries with him immense energy. I feel like fleeing when I see him, but I sense a great force pulling me back . . .

2

Killer had a frosty look as he stared at me coldly. His face was covered in coarse fabric—the same material as for a camel driver's short jacket—showing only his eyes, which seemed filled with hatred. I didn't know why. I asked him, "Why are you looking at me like that?"

"Don't you know?" he asked.

I did not.

"Not knowing your own crime is a crime in itself. A kind of original sin."

He dragged me out of the small room. I didn't know if he was the same hanging man, but it shouldn't be him. They looked different, but then again, I felt they were one and the same, for they both emitted waves of hate. I felt a prickly pain when the wave came at me. It was heavy and deep, very uncomfortable. He didn't even have to explain why he hated me, for the wave told me of his loathing for me. I thought he must have a reason if he harbored such profound hatred. To be honest, under the pressure of the wave, I even felt I was guilty of a crime for which even death couldn't atone. I didn't ask again. I must have done something terrible to him; maybe I owed him a serious debt in our previous lives, so why bother to ask? Over the many rounds of transmigration, I would surely have done something; he could be an ant that I intentionally stomped to death, maybe a fly I pinched in half, or an animal whose legs I lopped off once when I was driven by hatred . . . there were many "maybes," so I told myself to accept what was coming. I was reminded of Dharma's "Retribution," and decided to treat anything going against me as a karmic debt that I must repay.

So why ask?

I saw when he dragged me outside that the small house was just an illusion. It was actually a tent sitting on a rocky gobi, surrounded by blistering sunlight. Steam rose from the ground, like a raging fire. There was no one else but him and me. I wondered where the caravan had gone. Oddly, it felt to me that this was what it should be. Most of the time the caravan wasn't on my unfettered mind, and I often felt myself walking alone. I spent a lot of time with the caravan, but it had always been out of my mind.

It was just a feeling. Could it be what Lu Fuji called a delusion? I didn't know.

I sensed him looking at me, and felt like a mouse being watched by a cat. I was sure he felt like a cat. Recalling what Balte had told me about chasing to kill a cat, I could now imagine how the cat felt. It had to be completely helpless in the shadow of countless whips. But the cat obviously didn't know how helpless a mouse felt when it was being chased. Later, during the massive sandstorm, Balte was a mouse of a different sort.

Yes, we were all mice and we were all cats. When the day came, we'd surely be mice under a cat's paw. We would look around us helplessly, and, like now, with no one to rescue us.

On many occasions, as we look around in despair, there is really no one who can help us.

I felt that way at this moment.

I looked around me. I didn't see anyone. What I saw was fiery sunlight that told me I wasn't dreaming nor was I in bardo, an intermediate body between death and rebirth. I heard that the part of our brain that detects light and colors was in a state of rest when we slept, which was why our dreams are black and white. Which meant I wasn't dreaming, because I could see sunlight; I wasn't in bardo either, because our eyesight no longer functions after death. One cannot see the light from the sun or the sun itself when one is in bardo. At this moment, I could see sunlight, which could only mean I wasn't in bardo.

But I couldn't see anyone or anything I wanted to see. Where was my caravan? Where were my friends? How about the many things I owned? I couldn't find any of them.

Next to me was only Killer.

But I didn't want to see him.

I knew he was a killer whether I wanted to see him or not. He wouldn't turn into a Buddha just because I saw him. So why should I look at him?

Up to this very day, he felt to me more like a kind of *qi* that I couldn't shake off. He was sending me message after message that he wanted to kill me.

Go ahead and kill me then, I was thinking.

But I didn't want to die yet.

Because there were still things I wanted to do.

3

Yes. I was looking for the Hu Family Mill. And the Wooden Fish Incantation.

But you weren't aware that I was still looking for something else when I was in the Mill. What was it? Something that could change fate.

What fate?

The caravan's fate.

To be frank, I knew the caravan's fate already. I didn't know kālacakra, so I wasn't able to predict the end of the world. Yet I knew the caravan would meet with a terrible end. I could see it clearly.

It was a hard end to change.

No wonder some believed it was the end of the world. To some it was, of course.

Our beliefs were what set me apart from them; they thought the end of the world could not be changed, while I believed the opposite. I even held the notion that no matter how dire the situation, there was always a remedy. If you could find it, that is.

Based on what the ancients said, the key was in the Hu Family Mill, and they called it the Wooden Fish Incantation. But none could tell me what it looked like. Was it a talisman shaped like a tiger or some other sort? I had no idea. But I believed there existed in the world something that could change what was originally unchangeable.

And I came here looking for it.

I was convinced that any predestined outcome could be altered once I found it.

It was a message passed down by a holy person who practiced asceticism in the desert. I heard he'd actually found it, but no one believed him, so he hid it in the Hu Family Mill. No one knew where it was, and all anyone knew for sure was what would happen after it was located—all the enmities would be resolved, all the revenge killings would end, and all the outcomes would be changeable.

To many people it was just folklore, but not to me.

Neither did the ancestors in my family. In every generation someone in our clan was given the mission of finding the incantation. They followed a caravan and traveled all over China, and found many wooden fish incantations, but none seemed to be the one. It was very easy to check its authenticity—you'd suddenly no longer have enemies. Based on the lore, possession of the real incantation would vest in you a power and benevolence like Cakravartin.

Those found by previous generations in our clan didn't change much of anything. They couldn't even resolve minor disputes, like those between the Chinese and the Mongolian caravans, let alone major conflicts such as revenge killings between the Han and the Hui, or armed battles between Hakkas and the locals.

Every one of them was ecstatic at first when they found it, then became despondent and died depressed.

Even now, those incantations were installed in our family hall, some gold, some silver, some purple sandalwood, some glazed, all in various, endless styles. But I wanted to find the real one.

Naturally, I loathed having run up against Killer before I found it.

4

I didn't want to die.

The me who didn't want to die was naturally afraid of dying. I knew life was but a dream, but still I preferred to be alive. Besides my unwillingness to die, as I stated above, I felt something else I couldn't explain clearly. For sure that would be my habitual nature. There might have been people in this world who are not afraid to die, but I wasn't one of them.

My fear of death began with the advent of that unwillingness. The coolness derived from Dharma's "Retribution Code" receded into the distance. I realized that whatever wisdom I'd possessed lost its power at the instant my fear arose. Which I found most disheartening. Before Killer's appearance, I'd thought I'd been able to transcend death. It seemed I'd seen through the cycle of life and death, but at that moment I was just an ordinary human being. I was a holy person when death was far off on the horizon, because I thought I had transcended death. When death closed in on me, I realized that my transcendence was a wishful thinking, an illusion. It showed that the so-called wisdom I'd attained was simply knowledge; I understood the concept, but it couldn't change my behavior.

Which was why I felt the impact from the fear aroused by Killer.

He seemed to have said a lot while I was lost in a quiet trance, but my brain was sticky and left no space to take in anything else. Yes, my mind was a blank, but that's not all there was to it. I couldn't hear clearly what he was saying. I did know, however, that no matter what he was saying, he was offering me a reason. I was also aware that slaughter needed no reason. His intention to kill me was reason enough. The reason for violence is powerful violence itself. Everything else is desire. Humans have endless vocabulary, and any given word can help them manufacture a reason.

He was talking too much for my liking, even though I was afraid to die.

I was reminded of the little lamb trying to defend itself in the teeth of a wolf.

I looked up at the sky. The sun was still shining down noisily, *ri-*

ri-ri, and sending out waves. It had been doing that since I was little, and it continued even when I was older. It was a familiar noise, making imminent death seem less pressing, for I was accompanied by a familiar sun, after all.

Killer stopped chattering when he read my mind. He walked up to a camel. Where had that come from? I don't recall seeing a camel. It was hiding in a shallow spot. At first glance, it looked just like a mound of dirt. It was skinny, like Long Neck Goose in the caravan, but he was actually heavier. Long Neck Goose would be just as scrawny if he was deprived of food for a long time or if he was sick. I wanted to ask, "Are you Long Neck Goose?" Then again, it made no difference at a moment like this, I told myself.

He tugged the camel over. He had such a powerful hand that simply twisting the camel's nostril sent it to the ground like a bundle of wheat. He was unbelievably strong, for the move looked more like hurling a frog than toppling a donkey. I even heard a slapping sound, like a frog's belly hitting hard ground.

The camel panicked, crying out to me urgently. It made a strange sound, like a saw blade dragging back and forth across my heart.

"Go ahead, kill me," I said to him. "But spare the camel."

He smiled coldly, sneered, actually. I felt a chill on my face.

"You can kill me, but don't sneer at me." I added.

The camel stopping crying when I said that, and instead looked at me with pity. It must have been moved by my remarkable compassion, I thought. I was touched by it too. "No matter what, I must save the camel's life," I said to myself. Whether I succeeded or not was a different matter altogether. What I was trying to save was actually my heart, because it would be dead if I didn't think of saving the animal.

I ran at Killer, though I couldn't be sure he would kill the camel. I didn't want to die, but I would if my death could save a life.

His hands seemed capable of toppling mountains and overturning seas, and I flew off like a kite. I was very disappointed in my body; I'd entertained the ambition to take down heaven and earth, but my body rebelled. It couldn't be helped. Our bodies always place a restriction on our will. Laozi was right when he said a man's biggest misfortune was his body.

Killer plunged his knife into the camel's chest before my soaring body hit the ground. I saw squirting blood smear his face. His skillful handling with the knife told me he was highly experienced in killing. A single thrust aimed unerringly at the animal's heart. I remembered that slaughtering a camel was a major event requiring several people. Some held a pole or a rope to stop the camel from struggling before a knife went in the right spot. But this killer did away with a camel as effortlessly as killing a lamb. He truly was a seasoned and talented killer.

He went on to skin the camel, so deftly I was astonished. With one hand pulling and the other wielding a knife, he took no time to remove the pelt from the animal. Only when he was turning it over did he seem to strain a little. He used a pole as leverage to pry and pry to turn the animal around. I had no idea where he'd found the pole, but that wasn't worth my time thinking about it. I knew that you could always find a reason to kill and the tool you needed when you set your mind to do it.

He stretched the pelt with both hands and, with a flick, sent it flapping, like Yamāntaka pulling at an elephant pelt that symbolized fearlessness and deliverance. Killer looked fearless too, but he didn't do for deliverance. Like a flag in the wind, the camel pelt fluttered noisily as it spread out, filling the air around it with a bloody stench. It was terrifying. Fear overtook my mind; when terror reached its height, my mind had no more room for it. I could only stare at him blankly. The sun had just risen behind him, the rays still bright and red. I knew I wasn't dreaming despite what people said later, because, as I mentioned, dreams are in black and white.

His back against the sun, Killer continued to shake the pelt, a spectacular sight. The scene is as clear to me now as if it were yesterday. I also saw sand and distant mountains. I didn't recall any mountains in Wild Fox Ridge; instead, there was nothing but sand, as far as the eye could see, like the two poetic lines, "Flying sand in the great desert obscures the sun/on the desolate plain I stopped my horse to listen to the sad song"—you think it's a good poem? Of course, it is—now there were mountains in front of me. Was a Wild Fox Ridge with mountains still Wild Fox Ridge? I wasn't sure. The Hu Family Mill was nowhere to be found. I recalled finding it, but then I lost it. When I had it, I could enter it without trouble, but once it was gone, I couldn't find it again. I didn't know its general location and even doubted if I'd actually been in it. There was no sun when I went in, and no color. Now I wondered if my being there was, in reality, a dream.

But Killer was real. He was flapping the bloodied pelt the way a butcher would a sheepskin. Likely showing off his strength. You know, a camel pelt is not sheepskin, it's really heavy. But he was flicking it like a flag—*shua—shua*. I recalled how my sky darkened in the swooshing noise.

The sun was swept away by a fetid wind while a humongous tongue tore at me. I seemed to be falling, but not really; I was just in motion. A stench wrapped around me. Now I knew he had bundled me up in the pelt, but I had no idea why.

My body was tightening up when I noticed a bone needle coming and going around me. The long thread on the needle, I saw, was made of camel hair. Camel drivers used thread like that when sewing a sack, for it was sturdy and held up well in the elements. The pelt was getting tighter around me as the needle threaded in and out. My face was smeared with blood and other sticky liquids. I'm sure it would make you retch just thinking about it. Even now I feel a lump in my throat.

It finally dawned on me what he had in mind, as my body was wound tighter and tighter. The realization made my scalp numb. My family had meted out a similar treatment to thieves, particularly habitual thieves. We skinned a camel and sewed the thief inside to bake under a hot sun. As the elastic, wet pelt dried, it developed creases. From inside the pelt would come a mad struggle and mumbled groans that would slowly die down as the pelt dried up. In the end, there would be no more struggling. The thief was tortured out of shape by the creased pelt. I was amused as a child when the adults carried out the punishment, even hoped to see it more often. Now it was my turn.

Later I learned that praising or identifying with evil was the worst crime, and what happened to me on this day was surely retribution.

I detected the blood stench and odor of solid waste at first and I retched. Whatever I threw up soiled me, turning me into the source of pollution. Then I smelled nothing. I was hot and suffocating. I wondered, later on, whether one felt this bad inside a mother's womb. It's tough being human. If everyone shared the same experience, we'd all be able to feel the hardship of life with immediacy. Avichi Hell was probably not much different from this.

"Kill me," I screamed. "Go ahead, kill me."

My voice just swirled inside the pelt. It wouldn't soften Killer's heart even if he could hear me.

I had to resign myself to the thought that he must have his reason to treat me this way.

I stopped struggling.

The pelt was shrinking, and stiff, ridge-like creases were biting into me. Every breath required a great deal of effort. My lungs were filled with something viscous, and a large gong was banging in my head—*kuang!—kuang!* I didn't think I'd last much longer. I wanted to ponder something important; I could think about the Wooden Fish Incantation during the remaining moments of my life. But my mind was so sluggish I couldn't think of anything. I just knew I wanted to think, but there was nothing there. All I knew was my imminent death. I wanted to express my reluctance to resign myself to my fate, but at this moment, it was more feelings of despair.

The gong in my head was banging relentlessly. *Kuang—! Kuang—!*

The pelt continued to tighten. It turned hard and stiff from the blistering sun; its creases became knives. I felt my ribs cracked by the powerful pelt, that and my spine and my head. The pain around my head was most acute, probably because he'd placed more stitches around there. I got a taste of how the Monkey King felt when Tripitaka recited the head-tightening incantation. I screamed at the top of my lungs when the pain reached its apex, for I recalled someone saying that screaming can help relieve pain. But it was just a thought, since there wasn't enough breath in my lungs to shout.

I was suffocating, in the dark, besieged by heat and pain, as if there were screws tightening on me. Again and again, I passed out, and again and again. the pain brought me back, until all of a sudden I was shrouded in an even more massive darkness.

Finally a lightness came over me.

5

I saw light slanting in, accompanied by fresh air.

I heard a knife sawing on the pelt. Where am I? I asked myself. It took me some thinking to recall Killer and what he'd done. Maybe he changed his mind and chose to use a knife on me. That was fine. I'd take whatever fate had in store for me.

After taking a long, deep breath, I slowly opened my eyes and saw another pair of eyes on a familiar face. I racked my brain before finally it came to me. It was Wooden Fish Girl.

I was not surprised to see her there, but then quickly recalled something else. Hadn't she been kidnapped by a desert outlaw? How did she show up here? I wanted to ask her, so I did.

"I escaped," she said.

I wanted to ask her how she did it, but I didn't. You all know I hated being talkative, especially when I was with a girl.

She cut away on the camel pelt with a small knife. The side facing the sun was nearly dry, and the knife moved with difficulty.

"Why are you playing a game like this?" she asked. "Look at you. You'd be human jerky if I hadn't showed up in time."

It took me some effort to crawl out of the camel pelt shell. "Where's Killer?" I asked.

"I didn't see any killer," she said. "I heard someone screaming, so I came over to check it out."

Killer must have thought I'd die for sure, I said to myself.

Exhaustion overtook me, so I leaned back on the sand to catch my breath. As if venting her spleen, she cut the pelt into pieces and threw them all around.

My mind had stopped working after the near-death experience.

"Is the Young Master awake?" someone asked.

I knew the voice. I looked over. It was Feiqing. He and the other camel hands were drying tea leaves close by. Such a wonderful sunny day was perfect for that. Tea leaves easily turned moldy if exposed to rain or moisture. Back then, we used to dry tea leaves whenever we had a sunny day.

"You've been sleeping for days. We were so worried," Lu Fuji said. The drivers were happy for me and offered their own concern.

What a terrifying dream, I said to myself.

6

Obviously, I'd slept for a long time, for I was seeing different typography.

In my previous memory, we had been traveling in the desert, but now we were surrounded by mountains, soaring mountains with brownish yellow slopes, like a head scarf with brown dots. There were rocks eroded by wind that frequently fell off the slope and into a deep gulch, but a long time would pass before we heard them break the surface of water.

"Let's go." Some men were shouting.

We got on the road.

"We lost some camels and the feet on some of the surviving ones haven't healed completely. So, we switched to mules and yaks," Lu Fuji said. "We couldn't wait any longer. Certain things can't be delayed. Sometimes you can wait until the cows come home, but you don't necessarily get the result you want."

"That's fine," I said. "But the mules are no match for camels in transporting goods."

"Wild Fox Ridge has many different geological features—mountains, streams, desert, and a roaring river. All strange landforms. On mountains mules are better than camels." Lu continued, "We need both mules and camels. Camels work harder when we're in the desert, and on mountain roads we rely on the mules. We can move faster when we have both."

"We have to get some salt first," Feiqing said. "Besides having salt for our own use on the road, we can trade some for animal feed. Our animals won't get sick easily if they have some salt every once in a while. When we left, we only brought enough for ourselves, nothing for the animals. We ran out after giving some to the sick camels. If we're lucky, we'll travel by salt-makers along the way."

Let's get moving then.

We set out. Our procession looked different now. The camel hands transferred a lot of the loads onto the yaks, which were great for transporting, for they could carry a heavy litter. Mules weren't as strong. We had fewer camels now; those that couldn't make the long trek had been replaced. With their large bodies, camels were meaty, and some butchers were happy to trade camels for the mules and yaks they intended to kill for food. I felt terrible when I thought about the camels that had made great contributions to the Ma family fortune, and how they were being turned into food. I never ate camel meat. It's too stringy, and chewy, not very enjoyable. Besides, I didn't want those decent animals to be my food, which set me apart from other camel hands. I wasn't a holy man, but I didn't want to be an ordinary camel hand either.

That was the only option I was free to make.

7

I heard the rumbling roar of water in a river, and it did sound like what later was described in a song: The wind howled, the horse neighed, and the Yellow River roared. Heh-heh, the songwriter did a great job writing what I felt in my heart. My heart was like that. Sometimes desire is good, for it can fill a man with vitality. I wondered if a Buddha, devoid of desire, lived a boring life. Or take the Monkey King, for example. He was clever and adorable as an impish monkey, but was no longer likeable when he became a fighting Buddha that never lost. He had no more story to tell, and anyone without a story was boring.

Mountain after mountain appeared before me as the caravan traveled down the path between them. What I found odd was the mules. I asked about them and was told that some of the camels had ruined their feet and that mules had been hired to carry their loads. Sure, camels were meant to travel in the desert, and were no good at climbing mountains, for their feet would soon be bloodied. Why didn't they put leather pads on the feet? Wouldn't they protect the feet on the mountain paths? Hei, they did. They said the feet were actually destroyed when pebbles got caught in the pads. That made it hopeless.

But I don't understand why you said I was hallucinating. To me, what I said had really taken place. You kept saying I was delusional. Maybe. There are so many things I can't explain. I remembered we later added mules, but you all said no. There were also mountains and rivers in my memory, but you said no to that too. You don't remember what I remembered and remembered what I didn't. But I'm going to tell the story from my recollection.

With a heavy load, the mules had a tough time going down the mountain path; they were huffing and puffing, breathing hard. The sound seemed to fill my lungs with gummy liquid.

There were different versions about that trip. Some said the Chinese Revolutionary Alliance sent the caravan with tea to Russia, some said the tea was to trade for weapons, while others said it was a normal journey into the desert. No matter what they said, it was a revenge voyage to me. My goal was revenge.

Ai, my head is all messed up. I'm Ma Zaibo, so why do I have Killer's thoughts?

Could it be that was me?

I discover a problem at this point. Based on the development of the story, Wooden Fish Girl has already been kidnapped. The story she tells later actually happened before what she remembered taking place in Wild Fox Ridge. In those scenes, she did not make an appearance after she was taken away by the crippled outlaw. Feiqing and several drivers even went looking for her. Did she really show up to save Ma Zaibo, or was it part of his hallucination?

Ma has a blank look when I raise the question.

"Did it really happen? Was she kidnapped?" he wonders.

When I turn to Wooden Fish Girl, this is what she says,

"What's so strange about it? I can come and go as I please."

I ask her where she's going, she says, "To where I'm going."

I ask her where she came from, she says, "From where I came."

I have to stop asking her questions after that.

Nineteenth Session
Imminent Bloodshed

    The drivers all know about my predicament now, and everyone brings me water in their own containers. Some use a sheepskin sack, some a canteen, some a wooden basin. The water is sparkling, so fresh and refreshing it's beyond words, as nourishing as "bean water," as they say. It cools my heart the moment I see it. I have a little at first, but not too much, they cautioned me. If you drink too much after prolonged thirst, your stomach will be painfully bloated. I give some to the camels. The yellow camel spits when he sees it, but oddly the white camel also refuses to drink. I bring the water right up to him, but he refuses to even look at it. I can't do anything except untie his tether and say,

    "Go find something you like to eat. But be sure to stay close."

    He goes off on his own.

    I want to give water to the dog too, but it's nowhere to be found. I don't know when it took off. After getting up to a high point, I shout its name over and over, but only get blowing wind for an answer.

    I feel comfortable letting the white camel graze on his own, but not the yellow one. I'm convinced he'll run away the moment he's not tethered. And the old wolf will kill him, I fear. It can't easily have its way if the yellow camel is alert enough—the wolf seems quite old, too old to take a camel—

but even a tiger dozes off sometime. If the wolf pounces when the yellow camel is napping, it's likely it can make the kill.

The white camel won't run away; he's a loyal animal. The driver I borrowed him from told me, "This white camel would die with you. He's the Master Guan of camels." He must have his own reasons for not drinking the water. Is it not clean enough? Maybe. Well, let him be. He can eat what he likes. Maybe he'll find some cistanches. Camels have a keen nose, if downwind they can smell something ten li away. He might find some cistanches and water on his own.

I continue my interview in the Hu Family Mill.

The mill house I see is different from the one in their stories: a lot of stuff inside is in tatters and everything is under a thick layer of dust. It makes me wonder if this is really the millhouse. In the lore I've heard, the millhouse is always neat and clean, spotless. But this one is dusty. Could it be climate-related? Maybe sandstorms weren't as frequent a hundred years ago? Could be.

It doesn't matter whether it is or not, as long as it is for me. Besides, in the lore there was only the millhouse, no other structure, so this has to be it. I do see a broken millstone, its base worn thin. Grooves of various depth were all over the wood supports, as if formed by scratching fingers. If it's true, it has to be ages old. Think about it. How many times did people have to scrape against the wood when they scooped up the chaff to create such deep marks? And the basket pole is very thin; it had been thick, but now about to snap in two.

My thirst has abated, thanks to the water brought by the drivers, so I begin the interview.

This time I see a white camel, very much like mine, except this one is bigger and larger. I know it's Yellow Demon in the story. His image keeps shifting. He returns to his original figure of a camel when he's pleased with itself, but changes back to the hunch-backed Camel Deity when he's more reserved. It's amusing that his constant changes represent the mental state of the moment.

I find myself suddenly taken by Yellow Demon, hoping he was me in my previous life.

One. Yellow Demon

1

I didn't expect Brown Lion to lose his mind, just as I was surprised to have Long Neck Goose challenge me.

In my eyes, Long Neck Goose was always an impetuous little camel. Someone even thought he was one of mine, because he had a similar build, but I was certain he wasn't. You see, I hadn't mated with his mother. Back then it was the previous King Camel who had the prerogative to mate, the old one with the cleft nose. He fell on the ice and couldn't get up one year when we were crossing the river. I suspected he was ill, but was hiding that, probably because he didn't want to fight me over the position of authority. I wouldn't have had the strength to fight him if he hadn't been sick.

Long Neck Goose was only a few years my junior. He was big but had yet to grow strong enough to fight me. He was aware of that, which was why he ran off when I challenged him.

But this time he didn't run. He'd managed to mate several times while Brown Lion and I fought it out. He grew to like it so much it turned his head, and he was no longer contented. I saw he was forever stealing looks at me, which told me he had the intention but not the nerve to do what he wanted to do. But you should know that the hardest thing to tackle is sexual desire, which can sometimes drive someone to commit unspeakable crimes. Those who kill over sex know they'll pay with their lives, but they are so overpowered by their desire that they lose self-control. They kill someone and in turn are themselves killed. Back and forth, an eye for an eye, there is no end to the cycle.

I didn't know until later that Brown Lion and I were enemies from a previous life. I gained the insight only now. As an animal I lacked wisdom. You ought to know all animals are the products of stupidity and foolishness. Even a wise person would have his intelligence obscured by innate stupidity once he enters the other transmigration track—the animal plane. I wouldn't have done all those stupid things I did had I enjoyed the wisdom I have now.

But I was a male camel back then, wasn't I? I'd likely be rolling in hell if I hadn't been saved by a kind thought during my last moments.

Animals can only do bestial things. In those days all I wanted was to mate, and, to fight Brown Lion and Long Neck Goose. I was a beast, I couldn't help it. I was a beast who feared no one. Hei-hei.

I knew where Brown Lion had gone.

I knew, because my keen nose let me smell water and grass twelve *li* away, two *li* more than the average camel. I knew he was sleeping in a large sand trough. The wound on his head had healed; he looked hideous, but he hadn't died. He was sleeping after eating and drinking his fill, for he was exhausted, overpowered by sleepiness. Once he'd gotten enough sleep, he'd stir up big trouble.

But I didn't feel like telling anyone.

I felt sorry for Brown Lion—listen to me. I'm no longer calling him Brown Ass—but sympathy wouldn't change my desire to castrate him with my foot, if we could turn back time and I got another chance. I knew he'd do that to me if I didn't do it first. Didn't that foreigner say something like, "Natural selection and survival of the fittest?" I didn't like talks like that, but that was the truth, especially in the other track of transmigration, the animal plane. I was always tough when dealing with opponents. Hei-hei, I had the talent of a statesman. What talent? Thick skin and a black heart. The master theorist of "thick-black study," just a twinkle in his father's eye, yet to be born, but I already understood the truth he espoused. You need to know that he didn't invent it, he just discovered it. Truth exists despite all else.

I had to be swift and resolute to rebuff Long Neck Goose when I realized he could be a threat to me.

I had to strike before he reached maturity. I knew age was his edge. I wouldn't be able to take care of him when I grew older and he got stronger in a few years. I employed a method used by a regent in Tibet. I heard that particular kinds of Living Buddhas usually died in the teens or twenties, for a long period in their history. They never lived long enough to gain control, because if they had, the regent would have to step aside. Hence, the Living Buddhas always died of unknown causes before they could assume the position. Then the regent would replace him with another child, a reincarnate, who knew nothing.

The old Camel King, the one with a cleft nose, used the same ruse to remain in power longer than any other one. He nipped in the bud those who could pose a threat and kicked at least fifteen male camels in their nuts—their scrotum, that is—most of them big and powerful. With others, he provoked them into action for the drivers to castrate them. I wanted to try the same method on Long Neck Goose, but his crotch never managed to meet my hind foot. He ran off every time I raised one of my hind legs. Instead he preferred neck fights. We went at it a few times, and I saw the young camel had a powerful neck. I wasn't sure how I'd fare in a fight like that. A real gentleman competes with intelligence, not brute force.

I discovered that he'd been giving me funny looks, as if plotting a coup, which wasn't unlikely. Oftentimes, a coup was what divided an old camel king from a new one. The successful challenger would be the new camel king, but it was no big deal if he failed, unlike humans, among whom the successful one would be the king or noble while the failed one would be a traitor. Sometimes the failed challenger would lose his life. But not camels. For us camels, fighting now and then was like humans exercising. The loser would slink around for a while and, with no need for nonsense such as psychological victory, quickly forgot it, like water under the bridge.

Long Neck Goose and I had a real combat once and I nearly castrated him. It was one of my best skills. Ever since I was little, I'd been given to running around, and I'd run and kick, like a human working on leg strength. One day of practice increases one day's skill level, but missing one day voids ten day's effort; given enough time, you'll got the skill you need. Too bad none of my superb performances couldn't have been frozen and taped for people to see; I bet it would be as fantastic as stars in a circus.

By the way, let me explain why they called me Yellow Demon. You see, I kicked up dust when I ran. Why was that? Because I'd been working on my legs; I kicked up the yellow sand with my hind feet, which, seen from behind, resembled a sandstorm.

Later that style became a habit. Like a king rabbit kicking up sand, I had well-developed leg muscles. Think about it. How could I not after practicing for ten years? Everyone in the Chinese and Mongolian caravans knew about it. One year, when we came under attack by wolves, I kicked off several of them, like soccer players of a later time. Ah, the days of raging passion.

Long Neck Goose knew all about this. But he had his strong point too, his neck, that is. He had a powerful neck. Once, when we were going downhill and his litter came loose, a woven sack slid down his neck and frightened the camel driver out of his wits. An average camel would have been crushed, but all Long Neck Goose had to do was flick his neck to fling the sack back on to the litter. To be honest, I had to yield to his neck strength. Hard to say if I could have done that. And after that, the camel hands called him Long Neck Goose. Hei—it did look like a long neck goose.

When long neck geese flew over us, just before we took off, the village boys would all shout, "Long neck goose, long neck goose fly into the air/we'll knock you off and roast for all to share." Right, that kind of goose. We saw flock after flock flying south every year. If they were loud, we knew we'd have a harsh winter. I can't tell you why, but I found it to be a true rule. We did have long hair, but we didn't like cold winter either. We never liked the knife-like sharp wind, especially when the litters were being unloaded. The icy wind assaulted our sweaty backs, and we might come down with a cold if we were unlucky. When a camel gets a cold, it coughs like an injured mule, and it will be too weak to carry a litter, which will then be shared by other camels.

Humans forget their roots all too easily, and so do animals. I can hardly believe how I managed to survive when I think about those days. It's impossible for me to tell you how many trips I made along Baosui Road. Simply impossible. I can't tell you how many loads I carried. I find it hard to imagine the hard lift. Luckily for me, I was a camel and could only think camel thoughts, which was to carry the load and start walking, as dictated by my destiny. I'd be frightened if I had to relive that kind of life now. I didn't feel that way back then, of course. People say the animal plane entails hardships, but that's what humans think; the animals never know. Oftentimes, you know life was hard only when you're no longer an animal.

You think I'm getting off track? Hei-hei, you're right.

Let me go back to my fight with Long Neck Goose.

2

It happened on a rock patch of the desert. The grass in the neighboring sand trough was gone by then. Imagine several hundred camels chomping away. However, the desert rice there wouldn't last. We had to go farther away for bunchgrass, which, as I recalled, was abundant, mostly old growth. Obviously, the drivers were not in the habit of weaving bunchgrass. In my hometown—what a heartwarming term—the villagers never let it go to waste. They made mats, baskets, and winnows out of it. There was never any old growth bunchgrass, because it was used up in the same year; it couldn't grow old if it wanted to. But not here. Here you saw old growth bunchgrass everywhere; It was too tough to chew, all but for the leaves.

Rocky gobis and deserts always exist side by side. Southerners can't tell them apart. But you'll know by texture alone. A desert is made of sand, while a gobi has sand and dirt mixed together. The sand has hardened after thousands of years of rain, and is hard on camel feet. That was why Ma Zaibo, a self-prescribed clever man, came up with the idea of protecting the feet with leather pads. Unfortunately, that ended up ruining the feet of hundreds of camels.

It couldn't be helped. We had to keep on when we were in a rocky gobi. We were camels, and that was what we did.

There's a reason why I have to explain the difference between the two; you'll know soon enough.

Long Neck Goose and I had our fight in the gobi. Hei, I'd rather not talk about it, a not so glorious past. But I will tell you the story, as a kind of repentance on my part. If I don't sound right in places, please understand it was the me of the past talking. I was an animal, and animals have bestial thoughts, don't we?

Long Neck Goose started it that time. He charged at me while I was inching closer to Pretty Widow. It was a sneak attack, which meant he was immoral first. If someone attacks, I'll fight back, doesn't that make sense?

Pretty Widow was prettier than ever, after Brown Lion lost his mind; at least she appeared that way to me. When I think about it now, I realize that she was pretty in her manners, not her figure. She seemed somewhat sorrowful, with a hint of melancholy. You ought to know that with sadness—not too much, or it will look doleful—a female camel, and, for that matter, a female of the human race, will be graced by the capability to rouse sympathy from a male.

I have tender feelings toward females, which is quite grand, don't you think?

Motivated by precisely the grand feeling, I edged closer to Pretty Widow. It—I think I ought to say she—didn't react to my approach. Like encountering a stray dog on the street, she showed no anger, no sadness, and, especially, no happiness. She was immersed in her own emotional realm and shut out the outside world. I knew she still favored Brown Lion, a discovery that pained me. Why are you still thinking about that crazy old camel? I said silently to her. I couldn't see what made him stand out, maybe except for his organ—but mine wasn't necessary inferior.

I had always liked her. In my recollection, she seemed to be forever melancholic, which was why the humans called her Pretty Widow, not because she had a dead husband, you see. But the cleft-nosed old king camel did try to get near her—I had no idea if he had succeeded. Back then, he had tried his luck on some other female camels, so he could not be considered her "husband," nor could his death make her a widow. Many people called her that because she had the sorrowful air of a woman who had lost her husband. That was why I liked her, but so did Long Neck Goose, I knew. I saw him often stick his long neck out at her, and over recent days he didn't even care how I felt about his action.

I wasted no hesitation as I approached her. I wanted to mate with her even though she didn't look to be in heat—a camel in heat has a unique smell. Maybe that was why she ran off. I asked her why she was running; she could put up with me for the little time it would take. But she kept running. Pretty Widow ran in such an alluring way that I got even more excited. Then I got angry. I have to admit I behaved badly at the time, but you can't ask a camel to act like a gentleman, can you? Even humans can't rise above their upbringing and environment. I wouldn't want to get angry now, even if you asked me to. There's no need to turn into a scary demon over a female, don't you agree?

But at the time anger raged inside me, blood roared in my head. Holding back my wrath, I called out to her. Humans couldn't understand the call, but camels all knew what it meant. Translated into human language, it would be: why are you running like that? Why? Stop running or I'll show you what I'm capable of. As I called out, I gently bit her hind leg—maybe "gently" is a bit modest. I couldn't drag her down if I did it gently, you see, so I could mount her when she was down. To my surprise, before I was on her, she nimbly rolled away—like a graceful dancer, no less—and took off until she was several *zhang* away. I was truly outraged when she did that three times. I was reminded of the time when she and Brown Lion mated; he chased and dragged her too, but a light touch from Brown Lion had her lie down meekly so he could have its way with her. She didn't really put up a fight. Now, see how she treated me. Tell me, how could I not be angry? Don't many people commit murder when they lose their temper? I was just an animal. Can you understand how I felt back then?

The flames of rage burned off all reason, and I stopped biting gently. Instead I clamped down hard. I could even hear her leg bone screaming in pain, the sound of teeth on bone. I wondered if my teeth had left a mark on her bone, but that's not important. An acrid liquid spread in my mouth, which only intensified my wrath, but the taste made me let go of her leg. I knew I'd be another Brown Lion in people's eyes if I didn't. I couldn't make mistakes in matters of principle. The people wouldn't mind it if I mated with a few female camels, but they'd have the right to finish me off with one of their muskets if I became a killer camel. I'd seen them use the weapon on a wolf, whose body was covered in bloody holes. It was horrifying.

What I hadn't expected was how she tried to get up and run again, even after I drew blood on her leg. Maybe she was angry too, for she kicked me. It didn't hurt—you see, not everyone was as good as me when it came to swift kicks—one minute of performance on stage requires ten years of training, as they say these days—but I grew angrier from the humiliation. I was like a man who's been slapped by a woman. Mad with anger, I ran up and rammed my shoulder against her, knocking her to the ground.

And that was when Long Neck Goose made his move, I recall.

Darkness blinded me as I felt a powerful force pressing down on my neck.

3

Frankly, even today I refuse to believe that Long Neck Goose did it for her sake. No, he just picked the right moment; the opportunity couldn't have been better for him. He'd be the king camel if he won, but wouldn't lose face if he lost, because he was acting heroically for a just cause. He seemed to be equally calculating, which was precisely how I realized that I'd underestimated this camel. I thought he planned to launch a sneak attack, and I wouldn't have been engaged in a positional warfare with him if the circumstance had been different. Neck fighting was clearly his strong suit, while mine was my fast leg. He sneaked up on me, stayed clear of my legs, and struck at my weak point, playing to his strength while avoiding exposing his shortcomings. What would you call that if not scheming?

But, to be frank, he did live up to its nickname; his neck was likely as strong as Brown Lion's. I really had underestimated him; I was even convinced that he'd have taken over from me if I hadn't had such fast legs. He was a formidable opponent, not one I encountered often.

I might have been weakened by too much mating or his neck was simply too powerful—more likely, I'd used too much energy dealing with Pretty Widow—but I did feel his neck press down on me with a spectacular force, as I weren't facing a neck but a python, for there was an unusually powerful force surging in there. Onlookers would see a static scene, which was in effect two forces fighting for dominance, momentous combat. My neck shook more often than I cared to count; it was hard to detect, but I knew it was shaky. You ought to know that camel neck wrestling doesn't end until one bends the other's head. The neck is just a troop flag that, once toppled, drains the morale, and any more fighting after that would be more like harassment.

I cursed under my breath. I was certain that my frenzied mating in recent days had seriously depleted my vitality. Normally, I refrained from mating after setting out. The long trek lasted so many days, they were like countless leaves on a tree, and I was too exhausted to even think about mating. But this time we spent a long time resting, and I let myself go a bit; as a human saying goes, lechery springs from warmth and nourishment. If not, I wouldn't be so useless. I wouldn't have lost even at positional warfare if I'd had my usual energy level. Don't you agree? You forget that Brown Lion—no, Brown Ass—and I had had several neck fights, and I'd never looked seriously overpowered, had I? I don't believe Long Neck Goose was stronger than Brown Ass.

I had a feeling Brown—that wasn't his family name—and I were born enemies. Even thinking about it now puts me in a bad mood and I feel uneasy. I feel at ease regarding any other enemies, even the mortal ones—such as the cleft nose old camel king that had bitten me in the leg and given me the scar—for the so-called hatred dissolved like frost under the sun, after the trial of life and death. Except for Brown Ass. Each time I think about him, I get so emotional it's hard to get over. Maybe this is what people mean by karmic enemy and retribution. There is, however, another possibility: whenever I think of the Mongolian camel, I'm always reminded of how I had pretty much castrated him with a low blow. Sometimes a behavior that diminishes one's self-image can hurt like touching a tender spot. And the pain may twist one's mind and turn into everlasting hatred for the opponent. It surely is likely, because I still feel hatred when I think of him. I can never fully set myself free from that hatred, even though the circumstance of our shared existence had long changed and a great many materialistic aspects are different now, with just a tiny, almost indistinct shred of spiritual energy left.

No more idle chat—I'm not a chatterbox—let's move on to the fight.

Our necks froze in the air for who knew how long. It was a tense situation, and one minute felt like a hundred years. Long Neck Goose pressed his neck down on mine to bend my head, while I forced my neck up to flip him over. A stalemate developed and lasted several hours. I didn't know until later that he wasn't necessarily stronger; I felt his overwhelming power because his weight had added strength as he pushed his neck down on me. He had neck power and body weight, which meant he was aided by additional strength, while I was using only my neck. Based on your human war craft, he "occupied the ground with irresistible force," so he surely had the advantage.

Sweat flowed freely down my nape, my neck was numb, beyond sore. I knew I'd lose at any moment. Just his weight of several hundred *jin* was enough to overpower me, let alone the fact that he was well rested. It dawned on me later that he had clearly been plotting for a long time. He'd picked an advantageous moment to charge at me and launch an attack in a method favorable to him.

It was a competition that had started out unfair. Brown Lion and I had had similar contests, which were like human arm wrestling, except that we used our necks. Standard combat usually had me pressing to the left and him to the right or vice versa. We always pushed away from each other. But this time Long Neck Goose was pushing down and I up. Put aside the gravity you humans talk about, just his body weight alone—hei, I'll keep it short. It has been so long; it's pointless for me to go on and on about it. I just want to tell you I had no choice later when I did what I did.

Don't look at me like that and don't think I was born bad. Don't say I ruined Brown Lion and Long Neck Goose. I want to stress that Brown Lion started an unfair fight, so I'd had to counter with equal measure.

I felt my feet were sinking. Can you imagine the hard gobi surface giving way? It showed how powerful we were. My front feet went about five *cun* into the ground, deeper than the back ones. The sunken spots were wet, from my sweat; it could be from Long Neck Goose, but it was sweat and it wet the spots, no matter where it came from. Some rocks were exposed, black ones, though they could have different colors and only turned black after baking in the sun for a thousand years. You have to add "black" to any gobi with these rocks and call a desert like this black gobi.

On the black gobi were two camels, one white and one yellow, fighting, an interesting tableau. This is what Big Mouth would be saying frequently after that.

At the moment I was suffering; darkness flickered before my eyes and a bright, black light kept flashing before me. I didn't want to pass out. Then a light went on in my head.

I had the light going on in my head all the time, which set me apart from ordinary camels.

Is it what writers like you call inspiration?

4

I relaxed my neck.

I used all my strength to push up before relaxing. I immediately saw him panic over the sudden spurt of force, and he was ready to mobilize greater power to push down on me.

I abruptly lowered my head and moved it back.

You all know what happened after that: Long Neck Goose couldn't react fast enough and rammed his head against the black gobi; his jaw was broken in a straight line and blood gushed out.

I heard an agonized scream that sounded like a black log spewing out of his throat. It soared in the time and space of my life till this day when it still hits and hurts me now and then.

Long Neck Goose crumpled to the ground, where, overcome by the sharp pain, he squirmed.

His jaw had hit a rock, also a black one lodged in the gobi for a thousand years. It had been waiting for Long Neck Goose's chin. That was how I felt. It's true; for it was strange. The black gobi was strewn with rocks, but they were mostly small. A large one that could smash a camel's jaw was uncommon. I didn't even notice a large black rock lying in wait when we were fighting. It was the one that had been plotting for a long time and eventually became my accomplice—hei, that's not right. It wasn't an accomplice. Everything I did was the product of that light going off in my head.

On the surface it seemed random for rocks to appear on the ground and rocks to fall from the sky, I often thought, but it might not be all that simple. In the vast universe, why would his jaw collide with the rock or a falling rock hit someone in the head? There had to be an unusual, unknown force controlling matters like these. With help from such a train of thought, I was able to lessen the guilt I felt about Long Neck Goose.

You ought to know that despite our rivalry, Long Neck Goose, unlike Brown Ass, and I were comrades-in-arm in the trenches most of the time. We fought the Mongolian camels together; back there fights often broke out between the Chinese and Mongolian camels, mostly over water and grass. We usually rested and recovered in the big desert upon returning to the ground, after finishing a caravan transport. There was a lot of grass and water, but the best was always in short supply, especially good water—the bean water that Lu Fuji talked about all the time. It must have what the humans called a mineral or something, because it was beneficial and energizing for humans and camels. A source could be found under a certain cliff, but it wasn't in abundance; it actually dripped a drop at a time onto a shallow spot on limestone. Not much would gather each day, which was why the two sides often got into a fight. The Chinese side rarely got the upper hand, but we didn't do too badly.

Long Neck Goose was my best helper in each battle, as we fought side by side and broke even with Brown Ass and his camel friends. Every time after the battle, I'd reward some of the good fighters and let them mate with the females. Long Neck Goose got more than any other males. To be frank, I couldn't mate with all the females, which numbered in the thousands; I could break my back and still fail to mate with all of them.

With a long history of camaraderie, Long Neck Goose and I forged a special bond that was different from my relationship with Brown Ass. And I felt guilty over what it had to go through later.

I wondered if the black rock might have been its karmic enemy from a previous life. The rock waited, ready for the opportunity to strike.

I don't care whether you believe me or not; that was the only way I could look at it.

Imagine how uneasy I would be if I had to hold a different view. You ought to know it doesn't matter what the world is like; what's important is how one sees and explains the world.

5

I heard Lu Fuji shouting. I knew he was screaming at me. I turned to see him running over with his whip. It was made of woven strips of cowhide, as thick as a grown man's thumb, with a soft tip of musk deer. I feared it the most, even though the whip was pliable, for it was tough and didn't break easily. It often exploded on my nose till I saw stars.

I should have taken off running at that moment, but I was too stunned by the horrible sight of an injured Long Neck Goose. Quite a few people believed that I'd been planning to harm him, but that wasn't true. All I wanted was to teach him a lesson. Think about it. Had he not used so much force, he'd only have gotten a thick lip or lose a few teeth even if his jaw hit the ground. He obviously put all his strength into the fight and clearly wanted to break my jaw—how could he contemplate something so violent? He didn't expect that by wanting to do me harm he ended up hurting himself more. He broke his own jaw. How could he blame me?

But I was stunned. I don't like to see blood, which was now flowing on the ground before me and smothered my mind. I didn't think of fleeing, even though I saw Lu Fuji running over with his whip.

A loud crack, and I felt a stabbing pain. I was sure a gash had opened up on my face—later I did see the mark left by the whip. I never forgave Lu Fuji because of that. I cursed him for being an old ingrate, a beast—don't glare at me. That was what I thought back then. Have you forgotten that winter when you got so drunk you laid in a snow-covered sand trough, like an old dog frozen stiff? Where would you be today if I hadn't covered you with my hair? There was another winter when we were stuck on river ice; you slept on a sack and covered with a leather coat. Fast asleep. But the coat was useless and you were about to freeze to death, though you weren't aware of it. You just felt sleepy; yes, you were only drowsy, but your blood was about to stop flowing and you'd have died in what you believed to be sleep—many people freeze to death in a similar situation—it was me again who covered you with my chin air and warmed you up. You were so touched when you found out later, you vowed to repay my kindness. You repaid me with your whip. You old beast.

The crack reminded me to flee. The whip would surround me if I stayed. The pain didn't bother me; what I feared most was the flying tip of the whip taking out an eye. A tip could easily do that; a single swipe on the eyeball would send fluid flowing. and I'd be a blind camel—I wouldn't like it even if you called me a one-eyed dragon. I had to run.

As I took off, the whip crackled on my back this time. It hurt, of course. Now I knew the old thief Lu Fuji didn't spare anything. He could carry at least five hundred *jin*. I told you before that he could carry two litters each weighing two hundred *jin*. My back nearly gave out.

I had to run.

Lu Fuji was out of his mind and very close; he seemed to have forgotten about my fast feet. But I was somewhat panicky because of the bloody jaw, so I didn't think of kicking him with my feet. Otherwise, he would surely die if I kicked him in the chest. But that could mean I'd lose my life too. They called a camel like that a killer camel and would take it out when it kicked someone to death.

I had to run.

I ran to a distant dune, not very quickly, because it felt like a loss of face to run. Listen to me. I cared a great deal for face, didn't I? But I had to forget about it before the whip made its tenth contact with my back. Compared to the pain, face was a rag.

Wind whipping past my ears told me I was running fast. An average camel couldn't catch up if I ran as fast as I could. I was leaving the sound of the whip behind, but I didn't feel like stopping. I felt so wronged, for I'd always thought Lu Fuji was nice to me. But humans are fickle and they change just like that. The sense of injustice even reduced my guilt feeling toward Long Neck Goose.

I kept running, all the way to a distant sand trough. As I was rounding a bend, I turned to check behind me and saw a large crowd surrounding Long Neck Goose, which reminded me of his situation. You shouldn't have used so much force, I thought. I wanted to say, "Suits you right," but that would make me look mean if I did.

Don't you think?

I swallowed the words.

6

I saw Brown Ass.

He was in the middle of a standoff with several wolves. A quick check came up with three, along with the bodies of two dead ones nearby. They could have been taken down by Brown Ass, but not necessarily, because wolves did die on their own sometimes—if they were sick, that is. I wasn't jealous of Brown Ass when I said that. I just thought people might not believe that he killed the wolves with its feet. But they might have different views if I said the wolves died on their own. This was what's known as letting something go in order to capture it, or covering something up to make it more conspicuous. Hei-hei, I have to show off my learning, or you'd think I've got no brains.

I never imagined I'd see wolves in Wild Fox Ridge. I'd heard that the place was teeming with them, but we hadn't noticed their tracks on the way. It was an even bigger surprise that we'd attracted so many of them. Later I'd even ponder whether they were coming to avenge the two Brown Ass had killed with his feet or teeth. Hard to say. If true, then the Mongolian camel could be a man—I mean, a camel—condemned by history.

That was the moment when I was convinced that Brown Ass was indeed crazy. Why? Because he didn't seem to fear the wolves. Have you ever heard of a camel who wasn't afraid of wolves? Only lions aren't afraid. Could Brown Ass really think he was a lion? People can call you lion if they want, but don't think so highly of yourself you begin to behave like one and act fearless. Then you are truly mad.

I didn't know long the standoff had been going on, a day, three days, maybe more, but they were well matched. Yet, the longer it went on, the better for Brown Ass. Why? Because the lumps on his back had enough fat to last him ten days or two weeks, while hunger is detrimental to wolves.

The wolves looked around uncasily when they saw me coming. They thought I was coming to save a fellow camel. Yes, I'd do that, but I was in no hurry. I could tell he was in no immediate danger.

I stopped a little distance away and lay down in a sand trough to enjoy the desert rice in there—I was a little hungry—and enjoy the show. I admit I'd forgotten all about Long Neck Goose, not because I had a special skill to put such things out of my mind, but because it was my nature. I was never too keen on using my head. It was pointless, no matter what I thought about, so I gave up.

Put at ease by my lack of action, the wolves went back to deal with Brown Ass. I wanted to leave, but did not want to draw them to me. I was afraid of wolves. Sure, I'd kicked a few to death, but the fear was always there. Once I saw a young camel with its humps gnawed clean by wolves; the bloody wounds made me shudder when I thought about it. I hadn't been afraid of them at first; my ignorance went hand in hand with my fearlessness, the circumstance under which I deployed my special talent of kicking a wolf like a soccer ball. But once I'd seen the young camel's humps, my pores tightened and twitched when I thought of wolves. There's nothing unusual about that; so many heroes in the world want to keep on living, you know. What makes them true heroes is doing what they do fearlessly in the face of death. Humans would be fools if they weren't afraid to die, and a fool is still a fool even if he does something heroic. I didn't admire Brown Ass for kicking the wolves to death, because that wasn't a normal behavior for him.

The camel hands thought Old Brown had lost his mind, but I was never quite sure exactly how crazy he was. He might have had a touch of madness, but how much was hard to say. My suspicions came about when I saw how he dealt with the wolves. He knew when to attack and when to retreat; he was poised and never lost his cool. White foam covered his lips—the mark of a mad camel—but his actions could not be summed by a single word: mad.

Old Brown—I called him that, instead of Brown Ass, when what he'd done with Pretty Widow slipped my mind; that also depended on my mood—being aggressive with the wolves was his strategy. He kept his mouth wide open. He had such a big mouth, so big you could probably stuff a mid-size watermelon in there. He was drooling so heavily the ground was getting wet. He did look like a lion, enough to freeze the wolves in their tracks. When he pounced, they dodged. A few rounds later, I worked out their scheme: they wanted to tire him out. They didn't launch reckless charges; maybe the two dead ones had been rash and tasted his mouth or foot. I figured he'd gotten one in his mouth and tossed it into the air, and then stomped it to death when it fell. That had to be what happened. Simply flinging a wolf up wasn't enough to kill it, while a wolf would never wait quietly for a camel to come up and stomp on it. Only after a wolf was thrown would it submit to a camel's feet so willingly. I'd done that myself. Just imagine, we weigh nearly a thousand *jin*; all that weight concentrated in one foot is lethal. It would surely turn a wolf's internal organs into mush.

The wolves naturally got smarter after two of their own had met untimely deaths that way. They changed tactics by luring Old Brown this way and taunting him that way, making him jump and pounce all over the place, waiting to tire him out before killing him. The surviving wolves were endowed with scholarly talent and incredible guerrilla skills; one advanced while the others retreated or one paused while the others provoked the camel; one attacked when the others were tired; one backed off while the others gave chase. Hei, it was a frightening yet enjoyable scene.

I began calling Brown Ass Old Brown as I watched the battle.

What happened then?

Then I saved Old Brown.

He was on his last legs. The humps on its back were still up and continued to supply energy, but he was clearly exhausted, which, I believed, was caused by anxiety.

The wolves were looking pleased. They leap when they're happy, the hopping action an expression of their upbeat mood.

Old Brown was about to give up the fight. His movements slowed. He was stumbling, as sweat poured down like rain, soaking him as if he'd been splashed. He was about to crumble. Even if he didn't, one of the wolves could simply jump up and go for his throat, and there would be no more Old Brown.

With a roar, I ran over.

Startled, the wolves came at me, but before they got near, I kicked up sand with my hind legs, sending a yellow fog their way. Hei, if only one speck got into their eyes, I'd be able to turn a wolf into a soccer ball. You don't believe me?

They were petrified. It was their first time witnessing Yellow Demon's stunt.

What happened after that?

After that the wolves left unhappily, once they knew they had no chance.

It came as a big surprise to me when a barely recovered Old Brown pounced on me with his mouth opened wide.

He really had lost his mind, I thought. Every living creature was his enemy now.

Two. Balte

1

My long neck camel, I felt so bad about you.

You were a Chinese camel, but I liked you the moment I saw you. Maybe it was what people call predestined connection.

Someone had wanted to ask for you as compensation if Brown Lion died. We never expected he would use such a sneaky trick on you.

Old Lu whipping Yellow Demon wasn't enough for me; I wanted to skin him myself. How could you use that kind of devious scheme on your own? I was so angry I could barely breathe. That was how my young brother was killed. He was a camel hand too. One day several camel hands were playing tug-of-war, and the other side let go at the same time just when my brother's side was about to win. Several of his teammates fell on him and broke one of his ribs, which punctured his heart—wasn't that the same trick you used?

How could you do that?

You said you hadn't planned it, but of course I didn't believe you. I did not believe you weren't aware of the consequences of your move.

I even suspected you intentionally lured Long Neck Goose to the black rock—sure, you can deny that. Later I had to eliminate that possibility when I learned he had attacked you first, but I couldn't stop hating you; I loathed you. I wanted to skin you, take out your tendons, and remove your bladder for kids to turn into a leather ball. My son loved kicking those.

I refused to think that Brown Lion's earlier mating attempt was the cause of all the subsequent problems, though it did look that way on the surface. You can't create an explosion without gunpowder, even if there is a detonator, am I right? I believed in cause and effect and retribution. I wasn't paying attention when Ma Zaibo talked about it, but I did believe good deeds will be rewarded. The concept is so simple it needs no explication, which was borne out by the popular story about Old Lu in Liangzhou. He had simply freed the blacksmith who stole Master Guan's sword. Later, when Lu was beheaded at Xiaojiaping in Lanzhou, the blacksmith bribed an official so he could sew the head back on to the neck before taking the body to Lu's hometown. It was a widely circulated story.

In Wild Fox Ridge Old Lu could not have imagined that the government would lop off his head one day, which is why he could swagger like some big prick. He might have been more restrained had he known. I didn't expect us to meet again here to rehash our past either. It's better we don't know the future, it would be terrible if we did. Feiqing, you'd have been worried awake or asleep if you'd known your future and you were aware of a chopper hanging over your head until it came down on your neck, aren't I right?

But even today, after so many years, I'm still upset over the pain Yellow Demon caused Long Neck Goose. My heart aches when I recall how he spent his last days with a broken jaw.

After Old Lu whipped and chased Yellow Demon off, it dawned on us that we should be trying to save Long Neck Goose, not taking a whip to his tormenter.

I ran to the sand trough. I remember it was overgrown with thorny nitraria that could easily draw blood. My hands hurt from the thorns, but I plucked a big handful of them and crushed them as I ran back to Long Neck Goose. My hands were covered in green juice. As I applied the crushed plants to his neck, I was hit by the realization that he wasn't long for this world. His jaw was mangled, bloody shreds of flesh. The thorns would not work, for blood continued to wash it away.

I was heartbroken, my Long Neck Goose.

I wanted to kill you, Yellow Demon, when I looked at the horrific jaw.

Don't laugh. I meant it.

With a mutilated jaw, Long Neck Goose could not chew. Old Lu told some of the camel hands to pluck green grass and pound into pulp in a mortar to feed the camel. He wrapped up the broken bones and flesh in a piece of cloth. I hoped it would grow back together, even if the camel ended up with a crooked mouth. But it wouldn't stop bleeding. Later, it didn't bleed as much, so he wouldn't die of blood loss. Still Old Lu was worried sick.

Over those days, Long Neck Goose went away from the other camels to a distant spot in the desert, where he couldn't stop shaking. I knew it hurt really bad but he never cried.

I'll never forget the way he looked, not even now. When I bring it up, I can still see him and I feel the heartache all over again.

2

As for Killer you're always talking about, I never saw him.

How come I never saw any so-called killer? Who knows. What do you think?

And, I have no idea what you were saying about mules. I never saw any mules either. In the caravans back then, there was only Feiqing's steed, no mules and no other horses. The mountains and rivers the Young Master brought up were even more out of the question. I think you're a bit crazy yourself.

But I rarely noticed you in those days. I had my eyes on Feiqing, because I believed Huozi's claim that you were planning to do away with us, that you weren't going to Luocha, that you wanted to settle there and become outlaws.

Yes, I did think you were going to be outlaws.

No, I didn't think that; you were planning to.

No, you didn't plan to; you had been outlaws all along.

I admit we were the ones who fired the first shot.

On the surface we'd fired the shot over water and grass—it was indeed one of the reasons, but mostly because of something else. I knew we couldn't make it out of Wild Fox Ridge alive. I can't tell you why, I just felt that way. I had a premonition that the end of the world was near. I hadn't believed it when someone first brought up the idea. I refused to think the world was ending, whether he used Kālacakra or some other divination method for prediction. Later I changed my mind. It was simple: I watched one Chinese camel after another die, for no reason at all. There would be a wound but it never healed; it continued to fester and rot, even after washed with salt water. Camel wounds usually healed after we washed them with salt water. But this time the wound was like ice under the sun; it kept breaking down and spreading. That was when I started to think the end was near.

Luckily, our Mongolian camels were unaffected. I wasn't sure if it was because of the genetic differences you were always talking about. But I'd rather believe that we were protected by our camel deity. We respected our camel deity and goat deity too, while the Chinese only offer obeisance to their goat deity. You don't pray to your camel deity, so naturally it won't protect you. We also had a Buddha we called Lakshmi, a Tantric Buddha, whose doctrine the Lama in our temple followed. She rode a mule with a hanging sack that contained plagues. I wondered if the Chinese camels were affected by a pestilence. You should have prayed to the same deity as we did.

Most of the Mongolian camels were fine and the damaged feet were pretty much healed, except for Brown Lion. It was the same, roaming the sand troughs, and getting bony. Every time I saw him, I felt a loathing for the Chinese caravan—Long Neck Goose excluded, and my heart ached. I was annoyed when I heard the word, Han, as hatred bubbled up inside me. I had wanted the job for the Mongolians only, not sharing it with the Chinese caravan. But someone had talked me into it with some grand idea. What grand idea? You should know. The rag called Overthrowing the Qing and Restoring the Ming that someone was always waving as a banner. To be honest with you, Qing or Ming, it had nothing to do with me. Our ancestors always had trouble with the Ming. You know our ancestors started another dynasty of our own during the period that you called the Great Ming dynasty. Led by a man called Wang Baobao, they whipped your Great Ming. Isn't that true?

Yes, I did want to overthrow the Great Qing, but not for the same reason as you. I had no grand concept; I just felt that some of the things the Qing did were outrageous. They signed so many treaties, all of them a loss of face. I found it galling.

The Mongolian caravan was a powder keg when I was ready to fire the first shot; I merely lit the detonator.

The reason was simple enough. We wanted to leave. Why? We didn't want to die at Wild Fox Ridge because of the Chinese camels. We wanted to move on. We didn't just want to move on; we wanted to keep going until we reached our destination. We wanted to accomplish by ourselves the task originally set for the two caravans.

Was that wrong?

You should know that the client who hired us was worried he couldn't trust one of the caravans. He came up with an idea when assigning the cargo; he divided items into halves, though they should all have been in one place. The Mongolian and the Chinese each took half and we'd get what we wanted only when both halves arrived and were verified by the buyer. If one caravan wanted to hog the deal or got the wrong idea, the buyer would refuse to conclude it. He was right, of course. The client wanted us to work together and there was nothing wrong with that. What went wrong was, no one had expected the Chinese camels to suffer so much and that might never end. We couldn't be expected to stick around as they deteriorated, could we?

Don't you agree?

We were young back then. We wanted do something big, to overthrow the Qing.

Don't you think it made sense for us to ask for the cargo they were no longer able to deliver? They should leave the toilet if they didn't want to shit, right?

I didn't expect them to explode like that when we brought it up.

They went to the extreme and accused us of evil intention, of stealing the cargo.

Was that reasonable?

3

We had to think of something else when you refused to listen to reason.

The something else was simple: either we grabbed it or we stole it.

We just didn't want to die in Wild Fox Ridge.

It was a bit like the organization you mentioned. They wanted to save the earth; they didn't want a human race that was reproducing unchecked like cancer cells to drag the earth to the abyss of calamity. They came up with the idea of exterminating a particular race. I find their idea appalling too, of course. But we were a bit like that back then. It was clear that the Chinese camels were in serious trouble, and it could only get worse. Some of the camels had been reduced to carcasses, and their flesh turned into waste. Hopeless. It was really hopeless.

We were lucky we left in time; otherwise we might have been affected too. You said it was germs that caused infection, but to me it was camel pestilence. Our ancestors passed down the story that it had happened about a hundred years ago, like leprosy for humans. To me it was leprosy; it looked just like it.

We did our best to advance our case, only to incur endless curses. We decided we'd act at night and secretly transfer the cargo to our camels. We'd endure the humiliation and carry the heavy load to Luocha and trade it for what we were promised. If we'd succeeded, what happened next would have been completely different.

It was a dark night, I recall, as if heaven and earth had both died. I can still feel how everything was shrouded in a pall of death. You probably haven't seen anything like it. I can tell you a pall of death had a gray texture; think about gray and dusty air like silk or satin. I realized that it spread over everything. We were in fact trying to save the caravan. Think about it. We'd die with them there if they were stuck.

I didn't want to die. Our lives were flowing east like a torrent.

I'd scouted out the location of the cargo. I need to make it clear that the cargo included animal feed, actual real cargo and valuable goods among the real cargo. We carried bricks of tea, gifts to Luocha. We could take our own share of tea bricks and let the Chinese portion rot with them.

We just wanted the box of important goods, gold, precious goods that the Ma family had amassed over several generations. That was what we wanted.

The gold had stayed with Ma Zaibo, who was accompanied by several men with terrific martial arts skills. Later I heard that Ma had a screw loose as he spouted nonsense. Feiqing then assigned a few people to guard the gold. I learned it was kept in the middle tent. There were more of us but I didn't want to win by numbers only. I wanted to take the goods by wit; or put differently, I didn't want an all-out fight with them yet—even though we'd already shed all pretense of cordiality, I didn't want to. Heh-heh.

It was a dark night, I recall. Like they say, a night dark enough to kill someone and a wind strong enough to set a fire. I didn't want to kill anyone, however dark it was, but I told my people to set a fire despite the lack of wind. I wanted to use the fire to draw out the one guarding the tent so I could get in to take the gold. I heard the Russkies accepted only gold, nothing else; they wouldn't deign to even look at silver.

As the fire rose, someone shouted, Fire, fire! The so-called grassy ground was just bundles of Artemisia cut by Qi Lu and other drivers. They piled the stems and leaves up for future use. Actually, it didn't matter if the bundles were burned; there was no need to save them. But you should know that the drivers wouldn't be thinking so carefully when they heard someone shouting fire. They ran over in the grip of emotion; they would be sure to put out the fire. It'd be easy; all they had to do was throw sand on the fire to put out a fire that lit up the night sky.

We stormed the tent at that moment.

I took ten men with me, all terrific drivers.

And sure enough, the Chinese drivers were all out there to put out the fire.

I saw ten average looking chests that were placed in a spot that was anything but average. A fur-lined blanket was placed on top of them. We tossed the blanket, picked up the chests, and walked out. I carried one too, and it was heavy, enough to trade for a considerable quantity of firearms. I was told even Liu Huzi's cavalry would be no match for this stuff. I heard that a firearm even took out a hero called Nurhaci, so Liu Huzi was nothing. Pulpy Plum would be nothing, and so would the prince who ruled us. I could almost see the scene when the firearms were fired, when many were rolling in the fire and screaming in pain. We met no resistance, because it took us virtually no time to enter and leave the tent. I imagined the firefighters had yet to reach the site.

It was a lousy trick, but still I was surprised they weren't prepared for it. Obviously, they hadn't expected an attack from us; maybe it never occurred to them that their fellow travelers would kick them in the back.

I quickly leapt over a fence made of camel litters and onto a waiting camel.

I did it, I said to myself.

I was thinking that I could be a national hero if I succeeded.

But so many matters in the world are unpredictable. Like they say, man proposes, God disposes. If I did make out of Wild Fox Ridge, would I be able to escape the sand storm?

4

I saw a pile of sticks, what people called donkey dicks, in the open chest. They were made of sand and soil, and shaped like cucumbers. I thought the Chinese had hidden the gold in them, so I smashed each of them and got a pile of sand for my troubles. They'd tricked me, obviously. I didn't know if they'd swapped them at some point or they'd used the donkey dicks as a cover-up all along.

I was humiliated.

Huozi tried to cheer me up, but I could see the mockery on his face.

The drivers came back from setting the fire, to see their work had gotten a pile of donkey dicks in return. They couldn't stop with their sarcastic remarks.

I knew Feiqing and his people would soon see through the fire. Maybe they'd even come and make demands. I asked Huozi what to do next.

He scowled and took a long time to say,

"The snow has melted and the body is exposed. It's out in the open now, so no sense in holding back."

What he meant to say was: our intention was out in the open now, so we might as well carry it through, whatever happens.

The Mongolian drivers were like gunpowder now. Forget about what happened in the past; the events after Brown Lion's injury were enough to make them itch for action.

They waited for my order with their weapons.

"Let's not be rash, let's wait," I told them.

I knew it was hard to say whether we could win an open fight. The Mongolian and the Chinese each had their own strength; they were good with martial arts and we had powerful arms. Club fighters didn't normally fare well when fighting someone stronger, but we weren't sure if we could overcome those men.

"We do one thing if we want to fight. We do something else if we don't," Huozi said.

"We can only fight now, since it's come to this. We can't die here with them, because we have things to do. Their camels are dying, and we can't stay here and watch ours die. We can go to Luocha on our own." I was reminded of *Journey to the West*.

"If the demons disguised as Tripitaka and his escorts did reach the magic mountain and got the sutras, would they attain enlightenment?"

he'd asked me.

I couldn't give him an answer. Later I went and asked Ma Zaibo, who said,

"Sure. Monkey King Sun Wukong was a demon at first. A demon who undertakes religious cultivation is a practitioner. They'd attain enlightenment if they had the sutras."

I believed him.

"As long as the end is right, the means isn't important. If you really want to accomplish something major, don't be bogged down by details," Huozi said.

I liked the sound of that. I never cared for grandiose concepts, but I still needed something, so I could do what I couldn't ordinarily do with a clear conscience.

We talked it over and decided to act again that night. Huozi had already talked to the marksmen and got them on our side, which was like controlling a country's army. With their participation, the Chinese drivers would lose even during an open fight, but we settled on a sneak attack anyway. We just wanted the gold; we didn't want any bloodshed. Unless it was absolutely necessary, we didn't want to be responsible for any deaths.

When the sanxing slanted west, we picked up our weapons and advanced toward the Chinese caravan. Our goal was simple: get the gold and go to Luocha alone; we'd take the "sutras" they wanted.

Yes, I saw no need to waste our lives at crazy Wild Fox Ridge.

Balte's story has made me thirsty. I discovered something familiar in the story. I took a few sips of the water they brought me and my thirst was slaked.

The problem of water has been solved, but another one crops up.

The chill.

I can't find my bag when I want to light a fire. There is a box of matches, a lighter, a few books, and my notebook. The notebook contains the interviews, so it's naturally important, but fire is more critical. Water and fire are equally indispensable in winter desert.

It's just awful.

Human hearts are peculiar oftentimes. You don't feel thirsty when you have water, but once it's gone, thirst comes at you like a ferocious beast. With something to make a fire, you can do so anytime you want, so you're not affected by the chill. Once it's gone, coldness attacks like a demon.

The cold wind surges from all four corners and bores into my bones. The fur coat is good for blocking out some of the wind, but not enough to stop the chill from seeping in. With a limited use, fur can keep you warm, but can't provide heat. If I had my dog with me, I could hold it in my arms and keep myself warm. But it never shows. I wonder if it's decided to go home by itself. If so, then it's a deserter. I don't think it can leave the desert on its own.

I'm disappointed in its behavior, but still I say a prayer for the dog, asking the Guru, Yidam, Dakini, and Dharmapala to protect its safe journey out of the desert.

The white camel isn't here either. He's probably gone out to look for water. But why doesn't he drink some of the water brought by the drivers?

Twentieth Session
Interrogation of the Flesh

There's no sun this morning. The sky is overcast, while the cold wind continues to howl. I survived a cold night because of the Hu Family Mill—the drivers told me last night that this is indeed the place.

After bolting down some food, I ride the yellow camel out to look for my bag. I'm sure I've lost it on the road. I've been riding the white camel, letting the yellow carry the load. In theory, camels are quite smart, and he should have known I'd lost something. He should have stopped on the track and stood still to let his driver know something has fallen off. Obviously, the yellow camel did it on purpose; he knew the bag had fallen off, but pretended not to notice—and there's another possibility: he intentionally shook off the bag, which wasn't hard to do. To be sure, the rope around the bag must have come loose. But still, he's a bad camel.

"You have to take me to where the bag fell," I say to the yellow camel. "Or I won't let you off the hook. You should know what you did amounts to murder."

The camel ignores me with an impassive look. It's hard to tell if he regrets his action.

I flick the reins for him to kneel so I can get off to wrap the sleeping bag around me under my coat. The chill has me trembling, but I get back up on the camel anyway. I still had the bag yesterday, so it has to have fallen nearby. Besides, camels are good at remembering the route, so the yellow camel must know where it is.

"We'll die together if necessary," I say to the camel as I brandish a knife at it. I'm just trying to scare him, of course, so he won't play more dirty tricks.

The camel is silent. I cannot tell what is on his mind, but he gets up and starts carrying me back.

The gusty wind blows relentlessly. I feel like I'm about to freeze. This is unbearable.

The sand dunes spread out into the distance and into the unknown. I can't see the end, nor do I know where I am. I only know this is Wild Fox Ridge, but there are more spots in the ridge. To me it feels like a hazy spot of light. I'm forever shrouded in an enigmatic fog.

I rise and fall along with the camel's movements as he climbs a hill or goes down a sand trough. I almost wish I could keep going like this through eternity. Exhausted beyond words, I feel drowsy, but I know I'd be in another world if I shut my eyes and fell asleep. The icy wind would quickly freeze my blood. The stories I've gathered through the interviews would be blown off, and no one would ever know what happened to the camel drivers. So many stories have disappeared like that in the world. On the other hand, so many worlds have also vanished like that, and the earth never stops turning.

I get off the camel whenever I'm about to doze off. I remove the coat and the sleeping bag and toss them over the camel's back. Leading him, I use his mane to help me along, and soon my body come back alive.

Alternating between riding and walking, I travel on. Luckily, the camel doesn't play a trick on me by taking the wrong route, for I can tell it's the way we came.

Don't ask me if I'll kill the camel if it doesn't behave. I won't, because a knife is a lethal weapon and one should never raise it too easily. But this is rational thinking; I don't know what I'll do in the heat of the moment.

I don't know how long we walk until I see something black.

You probably think it's my bag.

But it's not. I see the dog first and then the bag, not too far from the dog. The strap is in its mouth, trailed by a line into the distance. Obviously, it was trying to drag it back to the Hu Family Mill. It didn't have to, because no one comes here, and I'd have found it in my search. The dog must have thought someone would pick it up, so it decided to retrieve it, whatever the cost.

It's stiff. I don't know if it has died of the freezing chill or of exhaustion. Maybe both.

I'm choking up. Earlier I was grumbling about the dog, calling it a deserter. My mind is a blank, as a colossal sorrow wraps itself around me. But no tears.

I run at the yellow camel with the knife. I really want to kill the animal. Evidently, emotions change.

In my view, the yellow camel should have fled. I've let go of the rein at some point and my physical condition will not let me catch him if he takes off.

I'm afraid that I may lose self-control and kill him. So I yell at him instead, "Run! Why don't you run away? You damned animal."

He doesn't run. Instead he slowly walks up to the dog and kneels. Something sparkles in his eyes, like tears.

Tossing the knife aside, I pick up the bag and check inside and see that nothing is missing. I cry out loud when I spot the light and matches, like a wandering son seeing his mother. After that I put a portion on each of the camels and carry one on me as a safeguard. I'll always have a spare if one is lost.

I make a silent vow to build a temple called "King Dog Temple" if I make it out of Wild Fox Ridge alive. I want to write about my dog, so people hundreds of years later will know about it. I want to shame those unfaithful ingrates into blushing when they're reminded of my dog.

"Go on then," I say to my dog. "I'm still young and I'll wait for you if you can return.

"You can be my disciple if I attain enlightenment and we'll meet again to complete our destiny. You can be my friend, too. I have few friends like you; what I have more of is betrayal and defamation. I'm always searching for steadfast friendship. You can bring your other loyal friends, and we'll all be sworn brothers in your next life.

"You can be reborn as a woman and come look me up. She doesn't have to be pretty, but must be faithful, like you. What the world has most of are ingrates, immoral, greedy, and avaricious people. I want to have a woman like you to pass our long life together.

"You can be another dog, too. I'll treat you like family even if you're crippled. But there's no airplane that will take you, so you can't travel the world with me. It's better that you come back as a woman. Pretty or not, you'd be the only one for me.

"Go on. You can go now. I'll wait for you for as long as it takes."

I talk and cry, with my arms around it like holding the dearest person in my life. I'm dehydrated, but my tears are abundant and flow freely. My tear-streaked face feels icy when a cold wind blows.

I see its promise, and I'm convinced I'm not hallucinating. I see its soul float out of the body, but instead of hurrying off to be reborn, it follows me. It's worried about me, I know. "Do what you want," I say to the dog. "We're in no hurry. You can be reborn after I leave Wild Fox Ridge."

It is near dusk when I finally bury the dog in the sand. I break a thick piece of Artemisia and stick it on the grave—I work very hard to make a mound, even though I know the sand will be blown off by the wind. I do it anyway. If I can make it out of Wild Fox Ridge alive, I'm going to bring someone here to take the dog's body back and turn it into a specimen to be installed in King Dog Temple. I once saw an animal specimen receiving offerings in a temple. I'm worried, however, that the old wolf will come eat my dog if it finds out I've buried it here. I look around, but don't see the wolf anywhere.

I build a fire when I return to the Hu Family Mill. As the fire shines warmly on my face, I tear up again.

I continue with the interviews later that night. Some of the drivers bring me water, so I can drink to my heart's content. But the white camel is still missing, and that worries me.

By now all their faces are clearly visible. Maybe their memories freshen them up, or maybe I've acquired a different skill. After this, the interviews feel like face-to-face conversations.

I even see the anger on Lu Fuji's face.

One. Lu Fuji

Worse than pigs and dogs.

Really, far worse than animals.

I've only heard of desert outlaws raiding a caravan, but never camel drivers attacking other drivers.

You could come up with countless reasons, but none of them would cover the evil in your hearts. You're evil when you do something vile. Evil is evil no matter what kind of reason you have.

Luckily for us, Feiqing was prepared. The gold was indeed stored in the chests, but since you made the request, Feiqing told us to watch out.

So we did.

We didn't expect you to act so quickly, within a few days.

I didn't believe you'd leave for Luocha if you got the gold.

We saw the chests were gone when we returned after putting out the fire. We thought it had been outlaws at first. In our wildest dream we'd never imagine our own brothers—I don't know if you could still count as brothers—would stab us in the back. I didn't expect you to do something so despicable.

It was around midnight when I finally dozed off. Not long after that I sensed something cold against my neck. It was a knife, I could tell. I thought it was an outlaw, but I also knew I had to leave my fate to heaven. A flick of the knife and all my previous efforts would be pointless.

I found out it was you holding the knife once I surrendered.

Later I learned that you had taken care of one tent at a time. On the empty ground under the dim light of the lanterns I saw lots of our Chinese drivers, but Ma Zaibo wasn't among them. I can't tell whether what he told us was real or not. If he said so it must be real. What I'm telling you is real to me.

The Chinese drivers were all cursing the Tartars, Tartar this and Tartar that, cursing their mothers and ancestors. I don't need to repeat them for you. Curses like those aren't all that different, and they all have to do genitalia.

Balte started asking about the gold. It made me laugh. We'd buried the stuff where a common driver wouldn't know where to look.

Balte was sheepish enough at first to explain why they did what they did. Revolution was a vital reason, for sure. It was a modish term in those days too. You've all heard about a small booklet called Revolutionary Army, which sounded quite nice when sung by a blind storyteller. We were all familiar with what he was saying. I knew he was saying it for his own sake, as he found it hard to face himself. He was a terrific driver, but ended up doing something so shameful that he had to convince himself first.

But his initial unease quickly vanished, because he didn't get what he wanted from us. He was anxious, angry even.

I hadn't seen Huozi yet, but I knew he had to be the one who stirred up something like this. Balte couldn't have come up with such a vile idea.

Sure enough, Huozi made his blatant appearance after Balte failed to get the answer he sought.

And Huozi started up with all those grand concepts.

Two. Huozi

What grand concepts?

It was true and plain to see.

We had only three ways out at the time. One, you leave the camels with ruined feet behind and go home to feed your cats with your snot; two, we wait together until we're finished; three, we go to Luocha to fulfill our duty.

At least that's what we were thinking when we captured all of you. We just wanted you to hand over the gold so we could get on the road. We didn't expect to find nothing when we searched all the tents and the nearby area.

Why were you so stubborn? Didn't you know we also wanted to join the revolution? I'd heard of the rules and regulations of the Longhua Buddhist Society and it sounded wonderful to me too. You may not be aware that the Qing government was my enemy too, even though they didn't kill any of my ancestors. I'm Han Chinese. You all say that we Chinese are all one family, so when the Qing court killed a Chinese, it was like taking my ancestor's life. I shared your idea.

I joined the Mongolian's Laoyao Society—this, naturally was top secret, privy to a select few—not the Liangzhou Society of Brothers, because of the history between Feiqing and me. He and I were mortal enemies. I can't help it. A hundred years have gone by, but when I mention him I still feel righteous outrage—heh-heh—fill my chest. Can't help it. I'm even convinced that we were karmic enemies from a previous lifetime, or I owed him a karmic debt, or he was an enemy over eight hundred lifetimes. When I think back now, I can see that what happened between us was minor, but strangely the minor incident still fills my heart with loathing. I really can't help it, I have no control over myself.

I relayed to the Chinese drivers all my grand ideas. Naturally, I was trying to persuade the Mongolian side too. We'd shared food, and we ran into each other all the time, so at a moment like this, we couldn't act like enemies, eyes blazing with hatred. Feiqing was the exception, of course. But he ran away. Maybe he didn't spend that night at the tent site.

Where did he spend it, then?

I'd have skipped the big talk if he'd been there. My patience would leave me when I saw his face. I admit my heart was filled with loathing that usually lay dormant, but sprang up and burst into flames of hatred the moment I saw Feiqing.

Whether it was useful or not is beside the point. With all the things I said, I'd done my best to be meticulous in virtue and attentive to my duty, like being courteous before taking tough measures, wouldn't you say?

What happened next came as a surprise. Human hearts can change, human beings can change. When you have no control over your heart, you can't control yourself.

No visible effects came after I wasted my time talking. Balte was obviously out of options, and asked me what to do.

"Why are you asking that when it's come to this? Capturing a tiger is easy, setting it free is hard. If we let them go now, we'd all die a horrible death," I said to him.

He believed me, since he too had noticed how irate the Chinese drivers were.

"But they won't tell us even if we ask nicely." He looked at me, clearly seeking my advice.

I knew what he was after, so I said, "They won't tell us when we ask, so we'll have to force them."

And that was how it all started.

Three. Chain Smoker

It had never occurred to me that when a good man goes bad, he can be as mean as an evil man. Who could believe that someone you shared a meal with could be so vicious?

They slapped our faces first, and followed that with whips. All they wanted to know was one thing: the gold, where is it buried?

"How should they know where it was buried?" I said to Huozi,

"I wouldn't have wanted to know even if they'd decided to share the secret." Oftentimes the more you know, the riskier your situation. Best to know nothing at all. "I really don't know," I added. My answer got me a lot of "private planks"— in other words, "face slaps," but they preferred their own term for it, comparing our mouths to women's private parts. I couldn't get it through my head why they couldn't be more lenient with me because of my gray beard alone. I was old enough to be their father. But they didn't use a whip on me, probably because they knew my old bones couldn't take much before they had to dump my body in the desert.

They whipped every driver. Cai Wu and Qi Lu, along with a few more, cursed them at first, but then they began to beg for mercy. Wasting their breath. The screeching whips continued to fall on them, mostly on their thighs and hind quarters. What worried me most wasn't the pain they were suffering, but the wounds that, if they didn't heal quickly, would fester, like the camel feet, until they died. I'd seen enough people dying of tetanus.

For days on end, all I heard was the sound of a whip, even in my dreams. Even after they stopped slapping me, I continued to be tortured by the sounds of the whips and the screams of pain.

It was hell on earth, I tell you.

I noticed something unusual too. Only a few of the Mongolian drivers whipped us at first, as the others looked quite uncomfortable with the whole deal. But soon more and more of them picked up their whips, until nearly everyone was in on it. Moreover, the wicked look on their faces intensified. I wasn't sure if the sound of a whip triggered the evil in their hearts or they were just born cruel. The depravity spread, almost at lightning speed. The expressions on their faces changed too, fierce-looking now, and there was an edge to their voices. They added an angry tone to show they'd reached the limit of their patience. That is, they no longer sounded like their normal selves; instead they squeezed hateful words out through their teeth, even distorting some of the words.

Lu Fuji got the worst beating.

He was even whipped on the face.

The Mongolians knew he had to have the information they wanted.

"Looks like they have their minds made up, Fuji," I found a chance to say to him. "You probably should think about giving them the gold so they can go to Luocha—as long as they'll give us a receipt."

"How would I know where it's buried?" Fuji said. "I couldn't tell them even if I did."

"So it's all right for them to kill us then?"

"Feiqing doesn't survive on handouts. He'll find a way to save us," Lu Fuji said.

"He'll be like a clay Buddha crossing a river. He wouldn't be their match even if he was made of steel," I said.

"Don't worry. I can see the Mongolians just want to scare us. Can't you see they didn't strip us and beat us naked? It sounds terrible, but it doesn't hurt as much."

"That's because the hate hasn't reached a fever pitch yet," I said. "Wait and see what happens when it has."

Sure enough. The hatred took over after a couple of days.

Or to borrow your term, they were in character.

Their whips made direct contact with the flesh on the third day. Just the sound alone would set your teeth on edge, even without the actual beating.

Four. Big Mouth

I could not be happy during that time.

I realized that real happiness is conditional: besides having enough to eat and keeping warm, there is one important condition—safety. Without it, you cannot be happy.

They didn't beat me. Everyone knew I was like a wandering ghost outside Jiayu Pass. Even if they buried black goods, or white goods, or whatever goods, let alone yellow goods, they wouldn't tell me. What was I, if not a dust-devil that picked up a bit of offerings and a little water. That was fine with me, because it helped me escape the whip, at least at first. The Mongolians made Wooden Fish Girl and me cook for them. Chinese or Mongolian, everyone had to eat. We made big pots of food, and nearly died of exhaustion, but we didn't dare complain. I saw how they seemed to have different eyes now, with a strange, vicious glint. I was afraid of doing something to incur their wrath and suffer a beating.

The mood changed completely three days later. They started whipping just hard enough to land on the clothes, but then switched to lashing the Chinese drivers so hard it landed on bare skin. With each whack, strips of fabric and balls of wool, even coat leather, fluttered in the air, accompanied by screams of pain. The clothes on nearly everyone's back was turned into strips. I knew that besides trying to find the gold, they wanted to force Feiqing to show his face. I had no idea where he was though; it was like he'd evaporated.

And yet, no one revealed the secret, even after the Mongolians turned the Chinese drivers' back into bloody mats. It wasn't that they didn't want to tell, but that they really didn't know. Balte knew that too; he was trying to force the ones who knew to tell him.

Everyone had changed.

Balte turned into a true demon. Who knew that someone could change so fast or could be so evil just by wanting to? With one thought, he became truly evil. When he whipped a Chinese driver on the back, I saw not a human, but a madman. And the same was true with nearly every one of the Mongolian drivers.

The tent site was a cacophony of whacking lashes, screams, and angry shouts. It was really hell on earth.

I also discovered that they had obviously been planning this for some time. They had a strict division of labor: some standing guard, some patrolling the area, some interrogating with a whip, and others digging around. With such a detailed, quasi-military style of organization, they were almost like outlaws—no, they were outlaws. It just took them a while to transit from camel drivers to outlaws; they tried to cover it up first, but slowly they didn't care anymore. Following the shrieking whips, their greed roared and surged, spilling out of the sand troughs. Even the Chinese camels looked worried and cried constantly, a weighty, anxious cry, like a sigh or a plaintive expression of their helplessness.

It got colder. Luckily, there were no flies. If the weather was warm, the festering camel feet would draw swarms of flies to lay countless eggs. I didn't see any flies, but the feet weren't healing either. Some never scabbed, while the scabby wounds would ooze yellow pus when squeezed. I couldn't see any improvement at all.

The feed—beans—was going down fast. But at least we had foliage, an abundance of vegetation. Without the feed, they wouldn't grow much fat. Or maybe the whip and angry shouts from the Mongolian drivers had frightened the camels so much they were losing weight quickly. Of course, that could be just how I felt.

A sense of doom overcame me. Everything was enveloped in a dusty grayness.

What worried me even more was the possible abuse Wooden Fish Girl would suffer once the Mongolian drivers turned into true outlaws. I'd already noticed the leery look some of them gave her.

Every Chinese driver was lashed, but still the Mongolians didn't know where the gold was buried. When Cai Wu couldn't take it any longer, he made up a location. They found nothing, and he got a severe beating. To the Mongolians the lie was a humiliation, so they stripped him to the waist and lashed his back until not a spot of flesh was unmarked. His screams were so loud and so awful, he sounded worse than a mad camel; even the camels found it unbearable and cried, making a scary sound. Which was why I could forgive Cai Wu for his betrayal later. The pain was unendurable.

Honestly, I worried most about Wooden Fish Girl. Who was to say the Mongolians wouldn't do something to her when they became outlaws?

That's why I did my best to get on Balte's good side. You can call me a traitor if you want, but I did it for her.

To end the nightmare as soon as possible, I talked to all the Chinese drivers.

"Stop being so stubborn. They have no evil intentions. They just want to get the job done. They're not going to take the gold for themselves. Besides, even if they do, can we be worried about that now? Money is a worldly possession; you weren't born with it and you can't take it with you. It's not worth losing your life over." That's what I said to them at first.

What I said later didn't sound very noble, but I did it to please Balte. It was all I could do. I started out by blackening Feiqing's name, call him disloyal for running off alone and letting others take the whipping for him. It was true, though, because he'd have been the first they whipped if he'd stayed. I told them they'd taken his place. Slowly, what I said began to work on them, and Qi Lu started cursing Feiqing. Balte seemed quite happy with my work.

I knew Lu Fuji had to know where the gold was buried. For one thing, he was tight with Feiqing; they were like brothers. Secondly, the rules of camel drivers required at least two people present when burying something valuable. If something happened to one of them, the other would be able to retrieve it.

Lu Fuji denied his knowledge, even though everyone knew he had to know. Huozi ordered the Chinese drivers to be beaten one by one. I knew the result he was after: to have everyone hate Lu Fuji. The Chinese caravan would collapse once Huozi got what he wanted.

Sure enough. On the fourth day, after the whip landed solidly on Qi Lu, he yelled out, "Tell them where it is, Brother Lu. You can't eat it or wear it. They're going to Luocha too. A scary place like that gives me goose bumps just thinking about it. I'm not going. Let them go if they want to go. They're working for revolutionary causes too."

You see how clever Qi Lu was with his words. If Lu refused, Qi would be accused of being opposed to revolution. Qi was barely finished when everyone shouted "righto." In Liangzhou dialect, righto meant "that's right," a more forceful confirmation.

"We should back off at a moment like this and let the Chinese drivers interrogate Chinese drivers," I heard Huozi say to Balte. They untied Qi Lu and Cai Wu before telling them to pick a few of their good friends among the Chinese drivers. Then they turned Lu Fuji over to them, saying the others would be released when Lu gave them what they wanted.

People always said the Mongolians were trustworthy, which was true. They were not sparing in their use of the whip, but they employed no tricks. Seeing how the Chinese drivers questioned Lu Fuji was a real eye-opener.

Cai Wu and Qi Lu were the first to torture him. Cai, who was relatively tight-lipped, always wore a smile. Qi, on the other hand, was a grandstander and a troublemaker who loved to argue. Lu Fuji had been good to them, but being the impatient type, he could be tactless with words. I wondered if he had offended them.

Five. Lu Fuji

I never knew how a man could change without experiencing what I went through.

I could understand why the Mongolians did what they did. They'd been fighting us for decades, after all. Since the time of our elders, we'd fought until we were all bloodied. But the Chinese drivers were like brothers; we'd braved countless storms along Baosui Road together. We'd fought wolves and outlaws and gone through much together, sharing a fate, life or death. I never expected them to be crueler than the cruelest men imaginable.

They acted shy at first. "You can see, Master Lu, that we're like arrows on taut bows, with no say in what we do," Cai said to me.

"I really want to give them the gold," Qi said. "What are the yellow goods? They're a bomb. You don't believe me? Go out holding it in your arms and see what happens. Hei, believe me now? Everyone would want to kill you. I mean it, Brother Lu. I have no interest in revolution. I just want to go home. When we first set out, I said to myself, *My god, Luocha is out there at the edge of the sky, so far my corpse might not make it back.* But what choice did I have? I'm a camel driver, and I have no say about my life. But heaven has eyes and managed to ruin the camels' feet. I like it that way. I hope they never heal. I want the feet to fester until they can't move any more. Why? Because I don't want to go to Luocha. I don't want to be a revolutionary. I just want to go home to see my wife and children and sleep on my heated *kang*. I believe in fate. I believe heaven has eyes. It can make things happen. It can do it easily. There's no need for you or me to fight fate. I mean everything I say, Brother Lu. I couldn't have said all of this if the Mongolians didn't pick me to do this. They forced me to tell the truth."

That was what they said at first.

Then they acted.

Instead of beating me, they tried something else. It looked to me that they really did want to toss the hot potato to someone else. I knew they were worn out. I was too, exhausted, even without what the Mongolians did. I managed to carry on, because I didn't want to give up too easily. I'd have lived my life in vain if I had, I told myself.

They served me their first course.

They made a rack with three makeshift sedan chairs. The rack was turned into the instrument of my nightmares. Even now I shudder when I think about it. I can't help it. So much has bored into my heart. It gave me nightmares for next six months after that.

Qi Lu stuck a chopstick into each of my nostrils before they tied two thin hemp ropes on the chopsticks. The ropes were stretched over the rack and controlled by Cai, who tugged them over and over, sending pain shooting through my body.

Qi called it "Chang'e Flying to the Moon."

Each tug from his hands lifted me up on tiptoes, as if I were leaping for the moon.

"Tell us, Master Lu!"

"Give it up, Brother Lu!"

They were the only ones yelling at first, but soon the Mongolian drivers joined in. I sneezed uncontrollably and each sneeze created endless pain.

Heh-heh-heh-heh.

Ha-ha-ha-ha.

I cursed them, but barely got the words out when they were cut off by the ropes.

The Mongolian drivers who had been my tormentors were turned into spectators. Later even some the Chinese drivers joined in and shouted along with them, "Give it up, Brother Lu. Tell them, Brother Lu."

Tears and snoot smeared my face, which embarrassed the hell out of me. Self-respect is a big deal with me, and losing it was worse than any pain. If they hadn't tied my hands, I'd have taken hold of the chopsticks and jammed them straight into my brain.

I tried it a different way. Instead of raising on my toes each time the ropes were pulled, I lifted my head and hoped the rack would help push the chopsticks up into my head.

Houzi saw through my plan. He was laughing so hard he nearly split his sides as he came up and removed the chopsticks. "Enough. That's enough. You're not going to die that easily."

"Let's try something else," he said. Then he turned to the Chinese drivers and offered, "I'll untie whoever comes up with a new trick."

"Let me try," another driver responded.

"Sure, no problem." Huozi grinned as he untied the man.

Six. Big Mouth

Here, I'd better take over.

I don't think anything was harder for Master Lu to talk about than "lighting a sky lantern upside down." You just let on that self-respect was important to you and that you wanted to die when your face was streaked with tears and snot. I know after the torture they subjected you to, you had a life-changing epiphany, whether you wanted to or not.

I was sure that Qi Lu and the others were in character. Actually, I was too, not just them. What I wanted most had slowly changed at some point, I realized. At that moment, what I wanted most was not for Balte and the others to be conscience-stricken or for the camel feet to heal, but for you to divulge the secret. Human hearts are strange indeed. Everyone, the Mongolians and the Chinese, wanted you to give it up. They were all pinning their hopes to end the nightmare on you.

Without knowing it, we formed an alliance to make one thing happen. It was an interesting phenomenon.

Which was why we were all outraged when you let us down. Quite a few of the Chinese were disappointed in you.

Which was why we all had a great time over the torture technique "Lighting a sky lantern upside down."

A few more similar courses later, everyone was incensed by your obstinacy. You need to know it wasn't easy being a spectator, watching a show can be tiring. We went through the same pain you suffered. For instance, my nose felt terrible when I saw them use "Chang'e flying to the moon." I feel the discomfort when I think about it even now.

I even heard some complain about you not appreciating our kindness. You didn't, that's true. You should be condemned for acting morally superior when everyone else was degenerating.

A few more Chinese drivers joined in on the fun. At first, they'd just wanted to be untied, but then they entered into the spirit of the expected character. Soon only the Chinese drivers were torturing Master Lu, while the Mongolians were mere spectators, watching on high alert, hands gripping weapon, of course. I knew they really ought to relax. I believed the Chinese would not fight back even if they had the chance. Days of lashing had beaten the will and dignity out of them. From this you can see how fragile human will is. Naturally born heroes are few. Many people aren't afraid to die, but no one can take too much pain. Some who can look death in the eye may turn after a few days under the whip.

Maybe Qi Lu and the others could retrieve a little dignity when torturing Brother Lu, but more likely, they'd blame his obstinacy for the beatings they'd suffered over several days. That was undeniable. Balte and his Mongolian drivers wouldn't have been so cruel if Lu had been more sensible.

The Chinese drivers' hatred of Lu Fuji fermented little by little. At first, they felt awkward, for they'd known him for years. But slowly they adopted their expected character, after which they were even crueler than the Mongolians. After the first few "courses," Cai Wu and Qi Lu acted with bold assurance, pulling down Lu's pants and treating him like an ill-behaved animal. It was a lot like a butcher, who after slaughtering a goat, pants breathlessly as he pounds and tears to remove the pelt. I noticed that they were not just doing that to please the Mongolians; no, they appeared to be giving vent to something else. They were both from poor families, and Lu Fuji had often helped them out. Maybe that had gotten under their skin. Sometimes you feel terrible when you have no choice but to accept someone's help. Maybe they were wondering why they needed his help. Accepting too many favors can become a burden. Other than that, I can't explain the fervor they showed when torturing Old Lu.

"Chang'e flying to the moon" had made Brother Lu look terrible, but it hadn't done away with his arrogance. He continued to curse them, using the worst language possible, all about doing something to their parents in indecent ways. Exploding out of his formidable beard, the curses didn't sound that bad. Over those days, we grew inured to foul language.

His legs were layered with grime, but it didn't look unsightly because ours were the same. Just think. We were always on the road; our feet walked on dirt and we couldn't bathe often and were drenched in sweat. It would be unthinkable not to be covered in dirt.

He had muscular legs, which wasn't unusual either. Year in and year out, he wore heavy shoes and traveled long distances, so his leg muscles were very well developed. What was disturbing was the lump between his legs. He had always looked so prim and proper, so much so that it was impossible for us to imagine him having something like that.

His eyes bulged, he roared and cursed, pulling so hard he rocked Qi Lu and the others from side to side.

"Give it up. Come on." Everyone was shouting. No way to tell Mongolians from Chinese, who displayed a powerful unity of will.

"Fuck your mothers."

Lu's eyes looked bloodshot.

"Put his pants back on. Put them back. You can kill a soldier but not humiliate him," Chain Smoker demanded. He was puzzled and refused to give in, so he was still tied up. Some Chinese drivers joined in with their shouts.

"Fuck your mothers, Tartar. Put his pants back on."

"No way. Not until he tells us where the gold is buried." I was surprised to hear Qi Lu's voice. Obviously, he had forgotten he was a Chinese driver.

"We'll use 'lighting a sky lantern upside down,' if you don't tell us," Cai Wu shrieked.

"Call Wooden Fish Girl over to see what our Brother Lu has," Qi Lu said.

Cai Wu actually went to get her. Despite their hostile behavior, the Mongolian drivers still followed caravan rules; they told her to cook, but left her alone. Unaware of what was going on, she came over and ran off when she saw Lu's naked lower body.

"Fuck your mothers." Lu roared, sounding less human now.

Balte laughed like a beast, while Huozi's laugh reminded me of a musical instrument. The others were laughing or cursing. The cursing ones were tied up, the laughing ones were mostly freed. The Mongolian drivers, on the other hand, wore an impassive expression, as if they could not bear to see what was going on.

"See, Old Lu. We can do it the easy way too. We don't have to light the sky lantern, but you'll have to tell us where the goods are buried. We don't want to make it hard on you and we won't take the gold for ourselves either. We just don't want your rotten camel feet affecting the revolutionary endeavor. Don't be so stubborn, all right? Don't you know that many of our own are being killed by the Qing court while we're having this stalemate here? You don't believe me?"

"Righto, righto." The freed Chinese drivers echoed.

"I don't know where the gold is," Lu said with a sad smile. "I really don't know. I would have told you if I did know, a few days ago when you were torturing my friends. People are more important than anything to me. What's gold? Everything can be had when there are people around."

"No one believes you." Huozi added, "Everyone knows you and Feiqing are so tight you practically share a pair of pants."

"But he didn't tell me this time. I didn't ask either," Lu said.

"Horseshit. That's just horseshit," some of the Chinese drivers yelled.

"Fuck your mothers. How can't you not believe me?" Lu glared at them.

"Look at you. At a moment like this, how can you still be arguing?" Cai Wu said.

"Light his lantern! Light it!" Qi Lu continued, "I don't believe he doesn't know. We were whipped because of you."

"Righto, righto. Let's light his lantern first," some drivers echoed.

Balte and Huozi exchanged smiles and pulled over a sack to sit on. Since Cai Wu and the other Chinese drivers took over for them, they were spared the labor and no longer had to clamor for results. Balte saw that his Chinese replacements were doing a better job than the Mongolians, who only knew to wave a whip to little effect.

Qi Lu wound rope around Lu's ankles and wrists to string him up. Lu Fuji looked indecent with his pants off. Men roared laughing. Having been in the desert so long without any diversion, everyone was keyed up. A novelty like this was just what they needed.

"You're going too far. Too far," Chain Smoker shouted.

"Horseshit. Horseshit," Qi Lu screamed, laughing wildly.

I saw Wooden Fish Girl stick her head out from behind a litter, so I shouted to her, "Go back. What are you looking at? Stay out of men's business."

"Come watch if you like, little girl." Cai Wu said, "Not everyone gets to see Master Lu's family jewels."

Lu was no longer cursing as much, probably from hanging upside down; he was breathing hard.

"It's not too late, Master Lu," Cai Wu said as he rolled camel hair into a rope. "I want to go home. I don't want to die for that revolution of yours. I joined the Society of Brothers, but that was to fend off bullies. I won't be part of anything that would cause my death in the desert."

"Watch what you're saying. We do this so we can be better revolutionaries. I'll tie you up if you say anything like that again."

"I won't. Promise." Cai Wu grinned as he spat into his palms and continued rolling the rope.

"What are you doing that for? I've seen lighting a sky lantern before. All you have to do is wind a camel hair rope around him, soak him in kerosene oil and light it."

"That's no fun, no fun at all. He'll die as soon as you light the lantern. What's the point? Kill him and you'll never know where the gold is. You'll be like a tiger trying to swallow the sky," Cai offered.

"That makes sense." Huozi laughed. "Show me what trick you can come up with."

"What you talked about is to light a big one, while mine is to light a small one. They're different. The big one is used on thieves and once only. You wrap cotton waddling on a thief, douse him in oil and light the fire. It goes whoosh, and you get a ball of fire, the smell of burnt hair, screams, and it's over. Several years ago, an adulteress was treated the same way, but Master Lu isn't an adulteress. He's a hero and he deserves to be treated like one. And that's lighting a small lantern."

Lu was breathing hard, with his eyes shut.

I saw Chain Smoker had his shut too, when a thought occurred to me. Lu might not know where the gold was buried, but Chain Smoker might know, because he was close to Feiqing. The idea flashed past and disappeared. I couldn't bring it up again; I didn't want them to use the same torture on Chain Smoker. He was too old to take that.

"Done. I'm ready." Cai was finished with his rope.

"Look, Master Lu. You still have time." Cai said. "It'll be too late when I light it."

Lu was quiet before he yelled out, "You're an ass, Cai Wu. Go ahead and kill me."

"You can kill us too," Chain Smoker said.

"We'll die together." The others who were still tied up yelled.

"No, can't do that." Cai smiled. "Your lives are as worthless as lamp wicks. We want the gold." Now he was part of the "we."

I was disgusted by what Cai said. He was going too far. I'd often seen him following Lu with a fawning expression, but now he was acting like a bully. See how he behaves one way with Lu and another way with Balte.

Cai walked up to Lu with his newly woven rope. I'd heard of the torture before, but never expected it to be monstrously slow. I still feel an irrepressible nausea even when I talk about it now.

I won't go into details or I'll throw up.

Cai Wu—I hope he remains in hell and never gets out—ignored Lu's curses and struggles and shoved the roll of rope into Lu's ass. He had to use a chopstick to accomplish the extremely difficult task. I saw blood drip down to Lu's chest. He must have passed out from anger, which was how Cai got away with it so easily. I'd heard of people using a chopstick to relieve constipation, and I'd done it myself. It had been common during years of famine when we ate nothing but chaff. But this was the first time I'd seen a rope shoved in like that. Where had Cai learned such a nasty trick?

Lu had stopped struggling, and his eyes were wide open. He had fainted from anger. Many people averted their gazes, but I didn't. The sight was horrific, but I wanted to see all of Cai's performance.

After pushing a long section of rope in, Cai nudged Lu's head and said,

"Give it up, Master Lu."

Then he lit one end of the rope and blew on it for the fire to spread.

Soon Lu let out a bloodcurdling scream. Only once. He went quiet after that.

I thought he'd passed out again, but then I heard a gurgling sound in his throat. He was awake. He opened his eyes and seethed,

"You listen. I'll kill you. I'll be an ass if I don't."

Cai panicked. He knew Lu always meant what he said. He turned to Balte.

"I did this to help all of you. You have to promise me one thing. Take me with you once we get the gold."

Balte glanced at him through slitted eyes, like looking at a pile of garbage. But he kept quiet. Huozi was the one who spoke up,

"Of course. You don't have to ask."

"You mean it?" Cai asked.

"Yes, absolutely." Huozi chuckled.

That's enough. I can't go on. It's disgusting.

Let me make a long story short. They had prepared sixty-four "courses" for Lu, and these were the first two.

With only two, Lu no longer looked human.

"Stop torturing Master Lu," finally Chain Smoker spoke up. "I know where it is."

"Don't be a fucking big mouth." Lu shouted angrily.

Twenty-first Session
Cacophony of Souls

I get familiar with the Hu Family Mill now that I have no interviews.

It's not just a mill. I find an opening and go in to find a large space. There are many odd-looking rocks, as well as water that feels similar to the water the drivers brought me. They must have gotten it from here. Maybe this is a secret spring connected to an underground waterway.

The sun is still nowhere, I'm still under the assault of the icy wind, and above me is the same dusty white sky. The sun must be obscured by clouds, I think.

I'd like to see the moon too. I saw a glimpse of the moon when I first got here; later, it turned into a crescent and gained weight each day. I haven't seen it over the past few days. I wonder if it's the wrong time of the month or if the clouds have blotted it out too.

I saw some drivers engaged in their own affairs. Now I don't need to wait till nightfall to interview them if I feel like it. I can chat with anyone who interests me whenever I want, which is clearly more convenient.

The wolf is out of sight, but even though I can't see it, I'm fully aware that it can see me. I feel its eyes on me at all times.

One. Chain Smoker

1

Don't be unhappy with me. I knew Old Lu would be a goner if the torture continued. I noticed a murderous intent crept into Cai Wu's eyes when Lu said he'd kill him. Give him a reason, and nothing was beyond him.

Old Lu looked barely human at that point.

He was hanging upside down on the rack, beneath was a smoldering pile of camel droppings. Smoke continued to rise slowly and encircle Lu, who passed in and out of consciousness.

They had wanted to cut his Achilles tendons, something Cai took pleasure in doing. In the past he'd used it to punish camel thieves. If the tendon, which is connected to the heel, is broken, the victim is maimed for life. Lu would not be able to kill Cai if he lost the use of his feet.

There will be firewood as long as there are green mountains, I said to myself, and there will be gold as long as there are people around. I knew Old Lu would be dead if they kept torturing him. So I took them to the secret spot and dug up the gold.

The Mongolian drivers spiritedly followed me to the sand trough. Don't celebrate too soon, I said silently, because I saw the millstone was growing bigger. It scared me. It wheeled over and over and closer and closer. I could hear a rumbling noise from it, momentous, like mountains toppling and waves surging, a deluge, weeping ghosts and howling wolves, thousands of ferocious beasts grinding their teeth, millions of stone rollers spinning over a rocky gobi. Of course, you didn't hear it, because your brains were clouded by greed. The fat of greed smeared your hearts. I was living in a nightmare, so, compared with the millstone, the Mongolians' dirty tricks were nothing.

Desire burned so strongly in Balte that he was like a mad camel; red glints shone in his eyes, his nostrils flared like a slobbering dog. You've probably heard the Liangzhou analogy, "A horny dog chasing a wolf," haven't you? What a great image. An aroused dog doesn't realize that the animal it's chasing isn't another dog, but a hungry wolf. It is so consumed by desire it runs at the source of its temptation, like a moth flying into fire.

I saw Huozi. I knew he had caused all this. He was very much like the Eunuch who plotted for the Huns to attack the Chinese. Without them, there'd have been much less bloodshed in the world. They played with fire, wanting to burn down the world, but in the end, they were the ones who got burned. I knew all about the heavenly law of "reaping what you sow." You may not like the idea of cause and effect or retribution, but "reaping what you sow" shouldn't be too hard to accept, should it?

I noticed how the flying object kept shifting its shape, a wooden fish one moment, a millstone the next, as if the changes in human hearts caused the alteration.

Look, the massive millstone is circling over our heads, its gaping hole growing bigger. You couldn't see it, of course, because you had nothing but gold on your mind. Sure, gold is good. But was that really gold? No, it was a poisonous snake that would separate you from everything you had.

A blind storyteller once told a story: When the Buddha and his disciples saw a pile of gold one day, they said, "Ai-ya, snake." They left. Later a merchant saw the pile and took it home, only to be arrested by the king. Turned out the gold came from the King's coffers, where someone had stolen it from. The king thought the merchant was the thief and had his head lopped off. Naturally, the story can't illustrate everything I wanted to express. All I wanted to say was, sometimes gold or silver can turn out to be a life-threatening curse.

You don't believe me? Then take a hundred bars of gold and play with them on a Chang'an Street. You'll see that many people have murder on their minds.

Enough about that.

We kept walking.

Following a sand ridge that was a path but not quite a road, I led them forward. There used to be Artemisia on the ridge, I told them, but no more. It's now only a bare strip. From this point, we cross a rocky gobi, then a more level area before passing through a place once teeming with Artemisia, which is also gone. But their roots are still there. Sometimes something wonderful grows on the roots; you can call it cistanches, beneficial to your yang. But, just like the gold you want, this thing that is beneficial to your yang is not good for you. If your body is strong, but your mind is weak, that's a recipe for disaster.

There's a long row of Artemisia roots in an area graced by a green dragon when the Artemisia sprouts and grows. You can think of it as *magang*, but it isn't. *Magangs* are in the Tengger Desert, while this is Wild Fox Ridge. Use a different name here, but don't call it a *magang*. Why? Because this is not the Tengger Desert.

Starting from the direction of the Big Dipper, I counted south until I reached the thirteenth stump of Artemisia, then I turned west and counted to the seventh stump before heading north to the third. Start digging. You'll first come into contact with a pile of camel dung, but keep going and you will dig up some bones. They are wolf bones, and they might stink or they might not. If the body has dried up, there won't be any stink, they'll be mummies. Keep digging until you unearth a sack made of camel hair, inside of which is a pile of three hundred and sixty-one bars. Those are the yellow goods you want.

Take them if you want.

It would be great if you are indeed going to Luocha, but I don't care if you get greedy. I'm tired. Actually, I took part in this purely out of professional ethics. I was a member of the Society of Brothers, and I carried out my duties diligently, but this was just something I did. I had to do something in my lifetime. I did know, however, that it made little difference whether I did it or not. You often used a new term, swapping rebellion or uprising for revolution. But I knew they were all the same whatever they were called; it was all about taking power from someone else, or snatching riches from others, or being the master. But you'll turn out to be worse than the previous masters once you become one yourself.

I've seen plenty of that.

I've heard enough of that too.

I've listened to over a hundred storyteller's tales and I know the history of all the dynasties, from the three sovereigns and five emperors of myth and legend to the Qing court. In the early days of each rebellion, the rebels all said the right things, but once they were enthroned, they were all the same. All crows are black, aren't they? They were all black, or even blacker. Take the gold if you want. I don't want my good brother Lu Fuji to lose his life over this little bit of yellow goods. We did our best. We'll just pretend we were robbed, a different kind of natural disaster.

There, that's all we've got. Take it.

Balte's eyes were brighter now. Watch out. You're staring so hard your eyeballs may fall out.

Don't you hear the millstone?

Listen. It's thundering.

2

After the Mongolian drivers left with the gold, I untied my brothers. They wailed after learning what I'd done with the gold. I tried to make them feel better by saying, "I did it, it's on me. You have nothing to worry about." But they didn't stop crying; they were tough men who hadn't cried from the cruel treatment.

Cai Wu, Qi Lu and a few worthless drivers went with the Mongolians. They knew they'd be skinned alive if they stayed. But I knew they'd have a hard time with the Mongolian drivers, who disdained anyone with no backbone.

They led their own camels away, taking whatever belonged to them. I truly hoped they were going to Luocha, even though I knew the outcome would be the same whether they went or not. I was fundamentally dubious about the possibility that a revolution or two would save the people from suffering—I was reminded of the lines from one of the songs: Why change dynasties? You drive away a turtle and get a tortoise in return. With what had happened so far on this trip, I'd of course have loved for someone to take our place and carry out the mission.

I told one of the drivers to fry salt and melt it in water to wash Lu Fuji's wounds. He had stopped complaining, for he knew that what I'd done was the best option. There was no need for us to be tortured to death. Still the same saying: There will be firewood as long as there are green mountains.

I stopped talking to them about the growing millstone. They never believed me. They just thought something was wrong with my head.

It was like trying to explain what a sun is to a blind man.

But I was sure that, with the gold, the Mongolian drivers would no longer live in peace.

Two. Big Mouth

Who could deny that?

I followed Balte and left the Chinese caravan. I didn't want to go. I wanted to stay, but they wanted Wooden Fish Girl to cook for them, and

I had to go because I saw that Balte had begun looking at her in a funny way, and so had a few of his drivers. On the other hand, sometimes the Chinese drivers looked at her the same way. That was to be expected, since the men got a bit worked up after being in the desert so long.

I really wanted to stay behind, but I was somewhat ashamed and I felt terrible about Lu Fuji. I didn't do anything bad, and yet I felt like I'd been a traitor. I hadn't been tied up when they were torturing Brother Lu; they told me and Wooden Fish Girl to get food ready for them. As a man I should have said or done something, even though nothing I did would have had any real effect. I was beset by the nagging feeling that I wasn't acting like a real man. You probably don't know this, but at the time I was most worried about the possible evil designs they might have on Wooden Fish Girl. Just think. If they would do that for some gold, why wouldn't they want her too? I went with the Mongolian drivers in the hope that they wouldn't harm her. I can't stress this point enough.

I wonder if Cai Wu and Qi Lu felt guilty. On the surface they seemed overjoyed, looking like they were ready to do others' bidding. Maybe they felt a tinge of guilt; they were, after all, humans too, and no one is born bad, at least I don't think so.

As they headed back, the Mongolian drivers sang their songs. I didn't understand the words, but I could tell they were elated.

Wooden Fish Girl looked glum, she didn't want to go with them.

"Aren't you afraid the Chinese drivers will want to even the score?" I asked.

"Why would they?"

"Why wouldn't they? If you hadn't cooked for them every day, the Mongolians wouldn't have had the strength to torture the Chinese. Come on, let's just go. It doesn't matter who. Didn't you see how the Chinese camels are ruined? I don't want to die in Wild Fox Ridge."

She didn't object when she heard what I said, though she sighed. I knew she felt terrible. Our departure amounted to cutting off ties with the Chinese caravan. She'd been forced to cook for the Mongolians, but now, by leaving with them, she was doing it willingly.

We wouldn't have the nerve to go back. Putting everything else aside, I felt I'd let Feiqing down and couldn't bear to look him in the eye.

Huozi chatted and joked with Balte along the way, greatly enjoying themselves. They were happy, I knew that. But I also knew that after what they'd done, they were riding a tiger.

When we were back at our earlier tent site, they told me and Wooden Fish Girl to make them a meal of hand-pulled mutton to celebrate their victory. Too bad there wasn't any liquor. The few leather pouches of liquor they'd brought along were long gone. If there had been some, it would have felt more festive, but that was all right, since they could sing and sing until their hearts were intoxicated.

Amid the rousing songs by the drivers, I heard Huozi whisper to Balte.

"We can't stay here long. When they recover, they'll surely come after us."

"We'll leave tomorrow," Balte said.

"Where to?"

"Luocha, of course."

"Are we really going to Luocha?"

At that moment I finally knew what he had in mind.

"Let's talk about this outside," Huozi said.

They walked out of the tent.

Pretending I was going to relieve myself, I followed them out and saw them round a bend in the desert. I dared not keep up. You know, sometimes the less you know the better off you are. They were plotting something, but the body will be exposed when the snow melts, so I saw no need to try to figure out what they were up to.

Sure enough, the next morning after breakfast Huozi brought up what he and Balte had talked about.

His voice sounded hollow, so he cleared his throat loudly and said,

"Let's talk something over, brothers. We've planned to go to Luocha, but you all know that damned place is so far it might as well be the edge of sky. Some of the camels are still recovering from their foot injuries. It's hard to say if we'd actually make it there even if they were all fine. They say outlaws roam the northeast, but the northwest has plenty of highwaymen. We hid the yellow gold and kept quiet about it, but yesterday it was out in the open. It's so complicated, it just means trouble. Let's come up with something different."

"I gave it plenty of serious thought," Balte said, "and couldn't find a solution. We'll have to talk it over."

"We promised to go through with it. It doesn't seem right to change plans," one of the drivers said.

"He's right. I agree," another one said. "You can't take back shit that's already out. If we break our promise this time, we'll have trouble plying the same trade in the future."

"Let's not think too far ahead. We're not sure if we'll leave Wild Fox Ridge alive. If we're really heading out to Luocha, I'm afraid we'd litter the way with our bones."

"This isn't about our bones. We must follow a code of conduct while we're alive. Look, I prefer to keep going. That's my opinion," the first driver said.

"He's right. I agree with him. We told them we were going to Luocha when we took the gold from them. If we change our plans now, that'll make us outlaws."

"What's wrong with being outlaws?" Houzi laughed. "We'll be royals if we make it."

Cai Wu saw through Huozi's plan and echoed, "I'm not going. Not me. Whether we can make it to Luocha is beside the point. The road is crawling with outlaws, and one is enough to take our lives."

Qi Lu joined in. The drivers kept quiet after what the two of them had said. The atmosphere was oppressive. The drivers couldn't wrap their heads around the new plan, for, after all, they had been under caravan directives for years, and the suggestion was something they'd never considered.

After a prolonged silence, one of the drivers said,

"Let's ask the leader. He's in charge, and we'll do whatever he says. We're just doing our job. We have nothing to fear, the tallest ones will hold up the sky if it falls."

Many of them breathed a sigh of relief after hearing him.

I knew he'd just placed a heavy moral burden on Balte, who had to take responsibility for everything the caravan did.

Three. Feiqing

How could they have sunk so low?

Yes, you could say you were helping with the revolution. You would have been if you'd gone to Luocha after seizing the gold. You can say we were dragging you down, and you didn't want to cause injury to the revolution, so you took the gold to trade for weapons.

You could have done all of this. You could have left the tea behind and chosen the stronger camels to carry the gold. Yes, you could have done that. You'd have been national heroes if the revolution succeeded, but in the end, you lost the opportunity. You didn't have the nerve. Not many people were brave enough to travel with so much gold. Yes, you were right; it's hard to say how far a few people could go by themselves, so then why did you seize the gold? No one but a few lead drivers knew we were carrying it. After what you'd done, you more or less put targets on your backs.

I wasn't angry with Chain Smoker; I'd have done the same thing. I wouldn't sacrifice my brothers' lives for the gold. My only complaint was, he should have dug it up earlier to spare the brothers the torture. The gold was tied to a great many things, but to me nothing was more valuable than my brothers.

I did make it out, but I fled in order to return. I knew it would spell serious trouble if the Mongolian drivers had malicious intent. Now that they'd disregarded niceties, they would throw caution to the wind and carry through. I had to get out if I wanted to stop them; I was looking for an external power to change the destructive course.

We might have had a different outcome had I stayed. One of them could be that they would kill all of us to keep their action under wraps. Would they do that? They could. Huozi had no backbone, but he was cruel and ruthless and capable of anything. I was worried he'd do something else once he had got the gold. I was even afraid for the Mongolians' lives.

They were still thinking about going to Luocha after I fled. They needed the excuse, for they couldn't turn their backs on their own moral code, an excuse they could accept so they wouldn't have trouble dealing with the process of their degeneration. They were still wary of me at the time.

I had to flee. My horse was tethered next to my tent, out of habit.

My heart was heavy with sorrow. I'd imagined all sorts of scenarios, but not once did I expect to be stabbed in the back by my brothers—the Mongolian drivers were brothers to me. Brothers can argue or fight, but they do it face to face; you can't sneak an attack like that. Brothers can be bad, but not vile. A vile person is a spineless maggot, not a real man. Listen to me, I'm fuming even now when I think about it.

The horse could read my mind and slowed down after running awhile. It didn't know where to go, and neither did I.

Tell me, where should I go?

Before me was endless sand, and my heart was filled with nothing but bleakness. Everything I could think of felt like distant water that couldn't put out a nearby fire.

After thinking long and hard, I decided to go the Hu Family Mill to talk it over with the Young Master. I absolutely knew he was there. He was shut in for his meditation and shouldn't be disturbed, but so what! I recalled he had a musket, though he had no helper. I'd given it to him when he left, for protection against wild animals. It was a good weapon. I wasn't sure if he still had it though. If not, I'd only have to raise it against Balte to take care of the others. When the Mongolian drivers turned into a viper, Balte would be the proverbial spot to gain control.

In my impression, the Mill was far way and had taken me half the night to get there. I'd been there before. It was called a flour mill but it was also an oil press. After the oil mill was chopped down to use as firewood, only a millstone and tools were left.

The mill was odd, with strange occurrences, in camel drivers' tales. The most unusual aspect about the place was how clean it was. No one went to sweep the mill house, but it was spotless, as if someone came to dust it every day. It had been like that when I got there the first time. Everything I saw was smooth and shiny, as if lacquered.

Finally, I saw its dark shadow; I felt as I'd spotted my own house. In the tales told by camel hands, the mill house was a terrifying place. The shiny neatness was said to have been maintained by scary specters, who had many different identities in the stories about them. According to some, they were Rakshas, non-humans to some, vampires to some, or even man-eating Dakinis. Ma Zaibo concurred with the last one.

I heard that no one dared come here again after someone had smoked and killed over a hundred camel drivers hiding in the mill house during a fight. I also heard that the floor was strewn with human bones. Yet the bones in the house didn't affect its tidiness.

I went in just before dawn, where everything still looked hazy. The horse was snorting in an odd way, which it did when there was a ghost. Horses have a third-eye that lets them see ghosts.

An eerie, chilly wind enveloped me and bored into my bones as soon as I entered. It was an iciness that went straight to the heart, not in terms of temperature, but a feeling. My blood ran cold. You know I was known for my bravery, and I feared nothing. I could sleep in a graveyard in the summer and snore through the night. But on this day, the bone-chilling assault set my hair on end. Later, Ma Zaibo told me the same had happened to him. But he liked the place precisely for that. He said it was easier to enter an enlightened state of mind in a demonic spot like this.

It was getting light out, so I could see clearly. Yet I couldn't find what exactly was giving me the chill. Everything looked pretty normal.

I spotted Ma right off. Like the crazy man on Liangzhou's streets, he sat quietly. I felt under his nose but detected no breath. Next to him was some food, already covered in green mold.

I felt as if hit by thunder. What would I say to Ma Erye if he died?

"Young Master! Young Master!"

I kept calling, but got no response. I called because I believed he was still alive. If he was dead, I said to myself, his body wouldn't be intact the way it is now.

It took me a while to recall what he'd told me. He'd said not to cremate him if he was in a deep meditative state. He'd come out of it if I banged the chime by his ear.

I followed his instruction and struck the chime.

Four. Big Mouth

Everything changed when they got the gold.

They were planning to go to Luocha at first, but unexpectedly, Huozi had a different idea once they had the goods. What idea? To keep it for himself, naturally.

It shouldn't have happened, of course. Reputation was the bottom line for camel drivers; without it, you couldn't be one. But don't forget, they were human too. At normal times, a group of camel drivers who valued their reputation would follow the rules when they worked together. But would it remain the same if one or two schemers wormed their way in and egged the others on, while their lives were all being threatened?

I clearly sensed the difference.

First to change was Huozi's tone. Before getting the gold, he'd been adamant about going to Luocha, which served as his excuse to seize the gold. Without it, he couldn't have rallied any support.

"Your Chinese camels can't make the trip, so we'll go by ourselves. You can't sit on the toilet and not shit. Yes, that's right. We'll carry out what you can't do."

No one doubted him after hearing what he said. But later, the gleaming gold blotted out his conscience, and he changed his tune.

He started with talking about hardships during the trip. That was true, and everyone knew it. The distance was only one of the reasons why it was daunting; the most fearsome were the outlaws and mutinous soldiers. Besides that, the Qing government sometimes got a tip and sent its police and patrolmen to check things out. We'd be doomed if we ran into any of them.

Some of the Mongolians echoed Huozi's sentiment, while the others didn't react. They were still in the process of abandoning their roles as trustworthy camel drivers to become outlaws.

I realized that something worse might happen if we stayed, so I told Wooden Fish Girl to run back to the Chinese camp site overnight.

I couldn't worry too much, even if Brother Lu was unhappy with me, I thought. Worst case, I bang my head on the ground as an apology. I was certain Balte would force her to sleep with him if we didn't leave. A man became a real outlaw once his heart turned.

My interviews have been suspended for several days so I can search for the white camel.

I get on the highest sand mountain to look around. I see sand ridges extending into the horizon and Artemisia groves in a distant sand trough, but no sign of him. I shout commands used by camel drivers to call their animals. My voice ripples out, but I get only the sound of the wind in response.

The yellow camel, on the other hand, is different. He's still quiet, but his hostility is gone. I don't say anything to him, for I want him to suffer a few more days with a guilty conscience. I don't want to utter "forgive" too lightly. It's a luxury not to be dispensed too easily. I find that those who receive forgiveness too easily often repeat their offense just as easily. Some even know they'll be forgiven before they commit the crime, but don't consider the cost to their morals. Forgiveness can only be given to those who are truly repentant.

"Repent," I say to him.

He gives me a look, with eyes like deep wells. I can't tell what he's thinking.

I miss the white camel. The longer he's gone the more I miss him. I wondered why he wouldn't drink the water, why he stayed out of sight for so long. He shouldn't have left like that.

But I don't want to spend too much time looking for him. I came for the interviews not to search for a camel.

I see those green lights again at night. I don't know if they belong to the old wolf.

Twenty-second Session
Wooden Fish Girl

1

Why don't I start with my life in the small town?

It felt like a drama. You'd have thought I was acting on the stage if the events hadn't been recorded in history books.

I returned to the Temple after the interrupted stoning execution.

Lü Erye sent a message through Hu Gala, saying he'd like me to move to his house to rest until I gave birth. I didn't go. I didn't know why he'd decided to save me. Could it really be for the baby? Actually, I hadn't known I was pregnant at the time. I'd missed my period, but I was braving the elements and didn't always have three meals a day; besides, my practice required "severing the red dragon," so my periods were irregular. After what Hu Gala said, it did feel like I was carrying a child.

Tell me, should I be happy about this?

I felt like I was waking from a bad dream. After I got back, I slept for three days straight. I didn't cook for the people at the Temple. It seemed to me that I had walked a long time, and I was exhausted inside and out. I even wished I could just sleep forever. Stones flew at me in my dreams, that and screaming crowds. I was even slapped. I didn't suffer, really, except for the slaps, and the flung shoe soles and rocks.

Ma Zaibo moved out of the Temple and returned to his home after we were found out. I heard his father had imposed family discipline on him, but I had no idea what that was. It did make me feel guilty that he was punished, but my guilt feelings didn't even last as long as frost under the sun. I was so tired I wouldn't have cared if the earth exploded, and even what I'd have felt had nothing with me. Heh-heh, don't say I was heartless. Just give some thought to what I'd gone through. Even if he had been whipped, it would be nothing compared to what had happened to me.

Hu Gala told me he'd asked Lü Erye why he'd come forward. Lü Erye said he didn't want the girl to be stoned.

"He also said that he'd do that as long as I could give him a reason, even if you weren't pregnant, which you are," Hu Gala said. "It's a human life, and saving a life is better than building a seven-tier pagoda."

Hu Gala also said the Ma family was turned upside down over this. Lü Erye wanted to accept me as his daughter-in-law and would make Ma Zaibo marry me if I gave them a son. His reason was simple: Ma Zaibo did it and he must take responsibility, it had been his decision alone. Ma Zaibo was happy to comply, of course. The rest of the family objected. They were a prominent family. Years before, the Empress Dowager had sent two of her palace maids to marry into the Ma family. They could not possibly have a beggar as a daughter-in-law. Besides, they weren't quite sure of the beggar's background. Hu Gala said they were still fighting over it.

I was surprised by Lü Erye's attitude after hearing what Hu Gala said. But I knew he hadn't done it out of the goodness of his heart. He knew exactly who I was and wanted to lure me to his door, where he could have the leisurely pleasure of killing me, or play a dirty trick to do away with me without anyone knowing about it. Then I'd be the wandering ghost in

Liangzhou's lore. But he didn't scare me. You know I did want to enter his estate and who knew who would die first once I was inside. I had planned to set a fire.

2

When I finally had a quiet moment, I felt I was awake enough to think. I needed to confront an issue: did I want to keep the baby or not? That's easy to answer now, but at the time, it was like a life-and-death decision, not trifling at all.

Lü Erye's role in this alerted me; I was made keenly aware that I was pregnant with his grandson or granddaughter, a very troubling thought.

Keep it or not?

At the time, I had trouble thinking of him living under the same sky as me. Once the child was born, we would have a very tangled kinship relationship. I didn't want to live under the sky with a man who had burned my entire family to death. I refused to do that. For a very long time my only reason for living was to cause him a horrible death. Hear that? A horrible death. Don't hate me for thinking like that, I couldn't help it. You need to know that hatred is a source of incredible energy, so powerful that only the strong-willed can resist it.

Besides this concern, I also needed to choose a lifestyle, for I'd have a drastically different life with a baby and without one. I was used to living a life with but one concern: vengeance. It was challenging but not without its own pleasure. With a child, I was just not sure if I could live the way I had.

Big Mouth wanted me to abort the karmic spawn inside me. He didn't think badly of Ma Zaibo, but still that's what he called the fetus. Don't be harsh on him. I felt the same way sometimes, so I understood him. He was looking out for himself, because he really wanted to marry me. He couldn't divorce his wife, but he genuinely wanted to marry me.

He got his hands on some salvia, some sappanwood, leeches, and other herbs for increasing blood flow, told me to make a brew, drink it, and run away. Or I could run away with him and take the medicine after we got to Dengmaying Lake. But I had no interest in running away, and when I thought of Ma Zaibo, I knew I wanted to have his baby. That would make me very happy. I imagined the vague melancholic expression in his eyes, which then made the thought of abortion seem absurd. This is Ma Zaibo's flesh and blood, I told myself. Later, I intentionally blotted out Lü Erye when I thought of the baby, and gradually grew attached to it.

I no longer cooked for them. Hu Gala found a local woman to replace me. He generously told me to stop working so as not to hurt the baby. Locals kept coming to see me in the Temple. I didn't go out much, and they found it hard to see me, so that the flow of visitors slowly thinned out. After that, I enjoyed the most peaceful days of my life. Thoughts of what I'd gone through felt like a dream. I found myself under the spell of a strange power, and I was changing in strange and unusual ways.

For a diversion, I went to Ma Zaibo's old room to copy the unfinished lyrics. I was not much of a calligrapher, but I wrote carefully, stroke by stroke. I didn't expect the handwriting to be much to look at, and would be happy if it was good enough for people to read the lyrics. I wrote day after day, days as many as the leaves on a tree. I surprised myself by completing several of the long wooden fish songs.

The ambience created by the songs and the familiar objects in the room often reminded me of him and of the times we were together. Sometimes my face burned and my cheeks turned hot, but more often than not, it felt like looking back on a dream. Everything lost its effect in the wake of all the joys and sorrow I'd experienced.

Our hearts are like that. The more you go through, the less you care.

3

I was moved into an old house in the city when I was near term. Hu Gala didn't want blood to offend the deities and pollute the Su Wu Temple. To Liangzhou people, there was nothing dirtier than blood from a birthing woman, it was also what those skilled in heterodoxic practices feared most. Apparently, deities, even with the magical powers, were troubled by this type of women's blood—you're absolutely right, this does explain the workings of their differentiating mind. Later, I witnessed a Tantric fire rite, where the medium used was precisely this kind of blood. Obviously, the mind is the deciding factor in a great many worldly matters.

A patron of the Su Wu Temple provided a place for me to give birth. No one had lived there for a long time, so Hu Gala sent someone to clean it up. It was in decent shape. The heating spot under the bed was filled to heat it up and drive away the dampness on the bed. The room was toasty warm by the time I moved in. After my prolonged stay in the Temple, I felt like I was in heaven here.

Not long after moving in I fell into a state of lethargy, with nothing to distract me other than flipping through books about Kālacakra.

Stable living conditions breed idleness, and I was worried that I'd forget about revenge. So every morning I recited words that would keep hatred fresh in my mind. Yet to my horror, I discovered that the hate coming from deep down was fading, no matter how hard I tried to keep it up. The emotion incited by the word "hate," was "ought to" hate, though it was not "real" hate.

Before I moved in, Hu Gala came with another message from Lü Erye, who hoped I'd move into the Ma estate to give birth, for I was, after all, carrying an heir for their family. I didn't consent. If it was what

Ma Zaibo wanted, I might go, but his father had made the offer, which immediately provoked hostility in me. I couldn't bear the thought of going to Lü Erye's house. How odd. I had tried everything I could to get there, but now I felt that danger lurked everywhere, with a bottomless unknown and horror.

Hu Gala brought over a printed copy of wooden fish songs shortly after I moved in. He gave me the first volume, saying the woodblock printer was working on the other three. It was so well done I couldn't stop looking at it. Big Mouth said many blind storytellers had asked for a copy, so they could convert the songs into the Liangzhou style of storytelling. That was fine with me, for the songs would now have another form and the possibility to survive. I also found that many of the tales in the Liangzhou tradition could be found in wooden fish songs, with similar contents that differed only in the language.

I'd hoped but failed to see Ma Zaibo. I heard he was being guarded by someone sent by his father, so he wouldn't come to meet me. I believed it; otherwise, he'd have come long ago. I was convinced that he'd fallen in love with me and I with him, pleasurable knowledge that sustained me through those days. When the terror from the stoning disappeared—I have to admit I was terror-stricken that day—I was beset by my longing for him and felt terrible. It wasn't a mere emotional state, for it had a tangible feel, as if an uncomfortable object called lovesickness was lodged in my heart, hard, abnormal, terrorizing me by its teeth and claws. My longing for him canceled my hate to a considerable degree; when the longing reared its head, the hatred in my heart was rendered immobile. This is terrible, I told myself.

Big Mouth came to see me a few times, bringing food and a message from Feiqing, who told me not to worry about anything, to just rest and have a smooth delivery. He said they were trying to persuade Ma Zaibo to come, but he didn't elaborate. I knew Feiqing would come up with something.

"Winter is here. How's everyone doing at Dengmaying Lake?" I asked.

"They moved to a spot with lots of trees. They can't cut too many, or they'd be easily spotted," he said. "A while ago they thought they needed to get ready for winter, so they cut some wood and piled it in a hollow. Hei—the government knew what it was all about right away. Soon Liu Huzi's mounted troops showed up. But it didn't look like Liu was interested in fighting; they whizzed over and whizzed back, clearly just to put in an appearance. The cut wood was burned, and when they fled into the heart of the desert, Liu's people did not give chase. Big Mouth said he felt terrible about fleeing into the desert.

"Think about it. We can't even defeat a small mounted force from a township office. Overthrowing the Qing court would be like a tiger trying to swallow the sky," he said. "The Qing government is simply too big. I could follow a caravan heading in any direction and walk for months and still wouldn't reach the limits of Qing territory. Just a few of us trying to topple the government? Don't even think about it."

"Don't look at it that way. A city wall collapses when everyone joins in to push it over. It will never fall if no one even tries. But if it's rotting, then with you and me, and everybody else, we work together and it will fall. Even a towering building will crash to the ground. There were always only a few heroes who caused dynastic changes, but they were united, and soon many joined them, and it grew bigger and bigger until they became a force to reckon with," I said.

His mood lifted after that.

Actually, I didn't reveal everything in my mind. What I really wanted to say was, even if we could unite and work together to effect a dynastic change, then what? It would like driving away a sated wolf only to see a hungry one coming. Emperor Zhu of the Ming was more vicious than the Mongolians, who, unlike Zhu, didn't kill off those who helped bring about the Mongols Yuan dynasty before it. Even the wooden fish songs raised the same question. But I knew I couldn't say that, for it would greatly affect their morale.

With time on my hands, I started reflecting on many things. I kept going through what had happened a few years earlier. No matter how justified I was in making the Qing court my enemy, I realized that they weren't the real culprits of my family's calamity. During battles between the Hakkas and the locals, they were equally vicious in killing their opponents, Hakka or not. The poor always victimize the poor, and the Chinese persecuted their own too. The realization put me in a funk. If we could really make our dream come true, so what? Would the founding heroes of the Ming still have fought the Tartars if they had known their own fate beforehand?

You see, these were my thoughts in that room when I had nothing to do. It was funny. You may not know this, but I'd learned a lot about history through wooden fish songs. My heart had been so taken over by hate I hadn't had time to think these thoughts, and now questions like these came up frequently. And it was disheartening.

Did you know I continued this line of questioning for several decades after that? I lived a very long life; I survived Feiqing and others by many years. I'd seen a lot. Big Mouth, who had managed to leave Wild Fox Ridge alive, was branded as a rich peasant decades later, a member of the four bad elements—he shouldn't have used the money he'd earned as a camel driver to buy land. He suffered for nearly twenty years, and eventually died in one of the struggle sessions. I couldn't help but sigh when I heard what happened to him. Feiqing and the others had given their lives for nothing.

I'm digressing. Let me return to the story.

I'll tell you more about what happened in the old house.

Big Mouth stopped talking me into taking the medicine when he realized I'd made up my mind to have the baby. Little by little a distance grew between us. He was no longer as devoted to me as before and adopted a more business-like approach. It was what I'd hoped for also. Some things are hard to predict. Before my relationship with Ma Zaibo, I never thought Big Mouth was ugly even with his big mouth; I actually like the way he looked. But now his mouth was simply way too big, the thought of being kissed by that big mouth gave me the willies. And there was more. He rarely bathed and didn't wash his feet often, so he had a terrible odor. All these were unbearable—I even forgot that I'd looked and smelled worse than him. The comfortable life brought back many of my childhood habits.

I would instinctively compare Big Mouth with Ma Zaibo each time I saw him. It was unfair, but I couldn't help it. Since the moment I found myself repelled by his big mouth, I knew that the particular karmic connection between us had ended. My heart had a mind of its own, as it slid to another spot. I felt bad, but the sweet giddiness—when I thought about Ma Zaibo—would always cancel out my guilt.

Later, I learned that in those days Big Mouth had thought I was a woman who despised the poor and curried favor with the rich. Entirely understandable. He'd have held the same, wrong view about me for the rest of his life if it hadn't been for an incident later.

On the other hand, misunderstanding or not, everything would eventually vanish like cloud and mist.

The Ma family sent over an old maid servant to tend to my daily life. When I was near term, she opened a hole on the surface of the *kang*, following a local custom. After giving birth, I'd relieve myself through the opening so I could avoid exposure to the elements. Each time the *kang* was refilled with kindling the room was a bit smoky, but it wasn't very thick and had no lasting adverse effect.

Giving birth was easy for me. That might have had something to do with my martial practice or it could be because this was my second time. Nothing happened, except for the usual pain, and no serious complications. I went through what most women have gone through. That's all. The midwife hired by the Ma family was highly experienced, so everything followed normal procedures.

I gave birth, just like that.

It was a boy.

4

The night the baby was kidnapped was a nightmare I couldn't shake off for the rest of my life.

I felt a wrenching pain in my heart whenever I thought about it. I recall a rope around my neck when I was awakened by the baby's cries. The texture told me it was made of camel hair, resilient and sturdy. I barely struggled before someone growled at me,

"Don't move or I'll slit your throat."

The threat was followed by something cool against my neck.

I noticed several dark shadows in the room. A baby's cries came from the arms of one of them. "If you move again, I'll give you a rotten gourd." He raised the baby over his head, making him scream in terror. Liangzhou people called a toad a stinky gourd. I knew what he meant. I went limp thinking about how he might drop the baby like smashing a toad into mush on the ground.

I was scared. I might have great martial art skills, but I was still scared. I couldn't help it. In fact, in a situation like that, I would have been afraid to fight them even without concern for the baby. I'd also been frightened when the military police rode up during our battle with the police. It was a problem I had. Hopeless.

The lonely white moon shone down the papered window panes. I vaguely saw that they'd covered their faces, and were all carrying knives that emitted a cold glint.

"We don't want to kill you. We just want the baby. Don't look for him, because you won't find him. Don't worry. We won't harm him. We want to do something, and when it's done, we'll give you back your baby."

"How will I find you?" I asked.

"You don't have to look. You won't find us. We'll be back when the time comes."

"What if you hurt the baby? Or he's hungry?" I asked.

"Shut up." The one holding the baby barked, "if you don't shut up I'll smash him."

"Right. And the baby will be dead. He's a living, breathing being, and no one can guarantee that'll last," another said.

"We promise we won't kill him. Isn't that good enough for you? But we can't promise anything else. Babies are dying right and left in this day and age."

The more they said, the more it hurt, and I started crying.

"Why are you crying? I hate hearing a woman cry. Something bad happens to me whenever I encounter a crying woman. The shaman always says a weeping deity causes it."

"Shut up. Let's go."

They stormed off, plunging the room into emptiness and deathly quiet.

I wept and slept for several days in the room, during which time a few people from the Ma family came, in addition to the old servant. They all looked anxious.

"The baby was kidnapped. Ma Erye is worried sick, his gums are killing him," one of them said.

But he didn't come, because I hadn't been through the first three months of childbirth yet. A Liangzhou custom required three months of laying-in for a new mother. No one should see her before the three months were up, to avoid the ghost of filth and blood. Nor was a new mother allowed into any houses, because she was not clean and might offend some family's deities.

I cried myself to sleep and woke up to cry again for more than ten days. I hoped Ma Zaibo would come, but he never showed. I couldn't think of any reason for his absence.

Without the baby, there was no point in staying in town. When Big Mouth came, I left the room and went back to Dengmaying Lake with him.

5

The Lake was hopping with action.

The Mount Qilian Organization was formally established. It had had some members already, but not enough to be on its own, and had instead been part of a larger organization. They had suffered a great loss during the battle with the police, but had also made enough noise to draw attention; now people knew that Liangzhou residents had risen up. The uprising was staged by a loose group of participants, who rushed headlong into action and dispersed in confusion; they needed discipline and organization. Hence, some people hoped a larger band could be established in Liangzhou. With the strict, clear rules of the Society of Brothers, they could succeed if given enough training.

It was called the Mount Qilian Organization.

Their rite to become sworn brothers left a deep impression on me. The men had their hands on a rooster as they sang in one voice, clearly the result of extensive practice:

Touch a phoenix on the head, and nobles we'll become;
Touch a phoenix on the back, and we'll carry a gold sword on a horse;
Touch a phoenix on the tail, a high position we brothers will obtain;
Touch a phoenix on the feet, we'll be promoted as officials.

Then they killed the rooster to mix its blood in liquor; they all drank it to swear their loyalty and be brothers from now on.

I was amused. I found that they all sang about promotions and getting rich, with none of the grand ideas that Big Mouth had talked to me about, such as overthrowing the Qing, restoring the Ming, rescuing people from the sea of suffering. I wondered why, so I asked him. He said he didn't know either, except that it was stipulated in a book called *Sea Bed*. That was how the Society of Brothers functioned. Maybe the average members were more interested in official positions and wealth, and the distant matters of Qing and Ming didn't concern them. Promotion and wealth were naturally the best the ordinary people could hope for.

Then the rules and regulations were read, ten sections and ten articles, all very focused and strict: any violation would result in five kinds of punishments: death by dismemberment, beheading, buried alive, drowning, six holes by knives, and forty lashes drawing blood. These were severe punishments, much worse than those meted out by the Qing court.

Feiqing met with me when the rite was over. I burst into tears when I saw him.

"Don't worry. They won't kill the baby," he said.

The place had changed. It had once been a shelter, now it was a martial arts training ground. Obviously, they planned to have an open battle with the government. Spots were leveled for the brothers to practice. Many were still working with lasso poles, for it was handy and practical. The Society of Brothers had some highly skilled cudgel fighters, who helped each other improve, until everyone was good at it. Except for learning secret code words, they spent all their time practicing club fighting. It was a form of fighting that had rules for moves. When I saw them follow the rules in the moves they made, I couldn't help but wonder what they could do when the military police fought without the same rules. In our earlier confrontation, I'd already noticed how the moves the brothers had learned were impractical when dealing with the police. They wielded a sword or raised a rifle as they charged you, without regard for martial art moves or rules of fighting. They chopped and fired at will. The orderly club moves were useless.

To me they were a group of adults playing games.

I'd lost interest in games like this. My mind was on the child. I'd only been a mother for little over two months, but my maternal instinct had been awakened and my heart had softened. Years of hardship had encased my heart in a thick callus, but it disappeared when the baby was born. Now my heart was impossibly tender.

One question kept cropping up: who were the kidnappers?

At first, I thought they were sent by the Ma family. But they would have the baby after the initial three months anyway, so there was no need for them to take it now, though it was hard to say. When the baby went to live with them, I'd naturally move in with him. Those members who cursed and called me a food-scraper would surely not like to have me as a Ma's daughter-in-law. In their view, their ancestors would be so shamed they'd jump off the sacrificial table if someone in their family married a beggar woman. When the baby was taken, I'd have no chance to live in their house. So the Ma family remained a suspect in my mind; they wanted the baby, but didn't want the baby's mother to join the family.

This was only one possibility.

I thought about others, such as desert outlaws, or the Society, both of whom had their eyes on Ma's wealth. Big Mouth told me once that the

Society needed money to buy weapons. During the first battle, there were many members, but they had quickly fallen into disarray when charged at by a hundred military police. Things would be a lot easier if they were armed. He also said that Feiqing and the others had been trying to come up with a surefire plan. Whatever it was, I knew, the surefire plan depended on money. Would they then have thought of using the baby? It wasn't impossible, I thought.

I said goodbye to Feiqing and left Dengmaying Lake to look for my baby. It was a heartrending, unforgettable experience. I saw more in my search; I saw how the people of Liangzhou could barely survive. You're right; they wouldn't rise up so long as they could have some potato millet soup. But at the time, fewer and fewer families could afford even that; many more never knew where their next meal was coming from.

Like finding a needle in the ocean, I traveled to many places, but got absolutely no information after several months. I heard Ma Zaibo had hired many to search too. I wished he'd gone out to do it himself, and hoped against hope that we might run into each other in our separate searches. I missed him. I'd thought often about him before the baby was born, but now it was the baby who was on my mind most of the time. I had to stop begging after people knew about my relationship with him, because I didn't want them to say,

"See that food-scraper, that's Ma Zaibo's woman."

Begging wasn't a shameful act to me, but that was how they looked at it, so I couldn't resume my old profession. It made my search tremendously hard. I was lucky that Feiqing gave me some copper coins before I left. The money came in handy.

Then Big Mouth found me and told me to stop looking for the baby.

Now I knew why they'd kidnapped my child.

Everything is easier now that I see the specters in their complete form.

No need to worry about water or fire either; there are plenty of trees around. In the Hu Family Mill's backyard are several litters of dry kindling. They have darkened, but can still be lit to keep me warm.

When Wooden Fish Girl tells her story, I can also see her family. I liked her father best, and I call him Wooden Fish Papa. A thin, tall old man, he always looked at me sorrowfully, as if he wanted to say something to me. I'd very much like to interview him, but he never says a word, only gives me a sad look.

I'm drawn to his story and I even feel I could be him in a previous life. I've met quite a few down-and-out artists who were obsessed with their works. To me he may as well be Van Gogh, which was why I'd be happy to be him—no, even in this life I'd like to be him, but I don't want his wife—I can live without love, but I can't live with the betrayal of love.

My supply of instant noodles is running low, but I'm not worried. I have plenty of hardtack, which will sustain me until I leave Wild Fox Ridge, if the interviews go well.

I wonder why he's looking at me like that.

I'm curious to know if he's wondering why the writer is always looking at him with sorrowful eyes.

I still haven't seen the moon.

The green lights resembling wolf's eyes continue to tail me at a distance, however.

Twenty-third Session
Wolves

Drive the camels, up before dawn, head to the tenth stop.
Going to see the boss, to get paid for my work, was chased out the door.
Empty-handed, I went home, I was outraged and I was sad.
A dizzy spell, I fell down, and couldn't turn over for the rest of my life.
You see, this is, the life of a camel driver,
No way to make a living.

——Song of a Camel Driver

I find that my imagination has improved dramatically, besides being able to see my interviewees' faces. Earlier I would listen as they talked and later write down the main points, but now the drivers' narrations have brought their world back alive. I'm certain I was a member of the caravan, and I say to myself I'd be happy to be anyone but Huozi, Cai Wu or Qi Lu, and not Killer.

It's my belief that many things disappear on the surface, but continue to exist in a different way—no, I'm not talking about memory. In the Tang dynasty Śramana Zhiyi was born over a thousand years after Buddha reached Nirvana, but he said that Shakyamuni's Dharma service continued on. I'm having a similar experience. I mean, would anything that exists in visible matter (including actions) be transformed into dark matter and dark energy after it disappears? Could it be the same as the Buddhist karmic force? Obviously, these are just questions and guesses. In my view, it's the only way the natural law of cause and effect can exist, agree?

Now I can see many of the people from way back as they reenact their stories. Though they are narrating their stories now, what appears before me are images from that earlier time.

One. Feiqing

1

Let's go back to talk about Wild Fox Ridge.

When I think back now, I wonder if the wolves also knew the end of the world was near.

The sky-obliterating sand appeared around dusk, as dozens of camels raced toward us. I thought it must be Sha Meihu at first. In those days several outlaws attacked caravans in his name to grab valuables. Later I learned that the Sha Meihu I knew wasn't the real one. Of course, you know now who he really was, but back then Sha Meihu was a sandstorm. It was a massive entity and to see it clearly you wouldn't know where to start, like a tiger trying to swallow the sky.

My feelings toward the Sha Meihus were complicated. On one hand, I sympathized with them, for they were actually sick. That's true. They were foolish, greedy, full of hatred, and had no conscience. On the other hand, I hated them, because their evil deeds had brought tears and bloodshed.

"Hurry, grab your weapons," I shouted when I saw the dust.

The camel drivers preferred clubs made of ash and chain whips. They traveled the camel trails when they were working and practiced boxing and club fights when they were free. They were in top form and adept at using a few different weapons. I used a short club—a long rope tied to a section of hardwood—for portability; I stuck it in my belt and looked indominable as I whipped it out and swung it. There were repeater rifles, but they were reserved for the marksmen, while the ordinary camel drivers used weapons for hand combat.

"Wooden Fish Girl—Wooden Fish Girl—the outlaws are coming," Big Mouth shouted as he banged on a broken tin basin. She was tending sheep on a hill in the distance. She herded the flock back to the campsite when she heard the shouts.

I took out my matchlock and lit the fuse. It had been loaded with gunpowder and a small handful of buckshot. When I was in the mood, aimed at a grouse, with each firing producing enough meat to grease our lips.

From the wall I took down a horn that contained gunpowder and hung it on my belt before removing a sheepskin sack that carried pig iron balls the size of black beans. These I used for gazelles or wolves. I took out a ball, put it in the barrel, added some gunpowder, and tamped it tight. I'd take care of Sha Meihu first if he made a wrong move.

In the most popular story, Sha Meihu had a small band of expert boxers and club fighters. Exceptionally talented, they traveled in deserts and crossed valleys as if riding on flat land. They came and went like jackals, whizzing here and there; you found them wherever there was loot to be had. I also heard that his followers never slacked off; on the contrary, they were lightning fast in killing and raiding. Worse of all, he knew all the camel trails like the back of his hand and paid informers well, so the activities of many businesses were in his grasp. All these meant he carried out his raids as effortlessly as reaching into a sack for something.

The dust storm was getting closer; I could see a bouncing dot atop the lead camel. When there is no obstacle, distinguishing a camel from a person is limited to a range of four *li*. Any farther than that it would be only a blur. I heard the cries of nearby camels, loud enough to shatter the sky, it seemed, so I turned to check and saw all the camels around the campsite gathering together. In an instant, they had formed a battle formation, the mature ones facing out. The other drivers moved litters over to create a protective wall in front of them. It was a standard battle array against wolves.

Finally, it was clear to me that the rolling columns of dust were in fact raised by wolves. They had traveled along the rocky gobi, kicking up dust from the grass. The camels' keen sense of smell could tell them what was coming as far as ten *li* away, if they were downwind. Obviously, they had sniffed out the threat in the dust.

"Hurry!" Big Mouth shouted at Wooden Fish Girl. She was by the fortress when she noticed several white dots in a distant sand trough. Obviously, greedy sheep that had strayed too far for her to bring them back in time.

"Baa—baa—" She called out to them. She was about to run out to drive them back, but Big Mouth pulled her back behind the wall. "You'll be killed."

"They'll be killed too," she said tearfully.

The noise roused Ma Zaibo, who was sitting idly in the tent—he wanted to shut himself up in the mill house to meditate, but I insisted that he come back—so he walked out. His face was placidly blank when he saw what was happening. He had continued to meditate in his tent after returning and rarely went out—the search you talked about, Young Master, I don't know whether it happened during meditation or when you were out. Heh-heh, no need to explain. Wherever it happened, I know its essence was the soul's search, wasn't it? You were exhausted physically and mentally from the search, but the real search occurred in your soul, didn't it?

I'll return to the wolves. You've been attacked by wolves yourselves, but that's your experience. What I'm talking about now is what I experienced. There was a wolf attack in everyone's mind. The rest of you, feel free to jump in anytime you want.

The camels were getting close when Wooden Fish Girl got into the fortress. Finally, I saw it more clearly; the dot on the lead camel wasn't human, but was a big wolf. I'll be damned, it was dead, but still hanging on the camel hump, tossed from side to side, like a child's rattle. It must have aimed for the camel's hump and instead got its teeth stuck in the fat and couldn't get off. As the camel ran up and down sand troughs, the wolf died as it was flung back and forth. That happened a lot at camel grounds, and we often saw a dead wolf hanging from a camel's back. A camel's hump must be a rare delicacy for the wolf, but it will enjoy the taste but once, not realizing that tasty food can be lethal.

Another camel had several dots on its back too, all still squirming. A close look showed that a big chunk of the hump was missing. It was a young camel whose humps had yet to grow tough, which drew the wolves to gnaw on the tender, tasty fat. Luckily, there were other camels free of wolves.

What are you running for? I said silently to the camels. It's just a few wolves. Nothing to fear. You probably know that a few camels can take on a few wolves, so long as they're brave and calm; one on one, the camels will still come out ahead. Camels have several unexpected, lethal moves, like kicking, biting, spitting, stomping, and crushing, all enough to frighten wolves off. But if the camels panic and run, it's like putting down their weapons and turning themselves into a movable feast for the wolves.

Since the Mongolian caravan had their own plan, the caravans were like two countries, each with its own grazing ground and boundaries. They had a few marksmen too. In the past, there had been no strict demarcation lines when caravans were out in the desert. The camels grazed wherever there was good grass and water, and the camel hands pitched their tents by a water source and unloaded the litters for the camels to graze freely. All they had to do was check on the camels now and then. Usually the camels grazed wherever they wanted; they ate when hungry and drank when thirsty, roaming at will, very democratic. The camel hands needed to take care of several things: watch out for wolves, prevent pestilence, monitor camel mating, and so on. There was no need to take the camels out of the pen in the morning and herd them back inside at night. It was easy living, if somewhat lonely.

"Wolf pack!" Wooden Fish Girl cried out fearfully.

I sucked in cold air when I saw there were more wolves than just those hanging on camel humps. Many black dots appeared in the dust storm around the camels. They formed a tight circle. The wolves would not dare charge into it, for they knew that every camel foot was a potential death threat.

The camels ran to the protective wall. Humans were their best friends.

"Light a fire!" I shouted.

Several drivers brought over dry kindling and lit the pile. A big fire roared, the smoke blotting out the sky. I moved a camel to create a sort of gate to the fortress. The wolves stopped at the sight of the fire, while the camels ran into the fortress.

"Let's go after them." I blew on the fuse and fired a shot. The wolves still chasing the camels stopped when they heard the explosion. Some of the drivers went up with their clubs to beat the wolves hanging on the camel's hump. They yelped from the pain, but soon went quiet, while the white camel with the damaged humps collapsed and cried pitifully.

After watching awhile, the wolves went after the sheep that hadn't make it back in time. The sheep ran off shrieking, but the wolves floated over like a cloud and converged on them. Wooden Fish Girl wailed. Soon the wolves dispersed, the sheep were gone, and there was nothing but clumps of wool in the sand trough.

"I'm going to end up in a wolf's belly," a young camel hand cried out. "I'm not married yet."

I felt like laughing. The young man was always grinning cheekily, without a care in the world. And now when he thought he was about to die, instead of missing his parents, he wished he'd had a woman. That wasn't uncommon. Camel hands usually pitied men who were virgins; to them it was a shame for a man to die before he "saw the daylight."

"You've still got time. Young Master is here. You can find yourself a pretty camel and ask her to perform the rite. You'll see daylight once before you become wolf food," Big Mouth said with a smile.

"Stop the nonsense!" The young man blushed as he pounded Big Mouth, making the others laugh like beasts.

"Enough. Throw on some more firewood," I told them.

Then I heard a wooden fish song—

Desire causes a fire to engulf the body,
A wrongful death in a stone house did the harm.
Seven people with eight lives died innocently,
In one night women and children went to the underworld.
Such cruelty, so ruthless in committing the crime,
Don't they know the ones who set fire would be burned?

The officials at all ranks were hateful;
All they wanted was more gold ...

I didn't know why she decided to sing the song at that moment, but I did know it would help offset the fear in some of the drivers. They might not all understood the words, but her voice would surely help reduce their fright.

Two more camels showed up in a distant sand trough, a female and her baby. They had clearly grazed too far from the herd. The pack of wolves floated over. I knew the two camels were goners. Now I worried about the others. Who knew how many were still out there. A rough count of those in the fortress came up with slightly over half the total number. It would have been better if the wolves all came at us here. We'd suffer a tremendous loss if there were several packs and each attacked the stragglers.

"Burn some wolf dung, Lu Fuji," I shouted, my head sweaty from worries.

"Fuck. How could I have forgotten that?" Lu Fiji ran into a tent.

The pack surrounded the two camels and the circle tightened, when the female cried out, a cry for help from her human friends. They were too far for my weapon to be of any use, but I fired a shot at the pack anyway. A commotion broke out among them, but I couldn't tell if any was hit.

"Fight the wolves!" Several camel hands yelled out. They wanted to draw the pack over to save the two camels, but the wolves ignored them and pounced on the camels. The female raised her neck to spit out her stomach contents, a camel's most lethal weapon. It's a big sticky gob that would mat a wolf's hair and cause it to molt. If a wolf loses too much hair it will have a tough time making it through the winter. Even in the summer the spot will itch so badly the wolf must scratch and scratch until the spot is raw with exposed skin. Then bottlenecks converge on the wound and reproduce to cover the wolf with maggots. The wolf's body festers and it will soon die. Experienced older wolves usually steer clear of camels.

The stomach contents are lethal but not immediately fatal. The wolves continued to pounce. Knowing it was in a dire situation, the female kept spitting as she shielded her young and ran toward the camp site. The wolves were right on their tails, like magnets on iron.

I fired another shot. One of the wolves behind the camels fell to the ground and writhed, drawing away some of the wolves, but more still came after the camels.

Experienced camels seldom flee from wolves; they will either spit out their stomach contents or bite and toss, or kick their attackers. All these moves will frighten off the wolves. Fleeing means putting down their weapons and exposing their weaknesses, which is the diaphragm near the hip. Without protection from ribs, the spot can be easily ripped open by a wolf's claws. A wolf can then reach in to pull out the intestines and pluck out the other organs, all delicacies for a wolf. But these two were trapped in a pack, and the female was no match if she stayed put. She'd be a pile of bones soon.

A wolf jumped up onto the female, who twisted and turned violently to shake the wolf off. When another wolf, an impatient one, wanted to attack the young camel running ahead of its mother, it lowered its head, bit down on the wolf's back, tossed its head, and sent a dark dot flying into the air. The dot fell and rolled into a sand trough. Two more took the opportunity to attack, one on each side, and dug their claws into the humps. The female stumbled, and I knew the claws had opened her sides.

"Yow—" the camel cried out.

"Yow—" the camels in the fortress cried in response, sensing the danger one of their own was in, as a way to cheer her on.

The pain made the female camel take off running. One of the wolves dropped to the ground, but the other hung on like a maggot on bones. I sighed. She was done for, I knew. The pack went after the young camel, prompting its mother to turn back, bite down on a wolf and toss it into the air, nearly killing it.

A black shadow flashed past me. I turned to see my black steed leap out of the fortress and charge the pack. The horse grazed with the camels and got enough to eat that it had a shiny satiny coat. It must have formed some kind of bond with the camels and now, seeing two of them in danger, ran over to help. I panicked. A horse can deal with one wolf easily, but not with a whole pack. Two fists were never a match for four hands. It would surely die if it wasn't careful. I gathered that the pack had come to within shooting range, so I aimed at one of them and fired. It fell to the ground at the sound of the explosion.

When the black steed reached the young camel, it kicked up its hind hooves and sent several wolves to the ground before shielding the camel. They ran back together, followed by the mother, and the pack. Several cunning old wolves flanked the horse and ran ahead of it, obviously trying to cut off its escape route. It looked to be in dire straits. I wanted to fire another shot, but didn't have time to reload.

Then the female stopped running. I knew she was going to sacrifice herself to save her young. It was a common scene along camel trails. When camels met up with wolves and were in danger, some old camels would willingly turn themselves over to the wolves to save others.

The wolves pounced on the female and she was immediately covered with them. She stood still, watching her baby and the black steed run to safety.

I was so tense I could hardly breathe. Over my years as a camel hand, I'd encountered wolves many times, but none so treacherous.

2

Wooden Fish Girl continued to sing.

Chain Smoker burned wolf dung.

According to our ancestors, wolf dung could exorcise evil spirits. There were other things about wolves that could do that too, for sure. The drivers usually carried a wolf bone or a wolf tooth on them, and we usually traveled with wolf dung on long trips. We'd burn it when we reached a spot with too much yin, and the smoke would be a signal for help when we were in danger. I told a driver to set a seven-star fire, the signal for a wolf attack.

I hoped the Mongolian caravan would come help us out when they saw the smoke. It was a wolf attack, a natural disaster. The convention required everyone to render assistance during a natural disaster, no matter how deep the enmity was; otherwise they would be worse than animals. It was like a country with many factions that fought all the time but united against a common enemy, such as an alien race. As our ancestors said, when the lips are gone the teeth will be cold.

Seven columns of smoke curled into the air, like a whirling tornado, but I wasn't sure if the Mongolian drivers saw them. If they were downwind they should have heard the gunfire, except I'd been shooting grouse over those days and they might have gotten used to hearing it.

The sun sank below the sand mountains and all was quiet. I groaned inwardly as I looked at the wolves spread across the sand troughs like sesame seeds. We had lit several large fires, but they consumed lots of firewood. We usually cut enough for our use and we didn't have much dry kindling that was reserved for rainy days. Normally, we cooked with camel droppings, a fuel that burned slowly, but did not produce a large flame, and worked less well in frightening off wolves than dry kindling. I told the drivers to add some camel droppings so we wouldn't use up the firewood too quickly. I had no idea what we'd do without a fire.

Now I felt like kicking myself for letting the marksmen go with the Mongolians. They wouldn't have been so quickly turned by Huozi—I was convinced it was all his doing, or at least he was one of the masterminds—if the marksmen had stayed, so they could send the wolves running. Wolves are very clever and they know which way the wind blows.

The camel whose humps had been destroyed by the wolves cried once in a while, with tears slipping down its face. It obviously wasn't going to make it. I told Ma Zaibo to give the order to put it out of its misery. I could give the order too, but with him around I had to ask him as a courtesy, so no one would have anything to say in the future. After Ma gave his consent, Lu Fuji and several drivers went up to tie the camel with a coir rope to bring it down, drain the blood, skin it and remove the innards. Then they sliced off enough meat for Wooden Fish Girl to cook. We tossed the dead wolves behind the pile of firewood, for we had no time to skin them.

Night came. The red glow from the western mountains slowly bled into the night sky. Wooden Fish Girl came into the big tent. Nighttime is the wolves' time to play, as they can see at night and are on the prowl after dark. We humans, on the other hand, are blind in the dark. Luckily, camels can see at night too, and the drivers were on high alert, so the wolves wouldn't cause any damage, as long as we stuck together.

Besides the drivers assigned to stand guard at various spots, I also had a few patrol with clubs. Then I put some beans in a feedbag and hung it around the horse's neck, which I patted to show my appreciation. Horses have a magical connection to humans; a man will get a horse just like himself. The black steed's brave actions earlier gained me a great deal of face.

The wolves were howling. I knew they were trying to wear down the camels' will to fight. My horse raised its neck and whinnied, silencing the wolves right away. That made me smile.

Wooden Fish Girl looked sad as she gazed at the sheep, but she didn't know it was a sheep's fate to be killed by wolves.

Before we left this time, we'd rounded up several hundred transporting sheep, each of which could handle almost twenty *jin* of highland barley or soy beans. They feasted on grass when there was some and ate beans when there was none. As we traveled, they slowly became food for the drivers. Usually we didn't need sheep to help carrying loads, but this time I thought it wasn't a bad idea to have more meat sources. I was proven right by later events. Without the sheep, those of us who survived couldn't have left Wild Fox Ridge alive. The mutton jerky provided the much-needed energy for us to leave the desert.

Ma Zaibo looked at the bits of camel fur quietly after muttering something. I knew he was delivering the animal's soul.

Chain Smoker handed me a fast-loading musket. It was called that to differentiate it from a matchlock, where the flint sent a spark into the pan and ignited the gunpowder. There were three matchlocks and one musket in our caravan; the latter was kept by Chain Smoker and brought out only during an emergency. I got onto a platform made of litters to survey the situation, but the smoke was so thick and the darkness of the night obscured my vision. I maintained a calm appearance, but inside I was burning with anxiety and worry. We'd had wolf attacks before, but they usually came and went like a storm, leaving a trail of carnage; it was rare to have a siege like this. A few days earlier, Lu Fuji had spotted several dead wolf cubs and asked the drivers, who all said they hadn't killed them. Could an enemy of ours done it? I thought of Huozi. That would have been a terrible thing to do. Don't be upset with me; I'm just telling you what I was thinking at the time. If you did it or not, that's your business. Even if you did, so many years have passed that time has leveled the hate-filled chasm.

As I saw it then, the wolf pack did appear to be seeking revenge, and that even a minor slip could lead to a major catastrophe. I'd seen enough wolf raids, where they turned animals into carcasses in no time. There was usually a reason why they did that; wolves rarely attacked unless provoked by humans. On the plain, wolves are the Earth God's dogs, on the mountain, wolves are the Mountain God's dogs, and in the desert, they are the hunting dogs of the yellow dragon. They all serve their own masters. They are not headless flies. If they raided a farm, it had to be because humans had done something to provoke them. I hadn't known yet that even more horrifying events would occur later. Like animals acting abnormally just before an earthquake, wolves at a time like this weren't entirely in control of themselves.

I got down and called Lu Fuji over.

"How long will the firewood last?" I asked in a low voice.

"I told the drivers to use more camel droppings. We'll be in trouble if the marksmen don't come to rescue us. Wolves could be driven off with a fusillade of gunfire."

"I think they'll be here soon. They have to come. What happened before was in the past. This time it's different. We have rules." I tried to reassure him. "Go cheer up the drivers." A northern wind blew over a thick plume of smoke causing coughing fits.

"Are you smoking desert rats?" one of the drivers shouted.

"It's easy for you to talk like that. The firewood's almost gone. Why don't you come take care of the fire for a change?" Big Mouth retorted.

"Don't worry!" I yelled back before telling Big Mouth to search for anything that could be used as fuel. The camels spitting had managed to keep the wolves at bay for now.

It was pitch black out now. Besides the stars in the sky, there were many other stars floating back and forth in the sand troughs, green, like will-o-the-wisps. Wolf eyes. A heavy stench of blood came at me. I'd travel the desert often and seen lots of wolves, so I knew their nature and habits like the back of my hand. They are not only ferocious and savage, but highly wary. Old camel hands were always saying, "Use a hemp stalk on a wolf, everyone has something to fear." Judging by what was happening, I didn't think they'd risk an attack.

A long howl came from the wolves, like a bullet shooting into the night sky. More quickly followed, like fireworks being set off. They drowned out the spitting camels, sounded much closer.

"Oh no, the wolves are going to get me," a driver screamed.

"Shut your trap!" Chain Smoker yelled back.

"Scream again and I'll toss you to the wolves," Lu Fuji shouted.

I focused on locating the alpha male, so I could shoot it first. I'd seen it earlier in the afternoon. A big black one. I'd tried to shoot it then, but it was out of range. You have to grab the leader when catching thieves; the same goes for killing wolves. A pack like this had to have a clearly defined hierarchy, and every one of them followed the leader. An alpha male was usually ruthless, which was how it solidified its authority. If I could take it out, I'd reduce their aggression by half. But the sand troughs were dense with green lights, spark after spark, impossible to quickly make out the alpha. Having gotten tired of waiting, I fired a shot to where the first howl had come from. The pack stirred and the howling died down a bit.

"Ai-ya! The wolves are on the sand hills." Big Mouth shouted.

Stunned, I ran over with my weapon. Sure enough, both sides of the hill were dotted with green lights. The hill was chock full of dead vegetation, so we'd pitched our tents against it. Setting up a tent was no different from building a house, where fengshui was important. Feng, or wind, referred to the path of the wind; usually, to keep everyone healthy, we avoided a wind blowing straight at us. Shui, or water, meant a water source. When we picked the site this time, we chose the hillside near water. To keep the sand hill from shifting, the drivers frequently piled firewood on it to keep it stable. We hadn't expected the cunning creatures to take up the high point. A death-defying wolf could run along the ridge, one jump would take it across the wall of camels, and right into the middle of the fortress.

I quickly reloaded, and saw I didn't have much gunpowder in the horn. That was terrible news. The consequence would be unthinkable if we ran out of gunpowder after using up all our firewood. I filled only buckshot this time, since I meant to scare them off. After moving closer, I aimed at one of the green lights and pulled the trigger. A wheel-sized ball of fire climbed the hill. The buckshot seemed to chirp cheerfully as it bored into the creatures' fur. Green lights shrieked and quickly dispersed.

Wiping my sweaty forehead, I poured in gunpowder, but couldn't suppress a sigh of distress. The distant sky was frozen, with no sign of action. I ought to ride over to get help from the Mongolians, I said to myself.

"Come over here, Lu Fuji." I shouted. He came over and went inside with me. Wooden Fish Girl was scooping out camel meat and steaming up the place. Lu grabbed a piece of meat, and tossed it onto the table, and cut off two pieces, one for me. I told him to take one to Ma Zaibo.

"We can't just wait here. I want to break out with my horse to get help."

"That's too dangerous," Lu said.

After having some camel meat, I went back up to the high point and saw nothing but darkness, no light from a fire. We'd be better off if I rode out to get help instead of sitting here waiting to die, I said to myself. The Mongolians had behaved badly, but they'd come to help.

I talked to the drivers, telling them to pass out blankets, sheets, and old clothes and set them on fire when necessary to scare the wolves. Then I got on my horse and left the fortress with my rifle and club.

To be honest, I'm not a born hero, and I was frightened by the numerous eerie green lights in the darkness. I knew that hidden in the darkness was limitless danger. At such a moment I could only puff myself up, like someone pretending to be well-fed after his face was swollen up from being slapped. Dozens of lives were at the mercy of wolves, after all, and as the lead driver I was responsible for them. Don't you think?

3

The green dots of light moved toward me the moment I left the fortress. A sense of danger had me in its grip, but I wasn't afraid enough to lose my cool. I traveled through grassland often, and sometimes, when I was in a pasture, ferocious Tibetan mastiffs would bark and charge me. It wasn't all that different from what I was facing now. In those days, I'd urge my horse on while I put my club to work, which in the end earned me renown.

The club, made of sawtooth oak, was a couple of feet long and wrapped in copper on both ends. One end had a ring looped with a length of rope. By swinging the rope, the club describes a circle that whistles in the air, sometimes near, sometimes far. Experienced dogs would stay away when they saw it. Sometimes a reckless one would rush up and bark like crazy until the club flew at it and, bang, its eyeballs shot out into the distance. It wasn't hard to kill one; I just had to swing harder.

Urging the horse to go faster, I swung the club around to protect it. Originally an untamed Mongolian horse, the black steed had been in perilous situations several times and had fought off wolves. It had grown bold from the battles, and was not easily scared.

I much preferred riding horses over camels, which weren't spirited enough for me. To help the horse run in the desert as if on flat land, I'd taken the feet from a dead camel and asked the cobbler, Shi Xiaoluozi, to make leather pads for me. When we were on sand, I fixed those over the horse hooves so it could run without sinking and slowing down. It wasn't used to wearing them at first, but soon it could run at top speed.

After a while my eyes got used to the dark enough to see the green lights continue to trail me, but at a distance. Wolves share some dog characteristics; they both fear ropes. If you run into a wolf in the wild without any usable weapon, you can remove your belt and swing it over your head to keep it at bay. When shepherds set up a tent, they usually string a rope all around to keep the wolves away. Now I regretted not leaving the firearm with the drivers. I'd wanted to, but Lu Fuji insisted that I take it. Out here it was clearly more dangerous than back inside the fortress. Still I worried about them not having a firearm to protect them.

Suddenly, I heard a wolf in front of me. I looked closer and saw green lights in front and on the sides. I knew I mustn't stop at a moment like this or I'd be wolf food. I tightened my legs and urged the horse on, while putting away the club and taking down the musket. I fired into the green lights and reloaded when they darted here and there.

Then I recalled that the area was infested with rat holes, the mortal enemy of a galloping horse. The horse could break a leg if it landed on one. When I left set out, I'd been too focused on riding away from the wolf pack to remember the pitfall of rat holes. Now all I could do was pray for protection. Wolves were again howling like the wind.

"My dear horse. Please be careful, dear horse." I called out, though I knew I had little control over what happened. If heaven wanted me to feed the wolves, I'd have to accept my fate. Putting the rat holes out of my mind, I swung the club and filled the night with its whistles.

The green lights in front vanished, but I saw I was trailed by many more when I turned to check. They were so close I could hear them breathing, though they were careful not get too close when I swung the club. If this had been daytime, I could crush their heads. It would give me a good feeling to send those vicious eyes shooting out of the sockets, making an arc in the air, and landing in the sand to roll around. I rarely used a firearm when I ran into wolves, the club was my favorite weapon. Easy to use and effective; on a fast horse, I swung it around and took on several wolves.

I favored the club even as a child practicing martial arts. It wasn't flashy, and I could stick it in my belt and whip it out to make me feel powerful. It could be gentle or brutal, reaching far and near. With a few moves it would dance in the air in concert with the movements of my body and land where I aimed it. Its tip zipped through the air and landed with lethal effect. Dozens of wolves had died at my club.

Suddenly, I was flying through the air as I felt something different beneath me. The horse must have stepped into a hole. I shot out like a bullet. With no time to think, I made the natural adjustment and rolled a few times into a standing position on a dune when I landed. Frequent travel in the desert gave me plenty of horseback experience. My feet were barely in the stirrups, only the tips resting in them to give me enough push to stay in the saddle. If they'd been all the way in the stirrups, I might not have time to remove them at critical moments and, if the horse was startled, could be dragged to my death.

The horse struggled to get up and run toward me. I was relieved to see it hadn't broken a leg. Green lights were coming again, so I quickly got my musket, engaged the flint, and pulled the trigger. An explosion sent the lights dispersing again.

When the horse came up snorting heavily, I felt around its body and legs and found no injury. I breathed a sigh of relief as I jumped back on. The green lights were getting closer again.

"Does this mean I'm doomed to die in the teeth of wolves?" I lamented, but managed to shake off the depressing thought and swung my club. Although its legs were fine, the horse must have an injured tendon, for it could no longer run. Instead it walked with difficulty.

Then I saw a row of torches rounding the bend of a sand hill. I was overjoyed. Even the horse neighed. "Is that you, Feiqing?" someone asked and another voice replied before I could answer.

"Of course, it's him. Who else could get near that black horse?"

I turned to see the green lights backing off, though they still floated in the sand troughs. "Watch out. I've attracted a wolfpack."

"Don't worry. Wolves are smart enough to stay clear of the rifle muzzles," the man chortled as they fired off a few shots. The green lights vanished.

When we were closer to each other, I saw he looked like a man I'd met in Xiongwogou. There were also several men with muskets, one of whom was the man who had asked me to paint a snuff bottle for him. Later Big Mouth told me that he'd spotted him at the Festival. It was Sha Meihu, he said, but he thought he looked unusual, so he'd checked closely and saw he did not have an Adam's apple. That was no man.

With plenty of firearms and an overwhelming presence, they chased after the wolves as they fired, so the wolves had run off before we reached the campsite. I told the drivers to stay alert and asked Wooden Fish Girl to cook more camel meat for the men.

"Never mind the Mongolian drivers. We've been watching you for a long time, but we were afraid our mouths weren't big enough to take on two caravans. But everything is fine now. To us the Mongolian caravan is just a delicious meal—you were too, but not anymore. We did the right thing by rescuing you," Sha Meihu said.

He left behind two muskets and walked off with his men.

From what he'd said, he had obviously been following us. The realization made me break out in a cold sweat.

4

The female camel was nothing but a pile of white bones when I walked out the next morning. Clumps of her hair were scattered here and there, littering the place. Her innards had been gobbled up by the wolves, while the solid waste inside splattered and gave off a horrible stink.

Bits of sheepskin and wolf droppings were all over the sand trough. Usually a wolf left its dropping on the grass at a certain spot, where no livestock would dare get close. It was rare to see so much in such a large area. Their unique odor still lingered in the trough.

It was time to hunt the wolves after breakfast, as we'd done after every wolf attack back at the grazing ground. We'd kill as many as we could, but if that didn't happen, at least we'd chase them onto someone else's turf.

I took several marksmen and enough food and water with me as we followed their tracks. The horse's leg was fine. No more limping, so I rode it out.

A windless night kept their tracks visible in the sand. Wolf paws are like dog's, the shaped of plum flowers. When a large pack walked by, the path would be covered in sand they kicked up and only those trailing behind or trotting on the side would leave any visible prints. Wolves have their own independent world, with a strict hierarchy and order; they also have their set of rules. Attacks like this one constituted a fierce revolt against human dominance. The abnormal behavior this time could be attributed to the sandstorm that would come later. They'd acted like this one year just before an earthquake.

As we walked along, the prints no longer looked neat, with some coming this way and some going that way. Bits of animal fur were all over the sand troughs, and even the trees were draped with animal skins.

A few sheep were slumped in there also. There was still meat on their bones, but the wolves had been too lazy to finish the job; the dead sheep were left to stare with the whites of their eyes. Further on, we saw a herding Mongolian driver sprawled on a poplar.

"When did the wolf pack come through?" Big Mouth yelled at the man.

But he was quiet, so he asked again and got no response. "He's dead!' Big Mouth shouted when he went up to check.

Indeed. The man looked surprised, with wide-staring eyes. He had no pulse. But oddly his body was unharmed. We wondered why the wolves had left him like that.

I asked the drivers to dig a hole and bury the man. They took off his shoes to hang on the tree before burying him, so anyone coming to look for him would find the spot easily. Then we broke off a sturdy branch and stuck it in the spot as a marker.

Along the way we saw torn camel fur all over the place. Sometimes there were also half-eaten sheep. Wolves favored the intestines, so they obviously poked holes in the bellies for the innards and nothing else.

As we looked, we could see that the tracks led into the distant desert. Who knew where they ended? We turned around and returned to the site.

As for Sha Meihu, that was the last time I saw him, the one who looked like a man. I didn't know what had happened between him and the Mongolian drivers. They had all vanished like vapor. Nor did I know if they managed to escape the deadly sandstorm.

Except for Huozi, who made an appearance in the Liangzhou gazette, all the other Mongolians simply evaporated. Chain Smoker said they'd violated rules of caravan trail and offended the Shepherd God, who decided to let them die.

Chain Smoker had been suspicious of Huozi, saying he could be one of Sha Meihu's informers. But there was no proof to bear out his claim.

Twenty-fourth Session
The End of the World

Of all the narrators of their stories, Killer is the only one whose face remains blurry, except that it gives off a murderous feel. I'll use "it" from now on. I know it doesn't want me to see its face and continues to conceal itself. In its own way, it amasses an orb of gray vapor to wrap around itself. It looks very much like a moon encircled by gray clouds. That's fine with me. I haven't seen the real moon for some time now, so you'll be the moon.

I could see its face through a special means, but I don't want to do that. Normally, I can see only those who want me to see them, not the ones who don't want me to.

Very well, then. Those who don't want me to see them are the ones I don't want to see, I say to myself.

I see only a collection of murderous air, grayish black, every time I interview Killer.

I have a dream that night. In it I'm attacked by the old wolf. It comes after me while I'm asleep. Sneaking in softly, it goes straight for my throat and with one swift move sinks its teeth into it. In the dream I don't know that I'm dead and continue doing what I normally do.

When I wake up, I break out in a cold sweat.

In the dream I ask, "Is the wolf Killer?"
I continue with the interview in my dream too.

One. Killer

1

Wild Fox Ridge suddenly grew much larger, I discovered, just before the arrival of the end of the world you were all talking about.

I'd never seen such a big mountain. Grass and trees were sparse. Camel bells rang loudly and echoed in the mountain in tiny spurts. It should have provoked something poetic in my mind. When I think about it now, such a beautiful scene ought to have inspired poetry, but no, it didn't. It couldn't be helped. Humans can never transcend their environment; or in your words, they can't transcend their minds. I was just a killer, with the mind of one. My heart was filled with an intent to kill. All I could think of was where and when I unsheathed my knife. Other than that, I had almost no other thoughts.

I was indeed shrouded in resentment. Later I learned that it came from my dead relatives. What people call ghosts are merely *qi*, and when resentment gathers, there're the spirits of those who died wrongful deaths. I was surrounded by that resentment. Actually, I was just a vessel for air, my own self gone.

I was watching Ma Zaibo.

He must have known I was watching him.

I vaguely recalled that I had a chance to knock him off a rope bridge over a river. It was an enormous river, and red, obviously from silt. I didn't know if it was the Yellow River. It couldn't have been, rationally speaking, but that was hard to tell. Oftentimes, when one thinks about the Yellow River, then it will exist in that person's mind.

I was obviously wrapped in the murderous air that was a concentration of resentment. When so much bitterness gathers together it forms a murderous air, and sometimes, whoever the air rushes at would become a killer. Sometimes it will surround you and make you commit suicide. I tell you. All those murderers or suicides are merely vessels for the murderous air. Sometimes a person can't control it when committing suicide. Just think about all those ghosts of wrongful deaths in the world. They come near you once you have the thought to kill yourself or someone else; some of them are looking for a substitute, while others are seeking revenge. You can't help it. Your thought attracts something in accordance with the idea. The same with me. There were so many bitter spirits around me; they surrounded me, hoping I would make sure justice was served—heh-heh, what is justice? I don't know. Oftentimes justice is on the side of whoever is the loudest. Whoever laughs last is the one who is said to have justice.

I kept my eyes on Ma Zaibo, which was my destiny, and his destiny was to be watched by me. I wasn't the only one; he had a more formidable enemy observing him. I don't have to tell you; you all know what I mean.

My knife was aimed at him. I'd wanted to toy with him like a cat playing with a mouse, but I knew I was running out of time. Like Chain Smoker, I heard the footsteps of the end of the world.

I must use the blood from a Ma family member as a sacrifice to my ancestors before the end was upon us.

Quietly, I walked toward him and unsheathed my knife. A single plunge to the heart would send his blood spurting. The red bundle had been thirsty, waiting to drink the blood. I even heard the ghosts of wrongful deaths singing, reveling. The time for their deliverance was upon us, after all. I'd let them down so many times before—they knew I'd had lots of opportunities, but of course you know that one is not always in control of one's heart.

Besides the knife, I had a short-barreled musket, which I'd stolen along with some gunpowder. I was worried about running into wolves. Honestly, the wolf attack had cast a shadow in my mind, and I kept seeing a camel that had been gnawed into a bloody mess.

2

I saw Brown Lion just as I was about to carry out my mission.

He was staring at me coldly, I discovered, with the hint of a sly smile in his eyes.

A giant silhouette, he was creeping along a sand peak, an unforgettable image. I've lost my poetic inclinations and am no longer guilty of strange, sentimental outbursts, as before. Asked to choose between a rose and a pair of gloves, I'd pick the latter.

But I can't forget Brown Lion, a lonely figure creeping along waves of sand.

Think about it. Sand ridges crest into the horizon. Against a backdrop of sand meeting the sky was a brown dot—a camel—moving all alone. And not your average camel either; it was a male camel castrated by external forces.

I wanted to chase him away.

I didn't want any living being to witness bloodshed from my knife, even an animal that cannot talk. I would chase him off so I could take my time exacting revenge, I thought. Ma Zaibo must know why he had to die, don't you agree? I could not let him die with unmitigated grievances; I wanted to tell him many things, wanted him to understand that even if I didn't kill him, he wouldn't make it past the end of the world. I did not want him to die with too many unanswered questions.

Brown Lion was more like a wild camel by then. In those days there were lots of wild camels in the desert, but they had been domesticated.

Once they had no owner, they were called wild camels. But from a biological standpoint, they were no different.

I felt sorry for Brown Lion. When lecherous scholars read about the castrated historian Sima Qian, they must feel the same way I did now with Brown Lion.

My heart softened, and I decided against chasing him away. I'd wait for him to go off before I made my move, I told myself.

Imagine my surprise when he came at me.

Could he have seen the knife in my hand?

I was thrown into a minor panic, but I quickly recovered. He was used to attacking Chinese camels, but not people. I'd shoot and kill him if he dared attack me this time, I thought. No one would say I did anything wrong.

Kicking up sand along the way, Brown Lion charged at me. Yellow Demon was the best at kicking up sand; I didn't expect Brown Lion, now clearly a mad camel, to act like Yellow Demon. I told myself to be careful. It wouldn't end well for me if he bit, stomped, or crushed me. He could send me straight to hell.

I set the flint and fixed my gaze on the column of sand rolling my way—it was just a feeling I had at the time, but it was enough to show me that Brown Lion was mentally confused enough to affect his behavior, like a deranged human. Practice had turned me into a decent sharpshooter. When hunting animals, I usually used buckshot, but this time I loaded a steel ball. That would give me a greater range, but unlike buckshot, which covered a larger area, a single ball required perfect aim. It was truly a miss is as good as a mile. The charging Brown Lion would not allow me time to reload.

I saw that the camel was foaming at the mouth, proof that he had indeed gone mad. You see the same thing on people who have gone mad. I recall I was actually calm at that moment. I knew that panic would only make it worse; I had to hold my breath and fix my gaze on the leaping brown dot in the cross hairs.

I pulled the trigger when I was sure I'd hit my target.

The rifle went off.

Some may dispute what I just described. Earlier Feiqing mentioned two ways of firing, one with the fuse, a matchlock, the other with a flint, a flintlock. Later we used the same term for weapons that fired bullets. Every era has its own fast-loading weapon.

Brown Lion fell. I was sure I'd hit my target. I wouldn't have pulled the trigger if I hadn't been certain. I was aiming for his heart, as I didn't know I could hit his head because he was a moving target. I could hit him in the chest, I knew. So I aimed for the spot where a driver would plunge his knife in when killing a camel. Each time a knife went in there, arrows of blood would spurt. And that was where I wanted to hit.

I jumped up from the sand mound—I'd shot from a prone position for accuracy.

To my incredible surprise, the fallen camel also jumped to his feet.

His chest was blood stained but the blood wasn't spurting. It was bleeding, and that was all. The ball had entered his chest but missed the blood-filled heart. Now it was time to panic. I was about to face a terrifying demon.

3

I could not shake the nightmarish image of fighting Brown Lion, to the point where I considered him part of the end of the world. I kept dreaming about the camel charging me and woke up in a cold sweat. Sometimes I was startled awake just dreaming about the camel staring at me from a distance. The nightmare continued into my intermediate body later. The demon I saw looked just like Brown Lion. I ran and ran, but never escaped the omnipresent camel.

Just imagine what an impact that had on me.

I was clear-headed enough at that moment to know that running was not an option. He would give chase, and his gaping mouth would clamp down on my neck. He had more than enough ways to kill me.

I could not outrun a deranged camel.

I had to fight him. And the best way to deal with the animal was a firearm. I'd fired too soon, when I think back. If I'd waited until he was closer, everything would have turned out differently.

I could use the weapon as a club. It was actually quite comical. Our nickname for a musket was "stove club," and that is exactly what I was holding now.

It would have been easier to fight the camel on flat land, because I was skilled in martial art moves and good at dodging, turning, leaping, and shifting. But on sand, my feet kept sinking and would affect my speed. I was bathed in a cold sweat.

As I thought these thoughts, the mad camel pounced.

Raising my weapon, I waited for him to be almost on top of me so I could crack down on his nose and knock him out with a single strike. It is one of a camel's weakest spots, second only to its gonads, a term unknown to us back then. We called them nuts.

I was well aware that I had to simultaneously strike out with the club and dodge a hulking body that could thud into me and send me flying, like a kite with a broken string. He could easily shatter my breastbone and ribs. See how clear-headed I was? I'd worked hard on maintaining my composure.

In the blink of an eye, the brown mass charged, as sand exploded under his feet. I shut my eyes as the sand rained down on me. As a reflex, I jumped to the side. I hadn't seen anything to prompt the move, but it was good that I had. A wind blew over and the brown mass whizzed past me. My weapon crashed down on his rear end almost at the same time and I heard something crack.

Then I realized that my plan of smashing his nose could be carried out only on flat land. In the desert, he would kick up too much sand and could make it easier for him to kill me if even a few grains of sand got into my eyes. All he needed to do was stomp on my chest, turning it into a meat patty.

He turned and charged again. The foam sprayed in my face. It was sticky. When I was a kid, camel drivers told me that a camel's spittle was toxic and caused pockmarks. Later I learned that was something grownups made up to frighten children. A camel's spittle was like human spit, harmless, though slightly saltier. The stuff from the mad camel was gooey, really disgusting.

Each time he charged I struck out. My weapon was reduced to a metal tube. It did hit him, but with no visible effect, like scratching an itch on your foot through your shoe.

I was sweating profusely.

Now I felt I was confronting a true lion.

Two. Ma Zaibo

1

What happened later really did feel like the end of the world to me.

I just wanted to save a life.

I was scared when the mad camel pounced at me. I'm really not that brave. To be honest, I was ashamed beyond words later when I reflected upon the scene. My face burned when I compared myself with Shakyamuni Buddha, who cut off a piece of his flesh to feed a vulture and gave himself over to a tiger. I realized that I couldn't eliminate fear, no matter how hard I tried to treat the masses as my parents or imagined having myself killed to feed them.

What occurred later then became a hazy bad dream. I recalled tripping and falling to the ground, where drifting sand trapped my feet while my body kept shooting forward. So I fell, despite my effort.

Sand hitting my face was what I felt first. Experience reminded me that Brown Lion would next put his weighty foot on me.

I was afraid but calm, a benefit from years of meditative training. I kept my eyes almost shut. From frequent travel in a windswept desert, I learned to open my eyes a mere slit to get a view of what lay ahead without letting sand into my eyes. Which was how I could see the brown mass pressing down on me.

Other than rolling on the ground, I couldn't think of any move. I wanted to draw the camel away to help you escape, while keeping myself from dying under his feet. I didn't want to die yet; to me the body was a valuable treasure, a vehicle through which I hoped to reach true enlightenment.

I rolled down a sand trough. Sand poured into my nose, ears, and mouth. A momentous noise exploded, though it was more like a sensation than a sound, when I thought about it later.

Quickly, I reached the bottom of the sand trough. What happened next can only be described as total chaos. To me it felt more like a whirlwind, like numerous camel feet stomping on me. I could roll this way or that way but could not get away from the leaden hairy legs. As sand flew, confusion reigned, and I was trapped.

I will always remember the giant camel's feet pressing down on me. Like the twirling wooden fish in your destiny, the feet became an image I could never shake off.

Under such circumstances, I knew, rolling was the only thing I could do. Luckily for me, I'd learned a kind of boxing with the camel drivers. It was popular in Liangzhou, with many moves dealing with rolling on the ground during a fight. Using all my energy and skill, I dodged feet that never stopped pounding.

It was a terrifying feeling to be under all those feet. It was a mystery where they all came from. I wondered if it was the false impression from fear or the never-ending sand hitting me in the face.

As the many feet came down and columns of sand struck, the mad camel cried constantly, as if outraged or overjoyed, sounding like a male camel enjoying mating, a full-throated voice, almost with a texture. In between crying, he panted heavily. I couldn't see his mouth, but I could tell it was drooling as he huffed and puffed.

For readers of your book, you can use an analogy to help them understand my situation. Imagine the camel as a soccer player dribbling—right, I was the soccer ball between his legs. But the mad camel would seem comical in such an image, even adorable. You do know that a soccer player appears nimble and agile as he dribbles, and the arching ball may look graceful as it glides in the sky. I was in dire straits at the time, in contrast, and the camel was bulky and clumsy, frenetic and wild, no hint of a soccer player's manner.

My rambling may turn you off, for normally a writer will gloss over details like this and quickly move on. They focus on story lines, while I want to tell you how I felt, for which no substitute is possible. People who haven't experienced being a soccer ball dribbled by a camel always complain about my long-winded description. But I want to ask you if you can, from my lengthy chatter, see the marks the situation left on my life.

You should know that the value of one's life is in one's experiences. What I went through in Wild Fox Ridge was a terror-filled nightmare, but without being tempered by it, I'd be an average man of Liangzhou. I'd lie on a heated *kang* with my wife and children, and slowly grow old. I probably would not be aware that I was aging, but I would be, turning into an old man and then into my grave.

I became the man I was later because of my experiences. I would experience many wondrous encounters in the years that followed, but it was in Wild Fox Ridge where my truly meaningful meditative practice began. And what I went through under the feet of that mad camel was an indispensable part of that.

I loved to think. I was one of those people you call a lay philosopher. You were right when you said my actions and experiences made up my worth. That's so true. I discovered that when later generations talked about me, they always focused on what I'd done, not caring at all about my appearance and personality, my family background, or my physique and body type. They enjoyed relating the things I did, how I gave myself up to save others, how I reached a certain realm, and so on. Yes, I did all of that, but they forget why. Without its days roasting in the magical brazier, the Monkey King would not have the occult eyes that let him tell good from evil. Likewise, the camel feet were the magical brazier of my life.

All the unhappiness later in my life was nothing compared with the perils in Wild Fox Ridge. The plum flowers wouldn't smell so fragrant without the wind and frost.

See what I mean?

So just keep listening to me.

2

Your heart became immune to the perils, no matter how treacherous they were, after experiencing them over and over.

At first, it felt like raging waves crashing on the shore, and I was scared witless. It was in fact one of those moments when mistakes can easily occur. If I wasn't careful, I could be pulped under his feet, but I managed to escape that. My belief in destiny started at that moment. I believed there was an unknown force helping me, an existence greater than human. I realized that I had no rational thinking at the time, and that everything I did was instinctive. Instincts that were beyond my ability to plan and control saved my life. Which was why I was convinced later that the instinct was the power of destiny; it pulled me out from under the feet and sent me to the offering table to be a kind of symbol.

Dying under a camel's feet or in one's bed are both deaths, but the latter results in a ghost, while the former creates a martyr. People treat a martyr with awe and admiration, no matter what religious sects they belonged to or what ideologies they adhere to, because he's their martyr, right or not. Martyr is a grand sounding term.

Destiny be thanked.

Slowly I recovered from my panic.

Then I found out that the safest spot was the camel's feet, not any place without them. One foot would not step on another foot. I didn't escape from the foot—if I had, I would probably be facing his teeth, which at the moment would not be grazing, but would bite me—but slipping under his feet was a wise move, when I think about it now.

I rolled toward one of his legs. He had to stand there, didn't he? He couldn't put his legs on his shoulders, could he? You see, such a simple concept, and I nearly paid for it with my life.

I felt safer, but only for a moment. The camel quickly realized he wasn't seeing results, so he stopped stomping and started digging. Don't underestimate the difference between the two. With the former the force reaches the size of its feet, while with the latter it lets the feet control a larger area. The space for my survival instantly narrowed. Worse yet, the digging feet raised so much sand that everything before my eyes was blurred. Sand hit me in the face, numbing it. Hei, the mad camel looked even more like a dribbling soccer player. I can talk with such levity now, but back then my life was in serious jeopardy.

I rolled for a while in the raging sandstorm. The camel nearly succeeded. His feet scraped against me and tore my clothes to shreds. As the situation looked increasingly grim, I had a brainstorm and rushed at one of his hind legs, like a monkey leaping for a big tree, except I didn't look as lithe.

It was still an instinctual move. Why hadn't I picked one of the front legs? I had no time to think. Later I realized that there would have been no more me if I'd done that. A front leg would have made it easier for the camel to bite or crush me, while the hind leg was harder, pretty much beyond his reach.

I felt as if I was gripping a massive power, not a camel's leg. The power picked me up and flung me into the air, and I nearly let go. The camel joggled his hind leg, like an impish mule pawing the ground. I held on tight to keep from flying off. It was a comical sight, now that I think about it. If I'd let go, I'd have shot out like a bullet, with two possible outcomes. One, I escape, and he would start chasing to kill again. Or I'd be dizzy when I landed and his foot could end my life. I didn't think about these at the time; I just held on as tightly as I could so I wouldn't fly off.

I was in the grip of a massive force, tossed and flung into the air and back to the ground. Luckily it was sand, not a hard surface, or I'd have been a bloody mess before long. I tried to adjust my position to face his body with feet on the ground so I could leap up as he flung me and touch the ground when he brought his foot down. But I couldn't. The powerful, almost demonic force had my body in its grip. On the surface, it might have looked like his leg was carrying me along, but I felt the visceral impact of being struck by a massive force. My chest was beaten numb and sore, and my head was buzzing, but I wasn't sure if it was the wind or a ringing in my ears.

The wind roared by, which meant the camel was lifting and dropping its leg at a relatively high speed. I was being hit not just by the leg but also by sand that strafed my face as the sandy ground spanked me. The pounding was intensified by the weight of the camel and my own body. My insides were churning like a roiling sea; I was nauseous, my chest hurt so much it felt like it could burst at any moment, and my hind quarters were slapped virtually into pieces. Yet my mind was clear and I knew he would begin to flag at some point. This was a fight of patience and stamina. From time to time, I heard Wooden Fish Girl call out, obviously an attempt to lure the camel away.

How long it lasted, I had no idea—actually, it continued deep in my soul for a long time after that. I kept having the same dream. I already told you that it became one of the most important images in my life. I often wondered why we can be carried away by a strong force and rise and fall along with it, in spite of ourselves. Moreover, the force we cannot control might come from a stupid animal. I'm not trying to be profound; that was really what I was thinking. You might understand me better if we replace the camel with our desires. Liangzhou people called chasing after desire "a mad dog trying to screw a wolf," which to me is a wise analogy.

Carried along by the beast, I bolted, leaped, jumped, and plunged. I was beyond dizzy and my head hurt, so nauseous I could die. A real nightmare.

Then I was abruptly flung out.

3

Like a stone launched from a slingshot, I flew into a sand trough. Rationally speaking, I didn't fly very high, because there was a limit to the camel's strength, but it seemed to me that I'd been tossed high into the air, for I could see the sky arcing before me and hear the wind whipping by. My mouth landed on the sand first, a terrible way to fall. At least I had my eyes shut, or I'd have had a hell of a time getting it out of my eyes. Landing mouth first meant the sandy ground punched me in the face. My nose ached, convincing me it was knocked crooked. Massive amounts of sand seemed to have flowed into my ears, where grain rubbed against grain cheerfully to create the sound of waves crashing on the shore. It was probably more like a flood of sperm rushing toward a womb, which is a repellent analogy, but it's all I can come up with. Nitpickers will say I didn't have that kind of scientific knowledge at the time, and yes, there was no expression like that. But just because there wasn't doesn't mean there can't be now. I know all about it now, when I'm telling you my story. You can also say my narration is my own creation, and yes, that is indeed the case. It took some time to learn that all lives in fact will eventually turn into memories and all memories can be created. We're constantly being recreated by our own memories, which absorb experiences we might not have had into our lives. Looked at from this perspective, life is but an illusion.

Aren't we living in an illusion now?

I had a dreamy feel at the time, and could not escape it despite the solid feeling when my head hit the sand. Maybe that's how I envision myself back then, or you can, at least, interpret it this way.

Still in an unreal state, I got up and saw the camel was soaking wet. He was obviously exhausted. I weighed over a hundred *jin*, so it had to be hard for him to toss me for so long. Yet it didn't seem to affect its deranged state, for he was walking toward me now, slowly, but with determination. Apparently, he wouldn't let me go. I wasn't sure why he hated me so much. Besides his mental problem, I must have given him unpleasant memories over many lifetimes. There must exist in his indestructible bindu substantial life memories; he could blame me for his many unhappy memories from fighting Chinese camels. Camels have a great memory that holds on to the good and bad memories for years. Like an elephant. We'd had disputes with the Mongolian caravan and fought them many times. I'm sure Brown Lion had taken part. Fights over water and grassland between people and between camels must have planted the seeds of hatred for the Chinese in the crevices of his memory. It was a deep-seated hate planted in his subconscious and continued into future lifetimes. In his current mental state, the hatred couldn't be erased.

Maybe that was why he kept attacking the Chinese camels.

He was charging me, unsteadily but with a vicious glint in his eyes. Baring his teeth, he was drooping and foaming at the mouth. The sweat poured down his body like rain—I even saw the scar from Lu Fuji's firearm. I knew he'd want to bite me now. He might have lost his mind, but not badly enough to treat me like a soccer ball again. He was drained of energy.

I wanted to run, but I knew I couldn't outrun the camel. Each time I took off, my feet sank into the sand, while the camel was fast on the sand, like a dragonfly flitting over the surface of water. I would barely take a few steps before his teeth would clamp down on my neck, a spot big enough to fill his mouth.

But I didn't want to stay and wait for death to claim me. Looking around me, I tried to find a good weapon, but not even an Artemisia plant was in sight—I couldn't have broken it off to use as a weapon even if I'd seen one. They were worse to handle than a mad camel if I didn't have an axe.

Wooden Fish Girl's face was ghostly white, but she ran over to stand next to me. It was a touching move. For that alone I could forgive all her faults, yes, all of them. That was why I chose her later. At the time, I didn't know my choice would bring her so much suffering.

What had just happened sapped all our energy.

. We lost our heads, I can see now. I could have dealt with the camel if we'd been calmer. His deranged behavior scared me witless. But in fact, a male camel is still a camel, though we treated him like a real lion. We could have overpowered him if we'd had something useful to hand. We could use the metal tube that was my firearm and smack him on the nose, like a camel hand lashing an ill-behaved camel. But neither of us was able to see the piece I'd destroyed.

I could only take off my shoes. I wasn't a camel hand, but grandpa had trained me with the same demands. My shoes were heavy, weighing at least five *jin*. They were made of cowhide, commonly found on the feet of camel hands. What we called heavy shoes, which were what we wore when we led a camel by the reins. We wore them all year round, which you can consider a form of martial arts training. These ugly, clunky shoes had given us extraordinarily strong legs. There were layers of leather and the side next to the skin was soft camel pelt. The outside was stiff cowhide that could be mended over and over until they nearly weighed a ton. As a bit of weight was added each time without us noticing it, our legs grew stronger in a similar fashion. A younger Feiqing had used the same method in his training. He'd carried a piglet out into the wild every day. It grew bigger each day. He had no trouble carrying it when it weighed four hundred *jin*. With prowess like that he was able to be the lead driver.

I held the shoe and waited for the camel to come at me. As if he could read my mind, he didn't charge and instead circled me, like a Bagua boxing master sparring with his opponent. Slowly, I calmed down and didn't feel the same fright now. I really had little to fear, after the crashing waves that I'd just gone through. It seemed to me that the camel had run out of tricks. If he stuck his head out at me, I told myself, I'd swing the shoe down on his nose.

We had reached a stalemate. We stared at each other, but neither made a move.

The problem was, his humps had enough stored energy to last him ten days or two weeks, while we were famished.

4

Soon I was dizzy with hunger. Wooden Fish Girl looked like she was about to pass out. We couldn't help it. As the saying goes, an empty sack can't stand upright. I lost count of the last time I'd had a decent meal.

I wished the drivers would come looking for us, but I knew they paid little attention to me. There were so many people in a caravan that one less driver was like missing a few flies in the toilet. No one would notice. Or maybe Feiqing would. He'd come looking for me if he needed to talk something over with me, but I knew there wasn't much to discuss. There was nothing but sand as far as the eye could see and there were only so many things that required our attention.

Later I learned that something was happening in everyone's life even at that moment. Trivial matters for some were of utmost importance to those experiencing them.

Compared with the imminent end of the world, triviality was negligible.

Too much chatter for your taste, right? If so, just tell me. A writer should know that chatter like this is a sort of digression that may not help move the narrative along, but is useful in character presentation. What do you say, pal? Only through my chatter can your readers understand me the way they could if they heard me speak.

A vivid portrayal of me in your pages is the product of my chatter, so stop glaring at me. You have no eyes, but I can see you giving me a dirty look. Heh-heh, that's not nice.

I could go on and on about my hunger, you know, but I've decided against it, because none of you is a stranger to the sensation. What you haven't experienced is being hungry while a formidable enemy was staring at you. It was very bad. As it dragged on, I saw the vast differences between a man and a camel. As hunger got the best of me, the camel looked to be perking up. It quickly recovered as the fat from its humps gave it a new and continued supply of energy. Its hump was still upright, which meant it could keep at it until I turned into a mummy.

Now I wasn't quite sure if Brown Lion was indeed crazy. He looked deranged, but he seemed too clever to be mad. He was as smart as me. Can there be a mad camel like that? I had wanted to ask him about it, but he never gave me a chance. Could you pose the question for me when you have the good karma to run into him?

We were truly exhausted. If he had attacked while we were losing focus, he'd surely have been able to bite through our necks. But oddly, he just stared at us with his crazed-looking eyes, but never lunged at us. My arms ached like hell when he looked like he was about to charge. I'd been holding the shoe ready to smack him in the nose but an hour had passed, and it felt like it weighed a ton. I let my arm droop but held the posture that I could swing the shoe up at any time. This worked to my advantage, because if he did charge, I could swing it up into his jaw.

Little by little, the shoe gained weight, fifty *jin*, five hundred *jin*. I could no longer feel its actual heft. I felt I was about to collapse. I was dizzy; I was passing out.

I was collapsing.

I was teetering.

I vaguely sensed that he'd charged . . .

Three. Yellow Demon

You don't have to thank me.

You hadn't expected me to save you after your drivers whipped me, did you?

I'd noticed the stalemate for some time already. In fact, I could have run over sooner, but I didn't want to. Why? I wanted to watch your performance. I wanted most to see the frightened look on Ma Zaibo's face, but I was disappointed. You were a frail scholar, Ma Zaibo, but you were also a real man.

I had to charge, not just to save you; I was saving myself too. Think about it. When people talk about Yellow Demon now, their favorite story is me rescuing Ma Zaibo, isn't it? They'd have forgotten me long ago if I hadn't.

Sure, they still remember how I kicked and maimed Brown Lion. I can't help that. You have to accept corresponding outcomes for what you do. The outcome is the reacting force of your action, naturally. Or to borrow the Young Master's words, an outcome is a force of karma, or retribution. Based on what he said, it's one of the principles of the universe: for every action, there's an equal and opposite reaction. I didn't discover that principle, of course; a man called Newton did that. Naturally, I had no idea who he was at the time. Now free of the shackles of the physical body, I've acquired a great many faculties. People call my kind of ability the "five magical powers": all-seeing eyes, all-hearing ears, mind-reading, past-life understanding, and supernatural feet. I've heard that all forms of life gain these powers when they are free from the confines of flesh and blood. I accumulated enough powers that, as expected, I came to understand principles of the Dharma realm.

Sure, I did many things humans consider terrible—if you think animals fighting is bad, that is—but also performed countless good deeds. That's why I'm complicated. I saved your life as well as others' lives. I'm a national hero among Chinese camels. The grassland would have belonged to the Mongolians long ago if I hadn't led the Chinese camels in fighting them, don't you agree?

What puzzles me is how in the world did Brown Lion become

Feitian. You people disdainfully call it Asura, the demigod, but it enjoys heavenly blessings with no heavenly virtues. I can't figure that out. Was it just the last thought it had before death? Yes, I did have worldly concerns, but that's what made me great. Just think what I would be if my heart was as hard as a rock when my friends suffered misfortunes.

What I wanted to say is, it wasn't for your sake that I saved your life. I would have done it, whether you whipped me or not. It was part of my instinctual nature. I did not expect that it would be reason enough for later generations to build a temple for me. I'm no Camel God. I'm just a ghost with superior strength, and I've done my best to help others. Maybe they made offerings to me because I was willing to help.

I have to admit that Brown Lion would have bitten you if I hadn't come along, but it's was hard to say if he would have gone for your necks, or maybe just nibble your lapels. Don't always think the worse of others, all right? This is just what I think now. Back then, I firmly believed he meant to kill you. He had a vicious glint in his eyes and murder on his mind. He could run like the wind, and was fearless and invincible. I was afraid of his crazy behavior too, just like people are scared of violent madmen, but I ran up anyway.

I pushed him away with my shoulder and then a huge fight broke out.

It might have been huge, but wasn't especially dangerous. Brown Lion had used up too much strength fighting you and was no longer my match. I meant its strength. It still looked deranged, though the spirit was willing, but the flesh was weak. I didn't have to shove very hard to move him on. I didn't have to use my special swift kick skill, and oddly, he didn't try to bite me. I was ready for him though. I'd made up my mind that if he tried to bite, I'd handle him the same way I dealt with Long Neck Goose—I need to make one thing perfectly clear: I did not mean to injure Long Neck Goose—but Brown Lion didn't make a move. He slunk off after I shoved him away.

Slunk away, with no grace at all.

Then I saw you slumped in the sand, covered in sweat. Wooden Fish Girl looked at me gratefully. I knew you wanted to say something, but you didn't. I sensed remorse. Did you regret not treating me better? I hope so. Only through repentance can people gain the possibility of being good. I saw remorse in your eyes.

The end of the world came just as you took hold of my reins.

Four. Chain Smoker

1

There were clear signs the day the world ended.

A heavenly drum sounded, and the millstone descended.

Didn't you hear the crashing sound? Look, blood was oozing out of the stone, bright red blood. There were human thighs and arms in the opening, accompanied by painful screams that seemed solid, both in liquid and gel forms, as they were mixed with flesh into the opening and overflowing with bloody water.

Brown Lion must have noticed it too, or he wouldn't have cried so sadly, I thought. He cried day in and day out, virtually nonstop, as if he wanted a young pretty female camel. He wasn't ready to mate; his nuts were ruined and he came across as listless. He'd looked like that for days until he suddenly started crying. Everyone thought that was weird, but to me it made sense. I could hear the anxiety in his voice, as if he were calling out: The end is near! The end is near! The world is about to plunge to its end. Yes, he was crying like that. I'm sure you know I understand camels all too well.

It was a horrible sound. Imagine a mournful sound loud enough to reach all corners of the earth and into the sky, imagine hearing it day and night. It would make you lose control of your bowels.

The first sign of the end was a giant black bear leaping into the sky from Wild Fox Ridge and, with one bite, chomping off the northwestern corner of the sky. Then it started drinking it; it was really drinking the sky. It opened its mouth wide and inhaled, and the sky turned into a liquid that flowed into its mouth. One mouthful after another, and it didn't take long to finish the sky.

Countless lightning bolts interwove the sky, countless demons and countless ghosts, all holding swords or spears, hollered everywhere. I heard the grinding noise of tens of thousands of millstones crashing against each other, so deafeningly loud it set my teeth on edge. I thought I was about to wet myself.

Chaos broke out among the camels. They had never seen anything like this, so they screamed, sounding like poles poking at my eardrums or pig bristles pricking my bladder. An unnamable sound that was neither human nor animal crescendoed deep in my soul, and an immense fear came over me. Yes, all these and many other things gave me the feeling that the world was indeed ending.

I was sure the camels were scared out of their minds too. Usually they lay down when gusty winds blew; never would they run around. But this time, oddly, some of them ran off. They cried as they ran, as if the wind was carrying a large wolfpack. I could see the wind was different this time. In the past I could always tell where it came from, east, west, north or south, but now it felt more like a gaping hole had opened up in the sky to suck in everything below. It was beyond weird.

Lu Fuji got the drivers to keep the camels in check. Some that were untethered had already run off like frightened donkeys and were soon black dots visible only when lightning flashed above them. Seeing them was hard enough, getting them back next to impossible. Luckily, they weren't carrying litters, I thought, so our loss would be minimal if they never came back. It was a habitual thought, which showed that deep down I didn't think our prospects were grim. I was even thinking about cargo and their value.

The black bear was finally done swallowing the sky, and yellow dust and sand followed. It looked like a sandstorm. Nothing terrible about that. I'd seen so many sandstorms, I nearly wet myself each time, but we made it through in the end, didn't we?

"The end is near. The end is here," someone shouted in the wind.

It sounded like Ma Zaibo or Wooden Fish Girl. I couldn't tell.

Brown Lion's cries rang loudly. After a prolonged silence, his voice pierced the curtain of sand. It was an unusual sound, slightly deranged, willful, wild, and brash, giving the camel the low roar of a lion, which was partially the reason for his moniker.

I was hoping he'd regain his sanity. I did like that camel, a superb stud animal who could breed and enhance a caravan's vitality. But I only heard his call; I couldn't tell where he was. It made me wonder if the end of the world had also brought his cries.

Feiqing came running over. I vaguely heard him shout,

"Get them together. Get them all back together."

It was a great idea, but the camels had gone off in all directions; we couldn't get them back at all, let alone get them back together. We'd be lucky if we could get the humans together and ride out the storm, I said to myself.

Several drivers were tugging at the reins with all their strength, while the camels reared their heads to struggle away, so the men pulled hard on the nose rings, a camel's most vulnerable spot. They normally would tear up when the ring was pulled, but now they swung their heads, fighting hard to break the reins.

Then I saw a sand wall heading my way. It looked as if the sand on the ground had somehow managed to stand up, or Wild Fox Ridge had learned to walk. Countless dark figures were twisting and screeching within the wall, like numerous wild boars feeding.

I ran toward the drivers. I yelled as I ran,

"Hold on to each other. Form a circle. Don't get blown away." I wasn't sure if they could hear me though.

Flowing sand was coming down when I got near them. I shouted for the camels to lie down, but Feiqing said they couldn't do that or the camels would be buried in the sand.

He was right.

"Let's go to the Hu Family Mill," he said, but the wind carried his words away. I knew what he meant.

I counted three camels and five humans. The others were no longer visible.

"Should we go look for them?" I asked.

"Go looking for them would be like looking for a tomb for ourselves now. We'll head over there first. I've sent a message out, telling them all to go to the Mill."

The sand wall was almost upon us now. I saw it was actually a powerful gust carrying a huge amount of sand, like a tornado. I was afraid the wind might sweep me up into the air. I'd heard of people being blown into the air.

"Hold on, hold on to each other," I shouted as I grabbed hold of a camel's neck. I closed my eyes and let the sand lash my face, which burned as if on fire. Someone grasped me, and another joined us. In between gusts of wind, I could hear the heavy, weighty breathing of the camels, which at this moment was most comforting.

The sky was gone. I couldn't open my eyes, but even if I could, I wouldn't have seen the sky. It had really been swallowed up by the black bear, which was in the process of gobbling us up. The flying sand was so dense, like torrential water, crashing into us. We couldn't lie down now, for we'd be immediately buried if we did.

"Don't forget to shake your bodies!" I yelled out. "Keep shaking. Don't stop."

It was a technique our elders had passed down to us.

They also gave us a song: "Wooden Fish Valley beneath Wild Fox Ridge/Wandering souls fill the nine ditches and eight ponds/Go look for the key at the Hu Family Mill."

Before he died, my father said so many camel hands had lost their lives at Wild Fox Ridge that I should go to the Hu Family Mill when I was in trouble.

"You should normally stay away from the Mill; go there only at critical moments," he added.

"When is a critical moment?" I asked.

"When the world is right under your eyes," he replied. What he meant was, when the world was near, the end of the world. What he said was popular among camel hands, and even now the song could still be heard in parts of Liangzhou.

That was why I'd never been to the Hu Family Mill. Many times I looked at it from a distance. I'd like to go there, but since our elders advised against it, they had their reasons. With certain things, it's better to keep a distance; when you're too close, its mysterious and awe commanding airs would be lost. It remained forever sacred in my heart precisely because I'd never been there. Whenever I thought of the end of the world, I'd comfort myself: Don't worry. There's always the Hu Family Mill.

2

I lost track of time and didn't know how long we were blocked by the sand wall. It was all a sensation; the end of the world was nothing but a feeling, like a dusty gray pall had separated me from everything else in the world. I wondered if that was how those who suffered severe depression felt. But I felt something else too, a great deal of tactile sensations that you couldn't understand without experiencing them, such as the flowing sand roiling around me, the pebbles shooting all over, strange screeches, in any case a cacophony of terror. Yet at the same time I sensed an immense silence. Everything froze, and my thoughts, my heartbeats, my world, and everything in my eyes seemed to be under a glass dome.

Time stopped.

Except for the colossal terror—in fact, I was terrified, but more than that too. I'd had a premonition that the end of the world was near. You probably know that premonitions sometimes are anticipation. I can't really say I was waiting for the end of the world, that's for sure. But you see, you'll spend your days waiting for the arrival when you know something is fated to come. Some often forget what they're waiting for as they wait, and these are fools. The wise men make sure the inevitable thing is first and foremost on their minds and examine it constantly. Heh-heh, you're often saying things like this yourself. I no longer have ears, but if I did, my ears would grow callused from hearing you. You have no idea I'm next to you when you say these things. There are others by you too, those you call non-humans. Heh-heh, non-humans? You people are the non-humans. We are the real humans.

Enough of that. Let me continue.

I didn't know how long we were trapped by the sand wall. We didn't dare move, until we felt the force of the powerful sand flow letting up. I knew it was just the beginning. It should be noon by then, but the sky was still in the bowels of the black bear. Who knew what was hidden in darkness like an iron chest. I knew the end of the world couldn't merely be a wall made of quicksand; there had to be more to come, and more frightening too.

As the shifting sand thinned out slightly, I took the drivers with me and headed to the Hu Family Mill. I couldn't see the lay of the land, but I could still feel it; traveling in the desert, one often relies on feelings. Feiqing had a compass, of course, to verify our sense of direction, though sometimes my senses were more accurate. When my senses didn't correspond to the direction pointed by the needle, I'd often go with my intuition. Later the drivers would see the compass was wrong and I was right. The needle always deviated when it encountered a magnetic hill or iron mine. My intuition only dulled when I met a woman who could turn my head. Heh-heh, and that happened only once in my life.

It was tough going on our way to the Hu Family Mill, like trudging in a marsh. I was ahead, leading Pretty Widow; a camel smarter than all the others, it followed me docilely while the other camels tossed their heads and flicked their ears. An animal is smart when it knows it's an animal, when it's aware that it can never outsmart humans. Then it will behave and follow orders. The others tried to struggle out of the human hands, away from the end of the world, but they couldn't outrun their fate. Some foolish camels had broken away, and I had no idea where they were now. I could predict their outcome in the storm: dying of thirst and hunger or of exhaustion, being blown into lakes, ramming into hard objects like poplars. They could not escape fate. Pretty Widow and a few of her camel friends stayed with us. She trusted humans, and her camel friends had faith in her. So I led Pretty Widow, Feiqing and Lu Fuji each led one, while the other drivers held onto camel tails. Like that, we groped our way in the curtain of darkness, feeling our way toward the Hu Family Mill we hoped to see.

The Mill was a distant light in the total darkness and became a symbol, like the Land of Ultimate Bliss to an old lady who practices Pure Land Buddhism. But in fact, so what if we got there? I couldn't ask that question. So many things should never be questioned; every time you do, it makes sense at first, but if you keep asking, all meaning will be lost when life is over, humans disappear, and the universe implodes. All I did was silently chant the ancient rhyme from our elders. They said there was a key, so there had to be one, I thought.

We had to find the Mill first.

Then a question occurred to me. I could sense my way to the Mill when all was dark around me, but what about the other drivers? How would they reach the Mill on their own? Feiqing had sent them a message, and they would surely want to get there, so how would they find it when darkness reigned?

A heavy sense of unease and sadness spread in my heart.

We'll get there first, and then I'll go back to find the others, I told myself.

I had to go find them, even though I had no idea where they might be. The compassionate thought was how I am who I am now.

I worried most about those drivers who tried to dodge the sandstorm by lying or crawling. They would already be on the way to the underworld if they'd followed the usual maneuver.

3

Don't ask me how long it took us to find the Mill. I don't know.

I already said that we had no sense of time. We were hungry, so we ate some beans, which we'd taken along as camel feed in case we found no good grazing ground. Lu Fuji had been farsighted enough to have brought along half a sack of beans and a pouch of water. The beans were raw and had the texture of uncooked noodles, but they were one of the nutritious grains, and, even raw, were high energy food. Without them and the water, we wouldn't have made it far, and if we'd stopped or chosen to give up, we wouldn't be where we are today—no, that doesn't sound right. When I think about it, whether we looked for the mill or not, we'd be who we are today—ghosts. The difference is, we wouldn't be the same ghosts. We'd have wound up differently if we hadn't done a bit more when we were alive, don't you think? Without the many things we did, Feiqing wouldn't be Feiqing and I wouldn't be me. The same goes for you. Wasn't it because of what we did that he found it worthwhile to interview us?

It's impossible to describe how hard it was looking for the Mill. Naturally, you can imagine us fighting drifting sand, a moving sand wall, a crashing sea of sand, not your average sandstorm. We weren't taking a leisurely stroll in the wind; we were struggling with Death, fleeing for our lives, fighting for our survival—I'm sure you can find all sorts of expressions to describe what we went through.

Our lungs hardened as we traveled in flowing sand. I fought for air as I moved my feet as fast as I could, while currents of sand lashed at my face. Under the assault of flying sand wheels, I knew my face would soon be raw, so I took off my sleeveless jacket to cover my face. I turned to tell the others to do the same, but the wind blew my words away the moment they left my mouth. I had to stop and shout toward where their ears might be.

"Don't worry. Just keep going," Feiqing appeared to shout. "I told everyone to press up against the camels' backs and bury their faces in the fur. Just keep going. Don't worry about us. We have the camels."

Now I felt better. I knew I was a lot like a man clearing a path in waist-deep snow. The others would have an easier time traveling once I opened up the road. With Pretty Widow I continued to feel the way forward. She was a superb white camel who lived up to her reputation, keeping calm at a time like this. I wasn't sure if I could control her if she fought to get free. I was beyond exhaustion, yet I knew that the Mill we were looking for was a dream. In such a perilous situation, we had to do something; it was up to me to take the lead. We couldn't just wait to die, could we? We were just completing a process in a way. I was moving forward, but I had no idea where my destination was. Hu Family Mill, where are you? My Hu Family Mill?

A driver fell. Feiqing tugged at my hand and shouted for me to stop. I knew it was not just exhaustion, but also despair, that brought him down. I felt the attack of despair constantly, but I knew I must not give in. They were younger than me and could afford to be despairing, but not me. They kept their eyes on me, with the confidence that I'd find the Mill. They believed in me. I'd made so many trips down this camel trail, and every time they talked about me, they'd say Chain Smoker has spent more than half of his life on Baosui Road. That's true; I have spent a greater part of my life on this road, and the soft pads on our camels' feet had worn down the stone by half a *chi*. But they didn't know it was my first encounter with the end of the world. I could only make them believe I could get them there. That was all.

We stopped and put the nearly paralyzed driver on the back of one of the camels. We couldn't leave him behind. If we must die, we'd die together. I told him to bury his head between the humps so the flying sand wouldn't chew up his face. I heard the camel's labored breathing. It was tired too, carrying our beans and water. I was certain it was also frightened. I knew oftentimes one's fears lead to exhaustion; or you might say it was our hearts we couldn't control. Heh-heh, I was unaware of this concept at the time.

I had the sensation I was walking not on the sand, but in it. It felt like water, and I was swimming. But the watery sand was sticky, making for hard going. Maybe you can imagine a fly swimming in honey. That's what it felt like. Except the fly tastes the sweetness of honey as it swims, while I had only fatigue and despair. I tell you, I lost hope later, though I did not show any sign of it.

We moved in the boundless darkness. We had no idea what direction we were traveling. A din of strange noises was all we heard. I could not tell if it was day or night. I did not know what strange things awaited us after this, nor did I know how long this would last. We ate a handful of beans when hungry and took a sip of water when thirsty. We'd used up so much energy that our bodies no longer belonged to us. I found that we seemed to be walking in place even when we thought we were moving. I knew, of course, that we escaped the fate of being buried alive by walking like that. When surging waves of sand cascaded down on us, we were like fallen leaves in a tempestuous sea. The topography changed as the sand under our feet changed. Our movements allowed us to keep walking on the flowing sand.

I didn't know how much time had passed when the camel carrying the driver collapsed. It shouldn't have, but it did. Fatigue was one reason, but I think it had reached the limits of its mental capacity. It gave up trying. Once your heart gives up, fatigue can crush you like Mount Tai. When it fell, the driver rolled off its back. "I don't want to go on," he said, "you can just leave me here."

We stopped and tried to get the camel back up on its feet. I knew it wouldn't take long for the sand to bury it. Lu Fuji jerked the reins over and over to drag it up. Aided by a flashing light—I don't know what to call it. Lightning? Didn't seem right. The sun? Not likely—I vaguely saw the camel stretching its legs out.

"Let it be then," I said to Feiqing. We put the slack body of the driver on Pretty Widow, along with the beans and water. She cried out once, but I wasn't sure what for.

On that night—was it nighttime? I didn't know. Maybe it was another sort of night—I experienced a lot, but the most unforgettable were, one, the camel died, from exhaustion. Did it foam at the mouth? It should have. Two, Big Mouth's face was churned into a bloody mess by the sand. I'd told him to cover his face with his vest, but he wouldn't listen. The rest shielded their faces with our clothes, which were shredded. I told everyone to walk behind the camel, while I explored the way with my sleeveless fox fur jacket. I led Pretty Widow. Behind her, the others took cover behind her to stay out of the assault by the sand-filled wind. Otherwise, their faces would have been chafed and bloodied.

Are you asking if we found the Mill?

I don't know what to tell you.

I can't say we didn't, but I can't tell you we did either. On the day the world ended, we did not find the buildings we'd imagined were out there, but we managed to survive because of our search. We'd have been buried in the sand if we hadn't tried to find it. We looked and looked and we lived. If we hadn't made up our mind to find the Hu Family Mill, we could have tried but failed to escape the sandstorm. If we'd stayed in one spot somewhere, we'd now be buried in sand. We were saved by our determined search.

As the sky slowly lightened, I saw that everything around us was different, all re-sculpted by the sand.

I saw a new sand hill off in the distance. On it a stone mill hung high atop a poplar, on which Wooden Fish Girl and Ma Zaibo, one in front of the other, were leading a camel in circles.

The drivers all leave after the interview except for Wooden Fish Papa. He continues to look at me in his sorrowful way. I hear him sigh.

"Do you have something to say to me, Grandpa?"

He looks around before pointing at the water.

"Don't drink the water."

"Why?"

"Just don't drink it. It's water from the underworld. If you drink any more, you'll never be able to leave here."

I break out a cold sweat in fright, and it dawns on me that I haven't seen the sun for a long time.

"How about now, can I still leave?"

"You still have a chance. But you must promise to do something for me when you're out."

"Sure. I can do that."

"Do you remember the white stone at Fairy Blockade, the one Wooden Fish Girl mentioned?'

"I do."

"I dug a hole under it. In it is a wooden box containing several valuable wooden fish song books. I want you to find them. They're the only copies. When you find them, I'd like you to have wood blocks cut so they can be widely distributed."

"There's no need to do wood blocks now. They can easily be reproduced."

"That's fine too. Just don't let them be buried by time. They've been on my mind all these years." He added, "I sensed something terrible was about to happen, so I buried them, but the fire started before I had time to tell my daughter."

"I'll find them."

"Don't wait any longer, and don't drink the water. If you want to leave, all you have to do is fire a few shots and you'll be out. But the specters won't come back if you do that, because they fear the smell of gunpowder."

"I appreciate your concern, but I have to finish my interviews," I tell him.

"At a time like this you're still thinking about interviews?" He sighs and shakes his head.

"I don't have to drink the water, but I must see them."

He heaves a long sigh, shakes his head, and drifts off into the night.

The faint howl of a wolf sounds from somewhere.

Twenty-fifth Session
Setting Out

I take Wooden Fish Papa's advice and stop drinking the underworld water.

I remember the way to shake off its power over me: fire my musket.

I know about that. My father once told me a story when I was a child: one day someone came to hire a drama troupe in our hometown. They'd agreed on performing a lyrical play, not a martial one. On the third day one of the performers noticed in the audience his late wife and knew right away that the spectators were all ghosts. So he switched to "Sun Wu's Soldiers Fire Cannons," and lit off some gunpowder. Members of the audience vanished on the spot, and he realized they were performing in a graveyard—all ghosts fear burning gunpowder.

But I don't want to fire any shots. I don't want to harm my friends.

I eat one of the cistanches that the white camel found and brought back. I don't know where he found it, but it's wonderful. I'd like to go there, but I want to continue the interviews. I've decided that I'll ride the white camel there once the interviews are over.

Ma Zaibo is the narrator on this night.

I can tell that the story is coming to an end.

1

I'd like to continue with my story.

I was in the Hu Family Mill, but I failed to locate the wooden fish incantation. Everything in there looked like it but none of it was.

I didn't know what it was, still don't.

I don't understand why the ancestors passed down a story about the wooden fish incantation, saying that the key in "getting the key under the Hu Family Mill" is itself the incantation. But what it truly represents, I do not know.

Wooden Fish Girl said she'd found it, but it was what she thought it was, and I wasn't sure if it was the same one mentioned by the ancestors. I thought I found it too, but it was hard to say whether anyone would accept my version.

Some brothers asked me if they hadn't kidnapped the baby, if I'd still have joined the society, if I'd still have traded the camel field for gold, if I'd still have gone to Luocha to buy firearms, and if I'd still have entered Wild Fox Ridge.

"No!" I replied. Everyone knew you could lose your head when you joined the Society of Brothers. Who wants to lose his head?

Over the month after the kidnapping, I had a string of visitors, all forcing me to join by threatening to kill the baby. I didn't agree at first, of course, since I'd always been opposed to tongs and societies. Even now I'm not convinced that what you did actually meant anything. Sure, you overthrew the Qing and toppled the Manchus, but I didn't see you bring peace and prosperity. I knew the Qing government was bad for the people, but what happened over the next hundred years after your successful attempt? The Qing perished, replaced by the Republic. Then foreign invaders came, followed by troubled times, brothers killing brothers until blood flowed like a river, and after that, famine, struggle sessions. I didn't see many peaceful days. Wouldn't you too want to know the meaning of your earlier uprising?

When I saw through that, I decided to become a monk. Revolution did not interest me. But my father wouldn't let me do that, so I had to find something else. I worked on the wooden fish songs, simply as a way of alleviating my boredom.

I hadn't expected you to threaten me with the baby's life. I had no choice but to agree. I joined the Society and followed your rules. You made me a branch head, the equivalent of an advisor, but I knew you had your eyes on my family's wealth. You needed money. After suffering a resounding defeat, you wanted to buy firearms, which you planned to use to revolutionize the Qing court.

You achieved your goal, of course.

You threatened me with my son, but I didn't know what you used on my father. Maybe the same ruse, threatening him with his son's life? At the time, I was unaware of what you'd done in Lingnan. You said the end justified the means, and all I could do was laugh a bitter laugh.

You really didn't have to do that. When General Zuo Zongtang launched his western expedition, he came straight to us and asked for a hundred thousand in silver for military provisions. We gave it to him, didn't we? Likewise, you could have asked, in a more forceful way, and we'd have complied. It was dishonorable, even immoral, to use a baby as ransom, among other things. Heh-heh, but now, after so many years, it just feels ridiculous to talk about them, no matter how dishonorable your methods were. I'm no longer angry at you.

Yes, no one is angry now that we're in Wild Fox Ridge.

Everything feels like a stage play here.

2

We quickly got enough gold together, then sold two camel fields and opened a few silver chests to make up the total. You didn't say where you were going; you covered up your destination with various excuses, throwing a smoke screen over the whole endeavor. When you think about it now, you have to agree that all your careful, cunning plans amounted to nothing, and you failed to escape your destiny. I once heard the expression, "God laughs when humans start thinking." What an apt description. Even I, let alone God, laugh when I think about it.

After all the scheming, finally the caravan set out. At the time, you naturally did not know you were heading into a dead end. You could put one over on me, but not on Wild Fox Ridge; you might also be able to muddle your way through Wild Fox Ridge, but you couldn't fool your destiny. You set off toward the predestined end of your lives in high spirits. You could struggle over and over, but all your struggles were just that, struggles. An ant on the spinning millstone, you could twist and turn all you wanted, but you couldn't stop the stone from turning.

Isn't that right?

Think about it. Weren't your high spirits back then quite vapid?

On that day no one would be thinking about the end of the world.

Winter approached, but that didn't dampen the festive atmosphere. All branches of the Society of Brothers in the northwest's five provinces sent representatives, who brought along gold. They needed firearms too. They had a different status, a legitimate one, which helped cover up their true intent. At the time, I was in the dark about the larger background story of your actions.

Hu Gala was the Qilian Hall's master, also called "Master Zuoxiang," a secret status, of course. In public he was a Daoist master. Before the caravan left, he came to see us off in his usual capacity as Daoist master, reciting well-wishing sutras and offering auspicious words. He wore his robe, burned incense, and presented the offerings. There were several types of offerings, mostly rare objects brought over by the camel hands, such as walnuts, peanuts and wrapped hard candies.

Ma Siye came, representing all the owners. As a county magistrate in Xinjiang, Ma Siye had been kind, never a bully. When his term was over, he returned to Liangzhou with his family and their belongings. As they passed through a rocky gobi, an outlaw appeared out of nowhere and took those belongings. He was about kill the family, but when he asked their name, Ma Siye told him, and the man dropped to his knees and banged his head on the ground, saying he had once been wrongfully accused of a crime, and that Ma Siye, who presided over his case, gave a fair judgement. Ma Siye fully understood the principle of retribution, so he became a devout Buddhist.

Each time the caravan left, he'd tell the drivers the same story and exhort them to be good, stressing a good deed will be repaid with good.

Picking up a few pieces of yellow spirit paper, he burned them as he prayed: I hope all the Bodhisattvas and Guardian Deities will protect the caravan and ensure their safety. When thieves try to rob them, they will lose their way, when wolves come to attack, their mouths will be sealed. May there be neither disputes nor unhappy arguments, may calamity be averted and misfortune turned into blessing.

Custom required that the caravan owners give their men the gift of a large castrated ram, to be slaughtered when the caravan stopped to cook their first meal on the road. It would be offered to the Camel God, the Kitchen God, and the Earth God. The rite would be performed with only a few words, such as: Camel Deity, please come for your sacrifice! Then liquor would be poured into the ram's ear and, if the ram shuddered, it meant the Deities got their share. It would then be slaughtered, the meat would be cooked, and the camel hands would all have some. They ate the innards too, couldn't toss them away. When they washed them, they had to be careful not to scrape against the black skin of the intestines. If it was, odd events would take place along the way, and whatever happened would cost money, greatly diminishing the profits from the trip.

The black part of the intestines was not scraped this time, but strange things still occurred later. We followed the rules, yet they failed to save the caravan. The rules were like a drop of water, while destiny was a raging fire, isn't that right?

Similarly, I followed the custom of going to Su Wu Temple to fill a bottle of water from its spring on the morning of our departure. Like all the ancestors of Liangzhou residents, Su Wu was a man when alive, but a deity after he died. Each time before leaving, we got a bottle of water there. It was said to be auspicious water that could ward off a drought, strengthen the weak, purify filth, and reverse ill-fortune. But that was a tale. During the Great Han dynasty, our ancestors had tormented old man Su, forcing him to eat sheep's wool and drink snow, and now he was a deity to us. I've always wondered if he would actually help his enemy's offspring.

But I got some water anyway, because it was our custom. What's custom if nothing but a group of small-minded people. You can despise but never provoke them.

The goods were put in litters. I heard they were tea leaves. Of course, there would be tea, and mostly from our family, which was world-renowned. The producers had hills specially designated for tea plants, a special frying method, and a unique formula, which was now lost. I was told the formula included eight Chinese herbs. Which eight? I have no idea. There were other goods too, besides tea, all packed up. I heard they were local special products, but only the owners knew about them. You'd be visited by major disasters if you knew something you shouldn't know. I didn't care to know. All I knew was we were going to a faraway place, but I had no idea how far. We'd be heading north, all the way north, but to where? I didn't know, and didn't want to know. I might have bowed out had I known our destination. I wasn't planning on leaving my bones in the desert.

Besides the tea and other packaged goods, we also took women along. We shouldn't have, according to custom, because, you know, women are bad luck. Camel hands always left their women behind. Every man had a woman, but none of their women came with a caravan. It was our custom. Sometimes custom could be religious discipline, without which there would be no concentration, and without that there would be no wisdom. You know more about this than me, I'm sure.

Women are bad luck, so camel hands never brought any along, but if the women were a kind of goods, then they were allowed. Camel caravans, like your motor vehicles today, could take passengers along, but for a much higher fee. Goods had no life, while passengers were living people, and all living beings can die, so they required special care on the road.

There were many stories about Wooden Fish Girl, and few of us knew which was true. The versions were so disparate; in one she was an immortal, in another she was an ordinary woman; she could be an official, or she could be a commoner. All seemed to be totally different people, but turned into one because of these stories.

Some camel hands were against taking women along on this trip, but I told Hu Gala to convince them to have Wooden Fish Girl with us, claiming she and Big Mouth, Zhang Yaole, would be in charge of the sheep. Hu Gala found a few more reasons, though you know they were pretexts, something the world never lacks. No one raised any objection when Hu said to take her. I was happy, of course, but I didn't know she'd have found a way to come along even if I hadn't tried.

Hu Gala left looking fully human, a Daoist master. He couldn't have imagined one day he would be beheaded by the county magistrate, when his identity as the head of the Society of Brothers was exposed. But that happened later. When the caravan left, he was still Master Hu in both the secular and religious ways. But I think he knew it too; the end of the world he'd divined was actually the end of his own life. Or, you can call it the end of an era, for sure.

Listen to me. I'm so muddled-headed I'm losing my train thought. Heh-heh, or you could say I have no more differentiating mind.

We had two large wooden crates to carry the yellow goods, and they were very heavy. We didn't say what they were and no one asked. I think you know the camel hands were taciturn, their greatest asset. We said it was paraphernalia for shadow plays, gifts to our friends. Everyone knew that shadow play puppets were made of donkey skin and could weigh a ton when there were a lot of them—but that was just what we told everyone.

Have you ever ridden a camel? You have? Oh, good. Those who haven't think riding a camel is like sitting in a car, soft and comfy in between the two humps. Yes, it is soft and comfy, but that's when you first get on. It will no longer be comfy if you ride for a day, two days, or ten days. You'll feel as if all your bones have been shaken loose. The worst is your hind quarters, your tail bone will surely be shattered. Yes, it will be. So for long distance travel, we put two large crates on an oversized litter, one on each side of the camel's back. And that's where a rider sat.

Wooden Fish Girl sat in a wooden box—Big Mouth took care of the sheep when we were on the road, she herded them once we stopped—and the other carried my sutras and various Buddhist paraphernalia.

I sat in a camel sedan. Have you seen one? It's like a common sedan chair, but with two long, springy poles. One end is placed on the camel litter in front and the other end on the litter in the back. It bounces up and down as the camel walks.

There were quite a few people in the caravan. You've met them.

A fire was set in the afternoon, a must each time a caravan left. It was meant to drive away anything filthy and bring good luck. Camel hands all knew a burning opened the door to riches. If you dreamed about a big fire, you'd be rich even if you didn't want to be. When your luck was with you, the dirt clod that turned up next to your foot could be a gold nugget. We had to light a big fire.

It burned for a long time, roaring and crackling. I was used to observing signs for the future in a fire. I watched the flame tips before we left each time. Don't underestimate a fire. This one was like every other one, but its shapes went through countless transformations. Sometimes it was a tiger's head, at other times it was a dragon's tail; sometimes it was smoky, sometimes it crackled loudly. Each shape foresaw something different. This time thick plumes of smoke flowed out of the fire, so thick that the tips were invisible. I saw Hu Gala's expression change, but no one uttered anything inauspicious. He poked the pyre with a wooden stick and the fire rose up, hurling dark ashes all around.

This doesn't look too good, I said to myself. I stopped myself from thinking more about it, no matter how unlucky it appeared. I was worried that thinking about it would bring even worse misfortune.

3

Camel hands were mostly from the village, and their women came to see them off.

In those days the men would be away for half a year, but no one was allowed to cry. You know women's tears are unlucky, so it was a taboo when the caravan set out. They were all smiles; tears actually welled up in their eyes, but they strained to keep smiling. These were really good women. No one could say for sure that the camel hands' wives were all chaste and faithful, but that wasn't far from the truth. They lived their lives in committed fashion and none was said to have any affairs. If a man tried to seduce one of them, he'd hear her say, "I can't do things like that. It would disgrace him."

Women all knew that doing something like that was flinging excrement into their husband's face.

After the men left, the women stayed home to take care of the old and raise the young. The men left them with the capital to keep house. What capital? Four *jin* of cotton. Over the six months their men were away, the cotton would support the whole family. The women toiled away in the field in the day, at night they worked a spinning wheel to turn the cotton into yarn, which they used on a loom to weave into fabric. Then on sunny days they borrowed a donkey to take the fabric into the mountains a hundred *li* away to trade for food. Some of that was traded for cotton that would again be turned into fabric. Back and forth a few times later the money from the four *jin* of cotton would fetch eight *jin* of cotton. And on and on they went, spinning, weaving, and trading. When their husbands returned half a year later, their baby hadn't starved to death, had instead grown taller and bigger.

And that was the wife of a camel hand.

With my own eyes I'd seen the lithe, young body of a camel hand's pretty wife slowly become wrinkled and wizened after years of such hardship. A loom was hard on the weaver, like a mill that ages a person, just grinds her down. All these good women grow old amid the sounds of a loom shuttle, but they have no regrets or complaints. You may not know this, but camel hands were the most capable men in the village. They travel all over the place and gain extensive experience, and they bring home all sorts of rare objects that make other village women jealous. The camel hands were strong, or they could not handle the litters. It was every village girl's dream to marry one of them. After putting up with the months of the men's absence, they get their husbands back and can lean against the men and listen to them talk about the hardships on the road, or about their visits to an opera theater in the capital city. The best seats at the theater cost a solid silver piece, but no one was too cheap to splurge on the comfort, however briefly it lasted.

"You're such a big spender. You had a good time while your wife and child suffered," she might chide him. And he would chuckle. All the camel hands had seen Peking opera; like the tough journey on camel trails, going to the opera was a badge of honor in a camel hand's life. When village children had an argument, one would say, "My papa has seen the opera. Yours hasn't. All he has is a few stinking coins."

At moments like this, the camel hand's wife would look at her husband and smile.

4

We survived the sandstorm, but failed to escape our destiny.

As to what happened to Feiqing later, I heard only rumors. I heard he went to the south, met Sun Yat-sen, joined the Revolutionary Alliance, and became a revolutionary. I couldn't verify any of this, however. You do know that I was only a nominal branch head in their group.

I often thought about his head hanging on the city gate.

Many of us had learned about his arrest. I heard he'd sneaked back home that day. Why did he do that? Rumors abound. Some say he sneaked back to Liangzhou to start a new uprising after the successful one in Wuchang. Some said he came home because he thought the Qing was done for and no one would be investigating his crime against the police—in any case, he came home.

He was oblivious of a pair of eyes watching him.

Whose eyes?

Right, Huozi.

Huozi had been waiting for an opportunity to take care of Feiqing.

Now he found that opportunity.

He knew that Feiqing had a fast horse and, once he was in the saddle, he could gallop away as if he'd sprouted wings. So Huozi came up with a scheme; like an expert hunter, he would find his prey's habits.

With Feiqing, there were two, painting and chess.

He was a fanatical chess player.

Huozi found a chess master from Hexi Fortress to play with Feiqing. They played game after game and Feiqing couldn't stop, as Liu Huzi's cavalry surrounded his house.

The one called Li Tesheng—he and Feiqing were like brothers—walked in and bowed to Feiqing. When Feiqing returned the bow, the man grabbed his queue.

That was pretty much what happened. What I wanted to say was, Feiqing's real enemy wasn't the Qing court, but a petty man in Liangzhou. Remember, anyone who got punished by the government, no matter where he was, it was usually because he had antagonized a small-minded man, except for those who commit heinous crimes. A great many men's calamities were in fact orchestrated by petty men.

Feiqing was too talented, too flashy, too accomplished, too wealthy. If he didn't die, then who would?

Later, when I looked back, I thought someone like him could actually die in many different manners. If he'd lived long enough to be present during the revolution decades later, he would not have survived. He would not have easily given up and let people take his land, so he'd have been shot as a despotic landlord.

Quite a few landlords were executed then.

I'm being driven mad by thirst.

After I stopped drinking the water, I feel thirst in every one of my cells. I chew on cistanches, but that never slackens my thirst.

The drivers hold up the water and tell me to take a sip. They are genuinely concerned about my thirst, but maybe they are unaware that I would remain in their world forever if I had too much.

"Come have some water. Don't worry," they call out earnestly. Now I see they do know about the threat of the water to me.

Like Tripitaka, who refused the advances by the Queen of Xiliang, I turn down the water they offer me. I even give them an angry look to show my determination not to drink. They go off disappointedly. It makes me feel miserable to see the look on their faces. They really want me to stay, which can only mean they accepted me from the beginning. They hope I'll stay to help them through the lonely nights ahead. On my part, I know I'd have to stay to be one of them, even if I turn down their water when I can't find water that is safe to drink. Strangely though, the idea of "staying" doesn't scare me.

It suddenly turns colder that night. A northern wind blows and never lets up. I wish it would snow. There have been a few flurries, but no real snowfall. My water problem would be solved if there were a big snowfall. I pray to all the deities I can think of.

I light a big fire that night.

And snowflakes start to fall, whether on account of my prayer or something else, I can't tell.

It's snowing heavier and heavier as time goes by. The flakes are the size of goose feathers. I bring out containers to catch the snow in a sand trough. I'd like to stay up and watch it, the prettiest scene in the world at that moment, but I'm too tired to keep my eyes open.

I stay by the fire to wait for the sand to warm up before making a Tartar kang. I'm fast asleep before I feel the toasty warmth from the sand.

Twenty-sixth Session
Wooden Fish Incantation

The sand beneath me is still warm when I wake up in the morning.

I open my eyes and see snow over my fur coat and sleeping bag. The snow hasn't melted, and the coat is dry.

I'm covered in snow, all but my nostrils. A few shakes remove the snow from the coat and the sleeping bag, so I can get up. Everywhere I see is white. The tent has collapsed under the weight of the snow. The sky seems laden with clouds, and the northern wind continues to howl. My white camel is lying in a sand trough, also under a blanket of snow. The yellow camel puts his head under the white one's chin hair, a warm spot. I would have slept there if I hadn't made a Tartar kang, which meant I could do without the shelter of the chin hair.

Snow everywhere. I can see it's a heavy snowfall, something I haven't seen for some time. We used to have heavy snowfalls, but we've rarely had one in recent years.

The clouds hang low and blend in with the distant sand dunes. I pick up a branch to dig a hole in the dune, set up my pot, light a fire, and pour some snow into the pot. Soon I hear sizzling noise, the most beautiful sound in the world.

I thank the heavens for giving me the water of life.

One. Wooden Fish Girl

1

How I felt about the oncoming sandstorm remained a bad dream for me for a very long time. It felt like I was being assaulted by countless mad camels; sand flew, rocks skittered, and darkness reigned between heaven and earth. As currents of sand surged, sound waves crackled; beyond the sand, there was an indescribable terror—no, not just terror. The sword of death danced over my head, and terror was inadequate in describing what I felt at the time.

Ma Zaibo led Yellow Demon—I was so grateful he stayed with us even under the circumstances—and I held Ma's hand, like grasping a life-saving straw. The warmth from his hand was somewhat comforting, while a voice warned me: The end of the world is here! The end has come! Everything needs to be concluded.

The tablet against my chest turned hot; the voice was coming from there. Over those few days, the tablet grew hot over and over, which convinced me that it was where the souls of my family resided. At certain moments—an opportunity to kill, of course—it turned scalding hot, even giving me a throbbing sensation, like a single—no, like many—hearts pounding at the same time.

It was thumping now. I could tell it sensed that this may be the last chance. Were they thinking they'd never see deliverance if Ma Zaibo escaped or died before the world ended, I wondered.

Were they worried?

They must have been.

I was worried too, actually. To me the end was truly here, and I didn't believe I could make it out alive, of course—no, even now I'm not sure that I did make it out of Wild Fox Ridge. I'm trying to act like a profound thinker. It really feels that way to me.

The knife was in my hand.

I kept it all this time. It stayed with the tablet; they got along well, coexisting in peace. The knife was a sort of protection for the tablet, while the tablet waited for the knife's participation. I'm sure you can understand my ancestors' eagerness. In the eyes of a person with attachments, deliverance has its conditions. Naturally, they didn't know it was that stubborn streak that kept them in the form of wronged ghosts all these years. You know, their souls would be delivered immediately once they dropped their obstinacy. But there is nothing harder to give up.

I didn't understand that until later.

Ma Zaibo walked ahead of me. His palm was sweating, a sensation that continued to ferment in my life. It may have been insignificant, but it represented a measure of power, which you can understand as the power of love, which expressed itself through the sweaty palm. In addition, there was another force, the force to kill him, which was conveyed through a burning tablet that felt like a thudding heart. The two were both powerful, and it was hard to tell which one was stronger. The force to kill got the upper hand, only by using the end of the world as its rationale—he would die anyway, so it made little difference if he died a few hours earlier or later.

Which was why I clutched the knife tightly when I thought the world was really about to end.

2

We found the Hu Family Mill.

At the time that had to be considered a miracle.

Imagine, when it was dark all around and sand flowed like torrents, we were two fish swimming in an inky ocean—or like headless flies—

a boundless, black ocean, and were able to find a tiny cave, so tiny it was hardly worthy of the name. Can you see how hard it was? I even thought it was the result of Ma Zaibo's religious practice. Maybe he did have a supernatural sense or some magical power—if so, were you aware that a knife was waiting right behind you? Could you feel the complex emotions in the heart of a killer?

I forgot that Yellow Demon was the real guide. Camels have an extraordinary ability to tell directions even in the midst of a sandstorm. Ma had come to the Mill on the camel's back, so it remembered the route, of course.

We walked in and he closed the door, shutting the world out. He groped around to find a candle and lit it—I had no idea where he found it. The place was immediately infused with light. I saw it was a yellow candle—heh-heh, another yellow candle.

Everything in the Mill came into view. Sandy pebbles continued to pelt the roof, reminding us of the rumored end of the world. But I felt a sense of warmth, for this was a house, after all, and there was light— what a wonderful word—light.

I saw Ma's handsome face as he looked at me. I found the way he held the candle very attractive, but he maintained his usual aloofness. Sometimes I found that look off-putting and wished he'd act up a bit. On the other hand, I was always charmed by that look. I had to agree with people who said women can be contemptible. Big Mouth had been so good to me and yet I found him inadequate, while Ma treated me with indifference—even when he was passionate, there was still a barrier between us, especially compared with Big Mouth.

"The end is here," I said.

"The end of the world, or the end of me?"

"Both."

Now I knew he had been aware of my plan all along.

"Will you hate me?" I asked.

"No," he said after a brief silence.

"Why?"

"What needs to be repaid must be repaid. When the times comes, it has to be done, whether it was owed by the ancestors or by me."

"You admit it's a debt?" I asked.

"Of course. It's a debt whether my father did it or not."

"Why?"

"Because my ancestors did help out with military provisions. It was immoral however it was used. They talked about it with relish for years, and even their attitude was immoral. Everything immoral incurs retribution, and I'm willing to be the one to receive it."

I saw something else in him. I'd been to churches before, and I saw the same thing on the man hanging on a cross. It was a terrible thought, for it always dissolved the hate in my head. I shook my head to chase it away.

"Actually, I wanted nothing to do with this, but I came. Do you know why?"

"Why?"

"I knew we wouldn't make it to Luocha. I didn't want to trade the gold for killing instruments. And what you did has helped me fulfill my wish."

"Why?"

"I saw you do something before the caravan set out."

"What did I do?"

"You sent a message to Sha Meihu. I noticed early on that he had been following the caravan. I didn't want to find out why, but I didn't want to go against your plan so long as it could help me get what I wanted."

"Then why did you enter Wild Fox Ridge?"

"To look for the Mill. You can't see it without coming here."

"You saw it, and it's time for you to die."

"Dying like this is a birth from a different perspective, don't you think?"

3

An immense silence pressed down on me. The tablet was pounding like mad against my chest, burning hot, as if it knew a feeling was destroying its hope. I gripped the knife in its scabbard so tightly my hand was sweating. Even the knife felt hot.

I felt like I was in a bad dream, like mired in mud that pushed and squeezed my chest. I no longer heard the sandstorm outside. I believed the end of the world was near, but it was different from what I'd thought. To me the sandstorm wasn't the end; it had to be something else. Later I learned that there was indeed another kind; I just didn't know that what I'd presaged was the end of an era. It would take me time to see that.

From the candle, a yellow light danced and cast a giant shadow on the wall, Ma Zaibo's shadow. I couldn't see mine. It must have run off without me.

Worried that my resolve would shake, I clenched my teeth and unsheathed the knife. My palm was sweaty, and cold. I wasn't a professional killer. I could sound and imagine myself ruthless, but I couldn't do it when I was facing a living person. In my imagination, I'd plunged the knife into his chest countless times, and now I must carry it out in real life. I'd rehearsed it for years, and it was now time to actually do it. My ancestors' souls were dancing in a frenzy on the tablet. Were they celebrating or were they worried? I still felt the burning sensation, and the throbbing.

He turned around. With his back to me, I couldn't see his expression, but I knew it would be the same indifferent look. He wouldn't run—it was pointless to run, of course. I hadn't been as diligent in martial arts training since we entered Wild Fox Ridge, but I was still very good; it would be as easy as flipping my hand to deal with someone like Ma Zaibo, with his genteel upbringing. The thought incited pity in me. I feared people stronger than me, people like Lü Erye's personal maid, the thought of whom filled me with trepidation—to me she was demonic—but I couldn't bring myself to use violence on someone weaker. He had baby-like qualities about him, pure and clean, and I wasn't sure I could bring the knife down on him.

He stood there quietly, motionlessly. I closed my eyes so I wouldn't see his back. During the time I spent in Su Wu Temple, I always felt a warm current when I saw his back. Now the intensity of warmth had lessened, but its lingering effect continued to ripple in my heart. After all, this was the man I'd loved—no, not loved, love. Since we were in Wild Fox Ridge, I'd been pushing an emotion, the proverbial ball, down to bury it at the bottom of my heart. I forced myself to think hateful thoughts and produced countless reasons to hate him. I wanted to be absolutely cold-hearted and tough, as I waited for the right moment—such as the end of the world—to plunge the knife of hate into the enemy's chest—was he my enemy?

Was he my enemy?

Yes, he was Lü Erye's son.

But he was the man I loved most. After he appeared, the formerly charming Big Mouth turned ugly, and my hardened heart softened. With his presence, the West was no longer desolate, and my life gained a different meaning—something that transcended hate. Similarly, he had added color to the trip to Wild Fox Ridge—don't be deceived by the language I used. Yes, I was watching with the eyes of a killer; what I'd told you before came from thoughts I forced upon myself. In essence, it was no different from a woman who is deeply in love calling her beloved "a man who should die a thousand deaths."

How could I kill him at this moment?

How do you think I could kill him?

The tablet was burning hotter and hotter, leaping like a frog on fire.

I wanted, when the end came, to lie my head against his chest and die with him. But I had to offer his blood as sacrifice to the burning tablet.

A massive silence pounded violently at my heart.

4

He turned around. Under the yellow candlelight his face had its usual aloofness.

"Don't hesitate. I really do want to pay back the debt. What needs to be settled must be settled," he said coolly.

I remained silent. I didn't know what to say as I looked at the face I loved and hated—though I'd worked on the hatred.

"Besides, the end of the world is near. We don't have long to live even if you don't do it," he added.

Still I remained silent.

"An accomplished monk told his disciples just before he reached nirvana to sprinkle his ashes at an intersection for carts and horses to run over. They didn't follow his instruction and instead built a pagoda to offer their respect. So he showed up in one disciple's dream and screamed at them, telling him he would have been liberated had they done what he wanted. And all his debts would be repaid in this lifetime. Now he has to start all over because of their disregard for his wish, and endure the trampling of carts and horses for another lifetime."

"I was that monk. I must take what I need to endure. I don't want it to drag on to the next life.

"I'm not paying for what my father did. As I said, he couldn't have done something like that. And I told you I'm taking responsibility for something else."

"Do it," he said.

My hand was shaking as I clutched the knife. Do you remember the emotional state I mentioned before? Yes, I had hated, all the time, especially at first, but slowly I saw how love could cancel out hate, really erasing it. It was clear to me that my wish over these years would finally be fulfilled if I thrust the knife forward, but I couldn't do it. I was sure that the notion of revenge would be gone if the wronged ghosts could be liberated without the enemy's blood—particularly when I was with him. It was hard for me to associate him with the idea of enemy. I used to have been intent upon revenge, and I'd always thought about ways to carrying out my desire for it. But so much had disappeared from my heart since we fought side by side against the mad camel.

I discovered that the hatred in my heart did not vanish in an instant; instead, it was more like the smoke rings blown by a smoker. There has been a traceable progression, starting with the strong hatred of the early days and up to its diluted state of the moment. Besides the passage of time, something else seemed to intervene in my revenge attempt. Was it the wooden fish songs? I wondered. Had my heart softened when I recited them silently? Or was it love? Had the hate in my heart been dispelled when I fell deeply in love with Ma Zaibo? I wasn't sure. It was beyond total comprehension, but no matter what, I couldn't strike with the knife.

I heard the angry shouts of my ancestors. You can say it was an illusion, but I didn't think so, because I did hear their voices, all but Papa's. When he was alive, Papa had always said it was better to squash enmity than keep it alive, and he would forgive his enemies—actually he didn't have any. His heart really was softened by the songs.

Straining to recognize the voices, I found that they were coming from my heart, for they were the reason for my existence. They had sustained me through these years and I wasn't willing to let them go. Without them, I'd lived for nothing. My life had been under a tremendous weight, but without them, I would be rendered weightless.

I knew all this, and yet still I couldn't raise the knife.

I imagined the scene countless times, but now I can't re-enact it.

Then I cried out and threw it down.

Ma Zaibo actually panicked. He was calm under the threat of a knife, but now he lost his composure when I cried. He looked at me with a helpless expression.

"I'm a terrible offspring." I was sobbing now.

"Without your blood to offer them, they won't be liberated," I said amid sobs.

I brought out the tablet wrapped in red cloth. I untied the bundle to show him the piece of crimson wood.

"With my blood? But not my life?" he asked.

"Blood. No one said your life." I was confused, for I didn't remember which one, but I said blood anyway.

"That's easy," he said as he picked up the knife.

"What are you doing?" I asked.

"Don't worry. I won't kill myself," He said with a smile. He drew the knife over one of his fingers and dark red blood dripped down on the wood tablet. My heart ached at the sight, as I was surprised by my own transformation. I had been so hard-hearted, as if I could really kill someone without batting an eye. Now the sight of his blood brought pain to my heart. Was I really concerned for my enemy? That was unthinkable. A drama of revenge had been enacted in my head countless times over the years, and each time it was a bloody scene, with mutilated bodies strewn everywhere. I never conceived of my heart aching over a few drops of blood. Which was the real heart, the cold, hard one of the past or the aching one now?

The blood did not seep into the wood and nothing happened to the tablet. There was just an impassive silence. It had been thumping against my chest, searing hot.

"Is that enough?" he asked with a sweet smile. "Want me to do it again?"

"No, no." I ran up to grab his hand. I'd have put the finger in my mouth if I weren't worried about dirtying the wound. We'd be in serious trouble if he were to get tetanus out in the middle of nowhere—obviously, I'd forgotten the looming end of the world.

"If their deliverance fails, then the obstacle is the stubborn belief that only revenge will liberate them. Once they give that up, they will be liberated," he said.

Strangely I heard laughter.

I couldn't figure out where it came from, still can't.

5

Then we heard sounds of violent shaking and something breaking. Ma Zaibo brought Yellow Demon over. I detected something different in the camel's eyes. I couldn't say what it was, but it was there.

"I found an old book in the rafters, when I came here for meditation last time." He took out a book with yellowed pages and made with something like sheep's skin. It was a thin book, with scant few pages that had odd-looking drawings and writings that were equally unusual and ugly but unique.

"Look. Here it says when the end of the world is coming, put the harness on your camel to pull the millstone," he pointed at a line and said. "I wonder if it meant what we're having now."

"Never mind whether it is or not. Let's give it a try."

He put the book back into his pocket.

We harnessed the camel. The dry desert weather had kept the halter sturdy even though it hadn't been used for many years.

"It also says to remove the wedge first when the time comes," he pointed at a wood peg on the wall. On it were many objects, which we took off one by one. We tugged and tugged before finally dislodging the wedge. It was made of desert thorn, big, heavy, thick, and covered in marks. It could be keeping something in check.

Ma Zaibo called to the camel to get it moving. It appeared to be straining, and yet the stone remained immobile. He raised the whip and a loud crack sounded on the camel's back. I couldn't stand it—notice the words I'm using? Not like the ones a killer would use. I truly must have changed. But what caused the change—yes, it had just saved your life from the mad camel, so how could you lash it?

The camel's muscles grew taut, a sure sign that it was working hard. The stone seemed to budge a little.

"Come, let's help it out." He yelled at the camel and joined me working a lever.

The stone finally began to move after the three of us used all the strength we could muster. "Good. Once it starts moving, it will be easier and lighter," I thought.

The camel's muscles relaxed a little as the stone began to revolve. It had indeed grown lighter.

I didn't know the significance of the movement, but I was excited nonetheless. Then I heard a creaking sound; the revolving stone must have triggered some kind of mechanism to make the whole house quake.

"The mill house is collapsing!" I cried out, with a little exaggerated fear in my voice—no, that wasn't like me. It dawned on me that, since who knew when, I was acting girlish. It was incomprehensible to me. I'd been a timid child, but hatred had bolstered my courage and turned me fearless. Now I turned feminine. My new dependence on a man was the sign that I'd become a regular woman, and I was even acting weak. My face burned as I stole a glance at him, but he didn't seem to sense anything different.

The house was shaking. Someone must have set up an intricate trigger, for a camel and two people weren't strong enough to make it quake like that, I said to myself. On second thought, besides the stone, the millhouse was made of wood and wouldn't weigh much. Maybe there were gear wheels somewhere below. I even had the outlandish idea that many non-human beings were helping us, as in the line of the song, "Wandering souls fill the nine ditches and eight ponds."

A wind blew in amid the creaks. The yellow candle flickered a few times before going out.

Total darkness. I couldn't see a thing. The camel continued to turn, however—by now, we weren't pushing the lever; we were being led forward. I could feel the stone was growing lighter, and I also heard sounds of something breaking. The millhouse was indeed going to come down. But we couldn't care about that now. So many things were beyond our control, but I didn't doubt Ma Zaibo's theory. I'd worshipped books since I was a child, and every written word meant something.

I wasn't especially afraid, even though I couldn't see a thing, because he was next to me. My hands beside his as we pushed the lever, I could feel the warmth of his hands. I could hear his heavy breathing; he was still pushing hard. It is bliss to hear your beloved panting on a dark night like this, don't you think?

The camel was panting too, but not too much. The stone was even lighter now, and I felt an air current. I thought I was outside, no longer in the millhouse, because my face was being painfully pelted by sand. Ma took out something to cover my face, so he obviously was also being pelted. I reached up to feel it; it was his camel hair sash. I'd seen him use it before. Camel hands often wore ones like that, for they were indispensable in the winter, when they tied them around their waist to keep the wind from penetrating their clothes. I pulled his head over and wrapped the sash around it, but he took it off for me. We went back and forth, neither wanting to take it from the other. In the end we shared it by using one end each. It reminded me of the red satin sash a couple held at their wedding ceremony. Let's consider this our own wedding ceremony; I was infused in happiness at the thought.

The wind grew stronger and came at us freely. I was puzzled. Weren't we in the millhouse? When did we wind up outside? I asked Ma. He replied in a muffled voice,

"Don't worry about it. The book says not to worry about anything, just walk. We'll be able to dodge the end of the world if we keep following the camel."

What kind of end would it be, I wondered. Would the sky fall or the ground open up? Whichever it would be, I doubted we'd be saved by the camel. But at a time like this, there was no better prospect, so I told myself to keep walking. I didn't care if the world ended, I thought, it was happiness consummate as long as we could keep going like this. It was a wondrous feeling when everything was gone from the world but I still had my beloved next to me.

A powerful air current surged around us, and I could sense the sand in it. If the sash slipped off, the exposed skin would sting. I was actually used to coarse sand hitting my face; it happened all too often, but never this bad. Since coming out west, I'd endured hardships and braved the elements; I was used to sandstorms. But sandstorms in the past never came in such pervading darkness. See, even the sky was gone. The wind was much stronger—no, that wasn't wind; it was the surging flow of sand. What I'd experienced in the past was mostly sandy windstorms, while now it was a sandstorm, but more than that.

The camel cried out, a muted sound. It must be exhausted or perhaps stunned by what was happening. Was it warning us or was it complaining? Maybe it was a revelation only it could understand. I couldn't. Shortly after that it stopped moving.

Ma Zaibo was breathing hard. He called out to the camel and thumped its rump. It started moving again.

"We can't stop," he said. "If we do we'll be buried in the sand."

"Heavenly downpours do end, so do heavenly windstorms," he added.

I didn't respond. I wanted to tell him that when doomsday was here, the world would end even if the wind stopped. Strangely, I didn't feel bad, though I did believe the end was near. Yes, it was a true blessing to be walking toward the end with the one you loved. That was how I felt then, and you'll never understand women, if you don't get that.

The camel stopped again. It was drained. It had been pulling a heavy millstone and walking—I couldn't tell for how long exactly—so of course it was dead tired. But Yellow Demon had enough fat in its humps to give it an endless supply of energy.

I slumped to the ground when the camel stopped. I was sweating from all that effort. Ma pulled me up and shouted,

"Don't give up. Keep going. We can't stop now, or we'll be buried in the sand."

"I don't care. I can't take another step," I said.

"It's getting light out. There'll be light."

"So what if there's light?" I asked.

"Don't say that. Nothing will make sense if you keep asking questions," he said. "What's important about living is the process."

I understood the principle, of course. The problem was, oftentimes principle cannot solve problems. For instance, it could not remove the darkness around us, it could not relieve our fatigue, and it could not stop the sand from flying. It only worked when it involved the mind, but unfortunately, our bodies don't listen to our minds a lot of the time. I knew it was important to keep walking, but my body was so tired it was like made of mud.

Besides fatigue, I was thirsty and hungry, and out of energy. I hadn't recovered from the fight with Brown Lion, and I'd have collapsed if not for my martial arts training. I pulled myself together and got up. I had the training, Ma never had. I saw, however, he had great stamina, as good as mine, for, since childhood, he'd traveled all with caravans.

Ma called out to the camel again, in a firm and angry voice, almost like threatening the animal. Knowing the situation, the camel started walking again with our help.

I looked at the sky through slitted eyes. I didn't see any light. He was just trying to make me feel better, I knew. It could be midnight, for all I knew. You can't see light at midnight. But I couldn't worry about that now. The sky had its prerogative to be dark, and walking was our destiny.

We walked and we walked. We tripped and fell time and again, but always got up and walked until we fell again, and on and on, until I did see the horizon lightening up.

The wind died down and I found the lay of the land was different. The millhouse was still here, but not the same one. The old millhouse had several rooms, but this one had only the room with the millstone—no, it wasn't even a house, more like a wooden frame.

As we turned, the mill rose up higher and higher. No, we were rising and the cascading sand was now landing at our feet.

I saw the tip of a poplar. There had been a tall poplar by the millhouse. Now I could see only its tip. From a distance, the millhouse must have looked as if it were hanging on the tree.

We saw Feiqing and others shortly after the sun reemerged.

They too had been looking for the Hu Family Mill, and that saved them.

They gave us some water. They didn't have much, but it was enough to sustain us for three days.

On the third day there was a heavy snowfall.

Living on camel meat and snow and with great difficulty, we finally made our way out of Wild Fox Ridge.

6

After Feiqing's death, we continued our activities through the Society of Brothers. The Qing government was done for, but we failed to escape our fate.

I wasn't sure if we could call it offering blood as a sacrifice when Ma Zaibo dripped his blood on the tablet in Wild Fox Ridge. But I never dreamed about my dead relatives after that, nor did the tablet burn again.

After we were married, he put the tablet in the Ma family hall. It was the first outsider's spirit table installed in their hall. Strangely, however, no one in the Ma clan raised an objection.

"Sure. Back when the Hui and the Han fought, we'd let many outsiders in to live in our fortress. If the living ones can come, why can't the dead?" Ma Siye offered.

Later, more outsiders were installed in the hall, and a private family shrine turned public and grew bigger. One day, several decades later, a group wearing red armbands stormed the hall, bundled up several hundred tablets, and threw them all into the Dasha River, where they bobbed along with the current to who knew where.

Shortly after we were married, Ma Zaibo told me his father had known the cause of his younger brother's death, but had decided not to reveal it. His father believed it was an accidental death, so he didn't want to inflict any harm on me and Big Mouth.

"The dead are gone. No need to cause two more deaths," he said.

My heart ached after I heard that. I felt awful, a feeling that dogged me for years.

There were many versions about the big fire. One had to do with the Society of Brothers. Some people had thought the end justified the means, but it was just a rumor, never verified.

. . . No way out. I was yoked by the rope of fate, on a pre-set track, no matter how hard I struggled to break free.

If I'd accepted my fate, this would have happened to me: years later, Ma Zaibo was classified as a landlord and I the landlord's wife. The Ma family wealth became a karmic debt that we never managed to settle, which could be considered a different form of punishment exacted by Lü Erye. Compared with living as one of the "four elements," I'd had an easy life traveling on camel trails. I'd have often thought of Feiqing and each time I'd have been comforted by his early death. If he'd lived longer, he'd have his own nightmare of a life to go through. It would be less terrifying than the end of the world in Wild Fox Ridge.

But I opted for a different life. Soon after we left Wild Fox Ridge, Ma and I decided to steer clear of strife of the mundane world and return to Wild Fox Ridge. We had renovated the Hu Family Mill people saw. In there we continued our meditative practice and, like the ending of all fairy tales, lived happily ever after.

You know it was a great decision, for we managed to dodge the trials and tribulations of the following decades. We were able to attain our sublimation.

You can imagine the kind of stories we had in Wild Fox Ridge. Even now, few people know it is a world onto itself.

We found the Wooden Fish Incantation, of course. It helped me withdraw from the turmoil of the world. It may not be the one you had in mind, but it was ours. I considered myself very lucky, especially when compared with Feiqing and Lu Fuji, who returned to the mundane world and ended up losing their heads, or Big Mouth, who was labeled one of the four elements and got struggled against in his old age. Even now you can still find nourishment from Ma Zaibo's books, which meant that life has meaning.

But what I found was just what I found; everyone has what he finds, and neither can take the place of the other, though it's still better than not finding it at all.

In fact, finding it or not is something else beyond the search.

I still thought of Feiqing often, even after finding my Incantation. I felt a different sort of ache for him.

Stories about Feiqing continued to circulate in Liangzhou, like his painting and calligraphy, which had been passed around for years. He was almost an eternal subject.

I heard he'd been made a City God in charge of the underworld in Liangzhou. Later, Liangzhou had several corrupt officials, and the people complained to the City God in his temple when they'd had enough. Interestingly, the corrupt officials all died. One of them was Governor He Fantai, who had persecuted Lu Fuji to death.

I heard that every time someone lodged a complaint in the underworld, they would see whirlwinds, which were Feiqing and his troops. I wondered if the troops were his brothers at Wild Fox Ridge or those from the Society of Brothers. I never knew.

I no longer sighed over his death. I knew he'd traveled to the end of his life's journey when he died.

After that, I grew old and heard lots of things, all of which elicited emotional sighs from me. The Qing court was gone, replaced by the Republic and a great deal of killing, shedding more blood than during the Qing. Later, factions of people fought each other, permeating the land with the smell of blood. And then the smell grew stronger by the year.

It makes me ponder the meaning of the lives and deaths of Feiqing and people like him.

The village where he'd lived curled up in a lake. When he was alive, the lake had a commanding force, drawing snowmelt from Mount Qilian on the ground or under the ground to form a lake in his hometown. People called it Qijiadang Lake. The west side of the lake was Dahu, where many swans gathered each year. One autumn two swans came, a loving couple that never strayed from each other's side. The male died on the day a hunter's rifle fired a shot. The female stopped going south and stayed through the winter, crying night after night until she froze to death in the lake. People were still talking about the swan when I visited Qijiadang Lake.

Feiqing's house was at Qijiadang Lake. Their one-time wealth meant the offspring were labeled as landlords. His son was old when I went there; he didn't talk much, and lacked passion when the topic turned to his father. Maybe lots of people had asked him about his father, and he was tired of talking about him as time went by.

The people there all said that if Feiqing's uprising had succeeded, the city of Liangzhou would be installed in Qijiadang Lake. If that had happened, it would be great for the people, the land alone would fetch them a great deal of money.

Feiqing must have made plenty of preparations when he was alive. I was told he'd buried gold and silver for revolutionary purposes. One time, during tree planting, the locals dug out lots of copper pieces, weighing in at forty-six *jin*. They sold it all to a passer-by, keeping only one piece for children to play with. Later, someone determined it was gold, but they could not find the buyer. This was many years after his death. He'd obviously never imagined he'd be beheaded by the Qing Court when he buried the gold.

The village was suffering from famine when I went. The streets were littered with rotting corpses. The sight was worse than during armed battles or revenge killings. "Did Feiqing and Fuji die for nothing?" I asked myself.

Stories about him abounded in the area. One was about him in prison still trying to contact the Society to plot another uprising, by sending chicken feather missives. Back then the children sang songs like: "On the fifteenth of the tenth month, raid the prison to set the jailed free," "on the twenty-fifth of the tenth month, attack Liangzhou Township office, ride a horse into the ancient city, and take Zhangyibao." Feiqing's son denied everything.

"There were missives, but my father didn't send them. It wasn't the Society either. They were sent by local bullies. They were afraid the Township magistrate would set my father free, so they sent the missives out to entangle him. The Qing court had no choice but to behead him. Besides, the Society would never announce the dates beforehand if they were plotting an uprising."

I detected something in his tone of voice; he actually disapproved of what his father had done.

He didn't look particularly sad about his father's death. I asked him why and he said,

"Life would be terrible if he had lived. He'd either die during the wars or be executed by the government, since surviving members of the Society later joined the Revolutionary Alliances that became the Nationalist Party. Several of the bullies executed after the Liberation were members. If my father had lived, if the Qing court didn't kill him, someone else would. His temperament just about guaranteed that he would not have a good end."

"Would he still do what he'd done if he'd known these things that happened later?" he asked me.

I had no answer for him.

There were many other stories about Feiqing. Every narrator told his story with great relish. In one story, Feiqing even knew magic. Once, when Liu Huzi's mounted troops came and he could not flee in time, he jumped into a giant steamer. He knew fire-dousing magic, so he was cool as a cucumber inside, even though hot steam continued to rise. Liu's people left after a fruitless search.

There were many similar stories.

Feiqing was now living in Liangzhou's local lore.

7

I'll always remember the day he was executed.

In my memory, it was a cloudy day, dust devils blowing all over, carrying dirt, yellow dirt. Maybe it was the kind of sandstorm you modern people talk about, but it was cool, and the wind wasn't strong as I recalled.

In the stories later generations told, we were said to have prepared to raid the execution ground, but that was only wishful thinking on their part. We wanted to, but lacked the capability. In fact, the government was hoping we would so they could round us all up.

What happened in reality was, we were broken up, not just as a society, but also in terms of morale. The uprising was indeed a group of people rushing into action and dispersing in confusion. And that was that. Some hid out in Dengmaying Lake, but only to avoid arrest and execution by government soldiers. That was all. I wish we could have had an uprising described in ancient books, but there was none. It couldn't be helped but it wasn't meant to be at the time.

I heard that, after Feiqing's arrest, Liu Huzi asked Feiqing's brother whether he wanted "give up life" or "give up wealth," meaning Feiqing would be spared if his family was willing to spend some money. Liu was said to have even mentioned a figure. His brother did some calculation and concluded that the figure was worth three pawn shops, so he decided to let Feiqing die. Some disagreed with this part, because Liu had no authority to let Feiqing live. Maybe, maybe not. Liu and his people might not have been able to stay the execution, but they might have delayed it; Feiqing's life might have been spared, if the execution was delayed. Why? Because the Wuchang Uprising had succeeded by then, though the Shaanxi and Gansu areas had yet to declare independence and still recognized the Qing court as the legitimate government. Feiqing was being executed precisely because they still pledged allegiance to the Qing.

It was a regrettable shame to the Liangzhou people that Feiqing's younger brother decided not to give up money—not selling three pawnshops to save him. It was touching for them to wish it this way, but so what if he did live? It was a question that I came back to again and again. He would have been labeled a landlord, if nothing else, and he wouldn't be Feiqing any longer. It was time for him to die, just as Lu Xun was, and he is remembered in forever after dying like that.

The Qing soldiers brought him out of the prison and paraded him to the major intersection, where he would be beheaded later that day. The government chose the spot, not the usual execution ground, because, I heard, it wanted to set an example and frighten the people.

The streets were eerily grim that day, at least in my recollection. What the local storyteller songs said about his death was inaccurate. There were spectators, many of them, all looking impassive. That was Liangzhou people for you, timid and cowardly.

Feiqing didn't look too good, likely from being beaten. Customarily, someone like him would surely have been beaten. Members of the local gentry whose houses were burned down would bribe the prison guards to have him beaten. They would even spend money to make sure he was dead. So even if his brother had sold three pawnshops he couldn't have saved Feiqing; too many people wanted him dead.

The version with sticky jute was another charming story. It had a prison guard who wanted to save him so he glued jute to the blade. If Feiqing survived the first cut and someone yelled out "Spare the sword," he would be saved. I didn't believe it at all. At a time like that, anyone who spoke up on his behalf with the notion of "taking a prison's life with one swipe of the sword" would surely be arrested and condemned as Feiqing's accomplice.

Therefore, his death was an inevitable outcome.

I saw the executioner raise his sword. He had thick, muscular arms, a sure sign of his strength. Pairs of blank eyes stared at him, and I did too. I was hoping he'd lop off the head with one chop. I knew no one could save Feiqing. The government sent out a large number of soldiers, who overran the streets, looking prepared to fight a formidable foe. In Liangzhou back then, there was no force that could challenge the government.

The sword whispered as it came down on his neck. What people said was indeed true; the sword came down, but Feiqing's head remained securely on his shoulders. I saw the stunned executioner look around, which gave rise to another story. For years, Liangzhou people speculated on the look; some said Feiqing knew qigong, so the sword left only a white mark on his neck. In another version, the executioner didn't want to kill him so he was hoping someone would take the cue from his look and come forward to shout "spare the sword." The proponent of this version maintained that the Qing Code decreed only one swing for beheading. No second try was allowed, even if the condemned was alive. Liangzhou residents sighed over this version for nearly a century.

The story about what happened next was equally intriguing. The executioner said, "Master Qi, you've outlived your people." Then he held up the sword and wiped the sticky jute off the edge.

"The people of Liangzhou have a right to be poor," Feiqing said with a sigh.

Then he closed his eyes and stuck his neck out for the executioner, who tried three times, but failed to sever the neck completely and had to resort to sawing it off.

In fact, there was another plausible version: members of the local gentry loathed him so much that they bribed the executioner to make sure Feiqing didn't die easily. Swing the sword several times and let him suffer.

Everyone said he died a terrible death. They also mentioned a reed root in his ancestral tomb that presaged an outstanding offspring, but Liu Huzi chopped it off. Some even claimed that a man with supernatural abilities had seen his signature on his calligraphy and paintings and predicted that he would die a terrible death. Feiqing, in this version, showed off his ability and acted too much like a high-handed man.

Feiqing's dying scene continued to flash in my mind throughout my life. Hundreds of spectators had witnessed his execution, and they propagated the stories I've given.

But I kept coming back to his last words: "The people of Liangzhou have a right to be poor." I'm convinced that he did say that. But why? What was the mentality behind this line? Had he really made all the arrangements? Was there really the code of one sword strike? Was there still something impossible to explain. It was a giant puzzle; I mulled it over for years, but never figured it out.

Twenty-seventh Session
Alive in the Stories

"You think I deserved to die, is that it?" Feiqing asks.

"We're a bunch of muddled-headed ghosts. The stories we told are incoherent. We either messed up the sequence or we conflated two events. The uprising staged by the Society of Brothers, did it happen before or after our trip in the desert?"

"Listen to you." Wooden Fish Girl laughs. "Don't worry about the sequence, as long as the events took place. Whatever comes to a writer's mind happens to him."

"What you said about me was what you thought had happened, not really my story. I have to tell my own story, but then again, I'd just be telling a story about Feiqing, and I won't be sure if it's the true one," Feiqing says.

"You worry too much about what's real and what's not. In fact, what's real is false and what's false is real," Wooden Fish Girl laughs again.

"You talk too much, Wooden Fish Girl," Big Mouth joins in. "Can't you keep quiet and let others have a chance to say something? Besides, how could you take up so many roles and be one person one moment and another one the next?"

She covers her mouth and giggles.

"Enough, enough. Let's talk about the other events later," the others say.

Under the dark blue light of the fire, I see the camel hands warming themselves. They all appear in their original features from the time they were at Wild Fox Ridge, which means they and I are having a real-life encounter during an interview. We're no longer just communicating on a spiritual level; it is an encounter on an authentic level. They are sitting all around me. I believe they've been lonely for too long, so naturally they want me to stay in their world.

The Hu Family Mill they remembered has changed. After so many years, the elements and the passage of time have reduced it to mere dilapidated walls.

The drivers hope I'll share more of what later generations said about them. After so many years, they wonder how people will react to their stories. In reality, so much has been happening in the human world that nothing is being said about them anymore. At the present time people are focused on pragmatic matters and few of them care about history—besides, the drivers' history was nothing more than a period of life buried in time over the years.

Some mentions were made of their stories thirty years ago; I was still a child back then. Virtually no one knows about them now that I've come to talk to them thirty years later.

A different version circulated in Liangzhou thirty years ago. In it, Feiqing and the others survived the sandstorm because of the magical Hu Family Mill.

According to earlier generations, Qi Feiqing and several others who didn't die in the sandstorm had their belief in a legend to thank for their escape. In the legend, they weren't allowed to sleep or rest; they had to hold onto the camel's tail and follow it as it turned round and round with the millstone. They didn't know why, but they did it anyway. When they were too tired to move, one of them would keep his hand on the tail while the others clutched the clothes of the person ahead. A string of humans followed the camel and walked around the millstone.

In this story, those were dark, sunless days; countless grains of sand fell from the sky, splashing on them like water and lashing their faces like a whip. They turned their fur coats inside out for the fur to take the beating from the sand-whips. Wooden Fish Girl didn't have a fur vest. so Big Mouth gave her his and wrapped a shirt around himself. Later the shifting sand beat through his shirt and turned his face into a bloodied gourd. Which was why he had no nose ridge—there were just two big holes. He had no outer ears either—in its place were strange fleshy bumps. The only original feature that remained on his face was the big mouth.

There were said to be ten of them holding on to the camel's tail and clothes at first. Then some were too tired to move and slumped sleepily to the side before being buried in the flying sand. They didn't suffer; the sand continued to swirl when they closed their eyes, and by the time they woke up, they were already on their way to the underworld. When one of them fell, the others would call out, but their voices were blown away the moment they opened their mouths. As they made the first round, they could still see their fallen friends, but by the time they came around, there was only a human shape on the sandy ground, and the figures were completely invisible the third time.

The Hu Family Mill was said to have an unusual structure: the roof, shaped like an upside-down V and sharp as a knife blade, was said to be built from a single block of wood and integral to the millstone. People said the turning mill base was meant to shake off sand falling onto its surface. It was the turning of the base that sent the falling sand cascading off the mill, and they were walking on the fallen sand as they turned, rising higher and higher. In one of the Liangzhou stories, Chain Smoker saw a mill base spinning continuously above his head, which was, in fact, a hint from destiny.

In the story, the remaining few cheered each other to raise their spirits, and helped each other along as they walked. They didn't know how long they'd been walking; they only knew they had to keep going as long as the sand continued to fly. Luckily, Lu Fuji had a piece of butter with him. He loved buttered tea, and his addiction was a reason why they lived. They held a small piece of butter in their mouths when they were hungry and drank their own urine when thirsty. When they had no more urine of their own, they drank the camel's. Do you still remember the unique way a camel relieves itself? Right, that's it. It made drinking camel urine easy for the drivers.

They were seemingly walking forever under a blanket of darkness, but later it began to lighten up and the flying sand slowly died down. They saw sand had filled the gulches and ravines that they'd seen before the storm and the Hu Family Mill looked to be hanging from a poplar treetop. Neither the Chinese nor the Mongolian caravan could be found in Wild Fox Ridge after the storm; only a camel and several sand-covered men remained. They were lucky they knew the desert well and were versed in many life-saving tricks—I could go into detail about this later—they finally walked out of the place after uncountable hardships.

In these stories, Wooden Fish Girl was with Big Mouth during the sandstorm, contrary to what she said about being with Ma Zaibo. No one knows which version is true. Some even thought that Big Mouth, Zhang Yaole, was the source of the former version, for he was more than happy to add a heroic patina to his deformed face. But there was no corroborative evidence. Many had seen his round, gourd-like head, but no one associated him with Wooden Fish Girl, likely because they didn't want him to sully the Dakini in the story.

Later on, a scholar wrote a research article refuting the existence of someone called Ma Zaibo, claiming that Wooden Fish Girl had created him based on her own desire, just as she imagined herself being a killer.

The scholar's allegation was met with severe criticism, as there is more than enough proof that Ma was a historical figure. Besides, at least in the west, Ma Zaibo and Wooden Fish Girl were said to be the Mahasidha of the Dharma of the Five Glorious Tantras' Deities, and received widespread veneration. Any doubt of his existence amounts to negating the lineage. The two were said to have completed their pair cultivation years after the sandstorm, but no one was sure which year or what time that was. They were sure about where though, and it was in the Hu Family Mill, which was made an even more sacred locale, holier than in the stories. Ma Zaibo and Wooden Fish Girl were rumored to have found the Wooden Fish Incantation, but no one knew what it was like.

In yet another version, she married Ma Zaibo and they didn't go anywhere. Instead, they stayed home for private meditation. Years later he was labeled a landlord, and she a landlord's wife. Along with Big Mouth, who was labeled a rich peasant, they were put in the four categories of "landowners, rich, counterrevolutionaries, and bad elements." They underwent reeducation through labor for years, despite their old age. But unlike the average members of the "four categories," they continued their meditative practice on enduring humiliation, which then helped them attain Buddhahood.

All these bits of information originated from stories passed around in the human world, some matching what I learned from the interviews, others were drastically different.

My new friends found what I just said unsatisfactory, and have asked me to tell a story from my world.

"I'm not a good storyteller," I say. "But I can sing. I'll sing you 'Story of the Lasso Pole' from the Liangzhou storytelling tradition, if it won't bore you."

"Sing it," they shout. "Sing it for us."

I take the three-string zither from Wooden Fish Girl and start singing:

Picking up a three-string zither and setting the key,
I'll tell you stories from the Xuantong reign of the Qing dynasty.
After two and a half years on the throne, the Xuantong Emperor
Made life so hard for the Liangzhou people they lived in terror.

"Bravo!"
"Great voice!"
"Shut up and let him sing."
"Right. If your lips are itchy, get yourself a sandy donkey dick to scratch it."

. . . Qi Feiqing grabs Lu Fuji to stop him.
Brother Lu, let's go ahead with our plan,
And we'll carry it through even it means the end of us.
Brother Qi, don't you worry and put your mind at ease.
I'd rather my name known for generations to come,
Than have the people live under worthless officials' thumbs.
We'll flatten Wanping Township with one kick of our feet,
Escalate the situation and make it a great feat.

"Ai-yo! Brother Qi is amazing."
"And Brother Lu too."
"Don't be a chatterbox."
"You're the chatterbox."
"Shut up. Shut up. Keep going, Xue Mo."

They cheer loudly when I get to the part about beating the police. They are so keyed up they rub their hands, ready to join the fight—they have no hands. It's just how it feels to me. I know they like songs like this, but good things pass all too easily. Slowly scenes describing dispersing in confusion appear in the lyrics, and the drivers shout obscenities. Obviously, they also wish the people of Liangzhou had more backbone, though some of them took part in battling the police. They, too, recalled how to fight only after the fight was over.

I'm slowly getting to the part about Lu Fuji's death:

> . . . Governor He Fantai was outraged from embarrassment.
> He shouted for the guards to tie up Lu Fuji right at that moment.
> A banner of death stuck behind his back.
> A large sword, shiny with a ghastly bright glint.
> Lu Fuji was taken out to the execution ground.
> They traveled through town to Xiaojiaping.
> Where they waited for a full two hours.
> The execution would be carried out at a quarter past noon.
> The banner of death, flapping in the autumn wind,
> The life-taking cannon rumbled.
> Ka-cha, the sword came down viciously,
> The head tumbled and rolled on the dusty ground.
> A real man, a good man, of Liangzhou was dead,
> What a shame to lose a tough man, a real hero.

"What a pity. Brother Lu had great martial art skills."

"What so great about it? If he was so good, how come he died in the end?"

"That's nonsense. No matter how good he was, he had to die."

"Martial art skills make no difference. Even the emperor has to die at some point."

"Has anyone lived forever?"

"Ask Ma Zaibo."

"Shut up. Let him sing."

I notice a wistful look on Lu Fuji's face. Some of the lines must have touched a nerve, so I smile and say to him,

"Don't take it so seriously. This could be true or completely false; either is possible. True or false, it all depends on what you think. If you think it's false then it will be, even though it's true. Everything in the world is but a dream."

"He's right," Feiqing says. "We're listening to a story and we become a story."

"Keep singing. Don't stop." The drivers shout at me again.

It feels like a long night to me.

Thanks to the fire, I'm not cold. I don't know how much time has passed, but the sky remains dark. I can see in the dark pairs of eyes, nice clean eyes like children listening to stories, brimming with curiosity and longing.

"Go on. Keep singing." They are louder now.

I remember myself in the thrall of an incomprehensible power and I continue to sing:

On the thirteenth day of the eighth month,
A nine-strand hemp rope around Feiqing tightly wound.
A banner of death stuck behind his back flapped in the wind.
The executioner held a sword with a ghastly glint.
He was pushed and shoved, taken to the intersection.
The time had yet to come, but they'd get right to the execution.
The life-taking cannon was ready to turn him into a ghost,
The ghastly sword was shining, with a blinding glare.
One strike, but nothing happened,
Except for a bright red mark on the nape.
Second strike, still nothing.
Qi Feiqing sniggered,

"The corrupt official is a blind dog,
And even his executioner isn't worth shit.
Bring on a sharp sword if you want to kill me,
Give a nice clean death, that's what you should do."
Qi Feiqing secretly sends qi running in his body,
He's alive after three strikes for a death by one strike of a sword.
The official presiding over the execution panicked.
Worried that some might come raid the execution ground.
Quickly Feiqing was pushed down on the street,
A brick was placed under his neck,
Then a dull sword sawed back and forth,
A long time passed before it sawed through.
The head rolled into the street,
"Pu" warm blood spurted and shot ten zhang into the air.
The execution ground was completely deserted,
An eerie wind swirled at the intersection and the sun was pale.
What a shame to lose Qi Feiqing, a Liangzhou hero.
He died a horrible death over a wrongful accusation.
For a death by one strike of the sword, he should have died after one strike.
Why did he suffer the pain of having his head sawed off after the failed tries?
No one had the courage to demand an answer,
And no one came to raid the execution ground.
The corrupt official who had Feiqing's head sawed was mightily pleased.
Three cannon shots were fired and the city gate was opened again.
The country folk coming to watch the show surged through,
Mountains of spectators swarmed toward the intersection.
When they reached the execution ground and took a look,

They all said what a terrible thing to have happened.

The drivers suck in cold air and keep quiet. Worried that the lyrics might be too much for Feiqing to take, I'm about to say something when I hear him laugh.

"The pain is brief. Losing the head is really just gaining a bowl-size scar. If given another chance to live, I'd fight the government all over again."

Despite my admiration for Feiqing as a real man, I feel like asking him,

"What do you expect to come out of all these battles? Can battles bring about true world peace?"

I force back my question because I don't want to sour his mood. I would very much like to know about the Wooden Fish Incantation that could help dissolve hatred, but if he can't even eliminate his own hate he probably doesn't know.

I don't have any sense of time on this night, oddly. Darkness reigns in my world—later I recall that the fire continues to burn even without adding wood.

I have no idea how long I sing. I'm possessed by some magic. My fingers strum the strings in a frenzied rhythm. I'm getting hoarse, but my voice seems to have a life of its own and keeps pouring out:

Yang Chengxu, his heart aching, crawled through the dirt to the spot.
He wrote a touching essay to mourn the dead,
Every word is infused with blood and tears for the hero's soul.
"You were a true hero when you were alive,
To help out the poor, you lost your own life.
In this world, you were tough, an upright man;
In the underworld, you were a hero among ghosts."
When he finished, he quickly got up, to get the body buried.

Suddenly I hear a dog barking; then I see my dog—I should say my dog's ghost—run up and into the specters around me. It's barking up a storm as it pounces and nips at them. The darkness that shrouds me slowly lifts.

A dim light appears before me, like breath on a window pane in winter. The breath will disappear into itself though, while this one keeps expanding until I see the white camel. It's roaring angrily and spitting at the same time, like a raging machine gun.

Little by little, the darkness vanishes like smoke, until it's completely gone. I can see sand dunes. I don't know when the moon has risen to the top of the dunes; it isn't very bright, but I know it's the moon. I wonder why the moon is shut out of the world I was in earlier. I'm unsure if this is really the moon.

I notice the white camel soaked in sweat. It must have been crying for a very long time before it roused me from my delirious state.

Later the guru tells me that I was lucky to have the white camel and the dog with me; without them I wouldn't have been able to leave that night. I'm most grateful to my dog—lucky for me it had yet to be reborn—for protecting me in its own way. The specters were obviously eager to have me stay; they were simply too lonely.

My heart aches at the thought of them.

I even feel the urge to stay. They were wonderful friends. I seldom have carefree gatherings like this in my life, but I know it's a frightening thought, because I'd be hooked and could never leave once it took hold of me. I strain to recall things I care about to help me shake off the desire to stay. In the end, my mission has the upper hand. I tell myself that I can't let the story disappear into the passing of time. Without me, the worlds they inhabited would likely vanish forever. Besides, there are so many things I need to do.

The interviews are finished.

The moon breaks out from the clouds and the dunes are brightly lit, as if by a sun. Countless specters crowd on the dune, all eager to join in. I see they are mostly ghosts of those who died in battles between the Hakka and the locals. They are crying and yelling, raising a din. They, too, have many stories, and they, too, want me to stay. Grateful though I am for their sincerity, I know I have to go home. I need food from my world and I only have enough hardtack to last me till I'm out of Wild Fox Ridge.

"Next time. How about that?" I offer.

Countless voices sob, their reluctance to see me go plain to my ears, like a gale blowing over the tips of poplars.

"If you really don't want me to be away," I'm choking up, "then be my Dharmapalas. All of you drivers, shooters, and everyone else."

Waves of joy surge around me. I notice they're blending into the mandala of my life.

The interviewing trip is a great success, but sadly I fail to figure out who I was in my previous life. I feel I could be any one of my interviewed subjects. I could be a Chinese camel driver, or a Mongolian one, even a camel or a wolf. But there are three people I'd loathe to be associated with: Huozi, Qi Lu, and Cai Wu. That is, I don't mind being an animal, but I can't abide being a sneak in my previous life. It's a sunny thought, to be sure, but it's just a wish, and I have no way to confirm that I wasn't. I can choose only the future; the past is out of my hands. I know every present moment will soon be the past, so I must live every current moment well for a better future.

Naturally, I'd like to have been Ma Zaibo in my previous life. The person I feel closest to, however, is Wooden Fish Papa. Even now I can still feel a kind of pain deep inside his soul, and my heart aches every time I think about him.

On that moonlit night, I shout at him,

"Don't worry. I won't forget."

I want to hear his reply, but get a wolf's howl instead. It lingers and drifts in the air, like a long rope.

I'm grateful for the auspicious snow and for the cistanches the white camel found to sustain me through the interview. I'm finally out of Wild Fox Ridge after an arduous trek over many days. A year later, I go to Lingnan to carry out my promise. After going through a great deal of trouble, I locate the Fairy Blockade—it's now a reservoir—mentioned by Wooden Fish Papa and unearth the neat, flat boulder resembling a white jade stone from the Han dynasty. In the wooden box under the boulder are some yellowed books of wooden fish songs.

I don't go back to my lodging that night. I spread out my sleeping bag and spend the night on the white boulder. I hope Wooden Fish Papa will come see me, but he doesn't show after I wait the whole night. All I hear is a wind blowing through stone caves, like someone choking on tears.

I never see him again.

The old wolf, however, flashes past my life now and then.

Suddenly I hear a spooky voice,

"Are you finished? It's my turn to tell my story."

My scalp tingles. A tremendous suspicion creeps into my mind,

"Have I ... really ... left Wild Fox Ridge?"

Desert Rites

- Author: Xue Mo
- Publication Date: September, 2018
- Rights Sold: German, Spanish

Description:

Desert Rites (Desert Trilogy Book 1) took author Xue Mo twelve years to finish with elaborate effort, and finally earned him immense acclaim and launched his career as a nationally recognized writer. Set in the Hexi Corridor of Gansu province, this realistic novel is remarkable not only for its huge cast of characters and psychological scope, but also for its detailed descriptions of common people's lives in an extremely remote village, representative of the challenges faced by peasants in late 20th century rural China.

This full-length novel has later been adapted into the television series *Desert Ties*, which attracted wide attention across China.

The English edition of *Desert Rites* was a collaborative translation by a preeminent American sinologist Howard Goldblatt and his wife Dr. Sylvia Li-chun Lin, printed by Encyclopedia of China Publishing House. Its German edition, *Die Riten der Wüste*, was translated by Hans-Peter Kolb, a PhD student of the German sinologist Wolfgang Kubin, and published by Bacopa Verlag in 2020. Its Spanish edition is currently being translated by Liliana Arsovska, a famed Mexican sinologist and professor at College of Mexico.

Desert Hunters

- Author: Xue Mo
- Publication Date: January, 2017
- Rights Sold: German

Description:

Desert Hunters (Desert Trilogy Book 2) is an enthralling fable written in a realistic style. The novel centers on Pig's Belly Well, a tiny place seated in the heart of the desert that provides drinking water not only for the wild animals nearby but also for the herdsmen and their livestock. When water is plentiful, people live in peace; when it runs dry, conflicts instantly arise. Accordingly, a series of disputes and bloodshed take place one after another, reminiscent of the many wars and self-destruction caused by human greed.

The English edition of *Desert Hunters* was translated collaboratively by a preeminent American sinologist Howard Goldblatt and his wife Dr. Sylvia Li-chun Lin, and published by Encyclopedia of China Publishing House.

White Tiger Pass

- Author: Xue Mo
- Publication Date: September, 2018
- Rights Sold: German

Description:

White Tiger Pass (Desert Trilogy Book 3) revolves around the miserable experiences of three young village women, Lanlan, Ying'er, and Yue'er, as they navigate life with its ups and downs, joys and sorrows, loves and hatreds.

This staggering story offers a lifelike portrayal of the pains and hardships faced by Chinese peasants especially women amidst the social changes. The writing of survival suffering and tenacious vitality in this naturalist book features rich details, authentic experiences and compact structure, and touches upon essential issues such as life and death, love and eternity.

The English edition of *White Tiger Pass* was a collaborative translation by a preeminent American sinologist Howard Goldblatt and his wife Dr. Sylvia Li-chun Lin, published by Zhonghua International Media Publishing Group.

Curse of Xixia

- Author: Xue Mo
- Publication Date: May, 2017
- Rights Sold: English

Description:

Curse of Xixia (Soul Trilogy Book 1) is a magical realism novel that takes readers on a journey through a rarely-known legend of western China, exploring life and death, light and dark, and eternity and impermanence. This captivating story begins with the narrator uncovering eight pieces of mysterious manuscripts in an ancient grotto. These manuscripts tell an enchanting tale of a Tangut monk who breaks his religious vows and develops an outlandish romance with a girl, nevertheless, both of them actualize eternity in the end, defying everyone's expectations.

Through skillful interweaving of folklore, customs, historical events and present-day experiences, this compelling novel creates a giant metaphor of dreamlike reality. Its bold and innovative narration showcases writer Xue Mo's extraordinary imagination and powerful storytelling skills.

Legendary Wolf of Xixia

- Author: Xue Mo
- Publisher: Encyclopedia of China Publishing House (ECPH)
- Publication Date: May, 2017

Description:

Legendary Wolf of Xixia (Soul Trilogy Book 2) unfolds a romantic story of a young married woman who desperately falls in love with a devoted spiritual seeker. The heroine, Zixiao, embarks on her journey to find a descendant of Tangut Mastiffs in a strange city in western China, while the hero, Black Singer, are looking for immortality of spirit.

In addition, this novel also mirrors the diversity of Chinese regional culture.

The Holy Monk and the Spirit Woman

- Author: Xue Mo
- Publication Date: October, 2018
- Rights Sold: All Rights Available

Description:

The Holy Monk and the Spirit Woman (Soul Trilogy Book 3) is a biographical story of a great Tibetan master, Khyungpo Naljor, who pilgrimaged to India and Nepal in search of the ultimate truth, and eventually achieved full enlightenment after going through a series of unbearable hardships and alluring temptations. This captivating book, unlike many popular biographies, offers a secret map for common people to transcend the mundane world, and provides practical solutions to deal with the common pitfalls that one may encounter on his or her spiritual path.

Eternal Love

- Author: Xue Mo
- Publisher: Encyclopedia of China Publishing House (ECPH)
- Publication Date: April, 2021

Description:

Eternal Love is the author's first epistolary novel. The heroine, diagnosed with tongue cancer, narrates her painful struggle to her teacher via letters and diaries. As a trustful friend, the teacher engages in a long heart-to-heart conversation with her, touching upon philosophical issues such as the purpose of life and the ultimate truth.

Eternal Love is a truly uplifting read particularly for those patients who are suffering from terminal diseases, offering a profound insight into the fundamental questions of human existence.

Wild Fox Ridge

- Writer:Xue Mo
- People's Literature Publishing House
- Publication Date: July, 2017

Description:

Wild Fox Ridge is a captivating novel that challenges readers' intelligence. A century ago, two renowned camel caravans in western China, one Mongolian and one Chinese, disappeared at Wild Fox Ridge, despite a detailed account of their treks in the local gazette.

On a cold winter's night, the narrator arrives at Wild Fox Ridge and summons those deceased camel drivers with an unusual method, allowing them to release their old memories during twenty-seven interview sessions. This fascinating paranormal story artfully blurs the boundaries between Yin and Yang, north and south, good and evil, and humans and animals.

Liangzhou Ci: A Tale of Wulin

- Author: Xue Mo
- Publisher: People's Literature Publishing House
- Publication Date: January, 2020

Description:

Liangzhou Ci: A Tale of Wulin is a gripping novel that immerses readers into a world of martial arts. The story is about the love-hate relationship amidst the backdrop of conflicts between martial masters and daring bandits. Unfolding like a captivating movie, it can be considered as a tribute to the spirit of martial arts.

Moreover, it reveals a different side of Xue Mo, who is passionate about martial arts, showcasing his versatility as a talented writer.

The Arabic edition was translated by Fouad Hasan, published by Arabic Literature Center.

Qiang Village(Traditional Chinese version)

- Author: Xue Mo
- Publisher: Zhonghua International Media and Publishing Group Limited
- Publication Date: March, 2022

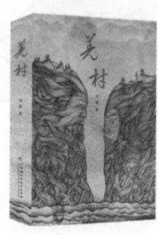

Description:

Qiang Village, located in western China, might resemble any other mountain stockade throughout history. However, this small village has etched an indelible mark on the annals of Chinese history due to its bizarre stories.

Over a century ago, a captivating show with lifelike characters, such as a macho man, an infatuated woman, and an avenging teenage boy, was staged in Qiang Village. Nevertheless, it could also be anything you can imagine: a fierce battle for power, a desperate search for love, or a cunning scheme for revenge, since its text is unlimited and contains infinite possibilities.

Author Xue Mo summons the souls of these men and women, young and old, with his pen and brings their encounters, passion, and faith back to life again. This village's tales may greatly astonish modern readers and challenge their outlook on life.

The Sound of Broadbeans Late at Night: The Secret Interview on the Silk Road

- Author: Xue Mo
- Publisher: People's Literature Publishing House
- Publication Date: April, 2016

Description:

The Sound of Broadbeans Late at Night starts with a Western sinologist sitting for an interview with a native Chinese writer, who is introducing the legendary Silk Road. Through nineteen intriguing stories, readers will meet with a diverse cast of vivid characters, and gain insight into their unique lifestyles, cultures, customs, and faith. Interwoven with dramatic plots and symbolic dialogues, these fascinating short tales reveal the worldview and spiritual outlook of western Chinese during that particular period of time.

Notably, this book has been hailed as "One Book to Understand the Silk Road" and "One Book to Understand People from Western China."

Selected Stories by Xue Mo(English Version)

● Author: Xue Mo
● Publication Date: May, 2018
● Rights Sold: Spanish, Romanian, German, Korean, Hindi, Nepalese, Sinhala, Turkish, Swedish, Russain, Hebrew, Arabic

Description:

Selected Stories by Xue Mo is a collection of short tales set on the ancient Silk Road, exploring love, hope, faith, life and death. The first three tales depict the lives and relationships of outsiders in rural villages, offering a contemporary perspective on the impact of rumour, pain and suffering. The last novella tells a gripping story of two sisters-in-law crossing the desert by camel to find hope, seek freedom and pursue dreams. These tales serve as a perfect introduction to Xue Mo's literary works.

Translated into more than two dozen languages, namely English, French, German, Korean, and Swedish, this book has been praised for its universal appeal. Its English version, translated by Nicky Harman, a prize-winning British sinologist and translator, was especially well-received, with the Guardian newspaper including one of its stories *Old Man Xinjiang*, in its list of the top five modern Chinese short stories. In 2022, its Sinhala version was awarded the National Literature Award in Sri Lanka.

Mother Wolf Gray

● Author: Xue Mo
● Publication Date: January, 2020
● Rights Sold: Swedish

Description:

Mother Wolf Gray is a compelling animal story adapted from Xue Mo's full-length novel *Desert Hunters*. It follows the journey of a mother wolf named Gray who seeks revenge against humans after her blind cub has been killed by accident. Her avenging quest leads to a gripping survival contest between humans and wildlife.

Through the eyes of wolves, livestock, herdsmen, poachers, and anti-poachers, this novel challenges the boundary between humanity and barbarity, testing the limits of the human mind. Filled with affectionate love and thrilling battles, *Mother Wolf Gray* is an inspiring yet fun read for young children, and a testament to Xue Mo's skill as a gifted storyteller.

One Man's West: A Biography of Xue Mo

- Author: Xue Mo
- Publisher: People's Literature Publishing House
- Publication Date: August, 2015

Description:

One Man's West: A Biography of Xue Mo is an autobiographical prose that depicts the author's childhood and adult years in his hometown of Wuwei, from the 1960s to the end of the 20th century.

Through a seamless blend of folktales, local customs, and social practices, author Xue Mo presents a panoramic view of the enigmatic cultural landscape of China's far west. Readers are taken on a captivating journey through a young village man's struggles and triumphs as he pursues his literary dream, providing an inspiring model for those who seek alternative paths to success and yearn for new possibilities in today's world.

Suosalang: The Ultimate Book (Volume I-VIII)

- Author: Xue Mo
- Publication Date: November, 2019
- Rights Sold: All Rights Available

Description:

Suosalang: The Ultimate Book, composed by Xue Mo, is the very first epic poem of the Han Chinese. Destruction is gradually approaching as the planet is lost in overindulgence and over-development. Five champions were tasked with saving their home world and were to be reincarnated on a distant planet known as Earth. In order to save her mother as well as her home planet, a brave and intelligent young goddess followed the five champions to Earth. Incarnated in a human form, she set out to awaken the champions from their earthly amnesia. During this process, she attained self-completion and lead others to enlightenment.

The journey was filled with challenges and hardships. They went through tests of romantic entanglements, life and death, fame and fortune, demons, and other evil forces, but eventually, they found the eternity that they are determined to find.

Suosalang touches on such enduring themes as the choices between good and evil, love and faith, excellence and mediocrity, war and peace, ego and universal love, and many more. Through the journey of the characters, you may see the wisdom that may guide you through tough choices like these in your own life. *Suosalang* is certainly a masterpiece that you might not want to miss.

Fox Worshiping the Moon: Xue Mo's Love Poems or Songs

- Author: Xue Mo
- Publisher: Central Compilation & Translation Press
- Publication Date: April, 2015

Description:

Fox Worshiping the Moon: Xue Mo's Love Poems or Songs is the first collection of writer Xue Mo's poems, characterized by its poetic vitality and philosophical insights.

The first part of this book outlines human yearnings for love, freedom, and kindness, exploring the mental struggles ordinary people may face on the path to enlightenment. In a strikingly imaginative way, author Xue Mo portrays these experiences, inviting readers to reflect on their own spiritual journeys. The final section is the author's creative reinterpretation of *The Diamond Sutra*. This collection encompasses various themes, such as life and death, humanity and nature, eternity and impermanence, making it more than a compilation of poems but a beacon guiding the direction of our life journey.

The Romanian version was translated by Constantin Lupeanu, a renowned Romanian sinologist and translator, and published by Ideea Europeana.

Laozi in Poems

- Author: Xue Mo
- Publisher: People's Literature Publishing House
- Publication Date: April, 2022
- Rights Sold: All Rights Available

Description:

Laozi in Poems is a new masterpiece by Xue Mo, displaying his remarkable creativity as he interprets *Dao De Jing* in a simple yet profound way. This book offers an overview of Laozi's eighty-one chapters, with each consisting of four parts: Original Text, Free Translation, Introduction, and Poem. Reading from the literal interpretation, one may gradually turn inward and explore the beauty of *Dao De Jing* step by step.

Using concise and poetic language, the author reveals the hard-to-describe wisdom embedded within Laozi's teachings, and provides guidance on how to incorporate Laozi's words of wisdom into everyday life. This is a book you will use time and time again as you understand the true meaning of the Dao and connect to the source of creation within.

Laozi's True Thoughts: Xue Mo Interprets Dao De Jing (I-IV)

- Author: Xue Mo
- Publisher: Encyclopedia of China Publishing House
- Publication Date: February, 2017
- Rights Sold: All Rights Available

Description:

Laozi's True Thoughts Series is Xue Mo's in-depth interpretation of the classic *Dao De Jing*. Using easy-to-understand language, the author uncovers the missed-out and misunderstood points, emphasizing the core of his profound teachings that may lead to spiritual awakening. The series offers a comprehensive guide for readers to apply this ancient wisdom to their everyday work and life, and meanwhile alleviate anxiety and reduce confusion on a daily basis.

Through this accessible and comprehensive book series, readers can gain a deeper understanding of the ultimate reality and transform their existence. Since its publication, *Laozi's True Thoughts Series* has gained immense popularity among Chinese readers, topping the charts for month online and offline.

Xue Mo Interprets Laozi's Dao: Make the Young Love Dao De Jing

- Author: Xue Mo
- Publication Date: July, 2022
- Rights Sold: All Rights Available

Description:

Make the Young Love Dao De Jing is a charming book designed to share ancient Chinese wisdom with today's teenagers.

The author provides solutions for young people to better navigate their real-life challenges. In this book, the author explains a good number of How-To's, such as how to behave properly; how to interact with the world; how to use wisdom to solve problems; how to be a better human, and how to set goals and change destiny.

To meet the specific reading needs of young learners, the author annotates rare words and key vocabularies, and recasts Laozi's insightful words with a light touch of humor and many relatable examples. *Make the Young Love Dao De Jing* is an exceptional selection for parent-child shared reading and family education.

Xue Mo's Wisdom Class (Volume I&II)

- Author: Xue Mo
- Publisher: Encyclopedia of China Publishing House (ECPH)
- Publication Date: August, 2020

Description:

Xue Mo's Wisdom Class is a remarkable book on Chinese philosophy that gifts the reader with a systematic approach to studying ancient wisdom and fostering cultural competence. Drawing from the fine traditions of Daoism, Buddhism, and Confucianism, the author integrates these philosophies to construct a multi-layered framework for self-cultivation.

The author begins by selecting "eight essential principles" from the Confucian foundation of his wisdom pyramid. These principles include "rectifying one's mind," "being sincere in thought," "cultivating oneself," "studying things to acquire knowledge," "regulating one's family well," "governing the state properly," and "bringing peace to all under heaven." For the higher stage, Xue Mo captures the essence of Daoism and Buddhism and establishes a road-map of self-refinement in six steps, serving as stepping-stones for one to progress towards the ultimate wisdom. These steps are Recognizing the Dao, Merging with the Dao, Observing with Wisdom, Complying the Middle Way, Being Your Own Creator, and Abiding in the Timeless Awareness.

Xue Mo's Wisdom Class provides guidance that can be applied to all aspects of one's life, making it a precious resource for anyone who seeks to learn the essence of Chinese ancient wisdom and gain personal excellence in workplace and beyond.

Sunyata and Beyond

- Author: Xue Mo
- Publisher: Encyclopedia of China Publishing House (ECPH)
- Publication Date: August, 2016

Description:

Sunyata and Beyond is acknowledged by experts the most celebrated writing on Mahamudra, or meditation on the nature of the mind over the past few centuries and beyond. Divided into two parts, this treasured book offers a comprehensive overview of the theoretical background and an unbroken lineage of this yogic tradition, and demonstrates a systematic path to initiating one's inner wisdom with step-by-step instructions.

Its English edition of *Sunyata and Beyond* was a translation by J.C. Cleary, who holds a PhD in East Asian Languages from Harvard University.

True Mind

- Author: Xue Mo
- Publisher: Encyclopedia of China Publishing House (ECPH)
- Publication Date: July, 2017

Description:

True Mind is an essential reading among *Xue Mo's Mind Series*. Using rather simple language, the author provides a comprehensive introduction and in-depth examination of the true mind, the source of wisdom. In this book, author Xue Mo also gifts the reader a systematic and feasible approach to discovering the true nature of mind.

For those are fond of philosophy, sinology and traditional culture, *True Mind* is a book that they should never miss.

Literary Mind

- Author: Xue Mo
- Publisher: Encyclopedia of China Publishing House (ECPH)
- Publication Date: June, 2017

Description:

Literary Mind is a writing-oriented collection among *Xue Mo's Mind Series*, consisting of creative essays, insightful prose, and literary dialogues. Throughout this book, author Xue Mo delves into various topics related to literature and innate wisdom, including the spirit of literature, the application of inner wisdom in literature, and the like.

By reading Xue Mo's *Literary Mind*, one will gain new insights into true literature and unlock their potential as a writer. In brief, *Literary Mind* explores new angles and new possibilities of literary creation and storytelling, which makes it a perfect choice for those who wish to improve their writing skills or become a master writer.

Enlightened Mind

- Author: Xue Mo
- Publisher: Encyclopedia of China Publishing House (ECPH)
- Publication Date: June, 2017

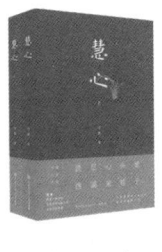

Description:

    Enlightened Mind is a thought-provoking read among *Xue Mo's Mind Series*, exploring multi-dimensional applications of innate wisdom in each individual's life and work. In this book, author Xue Mo shares his insightful views toward the myriad things, providing practical solutions for modern people to navigate life challenges in this ceaselessly changing world.

    Divided into two parts: *Life of Wisdom* and *Dialogues of Wisdom*, *Enlightened Mind* includes a range of Xue Mo's brilliant prose and many thought-provoking dialogues between Xue Mo and his readers. For anyone who wishes to access wisdom through reading and find strength amidst uncertainty, Xue Mo's *Enlightened Mind* is surely a book that can't be missed.

An Outline of Xue Mo's Mind Series (Traditional Chinese Version)

- Author: Xue Mo
- Publisher: Zhonghua International Media and Publishing Group Limited
- Publication Date: November, 2020

Description:

    An Outline of Xue Mo's Mind Series is an essential read for anyone who seeks to understand *Xue Mo's Mind Series*. This book not only provides a scientific method to deconstruct Xue Mo's philosophical system, but also serves as a key to unlock its profound teachings. Besides, it also briefly introduces other philosophical schools of mind, both ancient and modern, from China and abroad, providing readers with a broad cultural vision.

    This book examines Xue Mo's mind study in four dimensions: ontology, epistemology, methodology, and practice. Compared to other Xue Mo's works, it emphasizes academic aspect of his philosophy, offering precise explanations that are easy to understand. Therefore, it can also be used as a teaching and research material for higher education.

Buddha's Wisdom: Xue Mo Interprets The Diamond Sutra(Traditional Chinese Version Volume I-III)
- Author: Xue Mo
- Publisher: Zhonghua International Media and Publishing Group Limited
- Publication Date: May, 2019

Description:

In *Buddha's Wisdom: Xue Mo Interprets The Diamond Sutra*, the author has poured his heart and soul into a five-year cultural masterpiece that showcases his unparalleled understanding of *The Diamond Sutra*. Experts from the publishing industry have even praised it as an "unprecedented effort to interpret the classics." Xue Mo's profound wisdom and rich life experience are evident throughout this inspiring book, which is sure to leave a lasting impression on readers.

For those who prefer an audio format, the Chinese version of *Buddha's Wisdom* is now available on Ximalaya FM. Since its first release, this audiobook has gained a massive following among audiences from China and beyond.

Secrets of Mahasiddhas (Volume I-VIII)
- Author: Xue Mo
- Publisher: Zhonghua International Media and Publishing Group Limited
- Publication Date: March, 2019

Description:

Secrets of Mahasiddhas recounts the fascinating tales of 84 ancient Indian masters who lived between the 8th and 12th centuries. As author Xue Mo once said, "these stories have a direct bearing on our lives." Despite the passage of time and changing circumstances, the yearnings of human souls are always interlinked. Confusion, pain, worries, and expectations that we experience today are similar to those felt by people in ancient and modern times, in China and beyond.

The 84 mahasiddhas are relatable to each one of us, representing the various aspects of life. They were mostly common people with desires and emotions. What sets them apart is that they attained true freedom over a millennium ago, and their teachings have inspired many people to take control of their destinies. Today, however, we still face numerous problems, suffer from pain and miserable fates.

Entering the mystical world created by these stories, you will uncover your innate wisdom, seize control of your own fate, and become a free-minded and empowered individual. You will no longer be subject to your desires, the world, or your fate.

The World Is a Reflection of the Mind

- Author: Xue Mo
- Publisher: Encyclopedia of China Publishing House (ECPH)
- Publication Date: May, 2018
- Rights Sold: Italian, Hindi, Bengali

Description:

The World Is a Reflection of the Mind is a prose collection that explores the true nature of the mind and its vital role in shaping one's lives. Author Xue Mo argues that the phenomenal world is merely a fabrication of the mind; it does not exist on its own. What kind of mind you have, you will have that kind of life. What kind of mind you have, you will have that kind of world.

Through vivid anecdotes and straightforward examples, author Xue Mo demonstrates how the mind shapes the world and how, by altering our minds, we can change our actions and ultimately transform our lives.

This book was translated into English by J.C. Cleary, a PhD holder from Harvard University.

Be the Master of Your Mind

- Publisher: Encyclopedia of China Publishing House (ECPH)
- Publication Date: April, 2018

Description:

Be the Master of Your Mind is a potent guide for those seeking to see through the vanity of the world and look inward for solutions.

Following *The World Is a Reflection of the Mind*, this book further demonstrates how to cultivate self-awareness and develop insight in this restless world where people are bombarded with ever-changing viewpoints and values.

Using clear and vivid language, author Xue Mo gifts the reader a path to take control of their own mind and live a joyful, pain-free life. *Be the Master of Your Mind* is a must-read for those who are seeking the truth and looking to achieve a higher quality of life.

Give You a Wise Pair of Eyes

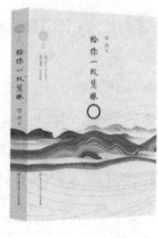

- Author: Xue Mo
- Publisher: Encyclopedia of China Publishing House (ECPH)
- Publication Date: April, 2018

Description:

Give You a Wise Pair of Eyes is one of Xue Mo's most popular collections of short prose, especially among young readers. In a rapidly changing world, discerning reality from illusion can be challenging, particularly for young adults who are just starting out in life and pursuing their dreams.

In this book, Xue Mo shares his personal experiences and profound insights on how to avoid getting lost in this fast-paced world, stay true to one's aspirations, and make the right choices when faced with difficult decisions.

Beyond the Hustle and Bustle

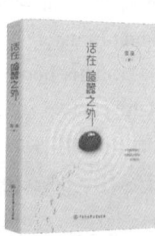

- Author: Xue Mo
- Publisher: Encyclopedia of China Publishing House (ECPH)
- Publication Date: June, 2019

Description:

Beyond the Hustle and Bustle, author Xue Mo's latest collection of short essays, delves into spiritual growth and mental healing. This book is divided into two parts, addressing mental health issues among modern urbanites and providing practical advice for effective treatment.

In the first part, *The World is a Tool to Tame Our Minds*, the author draws on personal experiences to explore how to cope with a restless mind in the face of setbacks and difficulties. The second part, *Life is a Theatrical Prop to Tame Our Minds*, investigates how individuals can use life experience to cultivate a more balanced state of mind.

This uplifting book, brimming with positive energy, is suitable for readers of all ages.

Live and Make A Voice

- Author: Xue Mo
- Encyclopedia of China Publishing House (ECPH)
- Publication Date: May, 2018

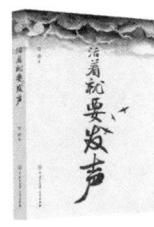

Description:

Live and Make A Voice is a new collection of ninety-four essays written for readers without enough time to read. The author shares his understanding toward the innate goodness of human nature and the essence of traditional Chinese culture, and provides practical guidance on how to choose the right books, how to perform acts of kindness, and how to make continuous progress.

Through his thought-provoking essays, readers will gain a better understanding of how to elevate themselves through reading and how to perform good deeds in a correct way.

Trials of Earthly Life

- Author: Xue Mo
- Zhonghua International Media and Publishing Group Limited
- Publication Date: July, 2019

Description:

Trials of Earthly Life serves as a beginner's guide to self-transformation, offering a glimpse into Tantric Buddhism and its relevant practices. Drawing from his decades of spiritual practice and deep understanding of the world, author Xue Mo employs insightful arguments and relatable examples to assist individuals embark on their spiritual journey, develop insight, and apply wisdom to their daily practice.

For lovers of Oriental philosophy, *Trials of Earthly Life* is a powerful guide that can assist them in overcoming obstacles and clarifying misunderstandings about self-cultivation.

For general readers, *Trials of Earthly Life* presents a refreshingly new approach that may help them elevate their spiritual awareness in terms of cultivating their inner worlds and aligning them with the outer ones.